# THE STARFISHERS TRILOGY

Also by Glen Cook:

*The Heirs of Babylon*
*The Swordbearer*
*A Matter of Time*
*The Dragon Never Sleeps*
*The Tower of Fear*
*Sung in Blood*

**Dread Empire**
*A Fortress in Shadow:*
  *The Fire in His Hands*
  *With Mercy Toward None*
*A Cruel Wind:*
  *A Shadow of All Night Falling*
  *October's Baby*
  *All Darkness Met*
*The Wrath of Kings (Forthcoming):*
  *Reap the East Wind*
  *An Ill Fate Marshalling*
  *A Path to Coldness of Heart*
*An Empire Unacquainted with Defeat*

**Starfishers**
*The Starfishers Trilogy*
  *Shadowline*
  *Starfishers*
  *Stars' End*

*Passage at Arms*

**Darkwar**
*Doomstalker*
*Warlock*
*Ceremony*

**The Black Company**
*The Black Company*
*Shadows Linger*
*The White Rose*
*The Silver Spike*
*Shadow Games*
*Dreams of Steel*
*Bleak Seasons*
*She Is the Darkness*
*Water Sleeps*
*Soldiers Live*

**The Garrett Files**
*Sweet Silver Blues*
*Bitter Gold Hearts*
*Cold Copper Tears*
*Old Tin Sorrows*
*Dread Brass Shadows*
*Red Iron Nights*
*Deadly Quicksilver Lies*
*Petty Pewter Gods*
*Faded Steel Heat*
*Angry Lead Skies*
*Whispering Nickel Idols*
*Cruel Zinc Melodies*
*Gilded Latten Bones*

**Instrumentalities of the Night**
*The Tyranny of the Night*
*Lord of the Silent Kingdom*
*Surrender to the Will of the Night*
*Wicked Bronze Ambition*
*Working Gods' Mischief*

# THE STARFISHERS TRILOGY

GLEN COOK

NIGHT SHADE BOOKS
NEW YORK

Night Shade books may be purchased in bulk at special discounts for sales promotion, corporate gifts, fund-raising, or educational purposes. Special editions can also be created to specifications. For details, contact the Special Sales Department, Night Shade Books, 307 West 36th Street, 11th Floor, New York, NY 10018 or info@skyhorsepublishing.com.

Night Shade Books® is a registered trademark of Skyhorse Publishing, Inc. ®, a Delaware corporation.

Visit our website at www.nightshadebooks.com.

10 9 8 7 6 5 4 3 2

Library of Congress Cataloging-in-Publication Data

Names: Cook, Glen, author.
Title: Starfishers trilogy / Glen Cook.
Description: New York : Night Shade Books, [2017]
Identifiers: LCCN 2016038962 | ISBN 9781597809009 (hardback)
Subjects: | BISAC: FICTION / Science Fiction / Space Opera. | FICTION / Science Fiction / Military. | FICTION / Science Fiction / Short Stories. | GSAFD: Science fiction. | Fantasy fiction.
Classification: LCC PS3553.O5536 S73 2017 | DDC 813/.54--dc23
LC record available at https://lccn.loc.gov/2016038962

Print ISBN: 978-1-59780-900-9

Cover design by Claudia Noble
Cover art by Daniel Dociu

Printed in the United States of America

## Dedications

*Shadowline*:
I dedicate this to Richard Wagner.

*Starfishers*:
This one is for Robin Scott Wilson, one-time spook
and erstwhile comrade/teacher.

*Star's End*:
This one is for you,
Sherry Lynne Manes.
Without your help no deadlines would be met.

# CONTENTS

# SHADOWLINE

# BOOK ONE
## ROPE

*Who twists the rope that dangles from the gibbet?*

# ONE: 3052 AD

Who am I? What am I?

I am the bastard child of the Shadowline. That jagged rift of sun-broiled stone was my third parent.

You cannot begin to understand me, or the Shadowline, without knowing my father. And to know Gneaus Julius Storm you have to know our family, in all its convolute interpersonal relationships and history. To know our family…

There is no end to this. The ripples spread. And the story, which has the Shadowline and myself at one end, is an immensely long river. It received the waters of scores of apparently insignificant tributary events.

Focusing the lens at its narrowest, my father and Cassius (Colonel Walters) were the men who shaped me most. This is their story. It is also the story of the men whose stamp upon them ultimately shaped their stamp upon me.

—Masato Igarashi Storm

# TWO: 3031 AD

Deep in the Fortress of Iron, in the iron gloom of his study, Gneaus Storm slouched in a fat, deep chair. His chin rested on his chest. His good eye was closed. Long grey hair cascaded down over his tired face.

The flames in the nearest fireplace leapt and swirled in an endless morisco. Light and shadow played out sinister dramas over priceless carpeting hand-loomed in Old Earth's ancient Orient. The shades of might-have-been played tag among the darkwood beams supporting the stone ceiling.

Storm's study was a stronghold within the greater Fortress. It was the citadel of his soul, the bastion of his heart. Its walls were lined with shelves of rare editions.

A flotilla of tables bore both his collectibles and papers belonging to his staff. The occasional silent clerk came and went, updating a report before one of the chairs.

Two Shetland-sized mutant Alsatians prowled the room, sniffing shadows. One rumbled softly deep in its throat. The hunt for an enemy never ended.

Nor was it ever successful. Storm's enemies did not hazard his planetoid home.

A black creature of falcon size flapped into the study. It landed clumsily in front of Storm. Papers scattered, frightening it. An aura of shadow surrounded it momentarily, masking its toy pterodactyl body.

It was a ravenshrike, a nocturnal flying lizard from the swamps of The Broken Wings. Its dark umbra was a psionically generated form of protective coloration.

The ravenshrike cocked one red night eye at its mate, nesting in a rock fissure behind Storm. It stared at its master with the other.

Storm did not respond.

The ravenshrike waited.

Gneaus Julius Storm pictured himself as a man on the downhill side of life, coasting toward its end. He was nearly two hundred years old. The ultimate in medical and rejuvenation technology kept him physically forty-five, but doctors and machines could do nothing to refresh his spirit.

One finger marked his place in an old holy book. It had fallen shut when he had drifted off. "A time to be born and a time to die…"

A youth wearing Navy blacks slipped into the room. He was short and slight, and stood as stiff as a spear. Though he had visited the study countless times, his oriental inscrutability gave way to an expression of awe.

*So many luxuries and treasures,* Mouse thought. *Are they anything more than Death, hidden behind a mask of hammered gold?*

And of his father he thought, *He looks so tired. Why can't they leave him alone?*

They could not. Not while Richard Hawksblood lived. They did not dare. So someday, as all mercenaries seemed to do, Gneaus Storm would find his last battlefield and his death-without-resurrection.

Storm's tired face rose. It remained square-jawed and strong. Grey hair stirred in a vagrant current from an air vent.

Mouse left quietly, yielding to a moment of deep sadness. His feelings for his father bordered on reverence. He ached because his father was boxed in and hurting.

He went looking for Colonel Walters.

Storm's good eye opened. Grey as his hair, it surveyed the heart of his stateless kingdom. He did not see a golden death mask. He saw a mirror that reflected the secret Storm.

His study contained more than books. One wall boasted a weapons collection, Sumerian bronze standing beside the latest stressglass multi-purpose infantry small arms. Lighted cabinets contained rare china, cut crystal, and silver services. Others contained ancient Wedgwood. Still more held a fortune in old coins within their velvet-lined drawers.

He was intrigued by the ebb and flow of history. He took comfort in surrounding himself with the wrack it left in passing.

He could not himself escape into yesterday. Time slipped through the fingers like old water.

A gust from the cranky air system riffled papers. The banners overhead stirred with the passage of ghosts. Some were old. One had followed the Black Prince to Navarette. Another had fallen at the high-water mark of the charge up Little Round Top. But most represented milemarks in Storm's own career.

Six were identical titan-cloth squares hanging all in a line. Upon them a golden hawk struck left to right down a fall of scarlet raindrops, all on a field of sable. They were dull, unimaginative things compared to the Plantagenet, yet they celebrated the mountaintop days of Storm's Iron Legion.

He had wrested them from his own Henry of Trastamara, Richard Hawksblood, and each victory had given him as little satisfaction as Edward had extracted from Pedro the Cruel.

Richard Hawksblood was the acknowledged master of the mercenary art.

Hawksblood had five Legion banners in a collection of his own. Three times they had fought to a draw.

Storm and Hawksblood were the best of the mercenary captain-kings, the princes of private war the media called "The Robber Barons of the Thirty-First Century." For a decade they had been fighting one another exclusively.

Only Storm and his talented staff could beat Hawksblood. Only Hawksblood had the genius to withstand the Iron Legion.

Hawksblood had caused Storm's bleak mood. His Intelligence people said Richard was considering a commission on Blackworld.

"Let them roast," he muttered. "I'm tired."

But he would fight again. If not this time, then the next. Richard would accept a commission. His potential victim would know that his only chance of salvation was the Iron Legion. He would be a hard man who had clawed his way to the top among a hard breed. He would be accustomed to using mercenaries and assassins. He would look for ways to twist Storm's arm. And he would find them, and apply them relentlessly.

Storm had been through it all before.

He smelled it coming again.

A personal matter had taken him to Corporation Zone, on Old Earth, last month. He had made the party rounds, refreshing his contacts. A couple of middle-management types had approached him, plying him with tenuous hypotheses.

Blackworlders clearly lacked polish. Those apprentice Machiavellis had been obvious and unimpressive, except in their hardness. But their master? Their employer was Blake Mining and Metals Corporation of Edgeward City on Blackworld, they told him blandly.

Gneaus Julius Storm was a powerful man. His private army was better trained, motivated, and equipped than Confederation's remarkable Marines. But his Iron Legion was not just a band of freebooters. It was a diversified holding company with minority interests in scores of major corporations. It did not just fight and live high for a while on its take. Its investments were the long-term security of its people.

The Fortress of Iron stretched tentacles in a thousand directions, though in the world of business and finance it was not a major power. Its interests could be manipulated by anyone with the money and desire.

That was one lever the giants used to get their way.

In the past they had manipulated his personal conflicts with Richard Hawksblood, playing to his vanity and hatred. But he had outgrown his susceptibility to emotional extortion.

"It'll be something unique this time," he whispered.

Vainly, he strove to think of a way to outmaneuver someone he did not yet know, someone whose intentions were not yet clear.

He ignored the flying lizard. It waited patiently, accustomed to his brooding way.

Storm took an ancient clarinet from a case lying beside his chair. He examined the reed, wet it. He began playing a piece not five men alive could have recognized.

He had come across the sheet music in a junk shop during his Old Earth visit. The title, "Stranger on the Shore," had caught his imagination. It fit so well. He felt like a stranger on the shore of time, born a millennium and a half out of his natural era. He belonged more properly to the age of Knollys and Hawkwood.

The lonely, haunting melody set his spirit free. Even with his family, with friends, or in crowds, Gneaus Storm felt set apart, outside. He was comfortable only when sequestered here in his study, surrounded by the things with which he had constructed a stronghold of the soul.

Yet he could not be without people. He had to have them there, in the Fortress, potentially available, or he felt even more alone.

His clarinet never left his side. It was a fetish, an amulet with miraculous powers. He treasured it more than the closest member of his staff. Paired with the other talisman he always bore, an ancient handgun, it held the long night of the soul at bay.

Gloomy. Young-old. Devoted to the ancient, the rare, the forgotten. Cursed with a power he no longer wanted. That was a first approximation of Gneaus Julius Storm.

The power was like some mythological cloak that could not be shed. The more he tried to slough it, the tighter it clung and the heavier it grew. There were just two ways to shed it forever.

Each required a death. One was his own. The other was Richard Hawksblood's.

Once, Hawksblood's death had been his life's goal. A century of futility had passed. It no longer seemed to matter as much.

Storm's heaven, if ever he attained it, would be a quiet, scholarly place that had an opening for a knowledgeable amateur antiquarian.

The ravenshrike spread its wings momentarily.

# THREE: 3052 AD

Can we understand a man without knowing his enemies? Can we know yin without knowing yang? My father would say no. He would say if you want to see new vistas of Truth, go question the man who wants to kill you.

A man lives. When he is young he has more friends than he can count. He ages. The circle narrows. It turns inward, becoming more closed. We spend our middle and later years doing the same things with the same few friends. Seldom do we admit new faces to the clique.

But we never stop making enemies.

They are like dragon's teeth flung wildly about us as we trudge along the paths of our lives. They spring up everywhere, unwanted, unexpected, sometimes unseen and unknown. Sometimes we make or inherit them simply by being who or what we are.

My father was an old, old man. He was his father's son.

His enemies were legion. He never knew how many and who they were.

—Masato Igarashi Storm

# FOUR: 2844 AD

The building was high and huge and greenhouse-hot. The humidity and stench were punishing. The polarized glassteel roof had been set to allow the maximum passage of sunlight. The air conditioning was off. The buckets of night earth had not been removed from the breeding stalls.

Norbon w'Deeth leaned on a slick brass rail, scanning the enclosed acres below the observation platform.

Movable partitions divided the floor into hundreds of tiny cubicles rowed back to back and facing narrow passageways. Each cubicle contained an attractive female. There were so many of them that their breathing and little movements kept the air alive with a restless susurrus.

Deeth was frightened but curious. He had not expected the breeding pens to be so huge.

His father's hand touched his shoulder lightly, withdrew to flutter in his interrogation of his breeding master. The elder Norbon carried half a conversation with his hands.

"How can they refuse? Rhafu, they're just animals."

Deeth's thoughts echoed his father's. The Norbon Head could not be wrong. Rhafu had to be mistaken. Breeding and feeding were the only things that interested animals.

"You don't understand, sir." Old Rhafu's tone betrayed stress. Even Deeth sensed his frustration at his inability to impress the Norbon with the gravity of the situation. "It's not entirely that they're refusing, either. They're just not interested. It's the boars, sir. If it were just the sows the boars would take them whether or not they were willing."

Deeth looked up at Rhafu. He was fond of the old man. Rhafu was the kind of man he wished his father were. He was the old adventurer every boy hoped to become.

The responsibilities of a Family Head left little time for close relationships. Deeth's father was a remote, often harried man. He seldom gave his son the attention he craved.

Rhafu was a rogue full of stories about an exciting past. He proudly wore scars won on the human worlds. And he had time to share his stories with a boy.

Deeth was determined to emulate Rhafu. He would have his own adventures before his father passed the family into his hands. His raidships would plunder Terra, Toke, and Ulant. He would return with his own treasury of stories, wealth, and honorable scars.

It was just a daydream. At seven he already knew that heirs-apparent never risked themselves in the field. Adventures were for younger sons seeking an independent fortune, for daughters unable to make beneficial alliances, and for possessionless men like Rhafu. His own inescapable fate was to become a merchant prince like his father, far removed from the more brutal means of accumulating wealth. The only dangers he would face would be those of inter-Family intrigues over markets, resources, and power.

"Did you try drugs?" his father asked. Deeth yanked himself back to the here and now. He was supposed to be learning. His father would smack him a good one if his daydreaming became obvious.

"Of course. Brood sows are always drugged. It makes them receptive and keeps their intellection to a minimum."

Rhafu was exasperated. His employer had not visited Prefactlas Station for years. Moreover, the man confessed that he knew nothing about the practical aspects of slave breeding. Fate had brought him here in the midst of a crisis, and he persisted in asking questions which cast doubt on the competence of the professionals on the scene.

"We experimented with aphrodisiacs. We didn't have much luck. We got more response when we butchered a few boars for not performing, but when we watched them closer we saw they were withdrawing before ejaculation. Sir, you're looking in the wrong place for answers. Go poke around outside the station boundary. The animals wouldn't refuse if they weren't under some external influence."

"Wild ones?" The Norbon shrugged, dismissing the idea. "What about artificial insemination? We don't dare get behind. We've got contracts to meet."

This was why the Norbon was in an unreasonable mood. The crisis threatened the growth of the Norbon profit curve.

Deeth turned back to the pens. Funny. The animals looked so much like Sangaree. But they were filthy. They stank.

Rhafu said some of the wild ones were different, that they cared for themselves as well as did people. And the ones the Family kept at home, at the manor, were clean and efficient and indistinguishable from real people.

He spotted a sow that looked like his cousin Marjo. What would happen if a Sangaree woman got mixed in with the animals? Could anyone pick her out? Aliens like the Toke and Ulantonid were easy, but these humans could pass as people.

"Yes. Of course. But we're not set up to handle it on the necessary scale. We've never had to do it. I've had instruments and equipment on order since the trouble started."

"You haven't got anything you can make do with?" Deeth's father sounded peevish. He became irritable when the business ran rocky. "There's a fortune in the Osirian orders, and barely time to push them through the fast-growth labs. Rhafu, I can't default on a full-spectrum order. I won't. I refuse."

Deeth smiled at a dull-eyed sow who was watching him half-curiously. He made a small, barely understood obscene gesture he had picked up at school.

"Ouch!"

Having disciplined his son, the Norbon turned to Rhafu as though nothing had happened. Deeth rubbed the sting away. His father abhorred the thought of coupling with livestock. To him that was the ultimate perversion, though the practice was common. The Sexon Family maintained a harem of specially bred exotics.

"Thirty units for the first shipment," Rhafu said thoughtfully. "I think I can manage that. I might damage a few head forcing it, though."

"Do what you have to."

"I hate to injure prime stock, sir. But there'll be no production otherwise. We've had to be alert to prevent self-induced abortion."

"That bad? It's really that bad?" Pained surprise flashed across the usually expressionless features of the Norbon. "That does it. You have my complete sanction. Do what's necessary. These contracts are worth the risk. They're going to generate follow-ups. The Osirian market is wide open. Fresh. Untouched. The native princes are total despots. Completely sybaritic and self-indulgent. It's one of the human First Expansion worlds gone feral. They've devolved socially and technologically to a feudal level."

Rhafu nodded. Like most Sangaree with field experience, he had a solid background in human social and cultural history.

The elder Norbon stared into the pens that were the cornerstone of the Family wealth. "Rhafu, Osiris is the Norbon Wholar. Help me exploit it the way a Great House should."

*Wholar. That's the legendary one*, Deeth thought. *The bonanza. The bottomless pot of gold.* The world so big and wild and rich that it took five Families to exploit it, the world that had made the consortium Families first among the Sangaree.

Deeth was not sure he wanted an El Dorado for the Norbon. Too much work for him when he became Head. And he would have to socialize with those snobbish Krimnins and Sexons and Masons. Unless he could devour the dream and make the Norbon the richest Family of all. Then he would be First Family Head, could do as he pleased, and would not have to worry about getting along.

"It's outside trouble, I swear it," Rhafu said. "Sir, there's something coming on. Even the trainees in Isolation are infected. They've been complaining all week. Station master tells me it's the same everywhere. Agriculture caught some boar pickers trying to fire the sithlac fields."

"Omens and signs, Rhafu? You're superstitious? They are the ones who need the supernatural. It's got to be their water. Or feed."

"No. I've checked. Complete chemical analysis. Everything is exactly what it should be. I tell you, something's happening and they know it. I've seen it before, remember. On Copper Island."

Deeth became interested again. Rhafu had come to the Norbon from the Dathegon, whose station had been on Copper Island. No one had told him why. "What happened, Rhafu?"

The breeding master glanced at his employer. The Norbon frowned, but nodded.

"Slaves rising, Deeth. Because of sloppy security. The field animals came in contact with wild ones. Pretty soon they rebelled. Some of us saw it coming. We tried to warn the station master. He wouldn't listen. Those of us who survived work for your father now. The Dathegon never recovered."

"Oh."

"And you think that could happen here?" Deeth's father demanded.

"Not necessarily. Our security is better. Our station master served in human space. He knows what the animals can do when they work together. I'm just telling you what it looks like, hoping you'll take steps. We'll want to hold down our losses."

Rhafu was full of the curious ambivalence of Sangaree who had served in human space. Individuals and small groups he called animals. Larger bodies he elevated to slave status. When he mentioned humanity outside Sangaree dominion he simply called them humans, degrading them very little. His own discriminations reflected those of his species as to the race they exploited.

"If we let it go much longer we'll have to slaughter our best stock to stop it."

"Rhafu," Deeth asked, "what happened to the animals on Copper Island?"

"The Prefactlas Heads voted plagues."

"Oh." Deeth tried not to care about dead animals. Feeling came anyway. He was not old enough to have hardened. If only they did not look so much like real people…

"I'll think about what you've told me, Rhafu." The Norbon's hand settled onto Deeth's shoulder again. "Department Heads meeting in the morning. We'll determine a policy then. Come, Deeth."

They inspected the sithlac in its vast, hermetically sealed greenhouse. The crop was sprouting. In time the virally infected germ plasm of the grain would be refined to produce stardust, the most addictive and deadly narcotic ever to plague humankind.

Stardust addicts did not survive long, but while they did they provided their Sangaree suppliers with a guaranteed income.

Sithlac was the base of wealth for many of the smaller Families. It underpinned the economy of the race. And it was one of the roots of their belief in the essential animal-ness of humanity. No true sentient would willingly subject itself to such a degrading, slow, painful form of suicide.

Deeth fidgeted, bored, scarcely hearing his father's remarks. He was indifferent to the security that a sound, conservative agricultural program represented. He was too young to comprehend adult needs. He preferred the risk and romance of a Rhafu-like life to the security of drug production.

Rhafu had not been much older than he was now when he had served as a gunner's helper during a raid into the Ulant sphere.

Raiding was the only way possessionless Sangaree had to accumulate the wealth needed to establish a Family. Financially troubled Families sometimes raided when they needed a quick cash flow. Most Sangaree heroes and historical figures came out of the raiding.

A conservative, the Norbon possessed no raidships. His transports were lightly armed so his ships' masters would not be tempted to indulge in free-lance piracy.

The Norbon were a "made" Family. They were solid in pleasure slaves and stardust. That their original fortune had been made raiding was irrelevant. Money, as it aged, always became more conservative and respectable.

Deeth reaffirmed his intention of building raiders when he became Head. Everybody was saying that the human and Ulantonid spheres were going to collide soon. That might mean war. Alien races went to their guns when living space and resources were at stake. The period of adjustment and accommodation would be a raidmaster's godsend.

Norbon w'Deeth, Scourge of the Spaceways, was slammed back to reality by the impact of his father's hand. "Deeth! Wake up, boy! Time to go back to the greathouse. Your mother wants us to get ready."

Deeth took his father's hand and allowed himself to be led from the dome. He was not pleased about going. Even prosaic sithlac fields were preferable to parties.

His mother had one planned for that evening. Everyone who was anyone among the Prefactlas Families would be there—including a few fellow heirs-apparent who could be counted on to start a squabble when their elders were not around. He might have to take a beating in defense of Family honor.

He understood that his mother felt obligated to have these affairs. They helped reduce friction between the Families. But why couldn't he stay in his suite and view his books about the great raiders and sales agents? Or even just study?

He was not going to marry a woman who threw parties. They were boring. The adults got staggering around drunk and bellicose, or syrupy, pulling him onto their laps and telling him what a wonderful little boy he was, repelling him with their alcohol-laden breath.

He would never drink, either. A raidmaster had to keep a clear head.

# FIVE: 3052 AD

My father once said that people are a lot like billiard balls and gas molecules. They collide with one another randomly, imparting unexpected angles of momentum. A secondary impact can cause a tertiary, and so forth. With people it's usually impossible to determine an initiator because human relationships try to ignore the laws of thermodynamics. In the case of the Shadowline, though, we can trace everything to a man called Frog.

My father said Frog was like a screaming cue ball on the break. The people-balls were all on the table. Frog's impact set them flying from bank to bank.

My father never met Frog. It's doubtful that Frog ever heard of my father. So it goes sometimes.

—Masato Igarashi Storm

# SIX: 3007 AD

BLACKWORLD (Reference: *Morgan's New Revised Catalogue of Stars, Planets, Astrogational Benchmarks, and Spatial Phenomena*, edition of 3007): Sole planet of white dwarf A257-23. Uniface body. Unique in that it is the only such planet colonized by mankind. A small population houses itself in seven domed cities, each essentially a corporate state. Economically important as a transport nexus and rich source of power metals. Major industry, mining. Major export, rare elements. Population, chiefly of negroid stock, of First Expansion origins. The name, however, comes from the fact that life is confined to Darkside. Major tourist attraction, the

Thunder Mountains on the western terminator, where slight perturbations in the slow planetary rotation result in tremendous tectonic activity due to heat expansion and contraction.

# SEVEN: 3020 AD

Blackworld as a reference-book entry was hardly an eyebrow-raiser. Nothing more than a note to make people wonder why anyone would live there.

It was a hell of a world. Even the natives sometimes wondered why anybody lived there.

Or so Frog thought as he cursed heaven and hell and slammed his portside tracks into reverse.

"Goddamned heat erosion in the friggin' Whitlandsund now," he muttered, and with his free hand returned the gesture of the obelisk/landmark he called Big Dick.

He had become lax. He had been daydreaming down a familiar route. He had aligned Big Dick wrong and drifted into terrain not recharted since last the sun had shoved a blazing finger into the pass.

Luckily, he had been in no hurry. The first sliding crunch under the starboard lead track had alerted him. Quick braking and a little rocking pulled the tractor out.

He heaved a sigh of relief.

There wasn't much real danger this side of the Edge of the World. Other tractors could reach him in the darkness.

He was sweating anyway. For him it did not matter where the accident happened. His finances allowed no margin for error. One screw-up and he was as good as dead.

There was no excuse for what had happened, Brightside or Dark. He was angry. "You don't get old making mistakes, idiot," he snarled at the image reflected in the visual plate in front of him.

Frog was old. Nobody knew just how old, and he wasn't telling, but there were men in Edgeward who had heard him spin tavern tales of his father's adventures with the Devil's Guard, and the Guard had folded a century ago, right after the Ulantonid War. The conservatives figured him for his early seventies. He had been the town character for as long as anyone could remember.

Frog was the last of a breed that had begun disappearing when postwar resumption of commerce had created a huge demand for Blackworld metals. The need for efficiency had made the appearance of a big exploitation corporation inevitable. Frog was Edgeward City's only surviving independent prospector.

In the old days, while the Blakes had been on the rise, he had faced more danger in Edgeward itself than he had Brightside. The consolidation of Blake Mining and Metals had not been a gentle process. Now his competition was so insubstantial that the Corporation ignored it. Blake helped keep him rolling, in fact, the way historical societies keep old homes standing. He was a piece of yesterday to show off to out-of-towners.

Frog did not care. He just lived on, cursing everyone in general and Blake in particular, and kept doing what he knew best.

He was the finest tractor hog ever to work the Shadowline. And they damned well knew it.

Still, making it as a loner in a corporate age was difficult and dangerous. Blake had long since squatted on every easily reached pool and deposit Brightside. To make his hauls Frog had to do a long run up the Shadowline, three days or more out, then make little exploratory dashes into sunlight till he found something worthwhile. He would fill his tanks, turn around, and claw his way back home. Usually he brought in just enough to finance maintenance, a little beer, and his next trip out.

If asked he could not have explained why he went on. Life just seemed to pull him along, a ritual of repetitive days and nights that at least afforded him the security of null-change.

Frog eased around the heat erosion on ground that had never been out of shadow, moved a few kilometers forward, then turned into a side canyon where Brightside gases collected and froze into snows. He met an outbound Blake convoy. They greeted him with flashing running lights. He responded, and with no real feeling muttered, "Sons of bitches."

They were just tractor hogs themselves. They did not make policy.

He had to hand load the snow he would ionize in his heat-exchange system. He had to save credit where he could. So what if Corporation tractors used automatic loaders? He had his freedom. He had that little extra credit at boozing time. A loading fee would have creamed it off his narrow profit margin.

When he finished shoveling he decided to power down and sleep. He was not as young as he used to be. He could not do the Thunder Mountains and the sprints to the Shadowline in one haul anymore.

Day was a fiction Blackworlders adjusted to their personal rhythms. Frog's came quickly. He seldom wasted time meeting the demands of his flesh. He wanted that time to meet the demands of his soul, though he could not identify them as such. He knew when he was content. He knew when he was not. Getting things accomplished led to the former. Discontent and impatience arose when he had to waste time sleeping or eating. Or when he had to deal with other people.

He was a born misanthrope. He knew few people that he liked. Most were selfish, rude, and boring. That he might fit a similar mold himself he accepted. He did others the courtesy of not intruding on their lives.

In truth, though he could admit it only in the dark hours, when he could not sleep, he was frightened of people. He simply did not know how to relate.

Women terrified him. He did not comprehend them at all. But no matter. He was what he was, was too old to change, and was content with himself more often than not. To have made an accommodation with the universe, no matter how bizarre, seemed a worthy accomplishment.

His rig was small and antiquated. It was a flat, jointed monstrosity two hundred meters long. Every working arm, sensor housing, antenna, and field-projector grid had a mirror finish. There were scores. They made the machine look like some huge, fantastically complicated alien millipede. It was divided into articulated sections, each of which had its own engines. Power and control came from Frog's command section. All but that command unit were transport and working slaves that could be abandoned if necessary.

Once, Frog had been forced to drop a slave. His computer had erred. It had not kept the tracks of his tail slave locked into the path of those ahead. He had howled and cursed like a man who had just lost his first-born baby.

The abandoned section was now a slag-heap landmark far out the Shadowline. Blake respected it as the tacit benchmark delineating the frontier between its own and Frog's territory. Frog made a point of looking it over every trip out.

No dropped slave lasted long Brightside. That old devil sun rendered them down quick. He studied his lost child to remind himself what became of the careless.

His rig had been designed to operate in sustained temperatures which often exceeded 2,000° K. Its cooling systems were the most ingenious ever devised. A thick skin of flexible molybdenum/ceramic sponge mounted on a honeycomb-network radiator frame of molybdenum-base alloy shielded the crawler's guts. High-pressure coolants circulated through the skin sponge.

Over the mirrored surface of the skin, when the crawler hit daylight, would lie the first line of protection, the magnetic screens. Ionized gases would circulate beneath them. A molecular sorter would vent a thin stream of the highest energy particles aft. The solar wind would blow the ions over Darkside where they would freeze out and maybe someday ride a crawler Brightside once again.

A crawler in sunlight, when viewed from sunward through the proper filters, looked like a long, low, coruscating comet. The rig itself remained completely concealed by its gaseous chrysalis.

The magnetic screens not only contained the ion shell, they deflected the gouts of charged particles erupting from Blackworld's pre-nova sun.

All that technology and still a tractor got godawful hot inside. Tractor hogs had to encase themselves in life-support suits as bulky and cumbersome as man's first primitive spacesuits.

Frog's heat-exchange systems were energy-expensive, powerful, and supremely effective—and still inadequate against direct sunlight for any extended time. Blackworld's star-sun was just too close and overpoweringly hot.

Frog warmed his comm laser. Only high-energy beams could punch through the solar static. He tripped switches. His screens and heat evacuators powered up. His companion of decades grumbled and gurgled to itself. It was a soothing mix, a homey vibration, the wakening from sleep of an old friend. He felt better when it surrounded him.

In his crawler he was alive, he was real, as much a man as anyone on Blackworld. More. He had beaten Brightside more often than any five men alive.

A finger stabbed the comm board. His beam caressed a peak in the Shadowline, locked on an automatic transponder. "This here's Frog. I'm at the jump-off. Give me a shade crossing, you plastic bastards." He chuckled.

Signals pulsed along laser beams. Somewhere a machine examined his credit balance, made a transfer in favor of Blake Mining and Metals. A green okay flashed across Frog's comm screen.

"Damned right I be okay," he muttered. "Ain't going to get me that easy."

The little man would not pay Blake to load his ionization charge while his old muscles still worked. But he would not skimp on safety Brightside.

In the old days they had had to make the run from the Edge of the World to the Shadowline in sunlight. Frog had done it a thousand times. Then Blake had come up with a way to beat that strait of devil sun. Frog was not shy about using it. He was cheap and independent, but not foolhardy.

The tractor idled, grumbling to itself. Frog watched the sun-seared plain. Slowly, slowly, it darkened. He fed power to his tracks and cooling systems and eased into the shadow of a dust cloud being thrown kilometers high by blowers at the Blake outstation at the foot of the Shadowline. His computer maintained its communion with the Corporation navigator there, studying everything other rigs had reported since its last crossing, continuously reading back data from its own instruments.

The crossing would be a cakewalk. The regular route, highway hard and smooth with use, was open and safe.

Frog's little eyes darted. Banks of screens and lights and gauges surrounded him. He read them as if he were part of the computer himself.

A few screens showed exterior views in directions away from the low sun, the light of which was almost unalterable. The rest showed schematics of information retrieved by laser radar and sonic sensors in his track units. The big round screen directly before him represented a view from zenith of his rig and the terrain for a kilometer around. It was a lively, colorful display. Contour lines were blue. Inherent heats showed up in shades of red. Metal deposits came in green, though here, where the deposits were played out, there was little green to be seen.

The instruments advised him of the health of his slave sections, his reactor status, his gas stores level, and kept close watch on his life-support systems.

Frog's rig was old and relatively simple—yet it was immensely complex. Corporation rigs carried crews of two or three, and backup personnel on longer journeys.

But there was not a man alive with whom Frog would have, or could have, stood being sealed in a crawler.

Once certain his rig would take Brightside this one more time, Frog indulged in a grumble. "Should have tacked on to a convoy," he muttered. "Could have prorated the damned shade. Only who the hell has time to wait around till Blake decides to send his suckies out?"

His jointed leviathan grumbled like an earthquake in childbirth. He put on speed till he reached his maximum twelve kilometers per hour. The sonics reached out, listening for the return of ground-sound generated by the crawler's clawing tracks, giving the computer a detailed portrait of nearby terrain conditions. The crossing to the Shadowline was a minimum three-hour run, and with no atmosphere to hold the shadowing dust aloft every second of shade cost. He did not dawdle.

It was another eventless crossing. He hit the end of the Shadowline and instantly messaged Blake to secure shade, then idled down to rest. "Got away with it again, you old sumbitch," he muttered at himself as he leaned back and closed his eyes.

He had to do some hard thinking about this run.

# EIGHT: 3031 AD

Storm placed the clarinet in its case. He faced the creature on his desk, slowly leaned till its forehead touched his own.

His movement was cautious. A ravenshrike could be as worshipful as a puppy one moment, all talons and temper the next. They were terribly sensitive to moods.

Storm never had been attacked by his "pets." Nor had his followers ever betrayed him though sometimes they stretched their loyalties in their devotion.

Storm had weighed the usefulness of ravenshrikes against their unpredictability with care. He had opted for the risk.

Their brains were eidetically retentive for an hour. He could tap that memory telepathically by touching foreheads. Memorization and telepathy seemed to be part of the creatures' shadow adaption.

The ravenshrikes prowled the Fortress constantly. Unaware of their abilities, Storm's people hid nothing from them. The creatures kept him informed more effectively than any system of bugs.

He had acquired them during his meeting with Richard Hawksblood on The Broken Wings. Since, his people had viewed his awareness with almost superstitious awe. He encouraged the reaction. The Legion was an extension of himself, his will in action. He wanted it to move like a part of him.

Aware though he might be, some of his people refused to stop doing the things that made the lizards necessary.

He never feared outright betrayal. His followers owed him their lives. They served with a loyalty so absolute it bordered on the fanatic. But they were wont to do things for his own good.

In two hundred years he had come to an armistice with the perversities of human nature. Every man considered himself the final authority on universe management. It was an inalterable consequence of anthropoid evolution.

Storm corrected them quietly. He was not a man of sound and fury. A hint of disapproval, he had found, achieved better results than the most bitter recrimination.

Images and dialogue flooded his mind as he discharged the ravenshrike's brainstore. From the maelstrom he selected the bits that interested him.

"Oh, damn! They're at it again."

He had suspected as much. He had recognized the signs. His sons, Benjamin, Homer, and Lucifer, were forever conspiring to save the old man from his follies. Why couldn't they learn? Why couldn't they be like Thurston, his oldest? Thurston was not bright, but he stuck with the paternal program.

Better, why couldn't they be like Masato, his youngest? Mouse was not just bright, he understood. Probably better than anyone else in the family.

Today his boys were protecting him from what they believed was his biggest weakness. In his more bitter moments he was inclined to agree. His life would be safer, smoother, and richer if he were to assume a more pragmatic attitude toward Michael Dee.

"Michael, Michael, I've had enemies who were better brothers than you are."

He opened a desk drawer and stabbed a button. The summons traveled throughout the Fortress of Iron. While awaiting Cassius's response he returned to his clarinet and "Stranger on the Shore."

# NINE: 3031 AD

Mouse stepped into Colonel Walters's office. "The Colonel in?" he asked the orderly.

"Yes, sir. You wanted to see him?"

"If he isn't busy."

The orderly spoke into a comm. "Masato Storm to see you, Colonel." To Mouse, "Go on in, sir."

Mouse stepped into the spartan room that served Thaddeus Immanuel Walters as office and refuge. It was almost as barren as his father's study was cluttered.

The Colonel was down on his knees with his back to the door, eyes at tabletop level, watching a little plastic dump truck scoot around a plastic track. The toy would dump a load of marbles, then scoot back and, through a complicated series of steps, reload the marbles and start over. The Colonel used a tiny screwdriver to probe the device that lifted the marbles for reloading. Two of the marbles had not gone up. "Mouse?"

"In the flesh."

"When did you get in?"

"Last night. Late."

"Seen your father yet?" Walters shimmed the lifter with the screwdriver blade. It did no good.

"I was just down there. Looked like he was in one of his moods. I didn't bother him."

"He is. Something's up. He smells it."

"What's that?"

"Not sure yet. Damn! You'd think they'd have built these things so you could fix them." He dropped the screwdriver and rose.

Walters was decades older than Gneaus Storm. He was thin, dark, cold of expression, aquiline, narrow of eye. He had been born Thaddeus Immanuel Walters, but his friends called him Cassius. He had received the nickname in his plebe year at Academy, for his supposed "lean and hungry look."

He was a disturbing man. He had an intense, snakelike stare. Mouse had known him all his life and still was not comfortable with him. *A strange one*, he thought. *His profession is death. He's seen it all. Yet he takes pleasure in restoring these old-time toys.*

Cassius had only one hand, his left. The other he had lost long ago, to Fearchild Dee, the son of Michael Dee, when he and Gneaus had been involved in an operation on a world otherwise unmemorable. Like Storm, he refused to have his handicaps surgically rectified. He claimed they reminded him to be careful.

Cassius had been with the Legion since its inception, before Gneaus's birth, on a world called Prefactlas.

"Why did you want me to come home?" Mouse asked. "Your message scared the hell out of me. Then I get here and find out everything's almost normal."

"Normalcy is an illusion. Especially here. Especially now."

Mouse shuddered. Cassius spoke without inflection. He had lost his natural larynx to a Ulantonid bullet on Sierra. His prosthesis had just the one deep, burring tone, like that of a primitive talking computer.

"We feel the forces gathering. When you get as old as we are you can smell it in the ether."

Cassius did something with his toy, then turned to Mouse. His hand shot out.

The blow could have killed. Mouse slid away, crouched, prepared to defend himself.

Cassius's smile was a thin thing that looked alien on his narrow, pale lips. "You're good."

Mouse smiled back. "I keep in practice. I've put in for Intelligence. What do you think?"

"You'll do. You're your father's son. I'm sorry I missed you last time I was in Luna Command. I wanted to introduce you to some people."

"I was in the Crab Nebula. A sunjammer race. My partner and I won it. Even beat a Starfisher crew. And they know the starwinds like fish know their rivers. They'd won four regattas running." Mouse was justifiably proud of his accomplishment. Starfishers were all but invincible at their own games.

"I heard the talk. Congratulations."

Cassius was the Legion's theoretical tactician as well as its second in command and its master's confidant. Some said he knew more about the art of war than anyone living, Gneaus Storm and Richard Hawksblood notwithstanding. War College in Luna Command employed him occasionally, on a fee lecture basis, to chair seminars. Storm's weakest campaigns had been fought when Cassius had been unable to assist him. Hawksblood had beaten their combined talents only once.

A buzzer sounded. Cassius glanced at a winking light. "That's your father. Let's go."

# TEN: 3020 AD

The Shadowline was Blackworld's best-known natural feature. It was a four-thousand-kilometer-long fault in the planet's Brightside crust, the sunward side of which had heaved itself up an average of two hundred meters above the burning plain. The rift wandered in a northwesterly direction. It cast a permanent wide band of shadow that Edgeward's miners used as a sun-free highway to the riches of Brightside. By extending its miners' scope of operations the Shadowline gave Edgeward a tremendous advantage over competitors.

No one had ever tried reaching the Shadowline's end. There was no need. Sufficient deposits lay within reach of the first few hundred kilometers of shade. The pragmatic miners shunned a risk that promised no reward but a sense of accomplishment.

On Blackworld a man did not break trail unless forced by a pressing survival need.

But that rickety little man called Frog, this time, was bound for the Shadowline's end.

Every tractor hog considered it. Every man at some time, off-handedly, contemplates suicide. Frog was no different. This was a way to make it into the histories. There were not many firsts to be claimed on Blackworld.

Frog had been thinking about it for a long time. He usually sniggered at himself when he did. Only a fool would try it, and old Frog was no fool.

Lately he had become all too aware of his age and mortality. He had begun to dwell on the fact that he had done nothing to scratch his immortality on the future. His passing would go virtually unnoticed. Few would mourn him.

He knew only one way of life, hogging, and there was only one way for a tractor hog to achieve immortality. By ending the Shadowline.

He still had not made up his mind. Not absolutely. The rational, experienced hog in him was fighting a vigorous rearguard action.

Though Torquemada himself could not have pried the truth loose, Frog wanted to impress someone.

Humanity in the whole meant nothing to Frog. He had been the butt of jests and cruelties and, worse, indifference all his life. People were irrelevant. There was only one person about whom he cared.

He had an adopted daughter named Moira. She was a white girl-child he had found wandering Edgeward's rudimentary spaceport. She had been abandoned by Sangaree slavers passing through hurriedly, hotly pursued by Navy and dumping evidence wherever they could. She had been about six, starving, and unable to cope with a non-slave environment. No one had cared. Not till the hard-shelled, bullheaded, misanthropic dwarf, Edgeward's involuntary clown laureate, had happened along and been touched.

Moira was not his first project. He was a sucker for strays.

He had cut up a candyman pervert, then had taken her home, as frightened as a newly weaned kitten, to his tiny apartment-lair behind the water plant down in Edgeward's Service Underground.

The child complicated his life no end, but he had invested his secret self in her. Now, obsessed with his own mortality, he wanted to leave her with memories of a man who had amounted to more than megaliters of suit-sweat and a stubborn pride five times too big for his retarded growth.

Frog wakened still unsure what he would do. The deepest route controls that he himself had set on previous penetrations ran only a thousand kilometers up the Shadowline.

That first quarter of the way would be the easy part. The markers would guide his computers and leave him free to work or loaf for the four full days needed to reach the last transponder. Then he would have to go on manual and begin breaking new ground, planting markers to guide his return. He would have to stop to sleep. He would use up time backing down to experiment with various routes. Three thousand kilometers might take forever.

They took him thirty-one days and a few hours. During that time Frog committed every sin known to the tractor hog but that of getting himself killed. And Death was back there in the shadows, grinning, playing a little waiting game, keeping him wondering when the meathook would lash out and yank him off the stage of life.

Frog knew he was not going to make it back.

No rig, not even the Corporation's newest, had been designed to stay out this long. His antique could not survive another four thousand clicks of punishment.

Even if he had perfect mechanical luck he would come up short on oxygen. His systems were not renewing properly.

He had paused when his tanks had dropped to half, and had thought hard. And then he had gone on, betting his life that he could get far enough back to be rescued with proof of his accomplishment.

Frog was a poker player. He made the big bets without batting an eye.

He celebrated success by breaking his own most inflexible rule. He shed his hotsuit.

A man out of suit stood zero chance of surviving even minor tractor damage. But he had been trapped in that damned thing, smelling himself, for what seemed half a lifetime. He had to get out or start screaming.

He reveled in the perilous, delicious freedom. He even wasted water scouring himself and the suit's interior. Then he went to work on the case of beer some damn fool part of him had compelled him to stash in his tool locker.

Halfway through the case he commed Blake and crowed his victory. He gave the boys at the shade station several choruses of his finest shower-rattlers. They did not have much to say. He fell asleep before he could finish the case.

Sanity returned with his awakening.

"Goddamn, you stupid old man. What the hell you doing, hey? Nine kinds of fool in one, that what you are." He scrambled into his suit. "Oh, Frog, Frog. You don't got to prove you crazy. Man, they already know."

He settled into his control couch. It was time to resume his daily argument, via the transponder-markers, with the controller at the Blake outstation. "Sumbitch," he muttered. "Bastard going to eat crow today. Made a liar of him, you did, Frog."

Was anybody else listening? Anybody in Edgeward? It seemed likely. The whole town would know by now. The old man had finally gone and proved that he was as crazy as they always thought.

It would be a big vicarious adventure for them, especially while he was clawing his way back with his telemetry reporting his sinking oxygen levels. How much would get bet on his making it? How much more would be put down the other way?

"Yeah," he murmured. "They be watching." That made him feel taller, handsomer, richer, more macho. For once he was a little more than the town character.

But Moira… His spirits sank. The poor girl would be going through hell.

He did not open comm right away. Instead, he stared at displays for which he had had no time the night before. He had become trapped in a spider's web of fantasy come true.

From the root of the Shadowline hither he had seen little but ebony cliffs on his left and flaming Brightside on his right. Every kilometer had been exactly like the last and next. He had not found the El Dorado they had all believed in back in the old days, when they had all been entrepreneur prospectors racing one another to the better deposits. After the first thousand virgin kilometers he had stopped watching for the mother lode.

Even here the immediate perception remained the same, except that the contour lines of the rift spread out till they became lost in those of the hell plain beyond the Shadowline's end. But there was one eye-catcher on his main display, a yellowness that grew more intense as the eye moved to examine the feedback on the territory ahead.

Near his equipment's reliable sensory limits it became a flaming intense orange.

Yellow. Radioactivity. Shading to orange meant there was so much of it that it was generating heat. He glared at the big screen. He was over the edge of the stain, taking an exposure through the floor of his rig.

He started pounding on his computer terminal, demanding answers.

The idiot box had had hours to play with the data. It had a hypothesis ready.

"What the hell?" Frog did not like it. "Try again."

The machine refused. It knew it was right.

The computer said there was a thin place in the planetary mantle here. A finger of magma reached toward the surface. Convection currents from the deep interior had carried warmer radioactives into the pocket. Over the ages a fabulous lode had formed.

Frog fought it, but believed. He wanted to believe. He had to believe. This was what he had given his life to find. He was rich…

The practicalities began to occur to him when the euphoria wore off. Radioactivity would have to be overcome. Six kilometers of mantle would have to be penetrated. A way to beat the sun would have to be found because the lode was centered beyond the Shadowline's end… Mining it would require nuclear explosives, masses of equipment, legions of shadow generators, logistics on a military scale. Whole divisions of men would have to be assembled and trained. New technologies would have to be invented to draw the molten magma from the earth…

His dreams, like smoke, wafted away along the long, still corridors of eternity. He was Frog. He was one little man. Even Blake did not have the resources to handle this. It would take a decade of outrageous capitalization, with no return, just to develop the needed technologies.

"Damn!" he snarled. Then he laughed. "Well, you was rich for one minute there, Frog. And it felt goddamned good while it lasted." He had a thought. "File a claim anyway. Maybe someday somebody'll want to buy an exploitation franchise."

No, he thought. No way. Blake was the only plausible franchisee. He was not going to make those people any richer. He would keep the whole damned thing behind his chin.

But it was something to think about. It really was.

Piqued by the futility of it all, he ordered his computer to lock out any memories relating to the lode.

# ELEVEN: 3031 AD

Cassius stepped into the study. Mouse remained behind him.

"You wanted me?"

Storm cased the clarinet, adjusted his eyepatch, nodded. "Yes. My sons are protecting me again, Cassius."

"Uhm?" Cassius was a curiosity in the family. Not only was he second in command, he was both Storm's father-in-law and son-in-law. Storm had married his daughter Frieda. Cassius's second wife was Storm's oldest daughter, by a woman long dead. The Storms and their captains were bound together by convolute, almost incestuous relationships.

"There's a yacht coming in," Storm said. "A cruiser is chasing her. Both ships show Richard's IFF. The boys have activated the mine fields against them."

Cassius's cold face turned colder still. He met Storm's gaze, frowned, rose on his toes, said, "Michael Dee. Again."

"And my boys are determined to keep him away from me."

Cassius kept his counsel as to the wisdom of their effort. He asked, "He's coming back? After kidnapping Pollyanna? He has more gall than I thought."

Storm chuckled. He killed it when Cassius frowned. "Right. It's no laughing matter."

Pollyanna Eight was the wife of his son Lucifer. They had not been married long. The match was a disaster. To understate, the girl was not Lucifer's type.

Lucifer was one of Storm's favorite children, despite his efforts to complicate his father's life. Lucifer's talents were musical and poetic. He did not have the good sense to pursue them. He wanted to be a soldier.

Storm did not want his children to follow in his footsteps. His profession was a dead end, an historical/social anomaly that would soon correct itself. He saw no future or glamour in his trade. But he could not deny the boys if they chose to remain with the Legion.

Several had become key members of his staff.

Of the men who had created the Legion only a handful survived. Grim old Cassius. The spooky brothers Wulf and Helmut Darksword. A few sergeants. His father, Boris, and his father's brothers and brothers of his own—William, Howard, Verge, and so many more—all had found their deaths-without-resurrection.

The family aged and grew weaker. And the enemy behind the night grew stronger... Storm grunted. Enough of this. He was becoming the plaything of his own obsession with fate.

"He's bringing her back, Cassius." Storm smiled secretively.

Pollyanna was an adventuress. She had married Lucifer more to get close to men like Storm than out of any affection for the poet. Michael had had no trouble manipulating her unsatisfied lust for action.

"But, you see, when he added it all up he was more scared of me than he thought. I caught up with him on The Big Rock Candy Mountain three weeks ago. We had a long talk, just him and me. I think the knife did the trick. He's vain about his face. And he still worries about Fearchild."

Mouse did his best to remain small. His father's gaze had passed over him several times, a little frown clicking on and off each time. There would be an explosion eventually.

"You? Tortured? Dee?" Cassius could not express his incredulity as a sentence. "You're sure this isn't something he's cooked up to boost his ratings?"

Storm smiled. His smile was a cruel thing. Mouse did not like it. It reminded him that his father had a side that was almost inhuman.

"Centuries together, Cassius. And still you don't understand me. Of course Michael has an angle. That's his nature. And why do you think torture is out of character for me? I promised Michael I would protect him. All that means, and he knows it, is that I won't kill him myself. And I won't let him be killed with my knowledge."

"But..."

"When he crosses me I still have options. I showed him that on The Mountain."

Mouse shuddered as a narrow, wicked smile of understanding captured Cassius's lips. Cassius could not fathom the bond between the half-brothers. It pleased him that Storm had circumvented its limitations.

Cassius was amused whenever a Dee came to grief. He had his grievances. Fearchild was still paying for the hand.

*These are truly cruel men,* Mouse thought, half-surprised. *My own people. I never really realized...*

He had been gone too long. He had forgotten their dark sides.

"To business," Cassius said. "If Michael has Pollyanna, and Richard is after him, there'll be shooting. We belong down in Combat."

"I was about to suggest that we go there." Storm rose. "Before my idiot sons rid me of this plague called Michael Dee." He laughed. He had paraphrased Lucifer, who had stolen the line from Henry II, speaking of Becket. "And poor pretty Pollyanna along with him."

*Poor Lucifer,* Mouse thought. *He'll be the only real loser if he manages to keep Michael from docking.*

Storm whistled. "Geri! Freki! Here!" The dogs ceased their restless pacing, crowded him expectantly. They were free to range the Fortress, but did so only in the company of their master.

Storm donned the long grey uniform cloak he affected, took a ravenshrike on one arm, strode off. Cassius trailed him by a half-step. Mouse hurried along behind them. The dogs ranged ahead, searching for the trouble they would never find.

"Mouse," Storm growled, stopping suddenly. "What the hell are you doing here?"

"I sent for him," Cassius replied in that cold metallic voice. Mouse shuddered. He was imagining it, of course, but Cassius sounded so deadly unemotional and lifeless... "I contacted my friends in Luna Command. They arranged it. The situation..."

"The situation is such that I don't want him here, Cassius. He has a chance to go his own direction. For God's sake, let him grab it. Too many of my children are caught in this trap already."

Cassius turned as Storm resumed walking. "Wait in my office. Mouse. I'll bring him around."

"Yes, sir."

Mouse began to feel what his father felt. An air of doom permeated the Fortress. A sense that great things were about to happen hung over them all. His father did not want him involved. Cassius thought he belonged. Mouse was shaken. A clash of wills between the two was inconceivable, yet his presence might precipitate one.

How could the Fortress be in danger? Combat simulation models suggested that only Confederation Navy had the strength to crack it. His father and Cassius got along well with the distant government.

Alone in the Colonel's inner office he began to brood. He realized he was mimicking his father. And he could not stop.

Was it Michael Dee?

The foreboding was almost palpable.

# TWELVE: 2844 AD

Costumed to the ears, wearing the heavy, silly square felt hat of a Family heir, Deeth stood beside his mother. Guests filed past the receiving line. The men touched his hands. The women bowed slightly. Pugh, the twelve-year-old heir of the Dharvon, honored him with a look that promised trouble later. In response Deeth intimidated the ten-year-old sickly heir of the Sexon. The boy burst into tears. His parents became stiff with embarrassment.

The Sexon were the only First Family with a presence on Prefactlas. They had the most image to uphold.

Deeth recognized his error as his father gave him a look more promising than that of Dharvon w'Pugh.

He was not contrite. Hanged for a penny, hanged for a pound. The Sexon kid would have a miserable visit.

The evening followed a predictable course. The adults began drinking immediately. By suppertime they would be too far gone to appreciate the subtleties of his mother's kitchen.

The children were herded into an isolated wing of the greathouse where they could be kept out of the way and closely supervised. As always, the supervision broke down.

The children shed their chaperones and got busy establishing a pecking order. Deeth was the youngest. He could intimidate no one but the Sexon heir.

Sexon fortunes would decline when the boy assumed his patrimony.

The Dharvon boy had a special hatred for Deeth. Pugh was strong but not bright. Only by malign perseverance did he corner his prey.

Deeth refused to show it, but he was terrified. Pugh was not smart enough to know when to quit. He might do something that would force the adults to take official notice. Relations between the Dharvon and Norbon were strained enough. Further provocation could escalate into vendetta.

The call to supper, like a god out of a machine, saved the situation.

Why did his mother invite people with grudges against the Family? Why was a social slight less easily forgiven than a business beating?

He decided to become the richest Sangaree of all time. Wealth made its own rules. He would change things around so they became sensible.

Deeth found the meal unbearably formal and ritualistic.

It was a dismal affair. The alcohol had had its effect. Instead of raising spirits and stirring camaraderie, it had eased restraints on the envy, jealousy, and tempers of the Families the Norbon were excluding from the Osirian market.

Deeth struggled to keep smiling down that long table of sullen faces. The meal progressed lugubriously. The faces grew more antagonistic.

During the desserts the senior Dharvon, *sotto voce*, expressed his animosity in words. His voice grew louder. Deeth became frightened.

The man was falling-down drunk, and had a reputation for verbal incontinence even when sober. He might say something that would push the Norbon into a corner of honor whence there was no exit save a duel.

The Dharvon was little brighter than his son. He did not have sense enough to avoid offending a better man. And the stupid pride of his heir would, of course, lead the Dharvon into vendetta. The Norbon Family would strike like a lion at a kitten and swallow the Dharvon whole.

But the mouth of a fool knows no restraint. The Dharvon kept pressing.

His neighbors edged away, dissociating themselves from his remarks. They shared his jealousies without sharing his stupidity. Sullenly neutral, they hovered like eager vultures.

Sangaree found feuds entertaining when they were not themselves involved.

Fate interceded just seconds before challenge became inescapable.

Rhafu burst into the hall. His face was red, frightened, and sweaty. He ignored the proprieties as he interrupted his employer.

"Sir," he said, puffing into the Norbon's face, "it's started. The field hands and breeders are attacking their overseers. Some of them are armed. With weapons from the wild ones. We're trying to get them under control in case there's an attack from the forest."

Guests buzzed excitedly. Heads and station masters shouted requests for permission to contact their own establishments. A general rising could not have been better timed. Prefactlas's decision-makers were far from their respective territories.

A few mumbled apologies for leaving ran from the table. What began as a babble of uncertainty escalated into a frightened clamor.

An officer of the Norbon Family forces compounded it. He galloped in, shouted over the uproar, "Sir! Everyone! A signal from *Norbon Spear*." *Spear* was the Head's personal yacht and the Family flagship. "A flotilla-scale naval force just dropped hyper inside lunar radius." A single sneeze broke the sudden silence. A hundred pale faces turned toward the soldier. "No IFF response. The ship types are those of the human navy. *Spear*'s signal was interrupted. We haven't been able to raise her again. Monitors show a sudden increase in gamma radiation at her position. Computer says she was hit in her drive sector and blew her generators."

The silence died. Everybody tried to leave at once, to escape, to flee to his own station. The great terror of the Sangaree had befallen Prefactlas. The humans had located their tormentors.

A gleeful wild devil spun circles of terror around the hall. Children wept. Women screamed and wailed. Men cursed and shoved, trying to be first to escape.

There had been other station raids. The humans had been merciless. They never settled for less than total obliteration.

Prefactlas was an entire world, of course, and a world cannot be attacked and occupied like some pitiful little island in an ocean. Not without overpoweringly vast numbers of ships and men. And, though sparsely settled, Prefactlas had a well-developed defense net. Sangaree guarded their assets. Normally a flotilla could have done little but blockade the world.

But conditions were not normal. The decision-makers were concentrated far from the forces responsible for turning attacks. No one had yet found a way around Family pride and stubbornness and formed a centralized command structure. The various Family forces, because their masters were far away, would be loafing far from their battle stations. Or, if the slave rising were general, they would be preoccupied. Attacking quickly, the humans could be down before defenses could be manned and effective interception barrages launched.

Even Deeth saw it. And he saw what most of the adults did not. Attack and uprising were coordinated, and timed for the height of this party.

The humans were working with someone on Prefactlas.

Their commander need only take the Norbon station to seize control of the planet. Having eliminated the decision-makers and gotten their ships inside the defensive umbrella, they could deal with the other holdings piecemeal. They could conquer an entire world with an inferior force.

The whole thing smacked of raider daring. Nurtured by treachery, of course.

Some laughing human commander, smarter than most animals, was about to make himself a fortune.

Over the years since their discovery of the Sangaree, and the fact that they were considered animals, the humans had created scores of laws designed to encourage one another to respond savagely. Billions in bounties and prize moneys would go to the conquerors of a world. Even the meanest shipboard rating would be able to retire and live on his interest. A developed world was a prize with a value almost beyond calculation.

The fighting would be grim. Human hatred would be reinforced by greed.

Deeth's father was as quick as his son. Defeat and destruction, he saw, were inevitable. He told his wife, "Take the boy and dress him in slave garb. Rhafu, go with her. See that he's turned loose in the training area. They don't know each other. He'll pass."

Deeth's mother and the old breeding master understood. The Head was grasping at his only chance to save his line.

"Deeth," his father said, kneeling, "you understand what's happening, don't you?"

Deeth nodded. He did not trust himself to speak. Once he had examined and thought out the possibilities he had become afraid. He did not want to shame himself.

"You know what to do? Hide with the animals. It shouldn't be hard. You're a smart boy. They won't be expecting you. Stay out of trouble. When you get the chance, go back to Homeworld. Reclaim the Family and undertake a vendetta against those who betrayed us. For your mother and me. And all our people who will die here. Understand? You'll do that?"

Again Deeth dared only nod. His gaze flicked around the hall. Who were the guilty? Which few would see the sun rise?

"All right." His father enfolded him in a hug that hurt. He had never done that before. The Norbon was not a demonstrative man. "Before you go."

The Norbon took a small knife from his pocket. He opened a blade and scraped the skin on Deeth's left wrist till a mist of blood droplets oozed up. Then he used a pen to ink a long series of numbers. "That's where you'll find your Wholar, Deeth. That's Osiris. The only place those numbers exist is in my head and on your wrist. Take care. You'll need that wealth to make your return."

Deeth forced a weak smile. His father was brilliant, disguising the most valuable secret of the day as a field hand's serial.

The Norbon hugged him again. "You'd better go. And hurry. They'll come down fast once they're into their run."

A raggedy string of roars sounded out front. Deeth smiled. Someone had activated the station defenses. Missiles were launching.

Answering explosions killed his pleasure. He hurried after his mother and Rhafu. White glare poured through the windows. The atmosphere above the station protested its torment. Guests kept shrieking.

The preparatory barrages had begun. The station's defenders were trying to fend them off.

The slave pens were utter chaos. Deeth heard the fighting and screaming long before he and Rhafu arrived on the observation balcony.

Household troops were helping the slave handlers, and still the animals were not under control. Corpses littered the breeding dome. Most were field hands, but a sickening number wore Norbon blue. The troops and handlers were handicapped. They had to avoid damaging valuable property.

"I don't see any wild ones, Rhafu."

"That is curious. Why provide weapons without support?"

"Tell them not to worry about saving the stock. They won't matter if the human ships break through."

"Of course." After an introspective moment, Rhafu said, "It's time you went." He gave Deeth a hug as powerful as his father's had been. "Be careful, Deeth. Always think before you do anything. Always take the long view. Don't ever forget that you're the Family now." He ran the back of a wrist across his eyes. "Now, then. I've enjoyed having you here, young master. Don't forget old Rhafu. Kill one for me when you get back to Homeworld."

Deeth saw death in Rhafu's watery eyes. The old adventurer did not expect to survive the night. "I will, Rhafu. I promise."

Deeth gripped one leathery old hand. Rhafu was still a fighter. He would not run. He would die rather than let animals shatter his courage and the confidence of his own superiority.

Deeth started to ask why he had to run away when everyone else was going to stand. Rhafu forestalled him.

"Listen closely, Deeth. Go down the stairs at the end of the balcony. All the way down. There'll be two doors at the bottom. Use the one on your right. It opens into the corridor that passes the training area. There shouldn't be anyone in it. Go to the end of the hall. You'll find two more doors. Use the one marked Exit. It'll put you outside in one of the vegetable fields. Go to the sithlac dome and follow its long side. Keep going in a straight line out from its end. You should reach the forest in an hour. Keep on going and you'll run into an animal village. Stay with them till you find a way off planet. And for Sant's sake make sure you pretend you're one of them and they're equals. If you don't, you're dead. Never trust one of them, and never get close to any of them. Understand?"

Deeth nodded. He knew what had to be done. But he did not want to go.

"Go on. Scoot," Rhafu said, swatting him on the behind and pushing him toward the stair. "And be careful."

Deeth walked to the stairwell slowly. He glanced back several times. Rhafu waved a last farewell, then turned away, hiding tears.

"He'll die well," Deeth whispered.

He reached the emergency exit. Cautiously, he peeped outside. The fields were not as dark as he had expected. Someone had left the lights on in the sithlac dome. And the slave barracks were burning. Had the animals fired them? Or had the bombardment done it?

Little short-lived suns kept flaring between the stars overhead. A long, rolling thunder of chemical explosions came from the far side of the station. The launch pits had been hit. The shriek of rising missiles was replaced by secondary explosions.

The humans were getting close. Deeth looked up into the heart of the constellation Rhafu had dubbed the Krath, after a rapacious bird of Homeworld. The human birthstar lay there somewhere.

He could not distinguish the constellation. There were scores of new stars up there, all of them too bright, and visibly brightening.

The humans were on the downward leg of their penetration run. He would have to hurry to clear the perimeter they would establish with their assault craft.

He sprinted for the side of the sithlac dome.

By the time he reached the dome's far end the new stars had swollen into small, bright suns. Missile exhausts rayed from them in angry swarms. He could hear the craft rumbling over the explosions stalking through the station.

They were just a few thousand feet up now, and braking in. His escape would be close. If he made it at all.

A flight of missiles darted toward the bright target of the dome. Deeth ran again, sprinting straight out into the darkness. Explosions tattooed behind him. Blasts hurled him forward, tumbled him over and over. The dome lights died. He rose, stumbled ahead, fell, rose, and went on. His nose was bleeding. He could not hear.

He could not see where he was going. The flashing of explosions kept his eyes from adapting as quickly as they should.

The assault craft touched down.

The nearest landed so close Deeth was singed by the hot wash spreading beneath it. He kept shambling toward the forest, ignoring the treacherous ground. When he was safe he paused to watch the humans tumble off their boat and link up with the craft that had landed to either side. The burning station splashed them with eerie light.

Deeth recognized them. They were Force Recon, the cream of the Confederation Marines, the humans' best and meanest. Nothing would escape their circle.

He cried for his parents, and Rhafu, then wiped the tears away with the backs of his fists. He trudged toward the forest, indifferent to the fact that the humans might spot him on anti-personnel radar. Each hundred steps he paused to look back.

Dawn was near when he passed the first trees. They rose like a sudden palisade, crowding a straight line decreed by the station's planners. He felt as though he had stepped behind a bulwark against doom.

Once his ears had recovered he had heard stealthy movements around him. He was not alone in his flight. He avoided contact. He was too shaken, and had too poor a command of the slave tongue, to handle questions from animals. The wild ones used a different language. He expected to have less trouble passing with them. If he could find them.

One found him.

He was a quarter-mile into the forest when a raggedy, smelly old man with a crippled leg pounced on him. The attack was so sudden and unexpected that

Deeth had no chance. His struggles earned him nothing but a fist in the face. The blow calmed him. He bit down on a tongue that had been damning the old man in High Sangaree.

"What are you doing, please?" he ventured in the animal language.

The old man hit him again. Before he could do more than groan, a sack had been flung over his head, skinned down to his ankles, and tied shut. A moment later, head downward and miserable, he was hoisted onto a bony shoulder.

He had become booty.

# THIRTEEN: 3052 AD

My father had an unusual philosophy. It was oblique, pessimistic, fatalistic. Judge its tenor by the fact that he read Ecclesiastes every day.

He believed all existence was a rigged game. Good strove with Evil in vain. Good could achieve occasional localized tactical victories, but only because Evil was toying with it, certain of final victory. Evil knew no limits. In the end, when the scores were tallied, Evil would be the big winner. All a man could do was face it with courage, fight though defeat was inevitable, and delay the hour of defeat as long as possible.

He did not see Good and Evil in standard terms. The Good and Evil most of us see he simply considered matters of viewpoint. The "I" is always on the side of the angels. The "They" are always wicked. He thought an absolute Islamic-Judeo-Christian Evil a weak, irrational joke.

Entropy is an approximate cognate for what Gneaus Julius Storm called Evil. An anthropomorphic, diabolic sort of entropy with a malign lust for devouring love and creativity, which, I think, he considered to be the main constituents of Good.

It was an unusual outlook, but you have to accept that it was valid for him before you can follow him through the maze called the Shadowline.

—Masato Igarashi Storm

# FOURTEEN: 3031 AD

Storm, Cassius, and the dogs crowded into an elevator. It dropped away toward the Traffic Control and Combat Information Center at the planetoid's heart.

Benjamin, Homer, and Lucifer whirled when their father entered the Center. Storm surveyed their faces grimly. The glow of the spatial display globes, overplayed by the changing light keys of the tactical computer's situation boards, splashed them with ever-changing color. No one spoke.

Storm's sons stared at their feet like shamed boys caught playing with matches. Storm half turned to Cassius, eye on the senior watchstander. Cassius inclined his head. The officer would have to explain his failure to report ships in detection. He would be reminded of his debt to Gneaus Storm. It would be a tempestuous admonition.

The officer's failure was beyond Cassius's comprehension. He never let his hatred of the Dees impair his trust. The Dees were a raggedy-assed gaggle of hypocritical thieves, boosters, and news managers. They were a waste of life-energy. But… Cassius suppressed his feelings because he had faith in Storm's judgment. This watch officer had not been with the Legion long enough to have developed that faith.

Should Storm ever fail, openly and dramatically… Cassius did not know what he would do. He had been with Storm so long that, chances were, he would bull right along in the official line.

Storm surveyed his sons again. He awarded Lucifer one of his rare smiles. The fool had been trying to kill his own wife.

Storm thought of Pollyanna, shuddered.

He had to let them off easy. This pocket revolt was his own fault. He should have passed the word about the woman.

He did not think much of himself just then. He had done his usual trick, not letting anyone know what he was doing or why. He was screwing up too much lately. Maybe he was getting old. In this business survivors eliminated the margin of error.

He locked gazes with Lucifer. His son stepped back as if physically shoved.

Lucifer was just six years older than Mouse. He was large and well built, like his father, but his mind had his mother's bent.

Lady Prudence of Gales had been a High Seiner poetess and musician in the days when her people, the mysterious Starfishers, had not completely retreated into the interstellar deeps. She had come to the Fortress as an emissary, recalling Prefactlas, begging for help to save her sparsely populated, remote homeworld from Sangaree domination.

She had touched Storm with naked trust. No man knew where to find the elusive Seiners. She had given him that secret in the naive hope that that would move him to help. She had cast the dice, betting everything on a single roll… And she had won.

And Storm had had no cause for regrets.

He remembered Prudie better than most of his women. A hot, hungry little morsel in private. Cool, competent, and occasionally imperious in public, and daring. Bedazzlingly daring. Never before or since had anyone cozened the Iron Legion into fighting on spec.

He had pulped the Sangaree on her world. She had given him a son. And they had gone their separate ways.

Storm had known countless women, had fathered dozens of children. His parents had had no concept of fidelity either. Three of his brothers had had different mothers. Michael Dee had had a different and mysterious father.

Frieda Storm was guilty of her indiscretions, too. She did not press Storm about his.

So Lucifer had been an artist born. And he was good. His poetry had appeared with that of giants like Moreau and Czyzewski. The visualist Boroba Thring had done a kaleidoshow based on Lucifer's Legion epic, *Soldaten*, using one of Lucifer's Wagnerian scores as background music. But Lucifer considered writing and composing mere hobbies.

He was determined to prove himself a soldier. It was a vain ambition. He did not, as they say, have the killer instinct.

The free soldier had to act without thought or remorse. His antagonists were professionals. They were quick and deadly. They would permit him no time for regrets or reflection on the barbarity of it all.

Storm forgave Lucifer's shortcomings more readily than he did those of sons with no talents. He had hopes for the boy. Lucifer might someday find and become true to himself.

Benjamin and Homer were twins. Storm's only children by Frieda, they were, in theory and their own estimation, his favorites. They were rebels. Their mother defended them like an old bitch cat her kittens.

*Probably my fault they're delinquents*, Storm thought. *They've been men for decades and still I treat them like boys. Hell, they're grandfathers.*

This extended life leached a man's perspective. The twins were as unalike as night and day. Storm sometimes wondered if he had fathered both.

Benjamin was a blond Apollo. He was the darling of the younger Legionnaires, who considered his father a historical relic. But did they turn to Benjamin in the tight places? They did not. Benjamin Storm tended to fold under pressure.

His mother and friends believed he was the Legion's Crown Prince. His father thought not. If the Iron Legion survived Gneaus Storm, none of his children but Cassius's favorite had what it took to rule and fight a freecorps.

Benjamin could win loyalties with a word, with a gesture. He had that knack for making each individual feel he was the only human being in the universe Benjamin cared about. But could he inspire faith?

Benjamin might command the Legion one day if his father did not appoint a successor. For one commission. Storm could see his son taking over on force of personality. He could not see him succeeding in the field.

Benjamin could play Piper of Hamelin to his own, but those hard cases across the battlefields, the Hawksbloods and van Breda Kolffs, would cut up his charisma and spread it on their breakfast toast.

Homer was Benjamin's antithesis. He was dark of mind and body, ugly, malformed, and congenitally blind. He repelled everyone but his twin. Benjamin was his only friend. He followed his brother everywhere, as if only Benjamin could neutralize the blackness in his soul.

In compensation for her cruelties Nature had given Homer a weak psionic ability that never did him any good. He was bitter, and not without just cause.

He was as sharp as anyone in the family, yet was trapped in a body little better than a corpse.

Storm's men saw the twins as living examples of the dualities in their father. Benjamin had received the looks and charm, Homer the hurt and rage and darkness of spirit.

Benjamin met his father's eye and smiled his winningest smile. Homer stared sightlessly, unrepentant. He was unafraid. There was no way to punish him more than life had punished him already.

He expected nothing but evil. He accepted it.

Storm hurt for him. He knew the shadow that ruled Homer. It was an old, ultimate companion.

At least once a day Storm turned to the book that time had forgotten, rereading and contemplating the message of a Storm dead four thousand years.

Vanity of vanities, says the Preacher, vanity of vanities! All is vanity. What does a man gain by all the toil at which he toils under the sun?

Gneaus Storm, even more than had Homer, had watched the rivers run into the seas, and knew the seas would never fill. Rather, they grew shallower with the ages, and someday would disappear. What did a man profit if, in the end, all his deeds were illusion? The Enemy could not be overthrown. Its resources were infinite and eternal and Storm knew he would only lose the long struggle.

Unlike the Preacher in Jerusalem, Storm refused to surrender. In spite of everything, there could be victory in the spirit. If he kept his courage he could scratch his memory on the cruel visage of defeat. Either to surrender, or to go to his fate with laughter on his lips. This was the only real choice he, or any man, was ever given in this life.

"There's a ship coming in," he growled at last. He jerked his arm upward. The ravenshrike fluttered into the shadows. No one paid it any heed.

No one argued. The truth was evident in the display globes.

"Michael Dee's ship, I believe. Contact him. Clear him a path through the mine fields."

The soldiers did not "yes sir" before returning to work. They would try to impress him with their efficiency now. Trouble lurked beyond the end of their watch.

"Traffic, contact the cruiser too. I want to speak to her master. All defense systems, move to standby alert."

"I have contact with Dee," said the man on Traffic Comm. "Clear channel, visual."

"Thank you." Storm seated himself at a visual pickup. Cassius moved in behind him. Michael Dee's fox face formed on screen. Worry lines faded away. A pearly-toothed smile broke through.

"Gneaus! Am I glad to see you. I was beginning to think you wouldn't answer."

"I had to think about it." Dee's smile faded. His was a con man's face, blandly honest, as reassuring as a priest's. But little folds uplifting the corners of his eyes gave him a sly look. "I could still change my mind. Did you bring my cargo?"

Dee was wearing his natural face. No makeup. No disguise. His dark eyes, narrow face, pointy nose, and prominent, sharp teeth gave him a definite vulpine look. *This is the true Michael,* Storm thought.

Dee was a man of countless faces. Seldom was he out of disguise, and his talent for shifting identities was preternatural. Given study time, he could adopt the speech habits and physical mannerisms of almost anyone. He found the talent useful in his trade. He was, supposedly, a free-lance newsman.

"Of course. I said I would, didn't I?" Dee sneered as if to say he knew his brother would not throw him to Hawksblood's wolves.

"Show me, Michael."

Exasperated, Dee backed off pickup. Pollyanna Eight showed her pretty face. A little sigh ran through the Center.

"All right. You're clear in. Out." Storm nudged the comm man. He took the hint. He secured the channel before Dee could come back on.

Lucifer sputtered behind his father and Cassius. Storm turned. He forbore any remark but, "Lucifer, go take charge of the ingress locks. Don't let Michael wander. Get him out of his ship and search it."

Dee was treacherous. From childhood he had thrived on sparking strife. The feud between Richard Hawksblood and his brother was his masterwork.

He could not help himself. Meddling and deceit were compulsions. One day his weakness would kill him.

Michael would be involved in more than just bringing Pollyanna home. He was not a one-track man. He always kept several balls in the air.

Storm thought he knew what Dee was up to. Richard's being interested in Blackworld was the giveaway.

Michael would try to involve the Legion. Merc wars made great holo entertainment. He had grown rich covering them. He had engineered a few to have something to tape.

Knowing what Michael wanted was inadequate forewarning. He was devious. His manipulations might not be recognizable.

The Traffic Comm man established contact with Dee's pursuer.

"Cassius. Who is he?"

"Lawrence Abhoussi. One of Richard's best."

"Richard must have sent him out blind. He's surprised to see me."

"Characteristic." Hawksblood was a demon for secrecy.

Storm keyed for sound. "Commander Abhoussi, you're entering restricted space."

The Ship's Commander replied, "We did note the automatic warnings, Colonel. But we were given explicit orders. We have to capture the yacht."

"Polite, anyway," Storm whispered.

"And scared."

The Legion had burned respect into Hawksblood's men. And vice versa.

"I know the ship, Commander. My daughter-in-law is aboard. I have to extend her my protection. Why don't you pursue your quarrel with her master after he leaves? If the ship is stolen, I'll let you send in a skeleton crew to collect her."

Abhoussi grew pale. Storm's defenses were formidable. "My orders are explicit, Colonel Storm. I'm to recover the vessel and everyone aboard her."

"This is getting dangerous, Gneaus," Cassius burred.

Storm nodded. "I know your employer, Commander. He's a disciplinarian, but he'll make allowances when you explain why you lost the yacht." Storm killed the sound. "I'm trying to give him an out, Cassius."

"He knows."

The Ship's Commander paused before replying. He kept glancing off screen. Finally, he keyed for sound and said, "I'm sorry, Colonel Storm. I have no option."

"Damn," Cassius said.

"I'm sorry too, then. Good-bye, Commander." Storm broke the link. "Fire Control, activate the passive defenses. Don't take the cruiser under fire unless she looks like she'll catch Dee." He rose, started toward the elevators. The dogs rose as he approached.

"Father!" Benjamin called. "Hold on. They've gone Norm." Storm turned. "Abhoussi's inherent velocity is aligned with Dee's and he's closing fast. He's accelerating. Catch point about nine hundred thousand kilometers out."

"Computer?" Storm asked the air.

"Active," a Cassius-like voice replied.

"You following the current situation?"

"Affirmative."

"Analysis please."

The machine confirmed Benjamin's assessment. It added, "Smaller target is decelerating on a line of approach to the ingress locks. Traffic Comm has docking control. Larger target still accelerating in line of approach. Probability nine-zero plus: Intent is to take hyper with the smaller vessel within its influential sphere."

"Free missiles," Storm ordered. "This Abhoussi is damned smart," he told Cassius. "He jumped on the only chance he's got."

By snagging Dee with his more powerful influential field Abhoussi could neutralize the yacht's drive and drag her beyond the range of Storm's superior weaponry. He could then drop hyper and deal with Michael at his leisure.

It was a tactic as old as spatial warfare, though a dangerous one. Both ships could be destroyed if either's drives were far out of synch.

"That man was a McGraw," Cassius guessed. "Only a pirate would have the nerve to try it."

"Free guns on the outstations," Storm ordered. "Commence action. You're right, Cassius. He's got guts. Pity he's wasting them."

"Some people fear Richard Hawksblood more than they fear Gneaus Storm," Cassius observed laconically. "Then again, he could know something you don't. You haven't analyzed his chances. He comped them while he was talking to you."

"Right. Computer. Analyze success probabilities for the assumed mission of the larger target, henceforth desig Enemy, Bogey One."

Practically trampling Storm's final words, the computer replied, "With Traffic control of Friendly, probability six five plus. Without Traffic control, probability four seven plus. Analysis of random minetracks incomplete."

"Pretty good," Cassius observed. "I'd buy those odds myself."

"And win. He's got the jump on us. Traffic, put Dee on his own hooks. Cassius, take the gun-control master."

Storm himself assumed control of the master board commanding the mines and missiles protecting the planetoid. "Computer. Probability of Enemy success with new board control." The machine was a cryocyborg unit. It could enter the skills of known human operators into its probability equations.

"With Friendly free of Traffic control and analysis of random minetracks complete, probability three one plus."

Storm was pleased. He and Cassius made a difference.

He did not like the ever-present plus. The computer was weighting the probability shift in Abhoussi's favor.

Storm examined his board. None of his active mines or hunter-killer missiles would pass close enough to Abhoussi to detonate. The weapons in line of approach were inactive for Michael's sake.

He blew several nearby mines. Maybe he could rattle Abhoussi.

He suspected the plus was being awarded because Abhoussi was performing better than the average Ship's Commander profiled in the computer. Richard did not hire average men. No merc captain did.

Storm punched more fire buttons. He did no good. Abhoussi was crawling into Michael's safety shadow. The only sure way to stop him was to activate weaponry in the approach path.

"Bogey One, probability of success, four two plus," the computer announced, and almost immediately raised its ante to four three, four four, and four five. Storm cursed softly and continuously.

"Time to jump?" he demanded.

"Twenty-three seconds optimum." Then the computer added, "Hit, beam, remote station twelve. Field anomalies indicate a temporary reduction of efficiency in Bogey One drives. Probability of Enemy success, three one steady."

Storm smiled. "Good shooting, Cassius."

Cassius was too busy to acknowledge the applause. He bent over his master console with the intensity of a virtuoso pianist, totally immersed in his art, webbing Abhoussi with beams of destruction.

Storm turned to his own master, secured it. He had not rattled Abhoussi at all.

He leaned back and watched Cassius while fighting off visions of Pollyanna being crisped by Abhoussi's weaponry. Hawksblood's man was firing only in self-defense, but might have orders to kill if he could not capture.

The odds against Abhoussi lengthened. Storm fidgeted. He placed little faith in computer analyses. He had beaten their odds when they had been five-to-one against him. The best games machines, with brains cyborged in, could not take into account all the human factors of a battle situation.

"Hit, beam," the computer announced. "Drive anomalies. Bogey One no longer accelerating. Probability of generator damage seven zero plus."

"Catch time," Storm asked. It had been telescoping, but Abhoussi had been hand-over-handing it up the slope.

"Eleven seconds."

Storm smiled. Abhoussi was climbing an ever-steepening slope. One more perfect shot from Cassius would do it.

Again he paid his chief of staff his due. The man was not just trying for hits, he was sharpshooting Abhoussi's facility for dragging Michael off to neutral space. And that at a time when he could have eased up and allowed his most hated enemy to perish.

Storm grabbed a mike, called the ingress locks. "Get a boat ready for rescue work. Have it crewed and standing by for astrogational instruction. Is Lucifer there yet?" He cut off before he received a reply. The computer was chattering again.

"Hit, beam. Major drive anomalies. Probability of generator damage nine zero plus. Probability of Enemy success, one three minus."

Storm moved to Traffic. "Contact the cruiser," he told the watchstander.

"Bogey One commencing evasive maneuvering," the computer continued. "Probability that Enemy is attempting to disengage, nine five plus." Abhoussi had accepted defeat.

Establishing the comm link took longer than the action had. Abhoussi was more interested in survival than in chitchat.

When the pale-faced Ship's Commander finally responded, Storm asked, "Can you manage your generators yourselves, Commander? Any casualties you can't handle? I have a rescue boat standing by."

Abhoussi gulped air, replied, "We'll manage, Colonel. We took no casualties."

"All right." Storm blanked off. "Cease firing," he ordered.

The order was unnecessary. Cassius had secured his gun board.

Was Abhoussi telling the truth? He had the feel of a man who would let his people die the death-without-resurrection before putting them into the hands of an enemy capable of using them against his employer later.

Storm called the ingress locks again. "Cancel the boat alert. We won't need it." Then, "Cassius, let's go meet Michael. He'll have an interesting story. Might even tell the truth."

"Good show, gentlemen," Cassius told the watchstanders. "Run a full systems check before you go off duty. See that Supply and Weapons know which mines and missiles to replace." His hard gaze darted from face to face. No one met it.

Storm peered into the shadows. The ravenshrike had concealed itself. It was alert.

"I think we did all right," he told Cassius as they followed the dogs into an elevator. "It was my kind of battle. Nobody got hurt."

"They should all be so chesslike."

A shadow moved in the shadows of a corner of Combat. The eyes of Storm's ravenshrike burned as they watched Homer and Benjamin. Homer slipped into the still warm seat before the mines and missiles board. The blind man caressed trigger switches and status boards with his sensitive fingers. He listened for his sporadic psi. He depressed an activation key, paused, tripped a fire switch.

Daggers of flame scarred the deep space night two light seconds from the Fortress. A swarm of hyper-capable seeker missiles went looking for Commander Abhoussi's cruiser.

The vessel had not traveled far.

Alarms screamed aboard the warship. Automatic weapons responded.

Constellations vanished behind a veil of fire. Abhoussi's engineers seized their only chance. They kicked in the damaged generators. The cruiser twisted away into hyperspace, leaving fragments of itself behind. The seekers, unaware of the cruiser's destination, began cutting lazy search patterns over half-light-year quadrants.

Homer's faint and seldom reliable psi touched upon a remote, short-lived scream. He leaned back and smiled at an aghast Benjamin. "It's done."

"Ah, Homer..." Benjamin could not think of anything to say. He could not meet the eyes of the watchstanders.

Their faces were long and grey. Storm was going to cut their hearts out for not stopping this.

The ravenshrike shuddered as it sensed the psionic scream and the pure disgust of the Center watch. It wrapped itself in wings and shadow, closed its eyes, and awaited its master's return.

## FIFTEEN: 3020 AD

Frog's rescue became high drama. Blake's crews reached him only after he had idled down and gone on intravenous and drugs in an extended, deep sleep free of the distress and pain of radiation sickness. He had emptied his oxygen tanks.

His rescuers had to tunnel under his crawler to reach his belly hatch. They found it fouled with splash scale. They stung a heated hose through his tractor skin into his oxy main. A couple of Blake hogs chipped the scale off his hatch. Others sprayed the tunnel walls with a quick-setting epoxy. They scabbed a pumper trunk over the tunnel mouth and flooded it with breathables.

They had to do it the hard way. Near the end, too pained to think straight, Frog had shed his hotsuit again. His stupidity came near costing him his life.

The expenses of the rescue came out of Blake's PR budget. The holonetnews snoops were on the scene, their cameras purring. The head office saw itself picking up a lot of cheap advertising. The name Blake Mining and Metals would get exposure all over Confederation.

Old Frog had gotten more than he had bargained for. He had not impressed just a little girl and the people of his home town. He was a seven-day news wonder Confederation-wide. His adventure was being broadcast live from Edgeward. Taping crews braved the Shadowline to get his rescue recorded for later broadcast.

He would have been amused and disgusted had he known about it. It was not quite the notoriety he had been seeking.

# SIXTEEN: 3031 AD

Mouse hovered on the fringes of Pollyanna's welcome-home party, attracted by the gaiety, repelled by Benjamin and Homer and what they had tried to do. Academy was all grey discipline and the absence of humor. He needed a little singing and dancing. The younger people were doing both, and building some mighty hangovers while they were at it.

Their elders frowned around the party's edges like thunderheads grumbling on grey horizons. Their faces were marked by an uneasiness bordering on dread. *They're standing there like brooding guardian idols in some Bronze Age temple,* Mouse thought. *Like the tongueless crows of doom.*

He tried to laugh at his own gloomy perception. His father's moods must be catching.

Storm, Cassius, and the other old ones had just come from a staff meeting. Mouse had not been permitted to attend. He guessed they had discussed the twins first.

There had been one hell of a traffic load through Instel Communications. Hawksblood had, apparently, been consulted. He could not guess what had been decided. Cassius had had only enough time to whisper the news that the cruiser had survived. Barely.

Then the Vice President for Procurement of Blake Mining and Metals, of Edgeward City on Blackworld, had made a contract presentation.

Mouse could guess the drift. Everyone had come from the meeting damp with apprehension. He could smell their anger and distress. Richard had not been understanding. Blake's man had tried a little arm-twisting.

A squeaky Dee-giggle rippled across the room. Good old Uncle Michael was the life of the party.

His loud, flashy presence was doing nothing for anybody's nerves. Amid the dour, ascetically clad soldiers he was a focus of peacock brightness, raucous as a macaw. At the moment he was a clown vainly trying for a laugh from his brother's staff. The sour, sullen, sometimes hateful, sometimes suspicious stares of Storm, Cassius, and Wulf and Helmut Darksword intimidated him not at all. Storm's sons he ignored completely, except for the occasional puzzled glance at Lucifer or Mouse.

Lucifer was more sour than his father. He moved with a stiff tension that bespoke rage under incomplete control. He watched Michael with deadly eyes. He snapped and snarled, threatening to go off like some unpredictable bomb. He should have been overjoyed to have his wife home.

Mouse's presence was a puzzling anomaly to everyone. He was enjoying their baffled reactions. They knew he was supposed to be at Academy. They knew that even midshipmen who were the sons of men as well known and respected as Gneaus Storm did not receive leave time without strings being pulled at stratospheric levels. Michael's nervous gaze returned to him again and again.

Dee was sharply observant behind his clown mask. His eyes never stopped roving. And Mouse seldom let his attention stray far from Dee.

Michael was worried.

Mouse sensed his uncle's nervousness. He felt a hundred other emotional eddies. He was enveloped by an oppressive sense of descending fate, as heavy as age itself.

Hatred for Michael Dee. Distrust of the Blake Vice President. Worry about Richard. Benjamin almost obsessive in his dread of what his father would do about his part in the attack on the Hawksblood cruiser. Lucifer, marginally psychotic, confusing his feelings about his wife, his father, Dee, Hawksblood, Benjamin, and distracted by suspicion, jealousy, and self-loathing. Homer… Homer was being Homer.

Mouse wondered if his father was making a mistake by letting Benjamin stew. Ben was not as well balanced as he liked to pretend. He had nightmares constantly. Now he seemed to be sliding into a daytime obsession with the dream.

Benjamin dreamed about his own death. For years he had laughed the dreams off. The attack on Hawksblood's ship seemed to have made a believer of him. He was running scared.

Mouse glanced at his brother. Benjamin never had taken him in. Ben was nothing but flashy façade. Mouse felt nothing but pity.

The brothers Darksword also had the disease of the moment. They were mad at everybody. Like Storm, they had expected The Broken Wings to be their last campaign. They had expected to live out their lives as gentlemen farmers on a remote, pastoral world far from the cares of the Iron Legion. They were overdue to leave the Fortress already, but ties two centuries deep had proven difficult to break.

Mouse looked at his father.

Storm had been motionless, brooding, for almost an hour. Now he was shaking like a big dog coming out of the water. He skewered the mining executive with a deadly glance. Mouse moved along the wall behind his father, the better to hear.

"We can buy a little time on this thing. Helmut. Wulf. Cassius."

Michael Dee appeared to lean slightly, to stretch an ear.

Storm said, "Kill the Blackworlder. Neatly. See that the corpse reaches Helga Dee. Without her knowing the source."

The condemned man was too stunned to protest.

"You did say Helga's World was mentioned in those papers Richard said he found, didn't you, Cassius?"

"Yes."

"And again on Michael's ship." Storm stared down at Michael Dee. One droplet of sweat rolled down Dee's temple. He looked a little pale.

Michael Dee was the financial power behind his daughter Helga, who managed that cold clerical principality called Festung Todesangst on Helga's World. He and his daughter had just been assigned a potentially embarrassing piece of property.

Mouse stared at his father's back. Not even he could so cold-bloodedly order a death!

"Blow Michael's ship, too," Storm ordered. "Make it look like Abhoussi got close enough for their fields to brush. Have Benjamin and Lucifer take care of it. It's time they paid their dues."

The brothers Darksword seized the executive's arms. They remained impassive as they marched the Blackworlder to his doom. They might have been two old gentlemen off for an afternoon stroll with a friend.

Mouse's guts twisted into a painful little knot.

Storm turned his back on Dee. He whispered, "Cassius, just confine him on one of the manned outstations. Officially, he never arrived. Pass the word."

"This won't buy more than a month," Cassius replied. "Richard is damned mad. And the Blake outfit is touchy about its people."

Mouse sighed. His father was not a monster after all.

"They'll be realistic. They want us bad. Let's stall and up their ante. I want a seat on their board and a percentage of their take on the Shadowline thing."

"You trying to price us out of the market?"

"I don't think I can. Keep an eye on the twins. We don't need any more of their crap."

"Uhn." Cassius followed the Darkswords and their victim.

Storm departed a moment later. He left his son Thurston, the warhounds, and the ravenshrikes to watch Michael Dee.

His eye narrowed in anger as he brushed by Mouse. He took a hitch-step, as if considering leaving his son with a few choice words about obedience. He changed his mind, resumed his angry stalk. Mouse's failure to return to Academy was the least of his problems.

Mouse sighed. There would be time for the idea to grow on his father. Time for Cassius to argue his case.

He watched his father leave, frowning. What now? Pollyanna had fled along that corridor a moment ago. Why would his father be following her?

# SEVENTEEN: 2844 AD

The old man's name was Jackson, but Deeth had to call him master. He was an outcast even among the descendants of escaped and discarded slaves. He lived in a fetid cave three miles from the animal village. He had parlayed a few sleight-of-hand tricks and a sketchy medical knowledge into a witch-doctor's career. His insane temper and magic were held in awe by his client-victims, who were an utterly mean, degenerate people themselves.

In less than a week Deeth knew that Jackson was a thorough fraud, that he was nothing but a lonely old man enraged by a world he believed had used him ill. His career was an attempt to get back. He was a sad, weak, pathetic creature, incontestably mad, and in his madness was utterly ruthless. Hardly a day passed when he did not torture Deeth for some fancied insult.

He brewed a foul grain beer in the rear of his cave. There were hundreds of gallons in storage or process. Deeth had to keep a full mug ready at all times. Inevitably, Jackson was partially drunk. That did nothing to dampen his free-wheeling temper. But what Deeth found most repulsive were Jackson's hygienic standards.

He came near retching often that first week. The old man refused to do more than stand and aim aside when he voided his bladder. He never bathed. The cave was more fetid than any animal's den.

He kept Deeth on a ten-foot leash knotted to choke at a tug. The boy soon learned that chokings had nothing to do with his efforts to please or displease. The old man yanked when he felt a need for amusement.

For him the sight of a small boy strangling was the height of entertainment.

Having identified a breakdown between cause and effect, Deeth abandoned efforts to satisfy Jackson. He did what he had to, and spent the rest of his time in sullen thought or quick theft.

Jackson made no effort to feed him. Indeed, he flew into a rage whenever he caught the boy pilfering from their meager larder. Nearly every meal cost Deeth a choking or beating.

He learned to endure in Jackson's cruel school. He began to learn the meaning of his father's and Rhafu's admonitions about taking the long view, about thinking before acting.

His initial lesson was the most painful, degrading, and effective. It came as the result of his first ill-considered attempt at flight, undertaken in sheer animal need to escape an intolerable situation.

His third night in the cave, after he had recovered from the immediate trauma of the station's destruction, but before he had become accustomed to maltreatment by the old man, he remained awake long after Jackson sent him whining to the moldy leaf pile designated as his bed. Jackson, seated in a rude homemade chair, drank and drank and eventually appeared to slip away into drunken sleep.

And Deeth waited, forcing himself to lie still despite a heart-pounding eagerness to be away. Hours trooped by in regiments. The last tiny flames of the cookfire died, leaving a small mound of nervously glowing embers.

He rose quickly, quietly, tried to untie the knot at his neck. His shaking fingers would not cooperate. He could not work a single loop of the tangle free. He crept softly to the old man's chair. The nether end of his leash was knotted around its leg.

The smaller knot, though only a simple clove hitch, defied him for several minutes. Jackson's proximity petrified him. His fingers became rigid, shaking prods.

He kept reminding himself that Rhafu had gone raiding at his age, that he was the first-born son of a Head, that he was heir-apparent to one of the oldest and greatest Families. He should have more courage than a common, possessionless Sangaree hireman. He made a litany of it, running it over and over in his mind.

On Homeworld he had been taught to give fear a concrete character, to make it an object to be fought. His choice of object was obvious. The old man was such a malign presence, so filled with evil promise…

The knot came free. He sprinted for the cave mouth. The rope trailed…

The loop around his throat jerked tight, cut off his wind, and snapped him to a halt. He went down, clawing wildly at his neck.

Jackson, good foot firm on the line, cackled madly. He seized a cane and began beating Deeth, pausing to jerk the neck loop tight whenever Deeth worked it loose enough to gasp.

Jackson's amusement and strength finally faded. He tied Deeth's wrists together and passed the rope through a natural grommet in the cave roof. Up the boy went.

He hung like a punching bag for two long days. Jackson subjected him to every torment his dim mind could imagine, including a foul wanting-to-be-loved, ineffectual homosexual pederasty. And through all those endless hours he whined, "Thought you'd leave poor old Jackson here alone, eh? You Sangaree whelp, don't you know you can't outwit a real man?"

Deeth was petrified. How could the old man know?

Eventually he would learn that Jackson was a reject slave who had understood his frightened outburst the night of his capture.

Through the pain and despair came the knowledge that he would have to degrade himself further to survive. He had to ingratiate himself lest the old man reveal his origins in the village.

When Jackson performed a kindness it was for profit or by oversight. Whichever applied, he never mentioned Deeth's background.

Hanging, aching, despairing, Deeth had time to reflect on the teachings of his elders. He began to understand the meaning of patience.

The old man did not break him. Maybe Deeth did not crack because the idea was too alien. He could not do what he did not know how to do.

On Homeworld they had a saying, "He's Sangaree." It meant, "He's a real man," only more so. It had overtones of unyielding determination and absolute inflexibility.

Deeth was Sangaree.

The old man tired of abusing him. He let Deeth down, seized him by the hair, hurled him into his pile of leaves. After an admonitory cane whack he bound Deeth's hands behind him and secured the nether end of the rope to the grommet, above Deeth's reach. Then he resumed his residence in his chair, chuckling into his filthy beard.

Deeth lay awake night after night, nursing his hatred and wounded ego. He nurtured his patience and determination to have his revenge.

# EIGHTEEN: 3031 AD

"Gneaus!" Pollyanna spoke his name breathily. "You've been avoiding me."

"Not really. I've had work to do."

Every curve of the woman, every patch of soft, smooth skin, bespoke sexual craving. She had that look of constant need seen only in young women in love and the most polished of prostitutes. Like the hookers', her eyes became vacant, cool, and snakelike when she was off stage. She posed, one hip thrown out model fashion. Her breath came in quick little gasps.

He was not playing the game today. "I want to hear all about your travels, little lady." He opened the door to her apartment. She tried the close, casual brush-past going in. He answered it with deliberate chill. A ghost of apprehension crossed her too beautiful face.

She pushed herself at him as soon as he shut the door.

Her pelvis moved against him. "I missed you. All of you. And the Fortress. But especially you, Gneaus. Nobody makes me feel the way you do."

"Sit down," he ordered. She backed away, more apprehensive. "Let's hear the story."

There were few men Pollyanna could not bedazzle and manipulate. Hawksblood. Cassius, who made her blood run chill. The Darkswords. And, she had learned the hard way, Michael Dee. But Storm… He had always been so amenable. He must have been using her when she thought she was using him. Her ego was bruised and aching from traveling with Dee. It was not ready for another blow.

Storm was positively grim.

These invulnerables were all old, old men from whom time and experience had leached all innocence, had abraded all boyish vulnerability. There was a darkness in them, a capital wickedness. It called out to the darknesses in her own soul. Their black flames reached out and pulled her like a candle pulled a moth. She was afraid.

"I didn't mean for anybody to get hurt, Gneaus! Honest. I just wanted to meet Richard Hawksblood."

"This is no nursery school, Pollyanna. This isn't polite society. We play by the rough rules. We had trouble enough without your meddling. Your actions can't be separated from ours. You're family. Richard won't grant you absolution because you're a nitwit. You've caused deaths that can't be recalled. Death breeds death. God only knows how many men are going to die because of you."

It was his fault too, he knew. He should have written her off. He should not have tracked Michael to The Big Rock Candy Mountain. But similar logic could be used to assign blame to Michael, Richard, and Lucifer. No, primary responsibility had to remain Pollyanna's. Hers had been the initiating decision.

"Tell me everything, Pollyanna. I don't want anything added. I don't want anything left out. I don't want you adjusting anything to make yourself look a little better. I just want straight facts. I want, verbatim, including descriptions of tones of voice and expressions, everything you heard discussed. Especially between Richard and Michael, and anybody they talked with. About anything. There's just a ghost of a chance we can still get out of this, or at least tone it down."

"That would take hours." She turned on the tears. Storm ignored them. Pollyanna interacted with reality through a studied repertoire of poses and roles. The real Miss Eight hid out somewhere way off stage, directing the play, pushing the buttons for whatever response seemed appropriate.

"I've bought time." The stricken face of the Blackworlder ghosted through his thoughts. The man had not doubted his fate for one instant. "I need to buy more."

She turned the tears off as quickly as she had switched them on. She began talking in a small, soft voice devoid of editorialization and emotion. She began at the beginning and told nothing but the bitter truth about everything except her motives.

She had seduced Dee and talked him into taking her to Old Earth with him. She now believed he had acquiesced for his own reasons. Their stay on the mother-world had been dull. The one thing that had impressed her had been the poverty of that gutted, overcrowded planet. Michael had been upset because the holonets had not been interested in his coverage of the action on The Broken Wings.

"From Old Earth we went to Blackworld. He kept me locked in the ship while we were there. The only reason I found out was he talked in his sleep. He wouldn't say squat when he was awake. He was worried and scared. Things weren't going right, somehow. He was a little paranoid, like he was afraid somebody might be after him but he wasn't really sure. After Blackworld we went to see Richard Hawksblood. He isn't such a big deal in person, is he?"

She had not been allowed to approach Dee and Hawksblood most of the time. She did know they were talking about Blackworld. What little she knew she had learned from Richard's underlings.

Then Michael had vanished. No one knew where he had gone. Some thought Tregorgarth, some thought The Big Rock Candy Mountain.

"It was The Mountain, Polly. Go ahead. You're doing great so far."

"I had to hang around and wait. It was boring. I hardly ever saw Hawksblood. He was working on the Blackworld project. I never realized how complicated your work is. You don't just jump in the ring like a boxer, do you?"

Storm smiled the weakest of smiles. If nothing else, Pollyanna had confirmed his intelligence about Richard. Hawksblood was in on Blackworld for sure.

"It was two months before Michael came back. That was a couple of weeks ago. He was really happy. Before, when his tapes were turned down and he thought somebody was after him, you couldn't hardly live with him. All he said was that he saw the man and everything was all right. He wouldn't even talk in his sleep."

Who? Storm wondered. Not him. Who else had been on The Big Rock Candy Mountain? Why had Michael been there, anyway?

"He was back about a week when he grabbed me and that yacht and took off for here. Every couple of days he locked me out of Command. Whenever he let me back in the instel set was warm. I don't know who he was talking to. Then we got here. And the rest you know."

And the rest he knew.

He checked the time. Her tale had taken an hour to tell. He had a few questions. He doubted she could answer them.

Pollyanna, he thought, was one hell of a puzzle. She was all surface and no depth. Even when you bedded a stranger she took on some kind of shape as bits and pieces of bed talk jigsawed together. But not pretty Pollyanna. She remained strictly one-dimensional. Her only real attributes seemed to be her beauty and her vagina, and her devotion to both. She had rebuilt her makeup while she talked.

She was a damned android built for modeling and screwing! You could penetrate her body, but not her façade.

Even Lucifer was baffled by her. She seemed to exist solely to be appreciated for her beauty, like a classic painting or cherished poem. Curious.

He had not thought much about Pollyanna before. She was like that painting. There to be enjoyed and otherwise ignored. It was time to start poking around, back in the silly shadows.

He would have to unravel her by reversing the usual process, by what he did not know.

Pollyanna had made a second point clear. The Blackworld affair was deeper than he had suspected. A potential mercantile war over trillions worth of radioactives did not excite Michael. Pollyanna said he seemed indifferent to the opportunity to tape the conflict. It was important to him for some other reason.

It had to be the Game.

That was Dee's label for the feud he had been engineering between Hawksblood and Storm. He did not know Storm knew that. The Game's goal appeared to be mutual annihilation. It had been going on since the founding of the two freecorps.

Storm still could not understand why.

He bullied Pollyanna. "Who did Michael see on The Big Rock Candy Mountain? Why?" The answer had to be important.

Pollyanna did not have it.

"Ah, damn. Damn." He let her kiss him once, then gently disengaged and departed. He returned to his study, put Cassius on call, and turned to Ecclesiastes. He found no solace there. The frenetic, helter-skelter flitting of his mind kept him from following the printed words. He tried the clarinet.

The soul-trying days had come.

Cassius listened without being noticed. "I've never heard you play so mournfully, Gneaus," he said.

Startled, Storm replied, "It's a dirge. I think we've reached the end. I grilled Pollyanna. She's a good observer. You wouldn't figure it considering how vacuum-brained she acts."

"I've sometimes wondered about that."

"You too? Then it's not my imagination. Could anybody be that shallow without working at it?"

"Possibly. Then again, a preoccupation with sexual encounter would make a mask few men, being egoists, would care to lift. You wanted me?"

Storm made a mental note to ask Frieda and his daughter for the woman's view of Miss Eight. "We're getting old, you and I. We're in our sundown days. Things are slipping past us. It's like we're caught in some backwater of time."

Cassius raised an eyebrow. Storm had difficulty expressing his feelings.

"We're on the verge of the nightfall of the Legion. Maybe of all the freecorps. I think we'll be both cause and effect of our own destruction, and I can't see any way out."

"As long as there are corporations and rich men who need us, and who won't be intimidated by the government, there'll be work for us."

"Time's catching up with us. Confederation is starting to flex its muscles. It's a historical process. It's inevitable. Democratic control and government regulation are coming on faster than the frontiers are moving out. They're about to catch up with us."

"You're too much the pessimist."

"Consider the past, Cassius. The block vote of pestholes like Old Earth will devour the capital approach. It's an old story. Goes all the way back to Rome. Why do something for yourself if all you have to do is vote for a guy who'll rob somebody else and do it for you?"

Storm's bitterness surprised him. He had not been aware of the strength of his own feelings.

He told Cassius what he had learned from Pollyanna.

"What do you suggest we do?"

"First, secure Dee here. Things will move slower if he's tied down. Have Thurston handle that. He doesn't have the imagination to be taken in by Michael. You go to The Mountain. Take Mouse. You won't send him back to Academy, and you tell me he's interested in intelligence work. The two of you, find out who Michael met there. Keep an eye out for Seth-Infinite."

"You're softer than you pretend, my friend."

Storm shrugged. "Ship him home if he gets in the way. Tell Wulf and Helmut to start getting ready for Blackworld."

"Why?"

"Looks like we'll end up there, like it or not. We ought to be in shape. Oh. Have the older sergeants think up jobs for Benjamin and Homer. We've got to keep them out of trouble. Lucifer I want to backtrack his damned bubble-brained wife. All the way to the place where she was born. Got it?"

"Got it. I take it you won't be here yourself."

"No. I'll rendezvous with you on your way back from The Mountain." He glanced around, half expecting to see Michael crouching in a shadow. "Where we keep Fearchild. I want to ask him a question."

"Where're you going?"

"Festung Todesangst," Storm murmured. "It was the only clue in Michael's papers. Pollyanna mentioned it. So did Richard."

By the raising of an eyebrow Cassius registered as much emotion as he ever did. "To the lion's den. To see Valerie? Or Helga herself?"

"Valerie. Michael will be using the facilities for all they're worth. And she will make sure Valerie handles the work. Valerie might know what's going on."

"I shouldn't presume… Nevertheless… Gneaus, it's too damned dangerous. If she lays hands on you…"

"I'm aware of the danger. But I have my edge. She doesn't expect me. There's an unmonitored landing pad near an out-of-the-way entry lock. I have her recognition codes. I spent a fortune arranging this way in back when they were building the place."

"Gneaus, I don't think…"

"You can't talk me out of it, Cassius. It's got to be done. Let's get on with it. Let's both go and get back before anybody misses us. We can't control Michael forever even if we chain him to a wall."

"I'm on my way."

Storm sequestered himself with the things he loved, strolling around his study, gently touching this or that, remembering, reaching out after timeworn feelings he had almost forgotten. He and Cassius, they were not emotionally normal.

Too many hard decisions, too many cruel losses, had turned them into calloused, indifferent men.

He worried about the young ones. Mouse especially. Would they follow the same doomed path? He hoped not.

His study tour was not a habitual practice. It reflected his appreciation of the dangers of Helga's World, and his uncertainty about his ability to get out again. "The risk has to be taken," he growled. "The thing has to be tried. The key is there somewhere. If it's anywhere."

He spent a few minutes with his wife, then collected equipment he had kept ready since the construction of Festung Todesangst. He said no good-byes.

Cassius would know what to do if he did not come back.

# NINETEEN: 3020 AD

Frog wakened in the Corporation hospital. Three faces hovered over him. One belonged to a Blake medic with whom he had dealt before. Smythe wasn't bad for a Corporation flunky. Another was a small white face with vulpine features and hungry eyes. He did not know the man. The third was Moira. Pretty little Moira. He tried to smile.

There were no officials around. He was surprised when his sluggish mind noted their absence.

He came up cussing like a stuttering Arab. He got his tongue under control, snarled, "Get the hell out of here, Smythe. I been getting away with it fifty years. Blake ain't going to break me with no phony medical bill."

"On the house, Frog."

"On the house, my ruddy red rectum. Blake don't give away no fourth-hand condom." He glanced at Moira, prim and blondly angelic, trying not to squirm worriedly on a hard chair. He misinterpreted her concern as embarrassment. He flashed her a weak grin. "We argue about it later."

He glared at Foxface. The man had perched on a low dresser, one foot on the floor. "Who the hell you be, guy?"

"August Plainfield. Stimpson-Hrabosky News. Pool man assigned to cover you here."

"Uhn?" He got a bad odor from the newshawk. Vulture-reek, maybe. His breed wallowed in it wherever there was human carrion.

He looked at Moira again. She looked anxious, frightened, and tired. Just the worry? Or the holonet people giving her hell?

He was no fan but he had watched enough HV to know the netmen pursued their stories ruthlessly, with a singleminded inhumanity.

He had half feared he would stir them up with his stunt, but had not foreseen that they would go after Moira. He had rehearsed a few choice lines for them. But Moira… She was a baby. She could not handle the pressure.

What did a child's comfort matter to a vulture like Plainfield? His kind saw everyone and everything as fodder for the camera-cannon they used to down the prey they fed their monster audience.

"Moira, you go outside a minute. I got a word to say to this critter." Pain was not making him feel reasonable. He was sure that Smythe, who had gone next door to check his metabolic monitors, was in a dither. The Doc was all right, but he took things too serious.

Hell, let him stew.

Moira crawled off her chair and left without a word. In her public reticence, and other ways, she was aping him. It was her way of showing affection. Frog found it disconcerting. Like so many men who maintain a tight rein on emotion, Frog longed for its expression in others. It provided him an excuse for opening a little himself. And it terrified him. He might get trapped into exposing an Achilles' heel of self.

He used some of his choice words on the newsman.

Then a few more, bloody-minded, colorful, and threatening. Plainfield endured them like a mountain weathering another of countless storms fated to lash its slopes.

"What did you find out there?" he asked when Frog ran down.

"Huh? Find? Nothing. More Shadowline. More Brightside. And if I did find something, I wouldn't tell no creepo like you."

"Thought so. You rambled a lot while you were under. About the yellow, the orange. Dreaming, Doctor Smythe thinks. I've got a notion you weren't. Dreams don't leave men radiation sick. Yellow has meant radioactivity for a thousand years."

Frog's face wrinkled in a frown so deep that for a moment he resembled a dark-eyed prune. "I don't remember so good. Oxygen starvation do things to your brain. Check my log." He smirked. Plainfield was not going to get near his rig till Blake's people checked it out. They might not bring it in for years.

"I did. I didn't find anything. In fact, I found so much nothing that it made me curious. Made me wonder why a man would tell his computer to forget a place that left him half dead of radiation poisoning. Made me wonder why a man would take the trouble to register a formal claim on the shade at the end of the Shadowline when he thinks he's dying. When he's never filed a claim before. And it made me wonder why he revised his will the minute the claim was notarized."

"I want to be buried out there," Frog improvised. "Somebody's going to do it again someday. I want him to bury my ashes on the only claim I ever had."

"Your diction and syntax are improving." Plainfield smiled a smile that made him appear more wolf than fox. "You may be telling the truth. Corporation people who think they know 'that crazy dwarf' figure it's something like that. Or think you're rigging a scheme to get them to throw money down a rathole in some cockamamie revenge. I don't suffer their preconceptions. I don't know you. I just know people. I think you found something."

"Just a place to be buried," Frog insisted nervously. This interrogation was not his idea of an interview.

Plainfield's smile broadened. "You might get there quicker than you want. El Dorados, dreams that come true, they have a way of devouring their dreamers."

"What the hell kind of newsman are you, anyway?" Frog was so nervous his customary act was slipping.

"Call me a dream shaper. I make fantasies come true. Mostly my own, but sometimes other people's, too. Those sometimes turn out to be nightmares."

Frog stopped being nervous and started being scared. He looked around for a weapon.

He was in over his head. Bluster was useless, and his condition denied him his customary alternative, attack.

Frustration kindled anger. Hadn't his flesh always betrayed his spirit? Hadn't he always been just a little too short, too small, or too weak? Why wasn't somebody from Blake doing the questioning?

"Why'd you do it, anyway? I mean, make the run. Reasons after the fact could be supplied, I suppose, but I want to know what makes a man try something impossible in the first place. I've studied everything known about Brightside and the Shadowline. There's no way you could have known that you'd find anything out there."

What *does* make a man throw himself into something for which there is neither a reasonable nor rational justification? Frog had done a lot of thinking during his ran. Not once, even remotely, had he been able to make his motives add up. Most of the time he had told himself that he was doing it for Moira, but there had been times whan he had suspected that he was doing it for Frog, to salve a scarred ego by showing humanity it was wrong about his being a clown. Yet that had not taken into account the probability of failure, which would have done nothing but underscore his foolishness.

Why, then? A badfinger for Blake? Because he had had some crazy, deep-down conviction that he would find something? No. Not one of those reasons was good enough in itself.

All that time alone and still he had not figured himself out.

Thr man who hides from himself hides best of all.

"What did you find?"

Frog strove to focus on Plainfield. And realized that his earlier assessments were incorrect. The man was neither vulture, fox, nor wolf. He was a snake. Cold-blooded, emotionless, deadly. Predatory, and unacquainted with mercy. Nor was he owned. This news business was cover. He was a dagger in his own hand.

Plainfield moved toward him. A slap hypo appeared in his palm. Frog struggled weakly. The hypo hit his arm.

*Wrong again,* he thought. *He's worse than a snake. He's a human.*

"What did you find?"

Frog knew he would not make it this time. This man, this *thing* that called itself August Plainfield and pretended to be a newsman, was going to strip him of his victory, then kill him. Even God in heaven could not stop him from talking once the drug took hold, and then what value would he have alive?

Frog talked. And talked. And, as he knew he must, he died. But before he did, and while he was still sufficiently in possession of his senses to understand, another man entered the dark door before him.

Smythe burst into the room, alerted by his monitors. Moira trailed him as if attached by a short chain. The doctor charged Plainfield, opening his mouth to shout.

A small, silent palm weapon ruined Smythe's heart before any sound left his lips. Moira, as if on a puppeteer's strings, jerked back out of the room. Plainfield cursed but did not pursue her.

A sadness overwhelmed Frog, both for himself and for Smythe.

On Blackworld, as on all but a few worlds, the dead never saw resurrection. Even the Blakes remained dead when they died. Resurrection was too expensive, too difficult, and too complex in social implication. And why bother? Human numbers made life a cheap commodity.

Plainfield finished with Frog, then disappeared. The murders went on record as unsolved. Corporation police hunted the newsman, but no trace turned up.

They wanted him for theft. They wanted him for destruction of municipal and Corporate property. They wanted him for suborning municipal and Corporate employees. They wanted him for a list of crimes. But most of all they wanted him because of Frog and Smythe.

Blake had a long, long memory.

Stimpson-Hrabosky News denied ever having heard of Plainfield. How, then, Blake's cops demanded, had the man reached Blackworld in a Stimpson-Hrabosky charter? How, if he was an unknown, had he managed to get himself elected pool man?

Stimpson-Hrabosky responded with almost contemptuous silence.

Their reticence was itself informative. Plainfield obviously carried a lot of weight outside.

In the furor of pursuit the killer's motives became obscured. Only a handful of men knew about Frog's claim and will, and they were the men Plainfield had bribed. They were on trial and no one was listening to them. They were sent into exile, which meant that they were given outsuits and put out of the city locks to survive as best they could.

Blake reasserted its contention that it never left a debt outstanding, though it might take a generation to repay.

Frog's original will left Moira more than anyone had anticipated. It set up a trust that assured her a place in Edgeward's life.

And life went on.

# TWENTY: 3052 AD

We were not a cuddly, loving family, but we had our moments. Most of them were a little bizarre.

—Masato Igarashi Storm

# TWENTY-ONE: 3031 AD

The Faceless Man smiled and reached out to Benjamin. He wore nothing. He had no hair, no sex. Benjamin cowered, whimpering. The Faceless Man came toward him with a steady, confident step.

Benjamin whirled with a weak wail, ran. The gooey street grabbed at his feet. He pumped his legs with everything he had, yet they barely moved, pistoning in slowed motion.

The streets and walls of the city were a uniform, blinding white. The buildings had no windows. The doors were almost imperceptible. He flitted from one to another, pounding, crying, "Help me!"

No one answered.

He looked back. The Faceless Man followed him with that smile and confident stride, hand outreaching, his pace no greater than before.

Benjamin fled again, along the molasses street.

Now they opened their little peepholes when he pounded. They looked out and laughed. He flung himself from door to door. The laughter built into a chorus.

His tears flowed. Sweat poured off him. He shuddered constantly. His body ached with his exertion.

He looked back. The Faceless Man was at exactly the same distance, walking steadily, hand outstretched.

He ran in a straight line, trying to gain ground. They laughed at him from the rooftops. They called his name, "Benjamin! Benjamin!" in a feral chant. "Run, little Benjamin, run."

He gasped around a corner into a cul-de-sac. He moaned in terror, whirled, and… The Faceless Man was coming to him, reaching.

He threw himself against the walls. He tried to find a foothold, a way to scale their ivory slickness. "Please! Please don't!"

A hand touched his shoulder. The palm and fingers were icy. Thumb and forefinger squeezed together. Fire lanced through his muscles.

He spun and flung himself at the Faceless Man, clamping his fingers around the throat beneath the unyielding smile.

An unseen hand slapped his face, back and forth, back and forth. He did not relax his grip. A tiny fist began pounding his nose and cheeks.

The real pain reached through his terror. He shook all over, like an epileptic in the first second of seizure.

His eyelids rose. He stared into Pollyanna's terrified face. His hands were at her throat. Her bed was a sweat-soaked disaster. She had scratches on her face and marks on her throat that would become bruises. She kept punching weakly.

He yanked the offending hands away. "Oh, Christ!" he murmured. "Oh, Holy Christ!" He slithered back out of the bed, stood over her for a moment. The shaking would not stop. The layer of sweat covering him was chilling him. He seized a robe. It did nothing to warm him.

"Polly, Honey. Polly. I'm sorry. Are you all right? It was the nightmare… It was worse than I ever had it. He caught me this time. I'm sorry. I thought I was fighting him. Are you all right? Can I get you anything?" He could not stop talking.

His heart hammered. The fear would not go away. He almost expected the Faceless Man to step into the apartment.

Pollyanna nodded. "Water," she croaked.

He crossed to her bathroom, found a glass, tried to fill it. He dropped it twice before getting it to her half full.

She had hitched herself up in bed. She was rubbing her throat with one hand while staring at him timorously. She accepted the glass. "You need help," she whispered. "No! Stay away."

"That's the dream… I run through these streets yelling for help and they all laugh at me. And he keeps on coming… He caught me this time. Polly, I don't know what it means. I'm scared. Honey, please don't pull away. I'm all right now. I didn't mean to hurt you. I thought I was fighting him."

Pollyanna relaxed, but not much. She edged away whenever he eased nearer, trying to draw comfort from her proximity and warmth.

"Polly, please…"

The apartment door opened.

It was night in the Fortress of Iron. The hall lights had been dimmed. They saw only the silhouette of a man standing with feet widespread and arms crossed. Anger radiated from him.

Lucifer, voice pitched an octave high, squealed, "You slut! You unholy slut! With my own goddamned brother!"

He flung himself into the room. The light of the bedside lamp caught his face. It was the face of a killer. He seized Pollyanna's arm and jerked her to her feet, hit her once in the gut, doubled her over. He planted another on her chin. He was swinging hard. Benjamin oofed when his brother's fist cracked the second time. He thought Lucifer had broken her jaw.

Lucifer broke his hand. He let out a little mewl of surprise and pain and looked at the fist, puzzled.

Benjamin reached Lucifer, hurled him away from Pollyanna. Lucifer stumbled over a chair and went down. He came up cursing. "You bastard. You leave my wife alone. I'll kill you." He charged Benjamin. His good hand clutched a knife.

Someone looked in the door, stared momentarily, then ran away.

Baffled and frightened, Benjamin crouched, waited. He blocked the knife stroke, punched Lucifer, tried for a grip on Lucifer's wrist above the blade. Lucifer danced back, crouched himself.

They had been taught in their father's schools. They were proficient killers. An uninvolved observer would have considered it an interesting match.

Lucifer feinted, feinted, stabbed. Benjamin slid aside, chopped down at the blade. It was not where he expected it to be. It drew a fine line of blood from the skin of his thigh as it withdrew.

"I'll take care of that," Lucifer snarled, nodding at his brother's groin. "You won't be bedding anyone's wife. Not even your own, you arrogant, pretty bastard." He circled. Sweating, Benjamin waited.

He kicked a pillow at his brother's face. Lucifer leaned out of the way, moved in.

A blast of icy water hit him, hurled him across the room. Benjamin turned. The water hit like the pummeling of a hundred fists. It drove him against a wall. "Stop it, goddamnit!" he raged.

The water stopped.

Two Legionnaires stood in the doorway, holding a fire hose. Frieda Storm pushed past them, her face aquiver with anger. She looked every bit as daunting as her father, Cassius. "Benjamin. Get your clothes on. Woman. You too. Lucifer. On your feet. Now!" She kicked him. It was no delicate female toe tap.

She did not ask what had happened. That was obvious.

"What the hell is the matter with you?" she demanded of Benjamin. "There a suicidal streak in you? First that crap with Richard's cruiser, now this."

"Mother, I..."

"Homer did it. Yes. And who's responsible for Homer? Who let him do it? Heinrich, take Lucifer to Medical. There's something wrong with his hand." She moved toward Pollyanna. The girl was getting dressed so fast she kept getting snaps lined up wrong. Frieda grabbed her chin, turned her head one way, then the other. Pollyanna avoided her eyes. "What happened to your throat?"

"I did it," Benjamin murmured.

"What did you say?"

"I did it, Mother. I had the dream... This time he caught me. I was fighting him."

Frieda's face changed slightly. It was not a softening, just a momentary shadow of fear. "I'll have to talk to Madame Endor. Get a new reading. She was afraid this would happen."

"Mother..."

"Benjamin, don't you have any decency? Don't you have any common sense? This is your brother's wife. This is your brother's home. Shut up! I know she's a damned public utility. I know that anybody who asks gets. You should have brains enough not to ask. You should, for Christ's sake, have brains enough to realize that he'd want to see her tonight. He's leaving the Fortress tomorrow."

"Leaving? I didn't know..."

"My father wants him to do something. If you paid attention to anything but your own precious self..." She turned to Pollyanna, "Get this place cleaned up. I'll send someone to help. And be warned. I'm taking this up with my husband when he gets back. Benjamin." She took his hand. "Come on."

Once in the citadel of her own apartment Frieda clutched him close, and whispered, exasperated, "Ben, darling boy, why do you do these things? I just can't keep getting you out of trouble. Your father is going to throw a bearing when he hears about this."

"Mother..."

"He'll hear about it. It'll be all over the Fortress tomorrow, for God's sake. Ben, stay away from her. She's like a cat in heat. She doesn't care."

"Mother..."

"Sit down. There. Good. I want you to think now, Ben. Really think. About you. About that woman. About Lucifer. About what all is happening here. The problems your father and grandfather have. And most of all, about Michael Dee. Michael Dee is here, Ben. Did you bother to wonder why? There's a reason. He doesn't do anything without a sneaky reason. And your father and grandfather made the mistake of leaving while he's here."

"Mother..."

"Don't move. Don't talk. Just think. I'll make you a drink."

She did, and while he nursed it she made comm calls. First she spoke with Madame Endor, the occultist she had imported from New Earth. It was a long conversation. She ended it wearing a pale face.

She placed the second call to the armory, waking the chief armorer. She ordered him to provide Benjamin with one of the lightweight weapon-proof "undersuits" Interstellar Technics had been trying to peddle to her husband for wear under ordinary garments.

"I don't care if we haven't bought them, Captain. I'll pay for it myself if the Legion won't. And make the modifications. He'll be down for his fitting in the morning." She ended the call angrily.

She went over and sat opposite her son, stared at him till he looked up and asked, "You called Madame Endor, didn't you?"

She nodded.

"About the dream? What did she say?" Frieda did not respond. "Was it bad?"

"Ben, first thing tomorrow I want you to go to the armory. Captain Fergus will fit you with one of the ITI personal suits."

"Mother..."

"Do it, Benjamin."

"Mother..."

"I mean it, Benjamin."

He sighed.

The fear hit him. It was the first time it had come while he was awake. Involuntarily, he looked back to see how close the Faceless Man had come.

# TWENTY-TWO: 2844-2845 AD

The Sangaree facility for bearing hatred like a torch against the night sustained Deeth throughout the grim months of his captivity. Jackson sometimes came close to crushing him, and assumed he had, but always, way back behind the meek exterior he adopted as protective coloration, Deeth nurtured his hatred. He thought, planned, and schooled his patience.

A week after his attempted escape Jackson took him to the village. The visit shook him more than had the old man's knowledge of his racial identity.

The village itself met his expectations. It consisted of a dozen filthy, primitive huts. The villagers were semi-nomadic hunters and gatherers. There were a hundred of them, ranging from numerous children to a handful of old folks.

The chieftain was about thirty Prefactlas years of age. That was barely adult by civilized standards. Here he was an elder. Life in the forest was brief and brutal.

About thirty Norbon workers and breeder fugitives had reached the village. Their condition astounded Deeth.

The wild animals were using their cousins as slaves, and far more cruelly than had the Norbon. The villagers were still exchanging jests about their gullibility.

Deeth followed Jackson as he went from house to house in search of patients. He saw Norbon animals being mistreated everywhere. There was a girl, no older than he, who had been confined in a storage pit for spurning the chieftain. There was a field hand nailed to a rude cross, moaning and coughing up blood. He had fought back. There was a corpse in the square, rotting away. Insects masked it. The man had been roasted alive.

Deeth's stomach churned all day. How could these beasts use their own kind so cruelly? They had no reason.

Was this why his elders held the human species in such contempt?

Jackson had done him an accidental kindness by frustrating his escape. He could have stumbled into something worse.

Jackson used steaming, fetid poultices to treat a growth on the chieftain's neck. Deeth squatted in the dust outside, beside the pit holding the girl. She hid in shadows and tangled, blood-caked, once-blonde hair. Her shoulders were scabby ruins. A cloud of insects surrounded her. She looked like one of the Nordic pleasure girls, a cheap, mass-market product.

There was a steady demand for Nordics. The Norbon raised them real-time. The Family had a good strain.

The Norbon claimed several excellent pleasure strains. Coffee Mulatto Number Three regularly placed in the shows.

Deeth shrugged. That was another reality, a billion light-years away and a thousand years ago. It was another Deeth who had learned pride in Family achievement.

"You," he grunted.

She did not respond. He kept squatting there. The sun crept across the sky, sliding his shadow across her. He felt her growing curiosity.

She glanced up, saw the rope around his throat. Fear and hope crossed her battered face.

Deeth did not recognize her. Clearly, she knew him. He smiled reassuringly.

He felt the caress of compassion, a gnarly, knobbly sort that had its roots more in classroom training than genuine emotion. He had been taught to cherish and maintain Family property. Abuse and waste were sins. Homeworld was a sometimes harsh, always poor planet. Its values and institutions were geared to conservation.

He could order a thousand slaves killed without a touch of conscience if there was a compelling need. He could not waste one, or destroy it out of malice. He could not abide waste or malice in others.

That was fitting in a Head.

He was the senior Norbon on Prefactlas now. The welfare and conservation of Norbon properties were his responsibility.

"Be patient, girl," he whispered. "Endure. We'll create our own good luck."

He felt foolish. His promise was meaningless. He was powerless to hurt or help. What would his father have done? Or Rhafu?

The same. Endure. Take care of their own.

An animal came howling into the village. He pointed behind him. The empty square filled. Animals hustled their valuables, especially the new slaves, into places of hiding. Bows and spears appeared.

Jackson grabbed Deeth's rope and fled. The old man cursed softly and continuously.

A pair of Marine personnel carriers clanked into the village from the far side. A support ship whickered over, hovered above the square. There were shouts and explosions. They faded as the old man kept putting distance behind them.

Were they looking for him? Deeth wondered. Did they know about his escape? He hoped not. Sant spare him, they would hunt till they got him. Humans were singleminded that way.

They reached the cave. Jackson beat him as though he were responsible for the raid.

He endured.

Months groaned by. Each staggered on like a wounded leviathan.

Deeth spent three-quarters of a Prefactlas year as Jackson's slave. They made weekly trips to the village. The animals had stayed put since the raid. They were afraid to migrate. Stronger tribes might prey upon them.

The slave girl Emily was the only Norbon animal not recovered by the Marines. Deeth visited with her whenever he had a chance. He kept repeating his promise of rescue.

He added the obligation to his hatred. Together they sustained him.

# TWENTY-THREE: 3031 AD

In 3031 the dead did not always stay down.

Human brains were in demand in an exploding cryocyborgic data-processing industry. Personality-scrubbed and inplugged to computation and data-storage systems, a few kilos of human nervous tissue could replace tons of specialized control and volitional systems.

No remedy for degradation in nervous tissue had yet been found. The cryocyborgic environment sometimes accelerated decay.

Nerve life had become the practical span limit for men like Gneaus Storm, who had power, money, and access to the finest rejuvenation and resurrection technology.

The number of brains available for cryocyborging never filled demand. The shortfall was filled in a variety of ways. Old Earth sold the brains of criminals in exchange for hard outworlds currency. A few were available through underworld channels. The bulk came of involuntary salvage.

There were a dozen entrepreneurs who jackaled around the edges of disasters and armed conflicts, snapping up loose bodies to resell organs. Confederation's armed forces often left their lower grade enlisted men where they fell. The soldiers themselves were indifferent to the fate of their corpses. Most were desperate men willing to risk anything to earn a long retirement outside the slums of their birth.

Gneaus Storm's agents dogged the service battlegrounds too, selecting men who had died well. Cryonically preserved, they were revived later and asked to join the Legion.

Most accepted with a childlike gratitude. A rise from a slum to the imaginary glory and high life of the Iron Legion, after having escaped the Reaper by Storm's grace, seemed an elevation to paradise. The holonets called them the Legion of the Dead.

Helga Dee used hundreds of scavenged brains in her business. Only the Dees themselves knew the capacity of her Helga's World "information warehouse." Publicly, Helga admitted only to capabilities in keeping with brain acquisitions that were a matter of public record.

Storm was sure she controlled a capacity twice what she admitted.

Helga's World was a dead planet. The human contagion had touched it only once, to create and occupy the vast installation called Festung Todesangst. The heart of Helga's far-reaching Corporation lay there, deep beneath the surface of that remote rock cold in the claws of entropy, orbiting a dying star. No one went in but family, the dead, and that occasional person the Dees wanted to disappear. No one came out but Dees.

The defenses at Festung Todesangst were legend. They were as quirky and perverse as Helga herself.

Men who went down to Helga's World were like last year's mayflies: gone forever. And Gneaus Storm meant to penetrate that ice-masked hell hole.

He did not expect Helga to welcome him. She hated him with a hatred archetypal in its depth and fury. Michael's children all hated Storm. Each had compelled him to recognize his or her existence and respond. His crime was that he had come out on top every time.

The Dee offspring were worse than their father.

Fearchild had raised his fuss, costing Cassius a hand. Storm and Cassius now kept him confined in a place only they knew. He was a hostage guaranteeing restraint by the others. The Dees were, unfortunately, all irrational, passionate people, apt to forget in heated moments.

Helga had tried to avenge Fearchild by capturing Storm's daughter Valerie and using her as part of Festung Todesangst.

Storm's response had been to capture Helga and deliver her to her own fortress so badly mauled that she had been able to survive only by cyborging in to her own machines. Forever damned to a mechanical half-life, she calculated and brooded and awaited a day when she could requite his cruelties.

Seth-Infinite, too, had given frequent offense. He seemed to be everywhere and nowhere, appearing openly some place like Luna Command, then disappearing before the swiftest hunters closed in. Half the things he did were nose-thumbings at the Storms. Like his father, he was slippery, and he always had several schemes in the air. Like Michael, he did nothing for a simple, linear reason.

It would be a fine, serendipitous thing, Storm reflected, if Cassius surprised Seth-Infinite on The Mountain.

# TWENTY-FOUR: 2354-3031 AD

Michael Dee's moments of happiness were tiny islands scattered in a vast sea. His life was a swift one. He had so much in the air that, when he found time to look around, he seemed to have surfaced in an alien universe. In the year of the Shadowline he had nothing but his schemes.

He always had been a little outside. His earliest memory was of a fight with Gneaus over his being different.

Gneaus eventually accepted him. He had less luck accepting himself.

Down on the bottom line Michael Dee did not like Michael Dee very much. There was something wrong with him.

That he was different he first inferred from his mother's attitude. She was too protective, too fearful.

Boris Storm, the man he thought was his father, was seldom around. Boris was preoccupied with his work. He had few chances to be with his family. Michael developed no bond with the paterfamilias.

Emily Storm hovered over her firstborn. She corrected and protected, corrected and protected, till Michael was convinced that there was an evil in him that scared her silly.

What was this dark thing? He agonized over it by the hour and could find nothing.

Other children sensed it. They withdrew. He studied people, seeking his reflection. He found ways to manipulate others, but the real secret eluded him.

Only Gneaus accepted him. Poor bullheaded Gneaus, who would take a beating rather than admit that his brother was strange.

Poor health complicated Michael's childhood. Boris spent fortunes on doctors. Bad genes, they would hazard, after finding nothing specifically wrong.

He was weak, pale, and sickly into his teens. His brother fought his battles. Gneaus was so strong, so stubborn, and so feared that the other children ignored Michael rather than risk a fight.

So Michael began spinning tall tales as an attention-getting device. He was amazed. His stories were believed! He had a talent. When he recognized the power he had to shape the truth, he used it.

In time he came to weigh every word, every gesture, before revealing it. He calculated its effect on his audience carefully. He reached the point where he could not be direct. In time even the simplest end had to be accomplished by complex means.

He never found his way out of that self-made trap.

He was blessed, or cursed, with brilliance and an almost eidetic memory. He used those tools to keep his webs of deceit taut and strong. He became a master liar, deceiver, and schemer. He lived at the eye of a hurricane of falsehood and discord.

In those days Academy's minimum-age requirement was fourteen standard years. As Gneaus's eligibility year approached, Boris Storm maneuvered to obtain favorable consideration for his son and stepson.

Boris was the scion of an old military family. His ancestors had been career people with the Palisarian Directorate, one of the founder-states of Confederation. He had departed service himself, but could conceive of no higher goal toward which to direct his offspring. He aimed them at commissions all their lives. Their early education took place in a private, militarily oriented special school he set up for the children of Prefactlas Corporation's officers.

Michael and Gneaus first encountered Richard Hawksblood there. He was Richard Woracek at the time. He took the name Hawksblood when he became a mercenary.

Richard was the son of a management consultant Boris brought in to improve his profit margin. The family had no service background. Richard was an outsider among children who saw civilians as a lower life form. Richard was, at the outset, smaller and more sickly than Michael. He was Dee's favorite victim.

Richard accepted slings and arrows with calm dignity and a refusal to be aroused. His imperturbability infuriated his classmates. He fought back by being better than anyone at everything. Only Gneaus was able, on occasion, to rise to the rarefied airs where Woracek soared.

His excellence only compounded his troubles with his peers. Gneaus, who was his closest acquaintance, often became exasperated because Richard would not fight back.

"The scores will even themselves," Woracek promised.

They did.

Eligibility time arrived, and with it Academy's grueling competitive exams. The youths flashed like spearpoints toward the target at which their parents had aimed their young lives. They streaked toward their chances to become card-carrying members of the established elite.

The battery lasted six exhausting days. Part was physical and psychological. A substantial fraction sampled general knowledge and tested problem-solving abilities. The candidates knew Richard would ace those forms. They were surprised to see Michael finish them almost as quickly.

Richard turned in his final test sheet and calmly announced that he had been deliberately answering incorrectly. The monitor asked why. Richard told him that someone had copied some of his answers. Could he retest in isolation?

Computer analysis indicated an unnatural relationship between Woracek's answers and those of Michael Dee. Richard was allowed his retest. He came in with the highest scores ever recorded.

Michael tried it the lazy way. The snake turned on him. He watched his dreams collapse like the topless towers.

He knew it was his own fault. Still, he had a perverse streak. Richard shared the blame. It was Woracek's fault, if you saw it from the right angle.

That was Michael Dee's watershed point. He had begun deceiving himself. His last bulwark of reality gone, he went adrift. He became a one-man universe whose ties to the larger existence were bonds of falsehood and hatred founded on untruth. He had chained himself in fetters so intangible and cunningly forged that even he could not define them.

He did bounce back from rejection. He found a new direction, in a field which valued men with his ability to restructure reality. He became a journalist.

The holonets, ratings foremost in the moguls' minds, had abandoned all pretense to objective reporting long ago. When Michael entered the trade drama was the bait that got the audiences to switch on. The bloodier the report the better.

Michael wanted to make it as an independent. He struggled hard for years. Then the Ulantonid War broke.

He showed a knack for being in the right place at the right time. He produced the best coverage repeatedly. His colleagues made tape after tape of disaster after disaster as the Ulantonid blitz smashed toward the Inner Worlds. Michael found the bright spots, the little victories and heroic stands. His coverage elbowed to the top.

While Boris, Gneaus, Cassius, and Richard fought for their lives in what looked a foredoomed effort to stall Ulant, Michael had fun making tapes. The Storms were impoverished by Ulant's occupation of Prefactlas. He grew rich. He set his own price for his material. In the wartime confusion he evaded taxation deftly and invested brilliantly. He bought huge chunks of instel stocks when commercial faster-than-light communication seemed nothing but wishful thinking. He got into interstellar data warehousing, a sideline that would lead to the creation of Festung Todesangst.

Everything he touched turned to gold.

He never forgave Richard. Though his fortunes soared, he was always the outsider at the party. Without that Academy diploma he could not rise above the second social rank. Service officers were the aristocrats of the age.

The war ended. Its chaos continued. Grand Admiral McGraw went rogue. Sangaree raiders continued to harry the spaceways. There were people to blame. Michael got into piracy.

He was careful. Hardly anyone ever suspected. He creamed information from his instel and data corporations to parlay a pair of broken-down destroyers into another fortune.

His extralegal adventures led him into another life-trap.

## TWENTY-FIVE: 3031 AD

Helga's World orbited far from its primary. Raging methane winds screamed across its surface. They were as cold as its mistress's heart, as unremitting in their savagery. Storm searched for the telltale heat concentration. Festung Todesangst was dug in deep, tapping the core's remaining heat.

He sent the stolen recognition codes, then injected his singleship into a low polar orbit. He went around three times before detecting the thermal anomaly. He took a fix and hit methane in a penetration ran.

Spy-eyes above and below ignored him. No missiles rose to greet him.

He had the right codes.

He smiled tightly, already worrying about the harder task of getting out.

He regretted spending an advantage that could be used but once. He hoarded those with a miser's touch. This one could be saved no longer, and could not be used again. Helga would eliminate the gaps in her protection following his visit.

He touched down. Already in EVA gear, he plunged into a violent methane wind. There was one instant of incredible cold while his suit heaters lagged in their effort to warm him.

"Poor navigation," he muttered. The doorway he wanted lay a kilometer away. The wind-chill might kill him before he got there.

It was too late to cry. Moving ship would tempt fate too much. Hobson's choice.

He started walking.

This lock had been an access portal during construction, a workmen's convenience that had not been sealed. One of Helga's weird guardians would be stationed inside, but she should be a half-century unwary. He thought he could surprise her.

He leaned into the gale, ignoring the bitter cold. Each few hundred steps he examined the glove covering his suit's left hand. He was not sure it would withstand the chill.

His odyssey went on and on. The wind and oxygen snow were gleefully malicious conspirators trying to contrive a disaster. Then there was a slackening of the gale's force. He glanced up. He had entered the lee of the lock housing.

The outer lock door stood slightly ajar. He forced himself through the gap and initiated the lock cycle.

Would the carelessness that had left the door open have allowed icing in the mechanism? The door shuddered, groaned, protesting. It whined shrilly. It broke loose and sealed. Frost formed on his suit and faceplate as breathable air flooded the chamber.

He batted the haze from his faceplate and found himself facing one of the more grotesque products of genetic engineering.

Helga's guardian was an amazon of skeletal thinness, with translucent skin, completely hairless and breathless. She was human and female only by virtue of her navel and the virgin slit between her sticklike thighs. And in her confusion at this unexpected apparition stepping from the lock.

Faceplate frosting made Storm briefly vulnerable but she wasted those seconds. She finally responded by switching on subsonics that caused an increasing dread as he approached her.

There was no humanity in her death's-head face. The little muscles under that deathlike skin never twitched in expression. Storm fought the mesmeric assault of the sonics, forced his fear to work for him. "Dead," he told himself.

He felt an instant of compassion, and knew it a waste. This thing was less alive than his most often resurrected soldier.

Storm approached the guardian, left hand reaching.

She looked frail and powerless. The impression was false. No man living could best her without special equipment. Pain, injury, and the normal limits of human strength meant nothing to her. She had been bred to one purpose, to attack till victorious or destroyed.

Storm's glove touched her arm lightly, discharged. The shock was supposed to scramble her neural signals and make her amenable.

It worked, but not as well as he hoped. She became less truculent, but far from docile. He took control, stripped her of her sonics, force-marched her down stairs and inclines. Every ten minutes he gave her another shock, expending more of the glove's power.

He worried. He was squandering his best weapon. If the charge went too soon he would have to kill her. He needed live bait to pass the next obstacle.

His path, as did all corridors from the surface, debouched in a dark, stadium-vast chamber, the ceiling of which was natural cavern. The floor had been machined smooth and covered with a half-meter of sand.

*This*, Storm thought as he crouched at the tunnel's end, *is the real gateway to Festung Todesangst. This is the real guardhouse.* Here the most powerful weapons were all but useless. The watchman was of a size in keeping with that of his kiosk.

Helga Dee had a bizarre sense of humor, a cockeyed way of looking at the universe. Her gateman was a reptilian thing, tyrannosaur-sized, from a world so massive that here it was as agile as a kitten. Only Helga herself, who had raised it from an egg and lovingly called it her "puppy," could control it. Through its love for her, she claimed. Storm believed she used implanted controls.

The thing subsisted on the flesh of brain donors and Helga's enemies.

As a defense it was primitive, crude, and devastatingly effective. And it was a glass-clear illustration of a facet of Helga Dee. Using it to back her sophisticated surface defenses was her idea of a joke.

The thing's bellow smashed at Storm. His ears ached. He saw nothing but a suggestion of shifting immensity inside the poorly illuminated cavern.

He was not here to ooh and ah at the animals in the zoo. The thing was an obstacle, not a spectacle. It required moving or removing. He took a kilo-weight packet from his tool belt, limpeted it to the amazon's back. He tossed a flare into the monster's chamber to get its attention. He hurled the guardian after it.

A vast, scaly head speared out of the gloom. The skeleton woman vanished into a fangy mouth. A huge yellow eye considered Storm.

The head rose. From the darkness came the sound of a vast bulk moving and of bones cracking.

Storm shuddered. The woman had gone to her death without a sound.

For an instant he wondered why he had not killed Helga when he had had the chance.

He waited. The munching faded. She *would* choose a monster that chewed its food.

The beast rumbled. Storm waited. Soon it was snoring like a healthy volcano. He waited some more, fretting at the delay.

It seemed he had been there half his life, and still he had not started. He still had to penetrate the fortress proper.

The drug was supposed to be fast, but it was old. And the poison with it was slow. He had to wait to be sure.

He wanted the monster asleep while he was below, and dead only after he made his escape. Helga might monitor its vital signs.

He made it three quarters of the way across the arena before the monster abandoned pretense. Its immensity bore down on him like some anachronistic blood-and-bone dreadnought.

It was not moving as lithely as earlier. The drug had had some effect. Storm did not panic, though fear raked him with claws of steel. He faced the charge.

He had rehearsed this confrontation for years. Rote reaction carried him through.

While backing toward his goal he set his glove to short in a single burst of power. The great head, the scimitar teeth, came down, slowly for the beast but incredibly fast in Storm's subjective perception.

He hurled himself aside, gloved hand reaching back like an eagle's talons. For an instant his fingers touched the moist soft flesh inside a gargantuan nostril. The glove blew. Charred flesh putrified the air. The beast flung back, screaming, falling over its tangled legs, tearing at its snout with its foreclaws.

Storm went sprawling. Up on adrenaline to a perilous level, he rose with a bounce astounding in a man of his age. He crouched, ready to dodge the next attack, hoping he could cat and mouse long enough to reach an exit.

The thing was preoccupied. Like a hound stung by a bee it had been snuffling; it kept pawing its nose. It tore its own flesh. When it ground its scaly snout into the sand, Storm laughed hysterically. He fled for the entrance.

The unbreachable gate had been broken. He had penetrated Festung Todesangst.

It took time to get hold of himself, to get his bearings. He wished he could quit. He wanted nothing so much as the peace and security of his study.

Giving in would not matter. He could not win anyway. Not in the long run. Why fight? Why not steal a little peace before the inevitable closed in?

That part of him which could not yield asserted itself. He resumed moving, downward, deep into Festung Todesangst.

The deeps of Helga's World were sterile and lifeless. He walked long corridors with featureless metal floors and walls, under blue-white lights. The only odor was a mild taint of ozone, the only sound a barely discernible hum. It was like walking the halls of an abandoned but perfectly maintained hospital.

The life of Festung Todesangst lay hidden behind those featureless walls. Thousands of human brains. Cubic kilometers of microchips and magnetic bubbles shuffling mega-googols of information bits. Helga's World had become the data warehouse of the human universe.

What unsuspected secrets lay hidden there? How much power for someone able to possess or dispossess Helga Dee?

Immense power. But no force, not even that of Confederation, could plunder Helga's empire. Her father had promised the universe that she would bring on the Gotterdammerung rather than surrender her position. Any conqueror would have to surreptitiously deactivate a dozen thermonuclear destruct charges and disconnect all the poison stores set to kill the brains in their support tanks. He would have to deactivate Helga herself, from whom all control flowed.

It was a setup characteristic of the Dees. What was theirs was theirs forever. Only what was yours was negotiable. No one, especially an avaricious government, was going to rob the family.

Storm meant to steal from a Dee. From the coldest, most hateful, and jealous one of them all. And he would accomplish it with the help of something stolen from himself. The great prize of the queen of the dead was going to become her most severe liability.

He was going to hurt her, and he was going to enjoy doing it.

Kilometers beneath the surface, beneath even the vast main fortress, so deep that his suit had to cool instead of heat, he found the terminal he sought.

It was the master for one small, semi-independent system. It existed for one limited, cruel purpose. It was the focus from which Helga meant to engineer her revenge upon Gneaus Julius Storm. Within it lay everything known about Storm and the Iron Legion. He suspected that it contained things he did not know himself. To it came every stray wisp of information, every gossamer strand of rumor, vaguely relating to himself.

To it, also, Michael Dee came when he had some scheme afoot.

Once upon a time Helga had been a wild-eyed wanton, rushing from thrill to ever more bizarre thrill with the frenzy of a woman condemned. Being locked into the endless boredom of Festung Todesangst was the cruelest fate she could imagine. She extracted compensatory bites from his soul every minute this bottom-most system ran.

The corebrain here, the overbrain that controlled the others, was that of his daughter Valerie. She had not been ego-scrubbed before being cyborged in. Every second that passed, in a vastly telescoped subjective time, was one in which she was aware of her identity and plight.

For this cruelty he would kill Helga Dee. When the time came. When the moment was ripe.

All things in their season.

He stared at the terminal for a long time, trying to dis-remember that the soul of the machine was a daughter he had loved too much.

Age, Storm would declare when the subject arose, did not confer wisdom, only experience from which the wise could draw inferences. And even the wisest man had blind spots, and could behave like a fool, and remain so adamant in his folly that it would strangle him with a garrote of his own devising.

Storm's blind spots were Richard Hawksblood and Michael Dee. He was overly ready to attribute evil to Richard, and too trusting and forgiving with his brother.

A long time ago, much as Pollyanna had recently, Valerie had vanished from the Fortress of Iron. Storm still was not sure, but suspected the machinations of Michael Dee. Nor did he know Valerie's motives for leaving, though beforehand she had spoken often of making peace with Richard.

His memories of Valerie's case colored his behavior in Pollyanna's. He went haring off to the rescue—perhaps unwisely.

Valerie fell in love with Hawksblood.

Word of their affair filtered back. Storm flew into a rage. He accused Richard of every crime a father ever laid on a daughter's lover. Michael arranged a meeting. Fool that he was, Storm disowned her when she refused to come home.

He was sorry the instant he spoke, but was too stubborn to recall words once flown. And he became sorrier still when Helga, after gulling her own father, snatched Valerie and hustled her off to Festung Todesangst.

Poor Valerie. She went into mechanical/cerebral bondage believing her father had abandoned her, that he had used her cruelly.

Storm had been working on Helga ever since. His vengeance thus far he deemed only token repayment for the destruction of a daughter's love.

They were hard, cruel, anachronistic men and women, the Storms and Dees, and Hawksbloods, and those who served them.

Enough, he told himself. He had crucified himself on this cross too often already. Hand trembling, he jacked his comm plug into a direct verbal input.

"Valerie?"

Came a sense of stirring into wakefulness. An electronic rustling. Then a return his equipment interpreted as "Who's there?" It contained overtones of surprise.

There was just one answer he dared give, just one that would not spark an explosion of bitterness. "Richard Hawksblood."

"Richard? What are you doing here?"

He felt her uncertainty, her hope, her fear. It hit him hard. He had an instant of nausea. Some foul worm was trying to gnaw its way out of his gut.

If he and Richard agreed on anything, it was that Helga should be punished for this.

Richard had loved Valerie. That love was one more unbridgeable gap between them.

"I came to see you. To free you. And to find out what Helga is doing to your father and me."

There was a long, long silence. He began to fear that he had lost her. Finally, "Who calls? I've slept here so long. So peacefully."

He could taste the agony of her lie. There was no peace for Valerie Storm. Helga made sure of that.

Storm replied, "Richard Hawksblood." He wished he knew their love talk, the pet names they had called one another in the night, or the all-important trivia that pass between a man and woman in love. "Valerie, what was that new complex I saw on my way down?" Between Helga's puppy and Valerie's pit he had encountered little but endless sterility and silence, except on the last few levels, where he had to slip through a construction zone as softly as a prowling kitten.

He wondered if Helga's zombie workers would have noticed if he had strutted through their midst. Personality-scrubbed, they were little more than robots. But they might be robots programmed to report anomalies.

"Cryocrypts for the sons of my father, whose deaths will be the first step of my mistress's revenge."

Storm subdued his anger response. "How? Why?"

"Helga and her father have decided that my father will fight on Blackworld. They intend to capture some of my brothers and hold them here till the fighting is done."

"Helga would never release them."

"No. Her father doesn't know that."

"How?"

"Michael Dee will capture them."

Storm recalled Benjamin's nightmares. Were they a valid precognition? Could both twins have the psi touch? Could the Faceless Man be Michael Dee? "How will they kill Benjamin?" he blurted.

He grimaced as he spoke Benjamin's name. Richard Hawksblood could not have known that anything of the sort was planned. He could not have done the sums.

"You! You didn't sound like Richard. So cold. He would've… Storm. My father. Here. Only he could suspect…"

She seemed too stunned to give an alarm—or did not want to sound one. Perhaps she had forgiven him just a little.

"Valerie, I'm sorry. I was a fool." The words came hard. He did not admit error easily.

He had to move fast. Helga would have made sure Valerie could keep no secrets. "Honeyhair… Forgive me." He had to do the thing that, when first they had learned of Valerie's enslavement, he and Richard had agreed had to be done.

There could be but one escape for Valerie Storm. He could free her no other way.

Flesh of his flesh, blood of his blood… He had trouble seeing. There was water in his eye.

Shaking, he reached for the large red lever prominent in the center of the terminal. The worm within his gut metamorphosed, became an angry, clawing dragon.

He had thought himself too old, too calloused to feel such pain.

He hesitated for just an instant. Then he pulled the safety pin and yanked the lever.

His helmet rilled with a sound not unlike that of someone slowly strangling. His hand strayed toward the comm jack. He forced it away. He had to listen, to remember. This dread moment would never have been were he not a bullheaded idiot.

One must savor the bitter taste of folly as well as the sweetness of wisdom, for wisdom is born of folly well remembered.

She was going. Faintly, she murmured, "Peace. Father, tell Richard… Please. Tell Richard I… I…"

"I will, Valerie. Honeyhair. I will."

"Father… Play something… the way you used to."

A tear forced itself from his eye as he remembered a tune he used to tootle for her when she was a child. He unslung the case on his back, praying the cold and encounter with Helga's guardian had not ruined his instrument. He wet the reed, closed his eye, began to play. It squealed a little, but yielded its child-memory. "That one, Honeyhair?"

Silence. The voiceless, bellowing silence of death.

He indulged in a frenzy of rage that masked a deeper, more painful emotion. For one long minute he let his grief take him. His music became an agonized howl.

Valerie was not the first of his blood he had slain. She might not be the last. Practice did not ease the agony. He could not do it without crying in the night forever afterward.

This Storm, the Storm of tears and grief and fury, was the Storm no one ever saw, the Storm unknown to anyone but Frieda, who held him while the sobs racked him.

He took hold. There were things to do. He had learned something. He had to move fast.

He used the dead face of Helga Dee as a will-o'-the-wisp to follow from Festung Todesangst's deeps. He stalked it with the intensity of a fanatic assassin.

He had thought that he hated Richard Hawksblood. That odium was a child's fleeting passion compared to what he felt now. His feelings toward Helga had become a torch he would follow through the darkness all the rest of his days.

He had not asked the questions that had brought him to Helga's World. But their answers were implicit in what he had learned.

They had come to the end of Michael's game. Dee was pulling out the stops, laying everything on the line, risking it all to get whatever he wanted. The Legion and Hawksblood were being pushed into Blackworld like cocks into the pit, to fight and this time die the death-without-resurrection.

Whatever obsession compelled Michael, it was about to be satisfied. Michael was about to attain his El Dorado. There would be war, and there would be feeling in it. The hatreds were being pumped up. The Gotterdammerung could not be averted.

The twilight of the Legion lay just beyond a near horizon. It might mean the end of all mercenary armies…

Storm made a vow. He and Richard might fight, and both lose, but they would go to the shadows with one victory to light their paths to Hell.

The Dees would go down with them. Every last one.

# TWENTY-SIX: 2845 AD

The last snow was melting in the forest shade when Deeth made his second bid for freedom. He had prepared for months. First he concentrated on convincing Jackson that he had resigned himself to his fate. He faithfully did all he was told, and cared for the old man beyond what was demanded. He made no effort to flee when apparent opportunities arose. Nor did he struggle much against perversions or the incessant maltreatment. He suffered in silence, stoically waiting.

He began decorating the stage of his revenge in the fall, under the guise of caring for Jackson. During autumn he carpeted the cavern floor with leaves. When the chills moved in and it became necessary to keep a fire burning, he gathered piles of firewood. While foraging wood he collected small, sharp stones that he concealed around the cave.

On the night he chose he cut his neck rope with an edged rock. Hours passed while he sawed, painstakingly avoiding rustling the leaves of his bed. When he was done he did not immediately flee.

Holding the parted rope round his neck, he rose and stoked up the fire. The old man wakened, as he always did when Deeth stirred. He cursed Deeth for disturbing him. Deeth bowed his head and went on with his work. Jackson settled back into a grumbling snore.

Deeth built the fire higher and higher. It began to roar, and pull a breeze into the cave.

Concealed near the fire were the things he wanted to take: a hide blanket, steel for fire-starting, a package of dried fruit. He tossed them out the cave mouth.

Jackson snapped to awareness, suspicious and crabby. He jerked the rope. It flew into his face. He stared at the frayed end in dull-witted surprise.

Deeth seized a forked stick and shoveled fire onto the dry, powdery leaves. He skipped back and toppled the huge kindling stack, carefully prepared for the moment. It slid into the flames. The fire gnawed at it, leaping higher and crackling louder by the second.

Deeth dumped piles of larger wood.

The old man, cursing, terrified, staggered out of his chair and tried to charge through before the barrier became impassable.

Deeth floored him with a thrown stone.

The power of hatred was in his arm. He whistled that rock into Jackson's chest with such force that he heard brittle old ribs crack.

Jackson rose for another try. The trap had closed. He retreated instead.

Deeth watched in fascination as Jackson screamed and danced in the fire. Eventually, crazed with pain, the old man flung himself at the barrier again. He crashed through and collapsed outside, twitching all over, feebly crawling toward his tormentor.

Deeth backed a step when necessary, and collected his supplies, but did not leave till Jackson died.

He felt no real emotion afterward. It had not been an execution, even, just an ending of misery.

He started toward the village.

The boy had been scarred. Something had been carved out of him in that cave. Never again would he feel true, whole, mortal emotion. He had become that fearful, wholly pragmatic monster which has no conscience, and no comprehension of emotion. Henceforth he would fake it, when necessary, as protective coloration, and would believe that everyone else was doing the same. The only things with meaning, most of the time, would be his own whims, fancies, and hatreds. Everyone else he would see as objects to be moved and used.

Deeth had acted now because the village chieftain had condemned the girl Emily to another week in the punishment pit. He could spirit her away without having to sneak her out of the chieftain's house.

He had to enter and leave the village past a guard watching for a night raid by neighboring tribes. Going in, the sentry was asleep at his post. Deeth crept past. Keeping to the deepest darkness, he moved to the chieftain's hut.

The pit had been covered with a lid made of hide on a wooden frame. Rocks weighted it down. Deeth removed it.

He lay on his stomach and whispered, "Emily! It's time." He could see nothing below, but knew she was awake. He heard her frightened breathing.

One of the village's domesticated beasts snorted nearby. It sensed his presence, but was neither noisy nor excitable. It did not give him away.

"Emily! Come on. It's Deeth."

She did not respond.

"Come on!" Time was passing. He dared not waste much on a frightened slave. He reached down, tried to get hold of her hair. His arm was not long enough. "Come on, girl. Give me your hand. We've got to get moving."

She whimpered.

He knew she had suffered, but hardly more than he. What was the matter with her? Was the spirit of these animals that easily broken?

"Your hand!" he snapped. He reached again.

And felt her touch and grab him. He braced himself and pulled. Wriggling and whimpering, naked, she slithered out of the pit.

"Now what?" he asked himself. She could not face the cold unclad, nor could she run through the woods naked. The underbrush would flay her. "Get something to wear," he ordered, indicating the chieftain's hut.

She shook her head.

"Move!" Deeth snarled.

Still she shook her head.

"Dammit, go!" He snapped fingertips against her cold bare buttocks. She yipped softly, then vanished into the house.

Deeth chewed his lip, crouched beside the hovel, watched the hills for the ghost of dawn. They had made noise. Had anyone heard?

The animal made more curiosity sounds, a kind of continuous questioning grunt. It could not leave its pen to investigate. The night creatures of the woods hooted and chattered and whistled.

What about those? He had heard of no large predators. That did not mean that they did not exist. He knew Prefactlas only by what he had seen. Jackson had not let him see much.

The girl returned. She had clothed herself in furs. "Yuloa's things," she whispered. She had stolen them from the chieftain's son.

Deeth chuckled softly, nervously. "We'd better get started. It'll be sunrise pretty soon."

"Where're we going?"

He did not know. He had not planned beyond getting her out of the pit. He just did not know enough about this world.

"Back to the station," he told her. He set off before she could protest. They had to go somewhere, if only to get away from here. She followed after a moment's hesitation.

The sentry had moved, but was asleep again. They passed him carefully.

Deeth stopped after another hundred yards. He did not know the way. The direction, yes, but not the paths.

Pride would not permit him to confess ignorance to an animal. He resumed walking before Emily asked questions.

An hour later, while they were struggling through underbrush on a steep hillside, she asked, "Why don't we use the trail? It's just over there." Panting, she added, "Doing it this way takes a lot of time. They'll be after us pretty soon."

Deeth frowned. Was she going to be a talker, all the time questioning and nagging?

She had a point. And had presented it without questioning his reasons for doing things his way. "You could be right."

He went in the direction she indicated. He encountered a narrow track. The going became easier. They reached the forest's edge as dawn began painting bold strokes of crimson and gold on a canvas of indigo clouds.

"We'll rest here," Deeth said. He settled down with his back against the trunk of a huge tree. Two giant roots made arms for his momentary throne.

Before him lay the plain the Norbon had cleared when first they had come to Prefactlas. It was lifeless now, except for a few feral grazers and the morning birds dipping and weaving after insects. Nothing but ruins remained where the Norbon complex had stood. Even the greathouse, which had been constructed as a fortress, had been smashed level with the plain. Grass and moss colored its fire-blackened remains.

Of the other structures there was even less evidence. The human Marines had done a thorough job.

And then they had gone. Not even a watch unit had been left behind. The baked landing sites of their assault craft had disappeared under new growth.

He stared and thought. There would be little here for him. Nothing lay behind but torture or death. He had to go on.

Where to? Any animals they encountered would treat them no better than those they had known. And if they reached an area controlled by Confederation humans? The girl would give him away.

Tomorrow and tomorrow. This was today. He had to meet the problems as they arose. Right now he had to keep moving.

"Deeth? Maybe we shouldn't stay here too long. They know I'm gone by now."

Deeth rose and walked toward the ruins. Maybe he could find something useful.

The lower limb of the sun cleared the horizon before they reached the site. Their path led them past scores of skeletons. Some had been scattered by scavengers. Shreds of Sangaree clothing clung to most. Deeth found one small one wearing Dharvon w'Pugh's bright party pantaloons. His skull had been crashed.

Deeth stood over his old enemy. That was no way for an heir to die.

He looked for the kitchens. They seemed the most likely source for something useful.

He poked around for an hour. It was useless. The ruins had been picked as clean as the Sangaree bones. Emily said all the nearby villagers had appeared once the Marines departed.

He came up with a battered aluminum cup and a butcher knife without a handle. He gave them to Emily. He scrounged a pointed, foot-long shard of glassteel for himself. He might be able to mount it on a handle or shaft. He moved to the armory, hoping to find a weapon. The raiders and scavengers had been thorough. He came up with nothing but a bottle of lasegun coolant he could drain for use as a canteen.

He was emptying the bottle when the girl shouted. She waved at the sky. A faint chuga-chuga-chuga came from high overhead.

A Confederation support ship was moving south. Deeth scrambled across the rubble, knocked Emily down. She kicked and screamed and…

The patrol dwindled into the distance. They watched it go. Deeth helped Emily up.

"Why?" she demanded. "They would've helped us. Oh. Well, *I* could've gone with them."

"You're Norbon." Deeth turned his back. He started kicking rubble around, remembering.

He had been on Prefactlas just one week when the raiders came. Not long, but long enough to have fallen in love with the station and staff. It had been his first trip off Homeworld. Everything had seemed romantic. Especially old Rhafu.

What had become of the breeding master? He had been a real man. Probably took several of the animals with him.

"Time to go, Emily," he said. "We should be off the plain before they track us here." He started after the copter. South was the only direction to go.

He was not ready to confront Prefactlas's conquerors, but had to be near their main base when he was. Their headquarters, he guessed, would be the Sexon holding. It was the biggest on the planet, most easily defended, and had the best communications facilities. It would make an ideal bridgehead for human occupation. It lay near the planet's main spaceport, a facility capable of handling the heaviest lighters.

That would have to be their destination. Only there could he get off planet.

There was one small problem. The Sexon holding lay more than a thousand miles away.

The journey took the youngsters three years. It was punctuated by interims of slavery as grim as their first. Adversity forged nickel-hard transethnic bonds between them. They became a survival unit.

Emily lost any desire to be away from or to betray him.

Years passed after their arrival. They begged. They were forced into schools or orphanages. They did odd jobs. Emily got work as a cleaning girl in the offices of Prefactlas Corporation. They survived. And Deeth almost forgot his father's parting charge.

They were sixteen when the wildly improbable happened. Emily became pregnant.

Deeth's world shifted its axis. He woke up. He began looking in new directions. He could not raise a child himself. He was Sangaree. He had a duty to the infant, wanted or not.

Emily's job had brought her into contact with the President of the Corporation. He was bemused by the girl. He kept plying her with little gifts.

Deeth went off by himself. He did a lot of thinking. And hurting. Emily's suitor was the man who had led the attack on his family. His orders had caused all the deaths at the Norbon station. The man was his dearest enemy. And the one real hope for his unborn child.

Sangaree prided themselves on their pragmatism.

"Go to him," Deeth told Emily. "Make him your man. Don't argue. He has what you need. Yesterday is done. Tomorrow we begin new lives."

She refused. She fought. She cried.

He put her out of their shanty and held the door till she went away. He sat with his back to it and wept.

# TWENTY-SEVEN:
# 3031 AD

The brothers Darksword looked like regimental file clerks. They wore that look of perpetual bewilderment of the innocent repeatedly slapped in the face by reality. Wizards of the data banks. Easy prey for the monsters in the human jungle.

They were short, slim, thin-faced, and watery-eyed. They had pallid skin and stringy brown hair so sparse it belonged on an endangered species list. Helmut affected a pair of pince-nez. The more bold Wulf had had his vision surgically corrected.

They were antsy little men who could not stand still. Outsiders pegged them as chronic hand-wringers, nervous little people who faced even petty troubles with the trepidation of an old maid bound for an orgy.

It was an act they had lived so long they almost believed it themselves.

There was as much ice and iron in them as in Cassius or Storm. Had Storm meant it, they would have killed the mining official without qualm or second thought. Disobedience was an alien concept.

A matched set of stringy old assassins.

Their lives, emotions, and loyalties had been narrowly focused for two hundred forty years. They had followed Boris Storm as boys, in the old Palisarian Directorate. They had attended military school with him, joined Confederation Navy with him, and became part of Prefactlas Corporation with him. When Ulant struck they returned to service with him, and afterward helped him create the Iron Legion. Following Boris's death they had transferred their devotion to his son.

They had been born on Old Earth and taken to the Directorate young. They had learned the motherworld's harsh lessons in Europe's worst slums.

Two things matter. Sign on with the gang with the most guns. Serve it with absolute devotion as long as it serves faithfully in return.

The centuries had garbled those truths a tad. They could not abandon the Legion now, biggest guns or no. One occasionally reminded the other that it looked like time to get out. Neither moved. They continued serving Gneaus Storm with the implacability of natural law.

Storm had left them in command of the Fortress. The simple fact of his absence presented them with enough problems, Wulf claimed, to frustrate a saint into a deal with the devil.

The Darkswords were curious in yet another way. They were that rare animal, the true believer in an age of infidels. Only they understood how they squared their actions with the moral demands of a Christian faith.

Michael Dee was human quicksilver. Pollyanna, without Lucifer there to compel discretion, seemed to have set herself the task of engulfing every functional penis in the Fortress. She had become a crude joke.

Lucifer had been gone only two days when she lured Benjamin back to her bed, with such indiscretion that everyone in the Fortress knew. Frieda became a volcano constantly on the edge of erupting.

The traditional morality had little weight in the Fortress of Iron, but one tried to avoid needless friction.

Pollyanna did not seem to care. Her behavior was almost consciously self-destructive.

Bets were being made. Would Lucifer return so incensed as to repeat the blood-spill he had attempted earlier? Would Benjamin's wife finally decide that she had taken enough and cut off his balls? It was a crackling tense situation made to order for a Michael Dee.

The preparations for Blackworld lagged. The Legion had no heavy equipment designed for use in an airless environment. For use in poisonous atmospheres, yes, but not for no atmosphere at all.

At least Richard Hawksblood faced the same problem.

Frieda's passion for the occult had become obsession. She spent hour upon hour closeted with her Madame Endor. She was convinced of the precognitive validity of Benjamin's nightmares. She was making herself obnoxious in her efforts to protect him. A dozen times a day she ran him down to make sure he was wearing the protective suit she had forced the armorers to prepare.

His dalliance with Pollyanna became his sole escape from, and defiance of, her insufferable mothering.

Among the troops there were dissensions explicable only in terms of the presence of Michael Dee. Rumors stalked the barracks levels. There were fist fights. There was a stabbing. The companies and battalions feuded in a manner unrelated to healthy, edge-honing competition.

Storm had been gone ten days. His stabilizing influence was severely missed.

Desperate, Wulf and Helmut decreed that any man not on duty had to report to the gymnasium for intensified physical fitness training. They established a round-the-clock roster of instructors. Exhausted Legionnaires had less energy for squabbling.

Wulf trailed Helmut by a step. They entered the gym. He growled, "The bastard don't have to do anything but be here to muck things up." He glared at Michael Dee. "Look at the damned trouble-monger. Sitting there smug as Solomon on his throne."

Helmut grunted affirmatively. "Would anybody yell if we shoved him out a lock?"

"Not till the Colonel got home. Ah. Look. There's Pollyanna. Want to help me with her?"

Pollyanna stood in a corridor mouth, watching the group around Dee. Her doe eyes were fixed on Michael.

They were filled with a surprising animation. It seemed to be hatred.

Homer and Frieda hovered over Benjamin, Frieda silently daring Pollyanna to come closer. Benjamin was directing the physical drill. The soldiers were not enthusiastic.

Michael watched in silence, unaware of Pollyanna's stare. He wore a contemplative smile.

"You handle her," Helmut said. "I'll take Benjamin and Dee." His voice carried overtones of distaste. Wulf might have asked if he wanted to share a swim in a sewer.

Pollyanna flushed when she saw Wulf approaching. He was pleased. He hoped she saw the thunderheads dancing on his brow.

Cassius, with his computerlike voice and metallic absence of emotion, was the one man Pollyanna normally feared. She seemed unable to remain afraid of a man who had been to her bed.

She had made advances to both Darkswords. They had not responded. She could fear them too. Wulf tried to look as grim as a suicide singleshipper. What he wanted to do took the same intense determination. Her amorality baffled and intimidated him.

"We walk!" he snapped, seizing her arm. She winced. He was stronger than he looked, and wanted to impress her with the fact. "You've got a lot to learn," he growled, propelling her along the corridor. "Only Michael Dee plays Dee games here. He can get away with them. He has Storm's safe-conduct. You've got nothing. You're just another daughter-in-law."

She sputtered. His anger hit her like crashing breakers, drowning what she wanted to say.

"I could put you into detention. I will if you don't start making like a nun. Stay away from Benjamin. And Homer. I've seen you sizing him up. Your pants come down again, it'd better be for Lucifer. Understand? You want to play games, get a deck of cards. This one the rest of us were playing before your grandma crapped her first diaper." They reached her apartment. Wulf pushed her inside.

"One more trick, girl, and you go in the can till the Colonel gets back. That's as plain as I can make it."

She relaxed. He sensed it. "Think you know him, eh? Count your beads. With him it's always the Legion first. A man who's had to kill his own children wouldn't hesitate to send an amateur Dee to Helga's World the way he did with that metal grubber."

His belief in his commander was so apparent that she had to accept its truth. He left her shaking and, he hoped, wondering why she had gotten involved with such terrible men.

Helmut approached the group observing the physical drills. He was only slightly less forbidding than his brother. Dee's smile became uncertain. Benjamin's charm aura faltered. Homer's sightless eyes turned his way, grim as the eyes of death. Frieda glared suspiciously.

She was a raw-boned, stringy-haired blonde, reminiscent of her father, without Cassius's self-confidence. She was alarmed by the purpose evident in Helmut's stride. Storm she could read and handle. Her father she could manipulate. The Darkswords, though, were beyond reach.

That was the impression they liked to give. Helmut threw himself into an empty chair with apparent violence. He glared at them in turn. "Captain Ceislak. Take over here. Benjamin, I've got a job for you. Directing vacuum drills. You start after morning muster tomorrow. Check with Wong. He'll fill you in on what you'll be doing."

Understanding passed between them. Benjamin was about to be moved out of temptation's reach. Putting the Legion through vacuum drills required weeks.

A man could do a lot of thinking if he was alone with himself in a spacesuit, Helmut reflected.

"But he could…" Frieda began.

"Get hurt?" Helmut snapped, bludgeoning her line. "Crap. He'll be safer outside. He's not suicidal, is he?" He glanced at Michael Dee, smiling a thin, bitter smile.

Benjamin reddened.

"Accidents happen!" Frieda had become neurotic about her son's safety.

"Relax, Mother," Homer said with heavy sarcasm. "You'd still have me to dote on."

Frieda winced. She forced a smile while coloring guiltily.

Homer's dead eyes glared at the floor. He knew. Even from his mother affection had to be forced.

"Accidents, yes," Helmut mused, smiling at Dee again. "I've been giving accidents a certain amount of thought. They're like mutations. Once in a while one can be beneficial. Wulf and I were discussing the possibilities a bit ago."

Dee's smile vanished. He had gotten the message. And he had noted the marks strain had left on Helmut. It was time he became more circumspect. Helmut had declared, albeit obliquely, that he no longer considered the interests of Gneaus Julius Storm and those of the Legion to be congruent. The hint that he and his brother were ready to eliminate Dee indicated a revolution in thought that could spread throughout the organization. When the old lap dogs stood on their hind legs and growled...

Helmut sat there and smiled as if reading Michael's every thought.

Frieda went on nagging. Helmut finally exploded. "You question my orders, madam? Complain to the colonel when he returns. Meantime, hold your tongue."

It was as harsh an admonition as ever he had given a woman. She shut up. Storm always supported those upon whom he bestowed the proconsular power.

Having delivered his messages, Helmut went to waken Thurston Storm. Thurston was his relief. Initially, Thurston's sole task had been to birddog Michael. With tension mounting, the Darkswords had been forced to saddle him with part of their burden. They worked staggered sixteen-hour shifts, one sleeping while the other two held chaos at bay.

"Friendly today, isn't he?" Michael observed as Helmut stalked away. "He'd turn on the gloom at a wedding. Put the groom to work before the party started."

Ah, his words were subtle. Benjamin was blind to their snare. "A party. That's an idea, Michael. We need to liven this place up. I'll put me on a going-outside party."

Michael smiled and nodded.

The party, through Benjamin's efforts, shed some of its early artificiality and turned fun. With the help of a few drinks the younger people forgot the pressures that had been building so swiftly and mysteriously. The occasional tentative spurt of laughter erupted from their midst.

Benjamin's mother hovered in the background, as grim as an old raven. She had opposed the party from its inception, purely on feeling. She had been unable to sway Benjamin. Madame Endor had failed. He was in revolt against mothering. He would not let them save him.

He could be as stubborn as his father.

Where were her husband and father? Frieda wondered. The Fortress was going to hell and they were off God knew where chasing women or something.

Dee watched the partiers with a disdainful, mocking smile.

Thurston Storm observed from a doorway. He was a huge, sullen, muscular redhead who looked too simple for even the most obvious subtleties. His appearance was an illusion. He was a dangerous man.

He resented having been left off the guest list. They thought him too boisterous. It did not occur to him that he could simply abandon his duties and invite himself in. He just stood there with his arms folded across his chest. His right hand clutched a needlegun made tiny by the size of his fist. It tracked Michael Dee as if computer-aimed.

Thurston puzzled everyone. He seemed almost a hollow man, entirely an appearance. He had the disquieting vacuity of a Pollyanna Eight. The appearances he presented sometimes conflicted. Occasionally he was a reflection of his father. Most of the time he appeared to be what people took him for, a big, dull, happy fellow who drank as if there were no future, ate for a company, brawled, bragged, and bullied his way through life. A mass of strength without a brain to guide it.

Wulf had absented himself from the party, pleading his work load. Pollyanna was sulking in her apartment. Helmut was asleep. Everyone else was there.

Benjamin looked splendid in a uniform of his own design. It was too ruffled and gaudy for the Legion. His father would not have approved. He was not pleased with it himself. His protective armor softened its effect.

That armor was the finest available. Energy weapons would feed its shields. Anything moving at high velocity would pillow out in its fields. Those fields would seize and wrench aside the metal of an assassin's blade. In a truly hostile environment he could button up and survive on his own air, water, and nutrient soup. He could not be touched. His mother bragged about his invulnerability when she was not being afraid he would find a way to get himself killed despite his protection.

Benjamin invented a game. He had his friends take turns shooting, hacking, and stabbing him. They ruined his uniform without harming him. He laughed a lot.

The point was to aggravate his mother.

Homer, alone in his blindness, shunned for his ugliness, sat and brooded. Another party, strong with the laughter of the beautiful women who gravitated to the Legion. Were they mocking him again? Women always laughed at him. Even that madwoman Pollyanna. Her real purpose for tempting him, surely, had been to mock him. And Frieda, that bitch who claimed to be his mother... She would like nothing better than to have him put away somewhere where she would not be embarrassed by him. She tried hard to pretend, but she could not hide from his flashes of psi.

No one cared. No one understood. Except Ben, his father, and sometimes that young, strange one, Mouse. And his father he could never forgive for having given him life. Surely, with all his power and money, he could have done something. Sight. Corrective surgery for his physical defects...

He knew his father had tried. The human mind in despair seldom responds to the soft persuasion of reason.

In fits, Homer hated Gneaus Julius Storm.

"Homer. You're unhappy," said a voice nearby. He was startled. It contained more compassion than he had ever before heard. He was primed to take advantage of someone's pity.

Odd that he had not sensed the speaker's approach. His eyes were dead, but his other senses were strong. This man was a ghost.

"Who is it?" He did not recognize the voice.

"Michael."

Of course. The sneaking and voice-changing should have cued him. "What do you want?"

"Only to cheer you up. The Fortress is becoming so terribly grim."

Homer nodded. He did not believe a word, of course. Dee was the Prince of Liars, and always oblique. He might indeed do some cheering up, but only as a means to an end.

Homer's suspicion was solidly grounded. His handicap betrayed him. Without vision he could not detect the evil Michael planned. Only on Dee's face was the wickedness obvious, and that for but an instant.

Dee had discovered Benjamin's Achilles' heel. He had gotten the information from the man's staunchest defender, his mother, simply by listening to her brag and worry.

"Would you like to get into the game, Homer? Benjamin is dueling. Maybe he'd give you a go."

"Duel a blind man? You're a fool, Dee."

"Oh, I'll help you. Here. Benjamin. Homer wants a try." Dee glanced over his shoulder. A droplet of sweat dribbled down one temple. Thurston's weapon still tracked him with deadly precision.

"Hell, why not?" Benjamin replied. "Come on, Homer. You'll probably do better than these clowns."

As was customary, the healthy stepped aside, condescending to allow the cripple his moment.

Glibly, smoothly, Dee talked Homer to his feet, placed a dueling knife in his hand, positioned him facing his twin. The gallery watched with amused smiles. Homer sensed their amusement. His temper soared.

"Count of three," Michael said, easing back, trying to place someone between himself and Thurston. "One..."

Benjamin, playing to his audience, presented his chest to Homer's blade. He could not be hurt. No known hand weapon could penetrate the protection of his armor.

"Two..."

Guided by Benjamin's breathing, Homer lunged. He wanted to knock Ben onto his showoff ass.

For a long moment after the drugged tip of the wooden blade slipped through armor proof against any metal there was absolute silence. The tableau became a freezeframe from an old-time movie. Then Benjamin and Homer screamed with one voice. Their psi forces locked. Their rage and pain reached out to envelop the Fortress. Benjamin folded slowly. Homer fainted, toppled onto Benjamin. His mind could not withstand the psi backwash from his twin. Women shrieked. Men shouted.

And as quietly as he had come to the blind brother, while even Thurston's attention was diverted, Michael Dee slipped away.

Pandemonium invaded the hall.

When Wulf arrived he found Thurston raging among a group of young officers trying to avenge Benjamin on Homer. The big man laid them out left and right while screaming for somebody to for God's sake get the twins down to Medical.

A man slipped around Thurston and, with the guilty wooden blade, as Homer recovered consciousness, exacted vengeance. Thurston whirled and cracked the man's skull.

Homer welcomed death with a smile. That dark lady was the only woman who could love him.

Wulf ignored the drama. With Medical a minute away nobody needed die the death-without-resurrection. He was looking for people notable for their absence.

Helmut roared in clad in nothing but underwear. He had a gun in each hand. "What happened?"

"Find Dee!" Wulf ordered. "Kill him. Cut him up and shove the pieces out different locks. The Colonel can't stop it this time."

Helmut looked at the bodies. He needed no more clues.

They separated, seeking a trail. They were hounds who would not be satisfied till the blood of their quarry stained their muzzles.

Wulf was too angry. He missed the most outstanding absence. Frieda. She should have been in the middle of things, screaming and weeping over her poor baby, preventing anything sensible from getting done.

Within minutes the entire Fortress was mobilized for the sole purpose of locating Michael Dee. But somehow, despite the planetoid's limitations, he managed to evade capture.

The brothers Darksword conquered their emotions, repaired to Combat, directed the search from there.

They arrived as the man on instel communications ripped off a printout. It was a frantic message from Storm. Wulf read it first, bowed his head in despair. "Twenty minutes, that's all it would have taken."

"Signal too late. Twenty minutes too late. Sign my name," Helmut said.

"I want Dee," Wulf grumbled.

"Set the hounds on him."

"Yes."

In minutes they had Storm's Sirian warhounds seeking a trail. They found it on Residential Level. It led to the ingress locks. Their questions baffled the duty section. They had seen no one but the Colonel's wife in hours. She and two corpsmen had loaded a pair of medical-support cradles aboard an old singleship…

"Oh, hell!" Wulf swore. "You think… ?"

Helmut nodded. He grabbed a comm.

It took two calls to confirm the worst. Dee, following Homer's killing thrust, had seized Frieda and dragged her to her apartment. He had stripped and bound and gagged her, and had assumed her clothing and identity. From there he had gone to Medical and, playing on Frieda's neurotic concern from Benjamin, had convinced the duty corpsmen to transfer the dead to a hospital with planetary resources backing it. Dee had played his part to such perfection that the unsuspecting corpsmen had helped move and load the cryo coffins.

Even those who had known the Darkswords for decades were awed by the rage they displayed.

"He isn't away yet," Helmut remarked after regaining his composure. "He didn't know where the Colonel went when he pulled this. Let's see what they say in Combat. We might have a shot at him yet."

They commenced the counter game backed by Combat's resources.

"He's headed straight out," Wulf said, indicating the Dee blip in the main global display. "Putting on a lot of inherent velocity while he's getting up influence to go hyper." He picked up a pointer and indicated each of a half-dozen blips chasing Dee. "They scrambled fast."

The senior watchstander said, "I sent everybody who was on maneuvers when I heard what the situation was, sir." He happened to be the man who had disappointed Storm and Cassius in the Abhoussi and Dee incident.

"Very good," Helmut replied. "That's thinking on your feet."

"I scrambled everything in dock, too, sir. I assumed…"

"You assumed correctly," Wulf said. "Anything that will space. They're starting to come on display, Helmut."

A wild spray of diverging tracks began to spread behind the Dee blip. Wulf glanced to one side. "Tactical computer have control?"

"Yes, sir. You can input whatever the situation seems to call for."

"Basal strategy?"

"Build a plane of no return behind Dee, sir. Put the fastest ships on the rim and move them forward to make a pocket."

"Very good. Helmut, looks like we've got him. It might take a while, though."

"We're going to have to get a command ship out. We won't be able to direct it from here for long."

The senior watchstander said, "I held the *Robert Knollys*, sir. I've given them a direct feed. They're running a parallel program. You can board and shift control."

"Good. That's a good start," Wulf said.

"I believe we have him," Helmut said, peering into the display tank. "Unless he's headed somewhere damned close. That's a damned slow boat he's running."

"What's the nearest planetfall that direction?" Wulf asked. If Dee made planetfall before the jaws of pursuit closed he would become impossible to find. He would vanish amid the population and marshal his own resources in the time it took to track him down. His resources were not inconsiderable.

"Helga's World, sir."

"Ah!" Wulf began to smile. He and the Colonel definitely had aces up their sleeves.

Helmut said, "Communications are the problem. The control. There's a lot of space out there."

"And?"

"So it's time to call in old debts. See if there's a Starfisher who can relay for us. They don't love Michael either."

Wulf turned to his instel operator. "Go on the thirty-seven band with a loop. 'Storm for Gales.' "

"They'll answer if they're out there," Helmut said.

Wulf shrugged. "Maybe. People can be damned ungrateful." He told the tech, "Let us know if there's a response."

# TWENTY-EIGHT: 3052 AD

I said my father had enemies of whom he was unaware. The same was true of friends. He was a hard man, but had a strong sense of justice. It did not move him as often as it might have, but when it did, it made him friends who remained loyal forever. Such friends were the High Seiners, the Starfishers, whom he saved from enslavement on Gales.

—Masato Igarashi Storm

# TWENTY-NINE: 2973 AD

It was pure one-in-a-quadrillion chance. *Glowworm* and her sister raiders had jumped into the gulf and gone doggo, hoping they could lose Navy, which had destroyed one of their band already. It had been a long, hard chase. The three ship's commanders were scared and desperate. On *Glowworm* the group leader nearly panicked when detection picked up approaching ships.

Almost, but not quite. Powered-down vessels are hard to spot unless a hunter gets close. He decided to see what Navy did.

His detection operator soon said, "That's not them, sir. Too big. I mean, we're getting them from too far out, and they're moving too slow."

The group leader studied the patterns. He had seen nothing like this before. In time, he murmured, "Holy Christ! There ain't nothing that big. Nothing but..."

Nothing but Starfisher harvestships.

Navy was forgotten. "Track. Get a fix on their course. And nobody does anything to show them we're here. Understood?" He took his own advice. Ship to ship messages were hand carried by suited couriers till the harvestfleet left detection.

Eight great vessels shouldering along at minuscule velocities... The group leader was tempted to abandon his employer then and there. A man could name his price for what he had found.

The Starfishers controlled production of an element critical to interstellar communications systems. There was no other source, and the source was terribly limited. He who won control of a harvest fleet won control of fabulous wealth and power.

In the end, fear drove the group leader to his master.

Michael Dee did the obvious. He gathered ships and went after the harvestfleet. The operation remained his secret alone. He saw not only the obvious profit but a chance to make himself master of his own destiny.

He gambled on a surprise attack. His forces were insufficient for a plain face-to-face showdown with eight harvestships. He gambled, and he lost. He squandered his raiders and barely escaped with his life. In his fury at being thwarted he left three harvestships broken, derelict—and a nation which would do him evil gleefully whenever the opportunity arose.

Poor Michael's life was a trail of bitter enemies made. And some day the pigeons would come home to roost.

# THIRTY: 2878-3031 AD

The world wore the name Bronwen. It was far from the mainstream. Its claim to fame was that it had been the first human world occupied by Ulant. It would be the last reabsorbed by Confederation. In the interim it resembled one of those gaudy, chaotic eighteenth-century pirate havens on the north coast of Africa. Sangaree, McGraws, and free-lance pirates made planetfall and auctioned their booty. The barons of commerce came looking for bargains in goods worth the cost of interstellar shipment. Freehaulers came looking for cargo to fill their tramp freighter holds. Lonely Starfishers came down from their rivers of night for their rare intercourse with the worlds of men. Millions changed hands daily. The state was not there to watchdog and steal a cut. Those were brawling, violent days, but Bronwen's rulers were not displeased. Fortunes stuck.

Michael Dee should not have visited the world. He should not have risked having his name connected with the rogues he employed. Success had made him overconfident. He did not believe anything could break his run of luck.

The Sangaree came to his flagship, the old *Glowworm*, that Michael had acquired through straw parties when war's end had thrown scores of obsolete ships onto the salvage market. The man did not pretend to be anything but what he was. Michael found him vaguely familiar. Where had he seen the man? In the background in press rooms during the war, he thought. And, possibly, once when he was a child.

Dee did not like puzzles. He did not like not being able to remember clearly. Memory was his best weapon. But the man had never impinged directly upon his reality… The Sangaree initially claimed to be a buyer. Michael watched the man pass through his security screens, wondering. He did not look the type. Too fat, too self-confident in that intangible way powerful men have. Fencing stolen goods would be a chore for fourth-level underlings. Dee secured his observation screen and waited.

The man entered his cabin, extended a hand, said, "Norbon w'Deeth. The Norbon."

Michael's underworld connections now extended into the Sangaree sphere. He had dealt with the race directly on occasion. They were sharp, cautious, and carefully honest in their business arrangements. They were paranoiac in their efforts to protect the secrets of Homeworld, Family, and Head.

This was a Head! And his Family's name was turning up everywhere these days. The Norbon had exploded into prominence wherever Sangaree operated.

He took the proffered hand. "An honor. How can I be of service?"

Michael masked his thinking well. He did not betray his consternation and curiosity. The Norbon was just another businessman for all the reaction he showed.

The man was damned young for a Head, he reflected. But you could never be sure in these days of rejuvenation and resurrection. He had the hard lines in his forehead and at the corners of his eyes. The man inside was old in thought if not in his flesh.

The Norbon eyed him. "How's your mother?"

The question took Michael by surprise. It came at him from the least expected angle. "Well enough, I suppose. I've been out of touch with the family."

"Yes. The war did disrupt things, didn't it? And helped some of us profit."

The slightest of frowns crossed Michael's vulpine face. He felt a case of nerves coming on.

"And the rest of your family?"

"Good enough. We Storms are hard to kill."

"I've discovered that."

Michael used a toe to caress an alarm button. In seconds a needlegun, in the hand of a reliable man, began tracking Dee's visitor from behind an apparently solid bulkhead.

"None harder than I, sir. You make me uncomfortable. Can you get to your point?" Michael was surprised at himself. He was never this direct. The Sangaree had him shaking.

"We have Family business. With the big F. Your Family and mine. There's an unsettled matter between the Norbon and Storms. No doubt you know the tale. I came to find out where you'll stand."

"You've lost me." The man had Dee totally baffled. It broke through to his face.

"I see I'll have to go back to the beginning. All right. Twenty-eight forty-four. Acting on information received from Sangaree renegades, Commodore Boris Storm and Colonel of Marines Thaddeus Immanuel Walters invaded Prefactlas. They destroyed the Family stations and slaughtered any Sangaree they found. My mother, my father, and hundreds of Norbon dependents were among the dead. Only a handful of people escaped. Norbon w'Deeth was one of the survivors."

Michael shrugged as if to say, "So what?" and did say, "Those are the breaks of the business."

"Yes. That's the human attitude toward risk and reward. Not that much different from our own except that those men felt compelled to make it a slaughter instead of a raid. It stopped being business when they took that attitude. It became vendetta. I survived. It's my duty to exact retribution."

Michael had begun to get the feel of it. His nerves were steadier. "There's a needlegun on you."

His visitor smiled. "I never doubted it. You're a reasonably cautious man."

"Then you're not here to kill me?"

"Far from it. I'm here to sign you up for my side."

Michael's jaw dropped.

The Norbon laughed. "That's the first time I've actually seen anybody do that."

"What?"

The Norbon shook a hand in a gesture meaning never mind. "You're in the middle, Michael. You've got one foot on each side. I want to get them both on mine."

"You confuse me. I don't have any special love for my family. That's common knowledge. But I don't have reason one to want them destroyed, either. In fact, it's a valuable connection sometimes."

"I understand. Yes. The problem is that I've been too obscure. I assumed you knew. Let's go back to your mother. She was slave-born, as humans say. You know that much?"

"Yes. So?"

"She was born and trained at the Norbon facility on Prefactlas. She was its only female survivor. For ten years she and I fought barbarians, Confies, Corporation beekies, sickness, and plain old bad luck together. And we made it through. Our relationship became as deep as one can between a man and a woman. We even parented a child."

Michael began to glimpse the shaggy edges of it. And it was a monster indeed. Yet… Yet it would explain so much that had puzzled him.

It was almost too simple an answer.

"You expect me to believe that crap?"

"It's happened before. It's genetically certain that human and Sangaree spring from the same ur-stock, sometime deep in proto-history. That both races are repelled by the idea doesn't alter the facts. There were races here before ours, Michael. Who knows what experiments they performed, or why, before they faded from history's stage?"

"And who cares?"

Deeth ignored his remark. "There's a curious thing about Homeworld, Michael. It's perfect for human habitation. A lot like Old Earth was before the Industrial Revolution. We Sangaree fill the human ecological niche there. But, and it's a curious big but, there's no archaeological or anthropological evidence of our presence before about the time Cro-Magnon appeared on Old Earth. There's no evolutionary chain. Nothing to connect with. No other primates at all. And we sometimes crossbreed with humans. What conclusion has to be drawn?"

That conclusion was irrelevant in an essentially emotional context. And Michael was responding to feelings, not reason.

He had grown up with an absolute presumption that the Sangaree were racial enemies. They were to be exterminated—unless momentary intercourse offered profit or advantage.

*I can't be my own enemy*, Michael thought.

"That's all I'll say about it now," his visitor said. "Think about it. It's a big bit to chew on. And don't forget. I'll help you as much as you help me. Oh. For what it's worth, you're technically my heir. You're my only child."

Numb, Michael pressed a button. It released the lock on the cabin door. The Sangaree departed.

Michael did not encounter the Norbon again for years. He had ample time to forget. He could not. His character took over. He began to scheme, to find ways he could use the Sangaree.

What he could not see, till it was too late, was that he was the one being used. Norbon w'Deeth was a gentle, subtle spider. He spun his natural son into webs of intrigue so soft that Michael did not recognize the chrysalis of doom enveloping him. In the time of the Shadowline some of the cobwebs were lifted from his eyes. And he wept. By then he could do nothing but follow instructions and try to deceive himself as to who was the real spinner.

Even his best-laid schemes betrayed him now.

Old Frog laughed in his grave. Michael had risked everything to kill the dwarf and suppress his secret till he could exploit it himself. The riches at the Shadowline's end would have gotten him out from under. They would have bought him a comfortable and anonymous new life free of the Sangaree and his family alike.

The Norbon found out. Somehow. And fed him orders that could encompass the destruction of the family Storm.

Dee squirmed. He writhed and tried to get away. The Norbon kept the pressure on, often through Michael's children by a marriage he had arranged, often economically. Michael could not wriggle loose. Perhaps his final defeat came when Deeth compelled him to drop the name Storm and adopt the subtle mockery of Dee.

Michael did not overlook the obvious. He did think of going to his brother for help. He rejected the notion. He knew how his brother would respond. If he believed at all. Gneaus would tell him to stand on his hind legs and act like a man. He simply would not understand.

And by staying in line he could even scores with Richard. That damned Richard. His little moment of spite had started this whole damned thing.

Michael had spun the anchor silk himself, then had lost control of his web to a bigger, nastier spider. In the year of the Shadowline he was caught on the back of a galloping nightmare. His only hope was that she would not deal him too brutal a fall when she reached the end of her run.

He denied hope. In his way he was as convinced of his imminent doom as was Gneaus of his.

# THIRTY-ONE: 3031 AD

It was a very exclusive toy shop. It even served tiny cups of coffee or tea with cutesy little cookies. Cassius was in hog's heaven.

"Not very exciting, is it?" he asked.

Mouse squeezed his eyes shut in a fierce squint. "No, it's not." He could not stay awake. They had been on The Big Rock Candy Mountain four days. Cassius had not given him much chance to sleep. "All we do is hunk around asking the same old questions."

"That's what intelligence work is, Mouse. You knock on doors and ask the same old questions till you get the right answers. Or you sit at headquarters and feed the computer the same old answers till it gives you the right question." He wound the music box again. It played a tune neither of them knew. A tiny porcelain mouse twirled and danced to the music. "Isn't that cute?"

"It doesn't seem worth the trouble."

"Mr. Russell. I'll take the music box: Can you have it shipped?"

They did have a few leads. Cassius had good, highly placed contacts on The Mountain, on both sides of the law. He had them asking questions too.

Michael had not worked hard to conceal his presence. They had unearthed a dozen people who had seen him here, there, or somewhere else, usually with Gneaus Storm. A few had seen him with one or two other men not locally known. They had had a hard look.

Dee had stopped being evident after Storm's departure, though he had not himself departed for several days.

"It's worth it. There's a pattern shaping up."

"What pattern?" Mouse signaled the sales clerk/waiter. "May I have another coffee?"

"That I don't know yet. I can see just a little of the edge. We've spread out plenty of money and eyes. Something will shake loose pretty soon."

"Speaking of eyes. Your friend the Captain has been watching us. Through the window and from next door. He doesn't look happy."

A hint of frown wrinkled Cassius's brow. He turned, gazed into the crystal shop connected with the toy store. His gaze met the policeman's. The officer took a deep breath, shrugged, and came through the connecting doorway. He seemed both angry and defensive.

"You might as well join us," Cassius said. "Easier to stay with us. What's the problem, Karl? Why do I suddenly need shadowing?" Cassius squatted, pushed a knobby plastic disk into the back of a caricature of a railroad train engine. The toy began chugging around the floor, tooting an old-time children's tune. "The only thing wrong with collecting these things is, if you want to do anything but sit and look at them, you have to special order the energy cells from an outfit on Old Earth. They're not even remotely like anything we use today. Russell! You sure this isn't a reproduction? Do you have a certificate?"

The waiter/clerk brought Mouse's coffee. He brought a cup for the policeman, who turned it slowly between his fingers before saying, "Maybe I'm watching you for your own protection. What're you up to, Cassius? A favor for a friend, that's what you told me. I owed you one. I didn't figure on getting caught in a crossfire."

"Something has happened."

"Something has happened, he says. You're so goddamned right. You've stirred up something I didn't count on."

"What's wrong, Karl?"

"We picked up five bodies this morning, my friend. Five. That's what's wrong. And I don't like it. The Mountain is a quiet place. People come here to get away from it all. They lease little houses in the outback, guaranteed to be fifty klicks from the nearest neighbor. Once a month they fly maybe halfway around the world to come in and pick up groceries or meet a buddy for a beer. If they wanted gang wars they could stay home."

"Karl, you'd better back it up. I missed something."

Mouse shook his head vigorously. Sleep had snuck up on him again.

"The word in the street is, you asked Clementine to do some poking around for you. Somebody took exception. Violent exception. Four of his boys went down this morning. We don't know who the hell the other guy is. An offworlder. No ID. Took a slug behind the ear. Clementine's old-time autograph."

"Curious," Cassius said.

"Curious, my ass. We've got a little unofficial kind of deal here, friend. We don't bother Clementine. He behaves himself and doesn't scare the tourists. We pick up enough hookers and gamers to pacify the strait-lacers, and the judges release them on their own recognizance. Clementine pays their fines. They're part of what brings the tourists in, so everybody comes up happy. He stays away from the stardust and windowpane and other heavy stuff and we stay away from him."

"A civilized arrangement." Cassius puttered with a toy steam shovel. "Don't you think so, Mouse?"

Mouse shrugged.

"Cassius," the officer said, "it's been four years since we've had a gang killing. There's no competition. Clementine keeps his people satisfied. So I get a friend come in doing a favor for a friend, and all of a sudden I've got bodies all over town."

"I'm sorry, Karl. Honestly. I didn't expect it. I don't understand it. You're sure it's because of me?"

"That's the feedback I get. Some high-powered out-worlders don't like questions being asked. They're sending Clementine a message."

"Who?"

"We don't know. Somebody important, I'd guess. From the Big Outfit. Maybe there's a meet on neutral ground. Nobody local would have the balls to push Clementine. He don't push."

"Yeah. I see what you mean. Russell? How much for the shovel?"

"I'm scared, friend," said the policeman. "Clementine is a peaceful guy. But when he gets riled he doesn't have sense enough to keep his head down. He'll fight. If it's the Big Outfit… Well, let's just say I like our arrangement. We get along. We don't have any trouble. We all know where we stand. If they move in…"

Something buzzed. The officer removed a handcomm from his pocket. "Heller." He pressed the device to his ear. His face became grave.

He put the comm away, considered Cassius momentarily. "That's three more down, friend. Two of theirs and one of Clementine's. It's got to be the Big Outfit. One looked Sangaree."

Cassius frowned. Mouse lost all interest in sleep. Baffled, he asked, "Sangaree? Cassius? Did we walk into something?"

"Sure as hell starting to look like it. Karl, I don't know what the hell is coming down. This isn't what we expected. We came looking for one thing and found something else. I'll talk to Clementine. I'll try to calm him down."

"You do that. And keep in touch. I don't like this. I don't want those people in here." Heller downed his coffee in a single gulp, started away. "Look out for yourself, friend. I don't want to scrape you up, too."

Mouse and Cassius watched him go. "What do you think?" Mouse asked. The boredom was gone. Sleepiness was forgotten. He was extremely uneasy.

"I think we'd better get back to the hotel and lay low. This doesn't look good."

Cassius paused at the hotel desk. "Suite Twelve," he said, requesting the key. "Any messages?"

Mouse leaned against the desk, watching the clerk hopefully. There might be something from his father. There wasn't. Nothing but a brief instelgram from the Fortress of Iron. Cassius read it aloud.

Mouse watched a lean old man come off the street. He had seen the man outside, watching them come in. There had been something strange about his eyes... "Cassius! Down!"

He dove toward the nearest furniture, drawing a tiny, illegal weapon as he flew. Cassius tumbled the other way.

Calmly, the old man opened fire.

A hotel patron screamed, fell, writhed on the plush lobby carpeting. A bolt hit Mouse's protective couch. Smoke billowed.

Cassius hit their attacker with his second shot. The old man did not go down. Wearing a mildly surprised expression, he kept hosing the lobby with beam fire from a military-type weapon. People screamed. Furniture burned. Alarms wailed. Diffused beams skipping off the mirrored walls made it impossible to see.

Mouse gagged in the smoke, snapped a shot at the old man. His bolt singed the assassin's hair. He did not seem to notice.

Cassius hit him again. He turned and walked out the door as if unharmed...

"Mouse," Cassius shouted, "call Heller. I'm going after him."

Mouse placed the call and was outside in seconds.

The old man lay on the sidewalk, curled in a fetal position, his weapon clutched to his chest. Cassius stood over him. He wore a puzzled look. Heller arrived almost before the crowds started gathering.

"What the hell, hey?" the policeman demanded.

"This man tried to kill us," Mouse babbled. "Just walked in the hotel and started shooting."

Cassius was kneeling now, studying the man's eyes. "Karl. Look. I think it's one of them."

Someone in the crowd said, "Hey. That's Cassius. The merc."

"Crap," a companion replied.

The word spread.

Heller snarled at a uniformed officer, "Get this cleaned up before the news snoops show. Take the body down to the plant. Cassius, I've got to take you and your friend down. I can't take any more of this."

Ten minutes later they were inside the police fortress. The street outside had filled with news people. The name Cassius had that effect.

"Just plan on sitting tight till we get this straightened out," Heller said, responding to Cassius's request that he be allowed to visit the man named Clementine. "He can come here if you've got to talk."

The shooting was all the news that evening. The net-folk were trying to establish a connection between the various murders. The editorialists were working the Legion over, insisting that The Mountain did not need its kind. Mouse listened halfheartedly while watching Cassius work.

Walters pulled out the stops. He used all his connections. He drew on the Legion's considerable credit to have the old shooter resurrected. The attempt failed because the man had been too old. He shifted his thrust to the instel nets, where he spent fortunes.

"Karl, you got that stuff ready to go out? I've got a connect with my man in Luna Command."

Heller was impressed despite himself. "Push the red button. It'll squirt when you do."

Cassius punched. "On its way. If there's anything on record about the old guy, Beckhart has it. He runs their Sangaree section. Good man. Taught him myself, years ago."

"I've heard of him," Heller replied. The last few hours had dazed the policeman. He was in over his head. Cassius had turned a local affair into an interstellar incident. He did not like it and did not know how to stop it.

Mouse watched with mild amusement till he fell asleep.

The sun was up when Cassius wakened him. "Come on, Mouse. We're heading home."

"Where?"

"Home."

"But..."

'We got what we came for. You do the flying. I need some sleep."

Heller escorted them to the port, which the police had closed till they got the crisis in hand. His okay was necessary before any vessel could lift off.

"Cassius?" Heller said as Walters was about to board. "Do me a favor, eh? Don't hurry back."

Cassius grinned. For a moment he looked like a boy again, instead of a tired, old, old man. "Karl, if you make me apologize one more time I'll puke. All right? I owe you one. A big one."

"Okay. Okay. You didn't bring them here. Go on. Get out of here before I forget I forgot to charge you with carrying illegal weapons."

Mouse glanced over as Cassius settled into the acceleration couch beside him. Walters said, "Set a base curve for Helga's World."

Mouse began the programming. "Why there?" He was baffled. By everything. "Cassius? What happened last night?"

Cassius answered with a snore.

He slept nine hours. Mouse grew ever more impatient. Cassius seldom slept more than five, and resented that, as if it were time stolen from his alloted span.

Mouse took the ship offworld, aligned the Helga's World curve, put her into a power fly while getting up influence to go hyper.

"Keep putting on inherent," Cassius said by way of announcing his return. "On this base you lose about a thousand klick-seconds on your inherent when you drop and we may want to make a fast pass when we get there."

"Now will you tell me what happened while I was asleep?"

"We got an ID on that old shooter. From my friend Beckhart. Turned out nobody else could have filled us in. The guy was supposed to have been dead for two hundred years."

"What?"

"Beckhart's got a computer that remembers everything. When he fed it the guy's personals it dug all the way back to personnel records we captured on Prefactlas. That's where it found him. His name was Rhafu. He worked for the Norbon Family. The Norbon station was where we caught them with their fingers up their butts."

Mouse examined the idea more closely than it seemed to deserve. Cassius's attitude implied that the information was especially significant. "What's the kicker?"

"Beckhart didn't just answer the question I asked. He went looking for the meaning. He instelled us an abstract of his printouts. This Rhafu wasn't the only survivor. The Family heir, a sort of crown prince, made it through too. They managed to get off Prefactlas and somehow reclaim their Family prerogatives. Very mysterious people. Their own kind don't know any more about them than we do, but they're mucho respected and feared. Sort of the Sangaree's Sangaree. They've turned the Norbon into one of the top Sangaree Families. Their economic base is an otherwise unknown First Expansion world."

"What's the connection with us? That old man didn't try to kill us because we had the wrong color eyes. He meant it personal."

"Very personal. You'd have to have Sangaree eyes to see it, though."

"Well?"

"They'd figure a personal involvement got started the night your grandfather and I spaced in on Prefactlas. Nobody has ever quite figured out how they distinguish what's business, what's the fortunes of war, and what's personal. It's a violent and volatile culture with its own unique rules. The Norbon seem to have decided the Prefactlas raid wasn't just war."

"You don't mean they've picked us for the other half of one of those Family vendettas?"

"I do. It's the only answer that makes sense. And our burning this Rhafu will only make them madder. Don't ask me to tell you why. They don't understand us, either. They can't figure out what makes us want to destroy them."

"I'm lost, Cassius. What's the connection with Michael Dee? Or is there one? Wouldn't there have to be? To have brought the old man out?"

"There may be one. I want to think about it before I say anything. You've got a red and yellow on your comm board. You might better see who wants to get hold of us."

Mouse did so. After listening a moment, "Cassius, it's a Starfisher with a relay from Wulf and Helmut."

"Shut up and listen to the man."

In fifteen minutes they knew the worst.

"Push your influence factor to the red line," Cassius told him. "Keep putting on inherent. I want to be going like the proverbial bat out of hell when we go norm again." He remained calm and businesslike while studying the displays the computer brought up on the main astrogational screen. He fed in everything the Darkswords had given them. He plotted alternate hyper arcs for Helga's World.

"But…"

"She'll take it. More if she has to. Check the register. I need the *c*-relative on the boat Dee swiped."

Mouse punched it up. "Old Mister Smart, my uncle Michael. He grabbed the slowest damned ship we had. Almost, anyway. Here're a couple of trainers she can outrun."

"One break for the good guys. About time we got one. Well. Look here. We're going to get him. About an hour before he sneaks under Helga's missile umbrella. Sooner if he has to maneuver to get around your father. Start a check down on the weapons systems."

Mouse fidgeted.

"What's the matter?"

"Uh… You think there'll be any shooting?"

Cassius smiled a broad, wicked smile. "Goddamned right, boy. There's going to be beaucoup shooting. First time for you, right? You just hang on and do what I tell you. We'll be all right."

The waiting bothered Mouse. He was not afraid, much. The hours piled up, and the hours piled up, and they seemed no closer than before…

"Here we go," Cassius said, almost cheerfully. "Got your father on screen. And there's your idiot uncle, hopping around like a barefoot man in a sandbrier patch. Give your guns a burst."

The hours became minutes. Cassius kept boring in. "Ah, damn!" he swore suddenly. "Gneaus, what the hell did you have to go and do that for?"

"What?" Mouse demanded. He shed his harness and leaned over. "What did he do?"

"Sit down, shithead. It's going to get rough."

It got rougher than Mouse could imagine.

# THIRTY-TWO: 3052 AD

My father was not a religious man. Nevertheless, he did have an unshakable faith in predestination. Till the very end he thought he was battling the invincible forces of Fate. You could sense that he expected no victory, but you never despaired. You knew that Gneaus Storm would never surrender.

—Masato Igarashi Storm

# THIRTY-THREE: 3031 AD

The Seiner got through just after Storm left the atmosphere of Helga's World.

"He's gone? Already?" The tension he had been riding like a nightmare suddenly dissipated. He found himself emotionally limp, hanging out to dry. His right hand snaked out, secured the instel receiver.

The limpness did not last. Rage and sorrow smashed down on him. It was a crushing emotional avalanche. The feelings were so powerful that a small, stunned part of him recoiled in amazement.

There in the privacy of his ship, locked away from all human eyes, he could safely open the flood gates. He did so, venting not only emotions engendered by his failure to save Benjamin and Homer, but his responses to all the frustrations that had been building since first he had heard of Blackworld and the Shadowline. He wept, cursed, asked the gods what justice there was in a universe where a man could not control his own fate.

The universe and gods, of course, did not reply.

There was no justice in that momentary eddy in chaos. There never had been or would be. A man made his own justice if he wanted any at all.

Storm knew that. But sometimes even the most strongly anchored mind slips its cables and refuses to accept reality. Once in a while, at least, it seemed the gods or universe ought to care.

Storm vowed, "I'll get a bit of justice of my own." He had been making a lot of vows lately, he realized. Would he survive long enough to see any of them fulfilled?

The shakes were going. The tears had dried. His voice was losing its tightness. He opened instel communications again. "Starfisher? Are you there? Why are you nosing into this?" Those people did not get involved in the troubles of outsiders.

There was a long delay. "Lady Prudence of Gales, Colonel. And other reasons involving the man you're chasing. Not subject to discussion. Do you wish a relay?"

"Yes. Fortress of Iron."

"Ready when you are, Colonel."

"Wulf? Are you there?"

In time, "Here, Colonel."

"Recall Cassius."

"He's finished already. He's on his way. I've inserted him into the pursuit pattern."

"Good. Anything new?"

"Dee is running for Helga's World. The Seiners have given us a projected course. He'll be coming right down your throat. I'm using box and plane and I'm tightening it up to keep him headed your way. I've got Cassius on an intercept that should catch Dee just after he spots you and sheers off Helga's World. The trap should close before he recognizes it."

The trap's mouth closed slowly. Even at velocities many times that of light it took a long ledger of days before the scale of action tightened enough to warrant Storm's taking his ship off auto control. For a while he lay motionless in relation to the nearest stars, listening to the Seiner's reports. He kept influence up so he could make a quick snake-strike at Dee as he came up. Essentially, he was pretending to be a singularity.

Michael did not fall for it. He could not know who was waiting to ambush him, but he did know that there were no singularities near his daughter's world. He shifted course into the one gap apparently open to him.

And there was Cassius, playing a trick not unlike Storm's but remaining in normspace with an inherent velocity approaching that of light.

Dee's nose swung toward the tiniest of cracks in the closing walls of the trap. He attacked it with every erg his ship could give.

Storm put way on. Cassius skipped into hyper. The quiet dance, that might but likely would not end in a blaze of weaponry, began. Storm wondered if his brother were desperate enough to fight. It was not Michael's style, but he might panic, not knowing who had blocked his flight.

Maneuver. Counter-maneuver. Feint and lunge. Dee tried to fake Storm out of position for the vital few seconds he needed to whip past and streak for the safety of Helga's World.

Wulf's pursuing box closed in while Dee surrendered straight-line velocity for maneuver.

Cassius arrowed in on a spear of a course, riding the fastest ship involved. His sprint would put him across Dee's bows if Michael took too long getting past Storm. Even separated by light-hours and without direct communication, Cassius and Storm worked as a team.

Storm became satisfied that his singleship would outperform his brother's. He could commit one narrow error and still not lose his man. In dealing with Michael a second was a treasure to be hoarded against the unpredictable, but Gneaus no longer felt like playing safe. He wanted Dee, and wanted him quick. He decided to risk his advantage.

Pushing as hard as his ship would endure without breaking up under hyper stress, he darted toward where he expected Michael to be next. He fed max power to his influential field. Dee's ship had the stronger generator and would take his under control, but then it would take Michael precious minutes in norm to disentangle the fields. Cassius would arrive. He would mesh his field with the others long enough for Wulf to slam the lid on the box.

Michael recognized his intention. He sheered off. Too late. The tracks of the singleships continued to converge.

Storm pulled closer and closer, at a steadily decreasing relative velocity, till his influential sphere just brushed his brother's.

His singleship screamed. Alarms hooted. An effect that could only be described as fifth-dimensional precession took place as both ships tried to twist away in a direction that did not exist. Storm's shipboard computer calmly murmured portents of disaster.

Swift as lightning and as jagged, hairline cracks scurried across his control-room walls. Even before he heard a sound Storm knew that his engine room's stressteel frame members were snapping, that his generators were crawling free of their mounts. His hand darted toward the manual override, to cancel his approach program, but he knew it was too late. Either his drive or Michael's was badly out of synch.

Dee had won again.

This might be the death-without-resurrection, his hope no more than a chance at a clone. It was no solace that Michael might share his fate.

His hand changed course and shot toward the disaster escape release.

Crystals and fog formed before his vision went. His skin protested the nibbling of a thousand hot little needles as vacuum gulped the contents of his control room. The locked vessels had precessed into norm space. Their conflicting inherent velocities were tearing them apart.

Before the darkness came there was a moment in which he wished he had been a better father and husband. And had had the sense to wear a combat suit going into a combat situation.

# THIRTY-FOUR: 2853-2880 AD

Deeth had thought he was immune to pain. Hell, the girl wasn't even Sangaree...

He walked. And walked, without paying any attention to where he was going. His feet responded to some instinct for the debts he owed. They carried him to the spaceport.

It had grown during the human occupation. Prefactlas Corporation involved itself in far more shipping than ever the Sangaree had. The port was furiously busy. The Corporation was gutting the world.

He paused to watch the stevedores unloading a big Star Line freight lighter. The Corporation employed natives and former slaves because human muscle power was less expensive than imported lading machinery.

A familiar face turned his way.

"Holy Sant!" he whispered, spinning away. "It can't be." He looked again. Rhafu's weathered face seemed to swell till it occupied his whole field of vision. The breeding master had aged terribly, but Deeth did not doubt his identity for an instant.

The old man did not seem to notice one curious boy. Back-country kids came in to stare at the wondrous port all the time.

It took all Deeth's will power not to run and hug Rhafu, to seize this one scrap that had survived a devastated past.

He fled instead, his mind a riot. The possibilities!

Rhafu's very existence set off the alarm bells. Was he a human agent, either human himself or someone who had made an accommodation to the animals? Someone had betrayed Prefactlas. The perfect timing of the attack on the Norbon station reflected possession of solid inside information.

If Rhafu were guilty why was he now a laborer, mildewing on the ass of the social scale? The humans would have killed their traitor the instant he was no longer useful. Or would have rewarded him better.

Deeth locked himself into the crude shack where he and Emily lived. Where he lived. Emily was no longer a part of his poverty. He would never see her again. He wrestled with his fears and suspicions.

Someone knocked. He had few acquaintances. Police? Emily?

Expecting a blow from the hammer of fate, he opened the door.

Rhafu pushed through, seized his left wrist, glared at the tattoo still visible there. The stony hardness left his face. He slammed the door, enveloped Deeth in a ferocious hug. "Sant be praised, Sant be praised," he murmured.

Deeth wriggled free and stepped back. There were tears in the old man's eyes.

"Deeth. I couldn't believe my eyes when I saw you at the pits. Thought my mind was playing tricks. I gave up years ago. Lad, what's been keeping you? Where've you been?"

Deeth babbled his own questions.

They hugged again.

The past had come home. He was Norbon w'Deeth again. He was Sangaree. He was a Head… Of a one-man Family?

"Hold it. Hold it," Rhafu said. "Let's get organized. You tell me your story, then I'll tell you mine."

"You make me green with anticipation," Deeth complained.

"And compel you to be brief if you want your questions answered," Rhafu countered.

Deeth wasted few words. When he mentioned finding the remains of the Dharvon heir, Rhafu chuckled but withheld comment.

"The girl," he asked when Deeth finished. "You're sure you can trust her? We can reach her."

"She'll keep her mouth shut." He saw murder in Rhafu's eyes.

"It's wisest to take no chances."

"She won't say anything."

"You're the Norbon." Rhafu shrugged as if to say he was acceding to Deeth against his better judgment.

"Tell me your damned story, you old scoundrel. How the hell did you manage to live through the raid?"

"Your father's orders. He had second thoughts about sending you off alone. Said he wanted you to have a bodyguard and adviser during the hard times after the raid."

"How you survived is what stumps me."

"It was grim. By then the Marines were dropping their perimeter. We killed all the breeders and field hands who knew me. I dressed up as a wild one. The first Marines in found me leading an attack on one of the guest cottages, howling and screaming and throwing spears around like a rabid caveman."

Deeth frowned.

"It was the Dharvon cottage, Deeth. By then your father had determined that they were behind the raid. They were supposed to get ten points in the Prefactlas Corporation, and all the Norbon holdings. They thought they could get Osiris that way. The animals might have gone through with the deal, too. Boris Storm is an honorable man. I suppose I saved him a lot of soul-searching by killing his Sangaree partners."

"All this because my father couldn't bring himself to share Osiris."

"Who sows the wind reaps the whirlwind. Your father was too jealous of his wealth, in hand or in prospect. Though he did judge the Dharvon correctly when he foresaw that a Wholar would be wasted on them."

"Where do we stand? As a Family."

"In vendetta with the Dharvon. I've resumed communication with your House on Homeworld. The Dharvon have recovered under a cadet line. The Norbon remain a House divided. There is a dwindling Deeth faction still hoping you'll return and lead them to Osiris. The other faction, naturally getting stronger by the month, want a new Head declared so they can control what the House has now. The human and Ulantonid spheres will collide before long. They want to develop a strong raid force and cash in."

"I see." As he remembered talk overheard during childhood, it sounded like typical in-House politics. Neither faction would be overjoyed by his reappearance. "But back to your escape. It couldn't have been that simple. These animals aren't fools."

"It did take some doing. They tried to double check every captive to make sure none of us got away by hiding with the slaves. I mostly outran them. I had a hard few years, then I got settled in here. Except for the occasional agent from off planet, you're the first of our people I've seen in nine years."

"We're the only survivors?" Prefactlas was irrevocably lost, then.

He had known that for a long time. The planet had been lost the moment a Dharvon had approached a human. He had been ducking the final admission. The denial was one brick in the wall he had raised to hide himself from the charge his father had set upon him. "How have you been keeping yourself, Rhafu? And do we have anything to build on?" His duty could be shirked no more.

Rhafu smiled. "I haven't been remiss. Once a field man, always a field man. Don't let my job fool you. I've become a very rich man. Being the only one of our people here has certain advantages. I've become the underworld here. I control it all. Without bragging, I can say the only man on Prefactlas with more power is Boris Storm. Nobody knows who I am, but everybody has heard of me."

"The Serpent?"

"In the scaly flesh."

"I'll be damned." Deeth laughed uncontrollably. "Why didn't we run into each other sooner? Years have gone to waste, Rhafu." The laughter evaporated. Rhafu had an empire of his own now. He might consider old obligations a liability.

"Were that true," Rhafu replied to Deeth's indirect question, "I wouldn't be here today. I would've gotten off Prefactlas as soon as I had the machinery running smooth. I'd have gone somewhere safe and collected my cut and shown my strength just often enough to keep the would-be independents in line. No. I stayed because I still haven't fulfilled my contract with the Norbon."

Deeth grinned. Rhafu was as sentimental as a Sangaree could be. "What should we do now, Rhafu?"

The old man grinned right back. "That's easy. We just reclaim the Family and its Homeworld power base."

"Really? That's going to take money and muscle, my friend. Do you have it?"

"No. Not enough. We'll have to liquidate here and use the cash to pick up a ship and some good men. We'll have to work Osiris till we're strong enough. We'll have to stay away from Homeworld but keep the Family informed so you don't get frozen out of your patrimony. Osiris will be our leverage. It'll bring them into line. Let's see. Maybe two years? Then at least another two to consolidate and fatten the Family on Osiris? Another five to settle with the Dharvon, defend ourselves in court and accommodate ourselves with any new enemies the feud stirs up, and to thoroughly develop the Osirian operation? Another year or two just for margin? Say plan on at least ten before we're solid, strong, and in any position to get down to the real work your father left us, the destruction of the animals who killed him and your mother."

"That's a lot of years, Rhafu."

"You had something else to do with them? Perhaps you went through all that business in that cave just so you could retire?"

The years rolled away into the dusty corners of time. Deeth and Rhafu made dream after dream come real. They recaptured the Homeworld Norbon.

They went to Osiris. They built a Norbon Family as strong and feared as any among the Sangaree. By cunning and guile they devoured several small Houses whom the Dharvon, aware of their Family's complicity in the Prefactlas disaster, tried to frame with forged evidence. When the Norbon rapacity had been sated and they were ready to settle with the Dharvon for all time, Deeth had a friend bring in damning documents lifted directly from Prefactlas Corporation files.

Emily stayed one day after her appearance before the assembled Heads of the First Families. She had become a stunning woman. Deeth felt the yearnings of their earlier life together. As did she. But...

Her years with Boris Storm had chipped the rough edges off her. She was no longer Emily the fugitive pleasure girl. She had become a lady, and one even a Sangaree must respect. She was a completely different person. She merely shared a few memories with Norbon w'Deeth's little Emily.

And Deeth was no longer an orphan boy surviving in a shack in a slum on an enemy world.

They spent a quiet afternoon walking the perfectly landscaped gardens of the Norbon Family holding, remembering when and trying to get to know the people they had become.

It was a ritual of ending, a final emotional endorsement of the separation that had taken place while they were still those other people. In their respective ways they agreed that there were no debts between them now, no enmities, and no tomorrows.

Deeth shed a tear for her when she left him. And never saw her again.

But the children that she brought with her, the sons, would cross his path again and again.

# BOOK TWO
## HANGMEN

*Who springs the trap when the hangman dies?*

# THIRTY-FIVE: 3052 AD

Some of the most unpleasant moments in life come when we have to face the fact that our parents are human and mortal. For me the revelations came in quick succession. They really rocked me, though I think I concealed my shock at the time.

I grew up believing my father a demigod. In an offhand way I knew he was mortal, but it simply never occurred to me that he could be killed. I suppose I should thank my uncle for removing those scales from my eyes.

I have only my father to thank, or blame, for making me realize that even the wise and noble Gneaus Julius Storm could be petty, arrogant, blind, unnecessarily cruel, and maybe even a little stupid. This latter revelation touched me far more deeply than did the other. After all, we all begin life under sentence of death. But nowhere is it written that our time on death row is to be spent compounding the idiocies and miseries of our fellow condemned.

Though I did not love him less afterward, I lost my awe of my father after witnessing his brush with my uncle. For a time just his presence made me suffer.

The loss of an illusion is a painful thing.

—Masato Igarashi Storm

# THIRTY-SIX: 3031 AD

Gneaus Storm gradually drifted up into a universe of gnawing pain.

Where was he? What had happened?

His dying hand had reached the switch in time. Or the automatics had asserted themselves. Somehow, he had been enveloped by the escape balloon before vacuum could take a fatal bite.

He knew that he had not died. There was very little pain in a resurrection. When you died the docs gave you a complete overhaul before they brought you around again. You came out with the vivacity, spirit, and lack of internal pain characteristic of youth. If you did not die, and you came back by more mundane medical processes, you had to play it by Nature's old rules. You took the pain along with the repairs.

More than once Storm wished they had let him go. Or that Cassius had had the decency to return him to the Fortress for proper medical care.

Storm once returned to consciousness to find a worry-faced, exhausted Mouse hovering over his medicare cradle. "Mouse," he croaked, "what are you doing here?"

"Cassius told me to stay," the boy replied. "It's part of my training." He forced a smile.

"He begged me." Cassius's voice, through the additional filter of the intercom speaker, sounded doubly mechanical and remote.

"Son, you've got to go back to Academy," Storm insisted, forgetting that he had lost this argument once before.

"It's arranged," Cassius said.

Perhaps it was, Storm reflected. He was not remembering clearly. The past month was all a jumble. Maybe Cassius had used his clout with the War College.

He tried to laugh. His reward was a shot of excruciating pain. Vacuum had done a job on his lungs.

"He needed somebody to watch you and Michael," Mouse told him, unaware that his father did not quite realize what was going on. "That's not a one-man job even with Michael sedated."

Storm remembered some of it. He smiled. Michael really impressed Cassius. Dee was only a man. He had been bested as often as not. His greatest talent was that of weaver of his own legend.

"He survived too, eh?" He remembered most of it now.

"He came through in better shape than you did," Cassius said. "He took some elementary precautions."

"It was his boat that was off tune," Mouse added. "He jiggered it on purpose. A trick he learned from Hawksblood. Hawksblood sets all his drives so they're off tune with everything but each other."

"His first intelligence coup," Cassius droned. "Though anybody with computer time and a little inspiration could have figured it out. Give him credit for the inspiration."

Mouse reddened slightly.

"We're headed for the asteroid?" Storm asked.

Mouse nodded. Cassius replied, "Yes. There're still questions we might put to Michael and Fearchild." Then, "We won't be able to reach Michael by the usual methods. He's been conditioned to resist drugs and polygraphs. Primitive methods may prove more efficacious."

"Uhm." Storm doubted that they would, though Michael, for all his bravado and daring, was a coward at heart.

How had Dee obtained an immunization course against the subtler forms of truth research? The process was complicated, expensive, and highly secret. Confederation restricted it to its most favored and highly ranked operatives and leaders in the most sensitive positions. Mouse, if he could stay alive for forty years and achieve flag grade, was the only man he knew who had a hope of attaining that signal honor. "Curious, that," he murmured.

"How curious you can't imagine."

Inflections in Cassius's speech were necessarily hard to grasp. This time Storm caught it. "You found something?"

"I think we learned most of it. It will be interesting watching the Dees while we discuss it."

"You can't tell me now?"

"We're fifty-one hours from the asteroid. Take time to recuperate. You're still disoriented. The discussion will be a strain."

"No doubt."

For two days Storm slept or endured his son's vague, intriguing hints about what he and Cassius had discovered on The Big Rock Candy Mountain. He tried to make the best of it by retreating to his clarinet and Bible. One of his sergeants had risked his life to salvage them from the phase-disrupted wreck of his singleship.

His eye was too weak for the book, his fingers insufficiently coordinated for the instrument. Mouse read some for him. Time did not drag. He slept a lot.

Mouse wakened him once, so he could watch while Cassius blurred their influential backtrail in the field around a star. Walters meant to make a complete orbit, take hyper briefly while masked by the star's own field, then drift for a day at a velocity slightly below that of light. The asteroid lay in the cometary belt of the chosen star.

The maneuver was intended to shed any unnoticed tail. Perforce, any such shadow would be operating at the limits of detection and would quickly lose contact.

Storm had Mouse move him to the control room for the stellar orbit.

"Cassius, roll her so the sun'll be topside during orbit," he said.

"You've got it." The star wobbled slightly as Cassius adjusted the ship's attitude. It swelled to the size of a sun. Cassius dove in, sliding around so close that the horizon curves vanished and they seemed to be drifting below an endless ceiling of fire. It was an Armageddon sky from which flames reached down with stately grace, as if to capture them and drag them into all that fury. Even smaller sunspots appeared as vast, dark continents surrounded by vaster oceans of flame. Cassius put all his filters up and let Storm stare, brooding, into that furnace that was the ultimate source of all other energies.

Storm said, "How like life itself a star is. It pulses. It struggles to maintain itself in a boundless ocean of cold despair. Every atom vibrates its little nucleus out, fighting the vampire night sucking its life. And the star fights knowing the struggle is hopeless, knowing that all it can do is die defiantly, going nova as its last grand gesture."

Mouse leaned forward, listening intently. His father seemed to be trying to create some order out of his own nebulous philosophy.

"Entropy and Chaos, death and evil, they can't be beaten by star or man, but in defeat there's always the victory of defiance. This sun is telling me, Gneaus, the mortal flesh can be destroyed, but the spirit, the courage within, is eternal. It need not yield. And that's all the victory you'll ever get."

Mouse watched with watery eyes as his father fell asleep, exhausted by the effort it had taken to put his feelings into words. The youth stared up at the fire, trying to see what Gneaus Storm had seen. He could not find it. He rose and took the old man back to his medicare cradle.

Being moved brought Storm back to a twilight awareness.

All his adult life Storm had been anticipating a fierce and final conflict from which he could win no mundane victory. With almost religious faith he believed that the manipulators would someday push him into a corner from which there would be no escape but death. He had always believed that Richard would be the instrument of his destruction, and that he and Richard, by destroying one another, would spell the doom of their kind.

The fires of the Ulantonid War had ignited a blaze of panhumanism of which Confederation was still taking full advantage. It was bulling its way into broad reaches of relatively ungovernmented space in apparent response to a set of laws similar to those defining the growth of organisms and species. Mercenary armies were among those institutions facing increasingly limited futures.

No government willingly tolerates private competition, and especially not competition which can challenge its decrees. The most benign government ever imagined has as its root assumption its right to apply force to the individual. From inception every government continuously strives to broaden the parameters of that right.

Storm believed he and Richard, if lured into a truly bloody Armageddon, would fight the last merc war tolerated by Confederation. The Services now had the strength and organization to disarm the freecorps. All they needed was an excuse.

Cassius's ship reached the chunk of celestial debris that Storm had long ago developed as a prison for Fearchild Dee. It was a living hell, Fearchild's reward for his perfidy on the world where Cassius had lost his hand.

That had not been a matter of the hazards of war.

Fearchild had been a dilettante merc captain commanding forces his father had hoped to turn into a Family army. The Legion had humiliated him in his field debut. He had tried using Dee tactics to recoup.

Merc wars were ritualized and ceremonial. Their ends were celebrated with a formalized signing of Articles of Surrender and the yielding up of banners by the defeated captain. Fearchild had smuggled in a bomb, hoping to obliterate the Legion staff prior to a surprise resumption of hostilities.

Appalled, his officers had turned on him and warned their opposites. Cassius had been the only Legionnaire injured. He had refused to have the hand replaced.

It reminded him that there were dishonorable men in the universe. He could consider its absence and remember just how much he hated the Dees.

It took Cassius and Mouse two hours to transfer Storm and Michael and their medicare cradles to the asteroid's single habitable room. They wakened the injured men only after completing the task.

Michael awoke with a whimper. The instant he discovered Storm's presence, he wailed, "Gneaus, that man is going to kill me."

Cassius chuckled. His prosthetic larynx made it a weird sound. "I will, yes. If I can."

"You promised, Gneaus. You gave me your word."

"You're right, Michael. But Cassius never promised you anything. Neither did Masato, and I've got the feeling he's mad about what you did to his brothers."

Mouse's attempt to look fierce fell flat. Dee did not notice. He was too involved with himself and Fearchild, whom he had just noticed.

"My God! My God!" he moaned. "What are you doing?"

"Thought he'd be up to his neck in houris, eh?" Cassius asked.

Michael stared, aghast. He was not inhuman. He loved his children. His parental concern overcame his trepidation. "Fear. Fear. What're they doing to you?"

"Plug him in, Cassius," Storm ordered. "It should make him more amenable."

Mouse and Cassius lifted a passive Michael onto an automated operating table.

Fearchild's situation did not seem cruel at first glance. He was chained to a wall. He wore a helmet that enveloped his head. A thick bundle of wires attached the helmet to a nearby machine.

That machine restricted Fearchild to limits that kept him barely among the living. Like Valerie in Festung Todesangst, he was permitted no lapses in self-awareness. Nor was he free to slide off into insanity. The machine enforced rationality with a battery of psychiatric drugs. At random intervals it stimulated his pain center with an equally random selection of unpleasant sensations.

They were all cruel men.

Mouse worked in a daze, not quite able to believe this place was real, not quite able to accept that his father had created it.

Cassius adjusted Fearchild's machine so the younger Dee could take an interest in what was being done to his father.

Mouse and Cassius strapped Michael to the table, rotated it till it stood upright. Storm watched impassively. Cassius positioned and adjusted surgical machinery which included a system similar to that which kept Fearchild sane. He added an anaesthesia system programmed to heighten rather than dampen pain.

"Do we have to do this?" Mouse whispered.

Cassius nodded. He was enjoying himself.

All cruel men.

"I keep my word, Michael," Storm said. His voice was soft, weak, and tired. "No matter what, I'll never kill you. I tried to make a point on The Mountain. You refused to understand it. I'm going to make it again here, a little more strongly. Maybe you'll get the message this time."

He paused for a minute, gathering strength. "Michael, I'm going to make you beg me to kill you. And I'm going to keep my promise and make sure you stay alive. You ready, Cassius?"

Cassius nodded.

"Give him a taste."

The machine whined. A tiny scalpel flayed a few square millimeters of skin off Dee's nose. A second waldo bathed the exposed flesh with iodine. A third applied a small dressing. The anaesthesia program intensified the fire of the antiseptic. Dee shrieked.

"Enough. You see, Michael? That rig is a little toy I put in when we slapped this place together. I had a feeling you'd make me use it someday. What it will do is skin you a few square millimeters at a time, here and there. You'll get plenty of time to heal so the skinning won't ever end. Think about that. Pain for the rest of your life."

Dee whimpered. His eyes seemed glazed.

Mouse turned his back. He kept jerking from the stomach upward as he fought to keep his breakfast down. Cassius laid a gentle hand on his shoulder. "Easy," he whispered.

Storm snarled, "Michael, Michael, you've just got to play your games. You can't claim you weren't warned. You can't say you didn't know the risks." He waved a weak hand at Cassius. "Do an eyelid now."

Dee flushed a pale shade of death. "My face…"

Cruel men. Cassius laughed. The sound was so malignant it seemed no artificial voice box could have produced it.

"There'll be scars," Storm promised. His voice was soft, musing. "Yes. That will hurt more than the skinning, won't it? Cassius, make sure there are plenty of scars in the program. Do something artistic."

Dee cried, "Damn it, Gneaus…"

"This isn't a pleasure spa, Michael. This is hell. Your own private hell. You brought it on yourself. Then you expect the rest of us to feel sorry for you. It doesn't work that way. We aren't kids now. You can't fool us the way you used to. We're on to all of your tricks."

"Gneaus, not my face."

"You want to tell us why Blackworld means so much to you?"

"It's my way out…" Dee shut up. He refused to speak again.

"Cassius, before we leave I want you to position them so they have to look at each other. Put a sound baffle between them so they can't talk. Now, before we tackle my questions again, tell me what you found on The Mountain."

Cassius sketched the story. Storm occasionally interrupted with a question or to make a point. When Cassius mentioned the elderly assassin, he asked, "Sangaree?"

Cassius nodded.

Storm turned to an attractive and frightened Michael Dee. "So that rumor is true. You *have* been dealing with them. That won't make you any friends, Michael." He shook an admonitory finger. "Go on, Cassius. This is getting interestinger and interestinger."

A minute later Storm muttered, "I've got a feeling I'll be eligible for Social Insurance after I pay your instel bill."

"Possibly. The man's name was Rhafu."

Storm sent a puzzled glance Michael's way. Dee seemed both disappointed and relieved. "It doesn't make sense, Cassius."

"It does. Keep listening." He explained what he had learned from his friend in Luna Command.

"Why would this mystery Sangaree wait till now to get even?"

"I take it he's really a low-key sort. Tries to get everything lined up perfect before he makes his move. He's probably been chipping away at us for a long time."

Storm looked at Dee. "That could explain a lot of things. But not too clearly."

"I've been doing some thinking. It was a long trip out, watch and watch. Not much chance to talk. Mainly, I tried to figure out why a man would want to destroy his brother so bad he would cut a deal with Sangaree. I didn't come up with anything. Each time I thought I had it, I came back to the same thing. The only things you've ever done were in reply to something a Dee did first. Our friend here is a son-of-a-bitch, but in the past he usually took his lumps when he deserved them. And until just lately he was always pretty impersonal about his crap.

"So I went back and thought it through from the beginning. There had to be a clue somewhere.

"I think it started because he wanted to get even with Richard Hawksblood. Including you was a sop for this Deeth creature. In others words, it's not really personal. It's an arrangement. Deeth helps him get Richard. He helps Deeth get you and the Legion."

Storm stared at his brother. Michael looked terribly uncomfortable. "Why the hell would he take up with this Deeth?"

"That's where I had to strain the old logic box. We have to go back to your father and mother to put it together. You know the family stories. He met her on Prefactlas. She was pregnant when they got married. Boris never found out who Michael's father was. Emily wouldn't say. Like that.

"Check my reasoning. Emily was born a Sangaree pleasure girl. Her genetic tagging was distinctly Norbon. We know she spent several years traveling and living with a boy who may have fathered Michael. He vanished completely once your mother moved in with Boris.

"There was a more notorious disappearance at the same time. The grand master of the Prefactlas underworld, a man we called the Serpent. My friend Beckhart tells me the Serpent and this Rhafu are the same guy. Starting to get a picture?"

"I've got one." Storm laid a finger alongside his nose. "And I don't like it. He's not just dealing with them, he is one of them. The son of this Deeth. Implausible on its face, but you found a few crossbreeds on Prefactlas, didn't you?"

"Too many. And from Michael's expression, I'd say we've hit it square."

"Ah, yes. So we have."

"Gneaus, I..." Dee shut up. It was too late for truth or lies.

The silence stretched out. Mouse began to move around nervously, glancing from man to man.

Storm murmured, "The thing takes shape. We know some whos and whys, and even a few hows. Enough to have upset them by recapturing Benjamin and Homer. But that doesn't really change anything. Probably too late to wriggle out."

"We can kill us a few Dees," Cassius suggested. "I grilled Beckhart on this Deeth. There's no way we can get to him. He's moved off Homeworld. His whole outfit is on his First Expansion planet. He's the only bastard in the universe who knows where it is. So how the hell do you bribe some fool Sangaree to go cut his throat? If we want him, we have to make him come to us."

"Michael stays alive. I gave him my word. He may not be as guilty as he looks, anyway."

"Stop making excuses for him, Gneaus."

Storm overlooked Cassius's remark. "He and Fearchild will be safe here. Remember Trojan Hearse? I'll order a go on it, and start hunting Seth-Infinite. If we nail him down too, this Deeth will have to come out if he wants to keep us running. He won't have any cat's-paws left."

"Helga," Mouse suggested.

"She doesn't get around so good anymore," Storm replied. "Warm your instel, Mouse. I've got to talk to Richard."

"We don't have one. We had our wave guides sheared off by friend Michael there," Cassius said. "And we've lost relay contact with your Seiner friend. It'll have to wait till we get back to the Fortress."

"Why are we fooling around here, then? Take me home."

Mouse turned his father's medicare cradle and pushed it into the passage to the ship dock. Michael started screaming behind him.

Cassius had energized the torture machinery.

Cruel men. All cruel men.

A small yacht drifted in normspace. Its pilot patiently watched her hyper scan. She had lost her quarry, but hoped to find it again.

Cassius went hyper. His vessel left a momentarily detectable ripple.

The yacht turned like a questing needle. In a moment it began to accelerate.

# THIRTY-SEVEN: 3028 AD

Moira was seventeen when she received the summons. It terrified her. She had heard stories… Not even Blake would force her. Would he?

She had no protector. She had had to do her own fighting since Frog's death. She was tough even for an Edgeward girl. But Blake? Fight a demigod?

Frog had, in his stubborn way.

She looked around the tiny room that had been the dwarf's home, that he had made home for a girl-child abandoned and unwanted by so many better able to provide. She turned an ear to listen for a ghost voice. "Frog, what should I do?"

"Go on, girl. And crank the bastard's nose up his butt if he tries anything."

She really had no choice. Blake was the great bull gorilla boss of Edgeward. They would come and get her if she did not go on her own.

As she prepared, making herself as unattractive as she could, she surveyed the room again. A cool tickle of irrational fear said it might be her last look around.

She had turned it into a museum. Almost a shrine, of and to the crazy dwarf called Frog, whose real name she had never known. There had been no way to show she cared while she lived. She had sensed that he would have been embarrassed by affection. Now, in her most romantic years, with her memories growing ever more vague and rose-lensed, she was, progressively, elevating him to godhead.

Moira did not fit. Edgeward was a black community. She was a curiosity and "old Frog's stray brat." The latter, with the ghost of the mad dwarf always peering over her shoulder, put people off more than did the former.

Old Frog had become a city legend. Edgewarders boasted about him to outsiders. The Man Who Ended the Shadowline. They had brought in his tractor and made a memorial of it. But he still made them nervous.

Dead and canonized was where madmen belonged. His mind had been diseased. They feared Moira might be a carrier.

They did not know what to say or do around her, so they did nothing. She was an outcast without justification, lonely, given far too much time to brood. The pressures of her fellow citizens' trepidations and expectations were creating the thing they feared.

Frog pictures on the walls. Frog things around the room. The ragged remnants of his hotsuit. A model of his crawler. Brightside charts which bore Frog's stamp, his openings of terra incognita. A diary in which Moira jotted what she felt were her most important thoughts, many of which orbited around her namesake, Edgeward's first woman tractor hog, The Girl Who Saw the Sun, a character saint of the same weird canon as Frog. Frog had claimed a relationship. Moira never had learned what it was. It was a mystery she was afraid to delve into. She had started in on the city records several times, and always stopped before she traced the link. She had a niggling little fear that she might find out her patron had had feet of clay.

She dithered. "At your earliest convenience," from Blake meant yesterday, and was that much more intimidating.

"Might as well get it over." She sighed, mussed her hair, and went.

Main offices for Blake Mining and Metals were in a huge old building at Edgeward's center, beneath the strongest part of the meteor screen shielding the dome. Years ago it had been City Hall and had housed city administrators' offices exclusively. Blake controlled that now. Edgeward was a company town. He might as well be in City Hall.

Moira arrived as the afternoon's programmed rain began falling. A light breeze drove mist into her face. Scents on the air brought back vague images of herself running across a grassy, wild-flowered plain under a friendly yellow sun, playing with the other children on the breeding farm. It had been a gentle, realtime operation run by a paternalistic station master. The youngsters had not known they were property to be trained and sold. She would not have cared had she known. She had been happy.

She paused on the steps of City Hall and stared upward, trying to glimpse the star-speckled black enemy besieging the city. She saw nothing but sunlights and the piping from which the rain was falling. Edgeward worked hard to deny the night.

The rain fell harder. She hurried through an iris door that would become an airlock should the dome fall.

She entered a small, comfortable reception room. Its sole occupant was a thin, elderly gentleman who reminded her of a grown Frog. He had the leathery look of a lifelong tractor hog forced to retire from outservice. He made her nervous. Retired hogs sometimes became antsy and unpleasant.

This man had not. He glanced up and noticed her biting her lip in front of his desk. His whole face broke into smiles. He made it look as if he had been waiting years just for her.

"Miss Eight? Moira Eight? So glad you could come." He thrust a dark, wrinkled hand at her. She took it in a bit of a daze. It felt warm and soft. She relaxed a little. She judged people by the way they felt. Soft and warm meant nice and no harm planned. Cold, damp, hard, meant unpleasant intentions. She knew body temperatures were nearly the same in everyone, yet she depended on the difference in hands—and later, lips—and trusted that part of her unconscious which interpreted them.

It proved right most of the time.

"What… What's it about?" she asked.

"Don't know. I'm just the old man's legs. So you're Frog's little girl. All growed up. You should get out more. Pretty thing like you shouldn't hide herself." As he talked and she blushed, he guided her toward an elevator. “Mr. Blake is in the penthouse. We’ll go straight up. He said to bring you right to him.”

Moira bit her lip and tried for a brave face.

“Now then, no need to be scared. He’s no ogre. We haven’t let him devour a maiden in, oh, three or four years.”

That’s the way Frog used to baby me, she thought. There was something about Brightside that made tractor men more sensitive. Everybody thought Frog was a crusty old grouch—maybe even Frog thought he was—but that was just people who didn’t know him.

Nobody bothered to get to know tractor hogs well. Their life expectancies were too short. It did not pay to get close to an enemy of the Demon Sun. Men like this one and Frog, who got old running the Thunder Mountains and Shadowline, were rare. Human beings simply could not indefinitely endure the rigid discipline and narrow attention/alertness it took to survive beyond the Edge of the World. Frog had broken down in the end, but he had been lucky. They had brought him out—to be murdered. Maybe this man had had his failure and been lucky too.

She began to grow angry. They had not done a thing about Frog’s murder. Oh, they had exiled those people, but the murderer hadn’t been caught. She planned to do it herself. She would be of age in less than a year. With Frog’s bequest, and the credit from the sale of the salvageable parts of his rig after Blake had deducted recovery costs, she would buy passage offworld and find August Plainfield.

The obsession had been growing from the moment she had looked through that hospital door and realized what Plainfield had done. The practicalities did not intimidate her. She was still young enough to believe in magic and justice.

Her plan was her one rebellion against the dwarf’s philosophy. Sour and grumbly as he had been, he would not have wanted her to hold a grudge so deeply it would shape her life.

“Here we are. Top of the tower. Be sure to ask if you can see the observation platform. Not many people get the chance. The view is worth it.”

Moira’s escort led her into an antechamber almost exactly reflecting her preconception of Blake’s headquarters. It smelled of wealth. Such spendthrift use of space!

A domed city like Edgeward used every cubic centimeter to some critical purpose. Even open areas were part of a grand design intended to provide relief from the cramped limits of living quarters.

Here space existed without function beyond announcing the wealth and power of its occupant.

“He’ll be in his private office, I believe,” Moira’s companion told her. “Follow me.”

“There’s so much room…”

“A big man with big responsibilities needs room to wrestle them.”

“Thank you. Uh… I don’t know your name.”

“It’s not important. Why?”

"Because you've been kind, I guess. And it is important. I like to know who's been nice so I can think nice things about them." She could not think of a better way to put it.

"Albin Korando, then."

"That's odd."

"For Blackworld, I suppose. My people didn't come here till after the war."

"No, I mean Frog used to talk about you. I was trying to remember your name just yesterday."

"I'll bet he told some stories," Korando said, and laughed softly. He wore a faraway look. Then he saddened. "Some stories, yes. We're here. And Miss?"

"Yes?"

"Don't be frightened. He's just a man. And a pretty good man at that. Very few of the street stories are true."

"All right." But as they paused before the door that would open on a man almost omnipotent, she became terrified of the sheer power she faced.

Korando pushed through. "Miss Eight is here, sir."

Timorously, Moira followed.

The man who swiveled a chair to greet her was not the fang-toothed cyclops she expected. Nor was he old. She guessed thirty-five. Maybe even younger. He had a slight frame which, nevertheless, had about it a suggestion of the restrained power of the professional fighter. His smile was broad and dazzling, revealing perfect teeth. For an instant she noticed nothing else.

"Forgive me for not rising," he said, offering a hand. With the other he gestured at legs that ended in stumps where he should have had knees. "An accident at the shade station in the Shadowline a few years ago. I haven't had time to grow new ones."

"Oh! I'm sorry."

"For what? I earned it. I should know better than to go crawling around under a rogue slave. I've got people who get paid for doing that sort of thing. Albin, bring the lady something. Something mixed, Moira? No, better not. Wouldn't do to have it get around that I'm getting young women drunk. Will coffee do?"

Korando departed when she nodded.

"Well, have a seat. Have a seat. And why this look of perplexity?"

"Uh..." Moira reddened. She had been staring. "I thought you were old."

Blake laughed. His laugh was a pleasant, almost feminine tinkle. She wished she had taken his briefly offered hand to see if it was warm. That hand gestured toward oil portraits hanging on a distant wall. "There they are. The real old ones. My father. His father. And the old pirate who started it all. Obadiah Blake." Three dark, hard faces fixed her with that look which is traditional in ancestral portraiture, a sort of angry calculation or cunning rapacity, as if each had been considering selling the artist into slavery. "They're old enough to suit anybody. I call them the Ancient Marinators.

They took everything so serious. They soaked in their own juices." He smiled as if at an old joke. "Greedy grabbers, they were. Had to have it all."

"I guess when you've got it all you can point fingers and say shamey-shamey." Moira was astounded at her own temerity.

Blake laughed. "You're Frog's brat, all right. Hardly knew him myself, but Dad had a few things to say about him."

"None of them kind, I hope." She smiled at Korando as he arrived with a silver carafe and china teacup on a silver tray. Silver and gold were by-products of Blake's mining operations. Both were common around Edgeward. Korando wore one large gold loop earring.

"Not a one. Not a one. And none of them fit for your pretty ears, either. No, Albin, stay. I think my guest would feel more comfortable with a chaperon, though God alone knows how I'd run her down if the fancy hit me."

"As you wish, sir."

Moira smiled gratefully, including both men.

"Well, then," said Blake, "pretty as you are, and much as I'd like to chat and look and wishful think, it's business that made me ask you here, so to business we must. How do you feel about the man who killed Frog?"

She did not have to answer. Her feelings burned on her face.

"That strongly? Albin, rummage through that stuff on the table there and hand Miss Eight the solidos we were talking about last night." Blake's office was a vast clutter. He seemed to be a man without time to keep order.

"Plainfield," she said, handling two cubes about ten centimeters to a side. There were little differences in appearances, but she felt no doubt.

"Those came in yesterday, from Twilight Town. I've got a man up there who watches out for things. Made these of a fellow who's been hanging around their brass. Thought he recognized him from back when. He was one of the ones we exiled when Frog was killed. He was lucky. Got picked up by one of their crawlers. But he wants to come home. Has family here. He's trying to earn his way back in."

"What about Plainfield?" Her voice was hard, her throat tight. Her stomach felt as though she were about to throw up.

"He's using the name Diebold Amelung now, but that's not his real one either."

"What're you going to do?"

"For now, nothing." He raised a hand to silence her protest. "For now. In time, what needs doing. I could have him killed, but then I wouldn't find out what he's up to. I wouldn't find out why he killed Frog. I wouldn't find out if he's connected with some strange phenomena we've observed Brightside. Albin, is that projector ready? Good. Moira, the man's real name is Michael Dee. We've known that for some time."

"And you haven't done anything?" She began to get mad.

"My dear young lady, Blake has done everything possible, consistent with its own interests. Which isn't much, I'll grant. This man, whatever name he uses, is no Old

Earth shooter, no crackdome cutthroat. He could buy and sell Edgeward City. He's a very old, rich, and powerful man. He's got a lot of connections."

"So?"

"For you it's simple. You could burn him. You've got nothing to lose. I've got an industrial empire and a hundred thousand people to consider."

"He can't be that important."

"No? He owns a planet. He almost controls the private instel trade. He has interests in all the shipping lines that carry our exports. His brother is Gneaus Julius Storm, the mercenary, who has a personal army of twenty thousand men and the ships to move it. He's associated with Richard Hawksblood, another mercenary. And he has friends in Luna Command who would put Blackworld under embargo simply on his say-so."

"I see. If he's such a big man, how come he's in Twilight?"

"Exactly. Now we're in tune, little lady. Let's watch some clips. Albin."

Korando lowered the lighting and started the holo projector.

"This is the shade cloud we send up from the outstation to cover the run from the Whitlandsund to the Shadowline," Blake said. The holo cube portrayed a tower of darkness, which, she realized after a moment, was dark only due to a lessening of an almost unbearable glare. "We've filtered it down to the limits of resolution."

The hologram changed. Another pillar of dust appeared, viewed from a slightly sunward angle, making a portion look like a tower of fiery motes. "A charter running fourteen hours north of the Shadowline caught this two years ago. We couldn't make anything of it then. Too far to investigate, and in Twilight territory. Somebody thought it might be dust blowing out of a volcano."

The third clip was a still of crawler tracks under artificial lighting. "This one's only about a month old. It was taken a little over two thousand kilometers out the Shadowline by another charter. He thought he'd stumbled across some side trip of Frog's. They didn't look right. Too wide. We checked against Frog's log. He didn't make them.

"Something was wrong. Obviously. It bothered me. Curiosities always do. I had Albin check the records. I had him talk to drivers. And he found out what I thought he'd find out. The only Edgeward man who ever went that far was Frog. So I had Albin make the rounds again. He found several charters who had gotten readings on, or sightings of, dust pillars in the north, especially way out west, where they could be seen from the Shadowline itself. Albin."

The holo changed to a small-scale chart of the northern hemisphere west of the Edge of the World. "Nobody thought they were worth reporting. Just another Brightside curiosity. Once we got interested, we plotted them. They all seem to have appeared along the black line there."

Moira understood. "A shade route to the Shadowline from Twilight territory. That would be expensive."

"She's quick, Albin. And the crawler track confirms it. It was made by a Meacham long-range charter. Twilight is in the Shadowline, at considerable expense in money and man-hours. More than they'd have available for a speculative venture. Putting a line of shadow generators across two thousand kilometers of Brightside is an awesome feat. The cost in equipment and lives must have been phenomenal. I checked with the engineers. They said it could be done, but somebody would have to be crazy to try it. So why did somebody?"

Korando changed clips twice while Blake was talking. The first showed an artist's concept of a peculiar tractor, the second an action sequence of the real thing, slightly different in its lines. The camera angle left no doubt that it had been shot in the Shadowline. Fine lines of intense light ran along the lip of towering cliffs in the background. "This was shot earlier in the week, not far from where we found the mysterious crawler track," Blake explained.

"This doesn't make sense," Moira told him. "There's no profit in it."

"Are you sure? There's got to be. Huge profits. Those Meachams are worse pirates than old Obadiah ever was. I was hoping you could shed some light."

"Me? All I know about the Shadowline is what Frog told me."

"Exactly. The only man who ever went all the way to the end."

"You mean he found something?"

"That's what I want to know. Did he?"

"He never said anything. But I only got to see him for a minute before he shooed me out. And then… Then…"

"Yes." Blake swept a hand around to include most of the room. "I've gone over every record we've got, trying to find something. Even those dreadful hours of broadcasts that went out before he made it back. I haven't found a thing. In fact, I've found too much nothing. It's like making a fly-by of a black hole. You know there's something there, but all you can tell is that it isn't. If you see what I mean. A lot of records were tampered with. You can't tell what Plainfield wanted to cover up. And more records seem to have been 'rectified' since. Like that black hole, there's so much nothing that you can tell it's something big and dangerous. And my only recourse is to some very fallible human memories of something that happened a long time ago."

"What about your spy?"

"I'd have to bring him home to question him properly. I'm trying, but I don't think I'll make it. The past few years the Meachams have gotten more paranoid than usual. Like maybe they've got something to hide. Getting the solidos of Dee was damned near impossible."

"You could put someone in, sir," Korando suggested. "Someone with a legitimate reason to come and go. Do the interview there."

"Easier than bringing someone out, I agree. But I'm afraid of how much trouble I might have getting my someone back out, legitimate business or not. My man there gives the impression that outsiders are watched pretty damned close."

"Then stage an ambush in the Shadowline," Moira said. "Use guns instead of cameras. Grab some of their people."

"I don't want them to know we know. That would bring on the war before we're ready."

"War?" Moira and Korando asked. The girl's voice squeaked.

"Of course. If there's something out there worth the trouble they've invested in stealing it, then it's worth our fighting for it to get it back."

Korando said, "Boss, you've got one hell of a subjective way of looking at things. On the map..."

"The Shadowline starts in Edgeward territory. As far as I'm concerned, the whole damned thing is ours. Doesn't matter that it wanders up above Twilight's south parallel."

*So there's a little pirate in this Blake, too,* Moira thought. She smiled. It took claim-jumper types to make money on Blackworld. "What's my part in this?" she asked. "You knew I couldn't help with what Frog found. So why drag me in?"

"You're right. You're right. Smart girl. I've got something in mind, something complicated. Do you think you could kill Dee?"

"Plainfield? Yes. I've thought about it. I could. I don't know how reliable I'd be afterward."

"Could you not kill him?"

"I don't understand."

"Could you be around him, exposed to him, and not do something to get even?"

"I don't know. Maybe. If there was a good reason. What are you driving at?"

"You think you could be friendly? Or more?"

Her breakfast slammed against her esophagus. She took a moment to force it down. Then it struck her that she could exact a much more satisfying revenge if she could get the man to love her before she killed him. The sheer cruelty of it felt good.

That was when she first realized how truly deep her hatred for Plainfield ran. It was an obsession. She would do anything.

She frightened herself. And did not like Moira very much. That was not the sort of person she wanted to be.

"What do you want me to do? I'll do it."

"Eh?"

"I'll do whatever you want me to do, as long as getting Plainfield is part of the deal."

Blake peered at her. "Don't let them turn you over to their women," he muttered. He seemed disappointed. "All right. Here's my thinking. It's still rough. We'll smooth it out as we go. First, we send you to Twilight Town. We're going to ticket you through to Old Earth. You can't get a through ship from any other port. We'll arrange a meet with our man there if we can. Then you'll take the first Earthbound ship out. You'll leave it at Weiderander's Station, cash in the rest of your ticket, and buy another for The Big Rock Candy Mountain under a different name. We're going to enroll you in the Modelmog. They've started taking rich kids in order to balance their books."

The Modelmog was the century's foremost study center for young artists, actors, and writers. As Blake suggested, the school had fallen on hard times. Rich no-talents were being admitted to carry the costs of subsidizing the talented but poor who made up the bulk of the student body. Substantial endowments were the price of the university's highly respected diplomas.

"What's this got to do with Plainfield?" Moira demanded. Her voice was plaintive. "It's awful complicated."

"Patience, child. Patience. I'm getting to it. At the Modelmog we want you to vamp a poet named Lucifer Storm. He's a talented young man, they say, and quite handsome. You shouldn't find him repulsive. Attach yourself. He'll be your passport into the Fortress of Iron. That's the headquarters of the mercenary Gneaus Storm. Dee is in and out of there all the time. You should have no trouble making contact. Become his consort."

"I see. Live with him and spy on him."

"Exactly."

"For how long?"

"There's more than Frog's paybacks to worry about, girl. There's Edgeward. I'm a big fish around here, but out there I'm just a minnow. I can't make enemies out of sharks."

Moira was intelligent. She recognized his problem, though she found it emotionally unpalatable. "All right. But you're making it too complicated. I'll mess it up for sure."

Blake chuckled. "I've been studying Moira Eight, too, dear. She's no dummy. Her acquaintances say she's a very good actress, both on stage and in her personal life. Dramatist White thinks he's made a real find."

Moira shrugged. Secretly, she was pleased. Mr. White never said anything of the sort to her.

"My Dad, and my grandfather, they treated old Frog pretty bad. If I'd been in charge, I'd have done it different. Frog was important. He reminded us that we aren't gods. He reminded us that what was good for the Corporation wasn't always good for Edgeward's people. He didn't realize it, and my Dad only saw the edges of it, but your old man kept Edgeward from turning into something like Twilight. You'll see what I mean if we send you. Blake and Edgeward still have a human side—despite my Board of Directors. I digress. I'm sorry. It's my hobbyhorse."

"May you never dismount, sir," Korando said.

"Albin is my conscience. He came from Twilight."

"I know. He was an exile. Frog brought him in. He's sort of my brother. That was a long time ago."

"A long time ago," Korando agreed. "Had a habit of collecting strays, didn't he?"

Grimly, Blake said, "I wish he were here today. I've got to present this to the Board pretty soon. He's the kind who could have bullied them into line. They were afraid of him. Still are, in a way. As if he might come back to haunt them."

"He has, hasn't he?" Moira asked. "When do we start? What do we have to do?"

# THIRTY-EIGHT: 3031 AD

Going home did nothing to brighten anything. The Fortress of Iron was gravid with bad news.

Wulf and Helmut had put a prize crewman aboard the singleship Dee had stolen. She and her escort had been attacked while returning home. The guilty warships had been of Sangaree configuration. Only one of them had survived. Wulf and Helmut had been forced to let it escape. Its crew had managed to recapture the medicare cradles containing Benjamin and Homer. The High Seiners had tracked the fleeing ship. They said it had made planetfall on Helga's World.

"We're right back where we started," Storm groaned from his own cradle.

"Oh, no," Helmut told him. He wore a sickly grin. "We're way worse off. The Fishers say Michael and Fearchild Dee arrived on Blackworld this morning."

"That's impossible." Storm's heart hammered so hard his cradle fed him a mild sedative.

"Not quite," Wulf said. "His wife got him out. She was on Helga's World. He instelled her during the chase. She spaced and followed you to the prison. That's the story they're telling on Blackworld."

"He's got a new wife?"

"All we know is what we get in the reports," Helmut growled. "It's the old wife. I thought she was dead, too. But our man got into their pockets while they were explaining to Seth-Infinite. He even found out how she followed Dee."

"How?"

"Limited range, general broadcast instel. A little node of a thing he swallowed before he was captured. It didn't last long, but it got her into the area of the asteroid."

"We get an ultimatum?"

"The minute that raidship grounded," Wulf replied. "No signature, of course. We take the Blackworld contract or we never see Benjamin or Homer again. I guess they'll try to frame Blake Mining with the snatch."

Storm lay back, stared at a pale ceiling. He needed no signature to know who had sent that message. Helga Dee. And she would not bother trying to cover her tracks. He was tempted to ignore it. Benjamin and Homer were his flesh, but he could balance their lives against those of all the Legionnaires who would die in combat. "What's our movement status?"

"Go. We can start any time."

"Activate Trojan Hearse," Storm ordered.

Nobody protested. Nobody acted surprised. He was amazed. They had done everything but laugh when, years ago, he had presented the contingency plan. They had seen no need to be ready to break into Festung Todesangst.

"The operation went active the day Michael left," Wulf said. "We've already located one of Helga's ravens. Ceislak took the ship yesterday. He's on his way to Helga's World now."

Storm smiled his first smile in a long time. Hakes Ceislak was a fine, bloodthirsty youngster with a flair for commando operations. If anybody could slip a shipload of Legionnaires into Festung Todesangst as pretended corpses, he could.

"How many? All volunteers, weren't they? I don't think she'd blow the scuttle bombs unless she thought she was dead anyway, but I don't like anybody taking risks if they don't want to."

"A full battalion. All volunteers. We turned another thousand away. They thought they might have to dig you out too. Ceislak picked the men he wanted."

"All right. We go to Blackworld. We stir it up there, and get their attention till Ceislak can do his job. He's going to need a lot of stall time. If he takes the raven in off schedule she'll smell us out."

"He needs almost five months." Helmut shrugged apologetically. "It was the only raven we could find."

"We'll miss Ceislak on Blackworld," Wulf said. "I've been studying the layout. Blake's position is so much better than what Richard has to work from that he's got to have a whole bag of tricks up his sleeve."

"Of course he does," Storm said. "He's Richard Hawksblood. He wouldn't have taken the commission if he didn't think he could win. If it gets hairy, we'll miss Ceislak bad."

Cassius said, "My friend Beckhart might be persuaded to take that job off our hands. If we can deliver proof of a link between Helga and the Sangaree."

Mouse had begun to feel lost. He asked, "Why would that matter?"

"He'd have to have an excuse to nose around in a private war," his father told him. "Then he'd jump on it so he can grab Helga's World for Luna Command. Sangaree would make him a great causus belli."

"I know they've done studies on the cost of taking her out," Cassius said. "Us, too, for that matter. The base plan was to saturate her defenses with missile fire. Go for overload and totalkill. They'd love to have us open the door and let them get their hands on all that sweet information."

"Arrange it," Storm ordered.

"You sure? He takes the place and the government gets a hammerlock on every corporation in this end of Confederation."

"I know," Storm said. "I know. No matter what way you go, it's no-win."

"What about Blake Mining?" Helmut asked. "They've been crying like babies for two weeks. I got a full-time guy in Communications giving them the stall."

"Keep him on the job. Meantime, start your preliminary movement. Surprise them. I'll be along as soon as Medical turns me loose."

"One more thing," Wulf said, as Mouse started to roll his father away.

"What?" Storm snapped. "What the hell other bad news can you hit me with?"

"Good, bad, who knows?" Wulf asked. "A message from Lucifer. He's a little embarrassed. Turns out his wife is an agent. For Blake, of all outfits."

"So? Does it matter anymore?"

"Maybe not. But answer me this, Colonel. Why was she planted on us? She hooked up with Lucifer before any of this broke. Which to me means she can't have anything to do with the Shadowline."

"Wheels within wheels," Cassius observed. He laid a gentle hand on Mouse's shoulder. "Some of us get born into the game. The wheels turn each other. Sometimes they never find out why."

"Ach!" Storm growled. "Take me down, Mouse."

The Fortress was a citadel of gloom. There wasn't a smile in the place. The Legion was a worm wriggling on a hook. A big fish was coming up to bite.

"It looks hopeless, doesn't it, Father?" Mouse asked.

"So it does, Mouse. So it does. But maybe we'll fool them all. It's always darkest before the Storm."

"Is that a pun?"

"*Me?* Make a joke of the family name? Horrors."

# THIRTY-NINE: 3028-3031 AD

Moira strained to get used to the name she was supposed to assume at Weideranders. She tried even harder to become a genuinely creative artist. She failed abysmally. She had absolutely no talent for anything but acting.

Blake grumbled, "I guess that'll have to do."

"Do? What's wrong with it? It's legitimate. And dramatist White says Janos Kasafirek..."

"I said all right." Blake smiled. "He's been at me harder than you have, pretty lady. He says it's your future."

She was thrilled. She would really get to do what she wanted... She began cramming classical drama, the Old Earth classics, especially the Elizabethans. She was mad for Shakespeare. Dramatist White actually broke down and told her she played an inspired Ophelia.

She was floating. Her mission was going to give her a chance to realize her wildest dreams. She would get to study with the great Kasafirek.

"Slight change in plans," Blake said one day not long before she was due to leave. "They've tightened security in Twilight. You're going to leave here as Pollyanna, instead of waiting till you get to Weideranders."

She was to be billed as the touring daughter of Amantea Eight, an under-minister in Confederation's Ministry of Commercial Affairs. The lady actually existed and was obscure enough to cause local officials some concern. The obscure career people were the real powers in Luna Command. The identity of surnames was serendipitous.

Moira thought the going would be easy once she left Blackworld. The character was more nearly the real her than the one she portrayed for Edgeward. Her daydreams often revolved around an acting career. She never had given that serious consideration before because Edgeward had such little use for actresses. She had not thought of leaving home except to go stalking after Plainfield.

It came time to leave. She went to the crawler locks reluctantly. This would be the end of one life and the beginning of another. The doubts had begun to hem her in. "Albin. What're you doing here?"

"Boss told me to go with you."

She spotted Blake, ran to his chair, gave him a quick little kiss. "Thank you. For Albin. I won't be nearly so scared."

"I thought not. And I thought we might learn something in Twilight. He knows the city. Be good, Moira. And be careful. You're going to be involved with some strange, dangerous men."

"I'll be all right."

She enjoyed the ride to Twilight. She had never been outdome before. She saw her world from an entirely new perspective.

Bleak ghosts of midnight landscapes slid by the crawler. Crewmen made garrulous by her beauty and exotic skin color provided her with a running commentary. This had happened here, that had happened there. Over yonder was a fantastic landmark mountain that stuck straight up a thousand meters, but you couldn't see it on account of it was dark. The crewmen were from The City of Night. They did not know her. She rehearsed her cover for them, as Pollyanna, telling outrageous lies about life in Luna Command.

She reached Twilight in a bright and cheerful mood. It quickly soured.

At first glance Twilight Town appeared to be a clone of Edgeward City. She started to say so to Korando. The human factor intervened.

Two hard-faced policemen began checking papers as the passengers started shedding their hotsuits. They were especially nasty to Edgewarders, but only slightly more civil to the Nighter crew and the citizens of Darkside Landing. They were revelers in petty power, the sadists who gave police a bad image everywhere. Pollyanna lost her temper when they started in on Korando.

"You," she snapped, using words as gently as a torturer uses small knives. "You with the face like a pig's butt. Yes. You. The one with the nose like stepped-in dog shit. We know your mother made a mistake when she decided against the abortion. You don't have to prove it. Go beat your wife if you have to mistreat somebody in order to feel like a man."

Korando flashed a desperate "Shut up!" look. She just smiled.

The policemen were stunned. The other passengers made pained faces.

The man she had abused grinned malevolently. He had found himself a victim. "Papers, bitch!"

Malice turned to uncertainty. He looked at her, at her travel pass. White. Meant offworlder. Youth and sex might mean she was the brat of power.

"These better be good, bitch," he muttered to himself.

"Give them here, Humph," his partner said. "And calm down."

"Can you people read?" Pollyanna demanded. "You can? I'm amazed."

She expected more trouble than they gave her. The one officer became very solicitous once he saw the seals on her pass. "Be cool, Humph. This fluff's straight out of Luna Command."

Humph grabbed the pass, flipped through it. His eyes widened slightly. He thrust the booklet at Pollyanna. "I'll be watching you, smartass."

"I do believe you take after your father." She was a little frightened now. She had to concentrate to maintain her snottiness. "He never forgave your mother either."

And, before he could reply, in a gentler tone, she added, "A little courtesy doesn't hurt, officer. If you're nice to people, they'll usually be nice to you." She stalked away.

Korando came over while she was eating a snack at the station canteen. "That wasn't very smart, Polly. But I appreciate it. He forgot all about me."

For possible watching eyes they pretended to become acquainted. Korando told her he was going to stick a little tighter than he had planned. She needed keeping out of trouble.

And stick he did, like a limpet. So tight that he got no chance to interview Blake's agent. He stayed beside her until he had seen her enrolled in the Modelmog.

The trip thither was an adventure, Edgeward having been her whole universe and most of his. The space flies were like a visit to a dome devoted to happy times. The big Star Liners were space-going hotels.

Weideranders Station was different. That vast space-going roundhouse was too alien. Pollyanna and Korando spent most of their layover in their rooms.

Pollyanna remembered Weideranders. She had been there before, almost too long ago to recall anything but the fear she had known then. They had been running from men who had wanted to kill the people she was with. She could not face all those corridors and shops and eating places filled with outworlders, Toke, the Ulantonid, Starfishers, and other strange people. Not without coming apart, without anticipating something dreadful.

She could not have endured it without Korando's help.

She was easing him into the role Frog had vacated by dying. He seemed to accept it.

The Mountain was terrifying too. Though it was the gentlest of worlds, it lacked that without which a Blackworlder never felt secure. It had no dome. Neither she nor Korando ever learned to face the open sky.

Lucifer Storm was almost too easy. She was sleeping with him, loving him, and married to him almost before she herself knew what was happening.

Janos Kasafirek was impressed with her abilities. She was astounded and delighted. He had a reputation as a savage, unrestrained critic.

For a time she was thoroughly content. Life seemed perfect, except that she did not get to see Korando as often as she would have liked. Albin was her sole touchstone with her past and home.

Then, a year after their arrival on The Mountain, Albin announced that he was going home. She protested.

"There's been trouble," he told her. "A skirmish in the Shadowline."

"What can you do?"

"I don't know. Mr. Blake will need me, though. Be calm, Polly. You've got it under control. I'm nothing but excess baggage now."

She cried. She begged. But he went.

Looking back later, she chose that as the day when everything started going wrong.

During her tenure at the Modelmog, Lucifer's father and Richard Hawksblood fought a brief war on The Broken Wings. Lucifer followed the news uneasily. She tried to comfort him, and quickly became engrossed in the action herself, seizing every sketchy report from the Fortress of Iron, skipping from newscast to newscast to find out the latest. It was her first exposure to mercenary warfare. She was intrigued by the gamelike action and by the odd personalities involved. Once she did become enthralled, Lucifer lost interest. He expressed a virulent disapproval of her interest.

She was disappointed because the war ended so quickly.

A few months later Lucifer announced, "We have to go home. I got an instel from my brother Benjamin. Something bad is in the wind."

"To the Fortress?" She became excited. She would be a step closer to Plainfield. And closer to the mercenaries she found so interesting. Lucifer's father had come to their wedding. What a strange, intriguing old man he had been. Two hundred years old! He was a living slice of history. And that Cassius, who was even older, and Lucifer's brothers... They were like nothing Blackworld or The Mountain had ever seen.

What had begun as an ecstatic honeymoon was fading fast. She did not mind leaving a scene that promised to become unhappy—except that she would miss Janos Kasafirek and her studies.

"I don't want to go," Lucifer told her. "But I have to. And it's cruel to take you away from your studies when you're doing so well."

"I don't mind that much. Really. Janos is getting a little overbearing. I can't take much more. We both need to cool down."

Lucifer looked at her oddly.

He changed after they reached the Fortress. His joy, youth, and poetic romance fled him. He became surly and distant, and ignored her more and more as he tried to fit into the Legion. The Legion tried to adjust to him. He could not meld in.

Inadequate to the mercenary role, he would be little help during the grim passage he had returned to help weather. Pollyanna could see it. Everyone else saw it. Lucifer could not. He was a fingerling among sharks, trying to believe he was one of the big boys.

Pollyanna became his outlet for frustration.

Knowing why he was hurting her did not ease her pain. Understanding had its limits.

Loneliness, self-doubt, her own frustration, and spite drove her into the arms of another man. Then another, and another. It became easier each time. Her self-image slipped with each one. Then came Lucifer's father. A challenge at first, he began to remind her of Frog. He gave her moments of real peace. He was gentle, considerate, and attentive, yet somehow remote. Sometimes she thought the body she clasped in their lovemaking was a projection from another plane, an avatar. The quality was even more pronounced in Storm's associates, spooky old Cassius and the Darkswords.

Plainfield, wearing the name Michael Dee, finally appeared. She met him with some trepidation, sure her hatred would shine through, or that he would remember her.

He did not remember, and did not sense her odium. Her scheme progressed with such ease that she lost herself in its pace. Before she knew it, she and Plainfield were aboard a ship bound for Old Earth and, eventually, Richard Hawksblood.

Her life seemed to become an ancient black and white movie. Jerky and depressing. Events followed Blake's script perfectly, yet she had a growing feeling that everything would fall apart.

She had lost a marriage that had meant a lot. She did not like the person she had become. Sometimes, lying beside Plainfield while he slept, she held discourse with Frog's ghost. Frog kept telling her nothing was worth the price she was paying.

It worsened. Storm forced her return to the Fortress. She would have killed Plainfield then had she not still felt an obligation to Blake, Korando, and her home city.

She became lonely in a way she had never known in Edgeward. She felt as if she had been dropped into the midst of an alien race. The men helped, for a few minutes each, but when a lover left her he took with him just a little more of her self-respect.

Then Plainfield was beyond her reach, running with the bodies of Storm's sons. She almost committed suicide.

Frog's ghost called her a little idiot. That stopped her.

She still had her duty to Edgeward. She had been living with soldiers long enough, now, to see herself as a soldier for her city. She could persevere.

# FORTY: 3052 AD

How important is a place? A place is just a place, you say. And I tell you: Not so! You are either of a place, or you are not. If you are, then it is in your heart and flesh and bones; you know it without thought, and it knows you. You are comfortable together. You are partners. You know all the quirks and bad habits and how to sidestep them. If you are an outsider…

It is the difference between new and old boots. You can wear both, but new boots can be trouble if you don't have time to break them in.

Blackworld was new boots for my father and the Iron Legion.

—Masato Igarashi Storm

# FORTY-ONE: 3031 AD

The spaceport crawler crested the pass through the White Mountains. Storm saw Edgeward City for the first time. "Looks like a full moon coming up," he murmured. "Or a bubble of jewels rising where a stone fell into dark water." Only half the city dome could be seen above the ringwall surrounding it. It glowed with internal light.

His aide studied him, puzzled. Storm sensed but ignored the scrutiny. He reached for his clarinet case, decided he could not play in this lurching, shaking, rolling rust heap.

He had to do something to ease the tension. It had been ages since his nerves had been this frazzled.

He returned to the reports in his lap. Each was in Cassius's terse, cool style. The data and statistics summed an impossible assignment. Meacham Corporation had gotten a long jump on Blake. Though they had the more fragile logistics, they had used their lead time well. They had put military crawlers into production years ago. Twenty-four of the monsters were laagered in the Shadowline a thousand kilometers west of Blake's shade station. They would be hard to root out.

Richard's supply lines, which also supported the Meacham mohole project at the Shadowline's end, could not be reached from Blake shade. They were too far into sunlight for even the hardiest charter to hit and run.

Cassius said there was a tacit agreement to avoid conflict Darkside. Blake would not hear the suggestion of direct strikes. He insisted that fighting be confined to the Shadowline.

"Idiots," Storm muttered in a moment of bloodthirst. "Ought to run straight to Twilight, kick a hole in their dome, give them something to breathe when they surrender, and have done." Then he laughed. No doubt Richard felt the same way.

Mercenary conflicts were seldom simple. Corporations, while willing to fight, seldom wanted to risk anything already in hand, only what they might someday possess.

The only positive he could see was that the Seiners were still out there somewhere, eager to ease his communications problem. It had been a lucky day when he had let emotion convince him that Prudie's people deserved his help. Those Fishers never forgot.

Darling Prudie. What had become of that sweet thing? She probably wouldn't let him see her now even if he could find her. Fishers didn't believe in fighting Nature. She would be an old woman. Storm shuffled reports, forced his thoughts back to the Shadowline.

He tinkered with Cassius's suggestion for cracking Richard's laager till the crawler reached Edgeward's tractor depot. He was sure it was a workable solution, though they would have to run it past their employer's Brightside engineers to be sure. And past the Corporate Board. Those sons-of-bitches always had to have their say.

Blake met him personally. It was a small courtesy that impressed Storm because the man had to impose on his own handicap.

"Creighton Blake," the dark man said, offering a hand. "Glad you're here. You're recovered completely?"

"Like a new man. I've got good doctors." He glanced at the man behind Blake. He seemed vaguely familiar. "We've got the best facilities at the Fortress. You might want to try our regrowth lab."

"You know, I don't think so. I don't miss the legs anymore. And not having them gives me one hell of a psychological advantage over my Board of Directors. They get to feeling guilty, picking on a cripple." He grinned. "You have to use every angle on these pirates. Ah. My manners. I'm not used to dealing with outsiders. We all know each other here. The gentleman with me is Albin Korando. He's my legs. And my bodyguard, companion, conscience, and valet."

"Mr. Korando." Storm shook hands. "We met on The Big Rock Candy Mountain. At the wedding."

Korando looked startled. He glanced at Blake. Blake nodded slightly.

"Yes, sir."

Storm smiled. "I thought so. We walk from here? Which way?"

"You've got a good memory, Colonel," Blake said. "I believe you met Albin for just a few seconds."

"Why?"

"Excuse me?"

"Why did you plant Pollyanna on me?"

"Ah? You know?" Blake chuckled. "Actually, you weren't the target. I had no interest in you at the time. Ground-zero man was your brother Michael. We almost stuck her to him, too. But you tipped the cart over."

"Long as we're being frank, would you mind telling me why?"

Blake explained. Before he finished, Storm again found himself regretting his contract to protect his brother. Michael had outdone himself here on Blackworld.

"About the Shadowline," he said, trying to ignore the curious hundreds watching them pass, "how much interference am I going to have to put up with? Cassius tells me you've ruled out direct strikes at Twilight, as well as any other armed action this side of the Edge of the World."

"This is between Blake and Meacham, not Edgeward and Twilight. We feel it's important to maintain the distinction. And we don't want civilians getting hurt."

Storm cast Blake a cynical glance, realized that the man meant what he said. The idea startled him. How long since he had worked for someone with a conscience? It seemed like forever.

Blake's humanitarian impulses could spell unreasonable casualties. "You didn't answer me."

"You won't have much trouble from me. I'm no general and I'm willing to admit it. But my Board won't make the same confession, as your Colonel Walters has discovered. They didn't want to release tractors for nonproductive employment. Maybe they thought you were going to fight on foot."

"How much voting stock do you control?"

"Thirty-eight percent. Why?"

"Any of the Directors your men?"

"I usually get my way."

"Will you assign me your proxy for the duration?"

"Excuse me?"

"One of my terms was five percent of the voting stock and a seat on the Board."

"That was rejected. Unanimously, I might add."

"Where's my headquarters?"

"Back at the depot. We set it up in an obsolete repair shed. Where're you going?"

"I'm going to pick up my toys and go home. I'm wasting my time here. I don't have a contract."

"Go home? Colonel Storm… Are you serious? You'd dump us now?"

"Damned right I would. Things get done my way or they don't get done at all. I'm not Galahad or Robin Hood. I'm a businessman. My comptrollers will compute what you owe for transport and maintenance. I'll disregard penalty payments."

"But…"

"Would you like to test your meteor screens against a heavy cruiser's main battery?"

"We thought that was a giveaway clause, Colonel."

"There were no giveaway clauses, Mr. Blake. You were presented a contract and told it was a take it or leave it. In a seller's market prices get steep. You're hiring an army, not buying one crazy Old Earth shooter. Do you have any idea what it costs to maintain a division even on a peacetime footing? Win, loose, or draw, the Legion gets five percent, twenty-year deferred payments, expenses, equipment guarantees…"

"To be honest, Colonel Walters told us the same thing. We hoped..."

"Get somebody else. Van Breda Kolff is looking for something. But he won't be much cheaper."

"Colonel, you have us. We've got to have you. They'll cry a lot, but the Board will give in. Their fussing has put us so far behind now that it's criminal."

"I don't have time for games, Mr. Blake."

"They'll come around. They see the Shadowline slipping through their fingers like fine, dry sand. They want to get back what's been lost. You could hold us up for more and get it."

Storm saw that Blake was straining to control his temper. His Directors must have caused him a lot of grief.

He understood, once he was introduced to those select old armchair pirates. They were the sort who would buck a young whippersnapper like Blake simply because they resented his having come to power at such an early age.

Storm repeated his prima donna performance and stalked out. After what must have been a bitter hour of debate, Blake came to tell him they had acquiesced with the grace of virgins bowing to inevitable rape. Storm returned to the boardroom long enough to remind them of what happened to employers who defaulted contracts with the freecorps. Their bandit eyes became angry. He knew they had not surrendered completely.

He wondered why he bothered. The premonition could no longer be denied. Blackworld was the end. The last page of his story was going to be written on this hell of a world. What matter a contract?

The Fortress, that was what mattered. Even if the Legion entire encountered its death-without-resurrection, there were still the people of the Fortress. The dependents and retirees needed support. He hoped Mouse could handle the asteroid. Dumping the administration of the empire into the boy's lap as he had...

His aide finished preparing his quarters. With Geri and Freki pacing him and the ravenshrikes watching with hooded eyes, he walked the floor and nursed "Stranger on the Shore" from his clarinet. He played it again and again, each time more mournfully than the last. He was exhausted, yet too keyed up to rest. His mind kept darting here and there like a fish trying to find a way out of its bowl.

Poor pretty Pollyanna. So young to be so driven. That Frog must have been something. He would have Mouse send her home. There was no point to her going on with her game.

Poor Lucifer. Played for a pawn. Pray it did not blind his sensitive poet's eyes. Maybe the boy would have sense enough to go with his talent now.

Poor Homer. Poor Benjamin. Gone to do hard time in the hell of Helga's World. Could Ceislak get them out? Hakes was the most perfect of commando leaders, but his chances were grim. The Festung in Festung Todesangst was an understatement.

Poor Frieda. She was about to lose a husband she never really had. He had not been much good for her.

Storm could not think of his wife without guilt, though she was a soldier's daughter and had known what she was getting into. Despite her peculiarities, she had been his best wife. In her way.

Poor everyone, Storm decided. There would be no winners this time. Not even the Sangaree Deeth. The shadow master was going to find the Shadowline a tool too hot to grasp. And poor Mouse was the dead-man's switch that would bring the Sangaree's folly home to him…

Storm finally relaxed enough to fall into a troubled sleep. His dreams gave him little peace. Only death itself promised that.

# FORTY-TWO: 3031 AD

Storm stayed clear of the tractor driver and asked no distracting questions. The briefing had made it clear that operators needed their full attention all the time. Storm's head and eye remained in constant motion as he both familiarized himself with the instruments and displays and observed the economy of motion with which the professional operator managed his crawler.

Storm gasped in awe when the convoy began its run to the Shadowline. He had never seen anything like this. Brightside in description was nothing compared to the hellish reality. He could not begin to imagine what it must be like beyond the interface of instruments and filters. A kilometer-long lake of molten metals slid past. He glanced at a rear-view screen and saw high-melting-point trace metals form a scum in the convoy's shadows. This much heat was impossible to conceive. The convoy consisted of fifty crawlers jury-rigged to transport troops and cargo. Ideally, they would have deposited their cargoes at the foot of the Shadowline and allowed the Legionnaires to proceed from the shade station under their own power. However, Storm and Cassius did not trust the vacuum-proofing of their equipment to withstand the punishment of the journey out to the Shadowline. They had elected to transport it all the way.

It would take months to move the legion that way. Every crawler outbound since Cassius's arrival had been ferrying, yet only half the Legion was in the Shadowline. The force Storm was taking out to the point of confrontation consisted of a battalion each of engineers, artillery, armor, and infantry. Support troops would be distributed along the way. He had no intention of fighting immediately. The combat troops were along only to protect the engineers, who would prepare his move against Richard's roadblock.

Cassius had been laying logistical groundwork from the beginning. He had set up major depots each hundred kilometers, scattered secondary depots in between, had erected hospital domes, recreation domes, and had set out thousands of small inflatable emergency shelters so men working in spacesuits stood a chance if something went wrong. He had set out a galaxy of communications repeaters and transponders, had widened the extant road, and had charted the most defensible terrain.

The more constrained the battlefield, the more meticulous and extensive was the preliminary work. Cassius was a sound detail man. Given the help of the brothers Darksword, and time, he would prepare down to the last shell for the explosive-type artillery Storm had selected as his main heavy weaponry.

*Already the Shadowline is cluttered*, Storm thought as he studied the screens. Near its foot every square meter of shade was in use. And the work had scarcely begun. It would be a month before they were ready for even limited action.

How much more trouble was in it for Richard? His lines were tremendously more extensive.

Storm's scouts encountered hostile pickets twenty-five kilometers from Richard's laager. He stopped and dug in while the infantry went out as skirmishers. He distributed the artillery so it could hammer any enemy probe. The armor he tucked away well behind his front, as a reserve to be deployed against any breakthrough.

For the present only Richard would be doing the attacking. And Storm thought that unlikely. Hawksblood's mission was defensive. His task was to prevent interference with the Meacham project at Shadowline's end. All he needed to do was sit and let things happen.

After establishing his position, Storm concentrated on outflanking Hawksblood from the more difficult direction.

Hawksblood would anticipate a circling strike. He would have his heaviest weapons positioned to repulse anything coming out of the sun.

Fifty kilometers to his rear Storm's engineers exploded charges which demolished a hundred-meter-wide stretch of bluff, spilling megatons of rock into shadow. The engineers had estimated that it would take a month to clear the rubble, then five to ten days to grade a crawler road to the high side of the cliffline.

Storm was not sure taking the high ground would help.

It would be pure pissing into the wind if Richard figured out what was happening—and it could turn into disaster if Hawksblood anticipated the maneuver and was waiting for it.

It was more promising than the alternatives. Attacking out of sunlight would be expensive and dangerous. Attacking straight up the Shadowline would be suicidal.

The positional and equipment advantages were Hawksblood's. Nevertheless, Storm believed he could win. One way would be to go all out, attacking with the Legion's full might. That would force a war of competitive consumption, of attrition. The sheer magnitude of Richard's logistics would betray and defeat him.

That way meant a bloodbath. Storm did not want one. Neither did his opponent. Theirs were wars of maneuver, not of slaughter. They were in the business for financial gain, not for blood and glory, not for some shadowy concept of honor or duty or patriotism, nor even for the latest in ideological fads. Their men were good soldiers. They knew how and when to keep their heads down. They knew how to stay alive and that was their primary bet in the battlefield sweepstakes. They would do their jobs with a cool professionalism and weigh each risk against the importance of the goal they were being asked to achieve.

They were the best and worst, according to one's viewpoint. A man could hire them and get a nice, clean, efficient job done quietly and quickly. A politician could rant and rave at them, exhort them, cajole them, inundate them with all the magic catch-phrases and righteous lies, and not get them to look up from their card games.

The characteristics of the Shadowline battleground left very little room for traditional mercenary finesse.

Hawksblood's detection equipment proved sensitive enough to isolate the explosion tremors from ambient thermal gradient noise in the planet's crust. He pushed a reconnaissance-in-force westward. Storm's artillery and mine fields stopped it. Hawksblood left a wrecked military crawler's slave sections behind. Storm studied them, comparing them with the handful Blake's crawler factory had produced.

He did not find much difference. Both manufacturers had stuck with a basic pumper design, modifying the slaves to carry armor and extrudable weapons turrets. The Meacham variety revealed somewhat less designer concern for the safety and comfort of the fighting crew.

"He may try flanking us now," Storm told Helmut Darksword, who was in charge east of the rockfall. "Watch for him coming out of sunlight. Keep him from spotting the fall."

"I think we'll get enough warning on the ground-noise sensors."

The command setup had been arranged so that Storm and Cassius would take turns controlling the schwerpunkt while the brothers Darksword would take turns directing operations in the support zone. The off-duty commanders would return to Edgeward City, to oversee the Legion's interests there. Storm's son Thurston directed the permanent communications and liaison team stationed in the city.

Helmut's defenses were anchored upon a battery of heavy lasecannon unshipped from a Legion cruiser. They were the only weapons Storm had which could engage a vehicle in daylight. Explosive shells, so effective in the shade, exploded a few meters after entering sunlight. Lighter laser weapons did not have enough power to punch through a crawler's heat screens.

What would Richard do if he discovered the notch in the cliffs? Move his laager back? Storm did not think so. That would be an admission of defeat. The maneuver could be repeated indefinitely, forcing Hawksblood to withdraw again and again. It might take years, but Richard would eventually run out of room to back up.

Would he come from Brightside, in force, to isolate the force screening the rockfall? That might work if he moved before the debris was cleared, so that units not inside crawlers could not retreat. But it would mean a bloody fight.

He might do nothing, hoping Storm would make a self-defeating mistake before his scheme came to fruition.

Storm favored the latter possibility. That was Richard. Hawksblood was a master of the art of doing nothing. He liked to wait till an opponent became committed before making a move himself.

Storm called the officer commanding the engineers. "Dahlgren, I hear you've got a problem back there. What's wrong?"

"Sorry, Colonel. It's bad news. We're going to take a lot longer than we figured."

"Damn! Why?"

"We didn't get a good enough picture of what was up top. We breached a metals lake up there. It's draining into the fall and hardening when it gets out of sunlight. We can't do anything till it stops."

Storm controlled his temper. "Very well." *I'm cursed*, he thought.

To someone at his end the engineer said, "Throw a spot up there, Henry, so we can show the Colonel what we're up against." His face vanished, was replaced by darkness.

In a moment the darkness gave way to a palely illuminated tumble of rock. Camera elevation climbed, revealing first a long rockslide, then an area where greyish material lay between the boulders, in places looking like leaden gobbets of hardened candle wax. Finally, the camera view rose to capture the dramatic, fiery frenzy of the liquid metal splashing and tumbling over the broken lip of the cliff.

"Awesome, Dahlgren," Storm said. "Do what you can while you're waiting." Storm secured comm, leaned back, stared at the wall of his specially-equipped command crawler.

Richard waited, as Storm had anticipated. Otherwise, that malicious, chortling little devil-god called Fate ragged the Legion with a special vengeance.

An attempt to run a line of shadow generators out to intercept Twilight's line collapsed when Blake's crews encountered a vast sea of heat erosion.

Heat erosion, which usually took the form of extremely fine powder, was not dangerous in and of itself. It was a mask hiding the real dangers over which it lay. It could conceal sudden drop-offs or spikes of hard rock that could open the belly of a crawler like a fish knife.

On Helga's World Hakes Ceislak failed in his initial attempt to penetrate Festung Todesangst. He did establish a surface bridgehead and seize control of her missile defenses. Cassius's friend in Luna Command, Admiral Beckhart, appeared to be in no hurry to commit his people.

Delays and delays. Obtaining vacuum-adapted equipment proved almost impossible. Confederation had a push on against the McGraw pirates. The Services were devouring everything being manufactured. And Richard was bidding in the same market.

There was no solace in knowing that Hawksblood faced as much trouble as did he. Richard had been born to trouble as smoke to a flame. Storm wished him a ton from the clutch of Dees he was letting camp in his back yard.

Storm still found it odd that the war did not carry over Darkside. Over there it was peace as usual. Intercourse between Edgeward and Twilight continued almost normally. They did not play psy-war games with one another's citizens. There was no trip-trip of spy over assassin. Neither city tried to whip its people into a war fever. Business followed its usual routines. Corporations controlled both cities, but only a small percentage of the population in each was involved in mining, and even of those each corporation was willing to risk but a minority. The war in the Shadowline was a risk operation. Neither Blake nor Meacham wanted to hazard anything but money.

*Well,* Storm thought, *that's why they buy soldiers. To avoid wasting their own people.*

# FORTY-THREE: 3031 AD

He returned to Edgeward after two grueling months Brightside. What had seemed a cramped, constricted city earlier now appeared so vast as to make him nervous. All a matter of viewpoint, he told himself as he tried to stretch and relax, free of the moment-to-moment survival worries of the Shadowline.

He discovered that he was a comparative unknown. Half the Edgewarders seemed unaware that the Legion was on Blackworld. The other half did not care. The war had not changed daily life.

Storm did not know whether to be pleased or dismayed. Blake had stirred up no hurrah at all. His employers usually went the reverse route.

He had a feeling Blake was a little ashamed of what he was doing.

His first day back he went through a rocky session with the Corporation's directors. They demanded action. Exasperated, Storm offered them weapons and transportation. "You know more about this business than I do," he told them. "I'm perfectly willing to run you out there and let you handle it yourselves."

After his initial aggravation, he enjoyed baiting them, delighting in their aghast expressions. He would love to have a chance to pull the same thing with the political pirates who ran Confederation. How many wars would there be if the warhawks themselves had to go put their fat asses on the firing line? The armchair warlord was one of the grotesqueries of post-feudal civilization. The Dark Ages were brutal, but then the ruling classes got out and whacked on one another…

There were no takers when he offered an inspection tour of his Shadowline operations, either. Blake, he discovered, was the only one of them ever to have crossed the Edge of the World.

*Typical of the breed*, he thought. *Never been out of their plush chairs.*

A week after his return Blake invited him to a City Hall party for Edgeward's elite. Pretty spy Pollyanna was on hand, looking more comfortable and vivacious than he had seen her since her wedding day. She was a different creature in her home milieu.

"Gneaus!" She greeted him with a kiss and an unselfconscious hug. "I hope you haven't been too miserable out there."

"Miserable isn't a word that will touch it. It's too good. I can't think of one that's low enough."

"Come on. I'll introduce you around."

"I hit Blake up pretty good on the contract, but I'm beginning to wonder if he isn't getting off cheap anyway. My men don't get to come in for these R-and-R breaks." Helmut, who had traded jobs with his brother, trailed Storm, looking like a grumbling thunderhead seeking a target for its spears of lightning. He was followed by the Sirian warhounds. Helmut scowled fiercely at those Board members who had a habit of sticking their long noses into the new Legion offices downstairs. Cassius had moved them there to take advantage of the Corporation's superior communications facilities.

The first person Pollyanna introduced was Albin Korando.

"We've met," Storm said. "How are you, Mr. Korando?"

"Still kicking, Colonel."

"Albin's sort of my brother," Pollyanna said.

"Must be a pretty thin genetic relationship."

"Oh, no. Not by blood. We were both adopted by Frog. Albin's an exile from Twilight. Frog brought him in. Got him into hogging. You should swap lies with Albin someday. He's got some stories to tell about the old days."

Korando grinned. "Anything before last week is the old days to these kids."

"Uhm. Maybe we should slip off and swap a few over a bottle. After the amenities."

"Oh, no you don't," Pollyanna told Storm. "I've got plans for you."

He began to fear that he had misread her, that she had not changed after all. "Lucifer..."

"The break is official. No hard feelings. It was good for a while, when we could both be ourselves. When we tried to be what we thought somebody else wanted, well... No. I don't want to bore you. Just say I don't regret it. Most of it."

Storm doubted that there were no hard feelings. This would mark Lucifer for years. The boy would throw himself into soldiering, trying even harder to become what he would never be. He did not disabuse Pollyanna. He could sense that she would hurt for Lucifer, knowing she had hurt him.

Next was Blake's wife, Grace, whom he hadn't known existed. She was a short, slim, retiring, elfin woman, who was socially ill at ease. She looked much younger than her probable age.

"Mrs. Blake." He put on his courtly manners, bowed to kiss her hand. A bit of ancient chivalry might put her at ease.

A part of his mind watched cynically. *How we love to play at being paladins*, he thought. *Hired killers pretending to be knights of the Round Table. Dragons slain. Maidens rescued. Ogres dismantled. No, no, that's not really innocent blood taking the shine off the old armor. Just a spot of rust.*

"Is it?... Is it dangerous?" Mrs. Blake said, staring at the ravenshrike on Storm's shoulder.

"Only if he decides you're edible." He tried a boyish smile. "Nothing to fear. He's not fond of sweets."

She became flustered. He moved on to Blake, who gave him a frosty, "Good evening, Colonel." He seemed painfully aware of Storm's philandering reputation. His gaze darted to the warhounds. "I hear you're quite skilled with an ancient instrument called a clarinet. Would you favor us by playing?"

Storm became quietly reserved. He could not be comfortable playing for strangers. He seldom played to an audience at all.

Blake sensed his discomfort. "Oh, not for the mob. For Grace and myself, after dinner. And Pollyanna, of course. Grace's request. She's a musician herself. Favors classical strings."

"An honor, then. Perhaps the lady will join me in a piece or two?"

Grace Blake stared at the floor and nibbled her delicate lower lip. She really was a timid creature. Pollyanna squeezed his arm. She whispered, "You're overdoing it."

People were watching. Several faces betrayed the thinking behind them. A few women were eyeing him speculatively. Men turned up their noses at his menagerie or calculated their chances with Pollyanna. Both sexes envied his access to the throne.

He spotted a grim face behind the partiers. Thurston pushed through the crowd, trampling toes and egos alike. He was supposed to be on duty downstairs.

Storm murmured, "Dinner and music may have to wait."

# FORTY-FOUR: 3031 AD

"Father, Cassius needs you," Thurston boomed from ten meters away.

"What is it?"

Thurston shrugged. "Something's shaping up." Evidently, he did not want to talk in front of civilians.

"Mr. Blake. Mrs. Blake. If you'll excuse me?"

"Of course," Blake replied. "Wish I had an excuse to slip out myself."

"Creighton, Colonel Storm," Grace said, her tiny voice quavering, "could we go along?"

"Of course," Storm replied. "Your husband is the boss. I'd look silly keeping him away."

"Albin, make my apologies," Blake told Korando. "Then join us in Colonel Storm's war room."

The war room was lively when they arrived. The Legion had added a massive amount of specialized equipment to Blake Mining's Comm Center. The heartpiece was a gigantic display board on which was imposed a computer-mastered chart of the Shadowline. The long, dark river of the rift was alive with shoals of tiny moving lights. Each represented a particular unit. A susurrus of soft communications chatter filled the air as commtechs monitored Shadowline radio traffic. The theme of the moment was confusion on the firing line, questions racketing back and forth among "Foxbat," "Mirage I," and "Damocles." The chatter was clear, but couched in jargon that Storm's companions could not interpret.

Cassius was on visual, and clearly impatient. "Command clear trunk, scrambled," the technician told Storm. Storm nodded.

"Gneaus," Cassius said the instant Storm moved in front of the pickup, "they're starting something. We don't know what yet, but it looks big."

"What have you got? I don't see anything on the big board."

"They started probing with infantry and armor two hours ago. Pushed our observers back. We've had to withdraw past the limit of reliable sonic discrimination, so nothing's sure. The computer enhancements make it look like there's a lot of heavy stuff moving."

Storm glanced at the pictures from the sky-eye orbitals. The damned satellites were next to useless. The demon sun burned them out in a few days' time, and what pictures they did send down were no good. Too much contrast between the sunlighted plains and the darkness of the Shadowline. "You get anything from Intelligence?"

"There hasn't been a crackle from an open carrier since this morning. Looks like they've shut down communications completely. Yesterday we did get confirmation of your notion that Richard went back to Twilight."

"Who'd he leave in charge?"

"Doskal Mennike. The younger."

"Richard wouldn't set up a push and then leave."

"That's why I called. He's been gone awhile, near as we can tell. He wasn't here for their spoiling raids last week, either. Something strange is happening."

"Where are they up top?" Storm's own forces had begun moving to break the laager that morning, after the engineers, a month behind schedule, had completed the incline to the upward side of the Shadowline cliffs. Any attack by Hawksblood would catch the Legion overextended.

"About ready. They were getting into position the last report I had."

"You have comm with Wulf?"

"A bad link. The sun is distorting the relay beam."

"Patch me in on Tac Two." While he waited, Storm asked, "Mr. Blake, is there any way we can find out what's going on in Twilight?"

"I have a man there, but I can't get in touch in a hurry. We have to wait till he finds some way to smuggle his microtapes out."

"That's no good. I need an idea of what's happening right now, today, not what was going on last month."

"Why?"

"I smell something rotten."

"Patched, Gneaus," Cassius said. "You won't get anything but snow on visual."

"I'll see if we can enhance. Switch it." He waited a few seconds. A 2 appeared momentarily. "Sky Writer, Sky Writer, this is Andiron, over." No response. "Sky Writer, Sky Writer, this is Andiron, do you read me, over."

"Andiron, Andiron, this is Blackwood. Sky Writer has lost lase-comm, over." The response was barely audible.

Storm whispered to a tech, "Who's Blackwood?"

The technician checked his charts. "Bill Allen, sir. In one of Colonel Darksword's crawlers."

"Blackwood, Blackwood, this is Andiron. Relay to Sky Writer. Query your position. Query can you relay visual of laager, over."

"Andiron, Andiron, this is Blackwood, relaying to Sky Writer. I read you loud. Am at point Romeo Tango X-Ray, engaged. Visual follows, over."

"Picture coming in," Storm said. "Enhance it."

A deep darkness, waxing and waning behind static snow, appeared before Storm. It wavered till the computer found how best to enhance it.

The darkness was broken occasionally by the fire-lances of lasecannon or the flash of explosives. The view was down from the rim of the Shadowline. Richard's laager was spread out like toys on a sand table. Here and there, jerkily in the flashes, movements suggested armor and mobile artillery scuttling for better cover. The visible crawlers began to glow.

"Why are they lighting up?" Storm asked. From behind him, Korando replied, "They're putting up their solar screens. That will stop the lighter lasecannon."

Storm leaned closer. "Those rigs look smaller than their military crawlers. Korando. What kind of units are they?"

"Pumpers and charters. Mostly old stuff. What I'd guess they'd be using for hauling supplies."

"Blackwood, Blackwood, this is Andiron. Query, classes of defensive fire received, over."

"Andiron, Andiron, this is Blackwood. Receiving light projectile fire. Have silenced one lasecannon. Over."

"Wormdoom, Wormdoom, this is Andiron, do you read me? Over."

"Andiron, Andiron, this is Wormdoom," Cassius replied. "Switching to secure comm. Wormdoom out."

Shifting to the scrambled trunk, Storm said, "Cassius, they've replaced their heavy stuff with obsolete mining equipment. Watch for something coming out of sunlight. You might move up some artillery and armor. Go ahead with the blast. It's too late for Wulf to help you anyway. Try to get this lot to surrender. If you don't get hurt, and can push far enough past them, a sunlight sweep wouldn't be able to get back to friendly territory."

"I'm working along those lines already," Cassius replied. "Gneaus, if that's it, it's likely to be bloody. What's wrong over there? This isn't Richard's style. There's no need for an attack. And Mennike isn't any glory hound either."

Remembering what it had been like out there, penned in a suit most of the time and always surrounded by natural dangers as well as enemies, Storm posited, "Maybe he went around the bend."

"Maybe. But I can think of a more probable cause. There are enough Dees over there to wreck a galaxy. I've got to get back and stay on top of this. Keep watching. I'll check in later."

"Later." Storm rose, surveyed the room. He moved a chair to its center, seated himself. From there he could hear all the monitors and see the big board. He completely forgot his guests. Thurston received a curt nod when he brought a tankard of coffee.

The razor's edge of Now swept forward, turning future into past. Hours groaned away, creaking on rusty hinges. Wulf took the laager under heavy fire. One of his crawlers ran on out along the cliff top, planted charges that would drop a rockfall behind Hawksblood's men. Wulf's fire wrecked several Meacham crawlers. The laager broke. The big units, manned by flighty civilians, fled into sunlight, abandoning everyone not already aboard. Cassius immediately applied pressure with his armor. Hawksblood's people withdrew till Wulf's rockfall barred farther retreat.

The Twilight fighting crawlers swept in from sunlight on a well-organized front two hundred kilometers wide, far behind Cassius.

"No doubt about it," Storm muttered as he watched the situation develop.

"Father?" Thurston asked.

"There's a crazy man running things out there."

The thirty Meacham crawlers attacked everything man-made, including hospitals, refuge stations, and recreation domes, all of which had been clearly marked for what they were. The crawlers maintained a grim comm silence throughout the action.

Albin Korando observed, "It looks like they don't want each other to know what they're doing. It doesn't take any military genius to know that our comm nets would let us watch every one of them."

"Curious, isn't it?" Storm said.

The Legion bent. Forewarned, it broke nowhere. The attack was still on when Storm said, "We've got them. They're going to be sorry they tried this. This might mean the whole war."

Before long the others began to see what he meant. One by one, Hawksblood's military crawlers were being disabled or forced back into sunlight. The specially designed military units were Richard's most potent tool. He was losing them fast, and would lose more when the retreating units tried to get back into the Shadowline.

A Lt. Col. Gunter Havik commanded the forces opposite Cassius. He had been Walters's student in Academy and had served with Storm in Confederation's Marines. He was the archetypal mercenary officer. He surrendered the moment it became clear that his position was untenable.

The modern freecorps would fight no heroic, doomed Stalingrads. Not when there was no known tactical or strategic justification. Glory was an epitaph for fools.

Cassius immediately started ferrying troops round the rockfall and digging them in for the return of Hawksblood's fighting crawlers. He did not expect to have much difficulty forcing their surrender. Most would be running near their limits of solar endurance and would be short of munitions. They would be eager to get into shade, and unable to shoot their way in.

Wulf's force withdrew to the Shadowline to recuperate from its extended exposure to the demon sun.

Storm glanced at a clock and realized that he had been in the war room, awake and intensely attentive, for twenty-two hours. Even iron man Thurston had taken a few hours to nap. Thurston started to suggest that he do the same.

"I was just thinking that," Storm told his son. "I can't do anything here anyway. It's all on Cassius right now. Get me up if it begins to go sour."

In the Shadowline, of course, the only sleep for the men involved was the big one. No one would rest till the issue was decided.

Blake was on hand when Storm returned. He did not seem pleased.

"What's his problem?" Storm asked Thurston.

"Casualty figures been coming in."

"Bad?"

"Not good."

Battle's confusion had begun to resolve itself into a grim statistical portrait, Storm saw when he checked the unit reports.

The first big battle in the Shadowline, still under way, would be a resounding victory for Edgeward. The laager had been broken. All but a handful of the attacking battle crawlers had been taken out. Cassius, with every available man and machine, facing light resistance, was racing toward the point where Twilight's supply line intercepted the Shadowline. He would reach it in four days if Hawksblood could not stop him. The war could be over before the end of the week.

And a thousand Legionnaires had died the death-without-resurrection. More were missing. The survivors were sifting the rubble. There were as many more injured and resurrectable dead.

Storm was appalled. He was dazed. He could not accept the figures. He had not encountered this much killing since the Ulantonid War. "Richard didn't do this," he murmured several times. "This's the work of a madman." Michael's face seemed to laugh silently from nowhere and everywhere.

Only a Dee stratagem could have spilled so much blood.

He circulated around the war room, trying to find some positive spark amid all the negatives. He found no promise anywhere but in Cassius's headlong sprint.

Suddenly, he caught one strained thread from amid the constant babble being monitored. "... you read, Iron Legion? I've hit heat erosion fourteen kilometers off Point Nine Hundred. Main track in. Can't drop my slaves. I have thirty-two men aboard. Can you help? Mayday, Mayday, this is Twenty-ninth Brightside Main Battle Tractor, can you read, Iron Legion? I've hit heat erosion..."

"How's he sending?" Storm asked.

"Pulse-beam laser, sir. He's bouncing it off the cliff face."

Storm turned to the big display board. It portrayed incredible confusion. He wondered if even the computers were keeping track.

Point Nine Hundred would be nine hundred kilometers out the Shadowline, only about fifty kilometers east of the incline Wulf had used to scale the cliffs. "How long have we been getting this?"

The monitor checked the log for the previous watch. "Nearly four hours, Colonel. Colonel Darksword began rescue operations as soon as the message came in."

Storm turned to Blake. "What're the chances of bailing them out?"

Blake shook his head. "About zit. We haven't had a successful daylight rescue since Moira Jackson brought her father in. That was right after the Ulantonid War. And we get several chances a year. Finding them is the hard part. Point Nine Hundred and fourteen out don't mean that much. It's a dead-reckoning guess. DR gets pretty loose after a few hours in sunlight. If we ever develop the technology, we'll put out navigation beacons... Anyway, you have to be right on top of another crawler to spot it. The charters have the best instruments, and even they can't see far. But we always try, if only because we hope we'll learn something."

The drama unfolded with painful slowness. Wulf had committed all his units to a computer-mapped search spiral around the trapped crawler's estimated position.

The tractor's commander grew more and more desperate as his screens drew nearer overload.

Suddenly, "Hey! Got him! Hey, over here!"

Storm chuckled nervously.

Soberly, the same voice said, "Intrepid, Intrepid, this is White Wing One. We have a contact bearing three four seven at six one zero meters. Over."

"White Wing One, White Wing One, this is Intrepid. Hold your position, over." Intrepid was Wulf on his own tactical net. "Storm King, Storm King, this is Intrepid. Assemble on White Wing One, immediate execute, over." Wulf shifted to command net. "Wormdoom, Wormdoom, this is Sky Writer. We have a positive contact. Request instructions, over."

There was no response from Cassius. Walters had outrun his communications engineers.

Storm bent to a pickup. "Sky Writer, Sky Writer, this is Andiron. Proceed with caution. Let one of the miners direct the rescue. Andiron out."

Storm stared at the big board again. He had a sudden bad feeling about this. Something told him he should let it go. Yet he could not overcome his feeling of moral obligation to a brother soldier. He could not make himself call Wulf off.

"Andiron, Andiron, this is Sky Writer. Acknowledge proceed with discretion under native direction. Sky Writer out."

Storm told the tech, "Keep a close monitor. Let me know if you smell anything funny."

The communications technician frowned questioningly. Storm did not expand.

The rescue attempt followed procedures which were little more than paper theory. It went smoothly, according to Korando and Blake, one or the other of whom was always present.

Charters moved into position sunward of the stricken crawler. They set up portable shadow generators which were themselves protected by a series of disposable molybdenum-ceramic ablation sails. Pumpers, the leviathan crawlers which took liquid metals aboard and hauled them in for processing, ran their pump trunks to emergency locks designed to receive them. The inner diameter of the trunks was large enough to permit passage of a small man.

"Makes a hog more comfortable, knowing he has a theoretical chance," Korando observed. "Even if it's so slim it only pays off once a century. Knowing somebody will try means a lot when you're crawling Brightside."

"Andiron, Andiron, this is Sky Writer. We're getting no response from the crawler. We're sending a man from Main Battle One. Over."

Storm turned to Blake, frowning a question. "The battle crawlers are modified pumpers," Blake told him. "The first few have converted pump slaves."

That was not the question Storm wanted answered. But Wulf was waiting. "Sky Writer, Sky Writer, this is Andiron. I read you, over."

Wulf had the man carry a hand comm and patched him into the comm net. There was a lot of back and forth about how to open the escape hatch from outside. Wulf had a lot to say about hurrying it up because the shadow generators would not last forever.

"What I wanted to know," Storm told Blake, "was why you couldn't have used this method to rescue that man Frog."

"Because his tractor was built on the other side of the hill where Noah was building the Ark. His only escape hatch was under his cabin. The high-hatch modification came about because of the trouble we had getting to him. Meacham picked up the idea the same time we did."

"I see."

"I don't see anything but dead men, Colonel," Wulf's investigator reported once he had effected entry. "I'm starting forward to the control cabin."

There was a minute of silence. Storm waited tensely, something raising the hair at the back of his neck.

"Can't figure what happened here, Colonel. They're all bluish and puffy-faced. Their screens are still up and the oxy levels look good…"

"Wulf!" Storm thundered, ignoring the code rules. "Get the hell out of there! I mean now!" The bad feeling had bloomed into an intuition. "It's some kind of trap!"

His order came too late. It had been too late for an hour.

There was an instant of thunder on the net, then a silence punctuated only by static.

"Andiron, Andiron, this is Honeycomb," a tight voice said, breaking the silence. "We have a visual and lase-radar on a nuclear cloud at approximately Point Nine Twenty, fifteen kilometers out. Over."

And, "Andiron, Andiron, this is Charing Cross. I'm getting heavy richters epicentered at approximately point Nine Seventeen, fifteen kilometers out, accompanied by heavy gamma radiation. Over."

Similar and related reports came in from a dozen observers. Storm responded to none. The communications technician acknowledged in a dull voice.

Wulf. Dead. Along with hundreds of his men. Because of a humanitarian impulse. It had been a trap. Dee work for sure, predicated on a knowledge of mercenaries and miners.

Storm told Thurston, "That was Fearchild's doing."

Thurston nodded sadly. "It's his style. What are we going to do, Father?"

Storm paused a moment before answering. "You take over here." His stomach felt as though the great-granddaddy of all ulcers were trying to gnaw its way out. "I've got to tell Helmut. Try to get through to Cassius. He has to know."

He was surprised at himself. He should have been in an insane rage. Instead, he was emotionally numb, still trying to convince himself that it really had happened. Part of him kept thinking Wulf would call in and say it was all a bad joke.

He scanned his people once before going to Helmut. Their faces were all reflections of his own, he suspected. Each portrayed shock and an inability to believe.

Nuclears had not been used on-planet, against people, even during the most critical days of the Ulantonid War. They had joined the list of banned-by-gentleman's-agreement weapons ages ago. One would expect chemical and biological weapons to see use first. Their effects were less long-lasting…

He had been right. The Shadowline war was the swan song of the freecorps. Confederation would move in and disarm them for sure, now. The public outcry would leave the government no choice.

He overlooked one small fact while thinking that. The media were completely indifferent to the Shadowline war. No one was covering it. Hardly anyone off Blackworld knew anything about it. He, the people in the war room, and perhaps a handful of men in Twilight, were the only folks Darkside who knew that proscribed weaponry had been employed.

# FORTY-FIVE: 2860-3023 AD

Only months after they had overcome the last Dharvon, Deeth growled, "I'm bored, Rhafu. I think I've figured out why my father was always so damned cranky. There's no real challenge in trying to boost a profit margin a tenth of a percent."

Rhafu looked at Deeth, perhaps thinking the young Head was fooling himself. "Your peers would argue the point."

"That's their lifestyle. The Haug and Gaab haven't ever done anything else. I might be happy if I'd had a normal childhood. But I didn't. The normal life makes me feel caged."

"We have a mission your father bequeathed us."

"We can't do anything about it. We're stuck with the tedious stuff here. By the time we clear it up, the animals will be warring with Ulant, and we'll have to wait them out. That could last twenty years. The Ulantonid are stubborn."

"I don't recall your father saying revenge had to be instantaneous. Even so, I have to admit to a certain restlessness myself."

"Any ideas?"

"Some."

"Let's hear them."

"I think we should divide ourselves into a greater and lesser House. One to go on being traditional Norbon, the other to exploit Osiris and pursue our vendetta with the animals. Creating a dual structure would isolate risks. If we fail, we wouldn't take the Family down with us."

Deeth eyed Rhafu uncertainly. They had built a very responsive, monolithic structure in order to destroy the Dharvon. He did not want to relinquish any of the power he had acquired.

"Your cousin Taake hasn't much imagination, but he's a competent administrator. Put him in charge of the Homeworld arm of the Family. Collect up our more venturesome people and move to Osiris. You'll find plenty of excitement there. And all the work you want, too. We can build puppet empires. We can develop broader markets. Raise sithlac domes. Construct breeding stations. Hell, we could even get into ordinary commerce and industry. It's a whole planet, and we don't have to share it with anyone."

*A primitive, medieval world,* Deeth thought. *We can play God, if we want. What more could I ask?* "I'll consider it. Any other suggestions?"

"We could exploit this war. We've collected a lot of new dependents since we came home. We have to employ them somehow."

"Build a raidfleet? Rhafu… When I was little, when I first went to Prefactlas, that was all I ever thought about. Growing up to be a raidmaster."

"Don't think it's all adventure and romance, Deeth. Even piracy is plain hard work if you're going to be any good at it. Ships have to be bought or built. Arms have to be acquired. All that takes financing. You have to assemble reliable intelligence sources. You have to find men who'll work together without letting too much pride get in their way. Men without Family loyalties who would become loyal to you and one another. That's not easy with our people."

"Yes, yes. I see. More of the same old administrative hoohaw. But at least with an interesting end in sight." Deeth began to recover some of that awe and excitement he had felt when, as a child, he had studied the adventures of the great raiders.

If the Sangaree race had one outstanding weakness, it was a cultural bias against tight, devoted administration, a cultural aversion to administrative detail. They pictured themselves as a people of action and behaved accordingly. The sprawling, suffocating, ever-growing bureaucracies characteristic of human enterprises were unknown to them. They strayed to the extreme in the opposite direction, sometimes so far that the lack was as crippling to them as was the excess to humankind. Critical records might amount to nothing more than a few handwritten notes on scraps of paper soon lost… What did not exist in the minds of the Heads and their immediate assistants could be extremely ephemeral, and setbacks frequently came about simply through failure of communication or absence of administrative precision or reliable records.

A Family's most prized retainers were those few Sangaree capable of being clerkish and detail-conscious. The Families scrambled for them aggressively and traded them carefully.

Deeth's raiding and Osirian operations prospered. In time the Norbon were accepted, grudgingly, as one of the Sangaree First Families. Deeth and Rhafu earned a reputation as a team with a golden touch. Their projects usually sprang from

Rhafu's fertile mind. Deeth's carefully recruited employees and agents put them into effect. The old man did his best to remain obscure and play his own role.

In a sense Rhafu was the power behind the throne, the real genius of the Family. Deeth simply manipulated hands.

Deeth did not want to be the brains. He dared not be. Despite all the lessons of Prefactlas, he remained impulsive. Rhafu usually softened the impact of his impetuosity, but there were times when the Family welfare suffered because of some ill-considered scheme Deeth launched without consulting the old man.

Though one of the First Families now, the nouveau riche Norbon were never fully accepted as such. They were a little too crude, too rough, too much involved in the more barbarous ways of garnering wealth. And Deeth employed outsiders.

He did not use them in the traditional way, as cat's-paws among their own peoples. He found good men and brought them into the Family operations on Osiris and, occasionally, Homeworld. Accountants. Economists. Data-processors. And soldiers, hard men who became the fist of the Family, led by trusted Sangaree retainers.

The more traditional Families were appalled. And not a little jealous of the wealth-accumulating and fighting efficiencies of the Norbon.

Deeth received few social invitations, but even fewer slights that might be viewed as invitations to bad feelings. He did not miss the social life. He remained unregenerate in his distaste for parties and the people who frequented them.

During the war he saw occasions when he thought he could fulfill his father's charge on the cheap. He moved without consulting Rhafu, hoping, like a child eager to surprise a parent with an accomplishment. His enemies were cunning and slippery. They seemed to smell danger from light-years away. They evaded him every time, and so effectively that they remained unaware of the nature of the threat.

During the war, from a distance, he re-encountered his son, and could not shake the Sangaree sense of Family. He applied a few helpful nudges where the Norbon had the power, and helped create a rich man. And an instrument by which, Deeth hoped, Norbon influence might be intruded into the heart of human power structures.

Much later, long after he had revealed himself, Deeth began spiriting Michael off to Homeworld and Osiris for a belated Sangaree education.

There were grave deficiencies in Michael's character. Deeth was disappointed. He never let on. Michael was his only child.

Deeth did not marry. That he did not, and remained untempted by the prizes steered onto his path, caused quiet comment. There were ungrounded speculations about the nature of his relationship with Rhafu, and questions about Michael.

Only Rhafu suspected the truth, and even with his oldest friend Deeth refused to discuss the question.

Norbon w'Deeth was carrying a torch for an animal woman called Emily Storm.

For a bred pleasure slave.

That one dread secret could topple his empire. A physical relationship could be tolerated, could be winked at, but an emotional involvement could not. Not ever. Such weakness could not be accepted in a Head.

He dared not share his feelings for fear that it would, like a Frankenstein monster, get loose and destroy him. His own House would repudiate him.

He had won the loyalties of his relatives. They would go into hell for him if he ordered it, but for the sake of a perverted love they would not follow him to a new Wholar.

Yet he walked the edge. He dared bring Michael into Sangaree society. He formed an alliance with the Gaab by wedding his son to one of their daughters. He dodged all questions about Michael's mother by saying that she had perished on Prefactlas.

Rhafu, sensing the mild, unformed suspicion of the Heads, spread a tale of a companionship with a Sexon girl. He used the whole true story of Deeth's youth, merely changing Emily's name.

Time marched. Decades dwindled into the past. Deeth suffered severe and extended depressions whenever he withdrew from his work and realized that he had, again, become an administrator. Fulfillment of his great obligation to his father seemed to be ever more remote. There just was no time to plot against the Storms.

A sudden and unexpected opportunity arose on a world the humans called Amon-Ra.

Michael sent word that his brother, who had just assumed command of the Iron Legion, had agreed to help the underground human government oust the Sangaree Families controlling the world.

The Amon-Ra Families were all small and weak. They would stand no chance against the Legion.

Deeth decided to help them. Over Rhafu's protests, without adequate preparation, he threw in his raidships. Aboard them he sent the quasi-military forces he had developed on Osiris.

He lost everything. Every man, every ship, every weapon. It was a hard way to learn the truth about his officers. Landless, Houseless, Familyless Sangaree simply were not disciplined enough to make war in human terms.

Rhafu treated him to an extended lecture on those cultural biases which made it impossible to fight the Storms heads up…

"All right!" Deeth finally snarled. "I can see that for myself. And I'm going to correct it. We'll build a real fleet and real army. And if our own people won't do, we'll use animals. All animals." They had used humans and Ulantonid from the beginning, but never in command positions.

Amon-Ra slipped away. The years and decades rolled on. Deeth buckled down, subjected himself to an intense self-discipline, did not let up till the Norbon had recovered from the Amon-Ra disaster.

When he did pause to look around he found himself blessed with an excuse for ulcers. Michael and his children… They carried on as if they were alone and immune to anything. Time and again, one or another endangered his plans for the future of the Storms or threatened to scuttle one of his profitable intrusions into the human business sphere. The children were the despair of their mother, who was a stolid First-Family woman completely uninterested in bizarre adventures. She came to him, as the Norbon, again and again, pleading for his intercession.

What could he do? He dared not overcontrol them for fear of losing an invaluable bridgehead in human affairs.

With his financial backing they were pushing tentacles into every corner of Confederation, and those tentacles were channels along which Norbon influence flowed. And when the Norbon prospered, all Sangaree eventually profited.

Following Amon-Ra, Deeth became an avid follower of the human wars, especially the Storm-Hawksblood contests, which contained so much genuine animosity at the command level. "Rhafu, I think this is what we need. We bend their own wishes and guide them into a to-the-death struggle…"

"They're too intelligent to fall into that trap. They don't let personal feeling interfere with business."

"Nevertheless…" Deeth tried putting agents into both mercenary forces. He failed. He had to rely on his son for inside information. And Michael was both unstable and the possessor of a strong streak of Sangaree self-centeredness.

The creation of Festung Todesangst strengthened the Norbon immeasurably. It freed the Family of the old Sangaree administrative bugaboo, and allowed Deeth to pirate invaluable commercial information. In a very few years the Norbon had as much power and wealth over the First Families as the First Families had over the average Sangaree Family.

Deeth's secret monitoring facility inside Festung Todesangst, existing outside the knowledge of his son and granddaughter, apprised him of Michael's discovery on Blackworld. It screamed a priority instel when Michael first ran his numbers.

# FORTY-SIX: 3032 AD

It was not much of a New Year. The Legion did not celebrate. Edgeward City tried, but events in the Shadowline had killed any spirit of optimism. The various parties fell flat.

Storm spent New Year's Day and the following week alone, or, when he craved company at all, with Helmut Darksword. Helmut was taking Wulf s death badly.

Cassius was ripping Twilight into bloody chunks in the Shadowline. Hawksblood's leaderless troops were falling apart. Storm could not refresh his interest in the Legion's advances nor in the enemy's mysterious vulnerability. He played his clarinet, read his Bible, and sat and stared at his old .45, twirling the dark steel cylinder as he did so.

Cassius had cut off the Meacham crews at Shadowline's end. He was having no trouble repelling relief forces attacking from the shade of the Twilight shadow generators. His men, despite orders to the contrary, frequently refused to play the old mercenary games of fire and maneuver. While Walters remained cool and professional, they went and slugged it out with the enemy, determined to teach lessons that would remain forever unforgotten.

Thurston had been making a career of trying to suppress the news of the nuclear blast. He was, like the Dutch boy, trying to save a dike with a finger. His luck was worse. The whole Legion knew how Wulf and his men had died. That was why they were out for blood.

Storm did not interfere. He believed that the whole thing had gotten beyond any chance of control. Like a cold, it had to run its course.

He had won another war. Resoundingly. And, probably, had stumbled right into a Michael Dee trap.

He thought a lot about his brother, and about the promise he had given so lightly, so long ago. Michael was on his mind whenever that old revolver rested in his hand… He often wished that, sometime, he had turned his head while Cassius or his sons had worked their will.

Keeping his word had cost too much. Far too much. And yet, even now, he knew he would shield Michael if Dee came begging for protection.

He returned to City Hall only when the first band of prisoners came in. He wanted to talk to Lt. Col. Havik.

Havik spotted him first. He rushed over, face drained and worn. "Colonel Storm. I want to offer my apologies. I know they're not worth a fart in a whirlwind, but I've got to say something. That thing is eating us up. I want you to know that if any of us had known, we would've refused our orders."

Storm, standing cold and silent, watched Havik's face. He knew the man was telling the truth, yet it was hard to separate the action from the enemy…

"My men and I have had a lot of time to talk, Colonel. One of the corporals made a proposal. We've all agreed. The whole battalion wants to offer its services in bringing to justice whoever is responsible for the atrocity."

Storm inclined his head slightly in acknowledgment. Havik was professional to the core. Like so many Academy products, he was an attempt at a carbon of Cassius. "Thank you, Colonel. If there's any way you can help, believe me, I'll yet you know. And without trying to get you to compromise your commission. But if I can, I mean to handle this myself. It's become personal."

"Uhm." Havik nodded his head. Perhaps he had seen Dees floating around Twilight. Maybe he understood.

"What's happened to Colonel Hawksblood?" Storm asked. "I just don't understand how this could have happened in his organization."

Havik frowned, shrugged. "Colonel, nobody has heard from the Commandant since Colonel Mennike took over. We've started to wonder if he hasn't met with foul play. He'd been having a lot of trouble with the Twilighters. And now your men have found Colonel Mennike."

Storm sent a questioning glance Thurston's way.

"They found him the day before yesterday," his son told him. "In a one-man shelter near where the Twilight route enters the Shadowline. He'd been dead better than two weeks. Stabbed."

"Colonel Havik," Storm said, "I still won't ask you to compromise your commission, but if you'd volunteer a little information it might help."

"Sir?"

"What sort of communications did you have with your headquarters in Twilight?"

Havik did not think before replying. "We used microwave relay in the Shadowline, Colonel. Pulse-beam laser repeaters across Brightside. The system wasn't reliable. The laser's been down all month. The shadow generators are too far apart. The power you need to punch a beam through overloads the equipment. We've been using messengers between the down stations."

Storm eyed Havik. The Colonel's statement was a clear-cut betrayal of his employer. The nuclear must have touched him where he lived. "Then Commandant Hawksblood could be perfectly healthy, crossing Brightside somewhere, completely ignorant of what's happened?" Storm hoped so. He did not want Richard taken out of his life by one of Michael's stratagems.

"Possibly. We were set up to be as independent of Twilight as possible. There wouldn't be much traffic. He'll eat heads when he gets back and finds out."

"Thanks, Colonel. We'll make you comfortable. I hope this won't last much longer."

"It shouldn't. You've won. Before the blast. That's what makes it so senseless. You lost a lot of men, but it didn't change anything."

Storm went to the war room to check the daily reports from Mouse and Hakes Ceislak. The Fortress was quiet. There was good news from Helga's World. Ceislak's engineers had sapped a tunnel into Festung Todesangst. His men were occupying the upper levels.

Where was this Beckhart, this friend of Cassius who had promised to land Marines as soon as the Legion established a bridgehead? He seemed to have vanished from the universe. And Storm wanted Ceislak on Blackworld.

He went on to Blake's penthouse. "Mr. Blake, I want to make a direct strike at Twilight."

"I've told you that's impossible, Colonel."

"Hear me out. That blast out there was a setup. That bomb had to come from their mining inventory. That means there was collusion by somebody up high in Meacham Corporation. And it means that Hawksblood has lost control. He wouldn't try anything like this. If he makes it back from Brightside, he'll end up dead or in a cell. They're not playing by the rules anymore. I'm telling you we've got to quit before they eat us up. The scenario I see is this: Richard will be the scapegoat. He'll probably get killed trying to escape after he 'orders' somebody to put a bomb in on Edgeward itself."

Blake looked baffled. "Colonel, I absolutely refuse to allow you to endanger civilians."

"I don't think you understood me. The civilians are in danger now."

Korando cleared his throat. "Mr. Blake, pardon me for butting in. I think you'd better give the Colonel's suggestion more thought. That nuclear was a storm warning. We can't ignore it. We'd better be ready for anything. Logically, the next step would be a move against Edgeward. They have to get rid of witnesses. And it's the only way they have left to get control of the Shadowline. You can't bet they won't do it. They've already gone further than any of us would have believed possible a month ago."

"Right!" Storm growled. "You people are going to be up to your ears in Confie snoops when this gets offworld. Personally, I want to keep you around to answer their questions. Mr. Blake, believe me, I know the man responsible for this. We slept in the same room for ten years. If you give him time, he'll not only destroy you, he'll get away with it. You know that. When you get down to it, it's not that much of a jump from Frog to Edgeward."

"You think it's Dee?"

"Absolutely. And backing him is a Sangaree Head named Norbon w'Deeth. And the Norbon seem to be top dog among the Sangaree Families."

"Sangaree?" Blake was baffled. "What have they got to do with this?"

"It's too complicated to explain. Take my word. This confrontation was engineered from offworld. It started when Dee murdered your man Frog. If we don't scratch and claw, it'll end up with the Sangaree in complete control of Blackworld's mining industry. And they won't leave any witnesses to testify against them."

Blake slowly shook his head. "I'll consider what you've said, Colonel."

"Don't take too much time. They won't. By now they know their attack failed and they're being overrun. That bomb was probably meant to go off somewhere else, making the whole thing work. They'll do something, just to find out if it blew at all, then to cover it up. You'll find me in the war room."

Storm went back downstairs, settled into a chair facing the big board. The confusion of the previous week had begun to disappear. Unit lights had appeared throughout the territory Cassius had occupied. There was a big concentration a hundred kilometers west of the junction with the Twilight supply line. Cassius planned to sit there and wait for the Meacham people to come in and surrender.

Had this been a normal merc war it would have been all over but the prisoner exchange. Richard could do nothing to dislodge Cassius. His logistics were too precarious and there was no shade where he could assemble sufficient forces.

But if Michael had Meacham's ear, war would break out Darkside as soon as news of the Brightside defeat reached Twilight. Michael had cast the dice. He had no choice but to escalate his bets.

Storm issued orders. He wanted a new board set up to represent the Darkside territory between Edgeward and Twilight, and wanted all available personnel planting observation devices on likely approaches to the city.

How would Michael avoid the mutiny that was certain when Richard's men found out what had happened in the Shadowline?

Simple. He, or whichever of his sons it was who had taken Mennike's place, would destroy shadow generators while returning to Twilight, cutting communications with and abandoning Hawksblood's forces. It was a harsh move, but Dee-logical.

He had better warn Cassius to watch out for nuclear booby traps. The Dees would want to reduce the witness population fast.

"The Whitlandsund!" he growled. People turned to stare at him. "Of course!"

Edgeward's pass to Brightside was the key. Michael would want it bad. By capturing it, Dee could trap almost everyone who could damn him Brightside. In its tight, twisting confines he could play Thermopylae. If Edgeward were destroyed and he held the pass till everyone Brightside perished, who would be left to speak against him? Only his accomplices.

Storm had no one to send to defend the pass. How long to travel from Twilight to Edgeward? How long from Helga's World to Blackworld? He calculated quickly. Not long enough, and too long. There was no point to having Ceislak abandon his mission.

"Thurston. Go find Havik. Bring him here. Then get Blake." He retreated into his speculations. The nuclear blast had to be part of a greater Dee plan. It could not have been an end in itself because it had not altered the field situation in the Shadowline. Was it a diversion? Something to grab the attention while Michael snuck up on Edgeward and the Whitlandsund?

The idea deserved more thought. How had Michael arranged it? On timing? If so, then the southward movement toward Edgeward would be under way now…

*The fox. The fool fox,* Storm thought. *I should have known he wouldn't be content to stay in the background while Richard and I tried to fake each other out with fancy footwork.*

Michael might be fated to win his game, but, damn it, there must be ways to make his winning expensive and painful.

Havik appeared. Storm said, "Colonel, I've got one hell of a problem." He retraced the path of his recent thoughts.

Havik suggested, "Put scouts out, of course. Fortify the pass. Hold a reserve to ambush them on their way down. Unless they've brought in someone from outside, there won't be many of them. We had almost everybody in the Shadowline. Meacham handled our logistics."

"The Legion is in the same position, Colonel," Storm said. "All I've got here are communications people and a liaison crew. And I expect Dee to use his own people. He won't want men who'll kick much about breaking the usual rules."

"I see." Havik remained thoughtful for more than a minute. Then, "The only help I could give you would be passive. I could go out and squat in the pass. If they attacked, I could consider that a move against my employer. I'd feel justified in resisting. But... What would I use for weapons? We turned ours over out there."

Blake had arrived and had been listening during Storm's speculations. He still did not want to believe, but had begun to recognize the potential for disaster. "Colonel Storm, do you really think Dee is such a demon?"

Storm snapped, "I grew up with him, remember? I think I know what he's capable of, and that's just about anything." He turned to Havik. "I don't know what we can do about arms. There're some personal weapons, but the only heavy stuff we have is what came back for maintenance work."

"We have our own weapons cache," Blake said. "It's obsolete stuff, though. It was used by the Devil's Guard during the war."

Storm made a face. He prided himself on keeping his men equipped better than Confederation's armed forces. "Any of it functional?"

"We've kept it up. We have a few men who play-act at being a militia."

"Colonel Havik?"

"I'll look it over." He did not sound excited. "But I want you to know, this is something I'll have to take to my men. I can't just order them to help the Iron Legion."

"I realize that, Colonel. Just ask them to hold the Whitlandsund till we can send someone to relieve them. They're your people caught out there, too. If you have doubters, send them to me. If I can't convince them, then I don't want them involved. It shouldn't be for more than a few days anyway. Mr. Blake. Do you have any people capable of managing the war room?"

"What're you planning now?"

"I'm going to do my job. I'm going to defend Edgeward City. I'm going to take my people out and ambush Michael Dee. I'll need somebody to keep track of things here."

"I have my communications people. You'd have to have somebody familiarize them with the equipment."

"I'll leave Helmut Darksword." Helmut was not yet ready for combat. "Thurston, how are your preparations coming?" His son had begun them immediately after contacting Blake and Havik.

"Half an hour, Father. They're loading the crawlers now."

Blake sighed, smiled a thin, worried smile. "I almost hope you've guessed right, Colonel."

Korando offered one of his rare observations. "Better a live fool than a dead skeptic, sir."

Storm smiled. He wished he had time to get to know Korando. The man interested him. "I'll keep in touch, Mr. Blake. I'm going to try to find Colonel Darksword."

It was a ragtag force he took out to meet the Dees. He had some three hundred men armed primarily with equipment that had been sent in for repairs. Their small arms were their only reliable weapons.

Still, if Michael did appear, the ambush should buy Havik a few more hours to get dug in in the Whitlandsund. Havik, in his turn, would stall Dee till the units Storm had recalled from the Shadowline arrived.

# FORTY-SEVEN: 3032 AD

Storm, wearing a standard infantry combat suit, stood on a hill overlooking the place where his men would fight. Silence and darkness surrounded him. To the west there was a hint of glow limning the Thunder Mountains, illuminated ions blowing on the solar wind. Before him, invisible to the eye, stretched a long, narrow plain flanked by the ringwalls of two immense meteor craters. The hill on which he stood was the wall of a third and smaller crater, which narrowed the nearer end of the plain to little more than road width. It was a nice tight place to defend.

The region had suffered intense meteoric bombardment over the ages. The plain, over which the customary Twilight-Edgeward route ran, was the only safe passage through the craters—unless Michael swung hundreds of kilometers eastward to come in along the route from The City of Night. Storm was sure Michael would be too arrogantly self-certain to come in by the less obvious path.

And he would be too arrogantly sure of himself to charge south as fast as he should. While he was tootling along, smirking about having put one over on the best, his brother would have anticipated him and would have chosen their place of battle.

*My brother*, Storm thought. *That's what it comes down to out here. A fight between me and my brother.*

He now knew that Michael was coming. Dee's convoy had been detected by remotes an hour ago, ten kilometers to the north, rolling south at a steady eight kilometers per.

Storm smiled grimly when he saw the first running lights appear at the far end of the plain. The battle crawlers were leading. Michael had six of the monsters. If those could be wrecked…

Though it was pointless, he turned to survey his dispositions. He could see nothing, of course, though he could vaguely sense the presence of the gun crew in front of him and Thurston there beside him.

*Here I stand,* he thought. *The Black Prince once stood like this on the hill at Poitiers. I know my soldiers are the best that ever were, but...* He wondered how sure Edward had been. From the literature it seemed that he had known his Englishmen could handle ten times their weight in French, but those histories had been written after the fact, with the outcome no longer in doubt, and mainly by Englishmen. The Black Prince had stalled for days, trying to negotiate his way out of the mess.

There would be no negotiation today. And these enemies would be no gentlemen burdened by generations of chivalric tradition. If, as he had begun to suspect when he had learned the size of Michael's force, these were Sangaree troops spirited in through some city other than Twilight, he faced some rough fighters. They would not be familiar with the terrain or their equipment, but they would be as case-hardened as his own people.

The fifteen-minute wait seemed endless. Storm caressed his lasegun. It felt cold and hard through his suit gloves. He hummed "Stranger on the Shore," and wondered why he had never learned to loaf through these final minutes. He had had a long life in which to grow calloused, yet he was as nervous today as he had been while waiting for the opening shot of his first battle.

"A time for living and a time for dying," he murmured. The leading Meacham crawler had entered the narrows between ringwalls.

His one lasecannon flashed blindingly, drilling a neat hole through the face of the lead tractor. It was a point-blank shot. In the second flash Storm saw frozen air spewing from the wound.

His artillery opened up. His armor, using radar and the enemy lights as guides, began scratching deadly graffiti on the crawlers' flanks. Their tracks were favored targets. His infantrymen, bouncing in on their jump packs, concentrated completely on tracks. Their guns and rocket launchers scrawled a thousand bright lines on the face of a startled night.

A secondary explosion ripped the guts out of a slave in the third crawler in line.

"A complete surprise!" Storm growled happily. He descended the hill in hundred-meter bounds, the compressed gas of his jump-pack rockets rippling the back of his suit stingingly. To his right Thurston was bouncing mightily despite the heavy load of satchel charges he carried. Thurston veered across Storm's path, heading for the stalled lead crawler. Storm followed him. The lead vehicle was the most important target. Properly wrecked, it would block Michael's advance for a long time.

The Twilighters started shooting back. Their fire was wild. Storm chuckled. They must have been riding along like tourists, bored, sleeping, completely indifferent to the world outside.

One of his tanks took a bad hit. The crew scrambled out before the ammunition blew. They joined the infantry, going to skirmish with bewildered enemy troops disembarking from the transports up the line.

The lasecannon disabled another battle crawler before dying of its own illnesses. That put the lead three out. The others put their solar screens up. The energy of the small arms could do nothing against those.

Storm stayed close to Thurston. Almost fifty men converged on the lead crawler. Though stalled, the machine was far from dead. Its weapons spit shells and coherent light. Storm's rocket men concentrated on suppressing that fire.

He and Thurston reached the tractor. His son cut his jump pack, tossed him a charge, then ran along the monster's flank, below its fire, limpeting charges to each slave. Storm attached his own over the hole drilled by the lasecannon, dove for cover.

He felt the explosion in his hands and feet. There was no sound and almost no concussion. He leaped up, yanked himself through the hole he had blown. He used his weapon like a firehose.

The cabin was an undefended shambles. Storm sabotaged the power controls. The men who followed him in moved to the hatch connecting with the first trailer. Storm began moving from chair to chair, peering into the faces of dead crewmen.

He could not tell. They looked human enough. He would have to take a few back for dissection.

Would Michael really take that risk? he wondered. The provable presence of Sangaree would bring Navy and the Corps whooping in here as if they were a day late for Armageddon. It probably would not be worth the trouble of lugging the bodies around.

Then he found the blue man.

"What the hell?"

He had seen blue men before, a long time ago. A lot more of them than he had wanted during the Ulantonid War. There were no Ulantonid in Richard's forces, nor did any reside on Blackworld. Cassius had said that the Sangaree Deeth employed men of several races.

The crawler rocked as Thurston's charges exploded in series. His men burst through into the first slave. There was a brief bit of gunplay. Storm ignored it. He pitched a corpse out of the cabin, broke radio silence long enough to call a crawler in to pick it up. He returned for another.

What would be going on in Michael's head right now? Would he be raging against the fates, the way he always did when things went bad? Or would he be wondering why resistance was so light?

He chose a half-dozen corpses all told. His men loaded them aboard the same crawler that had done passenger duty on the Edgeward-to-Twilight run. The operator became increasingly nervous as Dee's infantry pushed closer and closer, but held on even after spears of light began stabbing all around.

Storm's force got mauled, as he expected. But even his clerks and commtechs were Legionnaires. They delivered far more damage than they took. When Storm had his corpse collection and was satisfied that the lead battle crawlers were thoroughly disabled, he withdrew in good order.

The mass of armor and infantry that poured around the lead crawler, pursuing Storm, suddenly ceased to be, as a garden of mine explosions devoured them. Dee's caution afterward allowed Storm to finish disengaging.

"Now we'll see what Michael's made of," he told Thurston.

"Father?"

"We'll find out if he can control his temper. If he can, he'll go after the Whitlandsund. If he can't, he'll come after Edgeward to get even."

"He wouldn't have much trouble taking the city."

"No. But he'd have to spend a week making sure it was pacified. And he doesn't have a day to waste. Go up and tell the driver to stop at the top of the crater wall. We'll sit up there and see what Michael decides."

Storm sat on that hill for a long, long time. He had done a superb job of blocking Dee's path.

Thurston wakened him. "He's coming, Father."

Storm went to the control cabin to watch the screens and displays. Crawler after crawler came from the north, lumbered past, and turned west. "Good. He had time to think it out."

"I feel sorry for Havik," Thurston said.

"So do I, Son. But he's got a better chance now than before. Driver, take us in to Edgeward."

An antsy Helmut awaited him at the depot. "Looks like trouble," Storm told Thurston.

"Gneaus, we've got trouble," Helmut said when Storm went to him.

"What now?"

"Ceislak has his ass in a bind. A Sangaree bind. They ran a big raidfleet in on him. Our ships had to haul out. He's holding them off with the captured batteries, but he says they can force a landing if they want to push it."

"Looks like Cassius got his wish, then. We've pulled the head spider into the game. Any word from Navy or Luna Command?"

"Not peep one. Cassius is on his way in."

"Eh? Why?"

"He said that if Dee means Richard's people to be trapped out there, he's cut the line to Twilight, so there's no need for us to hold on west of the shade station. They'll come to us. He's just leaving a few men to help them evacuate."

"I wonder… You think Michael figured Cassius would think that way? That this Darkside thrust is just a feint to pull him in?"

"No. The nuclear…"

"Of course. That changed everything. He's playing for all the marbles, not just the Shadowline."

They reached the war room in time to receive Ceislak's message that he was being attacked by Sangaree. Storm connected Cassius, brought him up to date on Helga's World, Havik, and his own recent action.

"Gneaus," Cassius burred, "I have a suggestion about those corpses. Send them over to Darkside Landing or The City of Night for the autopsy. The more you spread the proof around, the harder it'll be for Dee to eliminate all the witnesses. And they'll pressure Meacham to stop backing him."

"Good thinking. I'll do it. Got to go. Havik's in action now."

"Father," Thurston called across the room, "instel from Helga's World. Ceislak has Sangaree on the ground now. Any special instructions?"

"Tell him to hold out as long as he can. Cassius's buddy will turn up one of these days. Helmut. Bring down the scale on the Whitlandsund there. Michael's dispositions look a little strange."

A half-hour later Thurston bellowed, "Yahoo! Hey, Father! Hakes says he's got ships in detection. They show Navy IFF, and there's a skillion of them."

Storm chuckled at his son's enthusiasm. "Calm down and keep an eye on it. Tell Ceislak to keep the comm open." He felt like whooping himself. "Helmut, this friend of Cassius's is as crafty as a Dee. He had me scared, but he knew what he was doing. Caught them with their pants down, making an assault. Bet none of them get away." Darksword's face lit with grim pleasure. Storm reveiwed the Whitlandsund situation again.

Michael's dispositions were not unusual after all, just unimaginative. Havik would not be in bad trouble for a while.

Thurston called, "Ceislak says he has contact with Navy. They brought in a full battle fleet. They've got them bastards nailed to the wall."

"Good. Good. Everything looks beautiful. I'm going to my quarters. Before I collapse."

He dreamed awful dreams. Something was nagging him. He had forgotten something. He had overlooked something, and one dared not do that when dealing with Sangaree and Dees.

Thurston shook his father. "Dad. Come on. Wake up."

Storm opened his eyes. "What is it? You look awful."

"They're attacking the Fortress. The Sangaree are. Another raidfleet. The Fishers just told me. They're watching and can't do anything to help. They've lost touch with Mouse."

# FORTY-EIGHT: 3032 AD

Mouse sat in his father's chair, behind his father's desk. His eyes were closed. He felt much as his father looked the day he had returned from Academy. How long ago? Just a few months… It seemed like half a lifetime.

So much had happened. So much had changed. The Fortress had slipped quietly over some unseen boundary into a foreign universe, a hateful, actively hostile universe.

He had changed with his home. He had seen things. He had helped do things. None of them left him proud. He had turned a sharp corner on the yellow-brick road and had caught a corner-of-the-eye glimpse of a side of his family he had not known existed when he had gone off to Academy.

"I was a child then," he murmured. "This is just growing-up pain. Just reaction to a head-on with reality."

With reality. With a special reality unique to the family and Legion, with their bizarre array of problems and enemies.

He opened his father's comm drawer, punched for Combat. "Anything new?" he asked.

"Ah, negative, sir. Situations appear static."

"Keep me informed."

"Will do, sir."

"You're very good," Mouse whispered after breaking the connection. "If I were you I would've lost patience with me last week." He rose and began prowling the study.

He could not shake a subtle conviction that something dreadful was about to happen. He was restless all day. He had been unable to sleep well the past several nights.

"If there was just something to do around here."

He began strolling from cabinet to cabinet, looking into each, re-examining his father's collections. He did the rounds at least once a day. The circuit had a curiously calming effect.

He wondered if his father used them for the same talismanic purpose.

The coins, the dolls, the china, the books—they were all evidence of a past, of a connection with and a part in a vast, ongoing process. You could reach out and touch them and feel that you were touching part of something larger than yourself. You pulled in endless, invisible strands of humanity and spun yourself a chrysalis… It was all very subjective and emotional.

Still restless, he quit the study and went up to Cassius's office. He met no one along the way.

The tiny, empty world of the Iron Legion made him think of still, abandoned cities, deserted for no reason history bothered to remember. Take twenty thousand people out of the Fortress and it became a self-contained desolation almost timidly murmuring to itself.

These days he heard sounds he had never noticed before, all the background noises of supportive machines that had been drowned in the chatter and clatter of human presence. The sounds left him with an eerie, spooky feeling. Sometimes, as he strolled the empty hallways of the office levels, he would freeze suddenly, for a fraction of a second completely convinced that he was alone, trapped in an empty structure seven light-years from the nearest human being.

In those instants he staggered with the impact of a very vacant, very hollow feeling, inevitably followed by an instant of panic. Alienation was not the same as being alone. The alienated man moved in a bubble, but could see other human beings outside. The soul of him knew they were there, accessible if he could find the enchanted key. The separation was emotional, not physical. The truly alone man was barred from human intercourse by insuperable physical barriers…

Mouse would never forget the look on Fearchild's face when he had entered the torture chamber in that asteroid—such pathetic joy at the appearance of another being, an almost eager anticipation of torment that would reaffirm his membership in a fundamentally gregarious species.

Mouse decided that he had had an insight into the human animal. The bad marriages that went on, the cruel relationships that persevered beyond all logic—most people preferred pain to being alone. Even pain was an affirmation of belonging.

"The beast isn't really a solipsist," he muttered. Cassius's toy purchases from The Mountain were still in their shipping packs. He considered unwrapping them, setting them up, abandoned the idea. They were Cassius's private pleasure. He had no right to interfere.

He spent an hour playing with an ancient electric train, just running it around and around its track, making switches, stopping at stations, restacking the boxcars, wondering how the original owner had differed from people of his own age.

Beliefs and values made him think of his Academy classmates. Drawn from Confederation's farthest reaches, they had brought with them an incredible range of ideas and attitudes, some of which he had found wholly alien.

Tommy McClennon, with whom he had crewed and miraculously won in the Crab Nebula Sunjam Regatta two years ago… Tommy was Old Earther and more alien than most of the racial aliens attending Academy. Those aliens were of the same caste, the warrior, as the Storms. Tommy's ancestors had been nonproductive wards of the state for centuries. Tommy's different ideas went right to the bone.

A beep-beep-beep sounded from a silver button on the breast of his tunic. An elf's voice repeated a number three times. Mouse opened Cassius's desk and punched it on Walters's comm. "Masato Storm."

"Sir, word from Ceislak. He's just had a Sangaree raidfleet drop hyper…"

"I'll be right down." He ran to the nearest elevator, feeling foolish as he did. What could he do, really? Nothing but listen while this Helga's World disaster developed.

"I was right about something bad coming on," he told himself.

Frieda Storm stepped from another elevator as he left his. "You got the word?" she asked.

"The Sangaree? Yes."

"What the hell happened to that nitwit admiral who said he was going to help?"

Two big boards had been set up in Combat. One tried to follow operations on Blackworld, the other Ceislak's Helga's World action. They were not fully computerized, nor were they up-to-date. A mob of old folks and youngsters did their best with sketchy information.

"What's happened?" Mouse demanded.

"Donninger's trying to hold them off, but he's going to have to run. There's way too many of them."

Mouse glared at a newly activated display globe. At its heart lay a cue-ball-looking orb which represented Helga's World. Combat was receiving a data relay from Legion ships orbiting the planet. Mouse watched the blips a while.

"What's our real-time lag?"

"Five minutes and some seconds. Pretty good, considering. Your father's Fisher friends must be right in on top of it. Close enough to risk getting shot at."

Mouse considered the trend. "Tell Donninger to get the hell out. Ten more minutes and he won't be able to." A Legion ship winked out of existence while he spoke.

"They brought in some heavy stuff," someone said. "Bigger than anything on the ID lists."

Mouse tried to watch several screens at once as specs came through and the computers tried to build images of the enemy warships. "They are big," he told Frieda. "Something new in the way of raidships."

"I hear the Norbon are something new in the way of Sangaree."

"You think it's them?"

"Who else?"

"This's what Father and Cassius wanted, then. To draw that Deeth out of hiding."

Frieda sniffed. "He wasn't terribly cooperative about timing his appearance."

"Uhm." Mouse found himself a chair. He did not move, except to use the toilet, till the engagement reached its bloody conclusion.

"Astounding," he murmured, rising at last. "I wouldn't have believed it if I hadn't seen it. I'm going to get some sleep."

He awoke to the insistent scream of the general alarm.

For a moment he could not understand what it was. He had heard it only twice before, long ago, during drills.

A booming voice echoed through the hallways: "Action stations. All personnel to action stations. We are about to be attacked. All personnel to action stations. We are about to be attacked."

"Holy Christ!" He grabbed clothing and ran.

He burst into Combat. "What the hell is going on?"

The senior watchstander indicated a display globe. His face was pallid. He gasped, "We got about two minutes' warning from the Fishers. They snuck past them somehow."

Red blips surrounded the Fortress in the tank. Tiny wires of fire lanced across the globe. Little stars sparkled. Diminutive sub-blips swarmed and danced like clouds of gnats on a still spring day.

"Eighty-two of them, sir," someone said. "There were eighty-five to start. Mostly light stuff. Sangaree."

"But…" He did not understand. It made no sense at all.

"They range from singleships to light battle, sir. Computer's still trying to project their assault plan."

Somewhere else, a computer voice murmured, "Kill. Bogey Forty-Six. Five thousand tons."

Frieda arrived. She had been asleep too. She was groggy and disheveled.

Mouse kept trying to make sense of the ship movements in the display globe. He could detect no pattern but an inexorable inward pressure.

"Just a raid?" he asked. "Or are they serious?"

The senior watchstander gave him a funny look. "Damned serious. Suicidally serious. They said so." He punched up something on his comm screen. A face appeared. The man said he was going to do to the Fortress what had been done to Prefactlas.

Mouse asked Frieda, "You think that's him?"

"Probably. Nobody's ever seen him, as far as I know."

"I've seen him before," Mouse said, suddenly remembering a moment on The Mountain. "He was there when that old man tried to kill us. In the crowd."

"Sir," the senior watchstander said, "the computer says they're running a randomed assault pattern. Some sort of command battle computer is controlling their ships. It looks like the ships' commanders have free manueuver any direction but backward. They've got to come after us whether they want to or not."

"Then it's a kamikaze attack."

"Sir?"

"A suicide thing."

"Definitely. Until whoever controls the battle computer turns them loose."

Mouse glanced at the display. An additional two enemy ships had been neutralized. "Are they going to break through?"

The watchstander sighed. "I think so. Unless we get a little more efficiency out of the automatic defenses."

"How long before they touch down?"

"Too early to predict."

"Tell the Fishers to contact Ceislak. Tell them to pass the word to Navy. Then have them get ahold of my father."

He could take only two hours of watching the claws of doom creep closer. The enemy kept coming and coming, despite one of the most sophisticated and deadly automatic defense systems ever devised. A third of their number had been destroyed, and still they came on with a dreadful, almost machinelike determination. Plainly, a madman was in charge out there.

He walked the silent halls of the office level, in some way making tentative goodbyes to the Legion and everything he had known. He visited his father's study again, thinking it would be a crime against history to destroy the collections gathered there. So many beautiful things...

He returned to Combat. "What's it look like?"

"Still bad, sir."

"We going to hold till *Hittite* gets here?"

"Yes, sir. You think they'll commit her by herself?"

"I couldn't say. There's nothing out there that can stand up to her."

"Empire Class could take on any ten, sir. But there're fifty-some still."

"When you get signals from her, you give her everything we know. Especially about their combat lock. They'll have to break it to engage her, won't they? Maybe some of the individual ships' commanders will make a run for it."

"Will do, sir."

An elderly officer, retired from Legion service, said, "Some figures, sir."

Mouse scanned them. They predicted that the Sangaree would overwhelm the outer defenses and land at least fifteen vessels on the planetoid's surface. "Not good. This makes *Hittite* our only hope."

"Yes, sir."

"Sir," said the senior watchstander. "We've just picked up another group of them moving in."

"*What?*"

"Easy, sir. They aren't fighting ships. Here. Five of them. Four big ones that scan out as transports of some kind, and one medium one that might be the command ship."

"Transports. Of course. So they can send troops inside."

Frieda eased up on the senior watchstander's far side. She studied the data momentarily, then stalked out of Combat. It was the first she had moved in hours.

"Pass the word to the Armory to stand by to issue small arms," Mouse said. "And tell them to run a check on all internal defense systems. You computation people. I want some kind of parameters on best and worst times we can expect them to reach the surface." More to himself than anyone, he added, "Father thought the Fortress could stand up to anything. I guess he never considered being attacked by a madman."

"Uhm. Sir, there never has been a perfect defense against someone who doesn't care what happens to himself."

Next evening Mouse mustered the entire population of the Fortress in the gymnasium. He explained the situation. He asked for suggestions and received none. There was little that could be suggested. They could but try to hang on till

Navy arrived. He bid them do what they could, and before he finished decided he had screwed up by bringing them together. It only rubbed everyone's nose in the fact that there were hundreds of children who would share the Fortress's fate.

Mouse's comm roused him from a troubled sleep. "Storm here."

"Contact with *Hittite*, sir. She's coming in."

"I'll be right down."

When he reached Combat, the senior watchstander told him, "We've fed them our data, sir. We've established a continuous instel link. She's got a couple of Provincials with her, for what they're worth. They're going to go for the command ship and transports first."

"How soon?"

The man checked the time. "They drop hyper in two hours and eight minutes, sir. They'll be coming in with a big inherent and only a couple degrees out of the slot to target."

"How much warning will our Sangaree friends have?" Mouse nodded at the red blips on the display.

"Depends on how good their detection gear is. Anywhere from five minutes to an hour."

It came up closer to an hour. "Damn!" Mouse spat. "Look. They're pulling back."

Within a half-hour it was obvious the raidships were being moved to protect the command ship and transports, and that they were still under that relentless outside control.

"I guess we'll see just how mean one of those big-assed Empire babies is," Mouse said.

"I suppose we will, sir."

*Hittite* dropped hyper and went into action in an awesome blaze of weaponry. She and her escort settled into a quiet, deadly routine of systematic destruction. The Sangaree seemed unable to touch her. But invincibility proved an illusion.

"Hello, Iron Legion. *Hittite* here. Boys, I don't want to tell you this, but I have to. We've taken some drive damage. We'll have to pull out or lose our screens. Sorry."

"Sorry?" Mouse snarled. "Sorry don't help nothing."

"At least we softened them up a little for you." *Hittite*'s Communications Officer had not heard Mouse. "We make it eleven solid scratches and a whole lot of bloody noses. Good luck, guys. *Hittite* out."

"Run the numbers," Mouse snapped.

"They're still going to get through, sir. Unless those bloody noses are worse than they look."

"Bloody hell! I didn't want to hear that."

Frieda made her first appearance of the new day. "What's going on?"

Mouse explained.

"Damn it all, anyway!" She flew out of Combat.

Mouse was returning to his quarters when he saw the body lying on the stretcher in the corridor. A girl of about fifteen. He did not recognize her. She had to be a daughter of one of the enlisted men.

"What the hell?" He knelt, felt her pulse. She was alive. Just unconscious. Or sleeping.

A sound startled him. He glanced up, saw two old men go into a cross corridor carrying a youngster on a stretcher. The one to the rear gave him a furtive look.

He started to run after them, became distracted when he passed an open dormitory door. The lights were on. A half-dozen retirees were lifting children onto stretchers.

"What the hell is going on here?" he demanded.

They stared at him. Nobody said anything. Nobody smiled or frowned. Two hunkered down, lifted a stretcher, came toward him.

He grabbed an arm. "I asked a question, soldier."

"Mouse."

He turned. Frieda stood framed in the doorway, not a meter away. She held a weapon and it was aimed at him.

"What the hell are you up to, Mother?"

She half smiled. "We're loading you youngsters aboard the *Ehrhardt.* We're sending you to your father. The Fishers will give you covering fire."

His thoughts zigged and zagged. That was a good idea. It should have occurred to him. Gets the children out. It would be risky, but *Ehrhardt* was one of the fastest ships ever built… But Frieda seemed to be including him in this Noah's Ark venture. He would not have any of that.

"I've got a job here."

She smiled weakly. "I relieve you of command, Mouse. Bring a stretcher, men."

"Don't try to pull anything on me…"

"Take your father a kiss for me, Mouse." Her finger tightened on the trigger.

Mouse tried to jump aside. He was not quick enough. The stun bolt scrambled his thoughts. He was falling, falling, falling… He never reached the floor.

## FORTY-NINE: 3032 AD

Storm flung himself out of bed. A real nightmare had closed in on him. An attack on his home… That was it. That was what he had overlooked. This was a war against his Family. He had left a flank unguarded.

"Is that true?" he asked, able to think of nothing else.

Thurston looked baffled. "Why would I lie about that?"

"Don't mind me. I'm just confused. Let's go."

Mouse had reestablished a continuous instel relay by the time Storm reached the war room. "Mouse, what's it look like?" he demanded.

The burst went out. The response came back, it seemed, no swifter than the speed of light. "It doesn't look good, Father. They're coming at us like they've gone crazy. No maneuver or anything. And it looks like they know our weak spots. We're holding, but we're losing outstations faster than the program allows. I think we need outside help."

Helmut whispered in Storm's ear while Mouse was talking.

"Okay, Mouse. Just do what you can. Helmut says we've instelled Ceislak and asked the Fishers to pass the word to Beckhart." He listened to Helmut a moment more. "Oh. You've done that, too. Good. Look. The arrangements are made. You've got a heavy battle group on its way from Canaan, two squadrons headed there from Helga's World, and *Hittite* somewhere in your vicinity on shakedown cruise. The whole damned Navy is headed your way."

Navy would, anytime, anywhere, drop everything else for a dustup with Sangaree.

"Hang in there, Son. The Fortress will see you through. I designed it myself."

Mouse laughed. "Thanks, Father. Mother sends her love. I've got to get back to work now."

Mother? Storm thought. Who?… Ah. He meant Frieda. How was Frieda handling the crisis? He shrugged. She would cope. She was a soldier's daughter and a soldier's wife.

Time would tell the tale. If the Fortress cracked before Navy arrived, he would be a poor man again, in several senses. All his treasures would be gone, with most of the people he held dear. He would be left with nothing but the financial wealth of the Legion… He forced his attention back to what was happening in the Whitlandsund.

Havik was taking a beating, but he was holding. An infantry battalion was assembling at the shade station. If Havik held till they crossed back to Darkside, Storm was sure he would win again.

He could do nothing but work up an ulcer here, he decided. "Thurston. Take over. I'm going for a walk."

"It's raining out, Father."

"I know."

After a while he realized he was no longer walking alone. Pollyanna, without intruding, was slouching along beside him. He had not seen her since the day Wulf died.

"Hello."

"Hi," she replied. "Is it bad?"

"They're attacking the Fortress."

"And nobody's there."

"Mouse is. And the families."

"But no one to fight."

"They'll fight. As well as any Legionnaire. It's mostly automated anyway."

"Couldn't you ask for help from Navy?"

"It's on its way. But it might take a week to get there. That's a long time to hold out if the raid-master is determined."

"And it's all because of Plainfield. Michael Dee."

"My brother is a pawn too. The shadow-master is a Sangaree named Deeth."

They walked a block in silence. Pollyanna said, "I like the rain. I missed that at the Fortress."

"Uhm."

"I couldn't go walking on The Mountain. The skies were too big."

"Uhm." Storm was not listening. His thoughts kept turning to the Fortress. "He must've gotten upset with the way things were going here. Or maybe because of Helga's World. I don't know. It doesn't make any tactical sense to move against the Fortress right now." He talked on, using a soft voice to describe how Helga's World had become a deathtrap for a major Sangaree raidfleet and how the Shadowline War might still go the Legion's way.

Pollyanna was not listening to him any more than he was listening to her. "Down here," she said, pausing at the head of a descending stairway. "I want to show you where my father lived. Where my heart still lives, I guess."

He followed her down to the tiny apartment she had shared with Frog. The dwarf's ghost was its only occupant now. Pollyanna now lived in quarters provided by Blake.

Storm felt right away that the place was a shrine. It made him uncomfortable. He remained carefully, neutrally attentive while Pollyanna told the story of each of her museum pieces. He felt like a voyeur peeping through the keyhole of her soul. The slightly dotty, obsessive monologue helped him understand Pollyanna Eight just a bit better.

From there they went to his rooms and made love, then lay curled together in the twilight afterglow and murmured of nightmares that had come true and dreams that had turned into smoke.

"I want to go back to the Modelmog, Gneaus," she said in her tiny, weary voice. "I was really happy there. Lucifer… I think we could have made it if it hadn't been for the rest of this."

"That's life, pretty thing. It won't leave you alone. It keeps hammering away till it finds the weak places, then it starts yanking everything apart."

"Does it have to be that way?"

"I don't know. Some people slide right through. They never have any bad times, never hit that tough piece of road. Or so it seems."

"Can you play something on that funny black thing? Whenever you do, you know, I get this image of this lonely old man way up on a mountain… A hermit, I guess. He sits there looking down at this city wondering if maybe he missed something. But he can't figure out what it is because he used to live in the city and he did everything there was to do… Aw, you're laughing at me."

"No. I'm just a little surprised."

"Anyway, hearing it always makes me sad. I guess I want to be sad now. Because I guess I'm feeling like that guy on the mountain. I was there but I missed something."

"You've still got a lot of years to find it."

"It wouldn't be the same. I'm not the same Pollyanna anymore. I've done a lot of things I don't like me very much for. I hurt people. Frog taught me never to hurt people."

Storm moistened the reed of his clarinet, startled Pollyanna with a couple of rollicking Hoagie Carmichael pieces.

She smiled when he finished. "I didn't know that thing could be happy. You never…"

"It could be happier. I didn't have my heart in it."

"That was really strange music. Kind of wild and primitive."

"It's very old. More than a thousand years."

"Thanks. I feel better. Come here."

They made love once more, and fell asleep lying side by side, reading Ecclesiastes.

His comm's shriek wakened him. An almost incoherent Helmut blurted, "They took the Fortress! It just came in, Gneaus. From Frieda. She sent a personal message… You'd better come here…"

Grimly, Storm began dressing.

"What is it?" Pollyanna asked, frightened by the sudden hardness of him.

"We lost the Fortress."

"Oh no! Not… Your wife! And your children…"

"Be quiet. Please." Feeling numb, he finished dressing. He did not remember the walk to the war room. Suddenly, he was there. Something within him would not allow him to react completely to the news. It felt like another in a parade of disasters that had happened to somebody else.

"Bring me Frieda's tape, Helmut," he said when he realized where he was.

"Gneaus?"

He looked up. Helmut was standing beside his chair, holding the microtape. Time had stolen away on him again.

He loaded the cartridge with the exaggeratedly careful motions of a drunk. It began with a continuous status report from Fortress Combat. He advanced it till Frieda's pale face formed on screen. Her thin, severe, colorless mouth writhed, but he did not hear anything.

*What's happened to Mouse?* he wondered. He had not been visible in the Combat views.

*Don't take him, too,* Storm prayed. *He's our only tomorrow.*

Frieda was saying something about there being fighting on Dock Level. He upped the sound.

"... penetrate Residential. They're tough, Gneaus. Primitives, I think. Definitely human. I've put the kids into the *Ehrhardt.* She's set to boost whenever the computer decides she has her best shot at breaking through.

"The Seiners say they'll try to cover her. We'll lose contact with them soon. The raiders are getting close to our wave guides. There it goes. The cruiser. Wish them luck getting through.

"Gneaus, I'm going to cut this short. I want you to remember me as a good soldier, but I'm so damned scared I might make a fool of myself. Forgive me now for whatever hurt I may have done you over the years. Remember my love, such as it was. And remember me to Father.

"We'll hold them as long as we can. Tell Navy to come get them."

She smiled weakly, pursed her lips in a last long-range kiss, then secured her screen. The instel relay continued. An old man calmly chanted ordnance data from the Fortress's Combat Information Center.

Storm sighed and closed his eyes. Getting the youngsters out was something, anyway. He shuffled around the dark places of his mind, collecting the old scraps of rage and hatred and hiding them in an out-of-the-way dust bin for nonproductive emotions. More than ever, now, he needed to keep a tight rein on his feelings.

"Helmut, give me an update on the situation here."

The news from the Whitlandsund was little better than that from home. Havik faced virtual human wave assaults. Michael appeared to be growing desperate.

The shade station was sending reinforcements, but only in driblets. Most of the functional crawlers were still far out the Shadowline.

Helga's World was the bright spot. The Fishers said the Sangaree raiders had been obliterated. Marines were taking over for Ceislak's commandos. The latter were taking ship for Blackworld. Already.

Storm sent Thurston to find Blake.

"Mr. Blake," he said when the man arrived, "I'm down to my last gasp. The one option I have left is to scratch Dee's base of operations."

"Colonel..."

"It's not open to debate this time. We're not going to argue about it. It's past that stage. I'm going to do it. I'm telling you so we can observe the proprieties. I'm going to do it even if you insist on a vote. Remember, I control the proxies. One of my ships will be here soon. When it shows, I'll use it to jump to Twilight."

"Colonel..."

"Blake, it looks like we're going to lose the Whitlandsund. If Cassius is going to have any chance to break through and save your ass, I'm going to have to destroy Dee's logistics. Can't you understand that?"

"Won't he just grab Edgeward?"

"He might try. I can't guarantee that he won't. He'll have a lot of trouble doing it now. You're ready for him. And he's been outside a long time, without much coming down from Twilight to support him. Yet. He didn't count on heavy resistance."

"So?"

"So he's going to run low on munitions before he gets new stocks. I think he's going to take the Whitlandsund no matter what we do. But if we do hit Twilight, then we have him in the same position he has Cassius. In order to survive, he'll have to take Twilight or Edgeward. Either way, he'll have to pull me out of the pass. Enough, hopefully, so Cassius can break through. If we manage that, Dee is done for. Unless he uses nuclears again. Which I doubt he has with him, but which he'll have on tap up north. So from our viewpoint, taking Twilight has become an imperative."

Storm did not admit just how much he was guessing and hoping. Michael, even in predictable circumstances, could be unpredictable. There was a good chance he would go the easy way and spread nuclears around, if he had them. Or he might take a cue from Hawksblood and sit tight till his ammo was gone, hoping he could outlast Cassius. Walters's supply situation was just as iffy as Dee's.

Days groaned past. Men and arms trickled over from the Shadowline, but never enough to halt Dee's gradual conquest of the Whitlandsund.

There was a tremendous inertia in the westward flow of men and materiel in the Shadowline. It had to be overcome and turned around before a large and effective force could be mustered against Michael...

"Father, Havik wants to talk to you," Thurston said one morning.

"Bring him up over here." Storm faced a screen. "Yes, Colonel?"

"Colonel Storm, I can't do the job. I'm sorry. I'm too bad shot up and this obsolete equipment... Crying won't change it. Sorry, sir. What I'd like is permission to stop trying to be everywhere so I can concentrate on holding a bridgehead. We'll need some place to assemble a counterattack once you've brought enough equipment back."

Storm nodded. "I've been expecting it, Colonel. Go ahead and pull in your lines. And so you won't feel too bad, I want you to know I think you've done all you could. I'm sorry I couldn't give you more support."

"Thank you, Colonel."

"Thurston, where's Cassius now?" Storm asked.

"Still a long way to go, Father." Thurston indicated a light on the big board. "He's rolling around the clock, but those damned machines just don't move very fast. Do you want me to link you through?"

"Not now. It's too early in the morning for a squabble."

He and Cassius had been conferring regularly. Every conference degenerated into an argument. The loss of the Fortress had hit Walters harder than had anything else in the whole time Storm had known him. Finally, after ages, warfare had become a personal thing for Cassius. Storm anticipated a classic bloodletting when he came to grips with Dee.

He checked Ceislak's progress. It was a long fly from Helga's World. The Blackworld business might be over before Hakes arrived.

Storm spent much of his time alone, writing. He had a lot of thoughts he wanted committed to writing. He hoped Mouse would understand what he was trying to convey.

The *Ehrhardt* rumbled into Edgeward's crude little space port. Storm went out to greet her.

The pilot was one of his granddaughters. No one else aboard was conscious. He walked along the passenger aisles, looking down at Mouse, Lucifer, and others of his children and grandchildren, as well as the progeny of his men. He took a while, strolling along. This would be the last he saw them all.

Silly, lovely Frieda had surrendered her tomorrows on behalf of theirs. She was a soldier's daughter indeed.

"She tricked us, Grandpapa," his granddaughter told him. "We wanted to stay. Even the little ones. Grandmama drugged the water supply. I guess she cooked it up with the other old folks. They put us on the ship while we were out and sent us off on auto, with the Starfishers to cover us. It just isn't fair!"

"Did you want to die, Goldilocks?"

"No. But they needed us there. We should be there right now…"

"You'd be dead if you were. We haven't been able to raise the Fortress for days. Even the automatic signals are out." He did not entertain the slightest illusion. The Fortress had been taken, all the way down to the computers at its heart. And Deeth would have taken no more prisoners than had Boris and Cassius on Prefactlas.

"Oh." His granddaughter started crying.

"Hey. Hey, Honey. No tears now. They chose… We're the Iron Legion, remember?" He ground his teeth, afraid the tears would be infectious.

"I don't care!"

"Now, now, there're outsiders waiting out there."

She tried to stifle the flood.

"What about you, Goldilocks? Why were you awake?"

"They fixed me to wake up after it was too late to turn back. Somebody had to bring her in. I'm the best pilot. Mouse isn't rated on anything this big. What're we going to do, Grandpapa?"

Storm strained at being cheerful. "We won one, we lost one, Honey. Now we're going for best two out of three. We're going to settle with them here." His optimism fell flat. He could not force it through a very real despair. "They won't get away with it cheap, Honeycakes. We'll make them sorry they didn't leave us alone."

As with so many promises he had made lately, he did not see how he could make this one bear fruit.

The old shuttle crawler had to make three trips to carry all the youngsters into the city. Edgeward's people welcomed them warmly, not understanding that the city and its problems were not the real reason they found themselves orphaned and homeless.

The fourth trip out the crawler carried Storm's raiding party. Thurston. Lucifer. Helmut. Mouse. The best of the men who had survived the ambush of Michael's convoy. Pollyanna, whom no argument had been able to dissuade from going along in pursuit of a rapprochement with her ex-husband. And then there was Albin Korando, who wanted to go home, to help impose order and reason on the city that had sent him into exile.

Storm examined Korando before he started the liftoff checkdown. The man was a lean black eagle, grimly trying to familiarize himself with his weapons. He looked, Storm thought, much as Cassius might if ever Walters found himself a mission with special personal relevance. Much as Cassius must look right now, in fact.

They made a silent, grim band of commandos. There was no small talk, no nervous joking, no murmured rehearsals. On the edge of this action each preferred to be isolated with his or her thoughts.

Storm hit the go.

# FIFTY: 3032 AD

Storm took the cruiser in low and fast and put her down a hundred meters from Twilight's south lock. His weapons started talking while he was still aloft. Shafts of coherent light stabbed at everything outside the dome. Shellguns bit at the stressglass of the dome itself, chewing a hole through it two hundred meters west of the lock. Freezing atmosphere roared out, mixed with dust in violent clouds. His searchlights probed for enemies who never appeared.

The decompression was not explosive. The Twilighters would have time to get off the streets, into buildings that could be sealed. But time to insure personal survival was all Storm meant to allow them.

Helmut captured the lock before Storm finished cycling down. Darksword was moving the last of the raiders through it when Storm hit dirt himself. Accompanied by Korando, Pollyanna, Thurston, Lucifer, and Mouse, Gneaus set out for Twilight's equivalent of City Hall.

He had given orders to shoot anything that moved. He wanted these Twilighters cowed fast. The tininess of his force compelled him to hit hard and keep on hitting. He dared allow his enemies no time to regain their balance.

The only resistance he encountered was a lone sniper who surrendered the moment he received counterfire.

The entry to Twilight's City Hall, like Edgeward's, was a massive airlock. The outer door was sealed. "Blow it," Storm told Thurston.

His son placed the charges. "Stand back, people," he shouted just before the *Boom!*

Storm clambered through the wreckage, checked the inner door. It was not secured. "Rig something over that outer doorway," he ordered.

Mouse and Lucifer scrounged plastic panels and pounded them into place. "They'll still leak, Father," Mouse said.

"They'll prevent complete decompression. That's all I'm worried about now."

He did not want to hurt civilians. The ordinary people of Twilight, like those of nations at war at any time, were simply victims of their leadership.

He was in a generous mood. In other times and places he had been heard to say that people were guilty of their leadership.

Storm and Thurston poised themselves, ready for the inner door. "Go!" Thurston growled. Storm kicked. Thurston went through on his jump pack, rocketing at an angle across a chamber twenty meters by thirty. Laseguns probed for him. Their beams went wide.

Thurston let go an antitank rocket. Before the debris settled, Storm, Lucifer, and Mouse moved in, firing, and spread out behind furniture. Pollyanna and Korando had enough sense to stay out of action for which they had no training. They indulged only in a little supportive sniping.

Thurston's second rocket, accompanied by grenades from the others, convinced the opposition. They surrendered. They wore no combat suits. Only four of fifteen had survived the exchange.

Korando sealed the inner door before more atmosphere escaped.

"Where're the big people?" Storm demanded of the prisoners, after folding his faceplate back. "Where's Meacham?"

He received surly looks in reply.

"All right. Be that way. Lucifer. Shoot them one at a time till somebody answers me."

They looked into his one grim eye and believed him. He was not bluffing. He no longer cared, especially about Michael's men. The lives he valued most had been wasted already.

"Upstairs. Fourth level. Communications center. Yelling for help."

"Thank you. You're true gentlemen. Lead the way."

They balked.

A twitch of his trigger finger got them moving.

The elevators were dead. Storm shrugged, unsurprised. His guides led him to an emergency stairwell. Thurston blew the locked fire door. The big man could have achieved his end with a lasegun bolt, but he enjoyed the bangs.

A bolt poked through the smoke, stabbing a small, neat hole through Lucifer's right calf. The ambusher died before he could take a second shot.

"Pollyanna, take care of him," Storm ordered. "You four. Up the stairs. Smartly now."

Two went down before they reached the fourth floor. Three snipers joined them.

While Thurston prepared to blow the comm center door, Korando told Storm, "These men aren't Twilighters. They're not even Blackworlders."

"I didn't think they were. Blackworlders would be a little more careful about gunfighting in tight places. You spend your life worrying about vacuum, you don't go shooting where you might put holes in the walls."

"Exactly."

"Stand back. When that door goes we're going to get a lot of fire."

Thurston set off his charges. The counterfire came. Storm and his sons hurled grenades around the door frame, frags first, then tear gas, then smoke. After a brief pause they moved in.

Through the haze, using his infrared filters, Storm could see men trying to get out other exits. "Mouse. Stop those men over there. Korando, over there." He and Thurston bulled straight ahead, charging a group that looked like they could be troublesome. They were a tough-looking crew, and among them Storm saw his brother's son Seth-Infinite.

Thurston announced his approach with a rocket. Hands flew up. In all the smoke and tear gas the Twilighters could not determine the number of their attackers.

Seth-Infinite managed to slide away in the confusion.

Storm herded the gagging prisoners to the center of the room. He posted Mouse, Thurston, and Korando at doors. When Pollyanna, supporting Lucifer, arrived, he left the main door to her. He sat down and waited for the air to clear, for Helmut to report how it was going elsewhere.

The comm boards around him chattered wildly as people all across the city demanded instructions.

The air cleared enough. Storm opened his face plate. "Which one's Meacham?" he demanded.

A very sick old man, who fit Storm's notion of an elderly brigand, timorously raised a hand. The gases and smoke had left him puked out and aguey. From the corner of his eye Storm caught Korando's slight affirmative nod.

"Would you mind awfully, sir, explaining what the hell you've been trying to do? Would you kindly tell me why you broke your contract with Richard Hawksblood in favor of a deal with that bandit Michael Dee? Or Diebold Amelung, if you prefer? And, for the sake of heaven, why you've been using nuclears on my people in the Shadowline?"

Meacham's jaw dropped. He peered up at Storm in unadulterated disbelief. Gradually, an air of cynicism crept over his tired old body.

"Ah. I see," Storm said. "He's done it to you, too. Believe it or not, old man. It's true. I wouldn't be here otherwise."

Briefly, he sketched what had happened to Wulf.

"I didn't know..." Meacham mumbled. Then, "We lost communications with the Shadowline weeks ago. Equipment failure is what they told me. Amelung's son came back and said everything was going fine. He said our troops were holding you and work on the mohole was ahead of schedule."

"It isn't going fine at all. Not from your viewpoint. The fighting is over in the Shadowline. You lost. Because Hawksblood wasn't in charge. Because some nitwit Dee set it up that way. Now, tell me why the force that hit us Darkside? I thought that was outside the rules."

Meacham frowned. He was old, but obviously rugged. He was making a fast physical comeback. "What are you talking about?"

"About the convoy that's besieging Edgeward and the Whitlandsund. Somebody sent six armed crawlers with twenty-one mining units in support. Half of which are no longer with us, by the way."

Meacham stiffened. "Colonel Storm... I assume you're Storm? Yes? I don't have the faintest idea what you're talking about. I specifically forbade any action Darkside." The old man's spirits were rising fast. "Establishing a tradition of Darkside warfare would be insane, Colonel. It would be bad for business."

"And what's become of Hawksblood, Meacham? Why is Dee fighting me, leading Sangaree troops?"

The old man glared. "That's not possible." Then his spirits collapsed again. He dropped into a chair so suddenly Storm was afraid that he had had a stroke.

"Sangaree?" he whispered. "Sangaree? No. That's just not possible."

There was a stir among the prisoners. The offworlders were getting nervous. They knew, whether or not they were Sangaree themselves.

"You don't have to take my word, Meacham. Call Walter Carrington at The City of Night. We sent him some of the corpses we took in after fighting near Edgeward. He had his people perform the autopsies. The word's out to all the domes now. Twilight is using Sangaree troops."

"My nephew," Meacham said in a barely audible voice. "Talk to him. He was in charge of military affairs. A little too anxious for the old man to die, I thought. Responsibility would settle him down, I thought. That's why I put him in charge. He was too weak, I suppose. The devils. The bloody devils."

How pleased Dee must have been, finding such an ideally usable man, Storm reflected. "Divide and conquer. The Dee way, Meacham. Get them by the greed. No doubt there was a plan to wrestle stock away from your directors. But their plans went sour. We attacked when they were overextended. Their bomb crawler got caught in heat erosion. Where is your nephew now?"

No one there would admit to being Charles Meacham. Storm glanced at Korando. Korando shrugged. The elder Meacham surveyed his fellow prisoners, shook his head. Then he rose and slowly walked to the tumble of bodies near the door Thurston guarded.

"Yes. Here he is. Caught up by his own sins." He shook his head wearily. "Children. They never quite turn out the way you want."

Storm sighed. It figured. The one prisoner who knew anything had been killed. Probably by Seth-Infinite's hand. He did not check to see if the nephew's wounds were in front or back. It was too late to matter.

What now? "Mr. Meacham, I'm going to draw up surrender terms. They'll be simple. You'll abandon your claim to the Shadowline. You'll agree to cooperate fully in bringing to justice members of the conspiracy to use nuclear weapons. You'll agree to help ferret out any Sangaree on Blackworld. You'll aid in the rescue and evacuation of personnel now trapped in the Shadowline. You'll free Richard Hawksblood and any of his men who might be imprisoned here. I expect Richard will have terms of his own to discuss…"

"Gneaus?"

Storm turned. Someone was at the door guarded by Pollyanna and Lucifer. "Helmut?"

The old warrior came to him slowly, wearily, his helmet open, his face as pale and strained as it had become when he had learned of his brother's death.

"What is it, Helmut? You look awful."

"Won't be any more wars with Richard Hawksblood," Darksword muttered. He laughed. It was a soft cackle of madness. "We didn't get to him in time. They had him down in the service levels. Gneaus, it was the work of the Beast. It was like something from the Second Dark Age. Like the camps at Wladimir-Wolynsk."

"He's dead?"

"Yes. And all his staff. Beyond-the-resurrection. And death was a gift for them."

Storm stared into eternity, lost among disjointed memories of what Richard had been to him, of what Richard had meant. All their conflicts and hatreds… which had had their own formality and inflexible honor… "We'll take care of them," Storm said. "An honorable funeral. Send them home for burial. I owe Richard that much."

One of the foundation stones of his universe had vanished. What would he do without his enemy? Who, or what, could replace a Richard Hawksblood?

He shook it off. Richard did not matter anymore. He had his own plans… He drew his ancient .45, slowly turned its cylinder.

"Father?" Mouse said softly. "Are you all right?"

"In a minute. I'll be okay, Mouse." Storm looked into his son's eyes. Today and tomorrow… What seemed to be a depthless sadness stole into his soul. "I'll be okay."

"I evened scores a little," Helmut said. "Dee's wife. One shot. Through the brain. May the Lord have mercy on her soul."

"Gallant, chivalrous Helmut," Storm mused. "What happened to you?" The Helmut he had always known could not have slain a woman.

"I learned to hate, Gneaus."

There was no way of resurrecting a brain-destroyed corpse.

"Seth-Infinite's here in the city," Storm said. "We saw him."

"Fearchild, too. He did Richard in. He was there when we arrived. We're hunting him now. The citizens aren't giving us any trouble, by the bye."

"Good. Be kind to them. And watch all the exits from town. Dees always have a bolthole."

"We've accounted for most of their hired guns. We get an estimate of fifty on hand. What I didn't see anywhere else seem to be here, except for maybe five or ten and the Dees."

"Helmut, be careful. They'll be worse than any cornered rats if they think the game is completely up."

Worse than cornered rats. The Dees were intelligent, terrified, conscienceless rats who went straight for the throats of those who threatened them.

They attacked through the door where Thurston stood guard, coming hard behind a barrage of rockets that slaughtered the prisoners without harming Storm's people. They came in screened by a handful of Sangaree gunmen.

Thurston killed one attacker by smashing his skull with a rocket launcher. Seth-Infinite shot Thurston point-blank, through the faceplate.

Beams stabbed around the room. People scrambled for cover. A rocket killed Albin Korando. Frog's orphan had returned home only to die.

Storm's old .45 spoke. A Sangaree died. Beside Gneaus, Helmut gasped and collapsed. Storm fired again, dropped another Sangaree. He got down and tried to drag Helmut to cover.

He was too late. Beams had punched fatal holes through Darksword's helmet and chest.

Storm crouched and, unable to do anything, watched Pollyanna try to pull Lucifer out her door. Beams found them both. Hers was a minor wound. She got off a killing shot herself before fainting from pain.

*Me and Mouse*, Storm thought. *So it's finally here. The last battle. It's almost laughable. It's so much smaller than I thought it would be. Two of us against… How many?*

He peeped cautiously around the end of the console that concealed him. Seth-Infinite, casually, was killing the last of Storm's prisoners. Getting rid of witnesses, Storm supposed. Leaving no one who could repeat the name Dee. Startled, he realized they might nuke the city if they escaped.

"Mouse…" he moaned softly. His favorite son lay on the floor before his door, his suit badly discolored along one side. He looked dead.

"Uhn…" Storm gasped. Mouse's head was turning slowly, toward Seth-Infinite. Mouse's suit had withstood the bolt. He was playing possum.

"I should've left him behind," Storm muttered. He smiled grimly.

Where was Fearchild? Storm assumed the men who had come in with the Dees were dead, killed by their employers if not during the attack. None were in evidence, and no Sangaree would have stood by while Seth-Infinite slaughtered his captured comrades.

An explosion slammed the console against him, tumbled him backward.

He had seen the grenade arcing through the air, could judge whence it had come. He seized Helmut's fallen weapon, rolled, bounced up, fired with both hands. He narrowly missed ending Fearchild's tale. Dee scrambled for better cover.

Storm's .45 roared at Seth-Infinite. He plunged back behind the console. The cabinet crackled as a lasebolt spent its energy inside.

Storm moved to his left, to get near a wall that would make flanking him difficult, and to make them turn their backs on Mouse. He fired as he went, to hold their attention.

The .45 stopped thundering, cylinder spent.

Storm reached the last cover available. He paused to catch his breath.

Now what? They would be crafty-aggressive. They would be sure they had him. He would have to do more than stall… Was this the time for it?

He had decided there was a thing that had to be done before Michael's game could be beaten. The act would ruin all Michael's calculations, and blacken his heart with terror.

Now was the time to do it.

He was afraid.

Faceplate open, laughing at Michael's spawn, he rose and hosed lasegun fire over the area where they were hidden.

A bolt pierced his lung two centimeters from his heart. It did not hurt as much as he had anticipated. His weapon tumbled from his hand.

Fearchild and Seth-Infinite rose slowly, their faces alive with malicious pleasure.

Storm smiled at them. He croaked, "You lose, you fools!"

Mouse shot with preternatural accuracy, a single bolt stabbing through the back of each Dee skull. They did not have time to look surprised.

Storm smiled as they fell. And smiled. And smiled.

"Father?" Mouse had come to his side. The boy's hands were on his arm, urging him to sit.

"A time for reaping and a time for sowing," Storm whispered. "My season had fled, Mouse. The season of the Legion is gone. But the rivers still run to the seas…"

He coughed. Funny. It still did not hurt. "It's time for the young." He forced a broader smile.

"I'll take you to the ship, Father. I'll get you into a cradle." Mouse's cheeks were wet.

"No. Don't. This is something I have to do, Son. In my quarters in Edgeward. A letter. You'll understand. Go on now. Take command. You're the last Storm. I give you Cassius and the Legion. Complete the cycle. Close the circle."

"But…"

"Don't argue with orders, Mouse. You know better. Go help Pollyanna." Storm leaned against the console, turned his back on his son. "Don't rob me of this victory. Go on." Then, to himself, "Vanity of vanities, all is vanity. What does a man profit?…"

Death descended on quiet, silken wings and enfolded him in gentle, peaceful arms.

# FIFTY-ONE: 3023-3032 AD

One of the Osirian commtechs called out, "Lord Rhafu, I've got a red light on something from Todesangst."

The old man limped across the huge communications center whence the Norbon empire was directed. "Get me a printout."

A machine whirled and rattled. Paper spewed forth. Rhafu caught the end and read as it appeared. "Uhm!" he grunted. He balled the whole thing up and carried it into a seldom-used office where he studied and researched it for several hours. He came to a decision. He picked up a phone. "Number One." A moment later, "Deeth, I've got a critical here from Todesangst. I'm bringing it up."

Deeth looked up from the printout. Rhafu was old. Probably older than any Sangaree alive, and near the time when rejuvenation would no longer take. The shakiness of massive nerve degeneration had set in.

Deeth frowned. He would not have Rhafu much longer. How would he manage without the man?

He scanned the report again. "I must be missing the point. I don't see anything remarkable here."

"It came red-tagged. I wondered what Michael is up to, that's all."

"Send someone to check."

"I already have. Deeth, if I may?"

Deeth smiled a soft smile. That was Rhafu's bad news tone. "Yes?"

"It looks to me like he's trying to bail out on us."

"What makes you say that?"

"The figures. What they add up to. A hell of a lot of wealth if this thing can be tamed. That and the risks he took."

"I don't see…"

"Sir, your son is Sangaree by your will only. If the truth were known, I expect, he wishes you weren't his father. He grew up a Storm. Inside he still wants to be a Storm. Or, second-best, some anonymous human. We're a closet skeleton he'd rather forget. He could disappear if he wanted, but he's hooked on money and power. If he could be somebody else and still have those…"

"He's got all the money and power anybody could want, Rhafu."

"Sangaree money. Sangaree power. Tainted. And shared. We can control him. We can destroy him by exposing him. With the wealth of this Blackworld thing he could assume any one of several identities we don't yet know and leave us standing around with our fingers in our noses wondering what happened. Except that he was stupid enough to use his own computation capacity to run this feasibility study."

Deeth leaned back, closed his eyes, tried to banish the pain. Rhafu was probably right…

"Deeth, there are indications he tried this once before. Nothing concrete, but he apparently went after a Starfisher harvestfleet years ago. He's never told us about it."

"And he might have achieved the ends you're arguing?"

"Yes. I hear it was an eight-ship harvestfleet. That's a lot of wealth, and a damned good place to hide."

How could Michael prefer anything else to being heir of the leading Sangaree house? That was not logical. What more could a man want? He put the question to Rhafu.

"Respectability. Acceptability in Luna Command. Rehabilitation from the sin of youth that got him rusticated in the first place. You can smell on him how badly he wants to get into the humans' elite club. He'll do anything, including selling us down the proverbial river if the payoff is big enough."

"Rhafu… I can't accept that. I refuse to accept that."

"I have the same emotional responses you do. Intellectually, I see how his emotions are driving him, but I don't understand." Rhafu stared over Deeth's shoulder, out a vast window, at Osiris. Deeth turned, also considering that slice of world.

"He wants to be loved. By the species which rejected him. Is that what it boils down to, Rhafu?"

"Perhaps. And does anybody love Michael Dee? Not really. Not unless it's Gneaus Storm. To everyone else he's a tool. Even us. And he knows it."

Deeth nibbled his lower lip. Put that way, he could feel some empathy… "Let me see that printout again." After a glance he said, "He won't evade his Family responsibilities."

Rhafu stared out the window while Deeth examined the numbers for the third time. After a time, he said, "Deeth, this Blackworld thing may be what we've been looking for. I checked it out before I came here." He dropped a chart onto Deeth's desk.

"It has some peculiar physical characteristics. Look how it lays out. A pot of gold here. In this Twilight Town's territory, but it's accessible only from this Edgeward City's territory. The pot's big enough to fight over. I would if I were in their shoes. And engineered right, we might end up controlling it. Here's my thinking. We engineer a war. We manipulate it so these cities hire Storm and Hawksblood. If the fighting is confined here on the dayside, we might trap both gangs. Suddenly, no Storms, no Thaddeus Immanuel Walters. And no Hawksblood, which would be Michael's payoff for running the show. That's just rough thinking, of course. It would take a long time and a lot of money and research to set it up right."

Deeth smiled. "I see it. I think you're right." He scrawled his name across a piece of paper, wrote a few words. "Take this to Finance and get whatever you need to do your own feasibility study. I'll cut loose whichever people you want. But don't get carried away. Just map it out and see how it looks. If it'll go, then we'll set up a special organization."

"All right."

"Rhafu? Go as carefully with this as you did with the Dharvon. For the same reasons. If there's that much power metal there, let's come out on the far end not only finished with the Storms but controlling that mine."

Rhafu smiled, apparently considering the Homeworld impact of yet another quantum jump in Norbon wealth. "Don't overreach, Deeth."

Deeth was not listening. The possibilities had revivified his childhood dream of restructuring Sangaree society to suit himself. "Call Michael in before you do anything. It's time for face-to-face. And you'll want his first-hand impressions."

If there had been any doubt that Dee was up to something, it vanished when Rhafu tried to summon him to Osiris. Michael dodged messengers the way lesser men dodged process servers. Rhafu had to collect him in person.

Deeth was appalled by the sullen creature Rhafu brought in. Michael snarled, "I've had enough. I didn't want to get involved with you in the first place."

"You're part of the Family."

"I don't give a damn about your Family. All I want is for it to stay out of my life."

"Michael… Look at all we've done. We've made you one of the richest men alive."

"Yes. Look what you've done to me. My children… belong in asylums. My people hate me. They think I'm a monster. And they're probably right…"

Deeth snapped, "We're your people."

The usually evasive, cowardly Michael looked him straight in the eye. He did not speak.

He did not have to. Deeth recognized his failure. He did not have a son. He had an unwilling accomplice. "All right, Michael. What do you want?"

"I want out. OUT. Nothing to do with you, and you nothing to do with me or mine, now or ever."

"It's not that simple. I still haven't settled with the Storms. That's why I brought you here. This thing on Blackworld…"

"Not that simple. Forget it. They're not that simple. Your buttboy here explained on the way. The scheme won't work. You're not dealing with some First Expansion primitives or tenth-generation pleasure slaves. You're talking about people even tougher and nastier than you. And smarter."

Deeth bolted up from behind his desk, face puffing with anger. He swung hard. Dee leaned out of the way. "You see? You can't control your temper."

"Rhafu!"

"Sir?"

"Explain it to him again. I'll come back when I calm down."

When Deeth returned he found Dee no more receptive. "Michael, I've considered everything. Here's my offer. Help us put this thing through and we're quits. We'll divvy up the organizations and go our own ways."

"Sure," Michael replied, voice dripping sarcasm. "Till the next time I'm a handy tool."

"Quits, I said. My word. The word of the Norbon, Michael. I even keep it with animals."

Dee gave him an odd look. Deeth realized that by tone or expression he had betrayed his secret pain. He massaged his face and forehead. Michael wanted to break all ties. He wanted a son. They could not both have their way.

"That's the deal, Michael. You're either with me or against me. No in between. Help me destroy the people who destroyed Prefactlas, or be destroyed with them."

Michael stared at him with that defiant, fearless look once more. Very, very slowly, he nodded. Then he turned and started toward the door.

He paused, took a priceless piece of Homeworld carved jade off a shelf, examined it. It was better than two thousand years old, and so finely carved that in places it was paper thin. He held it at arm's length and let it fall. Fragments scattered across the tile floor. "Damn. Am I clumsy."

Deeth sealed his eyes, fought his anger.

"That's going to be a very difficult tool to control," Rhafu observed.

"Very. Answer this. Was that bit of vandalism a message, or just the spite of the moment?"

"I don't think we'll know till the dust settles. And that's probably why he did it."

"Watch him. Every minute. Every damned minute."

"As you will."

Rhafu put the operation together with his usual genius. It rolled along with such perfection, for so many years, piling and building like the growing crescendo of a great orchestra, that Deeth became convinced of the inevitability of a Norbon success. The little setbacks were there, but carefully accounted for in a program put together with all the information and computation capacity of Helga's World. An absolute and unavoidable doom loomed darker and darker above the murderers of Prefactlas.

Then word came to the hidden headquarters chalet on The Big Rock Candy Mountain. A puzzled Rhafu announced, "The man called Cassius is here. Asking questions about Michael."

"I don't understand. How could they have gotten wind of us?"

"I don't know. Unless..."

"Michael?"

"Does anyone else know we're directing it from here?"

"Not a soul." Deeth considered. He had monitored Dee's dealings with Storm. Michael had kept his mouth shut. "Maybe we left tracks without knowing it."

"Possibly."

"Cut off his sources of information. We'll tend to friend Cassius ourselves."

"Deeth… Never mind."

Deeth studied the old man. Rhafu's nervous degeneration was so advanced he had trouble managing a drinking glass.

"I want this one, Rhafu. We'll hit them and move somewhere else."

"As you wish."

They entered the hotel by separate doors. Unfortunately Rhafu had the only clear shot.

The old man's nerves betrayed him. He missed.

Cassius did not.

Deeth's nerve betrayed him. He froze. He never touched his weapon.

Deeth found himself aboard his escape vessel without remembering how he had gotten there. Just one image remained clear in his mind. Meeting the eyes of Cassius's companion in the street, over Rhafu's body.

It went sour after that. He did not have Rhafu's enchanted touch.

Storm stunned Deeth by attacking Helga's World. He gathered the Norbon forces. His raidships blundered into a trap more disasterous than that at Amon-Ra.

Blackworld was becoming a debacle. Michael just could not handle his half of the chore.

Deeth remembered a shattered piece of jade and wondered.

He lost his temper. He ordered the attack on the Fortress of Iron. "I may not get them all," he told himself, "but they'll know they paid the price of Prefactlas."

He had abandoned hope of profiting from Blackworld. And he had abandoned Michael Dee.

"My son, if you've done your best, you deserve an apology. But I suspect you've subtly sabotaged the whole thing. Enjoy the trap you've built yourself."

His last few fighting ships reached the Fortress's surface. His troopships went in. His men forced the entry locks.

The fighting continued for days, cubicle to cubicle, corridor to corridor, level to level. His soldiers encountered only women and old people, but they too were Legionnaires.

Near the end one of his people told him. "Lord Deeth, enemy scoutships have been detected…"

"Damn!" The Fortress was almost clear. Only a handful of defenders remained, holding out in the old Combat Information Center. "Very well." He could not run now. He had to finish. For Rhafu. For his father. For his mother and the Prefactlas dead.

"All right. I want everyone out but the crew of Lota's raidship. Take space like you're in a panic. Let them intercept messages that will convince them that there's no one left alive here."

"Yes sir."

Deeth joined the one raidship crew in the final attack. His participation brought him face to face with Storm's wife, Frieda.

# BOOK THREE
## GALLOWS

*What are the carpenter's thoughts as he constructs the gallows?*

# FIFTY-TWO: 3052 AD

Never be amazed by me. My teachers were classics. Strategy and Tactics: Professor Colonel Thaddeus Immanuel Walters. Command and Administration: Professor Colonel Gneaus Julius Storm. Hatred, Vengeance, and Puppet-Mastery: Professor Sangaree Head Norbon w'Deeth. Cute Tricks, Cunning, Duplicity, and Artful Self-Justification: Professor Entrepreneur, Adventurer, and Financier Michael Dee. Between them they provided me a very solid background. Cuss the Admiral if you want. The most he did was give me an opportunity to do post-graduate work.

I was a stinker when he recruited me.

—Masato Igarashi Storm

# FIFTY-THREE: 3032 AD

Mouse crouched over his father for a long time, holding Storm's hand, fighting back tears. Someone came and rested gentle fingers on his shoulder. He looked up. Pollyanna had come over, using a laserifle as a crutch.

"He's dead," Mouse said. Disbelief distorted his face. "My father is dead."

"They're all dead. Everybody's dead but us." Her voice was as dull as his.

He rose slowly, mumbling, "Everybody. Helmut and Thurston. And Lucifer. And everybody." The magnitude of it slowly sank in. His father and two brothers. His father's friend. And all the people and family who had died already…

"I'll kill them," he whispered Then, screaming, "All of them!" He started smashing consoles with his rifle. But it was a delicate weapon. Soon he held nothing but a shard.

"We've got things to do, Mouse," Pollyanna reminded, indicating the corpses and wreckage. Her voice held no real interest. She was in such a state that getting on with the job was the only glue holding her together.

"I suppose." The dull voice again. "Will you be all right while I hunt up some of our people?"

"Who's left to hurt me?"

Mouse shrugged. "Yes. Who's left?"

He went hunting Legionnaires, using business like a sword with which he could fend off the madness clawing at his mind "All of them," he kept muttering. "Someday. Every Dee. Every Sangaree."

Withdrawing from Twilight took a day. Too many people, including Hawksblood and the brothers Dee, could not make it to the *Ehrhardt* under their own power. And the dome had to be patched, and someone had to be found who would take charge in Twilight, someone whose loathing for Sangaree was insurance that Michael would have nowhere to run, insurance that Twilight would not come under the worldwide sanctions being threatened by her Blackworld sister cities. Mouse found his candidate after a long search. Most Twilighters wanted shut of any identification with the seat of power. They seemed afraid the Sangaree disease was contagious.

Time to leave arrived. And a new problem raised its Scylla-like head.

"Polly," Mouse said, "I don't know if we're going to make it back."

"What? Why not?"

"I'm the only pilot left, and I'm not rated on anything like the *Ehrhardt*."

"Call for somebody to come up here."

"Can't waste time waiting for somebody to come overland. I'll just give it my best go myself."

"Don't be stupid."

"It can't be that much harder than piloting Cassius's corvette. I managed that fine."

"With him there to help if you got in any trouble."

"Yeah." He truly believed he could handle the cruiser. And he was determined to try. "Strap in, lady."

"Mouse…"

"Then get out and walk."

She grinned. "You're as stubborn as your father."

He grinned back. "I'm his son."

His liftoff was a little rocky.

"Gah!" Pollyanna grunted, nearly throwing up.

"We're off!"

"That was the part that had me worried. Anybody can come down. It's just how fast you're going when you get there…"

"A man does what he has to," Mouse told her.

For a few hours the pain and hatred did not touch him. The cruiser demanded all his sweat and guts and concentration.

He managed to get the *Ehrhardt* to and down on Edgeward's landing field without any irreparable damage.

Getting down required some careful maneuvering. A bank of ships had arrived during their absence. They were the battered bones of the Legion's once-powerful little fleet. They had brought Hakes Ceislak in from Helga's World. They were still off-loading the commando battalion.

Mouse had not informed anyone that he was returning, but the word was out by the time he entered Edgeward. Blake was waiting for him.

"Where's Colonel Storm?" Blake asked. His face was drawn. He feared the worst.

"My father was killed in action against Sangaree..." Mouse stopped to look inside himself. Somehow, for the outside world, he was removing himself from his feelings. He was reporting it as if it had happened to a stranger.

"And Albin Korando?"

"Killed in action, Mr. Blake. I'm sorry."

"No. That's terrible. I'd hoped... What about Colonel Darksword?"

"Dead, sir. If you don't see someone with me, he's dead. The cruiser is full of bodies. It was rough up there."

"Your brother Thurston, too?"

Mouse nodded.

"Who's going to take charge? Colonel Walters is cut off in the Shadowline..."

"I speak for the Legion, Mr. Blake. We have a new commander. Nothing else changes. If you'll excuse me?"

Blake struggled to roll along with Mouse. "What happened?" There was an almost whining, pleading note in his voice. The Shadowline War was tearing him to pieces.

For a moment Mouse could sense the man's feelings. Blake was thinking, *What have I wrought? What have I unleashed? What did I do that reduced Blackworld to this state?*

Mouse shut everything out. He strode toward City Hall, unconsciously imitating the walk of Gneaus Julius Storm. Knifing through his pain was a driving need to demonstrate his competence, to show everyone that he could step into his father's role.

Heads turned when he entered the war room. He checked the boards. Dee now held the Whitlandsund. Cassius's marker had reached the shade station. The unit markers were dense there. Only a handful lay more than five hundred kilometers west of the station. Those were all small units meant to aid the Twilighters in their withdrawal from the Shadowline's end.

The situation was in balance, in tension. Cassius was ready to jump off. It was discussion time.

"Get Colonel Walters on the scrambled clear trunk," Mouse ordered.

The man responsible, who seemed on the edge of exhaustion, gave him a brief who-in-the-hell-are-you? look before turning to his equipment.

Cassius came on quickly.

"Masato, Colonel."

"Mouse. How are you?" Then Walters got a better look at his face. "What happened?"

"Father's dead. And Helmut. And Thurston and Lucifer. Both younger Dees. And Richard Hawksblood. They murdered him and his staff."

Cassius frowned.

"All beyond-the-resurrection."

Cassius's features grew taut, grim.

"Cassius, we're the only ones left."

"It's ending, then. But first there's Michael Dee. And his Sangaree."

"Dee is trapped. We cleaned out Twilight. He can't go back."

"He doesn't know? Don't let him find out."

"Ceislak's here now. I'm taking over at this end. I can squeeze him…"

"Keep Ceislak at Edgeward. Protect the city. Don't let Dee hold it hostage. And get your ships off the ground. Don't give Dee any way out. Make him stand and fight. But let me take care of that part. I'll make the wasting of the Legion useful."

Mouse had never seen Cassius's face so expressive. His grief and hatred were primal.

"As you wish. I'll make my dispositions right away."

"Did your father… say anything?"

"Not much. He did it on purpose, Cassius. To give me a chance to get the Dees from behind. He left a letter. He wrote it before he went up. I haven't had a chance to read it yet. I have a feeling he knew he wasn't coming back."

"Let me know what he had to say. Soon. We'll be jumping off in a few hours."

"Right."

Blake, with his wife's help, arrived. The head of the Corporation seemed to have shrunk into a tiny old cripple. Before he could begin condolences that would only aggravate, despite their sincerity, Mouse told him, "It'll be over soon, Mr. Blake. We'll start clearing the Whitlandsund in a few hours. I'll be holding Ceislak's battalion in reserve in case Dee turns on Edgeward."

Blake started to say something. Grace touched his hand lightly.

"Pollyanna's in the hospital, Mr. Blake. I expect she'd appreciate a friendly face. I think her heart has been hurt worse than her body. She lost Lucifer and Korando both, and she was very fond of my father." He turned away from Blake. "Ceislak. I want a screen of pickets around the crater. I want all the listening devices out there doublechecked. If Dee turns on us, we'll need all the warning we can get. Donnerman. Where's Donnerman? Donnerman, I want your ships off planet as soon as possible. Gentlemen, I'll be in my father's apartment if I'm needed." He pushed out of the war room and went to Storm's quarters.

Geri and Freki whined pathetically. They rushed into the hall, ran back and forth anxiously, searching for their master. Finally, they turned on him with sorrowful eyes.

"He won't be coming back," Mouse whispered. "I'm sorry."

They seemed to understand. The whining grew louder. One let out what sounded like a low moan.

Mouse looked at the ravenshrikes. They had retreated into their little nest, into a tight, intertwined tangle from which they refused to be drawn. They knew. He tried coaxing them with canned meat from the store of delicacies his father had kept. They would not open their devil eyes.

He sighed, looked for the letter.

It lay on his father's desk, page after page of hasty scrawl beneath a plain sheet bearing nothing but the name Masato. Storm's Bible and clarinet weighted them down. The Bible lay open at Ecclesiastes, the clarinet book-marking.

"I should've guessed when he didn't take them with him," he whispered.

The letter, though addressed to him, sounded like an ecclesiastical missive from Gneaus Storm. It began: "Today I hazard the Plain of Armageddon, the blood-drenched field of Ragnarok, to play my part in a destined Gotterdamerung..."

Mouse read it three times before he returned to the war room, the Sirian warhounds tagging his heels apathetically. Their tails were between their legs and their noses were down, and they made strange snuffling sounds in their throats, but they stayed with him.

A whisper ran around the room. Technicians turned to watch his entrance. The Legionnaires took the behavior of the dogs as somehow symbolic, as a seal on the transfer of the mantle of power.

"Cassius," Mouse said, "he knew he was going to die. He planned it. So there wouldn't be any reason for the rest of us to coddle Michael Dee anymore. It was the only way he could keep from breaking his word."

Cassius's laugh was both harsh and sad. "He always found a way to slide around that promise. Too bad he couldn't find it in him to go back on it." Walters's mad humor faded. "Don't let Michael find out. That's got to be our most important secret." Walters's face became dreadful, something inhuman, something demigodly. Something archetypal. "It's time to jump off. Take care, Mouse." He switched off before Mouse could question him as to his intentions.

*What is he going to do?* Mouse wondered. He knew Cassius. It would be something unusual, something nobody would expect. Quite possibly something impossible... He settled into the chair his father had been wont to occupy. His gaze seldom strayed from the situation boards.

At times one or another of the technicians would glance his way and shudder. A slim, oriental youth of small stature filled the Colonel's chair, yet... Yet there was an aura about him, as if a ghost sat in the chair with him. The body of Gneaus Julius Storm had perished, but the spirit lived on in his youngest son.

# FIFTY-FOUR: 3032 AD

The man called Cassius, through holonet exposure in Michael Dee's merc war documentaries, was more widely known than Confederation's Premier. Yet he was a figure of mystery, an unknown even to his intimates. What made him tick? What made him laugh or cry? No one really knew.

He surveyed the Legion. He considered his public image, and reflected that he probably knew Cassius less well than did all those billions who watched the holocasts. They had an image of Thaddeus Immanuel Walters, and the tape editors maintained its consistency. But the Walters self-image rambled around centuries, and he had not had time to discover who and what he was.

The massed crawlers showed up well on infrared. There were thirty-five of them, in two long lines, idling, awaiting his commands. The longer line of twenty-five, led by eight captured battle crawlers, would run for the Whitlandsund. They would do so without benefit of shade, which would warn Dee that they were coming.

The remaining ten units would follow Cassius himself.

*No point in delaying any longer*, Walters thought. He picked up a mike, said, "White Knight, White Knight, this is Charlemagne. Go. I say again, go. Over."

"Charlemagne, Charlemagne, this is White Knight. Acknowledge go. Out."

"Charlemagne, out."

The larger force began rolling.

Cassius's group consisted of six long-range charters, three pumpers, and his own command combat crawler. The charters, carrying minimum crews, were expendable. They would find the way. The four big rigs were crammed with men and equipment.

Cassius shifted comm nets. "Babylon, Babylon, this is Starfire. Signals follow. Stray Dog One, go. Stray Dog One, go. Over."

A charter rumbled into sunlight.

The formations Cassius used crossing uncharted territory, once he entered it a few hours north-northeast of the Shadowline, he adapted from those of ancient surface navies. The charters ran in a broad screen ahead of the four important crawlers, ready to relay warning of any danger.

They ran far faster than was customary for explorers. The run Cassius was making was dangerously long. If the crawlers escaped sunlight at all, it would be with screens severely weakened.

He kept the crawlers rolling, knowing his chances were grim.

Maximum computation capacity and power in each vehicle was devoted to keeping in touch with Walters. He wanted to know what was happening every instant, hoping he could keep up speed and still not lose two crawlers to the same trap. Like a spider in hiding, waiting for something to disturb her web, he sat amid his comm gear, listening. Hour upon hour passed. He said not a word. His crewmen began checking to see if he was all right.

*The bad part of warmaking,* he thought, *is the 'tween-battles. There's too much time to think, to remember.*

He could do nothing but endure the pain, the care, the fear. He tried to banish the ghosts that came to haunt him, and could not. He discovered that he had acquired a new squad. His wife and daughter. The Fortress of Iron. Gneaus. Wulf. Helmut. Big, dull Thurston, who may have been the only happy man in the Legion. Richard Hawksblood, the ancient enemy, with whom he had felt a bond of spirit. He had not seen Hawksblood in so long he could not remember the man's face. Homer. Benjamin. Lucifer. The younger Dees, long might they burn in torment. Doskal Mennike, who had been his protégé at Academy. Someday he would have to explain to Mennike's father. What could he tell the old man? Only that, one and all, they had been played for pawns and fools by Sangaree. It was not an admission that would come easily.

A long-ago ghost came. Tamara Walters, a favorite niece whose ship had vanished without trace during the Ulantonid War. Why was he remembering that far back?

Hadn't he made his peace with the elder terrors? Were all his losses, injuries, and sins going to return and parade?

"Starfire, Starfire, this is Stray Dog Four. I've hit heat erosion. Can't back free." The voice was tight and rigid. The man talking knew there would be no rescue attempt. There was not enough time. To try would seal the fate of everyone else. But he had accepted the risks when he had volunteered. "My instruments show a streak running zero five seven relative, eighty meters wide, at least six meters deep. Good luck, Starfire. Stray Dog Four, out."

Cassius did not respond to the signal, merely passed the warning to the other crawlers, each of which slowed to skirt the danger. What could he say to a man he was leaving to die? He could do nothing but add a face and name to the list of men he had, through his own doing, outlived.

The media and his colleagues called him the ultimate commander. None but he realized that the ultimate commander was a pose, an image behind which Thaddeus Immanuel Walters concealed himself. Sometimes he managed to delude himself with the illusion.

Life, it would seem on remote observation, was something Cassius held no more holy than did the universe itself. Yet, like certain forgotten gods, he noted the fall of every sparrow, and put himself through silent, private purgatories for each. And still he went on, from battle to battle, without thought of becoming anything but what he was. Like Gneaus Storm, like so many mercenaries, he was a fatalist, moved by convictions of personal predestination. Unlike Storm, he did not fight and mock Fate, merely accepted it and sailed dispiritedly toward his final encounter with it.

At least a touch of solipsist madness was a must at every level of the freecorps.

Once past the heat erosion he redistributed his screen to fill the gap left by the lost crawler.

He lost another charter before he reached the Thunder Mountains three hundred kilometers north of the Whitlandsund, and yet another, through screen failure, while searching for a shadowed valley where the unit could hide from the demon sun. The crucial four heavy crawlers remained unharmed.

As soon as the charters had cooled down and loaded some gas snow, he sent them out again. Somewhere up here, according to the surveys done before the orbitals burned out, there was a possibility of slipping over the Edge of the World. A way to sweep around and beat Michael's game of Thermopylae. The pass had shown as a small, dark trace on a few photo printouts…

It was a long shot. The darkness might not be a pass at all…

While he waited on the charters Cassius played with the command nets, hoping to intercept something from the war zone. He got nothing but static, which was all he really expected in that cove of darkness on the shores of the sea of fire.

He thought Brightside was what the old Christians had had in mind for Hell. With the Legion here Blackworld certainly was a planet of the damned.

The charters returned two days later. They had found the way across the mountains, but did not know if the larger units could manage it.

"We'll give it a try," Cassius said. He had spent too much time with his thoughts and away from his command. He had to be moving, to be involved, soon, or he would go mad reliving his losses.

The pass was a tight, tortuous canyon, and the going was slow, but there were few real problems till they had crossed the Edge of the World. Then, after they had passed the limit of the original survey, they encountered a crack in the mountain which crossed and blocked the way. The crevasse threatened Cassius's entire scheme.

He refused to turn back. "We're going over these mountains here," he growled, "or we'll die here. One or the other. Let's find out how deep the son-of-a-bitch is."

His driver idled down. Cassius clambered out his escape hatch, approached the obstacle. The lead crawler had put lights on it, but they did nothing to illuminate its depths. He stared down into darkness. After a minute he fired his lasegun downward. The flash revealed a bottom much nearer than he expected.

He returned to his crawler. "Stray Dog One, this is Starfire. Maneuver your unit around parallel to the crevasse. Over."

It took two hours for the charter to wriggle into a position that suited him. "Stray Dog One, abandon your unit. Stray Dog Three, Stray Dog Six, push it over. Over."

The two surviving charters groaned and strained. The vibration of their effort shook the stone of the Thunder Mountains, made the big crawlers shudder. Their engines growled and whined, their tracks ripped at the earth. They injured themselves badly, but managed to topple the crawler into the crevasse.

Cassius offloaded his troops and had them gather loose rock. They dumped the detritus around the fallen charter. Hours crept away. The bridge grew, became level. Cassius sent a charter over to test and tamp, then an empty pumper. The fill held both times. One by one, the remaining units rolled.

That crevasse was the last serious obstacle. Abandoning the surviving charters because they could no longer keep pace, Cassius swung the big units onto the route between Twilight and Edgeward. He sped southward, maintaining radio silence. Near Edgeward he swung west, toward Michael Dee and the Whitlandsund.

His troops were exhausted. They had been cramped in their crawlers for days, racked by tension, constantly haunted by the fear that the next minute would be the one when a track went into heat erosion, or the mountain slid away beneath them. Even so, Cassius offloaded them at the eastern mouth of the Whitlandsund and sent them in. They made contact quickly.

Walters broke radio silence at last. "Andiron, Andiron, this is Wormdoom, do you read, over."

Mouse came on net only minutes later. "Wormdoom, this is Andiron. Shift to the scrambled trunk, over."

Cassius shifted. Mouse squeaked, "Cassius, where the hell are you? We've been trying to get ahold of you for six days."

"I'm right outside your door, Mouse. Moving into the Whitlandsund. I need Ceislak's men."

"You're on this side of the Edge of the World?"

"That's right. How soon can you get those men here?"

"How did you manage that?"

"Never mind. I did it. Send me those men. We can talk after we finish Dee."

"All right. They're on their way. I don't know how you did it…"

Cassius cut him off, turned to listen to the tactical nets once more.

He had been listening in since returning to Darkside, trying to assess the situation back in the Shadowline. It did not look good for those he had left behind.

# FIFTY-FIVE: 3032 AD

It was a very grim, very sour Masato Storm who watched the big board in the war room. It looked terrible.

Someone moved a chair into place beside him. He glanced up at at a commtech. He was holding the chair for Pollyanna.

Mouse smiled weakly. "How are you? Any better?"

"Ready for anything. Except I limp a little. They say it'll go away. How is it going?"

"Not good. I haven't heard from Cassius for days. I'm scared for him. And up there..." He indicated the board showing the Whitlandsund. "We made some gains when the first wave came over, but it's slowed down. Way down. We're still pushing them back, but not fast enough."

"But you outnumber them."

"We've lost too many tractors. We can't bring our people over fast enough. It looks like we've only got two chances. Either Cassius turns up or my uncle runs out of ammunition."

"Sir!" one of the commtechs yelled. "Sir, I've got Colonel Walters on Tac One."

"Put him on over here. Pollyanna, you're a good-luck charm. Maybe I'll strap you into that chair."

She smiled wanly. "I wasn't too lucky for Frog. Or Lucifer. Or..."

"Can it." Cassius's grim face came on screen. They argued back and forth about Ceislak's battalion, and Mouse tried to discover how Walters had gotten to Darkside. Cassius broke off.

"He's in a foul mood, isn't he?" Pollyanna asked.

"That he is. And he can be just as nasty as he wants as long as he does his job. I feel a thousand percent better now."

"Sir," commtech said a few minutes later, "I have Colonel Walters again."

"Put him over here."

"Mouse?" Cassius said, "Sorry about snapping. It's the nerves, I guess. It's grim out here. As your father would put it, the Oriflamme is up."

Pollyanna frowned a question. Mouse whispered, "No quarter given or asked."

Cassius continued, "We're in a bad spot. Nobody can back down. It's all or nothing, and the losers die the death-without-resurrection."

"I understand, Cassius. We're all under pressure."

"Your uncle has got what he wanted. His battle to the death." A nasty smile crossed Walters's mouth. "I don't think the fool counted on being part of it, though."

"No. One thing. He doesn't know about Father yet. I want to save that as a special surprise. Let him count on that last-minute protection till it's too late."

"But of course! That's why I wanted to keep it quiet."

"The Legion never fought this bitterly," Mouse said.

"Never before. We've got an emotional stake in this one, Mouse."

Had it not been for the topographical advantages, Michael's crew would have been obliterated long since. Dee's men were good fighters, but they were not soldiers, not in the sense that the Legionnaires were. They were unaccustomed to extensive teamwork and the complexities of large, enduring operations. Though largely of human origin, they were tainted with the Sangaree raid-and-run philosophy.

"Michael's people aren't doing bad."

"They're cornered. I've got to get back to it. I just wanted to say sorry for growling."

"It's all right."

Cassius's battalions shoved Dee deeper and deeper into the Whitlandsund. The lines facing Edgeward had been thin and unprepared for a heavy stroke.

The hours cranked along. Mouse sat that chair till his behind began to ache. Pollyanna remained beside him, partly because she was interested in events, partly because she sensed his need for a bridge to the Mouse that used to be.

Dee's resistance stiffened.

"He's figured it out," Mouse said. "He's shifting men now."

Cassius kept the pressure on. At the far end of the pass Legionnaires from the Shadowline began to make headway against defenses weakened by the removal of men shifted to halt Cassius.

Pollyanna touched his hand lightly. "You think we're going to do it?"

"Uhm? What?"

"Win."

"I don't know. Yet. I think the odds are shifting." He caught fragments of tactical chatter. Cassius was moving Ceislak's commando battalion into position.

Hours dragged on. Finally, Pollyanna whispered, "You've got to rest before you collapse."

"But…"

"Your being here or not won't change anything, Mouse. They can tell you if they need you."

"You're right. I won't be any good to anybody if I pass out from exhaustion. I'll stagger over to the apartment…"

Pollyanna went with him.

When he returned to the war room he carried a ravenshrike on his shoulder. The commtechs' eyes widened. A secret understanding seemed to pass among them. Mouse surveyed the boards as the warhounds began their fruitless search for enemies.

He sensed the change in the men. They had accepted the shift in power. It was not a matter of humoring the Old Man's kid anymore. He had become the Old Man.

The boards did not look good. Things had gone static.

"Sir," one of the commtechs said, "Colonel Walters would like to speak with you at your convenience."

"Okay. Get hold of him."

Cassius was on the scrambled trunk in minutes. "Coming up with a few problems, Mouse. We've pushed them from both sides till we've got them surrounded in a big crater. They've dug in on the outside of the ringwalls, where they can fire down into the pass. They've pulled back into a small enough circle so that they can run men from one place to another faster than I can make surprise attacks. I was going to cut them up one place at a time. Slice off a little group and take them prisoner. They've managed to keep me from doing it. Looks like it could turn into an old-fashioned siege."

"There're thirty thousand people in the Shadowline who don't have time for that, Cassius. They're running out of air."

"I've heard the reports."

The breathables situation was becoming dangerous. Food and water were good for weeks yet, with rationing, but there was no way to cut back on a fighting man's air. Recycling was never completely efficient, and lately the equipment had begun to deteriorate.

Mouse said, "I got the medical people started putting the wounded into cryo storage yesterday. We can resurrect them when we open the pass. They suggested we do the same to Meacham's people."

"They have the cryo storage facilities?"

"No. Not enough."

"I may start using some of Hawksblood's people. If I can get them over to this side."

"Why?"

"Sometimes you run out of ways to finesse. Then the only thing left is the hammer. Hit hard, with everything you got, and grit your teeth about the casualties."

"Your munitions picture don't look good for something like that."

"That doesn't bother me as much as the air situation. It looks like Michael will run dry first. His fire patterns show he's trying to conserve ammunition."

"That's a plus."

"I don't know. What I'm afraid of is having to offer terms so we can save the people across the way. I think that's what he's doing now. Trying to hold on till we're ready to trade his outfit for ours."

Mouse glanced at a depressing visual from Blake's shade station. The station was surrounded by a tide of emergency domes occupied by men waiting to be evacuated or sent into action. The encampment grew steadily as Hawksblood's men and Twilight's miners filtered in. Dee could lose his war and still win a Pyrrhic victory.

Mouse looked over at charts listing the various crawlers and their status. "Cassius, we're going to be in trouble no matter what. We don't have enough crawlers to get everybody out."

"So don't be proud. Ask your neighbors for help. Have Blake call The City of Night and Darkside Landing and beg for help if he has to."

"We've tried once. They say they won't risk their equipment if there's fighting going on."

"Keep trying, boy. I'm looking it over here. I'm going to try one more big push, then see what Michael is willing to dicker about."

"Don't deal. Not unless there's no choice."

"Of course not. I saw the trap that got your father into."

Mouse summoned one of the techs. "See if you can find Mr. Blake. Ask him to come down."

Blake joined him a half-hour later. Pollyanna accompanied him.

"Mr. Blake, could you try Darkside Landing and City of Night again? You can tell them the fighting will be over before they can get their equipment here."

The worn wreck of a man in the wheelchair showed a sudden interest in life. "Really? You've finally got them?"

"Not exactly. We're going to try one more push, then negotiate if it fails."

Blake protested. Boiling anger resurrected the man who had ruled the Corporation till the impact of the Shadowline War had driven him into hiding.

"My feelings exactly," Mouse agreed. "I don't want any of them getting away. But we may have no choice. It could be negotiate or let the men in the Shadowline die."

"Damn! All this slaughter for nothing."

"Almost. We could console ourselves with the thought that my uncle isn't getting what he wants, either. In a way, even if he negotiates his way out of the Whitelandsund, he'll have lost more than we have. He'll be on the run for the rest of his life. He used nuclears. He served the Sangaree. Navy won't forgive that. They'll confiscate his property…"

Pollyanna had been rubbing Mouse's shoulders. Now her fingers tightened in a surprisingly strong grip. "You negotiate if you want. You make a deal for the Legion. You make a deal for Blake and Edgeward. But don't count me in, Mouse. Don't make any deal for me. August Plainfield got away once. He won't again."

Mouse leaned back, looked up. Her face betrayed pure hatred.

"You been drinking snake venom again?"

She squeezed so hard his shoulders ached. "Yes. I drink a liter with every meal."

"Wait." Mouse indicated the boards.

Cassius was starting his attack.

"Sir, he's sending in everybody this time," one of the techs reported. "He's even stripped the crawlers of their crews."

Mouse stood up. "Mr. Blake, find me a crawler. Anything that will run. I'm going out there."

# FIFTY-SIX: 3032 AD

Cassius found himself a laserifle and climbed the crater ringwall.

The fighting was close, grim, and positional. Rock by rock, bunker by foxhole, his men flushed Dee's and drove them back. Man by man, they broke the Sangaree defense. The Legionnaires invested all their skill and fury. Dee nearly fought them to a standstill.

What had Michael said to make his people so damned stubborn? Cassius wondered.

"Wormdoom, this is Welterweight. I've got my hands on a prime chunk of ringwall rim real estate. Give me some big guns."

"You've got them, Welterweight."

Finally, Cassius thought. A break. He ordered all the artillery possible into the position Ceislak had seized.

The nets resounded with chatter about furious counterattacks and dwindling ammunition stocks. Cassius decided to join Ceislak. The man's position had to be held. It provided a platform from which the interior of the crater could be brought under fire.

He studied the fighting from the rim. It took time to fall into patterns. He had nothing but weapons flashes by which to judge.

"I think that last one was their last counterattack," Ceislak told him. "We're ready to finish them." Gesturing, he indicated the far rimwall. Heavy weapons flashes had begun to appear there. Legionnaires were coming over from the Shadowline side. Ceislak's bombardment had broken the stubborn defense of the ringwall.

A dwindling number of enemy weapons flashes indicated failing powerpacks and munitions supplies on the other side.

"Looks like we might manage it," someone said.

Walters turned slowly, wondering who had broken radio silence. One of a pair of figures, just joining the crowd and barely visible in the backflash of Ceislak's weapons, raised a hand in greeting.

"It's me. Masato. I said it looks like we've finally got them."

"That's Michael Dee down there," Cassius growled. "He'll still have three tricks up his sleeve. What the hell are you doing here? You're the last Storm."

"It isn't a private war," was all Mouse said by way of defending his presence.

Cassius turned back to the crater. The boy was his father's son. There would be no talking him out of staying.

A flash illuminated the face of Mouse's companion. "Damn it, Mouse! What the hell's the matter with you, bringing a girl out here?"

Pollyanna reminded him of that niece he had lost during the Ulantonid War. He felt strangely avuncular and protective. He was startled by an insight into his own ambivalent feelings toward Pollyanna. Tamra had meant a great deal to him.

The flashes on the far rim showed the Brightside troops making good headway. Michael's people seemed to be running out of ammo fast. Good. "Looks like we won't have to offer terms."

Mouse stuck with his previous contention. "She has as much right to be here as anybody. Her father..."

"Was I arguing? I've heard all about it." He caught a ghost of something in the timbre of Mouse's voice. The little slut had gotten her hooks into another Storm. "Let's stick to business. It's time to find out if Michael's ready to give up."

Michael contacted him first.

One of Cassius's officers called on Command One. "Sir, I've got Dee on a public frequency asking to parlay with Colonel Storm. What should I do?"

"I'm on the rimwall right now. Tell him he'll be contacted as soon as possible. And don't let on about the Colonel. Understand?"

"Yes sir."

With Mouse and Pollyanna tagging along, Walters descended to his crawler. He ran through the command nets, ordering his officers to keep the pressure on hard. Several units reported the surrender of individual human, Toke, and Ulantonid soldiers.

One commander reported, "Their munitions situation is so desperate they're taking small arms ammo from their troops and saving it for Sangaree officers."

"Good old Michael," Cassius said. "Really knows how to make and keep friends."

He started to signal Dee, suddenly stopped. "I just had a nasty idea." He went across the command net again. "Wormdoom. Gentlemen. I want a radiation scan on that crater. These guys used a nuke on us once before."

In two minutes he knew. There were two radiation sources not identifiable as tractor piles. They were nowhere near any of Dee's heavy units.

"Looks like my dear old uncle was going to close the pass after he made terms with Father."

Cassius smiled. "He's in for a surprise."

"He'll be asking merc terms, won't he?" Mouse asked.

"Of course. But he's not going to get them. If I end up dealing at all. I'm going to be against the wall hard before I let Sangaree get out."

"Better get hold of him before he panics."

Cassius found the band on which Michael was waiting. "Dee?"

"Gneaus? Where the hell have you been?" Only Dee's word choices betrayed his anxiety. His voice was cheerful. "I've been waiting half an hour."

Cassius silently mouthed, "He hasn't caught on about Twilight yet. That gives us the angle on him."

"Set the hook and reel him in," Mouse suggested.

"Been out directing artillery," Cassius said into the pickup. He kept the visual off so he would not correct Dee's presumption that he was speaking with Gneaus Storm. "What you want?"

"Keep it on the edge of the band or he'll recognize your voice," Mouse whispered. Cassius nodded, made a fine adjustment.

"Terms. We're beaten. I admit it. It's time to stop the bloodshed."

Cassius controlled a snort. "What reason do I have for giving them? We're winning. We'll have you wiped out in a couple hours."

"You promised…"

"I didn't promise your people anything. They aren't covered by any of the usual conventions anyway. They're not merc. They're Sangaree hired guns."

"But…"

"If you want to talk, come to my crawler. We'll sit down face to face."

Dee crawfished. He wriggled. He squirmed. But Legionnaires now held all the heights. Their artillery made an ever more convincing argument.

"You think he'll come in?" Mouse asked.

"Yep." Cassius nodded. "He isn't finished, though. He's got a trick or two up his sleeve yet. Besides the bombs. If he wants to have any men left to help pull whatever it is off, he's got to get them out. He'll come trotting over like a bad little boy expecting to get his hand slapped."

"I'm going to call Blake." Mouse cleared another channel, spoke with the city. "Cassius, he did it. City of Night and Darkside Landing are sending crawlers."

Cassius felt a century younger, knowing there was a chance.

"What about those nuclears?"

"I've got a plan. Stand back and be quiet. I'm going to call him again. Michael? You coming over here or not?"

"All right. But you make sure nobody shoots me on the way."

"You're clear. I'll leave the carrier on as a homer." Walters gave orders for one crawler to be allowed to leave the crater.

"Better watch him close," Mouse said. "He could have those bombs rigged to blow on signal. He won't give a damn if he loses his army."

"Maybe not. But he'll parlay first. Now listen close. Here's what I want. You two just be hanging around here when he comes in. I'll be back in the next section. You cover him and make him get out of his suit. Make him get out of everything, just in case. You don't know what he might be carrying."

Which was exactly what Mouse and Pollyanna did while Walters watched through the cracked door to the slave section. Stripping with a great show of wounded dignity, Dee kept demanding, "Where's your father?"

Michael had grown gaunt during his sojourn on Blackworld. He had spent so long in-suit that he was emaciated and pale. He shook noticeably. His nerves seemed to have been stretched to their limits.

Cassius watched, and searched his soul. He could find no sympathy for Michael Dee. Dee had made this bed of thorns himself.

He stepped into the command cabin. "Michael, you've got one chance to live out the day."

"Cassius!" Dee was startled and frightened. "How the hell did you get over here? You're supposed to be in the Shadowline." He whirled to face Mouse. "And you're supposed to be at the Fortress. What's going on? Where's your father?"

"Tell us about the nuclears you've got planted up there," Cassius suggested. "And I might give you your life."

And immediately Walters found himself fighting an intense desire to kill Dee. Wulf. Helmut. Gneaus. All the others who had died because of this fool... But Storm's ghost whispered to him of his duty to his men, to the thousands still trapped in the Shadowline.

He did not often run on his own emotions. He almost always ran on the feelings and ideals of his dead commander. His own inclination, at that instant, was to let the bombs blow and send the Legion off in one huge, dramatic stroke. It would be like the ancients sending their dead out to sea in a burning ship.

He had very little purpose left in life, he thought. Since leaving the Shadowline he had not looked ahead, beyond surviving long enough to exact revenge. He was no longer a man with tomorrows.

"Tell me about those bombs, Michael. Or I'll kill you now, here."

"You can't." Sly smile. "Gneaus wouldn't permit it."

"Oh, my poor foolish friend," Cassius said, wearing his cruelest, most self-satisfied smile. "Have I got news for you. Gneaus Julius Storm died leading a successful assault on Twilight Town. You and yours are all mine now."

Dee became more aguey and pallid. "No! You're lying."

"Sorry, boy. He died at Twilight, along with Helmut, Thurston, Lucifer, and your wife and sons." Metallic chuckle. "It was a classic bloodletting. And now you've got no exits."

Dee fainted.

"The circle closes, Michael," Cassius said when Dee recovered. "The cycle completes itself. The last revenges are in the wind. Then it begins anew." Wearily, Cassius drew the back of his handless wrist across his forehead. "Those were some of your brother's last thoughts."

Mouse picked it up. "A revenge raid on Prefactlas to even scores with the Sangaree, and from the ruins a survivor returned like a phoenix to exact a revenge of his own. Now Cassius is the only survivor of the Prefactlas raiders. And of Deeth's people there's only you."

The word had come, while Michael was unconscious, that Navy had caught up with the remnants of the fleet that had attacked the Fortress. No quarter had been given. None ever was.

Though there was no physical proof, Cassius wanted to believe that the Sangaree Deeth had died there. But there was no justice in this universe. His hope might prove mere wishful thinking.

"You and me, Michael," Cassius said. He laid a gentle hand on Mouse's shoulder. "Then it begins anew, with Gneaus's phoenix."

He was sad for Mouse. The boy was filled with hatred for his father's killers. He had done some tall and frightful promising during Michael's unconsciousness. "Mouse, I wish you wouldn't. I wish you'd just let it be," he said.

A stubborn, angry expression fixed itself on Mouse's face. He shook his head.

"Michael? About the bombs?"

# FIFTY-SEVEN: 3032 AD

Deeth waited till the woman was a step away, swinging her knife. He blocked the blow, stepped inside, sank his own blade into her chest. She clawed at his face as she went down.

He stood over her, watching her die. His stroke had been the only one he had struck himself. This was the first death he had dealt personally since he had killed the old man in the cave.

He felt no special satisfaction or joy. He felt almost nothing. The lack surprised him for only an instant. He never had been enthusiastic about fulfilling his father's plans.

What now? The Norbon revenge was nearly complete. The debt was almost paid. The final act, under Michael's direction, was beyond his participation. There was nothing left but to evade the fleet now passing the Fortress, pursuing his raidships.

Nothing remained but the mundanity of Norbon directorship. A huge loathing welled up within him. He never had wanted to be Head. He no longer needed the position's power. And without Rhafu, feeling the way he felt now, he might not be able to hold on.

He stalked through the Fortress of Iron, a thoughtful specter silently prowling a tomb. He paused in Storm's study, slowly poked through his enemy's effects. He began to feel a sense of spiritual kinship, to scent out a kindred loneliness. The man was not entirely alien. He was as much out of tune with humanity as his enemy was with his own people.

He found several undamaged, space-ready singleships on the shiplock level. He considered them. They were slow, but could travel almost indefinitely, seizing their power from the binding energy of the universe itself. A man who had the time could ride one forever.

Deeth summoned his remaining raidmaster, gave him a letter for his cousin Taake. It assigned Taake the duties of Head till his own return. The raidmaster glanced at it. "Where will you be, sir?"

"I'm going to make a pilgrimage."

"Sir?"

Deeth waved him away. "Go. Go on. Get out before they send someone back to check this place out."

Still not sure what he would do, Deeth boarded the ship he had chosen. It was a fat, slow vessel that had done small-time raven work. It carried both medicare cradles and cryobiological storage units. But no instel. Even the Legion had been unable to afford instel for all its ships.

The raidmaster spaced. Deeth spent more hours wandering the ruins of his enemy's home, wondering, at times, if Boris Storm and Thaddeus Walters had done the same after silencing the Norbon station. He finally took space himself, cutting a hyper arc for the center of the galaxy. He had no intention of going that far, only of running along till he had come to some understanding with and of himself.

His course sloped through the Centerward March of Ulant. He dropped hyper long enough to gather news of what had happened on Blackworld.

He could not be sure. It sounded like he had failed.

Without Rhafu there to push him he could not care. It no longer seemed to matter.

He apologized to his father's ghost, set his drives on auto, sealed himself into a cryo storage unit.

Someday the drive would fail and he would fall into normspace. Then he would waken and look out at a whole new universe… Or the ship might plow through the heart of a sun, where the field stresses were so great they would yank the vessel out of hyper. Or…

He did not care.

Staying alive did not much matter either.

# FIFTY-EIGHT: 3032 AD

Mouse sat in the crawler operator's seat, watching Cassius and Pollyanna. Polly kept zigging round, unable to stand still. She kept looking at Cassius strangely. And Cassius kept smiling that funny, boyish, embarrassed smile.

Mouse was a little surprised at Walters too. Cassius never thought out loud. Not about the way he felt.

Walters asked Pollyanna, "You know the character in *The Merchant of Venice*, the Jew, who does the soliloquy about his right to hurt like anybody else?"

"Shylock."

"Yeah. Shylock. That's me. I'm like him. I've got a right to be human too. It's just that I'm so old and been in this business so long that I don't show it anymore."

"But that wasn't what Shylock was really talking about. He was just trying to rationalize the revenge he was taking on…" She shut up.

Mouse did not know Shakespeare, but he got the feeling Pollyanna had reached the sudden conclusion that Cassius and this Shylock were alike after all. He lifted a leg onto the control panel, leaned back, chewed the corner of a fingernail. "You're not going to start singing your death song, are you?" he asked Cassius.

"Me? Never. I may not be completely happy with my life, but I sure as hell plan to stick around as long as I can. No, I've been thinking about getting out of the mainstream. If this kind of life has been in it. I might become a crazy old hermit on a mountain somewhere, coming down to prophesy at the villagers once a year. Or run off to the Starfishers. Or become a McGraw or a Freehauler. Anything to get away from the past. I'd just as soon do my fade before Confederation starts investigating the Shadowline, too. I don't have the patience to deal with those people. That's why I left the Corps."

"Somehow," Mouse said, "I can't picture you being anything but what you are. What about those bombs? Wouldn't you say Michael's had enough time to decide?"

Dee, still standing in the middle of the cabin, had not spoken for a long time. Only his eyes had moved, watching every muscle in Cassius, Mouse, and Pollyanna. And the weapon hanging with such apparent negligence in Cassius's hand. "What're you going to do?" he whimpered.

"Now, if it was up to me and I could do what I want," Cassius replied, "I'd kill you. But I won't. Unless you don't start talking about those damned bombs. You've had your time. Talk. And talk straight, because you're going to be out there beside me when we disarm them. How are they armed? How did you plan to set them off?"

The tractor's comm buzzed, demanding attention. "Mouse, get that. Michael, start talking."

"Guarantees, Cassius. I want guarantees," Dee countered. "You don't know what he's like. You don't know what he'll do if I don't set them off."

"Who?" Mouse asked.

Dee ignored him. "He'd destroy the whole universe to get you and the Storms. He's been a raving madman since you killed Rhafu."

"All right, damn it. I'll keep you in my closet if I have to. Just tell me how to get rid of those bombs."

"Your word?"

"What do you want? Me to cut my wrist and write it in blood? You're getting too good a deal now, and you know it."

"They're radio-controlled. My driver has the trigger."

"How long before he pushes the button?"

"He won't. He doesn't know he has it. I screwed up. I was too sure I'd find Gneaus here."

"Ah." Cassius chuckled evilly. "Fooled you."

"You promised."

"Cassius," Mouse said, "here's a little something to brighten your day. Helga's surrendered Festung Todesangst."

"What?" Michael demanded.

"That's the word from Naval Intelligence."

"For God's sake, why?" Dee demanded. "I don't believe it. She would have blown her scuttles…"

"I don't know why," Mouse said. "The report came from the Corps, filtered through Intelligence. They didn't explain. They just said it was a standoff, with Helga threatening to blow the scuttles and the Marines hanging on but not pushing her so hard she'd really do it. Maybe she got wind of what happened at Twilight and decided it wasn't worth it anymore. She suddenly just gave up."

Michael frowned and shook his head. "What the hell's the matter with her?" he muttered to himself. "The spoiled, self-centered twit. Just because she got what she wanted. We needed…"

Cassius was frowning, too. "It's got to be a trick. She put the bombs on timer or something. Dees are always up to tricks."

"Cassius, they got Benjamin and Homer out. They look like they'll be all right. We'll be able to resurrect them."

"Uhm? Good. Maybe. If she didn't have them programmed, or something. What kind of deal did she make? It can't be anything good for us."

Michael turned on Mouse. The Dee cunning took control of his face. He shook with anticipation, sure his daughter would have made a worthy trade.

Mouse smiled at him. "Nothing. No deal. Just plain surrender. Like she didn't have anything to live for anymore, so she quit."

"But?..." Cassius started to ask.

Mouse glanced at Michael, who seemed appalled. "They killed her, Cassius. Beckhart himself shut her support systems down."

"Dead?" Dee asked in an incredibly tiny voice. "My little girl? All my children? You've killed all my babies?" Mouse sat up as a mad light caught fire in his uncle's eyes. "You murderers. My wife. My children..."

"They all got a clean death," Mouse snapped. "Which was damned well better than they deserved. They brought it on themselves."

Cassius took a step toward Dee, staring into his eyes.

He spoke slowly, twisting the knife. "He's right. They should have died a thousand deaths each, in fire. And even then they wouldn't have hurt enough to suit me."

Pollyanna screamed. "Mouse!"

Dee plunged forward.

Cassius was not expecting it. He suffered from the lifelong misconception that a coward could not act in circumstances where he did not hold the upper hand.

Michael Dee was a coward, but not incapable of acting.

Cassius's instant of delay cost him his life.

Dee knocked the pistol from his hand, caught it in the air, fired one lucky, nose-destroying shot before Mouse slammed into him from the side and sent the weapon skittering across the cabin. Cassius fell disjointedly, slowly, like an empire, almost in pieces, as if different parts of his body were being acted upon by varying gravities. His mechanical voice box made skritching, clacking noises, but no sound that could be interpreted as anger or a cry of agony. He piled up in a heap, twitching, voice box still making those strange noises.

Mouse and Dee thrashed about on the deck, the youth cursing incoherently and weeping while he tried to strangle his uncle.

At first Dee fought in pure panic. He scratched, kicked, bit. Then reason set in. He broke the stranglehold, writhed away, unleashed a kick that hit Mouse over the heart.

Mouse got onto hands and knees. He put all his strength into attaining his feet. The deck rushed toward him instead.

Dee poised for a killing kick to his throat.

"No."

He turned slowly.

Pollyanna held the weapon that had killed Cassius. Her hands shook. The weapon's muzzle waggled uncertainly, but threatened.

"Pollyanna, dear, put it down. I won't hurt you. I don't want to. Promise. This's between them and me. You're not part of it."

He used his silkiest voice. And he may have meant what he said. He had no real reason to harm her. Not then.

"Stand still," she said as he started toward her, hand reaching for the weapon. She was terrified. This was the moment for which she had been living. This was the instant for which she had put herself through a personal hell. "I *am* part of it. I owe you, August Plainfield."

Dee's whole face seemed to pucker with consternation.

"You don't even remember, do you? You bloody, cold-hearted snake. You don't even remember the name you used when you murdered my father."

"What on earth are you talking about, child? I've never murdered anyone."

"Liar! You damned liar. I saw you, Mr. August Plainfield of Stimpson-Hrabosky News. I was there. You gave him drugs and made him tell you about the Shadowline, and then you murdered him."

Dee went pale. "The little girl at the hospital."

"Yes. The little girl. And now it's your turn."

Dee attacked, diving first to one side, then bearing in.

Had he remained where he was, waiting, Pollyanna might never have pulled the trigger. In the crux, when it came time to take a life in cold blood, she was not as ready as she had thought.

Dee's sudden movement panicked her. She shot wildly, repeatedly. Her first bolt hit the control console. The second pierced Dee's leg. He pitched past her with a shriek of pain and despair. She fired again, wounding him again. Then again. And again.

Groggily, not even quite sure where he was, feeling like someone had tied an anvil to his chest, Mouse again forced himself up off the deck. He shook his head sharply, to clear the water from his eyes and get them into focus.

He saw Pollyanna pounding Dee's ragged, almost unrecognizable corpse with the butt of the spent weapon while babbling incoherencies about Frog. He dragged himself over, took the weapon away, folded her up in his arms and held her head against his chest.

"It's over now, Polly," he murmured. "It's over. It's all over. He's dead now. They're all dead but us." She cried for almost an hour, the hysteria-sobs gradually becoming the great, deep, soul-wrenching grief-sobs, and those eventually diminishing to sniffles, and finally, to nothing but the occasional whimper of an injured animal.

"You just stay here," he whispered when she finished. "I've got work to do. Then we can go away." He rose, went to the comm panel, found a frequency which worked, and resumed command of the Legion.

# FIFTY-NINE: 3032 AD

In the deep black gulf great engines throbbed. A ship more vast than many planet-bound cities began to move. Her commander ordered maximum tolerable acceleration. She had fallen months behind her sisters.

Clouds of smaller vessels gathered to her. They had finished their part in the Shadowline War. There were no more debts to pay.

The Starfisher decision-makers were saddened because the results had not been more positive. But history, like everything else, is seldom fair. The balance had been rectified, and that was enough.

The great ship fled ever farther into the deep.

# SIXTY: 3052 AD

Who am I? What am I?

I am the bastard child of the Shadowline. That jagged rift of sun-broiled stone was my third parent. Understand what happened there and you understand me. Stir that hard, infertile soil and you expose the roots of my hatreds.

The Shadowline and four men. Gneaus Julius Storm. Thaddeus Immanuel Walters. Michael Dee. Norbon w'Deeth. Stand me trial for what I am and you had better indict them too.

And that, my friend, is fact.

—Masato Igarashi Storm

# EPILOGUE
## HANGED MAN

*The Hanged Man represents sacrifice or ordeal.*
*Afterward, though, he may feel his card is really The Fool.*

# EPILOGUE: 3052 AD

"That's it?" McClennon asked. Captain McClennon now. Midshipmen Storm and McClennon crewed the winning sunjammer in that long-ago Regatta.

Captain Masato Storm, Confederation Navy (Intelligence), replied, "You asked about the Shadowline and why I hate Sangaree. I told you." The ghosts of earlier days haunted his eyes as he studied the night sky thirty degrees off galactic center. There, in a few thousand years, if anyone were around to see from this vantage point, a bright new star would bloom.

McClennon freshened his drink. "Want to finish this game before Jupp gets here?" He moved to the chess table. Their game had been deadlocked for hours.

"I suppose." Mouse kept staring at the sky. "I can't believe it, I know it happened, but I still can't believe it."

Seldom had McClennon seen Mouse so disconnected. "Cassius and Dee dying might look like the end of it to you. Because they were the last principals. But you weren't really talking about the Legion. Or the Shadowline War. You were explaining the survivors. Especially Mouse."

"Maybe. You're right. Okay. We had to round up Michael's men and defuse those bombs and get our people out of the Shadowline. We did it, with the help from Darkside Landing and The City of Night… Wait a minute. What do you mean, explaining the survivors?"

"Seemed to me you were really explaining Masato Storm."

Mouse's gaze shifted to a section of sky where a new war raged. Humankind and its allies were locked in a ferocious struggle with a nasty enemy.

"You know, my uncle really blew it. He could've gotten away if he'd kept his cool."

"How so?"

"He always had that one more trick up his sleeve. The last one surprised everybody. We never had a hint till we found out we had to storm Edgeward."

"What do you mean?" McClennon asked, just trying to keep Mouse talking. He had worked for the commission investigating the Shadowline war. He knew most of the answers. But his friend needed herding out of the depth-less morass of depression.

"That trick of Michael's. He had some minority board members in his pocket. They pulled a coup. It wasn't hard to change their minds, but Michael could've changed his face and disappeared in the confusion."

"Then the commission descended on you."

"Like vultures. Lucky for me, my father, Cassius, and Richard had heavy drag in Luna Command. They didn't hurt us too bad. The holding corporation is still in business."

"What about the girl?"

"Polly? She went back to the Modelmog. Found out she couldn't stand the Shakespeare thing anymore. Changed her name again and went into holodrama. You'd recognize her if you saw her. She's completely different now. Getting something you want bad does that, I guess."

"And the Sangaree? Deeth?"

"Who knows?" Storm left the window long enough to fix himself a drink. "Maybe he died at Helga's World. Maybe during the Fortress attack. Maybe during the chase afterward. Or maybe he got away. Sometimes I think he did."

McClennon finally selected a move. He offered a pawn trade. "Your move. Why's that?"

"The Sangaree fleet the Starfishers engaged at Stars' End. That wasn't just a Family raidfleet. A dozen Families must have gone in on the operation. Which should have meant chaos in the fleet's command structure. But they were damned near as efficient as any human fleet."

"So?"

"So Deeth had a thing about organization and discipline. And he had the willpower and stubbornness and sheer insane vendetta spirit to put a thing like that together. I'm not saying it was him the Fishers fought. I'm just saying that fleet had his feel."

"Then you think you're going around the circle again? That now it's their turn to get revenge?"

"Maybe. There's plenty of them left. If they could find a way to mate off Homeworld…"

"They've always had that, Mouse. Your move." Mouse accepted the pawn trade. "Your uncle Michael was conceived on Prefactlas. And he was no mule. They just need to overcome their prejudices."

Mouse dropped his drink. "Breeding slaves. Why didn't I think of that? I wonder if Beckhart knows?"

"He knows everything. That's his job. Drop him a reminder anyway, if it'll make you feel better."

Mouse snickered wickedly. "For a minute I thought I was unemployed."

"For a while I'd hoped you'd quit. What now?"

"Polly is going to be here next week. Some kind of tour. She's got our kid with her. Maybe we'll skip over to the Fortress and see my brothers."

"You said..."

"He didn't destroy it. He just killed everybody. Ben and Homer live there now. Couple of crazy old hermits. They keep the family business rolling. When's Jupp going to get here?"

"Tonight, I hope. What do you think? Should I accept that offer from Ubichi?"

"Resign? Beckhart wouldn't let you. There's a war on, you know."

"Suppose he did?"

"Then walk carefully. Luna Command is watching them. The merc forces are gone. Now they're looking for excuses to break up the company police forces."

"At least the companies are run by honest crooks, not sanctimonious bandits like Admiral Beckhart."

Mouse looked angry. He growled, "We'd better let the game slide. Call me if Jupp turns up." He stalked out of the room.

McClennon turned to stare at the night sky. Mouse conspired in the destruction of an entire Sangaree star system? That was a lot of revenge.

*Norbon w'Deeth, are you out there somewhere? Are you polishing your guns, getting ready to come to town? Will the cycle continue round, and never mind the greater, more desperate struggle down toward the galactic core?*

"Hate is the worst poison," McClennon muttered. "Mouse, your father was right when he told you to go back to Academy. You should have listened."

# STARFISHERS

# ONE: 3048 AD

## Operation Dragon, Carson's

In that frenetic, quick-shift, go, drop-your-friends-possessions-roots-loyalties like throw-away containers age, heroes, legends, archetypal figures, and values as well, were disposable. They were as brilliant and ephemeral as the butterflies of Old Earth. One day someone on the marches of science might burst the pale and wrest from Nature a golden, universe-rocking secret. A bold naval officer might shatter the moment's enemy. Either could be a hero, a legend for a fleeting hour. And then he would become one with the dust of Sumer and Akkad.

Who remembered on the seventh day?

Who remembered Jupp von Drachau's raid in the Hell Stars? Mention his name. Blank stares would turn your way. Or someone would say, assuming memory, "He's too old," meaning too long gone. Von Drachau had been relegated to the historical toy box with the Caesars, Bonapartes, and Hitlers. Half a year, Confederation standard, had passed. The Now People had abandoned him. The yesterday people, the Archaicists, would not pick him up for a hundred years.

Luckily, benRabi thought, Jupp did not need the adulation.

The Now People, the down-planet people, who rode the screaming rockets of technological and social change, bought their values plastic-packed, to be disposed when their usefulness was done. BenRabi found no satisfaction in that. He could hold on to nothing long enough to wear the rough edges off, to make it comfortable with time, like an old couch after years of use.

He thought those things as, toolcase in hand, he wandered toward the gate of Carson's Blake City spaceport. The name he wore felt a size too small, yet it could become a burden heavier than the cross the Christian god had borne.

He was going to hate this. He loathed pipes and plumbing.

He wore a union-prescribed commercial spacer Liquids Transfer Systems Technician's uniform. It consisted of tight, dull grey coveralls with green and yellow piping.

His sleeves boasted three red hashmarks where Servicemen wore chevrons. They indicated that his union rated him a Master.

He did have the training, though his acquisition of it lay nearly forgotten amid that of countless exotic skills.

His teaching-couch days seemed part of another age. Still in his thirties, he felt the weight of a thousand years. Lifetimes worth of knowledge had been pressure-injected into his skull. And the education would never end.

The Bureau was his surrogate mother, father, and wife. It insisted he be ready for anything. Just in case.

The Bureau was a family without love. It left him with dissatisfactions that could easily grow into hatreds. The things they did to him…

They never justified. They never explained.

But lately he had been dissatisfied with everything. The image of the gun had become merciless. He had developed a crying socket of soul-need into which nothing seemed to fit.

And there were the aches and pains.

He *hurt.*

Within him he bore a second set of nerves. *They* had implanted a complete instel radio powered by bio-electricity. A small, dying pain surrounded a knot behind his left ear. That was the largest lump of the radio.

He had other pains. His ulcer. A little finger he had bruised playing handball. A hint of the headache that had been with him most of his life.

Each slow step drove spikes of agony up the bones of his legs. They had been lengthened six centimeters, hastily. His arm bones felt no better. The skin on his stomach itched where they had trimmed off twenty pounds.

His fingers, toes, and eyes itched too. His fingerprints, toeprints, and retinal patterns had been too quickly changed.

Carson's was as back of beyond a world as he had ever seen.

The damned ulcer… The fast-push to Carson's had reawakened it. It was a hurry-up job from the go.

But, then, they all were. How long had it been since he had had time to catch his breath, to relax, play with his collections, or just loaf around that house he owned, unshared, on the quiet government retirement planet called Refuge? Or to tinker with his literary opus, *All Who Were Before Me in Jerusalem*?

There was no time to loaf. Nor to plan operations in advance. In a rush of maddening changes, civilization seemed to be hurtling toward an apocalyptic crisis. Nothing was permanent. There were no fixed points on which to anchor.

Moyshe benRabi's life had become like the flash floods of Sierran rivers in Thaw Time, roaring and cascading past too swiftly, too liquidly, for any part to be seized and intimately known.

But wait! In the river of life apassing there *were* a few solid rocks. They were the long-lived legends lying heavy on his mind. Like the boulders in the turbulence, they had endured a forever compared to anything else of his age.

Something was missing: fixtures, solids, foundations for his life. There had to be something for him, something real... *I want,* he cried to the corners of his soul. And here came the image of the gun, that sprang to mind at the oddest time. Bow, howitzer, rifle, pistol, whatever, always unmanned, usually in profile and firing. What did it mean? A goal? Some sexual symbol? An expression of his sometime want for heroism? A sign of a secret urge to kill?

Memories returned, of the day he had entered Academy. He had been nervous and polished and proud to be part of Navy, proud to be one of the rare Old Earth appointees, and scared they would hold that against him. A bee of uncertainty had buzzed his butter soul even then. He had taken his oath with private reservations. He had devoted a quarter of his short life to winning the appointment, and success had left him with the feeling that something was missing. But Navy had seemed to promise what his *want* demanded.

The Academy years had not been bad. Hard work, hard play, not much time for introspection. But the first few months of line service had brought the hurt back stronger than ever. Casting about desperately, he had put in for intelligence training without understanding his own motivation. He had told his wardroom acquaintances that he wanted more adventure.

Even then his words had rung false. There was adventure enough in the line hunting Sangaree and McGraws.

All of which had come to a head in the now, with Moyshe benRabi, a flying knight, being sent to find a dragon hiding behind the eyes of the night.

Ahead, he spotted his small, brown, Oriental, Manchu-mustached partner, Mouse. Making no sign, he entered the gate behind the man.

He slowed momentarily, staring across the field. The lighter from the raggedy-assed Freehauler that had brought them in from Blackworld was still on the ground. It should have lifted last night. They had caught the Freehauler at the end of a fast-shuffle through a procession of ships designed to cover their backtrail.

Mouse saw it too. Nothing escaped Mouse's little devil eyes. He shrugged, lengthened his stride so benRabi would not overtake him.

They were not supposed to be acquainted this time. That left Moyshe without any anchor at all. He did not need lots of people, but he felt desolate when he had no one.

He daydreamed about Stars' End and the High Seiners, the unchanging boulders that had ghosted across his mind before he had become distracted by his own past.

Sheer mystery was Stars' End, a fortress planet beyond the galactic rim, bristling with automatic, invincible weapons that slaughtered everyone fool enough to come in range. Not one of a dozen expeditions had produced a shred of why.

In the lulls, the deep, fearful lulls when there was nothing to say and nothing being said, people seized on Stars' End as strange country to explore, in litanies meant to exorcise the dreadful silence. They were intrigued by the godlike power there. Theirs were the eyes of the godless seeking gods in a majestically powerful unknown, a technological equivalent of an Old Testament Jehovah.

Or, if Stars' End was momentarily passé, they turned to the High Seiners. The Starfishers.

The Starfishers should have been no mystery. They were human. Stars' End was just a dead metal machine voice babbling insanities in non-human tongues, the toy of gun-toting pyramid builders so long gone no extant race remembered them. But, because of their humanness, the Seiners had become the greater, more frightening puzzle.

Landsmen did not comprehend the quiet, fixed culture of the Starfishers at all. They yearned for the Starfishers' obvious peace, yet hated them for their blissful stasis. The Seiner trail was a perilous one, wending tortuously among yin-yang pitfalls of envy and jealousy.

His thoughtful mood departed. Work came first. He had to be alert. Lives could hinge on his slightest misstep, and the life at the head of the list was his own.

He entered the Blake Port terminal. It was a massive plastic, glass, and steel cavern. Its vast floor was a crossroads of color and movements, its entrances and exits the mouths of tunnels opening on other worlds.

Moyshe had wanted to be a poet once, a spacefaring Homer like Czyzewski. A child's dream, that had been. Like the one about having secret powers if only he could find their handle.

An instructor had made him read Czyzewski critically, then had forced him to examine his own secret images of space and night and the womb. That had been a broomstick fly. Strictly from hunger. The backs of beyond in the shadowy reaches of his mind were lands of corruption and horror he would never journey again. His muse had abandoned him for brighter skies. Now he played with prose, *All Who Were Before Me in Jerusalem.*

This mission should give him time to polish it.

Light surrounded him. Human scent hung heavy around him. People rushed hither and thither like swarming bees who had lost track of their queen. Their effluvia was too much for the air fresheners. It was the same in every terminal he had ever visited.

The citizens were there in their multitudes, dancing atoms pursuing the rituals of terminals. The costumes of a dozen worlds mixed in a kaleidoscopic choreography.

A small, subdued crowd occupied one backwater of the waiting room floor. A long table had been set up there. Behind it a half-dozen men in off-white, undecorated jumpsuits fiddled with forms and questionnaires. A girl at table's end, armed with an arsenal of secretarial gizmos, reduced the forms for microstorage. She was pale, had blondish hair that hung to her shoulders. He noticed her because her hair was unusually long for a spacegoer.

The men, though, conformed to the spacer stereotype. Their hair was cropped to a centimeter's length. "Like induction day at boot camp," Moyshe muttered.

These people would be his new employers. The ones he had been sent to betray.

Mouse passed, small and brown, with a wink. Why he had that name benRabi did not know. He had carried it for years, and seemed to like it, though for lookalikes *Weasel* would have done better.

*A weird one, my partner,* benRabi thought. *But we get along. Because of commensality of obsession. In some areas.*

Mouse was a mad collector too: postage stamps from the days when they had been used, coins, bottles, mugs, wrought-iron, almost anything old. But the ends they were after varied.

BenRabi collected for escape, for relaxation, as a means of learning. Mouse had gone mad Archaicist during his recent stay in Luna Command. His collecting had become a means of slipping into the gestalt of departed life styles. He had fallen in love with the twentieth century, the last with a real spectrum of class, ethnic, and cultural differentiations.

BenRabi did not comprehend Archaicists at all. His opinion of them was, to use Mouse's words, lower than a snake's butt.

The old distinctions had changed. Race, sex, wealth, style, and manner of speech no longer set a person apart. Prejudices pivoted round origins and profession, with Old Earthers the niggers of the age, and Service personnel the aristocracy.

BenRabi, under his other names, had known Mouse a long time. But he just did not know the man. Professional acquaintance and even a budding friendship had done nothing to break down Mouse's defenses. BenRabi was Old Earther. Mouse was Outworlds and third generation Service. That was a barrier across which little could trickle.

BenRabi studied other faces, saw bewilderment, determination, malaise. A lot of these people were not sure why they were here. But he was looking for the nonchalant ones, the ones who did know. They would be the competition and beekies.

The Bureau was far from unique in its interest in Starfish. Half these people, probably, were spies… "Uhn!"

"Excuse me, please?"

He turned. A small blue nun had paused beside him, startled by his grunt. "Pardon, Sister. Just thinking out loud."

The Ulantonid woman wobbled off wearing a perplexed frown, perhaps wondering what sort of mind thought in dull monosyllables. BenRabi frowned himself. What had become of the human need for faith? The Christians he encountered were almost always conquered aliens.

His curiosity faded. He returned to that disturbing face.

Yes, it was Marya, though she had changed as much as he. Her hair, skin, and eyes had all been darkened. She had put on twenty pounds. There were other changes, too.

They were subtler, but did not prevent his recognizing her. She had not disguised her ways of moving, speaking, listening.

She never was much of an actress, he reflected.

She did have a talent essential to their profession. She survived despite the odds.

She noticed him looking. Her eyebrows rose a millimeter, then puckered in consternation. Then she smiled a wicked iron smile. She had recognized him, too.

How big a demotion had she earned for failing on The Broken Wings? How much had it cost, beyond the cruel, slow deaths of her children?…

Frost mites danced between his shoulder blades. She would be doing score-evening calculations already.

She nodded ever so slightly, politely.

It was a vast universe. There was no way he should have run into her again, ever. He was too stunned for rational thought.

Nothing could have shaken him more than her presence.

He did not fear her. Not in a cold sweat way. She would see Mouse. She would know she had to let be, or die, or make damned sure she got them both with the same hit.

Several other faces teased his memory. Trace recognitions trickled back from his studies of Bureau files. None of them were outright enemies. They were competitors, beekies from the Corporations. Or possibly McGraws.

He tried to view the crowd as an organism, to judge its composition and temper. It was smaller than he had expected. Not more than two hundred. The Seiners had advertised for a thousand, offering bonuses and pay scales that approached the outrageous.

They would be disappointed.

He supposed there weren't many techs romantic enough, or hungry enough, to plunge into an alien society for a year. That might mean returning to a home changed beyond recognition. After the lighters lifted there would be no turning back. No one would be able to quit because he did not like his job.

Moyshe shuffled into the check-in line four places behind his partner. Mouse was shaking.

Moyshe never ceased to be amazed. Glacial. Glassteel. Conscienceless. Stonedeath. He had thought Mouse many cold, hard things. Yet there were unpredictable moments when the man let slip the humanity behind the facade of adamant. BenRabi watched as if witnessing a miracle.

This might be the only time during the operation that Mouse would let the hardness fall. And that only because he was poised on the brink of a shuttle fly.

Liftoffs terrified him.

"Dr. Niven." A whisper. Warmth caressed benRabi's arm. He looked down into eyes as hard and dark as Sangaree gunmetal coins.

"Pardon, ma'am?" He put on his disarming smile. "Name's benRabi. Moyshe benRabi."

"How quaint." She smiled a gunmetal smile. "Candy, even."

She must be more widely read than he had suspected.

Moyshe benRabi was the protagonist of Czyzewski's sole and almost unknown trial of the novel, a cartoon caricature painted in broad strokes of Gargantua and Don Quixote. The critics had said too much so, stopping only on the edge of accusations of plagiarism.

Strange that a Sangaree should be familiar with *His Banners Bright and Golden*...

Sangaree. He had to remind himself. He had shared her bed. There had been feeling in it during those hungry days on The Broken Wings.

She might willingly share beds again, but...

In the end she would drink his blood. Sangaree nursed their hatreds forever. For generations, if rumor was true.

"And the Rat, too, eh?" Meaning Mouse. She would have a special hell set aside for him. But the feeling was mutual. BenRabi knew Mouse would plain love a date with her in a medieval torture chamber. "All you Confies and beekies and McGraws pretending you need Seiner money... Orbit in an hour, Gun. See you upstairs."

More gunmetal smiles as she took her gunmetal-hard body toward the Ladies.

She would see him upstairs.

No doubt. He wondered if he could conjure up a Mark XIV Combat Suit real quick. Or spider's eyes so he could watch his back. This mission was going to be Roman candle all the way.

And he had hoped for a vacation operation. For nothing to do but loaf and work on *Jerusalem.*

# TWO: 3047 AD

## The Olden Days, Angel City

A whisper swifted on lightning feet through Angel City's underworld. It said the Starduster was on The Broken Wings.

A private yacht had slipped into Angel Port after making a surreptitious worldfall. It was registered to a Dr. Gundaker Niven. The cognoscenti in the outfit remembered that name in connection with a blow-up on Borroway that had set the Sangaree back a billion stellars.

Port workers with connections started the excitement. The bounty on Gundaker Niven was immense. The Sangaree would not sit still for a billion-stellar burn from God Himself.

The dock workers passed the word that the *Lady of Merit* boasted just two passengers. One was Caucasian, the other a small Oriental.

That got their attention downtown. Niven had something to do with the Starduster. He might even be the Starduster under an alias. And the Starduster's number-one man was an Oriental, one John Li Piao.

These men, though, looked like Old Earth shooters, not the masters of a shadow empire rivaling that managed by the Sangaree.

Nevertheless, heads nodded in the board rooms of crime. Orders went out to the soldiers.

The Starduster was a unique creature. He was a man in limbo. A crime czar who had built a kingdom independent of the established syndicates. He preyed on his own kind rather than pay a single credit for Sangaree-produced stardust.

His was the most feared name on the Sangaree hate list.

Sentences of death had been pronounced on a dozen worlds. Open, often redundant contracts approaching a hundred million stellars existed.

Time and success had made of him an almost mythic devil.

He had been claimed killed a half dozen times. But he kept coming back, like a thing undead, like a dying wizard's curse. Hardly would the jubilation end before his invisible hand would again strike swiftly and viciously, ripping the guts from another syndicate pipeline of profit.

Was there more than one Starduster?

The Sangaree Heads, to whom most organized crime could be traced, sometimes suspected that he was not a man at all, but a role. Perhaps Piao was the real Starduster. The handful of men who had been pinned with the Starduster name were as diverse a group as could be selected from a good-sized crowd. Short, tall, thin, fat, white, black.

The Sangaree family dictators knew only one thing for certain. The Starduster was human. Sangaree might be contentious, piratical, greedy, and short on conscience, but only a human who hated would slash at them as bloodily as the Starduster did.

Even his motives were obscure. The narcotic he stole did not always find its way back into trade channels. Greed had no obvious hold on him.

The yachtsmen rented a groundcar and vanished into Angel City's warehouse district. Gundaker Niven was a chunky man of medium height. He had hard, dark eyes of the sort that intimidated civilians. He had thick, heavy hands. He jabbed with forefingers for emphasis whenever he spoke. A wide scar poured from his right ear down over his cheekbone to the corner of his mouth.

"Take it out with a kilo of D-14," he growled, punching a finger at a dilapidated warehouse. His words came out slurred. The right side of his mouth did not move. "Burn them and run."

His driver was a small man with Fu Manchu mustaches. He had the same cold eyes. "But this ain't no shatter run. All that would do is show us how good they die."

"Working for Beckhart is getting a meter too tall for me, Mouse. This underworld stuff isn't my specialty. It's too rough. Too complicated. Suppose the real Starduster has people here?"

The smaller man laughed. “He does. You can count on it.”

“Oh, Christ!”

“Hey! Working for the Old Man is an honor. When he asks for you, it means you’ve made it. Didn’t you get sick of that military attaché dodge?”

“No. I was drafted into this.”

“Come on! Engineering coups in the outbacks. How dull can you get? There’s no rise to give it spice. When things go broomstick you go hide in the embassy.”

“You think it’s all champagne and ballroom conspiracy? I got my spleen burned out on Shakedowns. Inside the embassy.”

“Still ain’t the same. Yeah. The Starduster has people here. But by the time the word floats up and the shit comes down we’ll be long gone.”

“That’s what you told me on Gorki. And New Earth was supposed to be a piece of cake.”

This was their third mission teamed. Admiral Beckhart’s specialized, secretive division of the Bureau of Naval Intelligence had found that they complemented one another well.

“So you should be used to it.”

“Maybe. Gundaker Niven. What the hell kind of name is that?”

“You take what they give you. This ain’t the diplomatic service. You’re in the big time now.”

“You keep telling me. But they don’t job you. You stay Mouse every go. They never crank you through the Medical mill. They don’t have the Psychs scramble your brain.”

“They don’t need to. I’m not the front man. I’m just around to drag your ass out of the fire when it gets hot.”

“I don’t like the feel of this one, Mouse. Something’s wrong. There’s going to be trouble.”

“Man is born to trouble as the sparks fly upward.”

“Holy shit! I’m looking for toilet paper and he throws the Bible at me. It’s sour, Mouse.”

“Because we got no backup? Hang tight, Doc. We don’t need it. The Sangaree outfit here wouldn’t make a pimple on the ass of a Family like the Norbon. They’ve only got five or six people on the whole damned planet. They get the work done with local talent.”

“Stickers can burn you just as dead as any Homeworld shooter. Beyond-the-resurrection. What’s out here, anyway?”

“Got to go with you there, Doc. Not a million people on this rat hole. Three lousy domes, and enough swamp to supply the rest of Confederation.”

“It even stinks in here.”

“It’s in your head. Going to circle the block.”

They idled on, learning the warehouse district’s tight, twisty out-of-the-ways first hand. Street maps and eidetic holo-memories had been given them, but only exploration made a place real. Every city had its feel, its color, its smell, its *style.* Psych's familiarization tapes could not capture the intangibles of reality.

Knowledge and preparation were the corner- and keystones of their trade.

"I need a bath," Niven complained. "I can smell swamp muck on me."

"Let's head back to the Marcos. My stomach's okay now. I'm hungry. And a game or two would get me back in the groove. Tomorrow's soon enough to take the case."

The Marcos was The Broken Wings' best hotel, and one of the best in The Arm. And that despite the limits imposed by the space and conservation regulations of a dome city.

Dome cities are planet-bound space vessels. Which translates as uncomfortable.

The lobby of the Marcos had been decorator-engineered to provide an illusion of openness. The wall facing the entrance was masked by a curving hologramic panorama from another world.

Mouse froze.

"What's the matter?"

The smaller man stared straight ahead. He did not reply.

"The Thunder Mountains seen from Edgeward City on Blackworld," Niven murmured, recognizing the scene.

It was a stark view, of black mountains limned by the raging star winds of a pre-nova sun. Blackworld was one of the least hospitable and most dramatically beautiful of the outworlds.

"Just surprised me, Doc." Mouse glanced around the lobby. "It was the Cathedral Forest on Tregorgarth when we checked in."

People stared. The two gave the impression of being invaders instead of guests. Their appearance labeled them hardcases barely able to get by on their wits. Men of that breed belonged in the warehouse district, not at the watering hole of the genteel.

The watery-eyed bellhop, who watched them stroll through the hologram to the elevators, did not belong either. He limped when he walked, but he was too solid, too *macho,* to be staff. His uniform was a size too small. His stance was a centimeter too assertive.

"Something's gone broomstick," Mouse said. The elevator doors closed with startling severity, as though issuing a declaration of war.

Meticulous preliminary research characterized a Beckhart operation. They had seen holos of, and reports on, all regular hotel staff.

"I saw him. What do we do?"

"Cut out a floor short."

Why not just get the hell out? Niven wondered.

"We'll take the stairs. We'll catch them from behind."

"You're taking a lot for granted."

"Anything to save a kick in the teeth."

Their floor was the fifth. The penthouse level. It contained four suites. Only theirs was occupied.

"The empty car will tip them," Niven remarked after Mouse had punched Four.

"Yeah. You're right."

"So?"

"Tell you what. Let's slide down and see if we can snatch the gimp. Shoot him with Nobullshit and see what he's got to say."

That was pure Mouse thinking, Niven reflected. Running was an alien concept.

They were both in Old Earther role. Holonet stereotype Old Earther role. But they had not received a full Psych-brief. Their speech patterns tended to meander between that appropriate to the role and that of Academy graduates. Their mission-prep had included only a limited Psych-brief. They remembered who they were. They had to think to maintain consistent images.

"We're getting sloppy," Niven observed. "Let's tighten up."

The elevator stopped on Three. They exchanged glances.

"Better stand back, Doc."

Mouse's eyes and face blanked. A subtle air of crouch, of tenseness enveloped him. He seemed to have gone to another world.

He had entered "assassin's mind." Which meant that he had become a biochemical killing robot.

Mouse was a physical combat specialist.

A dowdy, blubbery woman with two poodles and a make-believe fortune in cultured firestones waddled aboard. "Five, please." And, before Niven caught the wrong note, "You're new. Offworlders?"

Niven responded with an affirmative grunt. He had to think of some way to distract the woman while Mouse relaxed.

"How marvelous. Let me guess. One of the Inner Worlds?"

Niven grunted again. He stared at the door, hoping rudeness would be distraction enough. He took Mouse's arm gently as the door opened on Four.

"Stay where you are!"

A tiny needlegun peeped from a fat hand. The woman sloughed the dowager character. Suddenly she was as hard-edged as they.

"Move together." The doors closed. "Thank you."

Niven looked beyond costume and props and saw the enemy.

She was the Sangaree Resident for The Broken Wings, Sexon S'Plez.

*Christ, you're slow,* he told himself. *The fat alone should've warned you.*

Plez was suspected of being a proctor of the Sexon, which was one of the First Families of the Sangaree. That would make her the equal of a Planetary Senator…

The assignment of a heavy-duty Resident to a backwater world was what had stimulated Luna Command into sending in its shock troops.

How had she gotten onto them so fast? Niven wondered.

Two nervous heavies in ill-fitting hotel livery awaited the car on floor Five. They were a tall, pale, ginger-haired pair who had to be brothers.

"Which one's Niven?" the older asked.

"Out." The woman gestured with her weapon.

Wavering guns peered from all the brothers' four hands.

*Careful,* Niven thought. He raised his hands slowly. These men were amateurs. They might start panic-shooting.

"Chunky's Niven. The gook must be Piao."

The Starduster's associates were as shadowy as he, but one of the few names known was John Li Piao, reputed number-two man and chief bone-breaker. The face of the man who wore that name, though, was as much an enigma as the Starduster's.

"I don't want you should get upset," Niven said, trying to project terrified and outraged innocence, and having no trouble with the fear, "but I think you've got the wrong..."

"Stuff it, animal!" the woman snarled.

*The Old Earth cant is catching,* Niven thought.

The brothers' eyes narrowed. Their lips tightened. The insult included them. Animal was the Sangaree's ultimate racial slur.

Niven put on a bewildered face. "What's going on, anyway? I'm just a social researcher. Studying the effects of dome constriction..."

The brothers laughed tightly. One said, "Crap."

Mouse had gotten caught in the limbo between normalcy and assassin's mind. The state was one of semi-consciousness. It would take him time to push himself one way or the other. Niven knew which way Mouse would go. His stomach knotted.

"... to study the effects of dome constriction on immigrant workers." Mouse needed a distraction. "For Ubichi Corporation. This man is my secretary. We're not carrying any cash." That was the course, he thought. Protesting innocence of a connection with the trade would cause laughter. Protesting being robbed might make them hesitate the instant Mouse needed.

He did not feel that Mouse was doing the right thing. But Mouse did not know how to back down. He was a hitter. It would get him killed someday.

It might get them both killed, but he could not change Mouse's ways.

The older gunman wavered. "The yacht was a Ubichi charter."

"Cover..." the woman began. Too late.

Mouse exploded.

Flying, with a scream that froze them an additional second.

A fist disarmed the woman. Her weapon dribbled into the elevator. One foot, then the other, pistoned into the older brother's face. He triggered. Needles stitched the wall over Niven's head.

The younger brother managed only a half turn. Mouse bounced into him. He chopped weapons away with his left hand. His right went for the man's throat.

A gurgling scream ripped through a shattered windpipe.

Knowing what would happen did not help Niven. Mouse was *fast.*

The woman was running before Niven recovered her weapon. He crouched, trying to aim.

He was too sick to hold his target.

She had kneed him savagely. The agony numbed his mind.

He hit the button for One, left the brothers to Mouse. Maybe he could get her in the lobby…

Reason returned before the doors opened.

There was nothing he could do. Not in front of fifty witnesses. Aching, helpless, he watched the fat woman collect her limping accomplice and depart.

He began shaking. It had been close. Too damned close.

Mouse was human again when Niven reached Five. He was shaking too. "Get her?"

"In the lobby? With fifty witnesses?"

"From the elevator. They couldn't see you through the holo."

"Oh." That had escaped him. "What about those guys?"

"Got to do something with them."

"Hell, turn them loose. Won't make any difference…" He took another look. His sickness returned, centered higher. "Did you have to?…"

Defiantly. "Yeah."

Mouse was driven by a murderous hatred of everything Sangaree. It splashed over on anyone who cooperated with them.

He refused to explain.

"Better get them out of the hall. Staff might come through." He grabbed a leg, started dragging.

Mouse dabbed at bloodstains.

"The outfit won't like this," Niven said as he hauled the second corpse into the suite. "Number's going to be on us now."

"So? We've been on the bull's eye before. Anyway, we bought some time. They'll want to salvage the fat broad before they move. And they'll bring in somebody new. They're careful that way. We'll hustle them meanwhile."

"How? The number's on. Who'll talk? Anybody who knows anything is going to know that we're dead."

"You ain't dead till they close the box."

"Mouse, I don't feel right about this one."

"Doc, you worry too much. Let it stew. We keep our heads in and our backs to the wall, maybe a little something will blow our way. Just be on your toes. Like they said in the olden days, when you get handed a lemon, make lemonade."

"I don't think the hardcase course took," Niven said. "You're right, I mean. I shouldn't be so worried."

"Know what your problem is? You ain't happy unless you've got something to worry about. You're spookier than an old maid with seven cats."

## THREE: 3048 AD

### Operation Dragon, Blake City Starport

The terminal's sounds crowded benRabi. The smells and swirling colors dazzled him. The nervousness started.

It always did at the mouth of the lion's den. Or, this time, the dragon's lair. The briefing tapes had claimed that starfish, seen in space, resembled dragons two hundred kilometers long.

He shuffled forward with the line, finally reached the table. One of the Seiner men asked a few questions. He replied numbly.

"Sign and thumbprint this please, Mr. benRabi. Give it to the lady with the rest of your paperwork."

Shaking, he completed his contract. The Seiner girl at table's end smiled as she shoved his papers into the maw of her reducing machine. She said, "Just through that door and take a seat, please. The shuttle will be ready shortly."

He went, bemused. That pale Seiner girl, with her pale hair and harsh cheekbones, reminded him of Alyce, his Academy love. That was not good. More than a decade had passed, and still the pain could penetrate his armor.

Was that why he had trouble with women? Every affair since had, inevitably, fallen into emotional chaos. Each had become a duel with swords of intentional hurt.

But there had been no prior affairs to stand comparison. Maybe he was just consistent in picking unstable women.

He took a chair in the waiting room. Out came the tattered notebook, a traveling companion of many years. This time, he swore, he would finish *Jerusalem*.

> *The unbreakable fetters which bound down the Great Wolf Fenrir had been cunningly forged by Loki from these: The footfall of a cat, the roots of a rock, the beard of a woman, the breath of a fish, the spittle of a bird.*
>
> —*The Prose Edda*

Yes, the more he thought about it, the more he was sure that was the best possible opening quote. It had an indisputable universality.

Every life had its Loki capable of binding it with chains as tenuous but strong.

Those wormwood memories of Academy returned. They were indestructible memorabilia of an affair with a fellow midshipman who had been the daughter of the Vice Commandant and the granddaughter of the Chief of Staff Navy.

He had been an idiot. A pig-iron, chocolate-plated fool. How had he made it through? In the context of Alyce, he still thought his survival a miracle.

And the cost? What if he had not, as ordered, dropped the affair? What if he had persisted? She had demanded that he do so, defying what to him had been terrifying concentrations of authority.

To her those people had been family. Mother and grandfather. To him they had appeared as behemoths of power.

And the night beast with guilt-fangs longer than any of his other haunts: What of the child?

*Come on*, he grumbled at himself. *What is this? Let's ditch the memories and romantic nonsense.* He was a grown man. He should get back into *Jerusalem*; that would be a blow against the dread empire of his soul.

One of his favorites, from Pope's *Dunciad*:

*Lo! thy dread empire, Chaos, is restored;*

*Light dies before thy uncreating word…*

"Ladies and gentlemen."

He looked up. What now? Ah. A last-chance-to-get-out briefing.

It was conducted by an officer with a voice so infuriatingly scratchy that it had to be technically augmented. "We don't want you on our ship. You're not our kind of people," the officer said for openers.

"Why're you here? What are your motives?"

*Good questions*, benRabi thought.

"Two reasons. You're either bemused by the Seiner myth, which is a holonet fabrication, or you're here spying. I'll let you in on the secret now. This isn't going to be any romantic adventure. And you're not going to get at any information. All we're going to give you is a lot of hard work inside a culture unlike any you've ever known. We're not going to ease you into our world. We're not going to coddle you. We don't have the time."

The man was deliberately trying to upset them. Moyshe wondered why.

"We've assembled you for one reason. It's the only way we can meet next year's harvest quotas."

BenRabi had a sudden feeling. A premonition, he thought. The man had more than harvests on his mind. Some worry, or fear, was racketing around his brain. Something terrible and big had him half spooked.

Admiral Beckhart liked using benRabi because he had these intuitions.

Moyshe also sensed a ghost of disappointment in the speaker, along with a taint of distaste for landsmen. He spoke as if tasting the sour flavor of betrayal.

It was inarguable that these Seiners were desperate. They would never have sought outside technicians otherwise.

BenRabi quelled a surge of compassion.

The speaker's home was a harvestship somewhere out in the Big Dark. To survive it needed a massive input of competent technicians. The man was sour because of all of Confederation's billions, only two hundred people had come forward. And most of those could be considered suspect.

The Seiner fumbled in the pockets of his antiquated tweed jacket. BenRabi wondered if the man was an Archaicist. His preconceptions of the Seiners did not include the possibility that they were faddists too.

The man produced a curious little instrument. He thrust it between his teeth. He gripped it with his right thumb and forefinger, puffing while he held a small flame over its bowl. Only after he had begun expelling noxious clouds did benRabi realize what was happening.

"A pipe!" he muttered. "What the hell?" Tobacco stench assailed his nostrils. "I can't believe this much bad taste." He shuddered.

His reaction was not unique. His companions buzzed. A woman rose and started to leave, then gagged and returned to her seat. Even Mouse looked appalled.

How many of these crude horrors lay in ambush ahead? This was carrying Archaicism to the point of boorishness.

Much as the pipe disgusted him, benRabi applauded the psychology behind its appearance. The man was easing them in after all. The impact of later cultural shocks would be blunted a little.

"As I said," the Seiner continued, once his pause had his audience squirming, "there're spies here. Spy is a nasty word, I know. And spying is a nasty business. But a realist recognizes the existence of espionage, and we're all realists here. Aren't we? Espionage is all around us today. We're drenched in it. Up to our heinies in it. Because almost anybody with any power at all will do almost anything to get control of a starfish herd."

He assayed a little smile. It mocked them all. He was doing a show, putting on the pompous ass to prod somebody into reacting. BenRabi sensed a quiet, self-assured competence behind the showmanship. In fact, there was something about the man that screamed *Security Officer*.

"You spies won't learn a thing. Till your contracts terminate you'll see nothing but the guts of a ship. Even then you'll see only what we want you to see, when we want you to see it. Everybody. Hear this. Security rules will be observed at all times. That's the Eleventh Commandment. Engrave it on your souls—if you have any. Even a slight irregularity might spook us into hasty reaction. Since we're not sure what information the spy-masters would consider valuable, we're going to do our damnedest not to give away anything at all."

BenRabi grimaced. Was the fool trying to impress them with Seiner paranoia and xenophobia? He could rave for a week and not intimidate the professionals.

"I reiterate: outside agents simply won't be given a chance to contact anybody who might possess critical information. There'll be penalties for trying to reach such people. Am I making myself clear?"

Someone made a snide remark.

The speaker responded, "You've got to realize that we consider ourselves a nation unto ourselves. We're not Confederation. We don't want to be Confederation. We don't give a damn about Confederation. All we ever asked from it was to be left alone. Which is what we ask of any gang of strongmen. Archaicism is our way of life, not just a crackpot hobby. Just for example, we still execute people once in a while."

That blockbuster fell into an ocean of silence.

BenRabi wondered how many times Confederation had tried coaxing these strange, fiercely independent people into the government fold. Dozens, at least. Luna Command was persistent. It was a long-toothed hound that did not turn loose of a bone.

And for a century and a half the Starfishers had managed to evade Luna Command's "protection," mostly by remaining so damned hard to find, but also by making it clear they were willing to fight.

Luna Command had never given up. It never would. Even these people had to recognize that, benRabi thought. They had to recognize the government's stake.

Nervousness pervaded the waiting room, fogging in like some unexpectedly conjured demon. The briefing officer met pairs of eyes one by one. The romantic flinched before his stare. They were finding their legend had teeth and claws.

No one executed people anymore. Even the barbarians beyond Confederation's pale recycled their human garbage, if only through cyborg computation systems.

The civilians were learning what people in benRabi's trade learned early. Adventures were more fun when it was somebody else getting the excelsior ripped out of his crate.

"In view of what I've said, and knowing that your futures may not be exactly what you anticipated when you applied," the man said, "anybody who wants to do so can opt out now. We'll cover expenses as advertised."

BenRabi smiled at his lap. "Thought that's where you were headed," he whispered. "Trying to spook the weaklings, eh?"

There was a stir in response, but no one volunteered to go home. The weaklings seemed scared that they would look foolish. The Starfisher shrugged, collected his notes, and said, "All right. I'll see you all upstairs." He left the room.

Time to sit, to wait for the shuttle; benRabi returned to his notebook and *Jerusalem.*

He was having trouble with the story. His mind seemed to be too ordered and mundane to produce the chaotic, nonobjective symbolism of a McGuhan or Potty Welkin. His maliciously intentional obscurantisms refused to remain obscure. That could have been because he knew what he wanted to say.

Maybe he should do the story as straight narrative, Moyshe thought. He could strive for what the Archaicist reviewers called "a refreshingly anachronistic flavor." It might then survive the Archaicist marketplace, where the unsophisticated arts of the past still had appeal.

*Ykadabar Station is six months long and two years wide, fifteen minutes high and a quarter of nine forever; there are songs in its skies and trumpets in its walls. The Roads have neared their ends:...*

Was he wrong? Was he alone in his feeling that all people were exiles in time? No matter. What could he do about it? Not a damned thing. That was the passion that should drive the story. Raging impotence.

People began moving excitedly. The volume of conversation picked up. BenRabi dragged himself back to reality. He muttered, "Shuttle must be ready."

Yes. His companions had begun filing onto the field already. These Seiners were frugal. They had not bothered to lease an attached landing bay.

The air outside was cool and on the move. A raindrop touched his cheek, trickled like a tear. A ragged guerilla band of clouds hurried over, firing off a few scattered water-bullets that made little mud balls in the dust lying thick on the tarmac. An omen? Rainy weather at Blake City was almost a nevertime thing. Water was too scarce in this part of Carson's.

He laughed nervously. Omens! What was the matter with him? "Into the shuttle, caveman," he mumbled.

The ship had been an antique when his grandfather was wetting diapers. It was no commercial lighter, and never had been. Broomstick, from Century One, it was a go-powered coffin with no comforts from strictly-for-gun-power days. He saw nothing but stark functionalism and metal painted black or grey. It appeared to be Navy surplus, probably from the Ulantonid War.

The part of him that was still line officer noted that she was well maintained. Not a spot of dirt or corrosion showed anywhere. The ship had that used but kept-up look sometimes seen in rare antiques. These Seiners were lovingly careful of their equipment.

The passenger compartment was the antithesis of luxury. BenRabi had to suspend disbelief to credit it as suitable for human use. Yet the converted cargo bay did have ranks of new acceleration couches, and soothing music came from hidden speakers. It was old stuff, quiet, perhaps something by Brahms. It put a comforting gloss over the unsteady whine of the idling drives.

They would lift blind, he saw. Weedlike clumps of color-coded wiring hung where view-screens had been removed. They were taking no chances.

This seemed to be taking security a bit far. What the hell could the screens show if the Seiners kept them switched off? For that matter, what could they betray if turned on? He knew where he was. He knew where he was going, at least for the short run.

Was it some subtle psychological trick? A maneuver to accustom them to flying blind? He dithered over a choice of couches.

The knot behind his ear, containing the non-dispersible parts of the instel-tracer, seized him with iron, spiked fingers. He had been switched on by the Bureau.

Why now? he wondered, staggering with the pain. They were supposed to wait till the lighter made orbit.

The thin, pale girl who had done the form reductions rushed toward him. "Are you sick?"

Her expression was one of genuine concern. He was more shaken by that than by this Bureau treachery. He had lived under the gun for years now. He was unaccustomed to strangers *caring.*

Her concern was not the bland, commercially dispensed pablum of a professional hostess, either. She *wanted* to help.

*I want* fired across his mind.

"Yes. A migraine attack. And my medicine is packed."

She steadied him. "Sit down here. I'll get you something."

He dropped onto the couch. A devil kicked the back of his skull with a steel-toed boot. It was a vicious little critter. It kept hammering away. He could not restrain a groan.

The headache became a bass drumbeat overshadowing his other pains. He looked up into the girl's pale blue eyes. They were perfectly suited to her pale complexion and colorless hair. He tried a smile of gratitude.

"Be back in a minute," she told him. "Hang on." Off she hurried, her hips moving in a languorous way that belied her haste. BenRabi's head left him no time to appreciate the nicety.

His frayed nerves jumped. They had migraine tablets on hand? That was strange. And her curiosity. Why was she interested in his health? She had become intrigued and apprehensive the instant he had mentioned migraine.

He had stretched the truth this time, but he had had headache trouble all his life. He had gobbled kilos of painkillers in his time.

Still, he had not been bothered recently. The susceptibility was noted in his medical file as a cover for the pain his tracer would cause…

Why the hell switch him on now?

His headaches were a mental thing, Psych had declared. They were caused by unresolved conflicts between his Old Earth origins and the demands of the culture into which he had climbed.

He did not believe it. He had never met a Psych he trusted heaving distance. Anyway, he had had headaches even before he had begun to consider enlisting.

For at least the hundredth time he asked himself why the Bureau had implanted an imperfect device. He answered himself, as always, with the observation that the tracer was the only way they had to follow a Seiner ship to a starfish herd.

Completely nonmetal, the tracer was the only device that could be smuggled aboard without being detected.

There was no satisfaction in knowing the answers. Not when they were so damned unpleasant. He wished to hell that he could take a vacation. A real vacation, away from anything that would remind him of who and what he was. He needed time to go home and get involved in something with known, realizable, and comfortable challenges. He longed for the private universe of his stamp collection.

The Seiner girl returned with another of those big, warm smiles. She carried a water bottle in one hand, a paper pillbox in the other. "This should put that right," she said. That damned smile tried to eat him up. "I brought you a dozen. That should last the whole trip."

He frowned. How long would they be aboard this piece of flying junk?

"I asked if I could stay with you till we make orbit. Jarl turned me down. Too much else for me to do." She smiled, felt his forehead.

He had had a feeling she would report him to somebody. It was the way she had reacted to his mention of migraine.

What was so remarkable about a headache? Even a migraine? Something was wobbling on its axis and he could not get a grip. The pain just would not let him think.

Hell. He was probably just feeling the first ground tremors of culture shock. *Fly with it, Moyshe*, he told himself. *You've raced a sunjammer in the starwinds of the Crab…* What could the lady do that was less predictable, or more terrifying?

She was leaving. He did not want her to go. "Wait." She turned. His heart did a teenager's flop. "Thank you. My name's benRabi. Moyshe benRabi." Now wasn't that a gimp way of feeling for an opening? But she responded with a quick little smile.

"I know, Moyshe. I remember from your papers. Mine's Coleridge. Amaranthina Amaryllis Isolte Galadriel de Coleridge y Gutierez." She yielded a half-laugh because of his rising eyebrows. "Mother was a reader. Amy's good for everyday."

There was a long, unsure moment. It was that period of uncertainty preluding potential relationship where he did not know if he dared open up a little more. She said, "I'm in Liquids Systems too."

He nodded. She had left the door open a crack. It was plain that it was up to him to use or ignore it.

Some words finally came, but too late. She was walking away. Maybe later, then.

*I want* returned to his mind, stimulated by the girl's invitation. Could a woman be his need? No. Not all of it, though having one around might be oil on the seas of his mind.

He had been hunting his Grail for a long time. Though he believed himself a cripple when dealing with them, the occasional woman had fallen his way. None of them had been panaceas. Alyce's ghost usually got in the way.

The Bureau supported his quest, knowing he was searching. Psych did not miss much. They might even know what he needed. Whatever, his masters were certain they would show a return on their investment.

Few of the Bureau's agents were sane in the accepted sense. It recruited obsessives intentionally. BenRabi did not think that sane men would make good operatives.

It took a madman to want into Intelligence in the first place.

He smiled, mocking himself.

The lighter shuddered, rocked, shoved against his back. He was on his way to the orbiting Starfisher.

He watched Mouse, who was three rows ahead of him. The small man trembled as if suffering from a palsy. The getting off the ground part of space travel seemed to be the only terror his universe held. His reactions to everything else seemed as intense as those of a stone.

"So the Rat's chicken."

The Sangaree woman was on the other side of the aisle, smiling. He had not seen her sit down. Did he have to take this and the pain too?

# FOUR: 3047 AD

## The Olden Days, The Broken Wings

Mouse was right. The outfit didn't whisper for days. Niven's tension dissolved. He started living his cover.

He began reviewing psychiatric statistics at Angel City's medical center. Bureau planners had calculated the cover mission both to gather information of potential interest and to keep the opposition undecided.

On the surface there was no logical reason for a prime agent to spend all his time developing a mental-illness profile for an outpost city. And even less sense in it for the Starduster.

He found the data intriguing. He began enjoying it.

Then he met the woman.

She materialized at the edge of his vision for an instant. She was long, willowy, dark-haired. High, large, firm breasts locked a stunning holographic picture into his mind forever.

She vanished before he could get a better look.

His papers hit the floor. He grabbed, wondering if wishful thinking had bitten him. Those knockers…

It was lust at first sight.

Then she was peeking back around a grey metal cabinet in open-mouthed curiosity. Niven looked up into dark eyes. He dropped his notes again. Bewilderment danced across her features.

"Is something wrong?"

"Just clumsy. You startled me." He had never been comfortable with women. Especially those who attracted him so strongly, so suddenly.

It had been years since a woman had aroused him instantaneously. He considered himself with amazement.

The tough program did not keep his stomach from knotting, or his hands from shivering. It was silly. Adolescent. And he could not help himself.

He knew that he would bitterly recriminate himself for his weakness later. He always did.

He fumbled with the papers again.

She smiled. "Better let me do that." She knelt, shuffled his notes together.

*Mona Lisa*, he thought as he peered down her deeply cut blouse. *Her mouth is exactly the same. And her face has the same shape. But freckled.*

She wore no makeup. And didn't use anything but shampoo on her hair. She wore it brushed straight down. It hung wild and free, and had a hint of natural curl.

*She's turned me into gelatin*, he thought. He wanted to say something. Anything. He could think of nothing that did not sound juvenile, or insipid. But he wanted to know her. Wanted her.

"You work here?" he gobbled. His throat was tight and dry. He expected her to laugh.

He knew she was no employee. He had spent two days in Records already. She was the first person he had encountered, excepting the ratty old nurse who had explained the system, and who stole through now and then to make sure he did not leave obscene graffiti or drop a grenade down the toilet.

While he was keeping the cover, Mouse was alley prowling, searching for the key that would open the operation. Prepared sound tapes made it seem he was hard at work in their suite.

"No. I came in to do some research. How about you?"

"Research. A project for Ubichi Corporation. Oh. Gundaker Niven. Doctor. Social Psychology, not Medicine."

"Really?" She smiled. It made her that much more desirable. "I guess you've heard it before. You don't look it."

"Yeah." He did not have to force much sour into his reply. He was a born homeworlder. That much of the cover was easy to keep. "You're from Old Earth, everyone thinks..."

The social handicap of an Old Earth birth, properly exploited, could be converted to a powerful asset. For no logical reason Outworlders felt guilty about what had become of the motherworld. Yet Earth's natives had made it the hell it was.

Escape was available to the willing. The willing were few. People with adventure in their genes had gotten out in the first centuries of space travel, around World Commonweal's Fail Point, during First Expansion, and other early migrations. Modern departures came primarily through the Colonial Draft, as Earth's planetary government sold huge blocks of conscripted labor in return for forgiveness of indebtedness. Those few natives who wanted out usually chose military service.

Niven did not suspect that she might be Sangaree. He thought he had scored the Old Earth point.

"You must be an exceptional man… Excuse me. That's rude."

"That's prejudice."

She handed him his notes, huffed, "I said I was sorry."

"Forgiven. I don't expect an outsider to understand Old Earth. I don't understand it myself. Won't you introduce yourself?"

"Oh. Yes. Marya Strehltsweiter. I'm a chemo-psychiatrist. I'm doing my internship here. I'm originally from The Big Rock Candy Mountain." For an instant she fell back inside herself. "I have one more year to go."

"I've been there," Niven said. "It's magnificent." *Oops,* he thought. *That was a screw-up.* Dr. Gundaker Niven had never visited The Big Rock Candy Mountain.

"I miss it. I thought The Broken Wings would be exotic and romantic. Because of the name. You know what I mean? And I thought I'd get a chance to know myself. I never had time at home."

Niven frowned his response. He wanted to keep her talking, to hold her, but did not know what to say.

"The old story. I got pregnant young, got married, dropped out of school. Had to find work when he took off… Did that and went back to school both…" She smiled conspiratorially, winked, "It didn't do any good to get away. The pain came with me."

"Friend of mine told me you can't run away. Because the things you want to get away from are always inside you."

"An Old Earther said that?"

"We're not Neanderthals."

"Sorry."

"Don't be. You're right. It's down the chute. If it weren't for Luna Command and Corporation Center it would be back in the Dark Ages. I've had it. Want to duck out for lunch?" He surprised himself. He was seldom that bold.

"Why not? Sure. It's a chance to talk to somebody who hasn't spent their whole life in this sewage plant. You know what I mean?"

"I can guess."

"You on expense account? Don't get me wrong. I'm not trying to be mercenary. But it seems like forever since I ate in a decent place."

"We'll find one." *Anything, lady. Just don't fade away before I get organized and start talking my talk.*

"Where the hell have you been?" Mouse demanded. Niven had wandered in after midnight. "I was getting scared they'd burned you."

"Sorry, Mom. Won't happen again."

"Shee-it. Doc found him a girlfriend."

"Hey! You don't have a copyright on..."

"All right. I know. Be cool. But give me a yell next time. Just so I don't get hemorrhoids from worrying. I got it."

"What? The clap?"

"Why we're here. It's stardust."

"We knew that. Why else this silly-ass double cover?"

"Not little stardust. Not small-time stardust. Stardust big enough to rate a Family proctor in an outback Residency."

"You mean the fat broad?"

"Yeah. She was here because Angel City depots distribution traffic for this whole end of The Arm. I'm talking a billion stellars' worth a month."

"You're talking out your butt. There isn't enough ship traffic to handle that kind of smuggling."

"Yes there is. If you don't really smuggle it. If you send it out from a legit source labeled as something legit. If you own the Customs people and the ships and crews and shippers..."

"Start over. You skipped chapter one."

"What's Stink City known for? Besides the smell?"

"Organic pharmaceuticals."

"Point for the bright boy. All the good organics they dredge out of the muck outside. The main reason Angel City is here. The Sangaree have gotten control of the whole industry. And most of the local officials.

"They parachute the raw stardust into the swamp. The dredgers bring it in. The field traffic controllers are paid to ignore strange blips on their detection systems. The stuff gets refined here, in the best labs, then they ship it out along with the finest label organics. Their people at the other end intercept it and get it into the regular stardust channels."

"How did you dig that out?"

"Ran into a man who knew. I convinced him he should tell me. Now, figuring how the Old Man works, he probably guessed most of it before he sent us out. So what does he want? The source. Us to find out where the stuff comes from before it gets here."

Niven frowned over the drink he had mixed while talking. "It is big, then. So huge it would take a cartel of Families... And you tried to tell me the Sangaree outfit here was..."

"The biggest, Doc. We just might be on the trail of the First Families themselves. And I know what I said. I was wrong."

"I'm thinking about retiring. We're really in it, and that's the only way out."

The Sangaree were a race few in number. They had no government in the human sense. Their major form of organization was the Family, which could be described as a corporation or boundaryless nation led by persons who were related. So-called "possessionless" Sangaree formed the working class.

The Family was strongly elitist and *laissez-faire* capitalist. Sangaree cut one another's throats almost as gleefully as they chopped up the "animal" races.

A Family Head was an absolute dictator. His followers' fortunes depended upon his competence. Succession was patrilineal. The existence of proctors only mildly ameliorated the medieval power structure.

The First Families were the five or six most powerful Families. Intelligence had never accurately determined their number. As a consortium they determined racial policy and insured their own preeminence among their species.

Very little was known of the Sangaree that the Sangaree did not want known.

"Oh, hey," Mouse enthused. "Don't even joke about getting out. Not now. Not when we've got an opportunity like this. This might be our biggest hit ever. It's worth any risk."

"That's subject to interpretation."

"It is worth anything, Doc."

"To you, maybe." Niven nursed his drink and tried to regain the mood he had had on arriving.

Mouse would not let be. "So tell me about your friend. Who is she? Where did you meet her? She good-looking? She give you any? What's she do?"

"I ain't telling you nothing. You birddog your own."

"Hey! Don't get that way. How long you known me?"

"Since Academy."

"I ever take your girl?"

"I never caught you." He mixed another drink.

"What's that supposed to mean?"

"Jupp did."

Mouse flashed him a black look. "Who?" He shook his head, indicated his ear. The room might be bugged. "Carlotta, you mean? She came after me, remember? And he didn't give a damn."

Jupp von Drachau *had* given a damn.

Their mutual acquaintance and Academy classmate had been crushed. He had hidden it from his wife and Mouse, though. Niven had been the receptacle into which he had poured all his pain.

Niven had never told Mouse that he was the reason that von Drachau had abandoned wife and son and had thrown himself into his work so wholeheartedly that he had been promoted ahead of men far senior. Navy was the one institution that von Drachau trusted implicitly.

He was not alone in that trust.

The Services were the Foreign Legion of the age. Their people shared a hardy camaraderie based on their conviction that they had to stand together against the rest of the universe. Service was a place to belong. For people like von Drachau it became a cult.

Niven never would tell Mouse.

The evil had been done. Let the pain fade away.

It was not what Carlotta had done. Faithful, till-death-do-us-part marriage was an Archaicist fantasy. It was the *way* the hurt had been done. Carlotta had made a public execution of it, flaying Jupp with a dull emotional flensing knife, with clear intent to injure and humiliate.

She had paid the price in Coventry. She was still one of the social outcasts of Luna Command. Even her son hated her.

Niven still did not understand what had moved the woman. She had seemed, suddenly, to become psychotic, to collapse completely under the weight of her aristocratic resentment of her *nouveau-riche* husband.

Von Drachau, like Niven, was Old Earther. Even before the collapse of his marriage he had been climbing meteorically, surpassing his wife's old-line, fourth-generation Navy relatives. That seemed to have been what had cracked her.

"Well, don't get in too deep," Mouse warned, interrupting Niven's brooding. "We might not hang around long."

Later, as he drifted on the edge of sleep, trying to forget the trials of life in Luna Command, Niven wondered why Mouse had discussed their mission openly, yet had stifled any mention of von Drachau.

Protecting their second-level cover? Associates of the Starduster certainly should not be personal friends of a Navy Line Captain.

Or maybe Mouse knew something that Admiral Beckhart had not mentioned to his partner, Niven thought. The Old Man liked working that way.

The bastard.

"Probably both," he muttered.

"What?"

"Talking to myself. Go to sleep."

Beckhart always used him as the stalking horse. Or moving target. He blundered around, stirring things up for Mouse.

Or vice versa, as Mouse claimed.

He wondered if anybody had been listening. They had found only one bug in their sweeps. It had been inactive. It had been one of those things hotel managers used to keep track of towel thieves. But it was good tradecraft to assume that they had missed something live.

Niven was not in love with his profession.

It never allowed him a moment to relax. He did not perceive himself as being fast on his mental feet, so tended to overpress himself pre-plotting his situational reactions. He could not, like Mouse, just fly easy, rolling with the blows of fate like some samurai of destiny.

For him every venture out of Luna Command was an incursion into enemy territory. He wanted to go out thoroughly forewarned and forearmed.

Life had not been so complicated in his consular residency days. Back then friend and foe alike had known who and what he was, and there had been a complex set of rituals for playing the game. Seldom had anyone done anything more strenuous than watch to see who visited him and who else was watching. On St. Augustine he had worn his uniform.

There were different rules for scalp hunters. Beckhart's friends and enemies both played by the war rules. The blood rules.

And for reasons Niven did not understand, Beckhart's command was involved in a war to the death with the Sangaree.

Niven had had all the indoctrination. He had endured the uncountable hours of training and hypo-preparation. He even had the benefit of a brutal Old Earth childhood. But somehow his Academy years had infected him with a humanism that occasionally made his work painful.

A tendency to prolonged introspection did not help, he told himself wryly.

The campaign against the Sangaree could be justified. Stardust destroyed countless minds and lives. Sangaree raidships pirated billions and slaughtered hundreds. Through front men the Sangaree Families obtained control of legitimate business organizations and twisted them to illegitimate purposes.

The humanoid aliens had become a deadly virus in the corpus of human civilization.

Yet the very viciousness of Navy's counterattacks caused Niven grave doubts. Where lies justice, he wanted to know, when we are more barbarous than our enemies?

Mouse was fond of telling him that he thought too much and felt too little. The issue was entirely emotional.

Morning brought an indifferent mood. A depression. He simply abdicated all responsibility to Mouse.

"What's the program today?" He knew his partner meant to break routine. Mouse had had Room Service send up real coffee. Niven nursed his cup. "How are you going to get this past the auditors?"

"My accounts go straight to the Old Man. He stamps them ACCEPTED."

"Must be nice to be the Number-One Boy."

"It has its moments. But most of them are bad. I want you to hit the Med Center again. Business as usual. But try to audit their offworld drug traffic if you can. There's got to be records of some kind even if they only give us a side view. I think most of it is going out of the Center labs, so it's got to leave some kind of paper trace. If we can't find the source, maybe we can pinpoint the ends of the pipes."

"What about you?"

"I'm going to spend some of the Old Man's money. For hidey holes. For tickets out. You know. The insurance. That new Resident will show up pretty soon. We've got to be ready when it hits the ventilation."

"Are you getting close?" Feelings warred within Niven. He wanted out of Angel City and the mission, but not right now. There was Marya to get to know.

"No. Like I said, just buying insurance. I've got the feeling this'll get tight fast when they have somebody to tell them what to do."

"What do you mean, get tight? It already is. I had sticktights all day yesterday. Some of them stayed so close we could have worn the same shoes."

"That's what they get for using local talent. But I think that's part of their camouflage. We'd figure a place this important would have a battalion of high-powered types baby-sitting it. If somebody hadn't gotten onto S'Plez, they might have rolled along forever."

"I've got a feeling too, Mouse. And it ain't a good one. What happens if we get caught in a crunch between them and the Starduster?"

Mouse whipped a finger to his lips. "Let's not get back to tertiary cover yet," he breathed. Then he grinned. "Going to suicide? Look, if you have trouble, make the fallbacks. If I can't make them myself, I'll drop you a note somewhere. Otherwise, I'll catch you here tonight. It should be our last here, anyway."

Niven hit the lobby convinced that Mouse knew a lot more than he was telling. But that would be typical. Mouse was Beckhart's fair-haired boy. His perfectly expendable fair-haired boy.

He glanced back at the holorama. It was portraying one of the furious electrical storms in Ginunga Gap on Camelot. A herd of wind-whales quartered toward him through the rain and lightning.

For Beckhart the Bureau's work was a game. A vastly recomplicated form of the chess to which Mouse was addicted. The universe was his board. He would sacrifice his most precious pawn for a minuscule advantage.

He had been taking on the entire Sangaree race for a generation. And, with the implacability of a glacier, he was winning.

The prices of little victories left Niven appalled.

It took some sweet talk on his part to get to the Med Center's commercial records. He never was quite sure what made the old nurse give in. Somewhere along the line he said the right things. Pretty soon her death mask fell apart and reassembled itself in imitation of a smiling face. Then she fell all over herself explaining the data-retrieval system.

The information was there. A bonanza, and only thinly disguised. More than Mouse could have prayed for. This was the data center from which the whole operation was controlled. And it was not guarded by so much as a data lock.

The Sangaree were notoriously sloppy administrators. They had entered the interstellar community as predators, and had never really adapted to the demands of modern commerce. Action-oriented, they tended to ignore boring details, especially on worlds they believed safely in their pocket.

Like making sure no one without an absolute need had access to their records.

There had been a time when the need for protection would not have occurred to them at all, just as certain hues might not occur as existing to a color-blind man who had spent his entire life among others with the same affliction. But they were learning. Beckhart was teaching them via the Pavlovian method. The weakness was his favorite angle of attack.

The Sangaree did keep one secret. They wrote it down nowhere, and defended it to the death. The need to protect it was the one thing that could bring all the Families together. Even Families in vendetta would set aside their enmity long enough to keep Homeworld's location from becoming known.

On Borroway Sangaree children had murdered their younger brothers and sisters and had then committed suicide rather than face human interrogation, and that just because they had been afraid they *might* know something the human animals would find useful.

The hospital records were perfect. Niven unearthed few names, but did gather business intelligence pinpointing critical distribution points on more than two dozen worlds. Crimped there, the pipelines would require years of healing.

He found it incredible that a people could be so ingenious in marketing and so inept in administration. But the Sangaree were pure power people. They provided the muscle, money, guns, and merchandise. They let human underlings take most of the risks. And lumps.

From the Sangaree viewpoint their human associates did not much matter. The tips of the kraken's tentacles were nothing but ignorant, expendable animals. They could be replaced by others just as ignorant, greedy, and expendable.

Only one or two people on a market world could point toward Angel City. Only from the back of the beast itself could the entirety of the monster be seen. And the beast was solidly in Sangaree pay.

Marya caught him before he finished. "What in the world?" she demanded when she found him immersed in the data, far from his usual orbit.

# FIVE: 3048 AD

## Operation Dragon, Lifting Off

"Sorry I startled you." A she-wolf's grin made it plain that the Sangaree woman felt no remorse whatsoever. "I'm Maria Elana Gonzalez. Atmosphere Systems. Distributions Methods. Sometimes I do a little Hydroponics Ecology. I don't have a Master's for either, though. Too busy with other things." She smiled her gunmetal smile.

*Yes,* benRabi thought, *the lady has other interests. Stardust and murder.*

"Moyshe benRabi," he replied, in case she had forgotten.

"An unusual name." She smiled that smile. "Jewish?"

"So I'm told. I've never been in a synagogue in my life."

"You wouldn't be a writer?" She knew damned well that he was. Or that he pretended to be. He had whispered to her about it… "The name sounds so literary, somehow."

"I try, yes." Was she going to expose the Pale Imperator?

No. She did not push it. Nor did she thrust with anything from her arsenal of needles.

"What made you decide to sign up?" she asked.

"Unemployment."

"A space plumber? You're kidding. You must be on the blacklist."

"Yeah. Sort of. Somebody's. What about you?"

"The money."

The vibrations of hatred had begun mellowing out. She was controlling herself superbly.

BenRabi let it flow. He hurt too much to fence, or to probe about her mission. The armed truce persisted till the lighter reached the Starfisher.

Moyshe did not forget that she was Sangaree, that she would drink his blood happily. He simply tabled the facts for the time being.

Hundreds of her people had died because of him. Her children were dying. She *would* do something. The Sangaree tradition of honor, of Family responsibility, would compel her…

But she would not act right away. She had come here on a mission. She would complete that first. He could relax for a while.

As introspective and morality-stricken as he sometimes became, he could not feel guilty about The Broken Wings. Nor about its aftermath. Humanity and Sangaree were at war, and the Sangaree had fired the opening shot. That it was a subterranean war, fought at an almost personal level, did not matter. Nor did the fact that only humanity perceived a war, that the Sangaree were just in business. Battles were battles. Casualties were casualties, no matter how or why they went down.

Most of his associates and contemporaries hated the Sangaree, but to him they were just people. People he had to hurt sometimes, because of what they did and represented.

He snorted. The most bigoted man alive could say the same thing and mean it.

The whole stardust trade turned his stomach.

"The trouble with me is, I don't love or hate anything," he murmured.

"What?"

"Sorry. Thinking with my mouth in gear."

His mood left nothing counting. Nothing could move him. The pain tablets had kicked him into nirvana. Or into a depthless black pit where the light of emotion simply could not shine. He was not sure which.

He did not care. He did not give a damn about anything. Instead, he immersed himself in the mystery he called Mouse.

BenRabi believed he knew Mouse better than did anyone but the Admiral. A lot of one another had leaked across during their teamed operations. These little flare-ups in the secret war were slowly melting them, molding them…

And still Mouse remained a mobile enigma.

Mouse scared hell out of benRabi.

Mouse was the only man he knew who had killed someone with his bare hands.

Killing had not become a social dodo. But the personal touch had been removed. Murder had become mechanized, its soul and involvement eliminated. It had been that way for so long that most civilians could not endure the emotions they suffered if they entered a killing rage.

Their brains shorted. They went zombie. And nothing happened.

Anybody could push a button and hurl a missile to obliterate a ship of a thousand souls. A lot of timid little anybodies had.

The same anybody could sleep without dreaming the following night. The involvement was with the button, not the bang.

Ample opportunities arose in nice remote space battles with Sangaree, McGraw pirates, or in the marque-and-reprisal antics of minor governments, for that kind of killing. But to do a man face to face, with hands or knife or gun… It was too personal.

Confederation men did not like to get too close to anyone. Not even to end a life. A man knew he was in too deep if the urge arose.

The People of Now wanted no faces on their haunts.

BenRabi was free-associating, and unable to escape the flight of his thoughts. Mouse. Interpersonal relationships. The two joined forces to kick him into a pit of fear.

He had known Mouse as early as their Academy days. They had shared their moments then, both in training and the play typified by sunjammer racing in the wild starwinds of an old supernova. They had crewed their sunjammer victoriously, and had shared celebrations during leave. But they had refused, persistently, to become anything more than acquaintances.

Friends were strange creatures. They became responsibilities. They became walking symbols of emotional debits and personal obligations.

He was getting too close to Mouse. Growing too fond of the strange little man. And he suspected that Mouse was having the same trouble.

Friendship would be bad for their professional detachment. It could get them into trouble.

The Bureau had promised that they would not be teamed again after the operation on The Broken Wings. The Bureau had lied. As it always did. Or this *really* was a critical, hurry-up, top-man job.

He wondered. The Admiral apparently would do or say, or promise anything to get the work done.

Always there was a rush but he had no good reason to complain. Hurry was inherent in the modern social structure. Change came about so swiftly that policy, operational, and emotional obsolescence developed overnight. Decision and action had to be sudden to be effective.

The system shuddered constantly under the thundering impact of precipitous error.

BenRabi was now involved in one of the Bureau's few old, stable programs. Catching a starfish herd had been a prime mission before his birth. He suspected it would continue to be one long after his death.

He might die of boredom here. He now saw little hope that he and Mouse would be recalled early. The presence of Sangaree altered all the rules.

He had abandoned all hope of enjoying the mission.

Somehow, sometimes, because of the Sangaree woman or otherwise, he or Mouse would get hurt.

A *clang* rang through the shuttle. The vessel shuddered. BenRabi ceased flaying himself with the tiny, dull knives of the mind.

The lighter nosed into its mother ship like a piglet to a sow's belly. Moyshe followed the crowd moving to board the starship. He worked his way close to the pale Seiner girl. Could he pick up where he had left off?

He wondered why she intrigued him so. Just because she had been kind?

Guides led the way to a common room where several high-powered command types awaited them. *Another lecture*, Moyshe thought. *Some more shocks set off by a lot of boredom.*

He was half right.

Even before they were comfortable, one of the heavy-duty lads said, "I'm Eduard Chouteau, your Ship's Commander. Welcome aboard Number Three Service Ship from *Danion*, a harvestship of Payne's Fleet." That was enough ceremony, evidently. He continued, "We've contracted you as emergency replacements for technicians *Danion* lost in a shark attack two months ago. Frankly, Fishers haven't ever liked or trusted outsiders. That's because outsiders have given us reason. But for *Danion*'s sake we'll do right by you till we get our own people from the schools. All we ask is that you do right by us."

BenRabi felt that little feather tickle again. Half-truths were fluttering around like untamed butterflies. The man had something on his mind. There was a smoke screen rolling tall and wide, and behind it something he and Mouse just might find interesting. He made a mental note.

The Seiner schools were unique. Most ground-siders knew a little about them. They made romantic, remote settings for holonet dramas.

Those shows, naturally, had borne little relation to reality.

The Seiner creches were hidden in dead planetoids somewhere in deep space. The old and the young of the Fisher fleets dwelt there, teaching and learning. Only healthy Seiners of working age spaced with the fleets and hazarded themselves against disasters of the sort that had overtaken *Danion*.

Unlike Confederation parents, Starfishers yielded their children to professional surrogates out of love. They did not see their young as dead weight that might hamper them as they shot the rapids of life.

BenRabi had never seen enough of his father to have developed an emotional attitude toward him. And what could he think about his mother? She could not help being what she was. His mother was the child of her society, shaped by a high-pressure environment. The years and prejudice had devoured their tenuous umbilical link... They were of alien tribes now. The barrier between them could no longer be breached, even with the best will on both sides.

Visiting her had been a waste of leave time, but then there was the kid.

How was Greta doing? Christ! He might not know for one hell of a long time.

Why had his mother's behavior so horrified him? He should have known better than to have gone. He had come out of that world. All Old Earth was a screaming rat warren packed with people seeking new thrills and perversions as escapes from the grim realities of narrow little lives.

"Lightsl" the Ship's Commander snapped. BenRabi returned from introspection. A hologram took form in the center of the darkening common room. It developed like some fantasy magician's uncertain conjuration, flickering for several seconds, then jerking into sudden, awe-inspiring solidity.

"The stars you see here we retaped off a standard Second Level astrogation training module. Our holo people dubbed the ships from models used in an engineering status display at Ship's Engineering Control aboard *Danion*. This is *Danion*, your home for the next year."

The name *Danion* rolled off his tongue, freighted with everything the ship meant to him: home, country, refuge, responsibility.

A ship formed against the imaginary stars. It was a weird thing, making Moyshe think of octopi entwined. No. He decided it looked like a city's utilities systems after the buildings and earth and pavement had been removed, with the leavings flung mad among the stars. There were vast tangles of tubing. Here and there lay a ball, a cone, a cube, or an occasional sheet of silverness stretched taut as if to catch the starwinds. Vast nets floated between kilometers-long pipelike arms. The whole mad construct was raggedly bearded with thousands of antennae of every conceivable type. The totality was spectacularly huge, and dreadful in its strangeness.

In theory a deep-space vessel need not be confined in a geometric hull. Most small, specialized vessels were not. A ship did not have to have any specific shape, though the complex relationships between drive, inertial-negation, mass increase effect reduction, temporal adjustment, and artificial gravity induction systems did demand a direction-of-travel dimension slightly more than twice that of dimensions perpendicular to line-of-flight in vessels intended to operate near or above the velocity of light. But this was the first truly large asymmetric ship benRabi had ever seen.

It was a flying iron jungle. The streamlined ship had been preferred by mankind since space travel had been but a dream. Even now designers felt more comfortable enclosing everything inside a skin capable of generating an all-around defensive screen.

Even the wildest imaginings of novelty-hunting holo studios had never produced a vessel as knotted and strewn as this mass of tangled kitten's yarn.

BenRabi's astonishment was not unique. Silence died a swift death in that room.

"How the hell does that bastard keep from breaking up?" someone demanded.

"What I want to know is, how do you build something like that without a crew from every holonet in the universe turning up?"

Someone more technically smitten asked, "Ship's Commander—what sort of system do you use to synchronize drives? You'd have to have hundreds on a ship that big. Even with superconductor or pulse laser control systems your synch systems would be limited to the velocity of light. The lag between the more remote units..."

BenRabi lost the thread. Another surprise had jumped on him wearing hobnailed boots on all four feet.

He was aboard a ship he and Mouse had studied from the surface of Carson's. She was a typical interstellar vessel of an obsolete class now common only among the Rim Run Freehaulers.

A similar vessel had appeared in the hologram. It was approaching the harvestship.

The surprise was in their relative sizes.

The starship became a needle falling into an expanding, cosmic ocean of scrap. The service ship retained its holo dimensions. *Danion* swelled till she attained epic proportions.

Moyshe could not begin to guess her true dimensions. His most conservative estimate staggered him. She had to be at least thirty kilometers in cross-section, twenty thick, and sixty long. That was impossible. There were countries on Old Earth smaller than that.

And stretching far beyond the dense central snarl of the ship were those spars spreading silvery sails and nets.

Did she sunjam on stellar winds?

She couldn't. The Starfish stayed away from stars. Any stars, be they orbited by settled worlds or not. They stayed way out in the Big Dark where they could not be found.

The whole thing had to be a brag show. Pure propaganda. It just had to be.

He could not accept that ship as real.

His normal, understandable operation-opening jitters cranked themselves up a couple of notches. Till that ship had declared itself he had thought he could handle anything new and strange. Change was the order of the universe. Novelty was no cause for distress.

But this mission held too much promise of the new and unknown. He had been plunged *tabula rasa* into a completely alien universe.

Nothing created by Man had any right being so damned big.

Light returned. It drowned the dying hologram. BenRabi looked around. His jaw was not the only one hanging like an overripe pear about to drop.

Despite prior warning, everyone had believed themselves *aboard* a harvestship. Cultural bias left them incapable of believing the Fishers could have anything better.

Moyshe began to realize just how poorly he had been prepared for this mission. He had done his homework. He had devoured everything the Bureau had known about Starfishers. He had considered speculation as well as confirmed fact. He knew all there was to know.

Too little had been known.

"That's all you'll need to know about *Danion*'s outside," the Ship's Commander told them. "Of her guts you'll see plenty, and you'll have to learn them well. We expect to get our money's worth."

They had the right to ask it, Moyshe figured. They were paying double the usual spacer's rates, and those were anything but poor.

The man talked on awhile, repeating the security officer's injunctions. Then he turned the landsmen over to ratings, who showed them to their quarters. BenRabi's nervousness subsided. He had been through this part before, each time he had boarded a Navy warship.

He got a cabin to himself. The Seiner assigned to him helped settle him in. From the man's wary replies, Moyshe presumed he could expect to be aboard for several days. Payne's Fleet was harvesting far from Carson's.

Once the man had left and benRabi had converted his barren cubicle into a Spartan cell, he lay down to nap. After looking for bugs and spy-eyes, of course. But sleep would not come. Not with all the great lumpy surprises his mind still had to digest.

Someone knocked. Mouse, he guessed. The man never used a buzzer. He made a crochet a means of identification.

Yes. It was Mouse. "Hi," he said. "I'm Masato Iwasaki. Oh. You're in Liquids too? Good." He stuck out a hand. They shook.

"BenRabi. Moyshe. Nice to meet you." Silly game, he thought. But it had to be played if they wanted people to believe that they had just met.

"You wouldn't happen to play chess?" Mouse asked. "I'm looking for somebody who does."

He was addicted to the game. It would get him into trouble someday, benRabi thought. An agent could not afford consistent crochets. But who was he to criticize?

"I've been up and down the passage, but I haven't found anybody."

No doubt he had. Mouse was thorough.

"I play, but badly. And it's been awhile." It had been about four hours. They had almost been late to the spaceport because of a game. Mouse had been nervous about liftoff. BenRabi had been holding his own.

Mouse prowled, searching for bugs. BenRabi closed the door. "I don't think there are any. Not yet. I didn't find anything."

Mouse shrugged. "What do you think?"

"Broomstick all the way. Strictly from hunger. We're riding the mythical nova bomb."

"The woman? Yeah. Pure trouble. Spotted a couple McGraws, too. You think she's teamed?" He dropped onto the extra bunk.

"I don't think so. Not by choice. She's a loner."

"It doesn't look good," Mouse mused. "We don't have enough info. I feel like a blind man in a funhouse. We'd better fly gentle till we learn the traffic code." He stared at the overhead. "And how to con the natives."

BenRabi settled onto his own bunk. They remained silent for minutes, trying to find handles on the future. They would need every advantage they could seize.

"Three weeks," Mouse said. "I can handle it. Then a whole year off. I won't know what to do."

"Don't make your reservations yet. Marya… The Sangaree woman. She's one bad omen. Mouse… I don't think it's going to work out."

"I can handle it. You don't think I want to spend a whole damned year here, do you?"

"Remember what that character said down at Blake City? It could be the rest of our lives. Short lives."

"Bah. He was blowing smoke."

"Ready to bet your life on it?"

BenRabi's head gave him a kick. He was not sure he could take much more pain. And this compelling *need*…

"What's the matter?"

"Headache. Must be the change in air pressure."

How the hell was he supposed to work with his body in pain and his mind half around the bend? There was something to be said for those old-time sword swingers who did not have to worry about anything but how sharp their blades were.

"We'd better hedge our bets, Moyshe. Better start planning for the long haul, just in case."

"Thought you could handle it."

Mouse shrugged. "Got to be ready for everything. I've been poking around. These Seiners are as bad as us for special interests. They've got coin clubs and stamp clubs and Archaicist period groups… The whole thing. They're crazy to get into the past. What I was thinking was, why don't we start a chess club for landsmen? We'd have a cover for getting together."

"And you'd have an excuse to play."

"That too. A lot of Seiners play too, see. Maybe we could fish a few in so we could pump them socially." He winked, smiled.

The Seiners he was interested in hooking were probably female.

BenRabi could not fathom Mouse. Mouse seemed happy most of the time. That was disconcerting. The man carried a load of obsessions heavier than his own. And somebody whose profession was hatchet work should, in benRabi's preconceptions, have had a happiness quotient approaching zero.

BenRabi never had been able to understand people. Everybody else seemed to live by a different set of rules.

Mouse shrugged. "Fingers crossed? Hope Beckhart will pull it off? Wouldn't bet against him."

BenRabi *never* knew where he stood in the Admiral's grand, tortuous schemes.

"Hey, I've been here long enough," Mouse said. "No point attracting attention straight off. I saw you get pills from that girl. What was wrong? Head?"

"Yeah. Might even be my migraine. My head feels like somebody's been using it for a soccer ball."

Mouse went to the door. "A game tonight, then?"

"Sure, as long as you don't mind playing an amateur." BenRabi saw him off, feeling foolish. There had been no one around to hear his parting speech.

The public address system announced dinner for passengers. Mouse turned back. "Feel up to it?"

BenRabi nodded. Though it had ached miserably seconds ago, the tracer was not bothering him at all now.

Somebody was trying to impress them. The meal was superb. It was the kind Navy put on when important civilians came aboard. Everything was hydroponics and recycle, yet supremely palatable. Each mouthful reminded benRabi of the horrors of a Navy mess six months out, after the fresh and frozen stores were gone. From some angles the mission had begun to show promise.

He looked for the Seiner girl, Amy, but did not see her.

Lazy days followed. There was little to do in transit. He stayed in his cabin most of the time, loafing, toying with *Jerusalem*, and trying not to remember too much. Mouse, and a few others he had met, occasionally came to visit, play chess, or just bullshit about common interests.

The landsmen began to settle in, to get acquainted. The unattached singles started pairing off. Mouse, never inclined to celibacy, found himself a girl the second day. Already she wanted to move in with him.

Individual quarters had been assigned everyone but the married couples. There was room. The ship had been prepared to haul a thousand people.

Mouse immediately established himself as a character and leader among the landsmen. His notion of a chess club, while no fad, caught on.

One of the joiners was the Seiner who had striven to rattle them at Blake City.

His name was Jarl Kindervoort. He did not hide the fact that he ranked high in *Danion*'s police department.

BenRabi marveled again at the size of the harvestship. A vessel so huge that it had a regular police agency, complete with detectives and plainclothes operatives… Just incredible.

They called themselves Internal Security. BenRabi saw nothing in what he learned of their structure to remind him of a security unit in the intelligence sense. The function was doubtless there, cobbled on in response to the arrival of outsiders, but the agency look was that of a metropolitan police force.

Mouse's club inspired a general movement. Half a dozen others coalesced. Each was Archaicist-oriented.

In an age when nothing seemed as permanent as the morning dew, people who needed permanence had to turn to the past.

BenRabi looked on the whole Archaicist movement with studied contempt. He saw it as the refuge of the weak, of moral cowards unwilling to face the Now without the strategic hamlets of yesterday to run to when the pressure heightened.

Archaicism could be damned funny. BenRabi remembered a holocast of pot-bellied old men stamping through modern New York outfitted as Assyrian soldiery off for a sham battle with the legions of the Pharaoh of New Jersey.

Or it could be grim. Sometimes they started believing... He still shuddered whenever he recalled the raid on the temple of the Aztec Revivalists in Mexico City.

One morning he asked Mouse to read the working draft of his story. He had managed to push it all the way to an unsatisfactory ending.

Mouse frowned a lot. He finally said, "I guess it's all right. I don't know anything about non-objective art."

"I guess that means it isn't working. I'd better get on it and do it right. Even if you can't figure out what the hell it's about, it should affect you."

"Oh, it does, Moyshe."

His tone conveyed more message than did his words. It said that he thought benRabi was wasting his time.

Moyshe wanted to cry. The story meant so damned much to him.

## SIX: 3047 AD

### The Olden Days, Luna Command

He waited patiently in the line outside Decontamination. When his turn came he went to Cubicle R. No one else had done so. A sign saying OUT OF SERVICE clung to the door beneath the R.

That sign had been there more than twenty years. It was old and dirty and lopsided. Everyone in Luna Command knew that door R did not open on a standard decon chamber.

The men and women, and occasional non-humans, who ignored the sign were agents returning from the field.

He closed the door and placed his things on a counter surface, then removed his clothing. Nude, he stepped through the next door inward.

Energy from the scanner in the door frame made his skin tingle and his body hair stand out. He held his breath, closed his eyes.

Needles of liquid hit him, stung him, killing bacteria and rinsing grime away. Sonics cracked the long molecular helixes of viruses.

A mist replaced the spray. He breathed deeply.

Something clicked. He stepped through the next door.

He entered a room identical to the first. Its only furniture was a counter surface. On that counter lay neatly folded clothing and a careful array of personal effects. He dressed, filled his pockets, chuckling. He had been demoted. His chevrons proclaimed him a Second Class Missileman. His ship's patch said he was off the battle cruiser *Ashurbanipal.*

He had never heard of the vessel.

He pulled the blank ID card from the wallet he had been given, placed his right thumb over the portrait square. Ten seconds later his photograph and identification statistics began to appear.

"Cornelius Wadlow Perchevski?" he muttered in disbelief. "It gets worse and worse." He scanned the dates and numbers, memorizing, then attached the card to his chest. He donned the Donald Duck cap spacers wore groundside, said, "Cornelius Perchevski to see the King."

The floor sank beneath him.

As he descended he heard the showers go on in the decon chamber.

A minute later he stepped from a stall in a public restroom several levels lower. He entered a main traffic tunnel and walked to a bus stop.

Six hours later he told a plain woman behind a plain desk behind a plain room, behind a plain door, "Cornelius W. Perchevski, Missileman Two. I'm supposed to see the doctor."

She checked an appointment log. "You're fifteen minutes late, Perchevski. But go ahead. Through the white door."

He passed through wondering if the woman knew she was fronting. Probably not. The security games got heaviest where they seemed least functional.

The doctor's office made him feel like Alice, diving down a rabbit hole into another world.

*It's just as crazy as Wonderland,* he thought. *Black is white here. Up is down. In is out. Huck is Jim, and never the Twain shall meet…* He chuckled.

"Mr. Perchevski."

He sobered. "Sir?"

"I believe you came in for debriefing."

"Yes, sir. Where do you want me to start, sir?"

"The oral form. Then you'll rest. Tomorrow we'll do the written. I'll schedule the cross-comparative for later in the week. We're still trying to get the bugs out of a new cross-examination program."

Perchevski studied the faceless man while he told his tale. The interrogator's most noteworthy feature was his wrinkled, blue-veined, weathered hands. His inquisitor was old...

The Faceless Man usually was not. Normally he was a young, expert psychologist-lawyer. The old men in the Bureau were ex-operatives, senior staff, decision-makers, not technicians.

He knew most of the old men. He listened to the questions carefully, but there was no clue in the voice asking them. It was being technically modified. He reexamined the hands. They offered no clues either.

He began to worry. Something had gone broomstick. They did not bring on the dreadnoughts otherwise.

His nerves were not up to an intensive interrogation. It had been a heavy mission, and the trip home had given him too much time to talk to himself.

Debriefing continued all month. They questioned him and counterchecked his answers so often and so thoroughly that when they finally let him go he no longer really felt that the mission had been part of *his* life. It was almost as if some organ had been removed from him one molecule at a time, leaving him with nothing but a funny empty feeling.

Five weeks after he had arrived at Luna Command they handed him a pink plastic card identical in all other respects to the white one he had received at Decontamination. They also gave him an envelope containing leave papers, money, bankbooks, and such written persona as a man needed to exist in an electronic universe. Included was an address.

An unsmiling amazon opened a door and set him free.

He stepped into the public tunnels of Luna Command. Back from beyond the looking glass. He caught a bus just like any spacer on leave.

The room was exactly as he had left it—except that *they* had moved it a thousand kilometers from its former location. He tumbled into his bed. He did not get out again for nearly two days.

Cornelius Perchevski was a lonely man. He had few friends. The nature of his profession did not permit making many.

For another five days he remained isolated in his room, adapting to the books, collections, and little memorabilia that could be accounted the time-spoor of the real him. Like some protean beast his personality slowly reshaped itself to its natural mold. He began taking interest in the few things that made a unified field of his present and past.

He took down his typewriter and notebooks and pecked away for a few hours. A tiny brat of agony wrested itself from the torn womb of his soul. He punched his agent's number, added his client code, and fed the sheets to the fax transmitter.

In a year or two, if he was lucky, a few credits might materialize in one of his accounts.

He lay back and stared at the ceiling. After a time he concluded that he had been alone enough. He had begun to heal. He could face his own kind again. He rose and went to a mirror, examined his face.

The deplastification process was complete. It always took less time than did his internal mendings. The wounds within never seemed to heal all the way.

He selected civilian clothing from his closet, dressed.

He returned to public life by taking a trip to the little shop. The bus was crowded. He began to feel the pressure of all those personalities, pushing and pulling his own… Had he come out too early? Each recovery seemed to take a little longer, to be a little less effective.

"Walter Clark!" the lady shopkeeper declared. "Where the hell have you been? You haven't been in here for six months. And you look like you've been through hell."

"How's it going, Max?" A self-conscious grin ripped his face open. Christ, it felt good to have somebody be glad to see him. "Just got out of the hospital."

"Hospital? Again? Why didn't you call me? What happened? Some Stone Age First Expansioner stick a spear in you again?"

"No. It was a bug this time. Acted almost like leukemia. And they don't even know where I picked it up. You have anything new for me?"

"Sit your ass down, Walter. You bet I have. I tried to call you when it came in, but your box kept saying you weren't available. You ought to get a relay put on that thing. Here, let me get you some coffee."

"Max, I ought to marry you."

"No way. I'm having too much fun being single. Anyway, why ruin a perfectly good friendship?" She set coffee before him.

"Oh. This's the real thing. I love you."

"It's Kenyan."

"Having Old Earth next door is good for something, then."

"Coffee and comic opera. Here's the collection. The best stuff is gone already. You know how it is. I didn't know when you'd show up. I couldn't hold it forever."

Perchevski sipped coffee. He closed his eyes and allowed the molecules of his homeworld to slide back across his taste buds. "I understand. I don't expect you to hang on to anything if you've got another customer." He opened the ancient stamp album.

"You weren't out to the March of Ulant, were you, Walter?"

"Ulant? No. The other direction. Why?"

"Because of the rumors, I was curious. You know how Luna Command is. They say Ulant has been rearming. The Senators are kicking up a fuss. High Command keeps telling them it's nonsense. But I've had a couple of high-powered corporate executive types in and they say the Services are smoke screening, that there's something going on out there. A lot of heavy ships moving through here lately, too. All of them moving from out The Arm in toward the March."

"It's all news to me, Max. I haven't had the holo on since I got back. I'm so far behind I'll probably never catch up. These Hamburg... The notes all over the page. What are they?"

"Jimmy Eagle did that. Right after I picked up the collection. Lot of them are forgeries. The cancellations. Most of the stamps are good. He marked the reprints. You haven't heard any news at all?"

"Max, by the time I got back from Illwind I was so sick I couldn't see. I didn't care. I don't know why we've got an embassy on that hole, anyway. Or why they sent me there. The only natives I ever saw were two burglars we caught trying to blow up the Ambassador's safe. They need a military assistance mission like Old Earth needs another Joshua Ja. Their methods of killing each other are adequate already."

"Then you haven't even heard that Ja is done for?"

"Hey? What happened? This I got to hear about."

Joshua Ja was one of Old Earth's more noxious public figures. The holonet newscasters had dubbed him the Clown Prince of Senegal. The nets followed his threats and posturing faithfully, using him as humorous leavening for their otherwise grim newscasts.

The self-proclaimed Emperor of Equatorial Africa was no joke to his subjects and neighbors. His scatterbrained projects and edicts invariably cost lives.

"He invaded the Mauritanian Hegemony while you were gone."

Perchevski laughed. "Sounds like one gang of inmates trying to break into another's asylum."

Old Earth was a nonvoting member of Confederation. Both Confederation itself and the World Government refrained from interfering in local affairs. World Government held off because it had no power. Confederation did so because the costs of straightening out the home-world were considered prohibitive.

Earth was one of the few Confederation worlds supporting multiple national states. And the only one boasting an incredible one hundred twenty-nine.

World Government's writ ran only in those countries deigning to go along with its decrees.

Centuries earlier there had been but two states on Earth, World Commonweal and United Asia. United Asia had remained impotent throughout its brief, turbulent history. World Commonweal might have created a planetary state, but had collapsed at Fail Point, so called because at that point in time agro-industrial protein production capacity had fallen below the population's absolute minimum survival demand.

"You missed the best part of it, Walter. During the first week the Mauritanians shot down half of their own air force. And the Empire lost a whole armored brigade in a swamp because Ja ordered them to march in a straight line all the way to Timbuktu. The holonets had a field day. That's the lilac brown shade there. We've got a Foundation certificate for it."

Perchevski lifted the stamp and examined its reverse. "I already have a copy. I'm just looking."

"Anyway, the Mauritanians have been less klutzy than the Imperials. They're closing in on Dakar."

"What's the Council doing?"

"Laughing a lot. They're going to let him go down. The word's out that other countries shouldn't accept refugees from the Empire. Ja and his gang have done too much damage to Old Earth's image."

"Old Josh? You're kidding. How do you lower something that's already at the bottom?"

"You see anything you want?"

"You, my love."

"Smart ass."

"Wednesday night?"

"What've you got in mind?"

"A cribbage game."

"I'll call you. If it does any good. If you're not off to some weird place with a name like Toilet Bowl."

"Actually, I was thinking about going to the archaeological digs at Ley."

"Funny you should mention them. More coffee?"

"Sure. Why?"

"They broke into a new chamber last month. It was in pretty good shape."

"Is it open?"

"They put a transparent tube in. You can walk through and look, but you can't get close to anything or get in the way."

"Call me, then. If you want to go see."

"Excuse me, Walter." Another customer had come in. "Yes sir? May I help you?"

"How are you in Twenty-first Century France?"

Perchevski lost himself in the bits of paper that told tales of a remote, turbulent era. He finally selected seven pieces for his collection, paid for them from the Walter Clark account.

"Max, thanks for the coffee. And hold that Berlin piece, will you? I'll let you know as soon as I make up my mind. Like maybe Wednesday?"

"All right, Walter. I'll call you tomorrow."

"Leave a message if I'm not there."

"I will."

He clambered aboard a bus and returned the two hundred kilometers to his apartment.

*You're a fool,* he told himself. *To go all that way for an hour of gossip.*

But damn, did he feel better.

He had traveled a lot farther in the past. He doubted that Max had a ghost of a notion just what she meant to him. She was one of the few stable realities in his life. She was a landmark by which he guided himself back from the wildernesses of Bureauland.

He mounted his new stamps in his albums using a surgeon's care. He took down a notebook and marked their catalog numbers off his list of wants, noting the date and price he had paid for each. He entered the total in his cumulative ledger, then marked down the fact that two more album pages had been filled.

The detailed record keeping was necessitated by something within him, some compulsion to put down tiny proofs that he was interacting with the universe, if only through the hieroglyphics of numbers. He had other notebooks in which he kept other records. He did a lot of bookkeeping on the events of his life.

None of it ever left his apartment.

He wondered what the Bureau snoops made of the lists and notes. He was sure they checked them whenever he was away.

He finished his record keeping. He looked around the sterile room. It suddenly became very tight, very lonely.

He tried the holo, turning to the Luna Command news channel. He caught it in a low cycle. There was nothing on but an endless parade of public service messages, though once a commentator mentioned rumors of a forthcoming major news event involving Navy. Something big was expected, but its nature could not be determined. Security remained unusually tight.

"Sure," Perchevski growled at the cube. "The Chief of Staff will probably announce this year's winners in the Fleet Backgammon Playoffs."

Luna Command was heart and brain of Confederation. It was headquarters for the Services, which were Confederation's bone and sinew. It was the hub of a human enterprise kept unified only by its military. And the only exciting thing that had happened there in Perchevski's lifetime had been the discovery of the prehistoric alien base on the moon's dark side.

The military did not control Confederation. But the only obstacle to absolute military rule was a gentlemen's agreement among the generals and admirals to accept the forms of democracy. High Command could do anything it damned well pleased, any time it pleased, were it to ignore custom. Out in the remote reaches, far from senatorial eyes, it often did. There were few sanctions the civilian sector could exercise.

Aggravated, Perchevski killed the holocast. He checked the lunar calendar for the best viewing site, recovered his tunic, and hit public transportation again. He took the high-velocity electric train the six hundred kilometers to the tourist observation dome overlooking Tycho.

The crater was not the attraction there. People did not come from Confederation's one hundred thirty-four member planets, and more than a hundred dominions, protectorates, associated states, and outright colonies, to look at a hole in the ground. The allies and tributaries were not interested in a crater either.

Neither was Perchevski.

Tycho observation dome offered a magnificent view of Old Earth. His homeworld. A world he had not visited in eight years.

Tycho, or its sister domes, was as close as most tourists cared to get to their biological roots.

Perchevski lay back in a lounger and half-listened to the canned commentary.

"...where the race of Man began... possibly also the planet of origin of the Sangaree... first successful extraterrestrial landing, July 20, 1969, in the old dating. Neil Armstrong... ascension of World Commonweal following World War III... Fail Point, July, 2194, led to the Collapse. Reinhardt Ships carried Commonweal refugees to interstellar colonies from 2187 through the end of the Luna Wars in 2226. The Treaties of Jerusalem of 2228 led to the chaotic exploration and random settlement we now call First Expansion.

"A profligate expenditure of resources and racial will initiated a reactionary isolationism which spanned the twenty-fourth and twenty-fifth centuries. Space travel, even to Luna, was discontinued. Contact with the star worlds did not resume till 2613, when Vice-Admiral Takada Yoshimura brought New Earth's fleet back to Luna. A short time later Yoshimura encountered ships of the Palisarian Directorate.

"The old records in Luna Command revealed the locations of scores of settled worlds. The secondary colonies of the Directorate were under pressure from Toke at the time. The Directorate and New Earth concluded a xenophobic alliance, and began searching for other human allies.

"The concept, if not the fact, of Confederation had been created.

"We have our former enemies, the Toke, to thank for midwifing Confederation through its birth pains. The unrelenting determination of the Star Lords and Caste of Warriors united humanity. The conflict endured sufficiently long for Confederation to become a reality, with its military headquartered here in the tunnels of Luna.

"Confederation and Luna Command have been growing steadily since."

Perchevski stopped listening. He had heard it all before.

He knew he would hear it again. The viewing domes were the Meccas of regular hadjs.

He looked at the Earth and wondered how his parents were doing. He had not heard from either for a long time.

He slept while returning to his apartment. It had been a long day.

Two messages awaited him. The first was from Max. She wanted to see the xenoarchaeological digs Darkside. The other was from his employers. The printout said: SENIOR STAFF PARTY WEDNESDAY 8 PM ATTENDANCE MANDATORY CONTACT 864-6400-312 FOR FURTHER INFO.

He sighed, pecked out the number. Max would not like this. He tried her number after he had gotten the story.

"Max? Walter. Yeah. Thanks for calling. Hey, I've got a problem. Just got word from my boss. I have to go to a staff party tomorrow night. Can't get out of it. I know. I'm sorry. Hey! Want to come along? All the big wheels will be there. The Chief of Staff Navy is supposed to come out with some big announcement. No. I don't think it has anything to do with the March of Ulant. That's all smoke screen, if you ask me. It's at the Command Club. Can you meet me there? Okay. 'Bye."

He lay back on his bed and wondered what the news would be, and why he had been ordered to make an appearance. He was a senior operative, but certainly not senior staff.

He also wondered how long it would be before they called him down and stuck him behind a desk. It didn't look as if his vacation was going to go through, and they did not like people just loafing around while they waited for an assignment.

Again he thought about his parents.

# SEVEN: 3048 AD

## Operation Dragon, Engagement

He could not write. He had too much free time. He always worked better when the minutes were quick and crowded.

Something was wrong with his head. Skeletons were coming out of their closets in there. Especially the Alyce affair. The unbreakable walls of Tyre were crumbling.

It had been years since he had thought about Alyce. Why now? That hasty Psych programing before the mission? Or were the edges of his sanity just fraying?

He had two bad days. There were moments when he did not know where he was or why, or, sometimes, just who he was.

He sometimes felt his life was managed by guardian devils. The Fates pursued him like indefatigable hounds, with malice their only joy.

The ship dropped hyper without warning. "Are we finally there?" he asked the air. He stepped into the corridor. Most of the landsmen were there.

Jarl Kindervoort's voice filled the ship. "Passengers, remain in your quarters. Strap in for acceleration. We're about to engage a Confederation squadron that has been following us."

"Engage?" Moyshe said. "What the hell? Mouse? What's going on? Jupp's not supposed to move for two weeks yet."

Mouse shook his head warningly. People were listening. The Sangaree woman appeared to be in a black rage.

"Wheels within wheels," benRabi whispered. "Beckhart's doing it to us."

"Let's hope we didn't suddenly get expendable," Mouse said. "What's going on?"

"Oh, damn! I figured *you* knew. Beckhart? Maybe Jupp thought he saw a chance? Maybe that frontier thing broke?"

"What? That's bullshit. The Ulantonids know better. It's the Old Man. Got to be."

"Better strap in. Say any prayers you know." BenRabi had seen several battles while in the line. They had ruined his taste for space warfare. Defeats were too total and final.

The vessel shuddered while he was strapping in. He recognized a heavy missile salvo departing. The ship clearly mounted weaponry not customary for her class.

Would the nasty surprises never end?

For a few seconds his mind fell apart completely, into absolute chaos. A tiny part of him seemed to be outside, watching the disorder.

All-clear bells and his door buzzer sounding bracketed the reassembly process.

A crewman stepped into his cabin. "Mr. benRabi? Will you come with us, please?"

He was as polite as the spider inviting the fly.

There was going to be trouble.

A half-dozen people wearing guns backed him. BenRabi joined them in the passageway.

Another group had collected a stoic Mouse.

How had they blown it?

Kindervoort was directing the pickup himself. He looked like a man with a compulsion to explain. And to ask. Moyshe hoped he would not get primitive.

Mouse seemed to fear that. But hatchetmen lived by the Old Testament: eye for an eye, live by the sword...

"Got you, boys." Kindervoort grinned toothily. He had an overbite.

BenRabi had an irrational aversion to the man. It had nothing to do with the situation. More like loathing at first sight.

Kindervoort had a colorless, fleshless face. His skin lay stretched drumhead tight over prominent cheekbones and a lantern jaw. Shadowed hollows lay between. He achieved a deathshead look when the light was wrong.

BenRabi automatically disliked anyone with that gaunt, graveyard look.

"Ah, here you are," said the Ship's Commander as they shuffled into his darkly decorated office.

The furniture was of mahogany-toned imitation woods crafted in antique styles. The walls and ceiling had been artificially timbered to suggest the captain's cabin of a sailing ship. There were reproductions of antique ship's lanterns, a compass, a sextant, a chart of Henry the Navigator, framed prints featuring caravels, clippers, and the frigate *Constellation*. "Any trouble, Jarl?"

"No sir. The Bureau doesn't employ fanatics. May I present Commanders Masato Igarashi Storm and Thomas Aquinas McClennon, of Confederation Navy? They're senior field agents of the Bureau of Naval Intelligence. Commanders, Ship's Commander Eduard Chouteau."

BenRabi pursed his lips. He had been afraid Mouse's real name might be Storm. Mouse had been conspicuously absent from Academy during their final year of school. That had been the year of the Storm-Hawksblood war in the Shadowline.

Moyshe had visited Blackworld after that war's end. There had been a Masato Igarashi Storm there at the time, but their paths had not crossed. That Masato had taken command of his father's mercenaries after Sangaree treachery had killed his father, brothers, and most of the family officers.

Kindervoort certainly had *him* pat, though the name McClennon seemed like a stranger's, like that of someone he had known a long time ago, in an age of innocence.

He felt less like Thomas Aquinas McClennon than he did Moyshe benRabi, Gundaker Niven, Eric Earl Hollenkamp, Walter Clark, or… How many men had he been?

"Take seats, gentlemen," Chouteau said. "And relax."

BenRabi dropped into a chair, glanced at his partner, Mouse, who also seemed stunned. The simple knowing of a secret name bore so many implications… The spookiest was that someone might have penetrated the Bureau deep enough to have gained access to its primary data system. That meant a mole of a generation's standing.

"Worrying about your Navy friends?" Kindervoort asked. "Don't. They're all right. They cut and ran. And I mean fast. Guess they figured there wasn't any point to a slugfest when they couldn't gain anything even if they won." He chuckled. So did Chouteau.

Had to be a deep mole. Nothing else would explain their perpetual success at evading Confederation.

Kindervoort planted himself in front of benRabi. He leaned close, frowning. Moyshe avoided his deathshead face by staring at Chouteau.

The Ship's Commander leaned back in his fat, comfortable chair and half closed his eyes.

Kindervoort said, "But we're not worried about von Drachau or Admiral Beckhart, are we?" He chuckled, again, moved to Mouse. "Why we wanted to see you was these tracers you've got built in. Walking instels they inflict on us. Ingenious."

They *did* have a mole.

Moyshe had thought he was the only human instel. Beckhart had pissed and moaned like the expense of it was coming out of his own pocket. Redundancy had not seemed plausible after that.

He hadn't really wondered why Mouse was along. Beckhart had issued an assignment. Nobody questioned the Old Man. Not in any way that might look like contradicting his will.

Mouse looked like death warmed over. Swell. It would do him good to get short-sheeted sometimes too.

How come Mouse had not been hurting?

Knowing Beckhart, the Pyschs had programmed the headaches. Maybe to divert attention from Mouse. Had Mouse known?

They had some talking to do.

Beckhart clockwork, jerking along, often was oiled by the confusion of its parts. Only the master knew all the secrets of his machinery.

Would there be more?

Silly question.

Beckhart's nature semed to demand twists on twists and gaudy smoke screens that concealed truths as slippery as greased snakes. His plots, however, while labyrinthine, had their own tightness and logic. They were mapped by the finest computers in Luna Command. He ran simulation models against even the most ridiculous contingencies.

Had Beckhart calculated a mole into this scheme?

BenRabi suddenly intuited that he and Mouse were not partners after all. This time they were voyagers sailing parallel but distinct courses. They had been programmed to hide from one another as much as from their targets. And they had been intended for exposure from the beginning.

Beckhart knew about the mole.

He wanted them taken captive. He wanted them to spend a year in Seiner service.

Moyshe got mad. That was a year stolen from his life!

"The thing's all biological, eh?" Kindervoort asked.

"What?"

"This instel. Remarkable gimmick. Our detectors didn't quiver when you came aboard. 'Course, that didn't matter in the long run."

He was smug, damn him. So was Chouteau, chubby-happy there in his plastic-antique, made for the Archaicist trade captain's chair.

"How the hell did you get my name?" benRabi demanded. They were in the mood for talking. They might give him something the computers could use to pinpoint the mole.

Kindervoort ignored his question.

"We began monitoring the hyper bands when we broke orbit at Carson's. We wanted to see if we could catch anything from von Drachau's squadron. Imagine our surprise when we found out somebody was sending from the ship."

"You were plain lucky, Jarl," Chouteau said.

"It wasn't luck that we knew they were coming, just that they started broadcasting in a ship small enough for us to pinpoint them."

How had they gotten the word?

Moyshe remembered a raggedy-assed Freehauler boat that had not lifted on schedule. Had the Freehaulers been the mole's couriers? *Black Mirage.* Remember that ship. Somebody would have to have a talk with her people someday.

Was there a relationship between Seiners and Freehaulers? Both certainly refused to stop giving grief to Confederation's policy makers.

Chouteau called out, "Doctor DuMaurier, come in here. Let's get on with this."

Kindervoort darted behind Moyshe and seized his shoulders. BenRabi did not resist. There was nothing he could do.

A doctor pushed into the room. He poked, pinched, and sprayed Moyshe's neck with an aerosol anesthetic. He removed an unsettlingly ancient lase-scalpel from his medical bag. Then, quoting every doctor who had ever lived since the days when Incas trepanned one another with sharp stones, he said, "This will only take a minute. You won't feel a thing."

"That's what they told me when they put it in," benRabi grumbled. He could not go down without registering some kind of protest.

"We'll just pull the ambergris nodes," Kindervoort said. "Ed, what do you think? Is it proper to sell them back to Navy come next auction?"

Chouteau nodded amiably. "I think so. I like it."

Moyshe wished they would stop. It made him want to scream, "You're being unprofessional!"

They were not professionals. The harvestships apparently had no real intelligence-oriented security people.

There was justice in Kindervoort's suggestion. BenRabi and Mouse, and all the other agents aboard, irrespective of their allegiances, were after the same thing. Access to one of the herds of great nightbeasts that produced the critical element in the node being removed from benRabi's neck.

The Seiners called it ambergris. The name had evolved from that of a "morbid secretion" of Old Earth whales once used by perfumers. The word could mean anything anyone wanted now. The leviathans of the deep no longer had a claim. They had been extinct for centuries.

Star's amber, space gold, and sky diamond were other popular names. By any name ambergris was the standard of wealth of the age.

In the vernacular its name was short and pithy. It was the solid waste of a starfish. Crap.

This crap fertilized a civilization. Confederation could not have existed without it. Without it there would have been no fast star-to-star communication. Speed and reliability of communications ultimately define the growth limit of any empire.

BenRabi did not comprehend the physics of instel. He knew what the man in the street knew. A tachyon spark could be generated in the arc between an ambergris cathode and a Bilao crystal anode. The spark could be made to carry an FTL message. Neither ambergris nor Bilao crystal could be synthesized.

The crystal occurred naturally deep in the mantles of several roughly earth-sized worlds orbiting super-cool stars. Sierra was the only such world within Confederation. Mining the crystal, at depths exceeding thirty kilometers, was overwhelmingly expensive.

Bilao crystal was cheaper than ambergris. The Seiners had a monopoly. They were free market capitalists of the first water. Every node went to the highest bidder.

The demand for ambergris perpetually exceeded supply. Despite gargantuan capital demands, optimists often assembled the hard and software of an installation merely in hopes that an ambergris node would become available.

The combined Seiner harvestfleets, in their best year ever, had gleaned fewer than forty thousand nodes. Most of those had gone to replace nodes already burning out.

The Seiners sold their product at auction, on worlds declared temporarily neutral and threatened by all the firepower the fleets could muster. The bidders always went along with Seiner rules. The Starfishers might refuse to do business with someone who pushed.

Ambergris alone explained the flood-tide of operatives heading toward Carson's after *Danion* had begun advertising for groundside technicians. The agents had swept in like vultures, hoping to feed on the corpse of a betrayed Payne's Fleet.

*That's what we are,* benRabi thought. *Me and Mouse, we're vultures... No. Not really. We're more like raptors. Falcons flung from Beckhart's wrist. Our prey is information. We're to bring down any morsel that might betray a starfish herd.*

Moyshe tried to believe that Confederation *should* control the harvesting and distribution of ambergris. He tried hard.

Sometimes he had to tell himself some tall ones to get by. Otherwise he asked himself too many questions. He started worrying irrelevancies like Right and Wrong.

His soul, slithering past morality shyly, merely mumbled *I want.* There was a pain in it that he could not understand. It nagged him worse than did his ulcer.

BenRabi dreaded madness. He was afraid of a lot of things lately. He could not figure it out.

"There. One down." The doctor dropped Moyshe's node into a gleaming stainless steel tray. Plunk! Exclamation point to the end of a phase of the mission. He began suturing Moyshe's wound.

"How bad will that hurt when the anesthetic wears off?"

"Not much. Your neck should be a bit stiff, and tender to the touch. See me if it gives you any trouble." The doctor turned to Mouse. Mouse squirmed a little before he submitted. His conscience, benRabi supposed. He had to make a showing.

Doctors were another of Mouse's crochets. He had no use for them, as he often told anyone who would listen.

BenRabi suspected that was why Beckhart never had Mouse altered during his mission preps.

"We don't like spies," the Ship's Commander blurted. The way he said it made it sound both spontaneous and irrelevant, a non sequitur despite what was happening.

*We,* Moyshe thought. *These people always say* we.

The worm within him bit. He shifted uncomfortably. Somehow, Chouteau had taunted his need. Weird.

He tried to recapture it, to discover what it was that he wanted, but, like a wet fish, it wriggled through his fingers.

Nearly a minute later, Chouteau pursued his remark. "But *Danion* needs your expertise to survive. And we love her enough to give you another chance." He became less distant.

"Listen up. We're going to keep you alive. But you're going to work till you drop: till you forget why it was that you were sent here. And when we're done with you, we're going to ship you home just as ignorant as you were when you signed on.

"Men, don't give us any more trouble. Be satisfied being ignorant. We need you bad, but won't let you push. *Danion*'s big. A couple men more or less wouldn't make much difference. Doctor, aren't you finished yet?"

"Just have to sew him up, sir. One minute."

"Commander McClennon, Commander Storm, go back to your cabins. Try not to aggravate me for a while."

BenRabi rose, touched the small bandage behind his ear. The numbness had begun to fade. He could feel a mild burning. It made him think of bigger cuts on his body and soul.

The doctor finished with Mouse. "There you go, Commander. Try not to strain it too much. I suggest you let your lady friends do the work for a few days." He spoke with a gentle sarcasm that may have masked envy.

"Word's getting around about you, Mouse," benRabi said.

Mouse did not respond. He was in no mood for banter.

They beat an unescorted retreat, seeking their cabins like wounded animals seeking the security of their dens. In the passage outside benRabi's cabin, Mouse asked, "What do we do now, Moyshe?"

BenRabi shrugged. "I don't know. I was hoping you'd think of something. Go for the ride, I guess. They've stalemated us."

"Just for now." Mouse stood a little taller. "We've got a year. They can't keep their guard up forever, can they?"

"They probably can." But a little false encouragement felt good. "Still, you never know. Something might turn up."

"Look at that."

The Sangaree lady was watching them from her doorway. She smiled, waved.

"Gloating," benRabi said.

"Think she knows what happened? Think she helped do us in?"

BenRabi shrugged, looked at the woman. Their gazes seemed to ring like meeting swords. Her smile broadened. "Yes. I'm sure she did."

# EIGHT: 3047 AD

## The Olden Days, The Broken Wings

Hoping Marya would make no sense of the data before him, Niven told her, "I'm checking to see where people go when they leave The Broken Wings. If a statistically significant number emigrate to certain worlds, we can begin to infer both their fantasies under dome conditions and what it is that attracts them to a particular type world. If it's environmental, then we've discovered a way to ease the negatives of dome life." He hoped he sounded tutorial. He cranked it up a notch to be sure. "Ubichi specializes in negative environment, high-yield exploitation operations. Employee turnover has become a major problem because of the expense of training and transportation for some of our field operations. It's in the corporate interest to reduce those costs by keeping our employees happy and comfortable."

*Pretty glib*, he thought. He congratulated himself. "What're you doing here?"

"Looking for you. We had a date."

"Not till… Holy Christ! Look at the time. Hey beautiful lady, I'm sorry. I got on the track of something. I worked right through lunch. Give me a minute, will you? I'll finish up, call my secretary, and we can get moving." He grinned. "I have to check in. Education didn't wear the Old Earth off of him. You wouldn't believe the hell he gave me last night!"

He no longer felt the smile. She was turning him to gelatin again.

Mouse did not answer his buzz. Niven would have been surprised had he done so. The call was simply a ploy to get the data out of Marya's sight, and to seize time to create a plausible structure of lies atop those he had just told.

He needed no story. Marya asked no questions except, "What do you want to do?"

He almost replied with the hard truth.

"I've had it with work, but we about covered everything last night. Angel City isn't swing-town." Gallantly, he added, "I'm content just being with you. You pick."

She laughed. "And they say there's no romance left on Old Earth. How about we just go for a walk? I feel like a good long one."

"Uh…" His hands started shaking.

He had gotten out young, but the lessons of an Old Earth's childhood died hard. People who did not learn them young also died hard. Not to walk the streets without a gang of friends was one of the strictest lessons of the motherworld.

This was not Old Earth. Death did not make the streets its home here. But the sticktights did lurk there, and they might up the ante in the game at any minute.

"How come you're grinning?"

"That's no grin, lady. That's what they call a rictus. Of fear. I'm Old Earther. You know how hard it would be for me to walk down a street without at least fifty guys to back me up?"

"I forgot. But there's nothing to worry about here, Gun."

"You know it. I know it here in my head. But down here in my guts there's a caveman who says we're both liars."

"If it's really that hard…"

"No, don't get upset. I didn't say I wouldn't try. I've got to get used to it. Hell, I force myself to get out as much as I can. I just wanted to warn you so you won't think it's your fault if I get a little jumpy and quiet."

"You'll settle down. You'll see. This is just about the dullest, least dangerous city in The Arm."

A few hours later, shortly after The Broken Wings' early night had fallen, Niven snarled, "What did you say back at the hospital? Something about the safest streets in the galaxy?"

The darkness of the alley pressed in. His frightened eyes probed the shadows for movement. The lase-bolt had missed his cheek by a centimeter. He still felt the heat of it. "Even my toenails are shaking, lady."

Marya fingered her hair. A bolt had crisped it while they were running. Niven's nostrils twitched as they caught the sharp burnt hair odor.

Marya's face was pallid in the glow of a distant streetlight. She was shaking too. And apparently too angry to respond.

"You got a jealous boyfriend?"

She shook her head, gasped, "This isn't Old Earth. People don't do things like this out here."

Niven dropped to all fours and crawled to the alley mouth.

Heavy work was not his province, but he had had the basic programs given all field agents. He could make a show if he had to.

He had to do something now. The alley was a cul-de-sac. And the rifleman might be teamed. A deathtrap could be closing.

A bolt scarred brick above his head. He rolled away, growling, "Starscope. Damn!" But he had spotted the triggerman. The bolt had come from atop a warehouse across the street.

"Can't be much of a shot," Niven mumbled. "That isn't fifty meters."

If he could survive the sprint across the street…

There was a startled exclamation from the gunman's position, then a choked wail of fear and pain. A body plunged off the warehouse roof and thumped into the street.

Niven was across in an instant, shoving himself into the warehouse wall while he studied the corpse.

The weak light revealed the limper from the Marcos lobby. His windpipe had been crushed.

Every man's signature is unique. And an assassin leaves a grim sort of signature on his victims. Niven knew this one. He peered upward.

Why would Mouse be shadowing him?

Not that he objected. Not right now.

Marya arrived. She averted her eyes. "You must have a guardian angel."

"One of us does." He stared at her. Something clicked. It was nothing he could define, just a tweak of uneasiness because she had not asked him why anyone would want to kill him. A civilian would have asked that right away.

He looked for the assassin's weapon, did not see it. "I'm going to try to get onto that roof."

"Why? Shouldn't we get out of here?"

Another click. Civilians started screaming for the police. Outworlds civilians, anyway.

"Yeah, I guess. If he had anybody with him we would have heard from them by now." But where to go? he wondered. Not the hotel. Not with the number officially on. Not with the war rules proclaimed. And not to a safehouse. He did not yet know what Mouse had arranged. And he could not make the fallbacks to find out with Marya tagging along.

The death threat had alerted the professional in him. Had raised barriers that would wall off the whole universe till he had sorted the friends from enemies and noncombatants.

"We could go to my place," Marya suggested.

Memories of countless spy and detective dramas battled for Niven's attention. Was it all a setup? Three misses at fifty meters seemed unlikely for even a clumsy assassin. But he did not want to believe that Marya was involved. She was such a magnetic, animal woman…

Believe it or not, only a cretin would have ignored the possibility completely. Survival had become the stake on the board.

He dared not let her know he was suspicious. "All right." He looked around fearfully, having no trouble projecting shakiness and confusion. "But I've got to do a couple of things first."

Their eyes met. And he *knew*. He did not want it to be, but it was true. She *was* the enemy. Right now she was trying to find an excuse to stay close to him that would not arouse his suspicions.

She was not a good actress. Under stress she could not control the body language signals that betrayed her thoughts.

He felt betrayed and hurt, though he had known her just one day.

He had always needed to be wanted. Not for whom or what he was, but just as a human being.

Human. Was she even human? There was no sure way of telling without complicated tests. Geneticists were certain that humanity and the Sangaree shared a prehistoric ancestry.

She might even be the new Sangaree Resident. The last one had been a woman.

"Where do you stay?" he asked.

She chose not to push. She explained how he could get to her apartment.

"You don't have to do this," he told her, then cursed silently. By saying that, he had tacitly admitted being the sniper's target. But sometimes it was necessary to take chances. He could at least feed her belief in his lack of suspicion. "It might be dangerous."

"That's all right. I've never been involved in anything like this." Feigned excitement illuminated her face. "What have I gotten myself into, Gun?"

It was smoke screen time. "Sweetheart, I don't know. I really don't. This is the second time I've been jumped, but nobody bothered to tell me why last time either. They tried it right in the Marcos before. The day we got here. And we don't even know anybody here. But people have been following me all the time, and… If you're an Old Earther, you sense things like that."

"Maybe it's not you. Maybe it's your friend."

"John? I never thought of that. I guess it's possible. I don't really know anything about him. The Corporation sent him. Anyway, whatever's going on, I mean to find out."

He had yielded just enough distorted truth, he hoped, to leave her with doubts. A lot depended on whether or not the opposition had been able to evade Mouse's bug-scans.

"Will you be all right, Marya? Should I walk you home?"

"I'll manage."

"Probably be safer without me, anyway. See you in a while." He glanced at the dead man, then the streets. Not a soul was stirring.

It was odd how people sensed a gathering storm, then stayed inside where they would witness nothing and run no risks. Though this was a warehouse district, there should have been some traffic. Hell. Where were the security patrols? Where were the police cruisers?

He had seen the same thing happen on Old Earth, where the gangs went to their guns at the slightest provocation. Citizens and enforcers always kept a low profile till the stink of gunsmoke left the air.

Mouse was not at the first fallback, nor had he left a message. Niven did find a hastily scribbled message at the second. It told him that Marya was the new Sangaree Resident. And, as if in afterthought, Mouse went on to say that he was on the run from a dozen men who had gotten onto him after the incident at the warehouse.

Niven scratched a reply, explaining where he would be. The drop was large, so he left the notes he had taken at the Med Center.

Those had to be salvaged no matter what. Maybe by Chief Navy Recruiter for The Broken Wings. He was the Bureau Angel City station chief.

Niven began drifting, killing time in order to give Marya a chance to make a move that would illuminate the outfit's current thinking. After an hour he picked up a sticktight.

His shadow was a sleepy-faced thug pretending to be a derelict. A not-too-bright offworlder, Niven decided. Angel City was too young and thoroughly ordered to sustain even a one-man Bowery.

The man did not move in. They were hoping he would lead them to Mouse.

He observed his shadow's tradecraft more out of curiosity than concern. The man was a professional but unaccustomed to this kind of work. He was probably a shooter or runner grabbed simply because he was available. He could be shaken at leisure. Niven shifted him to the back burner of awareness.

He drifted toward Marya's apartment. His nerves settled. He decided what he was going to do.

He did not relax completely. They might catch Mouse. Then his life would be worthless. But while Mouse remained at large, he was sure, they would not harm him.

He shook the sticktight, found a public comm, woke the Angel City station chief, explained where the Med Center information was hidden. He used a word code the other side would need hours to unravel—assuming they were tapping at all.

He reached Marya's apartment as dawn began coloring the dome. The molecularly stacked plastic glimmered redly. As the sunlight changed its angle of incidence, the plastic would alternate between transparency and a progression up an iridescent spectrum.

He was tired but still alert, and exhilarated because he had handled himself well.

Marya responded to his knock instantly. "Where have you been?" she demanded. "I've been worried sick." She peered over his shoulder, along the second floor hallway.

Checking for Mouse? For her backup?

"Somebody started following me around. I didn't know what to do, so I just walked around till he gave up. Or I lost him."

"Gun, I don't understand all this. Why?..."

"Honey, I don't know. And I've been thinking hard. All I can figure is maybe one of Ubichi's competitors thinks I'm after something besides that research data..." He paused, pretending to have been startled by a thought. "Hey! They never did tell me *why* they want the data. I just assumed... Maybe it's for a project that's stepping on somebody's toes."

Had he been what he claimed, the possibility would have been real. Ubichi maintained its own armed forces. The frontier corporations played rough.

Uncertainty filled Marya's eyes for a moment.

*Bureau miscalculated,* he thought. He could have convinced her had he *looked* like a social psychologist. His cover could be checked all the way back to his birth. The Bureau was thorough that way. Especially Beckhart's section.

But Niven looked like an Old Earth heavy. And that was the death of any other credential a man could present.

"Mom? What's going on?" A dark-haired girl of seven or eight stumbled into the room. She ground sleepy eyes with the backs of her fists. She was small for her age, a breastless miniature of her mother.

"Brandy, this is my friend Dr. Niven. I told you about him."

"Oh."

Less than enthusiastic, Niven thought. In fact, her expression said he was a threat to her world.

She was a beautiful child. Straight out of a toy ad.

Niven could not frame a compliment that did not sound inane. "Hi, Brandy. You can call me Gun. It's short for Gundaker."

"Gundaker? What kind of name is that?"

"Old Earth."

"Oh." She wrinkled her lip. "Mom called you Doctor. Michael's sick."

He turned to Marya. The woman still stood at the door. "My son. Brandy's younger brother. He's got some kind of bug. Looks like flu."

"I'm not that kind of doctor, Brandy. But if there's anything I can do…"

"Do you know any good stories? Michael don't like the ones I make up. And Mom's never here." She glanced at her mother accusingly.

She was good, Niven thought. Better than Marya. "What kind of stories? Pirates? Olden days? War stories? Richard Hawksblood and Gneaus Julius Storm? Did you know they fought a war right here on The Broken Wings?"

He mentioned it casually, conversationally, fishing for a reaction. The war in the Shadowline, the last great mercenary war, had taken place on Blackworld not long after the encounter on The Broken Wings.

Sangaree interests had taken a beating because of the Shadowline. But one or two Families had begun recouping here before the shock-waves from Blackworld had died.

Getting caught with their hands in there had cost them control of numerous legitimate corporations and the lives of several Family chieftains. The disaster had been so huge and widespread that it had become Sangaree legend.

The girl just shrugged, implying that Blackworld meant nothing to her. "Pirates, probably." She seemed to lose interest.

She left the room. Cooking sounds followed her departure.

*Must not have heard about the Shadowline*, Niven thought. What Family did Marya represent? A minor one crowding the First Families because of their loss of face on Blackworld? Surely not one that had been involved there.

"She's a doll," he told Marya. "You thought about getting her into modeling?"

"No. She wouldn't. Sit down. Relax. I'll fix you something to eat. Then I'll move Michael in here. You can sleep in the kids' bed."

Brandy brought coffee. It was real.

He discovered what Marya had meant about Brandy. He had not caught it earlier because she had not looked his way.

The girl's one eye trained wildly walleyed and appeared blind.

He showed no reaction to her pained, defiant stare. Her sensitivity screamed at him. He supposed the damage was recent.

Niven indulged in tradecraft during the few seconds when Brandy had returned to the kitchen and Marya had not yet returned. He examined his surroundings critically.

The time would come when he would have to report, accurately, where every speck of dust had lain.

The apartment was cramped. That was typical of dome city living quarters. It was sparsely populated by ragged second-hand furniture. That was to be expected of poor folks. And Marya, clearly, was not an obsessive housekeeper. Cobwebs hung in the ceiling corners. Junk cluttered the chairs and floors.

Her sloppiness had nothing to do with poverty or lack of time, only with habit. Sangaree at home had animal servants who picked up after them.

Marya shared her roof with whole tribes of roaches. Dirt streaked the plastic walls. The curtains were frayed and soiled.

It was exactly the sort of place where a busy, impoverished woman would come to rest. She was crafty, this one. She had converted her ethnic liabilities into assets.

But would a poor woman serve real coffee? When coffee had to come all the way from Old or New Earth?

He did not call her on it. He might give something away by revealing that he recognized the real thing when he tasted it. Most Old Earthers would not, because every ounce went into export.

They were fencing now, subtly, with rapiers consisting of little tests.

One of the rules of his profession was never to yield anything concrete.

She was not giving him anything either. Certainly not enough to understand her.

Who could comprehend the Sangaree mind? The Admiral had been trying for decades. He barely got by.

Like Mouse, though, Beckhart did not want to understand. Not really. He wanted to destroy. Comprehension was just a weapon in his arsenal.

They sat in silence for several minutes. He watched Marya over his cup. She considered him. He wondered what strange thoughts might be running through her alien brain.

"I'd better check on Michael, Gun."

He followed her as far as the bedroom door.

The room was tiny. It contained two dilapidated beds. One for Marya, one for her children.

Marya settled on the edge of the one containing a pale five-year-old. The boy watched Niven warily.

"Michael, this is my friend Dr. Niven. He's going to stay with us for a while."

"Hi, Mike."

"Not Mike." The child's voice was weak but angry. "Michael. After my great-grandfather."

Marya winced.

Michael radiated pride.

Niven controlled his surprise. "Right. Michael it is."

He had been wrong. Almost fatally wrong. These Sangaree would know the Shadowline well.

There had been but one Sangaree with the human name Michael. Michael Dee. The man who had engineered the war. The man who had been both the pride and despair of his race.

The man who had paid the ultimate price for failing.

"Brandy says you like pirate stories. I knew a pirate once. Only he wasn't a pirate when I met him. That's what he is now. I grew up and went to school, and he grew up and became a pirate."

"I don't think he's ready for that right now, Gun." Marya seemed honestly worried. "I'm going to have to call a doctor, I think."

Niven was surprised at himself. He was concerned too. "You want me to call a cabcar?" What was he doing? The kid was Sangaree. His purpose in life was to help guide that species to a final solution. Little ones became big ones.

"Oh, no. There's one from the hospital who lives right upstairs. I don't know her very well, but…"

"Go get her, woman. I'll manage here."

She stared. Something within her softened momentarily. The hidden woman, the one behind the one behind the one she was trying to portray, showed through. She kissed his cheek. "Thanks, Gun." When he pulled her closer, "Later. I'll be back as soon as I can."

He had not been after a kiss. He had attached a tiny chameleon transmitter to the back of her collar.

She closed the apartment door behind her. Niven inserted a receiver into his ear while pretending to scratch.

Smiling wryly, he patted himself where she had touched him. Had she done the same to him?

There was no reason why she should have to go out for a doctor. She would have sufficient medical background herself—if there was any truth to her cover.

He smiled again. Marya was no tactician, either.

"Are you my mom's new lover?"

He was surprised. Little girls did not ask questions like that.

"No. Not yet."

"She needs one. Do you think she's pretty?"

"I think she's gorgeous." He was uncomfortable. He did not know how to socialize with children. The only child he knew was Jupp's boy, Horst-Johann.

"Maybe she should get married again. Are you married?"

Marya had reached a public comm. She was briefing someone. Following her part of a conversation and trying to guess the other half while carrying on another with Brandy proved impossible. He did hear Marya ask for a deep trace on his cover. That meant he had won a round. She had doubts. Or wanted to have them, which came to the same thing.

"No. I never met the right lady." This was one bold child. Did she know she was not human? Probably. From the little he had heard, Sangaree had no childhood in the human sense. Their children were shielded from nothing. They were treated as, and expected to behave as, miniature adults.

"Don't know if I'd like you, though."

*Honest, too,* he thought. He went to check on Michael. The boy still watched him with wide, wary eyes.

He was bad sick. Marya would not risk a human doctor otherwise. There were few greater risks the underground Sangaree could take. Physicians could sometimes spot the subtle differences between species.

Marya returned with the doctor before Niven's conversation with Brandy became impossible.

The doctor, he decided, was "tame." She worked with a confidence and quickness that betrayed her.

Niven whispered to Marya, "Brandy's been matchmaking."

She laughed. "Husband-shopping for me again? She never gives up."

"I don't think I passed the exam."

"Doesn't matter. I won't get caught in that trap again."

"Why'd you bring them out here?" On Old Earth parents usually put their children into public care as soon as they were born. Niven had had an unusual childhood in that he had spent much of it with his mother. He still kept in touch with her, but had lost track of his father years ago.

The shedding of children was a common practice on the tamed outworlds, too. Fewer than a quarter of Confederation's children were raised by their biological parents.

Marya was shocked. Her Sangaree sense of Family had been outraged. But she could not tell him that. "I forgot. You do things differently where you come from. Yeah, it would be convenient sometimes. But they're *my* kids."

"Don't try to explain. Just call it one of the differences between the Inner Worlds and the frontier. I'm getting used to them."

The doctor returned from the bedroom. "I gave him a broad-spectrum antibiotic, Marya. And an antiviral. It's nothing serious. See that he gets plenty of bed rest and lots of fluids, and keep an eye on his temperature. It'll go up. Give him some aspirin if it gets too high. Do you need a thermometer?"

Marya nodded. She portrayed embarrassment beautifully.

*You did that well, lady,* Niven thought. *Too poor to afford a thermometer. But you serve genuine coffee.* He smiled. She was doing a chemo-psychiatric internship, but had to summon an outside doctor… Was she driven by some secret death wish?

"Nice to have met you, Doctor Niven," the doctor told him.

"You too." He watched her go to the door. There was no pride in the way she walked.

"You want to get some sleep now, Gun?" Marya asked.

"Going to have to." But would his nerves permit it here in the heart of enemy territory?

They would. After he had skinned down to his underwear, had flopped into Marya's bed, and had told Michael, "Good night, Captain," the lights went out.

He wakened once, hazily, when Marya slipped into bed beside him. He mumbled foggily, then knew nothing for hours.

He wakened slowly. Gradually, he realized that The Broken Wings' truncated day had sped by. It was night again. He did not remember where he was till he rolled against the woman.

That simple movement initiated three tempestuous days.

Marya was insatiable. The only word he found to fit her was "hungry." He had never encountered a woman who had such a need for a man.

Niven astounded himself. Their lovemaking became so savage, so narrowly scoped, that it was more like combat. As if, "Let he who first cries 'Hold! Enough!' be damned forever."

They seemed to do nothing but sleep and copulate, making attack after attack in some sort of sexual war. The outside world seemed to have lost all meaning.

Yet there was method. There was rationality. In struggling to please Marya, who was struggling to distract him, Niven kept himself motivated by remembering who she was. He kept trying to convince himself that he was doing this to sabotage the enemy chain of command.

He knew Marya was not motivated entirely by lust either.

Oh, but they did have one hell of a good time on the rumpled sheets of that battlefield.

In the interims Niven sometimes wondered what had become of Mouse. Mouse, he reflected, sure had the free hand he always wanted.

Brandy, recognizing the way of things, had taken her brother out the first night. They were staying upstairs with the doctor. Michael, looking a little better, sometimes wandered in, moped around without saying much, then wandered out again. Brandy stayed away all the time.

"What are we doing?" Niven once muttered to himself. They were enemies to the death. That was the prime rule, the blood rule, by which he and she were supposed to live and die. Yet they were denying it, or sublimating it in the form of love…

He began to dread mission's end. Debriefing… He would have to answer questions. He would have to explain.

Niven was snoring. He had one arm beneath Marya's neck.

The building shuddered like a dog shaking off water. A window cracked. Tableware clattered onto the kitchen floor. The whole neighborhood reverberated to the explosion.

Niven jerked upright. "D-14," he grunted.

"What?"

"What was that?"

"An explosion."

They dressed, almost racing. Reflections of dancing firelight colored the cracked window. Marya looked out. "Oh, Holy Sant!"

"What?"

"The warehouse..."

"Eh?"

"I'll be right back... What's that?"

A yell had come from somewhere downstairs. Cries and screams followed it.

Niven knew that first yell. That was Mouse in assassin's mind.

Earlier, he had seen the shape of the needlegun lumping her underwear in a dresser drawer. He beat her to it.

The door crashed inward. A ragged, battered, bloody Mouse hurtled through. He was so keyed for action that he looked three meters tall.

"Easy," Niven said, gesturing with the needlegun. "Everything's under control, Mouse."

Mouse was not hurt. The blood was not his own. "Got everything," he croaked through a dry throat. "Message away. Got to bend the bitch and get out."

That was their business, but... Niven could not permit the woman's murder. That she was Sangaree seemed irrelevant. "No. There's no need. Not this time."

Mouse was coming down. Thought was replacing action. He glanced at Niven's weapon, at the woman. "All right. You're the boss, Doc. But I've got to get something out of this. Where're the damned kids?"

"Upstairs. But I won't let you kill children, either."

"Wouldn't think of it, Doc. Wouldn't even drown a puppy. You know old John. So tie her up, will you? Can't have her coming after us." He backed out the door.

Siren howls tortured the streets. The grumble of a gathering crowd slipped tentacles into the room. "Sorry it had to end this way, Marya. But business is business."

"I almost believed..." She stared at him. For an instant she looked small and defenseless. He reminded himself that she was Sangaree, that she would become instant death if he were careless. "I suppose you're soothing your conscience. I wouldn't if the tables were turned. You've hurt us too much already."

*Not a smart thing to say to somebody pointing a gun at you,* Niven thought. He shrugged. "Maybe. It's not conscience, though. A different weakness. You'd probably have to be human to understand." He left it to her to figure out what he meant.

Mouse returned with the children and doctor. In the process he had acquired a weapon. "Tie these three, too, Doc."

The doctor was more frightened than Brandy or Michael. Humans on the fringes of the Business generally imagined operations by and against the organization to be more deadly than they were.

Brandy asked, "What're you doing, Gun?" Straight out, emotionlessly. As if she were used to being under the gun.

"Business, dear."

"Oh." She sped her mother a disgusted look.

"He's the Starduster," Marya told her.

"And you fell for his story?"

Niven tore sheets into strips, tied the doctor, then the girl, then Michael. "Told you I knew a pirate, Captain."

"Good," Mouse said. "Let me have the gun, Doc."

"Eh? Why?"

"Because I need it."

Puzzled, Niven handed the weapon over. Mouse tossed it into the hallway.

Niven shook his head, said, "We'd better get moving. They won't stay disorganized forever."

"One thing first." Mouse shoved his weapon under his arm. He took a hypo from the doctor's bag and filled it from an ampule he carried in his pocket. "This one's for your great-grandfather, kids. And all his brothers and sisters, nieces and nephews."

"What the hell are you doing?" Niven demanded.

"Just business, Doc. Turnabout's fair play, right? We should expand our own markets." He raised Michael's sleeve.

Marya understood instantly. "No! Piao! Not my children. Kill me if you want, but don't…"

Mouse answered her with a tight smile. "Just business, lady. Gag her, Doc. Hurry. We got to get the stuff out before Navy pops to we've cut out the instel here."

Niven suddenly understood what Mouse was doing. "Hey! You can't…" He wanted to stop it, to protest, to refuse, got confused by the reference to Navy. "Stardust?"

Mouse nodded, smiling wickedly. His hand strayed toward his weapon.

"Oh." How could the man be so cruel? That was murder in the worst possible way.

Marya needed gagging desperately. Her screams could attract attention…

Dazed, Niven silenced her. Her flesh seemed icy beneath his fingertips. He felt the rage and hatred boiling inside her. She started shaking.

For an instant he thought she was having a seizure.

Mouse injected the children. That wicked little smile kept playing with his lips. He was blissfully happy in his cruelty.

Why did he hate so much?

"Come on, Doc. They're on their way down. Can't you hear them?"

The crowd noise and sirens were yielding to the rumble of assault landing craft descending on penetration runs. The Broken Wings' atmosphere howled its protest of the violation.

Jupp was on his way.

Someone stuck his head through the doorway. Mouse shot, missed, jumped into the hallway and shot again. "Doc, will you come on?"

"I'm sorry, Marya. Really. It's the way things had to be." He snagged the needlegun in passing, skipped a fresh corpse, and pursued Mouse into the emergency stairwell.

Later, as they waited in the crowd watching the invaders pour through the main city locks, Niven asked, "What was that crap about getting off before Navy finds out?"

"We're supposed to be the Starduster and Piao, remember?"

"But they'll know when…"

"Not yet. Look." The Marines entering the city wore uniform gear, but it was not Service issue. It was like nothing Niven had ever seen.

Mouse had chosen the waiting place with care. A man loaded with brass headed directly toward them. "Mr. Piao?" He avoided looking at Niven. His attitude seemed one of mixed awe, fear, and loathing. "You have the material for my officers?"

"That I do, Colonel." Mouse proffered a thick package. "Congratulations. Your men are as efficient as ours."

The Colonel reddened. His mouth snapped open, but he caught himself. Carefully, he said, "More so, Mr. Piao. As you'll someday learn."

"All things are possible to those who believe."

The Colonel riffled through a stack of copies. Other officers gathered behind him. He started passing them papers.

"Let's drift, Doc. They can handle it."

Niven did not miss the wariness in all those Marine eyes. "What was that all about?"

"Oh. They think we're Piao and the Starduster too. They think we worked a deal with Luna Command so we could knock over the Sangaree and take control of their nets."

"What's all the smoke screen for?"

"We've got to keep the Starduster story alive, at least till Jupp makes his hit. Otherwise they might evacuate their production facilities. By the way, I wanted to say you did a job digging all that info out. The Old Man is going to love you."

Niven did not follow it. "It's too Byzantine for me. Are the Sangaree supposed to find out that they're Marines? And then figure we didn't say anything about the production facilities because that would cut off our own supply?"

"Wait till you're in on one of the Old Man's complicated ones."

"Mr. Piao?" a Marine non-comm asked.

"Yes."

"If you'll follow me, sir. Your transportation." Marines surrounded them. A precaution against assassination, Niven supposed. Those bounties still existed.

Sounds of sporadic fighting came from the city. Believing the raiders to be Starduster men, the Sangaree minions would battle hard. The Starduster's viciousness toward collaborators was legend.

The Marines guided them into an armored personnel carrier. They had it to themselves. It rumbled away toward Angel Port.

"Mouse, I get the feeling the Admiral threw in a few twists just to make it interesting. What happens when the Starduster finds out that we've been using his name in vain?"

Mouse was in a bright, expansive mood. He had had a beautiful day. He had carved his initials on the Sangaree soul. He had vandalized their house of crime. "I'll tell you a secret, Doc. If you promise you won't ever let the Old Man know you know." He looked at Niven expectantly.

"All right. I give. What?"

"You really *are* the Starduster."

"What?"

"The Starduster. Piao. The Old Man invented the whole thing. The Starduster is whoever he points at and says, 'You!' "

"Well, shit. Mouse, I really needed that. Here you've had me scared to death that the son of a bitch was going to crawl out of the woodwork and cut my throat. I got a year's vacation coming after debriefing. And, dammit, as soon as it goes through, I'm going to…"

"Don't count on it, Doc. Not when you're working for the Old Man."

October 3047. Captain Jupp von Drachau, commanding Special Action Task Force IV, with a heavy siege squadron attached, surprises and commences reduction action against Sangaree manufacturing facilities hidden in the inner asteroid belt surrounding Delta Sheol, a white dwarf in the mini-cluster called the Hell Stars. Destruction is swift, savage, and complete. At the same time Confederation and local police agencies begin closing down the drug networks formerly rooted on The Broken Wings.

Admiral Beckhart has taken every point in a victorious round against his oldest and most favored enemy.

# NINE: 3048 AD

## Operation Dragon, *Danion*

BenRabi started to push into his cabin, still glaring at the Sangaree woman.

"I should've bent her on The Broken Wings," Mouse snarled. "You should've…" He had not forgiven Moyshe the weakness that had left her alive.

"I can't stomach contingency assassinations, Mouse."

"Yeah? Look over there and think about it some more. How much mischief could she do?"

"All right. So it makes a perverted kind of sense. If you figure a ghost like The Broken Wings will come back to haunt you."

"It will. It always does. Maybe I'll settle this up…"

BenRabi shook his head. "Not here. Not now. Not after what we just went through."

"I didn't mean right now. I'm not a fool, Moyshe. It would look like an accident."

"Let it be, Mouse."

There was no compassion in Mouse. *I should be flint too,* benRabi thought. *But I don't have his knack for hating.*

BenRabi found the things and people in his life too transient for more than mild aversion.

"She'd better move fast when we hit dirt again, then." Mouse growled. "One getaway is all she gets… I hope we find Homeworld before I check out."

BenRabi felt a twinge of jealousy. Mouse knew the nature of his Grail. His feet were set inalterably on the path that led to it, though it was a cup of blood.

"For your sake, I hope so." Moyshe laughed softly, bitterly. Sometimes he had to, or scream. "See you later." He pushed into his cabin.

He hoped their year cooped up here would soften Mouse, but feared there was no hope. Marya would not let time work. Memories of her children would lead her on…

Mouse's hate was old and strong, and deeper than Confederation culture usually ingrained. If he were indeed a Storm, that would explain it. The Storms of the Iron Legion had had an old-fashioned, Biblical way of looking at things.

Sangaree manipulations, during the war in the Shadowline, had destroyed the family.

But Mouse did not have to be a Storm. His hatred could be stardust-related.

"The joy that burns, the dream that kills," Czyzewski had called the drug only seconds before his own addiction had carried him into the big, endless dream of death. The drug was the leading plague of the age, and had touched virtually every human being. It had taken more lives than had the bitter Ulantonid War.

Stardust was the pusher's dream. It was immediately addictive. One flight and the user was hooked forever. An addict could not taper off. Neither could he withdraw cold. Nor could he substitute another, less fearsome drug in its place.

For the poor Inner Worlder addiction ended hard: by suicide, by being slain while trying to steal enough to finance another fix, or by finding death in the constant dogfighting among have and have-not addicts. And many times the end came slowly, screamingly, in an institution where the warders could do nothing but watch, protect the world by keeping the addict restrained, and try to develop hearts of stone.

The sordid facts of stardust addiction tickled the Sangaree conscience not at all. They had a product to market, a stellar to turn.

They were not innately cruel. They simply did not see humans as anything but animals to be exploited. Do the cattleman, butcher, and customer consider themselves cruel to the beef animal? Sangaree thought their customers better than cattle. More like what Renaissance Europeans thought of black Africans. Semi-intelligent apes.

BenRabi lay on his bunk and wondered about his partner. Mouse claimed his assignments were all counter-Sangaree. To date they had been, and Mouse had prosecuted them with a savage zeal, with cruel little touches, like the injection of Marya's children. But what was he doing here, now, working against the Starfishers? That did not compute.

Following the announcement of von Drachau's raid, Mouse had been in the clouds, as if he were a skying addict himself.

The Sangaree were the demons of the Confederation era. They passed as human easily. Their Homeworld lay somewhere outside The Arm. Compared to humanity, they were few in number. It was rumored that they could breed only under their native sun.

The Sangaree produced little for themselves. They preferred instead to raid, to deal in drugs and slaves and guns.

Confederation resented them bitterly. Man was their prime victim. The nonhuman races considered them merely a nuisance.

Someone softly knocked on Moyshe's door. "Come in," he said. "Mouse. Thought it was you." It was the first he had seen Mouse since Kindervoort's inquisition.

"The word's around," Mouse told him. "They've all decided that we're evil, mean, bad, wicked, nasty, crude, rude, and unattractive spies." He laughed.

"The Sangaree woman passed the word, I suppose."

"Maybe. Why don't you slide out there and see what's going on? It's good for a laugh. Hell, you'd think we were as rare as dodos and smelled like skunks."

"Don't we? Morally?"

"Ahh... Moyshe. What the hell is it with you these days? Hey! You should see the competition laughing up their sleeves. But we get the last laugh. They're on their way. Kindervoort's troops snatched a couple beekies this morning. Same way he got us. Knew they were coming. Looks like he knew about everybody, except Strehltsweiter."

"Mouse, they've got to have a mole in Luna Command. Somebody deep."

"That's what I figure. It's the only answer that adds up. Moyshe, you should see the kids with their holy attitudes. Like they think they're a plane above us. Poor innocents." Mouse smiled at a memory. "You know that Williams girl? I shocked the hell out of her. Asked her her price. She missed the point. That's real innocence."

"Ah, youth. Mouse, what happened to *our* innocence and idealism? Remember how it was in Academy? We were going to save the universe."

"Somebody found our price." He frowned, dropped onto the spare bunk. "That's not really true. We're doing it, you know. It's just that the mechanics of it aren't what we thought they'd be. We didn't understand that everything has to be a trade-off, that whenever we changed things to what we thought they should be, we had to do it at somebody else's expense... Hell, you've got me doing it."

"What?"

"Thinking. Moyshe, what's happening with you? You always were a moody guy, but I've never seen you like you've been lately. Ever since we left Carson's..."

BenRabi's defenses stood to arms. He did not dare open up. Two reasons: you just did not do that these days, and he was not sure what was happening himself. So he masked the shadowed walls of *Festung Selbst* behind a half-truth.

"I'm just depressed. Maybe because I didn't get my vacation. Maybe because of Mother… I had a bag full of things I wanted to take home. Some stamps and coins I picked up in Corporation Zone. Some stuff I managed to get back from The Broken Wings. This beautiful hand-carved bone trivet from Tregorgarth, and some New Earth butterflies that would be worth a mint anywhere else…"

"Bullroar, my friend. Bullroar." Mouse peered at him from beneath lowered brows. "I'm getting to know you, Moyshe benRabi. I can tell when something's got you by the guts. You better do something. It'll eat you alive if you keep it locked up inside."

Mouse was right about one thing. They were getting to know one another. Too well. Mouse was reading him now, and wanting to help. "Maybe. When's your next chess thing? I'll come lose a few games, tip a few brews with the troops."

Mouse frowned. He knew a light show when he saw one.

Getting too damned close!

Mouse glanced at *Jerusalem*, at which benRabi had been scribbling. "Well, I didn't mean to porlock, Moyshe." He rose. "I don't know if we'll have any more tournaments. Kindervoort says we'll make *Danion* sometime tonight. That's why I came over. Thought you'd want to know."

BenRabi brightened. "Hey, good." He pushed the *Jerusalem* papers back, rose, started pacing. "The waiting is getting to me. A little work…"

The rendezvous with the harvestship was anticlimactic. There were no brass bands, and no curious crowds at the receiving bay. The only Seiners around were those who had been sent to show the landsmen to their quarters and brief them about their job assignments. No one of any stature came to greet them. Moyshe was disappointed.

His guide did his work quickly and efficiently and told him, "You'd better turn in. This is the middle of our night. I'll be back early to help walk you through your first day."

"Okay. Thanks, Paul." Moyshe examined the man. Paul was much like the Seiners he had met before.

The man examined him, too, and struggled with prejudices as he did so. "Good night, Mr. benRabi."

"See you in the morning."

But he did not. Amy showed up instead, and took both benRabi and Mouse under her wing.

"Keeping an eye on us, eh?" Mouse asked.

She colored slightly. "Yeah. Sort of. Jarl said he wanted to keep you together so you'd be easier to watch."

"You don't have to be embarrassed. We understand."

"This isn't my kind of thing, Commander Storm. I'm a plumber, not a counterspy."

"Call me Mouse. Please. Or Mr. Iwasaki."

"Whatever you want. Mouse. Are you ready for breakfast?" She turned to Moyshe.

"I'm still Moyshe benRabi. All right? Yes. I could eat three breakfasts."

Work commenced immediately after tool issue and a brief class in how to find one's way around the harvestship. It never let up.

Moyshe forgot his screaming need in the pressure of the following week's labors. The memories that had been gnawing the underbelly of his soul vanished from consciousness. He flew easy, not thinking, not observing, not questioning. He stayed too busy or too tired. The Seiners were true to their promise to work the landsmen hard.

The mind-quirk he thought of as the image of the gun bothered him some, but only mildly, as he wandered through daydreams while replacing wrecked piping or damaged flow meters. He seized the vision, played with it, wrapped a few extended daydreams around it. It helped pass the time.

Kept busy, he began to enjoy life again.

"Something strange is going on here, Mouse," he whispered once when Amy was out of hearing.

"What's that?"

"This ship isn't hurt as bad as they want us to think. Look around."

"I couldn't tell. I never did any time in the line. All I know about ships is you get on, and after a while you get back off someplace else."

"What it amounts to is, there's a lot of damage, but nothing that would put something this size out of action. They could've handled it themselves. Just might have taken them a couple of years."

"So?"

"So, maybe we're here for some other reason. My intuition has been sniffing around that ever since Carson's."

"Why would they bring outsiders in if they didn't absolutely have to?"

"I don't know. The only reason you overstaff a ship is so you have personnel redundancy in case you take battle casualties. But on a ship this big two hundred people, or even a thousand, don't mean a thing. And who would the Seiners fight? Confederation? Not with a bunch of fifth columnists aboard."

"Give it time. It'll come to the top. No matter what they hope, they can't keep everything hidden forever."

"Can it. Amy's coming." Curious, he thought. Mouse did not seem interested in Starfisher motives at all.

BenRabi's first week did have its rough edges. Every encounter with the Sangaree woman became a crisis. And she could not be avoided. Her team, repairing air ducting, was working the same service passages as his.

She would not leave Mouse alone. And the certainty of purpose which made Mouse's responses predictable taunted benRabi with worries about his own incompleteness.

She did not bait him. She knew that he would do nothing but look at her soulfully, reflecting the pain-giving back at her.

She appeared from a cross-passage only seconds behind Amy.

"Damn!" Moyshe swore. "Her again."

"Restrain me, Moyshe."

"You got it, partner. Be my ass in the fire, too."

"Well, the Rat again." The Sangaree woman stood with her hands on her hips, defying him to act. Backing her were several idealistic youngsters. She had sold them a simple-minded anti-spy package. "What an unpleasant surprise. Butchered anyone lately, spy? There're lots of non-Confies aboard. You ought to be as happy as a hog knee-deep in slop."

*A curious metaphor,* benRabi thought. *She must have chosen it especially for the Tregorgarthian kids.*

The youths looked at one another, embarrassed. They shared her views, and were a rather rude bunch themselves, but their society had taught them that too much bluntness could get a person killed. Tregorgarth was a rough world.

"You could start with me. You know what I think about your fascist military dictatorship. Or don't you have the guts?"

She knew damned well that he had, but assumed that he would not respond in front of witnesses—or that she could take him if he did. She was fooling herself there, benRabi thought. She believed Mouse strictly a strike-from-behind man. He was a lot more. Two decades of training and several thousand years of combat experience had gone into making him the perfect organic killing machine.

Moyshe did not know of a weapon, or a system of close combat, that Mouse did not know as well as any man who had ever lived. Short of pulling guns, there was little she and her whole crowd could have done were he to lose his temper.

BenRabi could sense the aching in Mouse, could feel Mouse's need to show her. But his partner controlled himself. That, too, had been part of his training.

BenRabi had to exercise some self-control himself. The woman's behavior had eroded his compassion.

She was playing a more dangerous game than she suspected. It would backfire on her if she did not ease up.

BenRabi was sure the woman was working to some carefully prepared plan. Her acting had not improved. Her easy confidence betrayed.

But she was vulnerable. Her Achilles Heel was her hatred. BenRabi was sure Mouse would exploit it…

"Miss Gonzalez," Amy said. "If you're quite finished? *We* have work to do. And I suggest you return to yours before there's cause for an inquiry into the absence of your supervisor."

The Sangaree woman backed down. She was not ready to jeopardize her mission.

"I feel like a fool," benRabi muttered.

Eyes downcast, Mouse said, "So do I. I can't take it forever, Moyshe."

Then Amy told them, "I'm glad you restrained yourselves. Things are ugly enough without our getting physical."

She intrigued benRabi. He watched her a lot when she was not looking. He was glad she did not go for chest-pounders. He was not the type, and in the back of his mind he had begun formulating designs upon her.

Over a flow chart thick with black X's indicating trouble spots, while Amy was off requisitioning a special wrench, Mouse muttered, "It's getting hard, Moyshe. I know what she's doing, but… She's trying to make us take ourselves out of the play."

"Hang on."

"One of these nights…"

Indefatigable Mouse. When benRabi finished work he had barely enough energy to eat, then tumble into bed. But Mouse got out and mingled, made new acquaintances (mostly female), and found new interests. He sponged up every bit of information that crossed his path.

His latest thing was the Middle American football popular with Seiners. They had arrived just in time for the pre-season excitement. His interest gave him an excuse to move around.

Moyshe was afraid. Having established his pattern of mobility, Mouse might arrange a fatal encounter with Marya somewhere far from the usual groundling stomping ground.

Moyshe wondered if he should catch her alone and try to make her understand.

He remembered The Broken Wings.

He was her primary target. She was trying to get at him through Mouse. The hurt he had done her was more personal, more ego-slashing than what Mouse had done. By her reasoning, what had happened to the children could be laid at his doorstep. He could have prevented it.

He would have to watch his back. Mouse was not the only one who could arrange an accident.

"Is she alone?" Mouse asked. "They like lots of backup."

"I haven't spotted anybody yet. They could be playing it close. What I want to know is, why is she here? Everybody else has tried something. But she just keeps on being obnoxious."

"She's waiting."

"For what?"

Mouse shrugged. "We'll find out the hard way, I guess."

"Here's a notion," Moyshe said. "It just came to me. A way to warn her."

"How?"

"Tomorrow's recreation day, right?" They had been promised one day off a week. This would be the first.

"And?"

"Those kids. You know how Tregorgarthians are. They're challenging everybody to meet them in a martial arts elimination tournament. Think you could manage them? Without hurting anybody?"

Mouse thought. "I don't know if I can pull the punches anymore."

"It would be good for the boys, too."

Tregorgarthians away from home tended to become bullies. Their homeworld schooled them to believe that those who did not fight at the drop of a hat were cowards. Smacked around a little, they civilized fast.

"Might give them second thoughts about letting her suck them in," benRabi mused. "They've got to know she's up to something."

"They'd back off if they knew I was dangerous, eh?"

"I'm hoping. Sex seems to be her main hold on them. I see one sneaking out of her room almost every morning."

"Who's sneaking out of whose cabin?"

Amy had returned. "Just gossiping," Moyshe replied. "One of the girls has an assembly line going."

She bit. "Landsmen! They're right about you being immoral."

Moyshe forbore observing that the Seiners seemed to be just as loose as his own people. Amy's priggishness was personal, not cultural. She was the only Starfisher he knew who talked that morality nonsense.

Mouse did not forbear. "When did you lose yours, Miss Morality?"

"Huh? My what?"

"Your cherry. You're no more pure than Old Earth air."

She sputtered, reddened, mumbled something about all landsmen being alike.

"You're right. Satyrs and nymphs, the lot of us." Mouse licked his lips, winked, asked, "What're you doing tonight?"

BenRabi grinned. Mouse was teasing her, as he had been all week long, but she did not realize it. He used a subtler approach when he really wanted a woman.

Something within her clicked, as it did each time Mouse put her on the defensive. A different, colder personality surfaced long enough to carry her past the rough spot. "Sleeping. Alone. Did you decide where you want to cut that water main?" Then another quick change of subject. "Oh. Jarl said to tell you to sharpen your teeth. He's bringing some people to play you tomorrow. You too, Moyshe."

Mouse had become chess champion of Service Ship Three. The Seiners had been excited about it. They were fond of the game and eager for new challenges.

"Why me? I'm no good."

"Better than you think. Anyway, we like everybody to find their place in the pecking order." Her hardness faded as quickly as it had come.

"I wanted to go over to Twenty-three West. If I could get permission." He pulled the excuse off the wall, for the salving of his ego. He did not like losing all the time, even at games. "I heard there's a guy over there with some early English coins. Victorians."

She looked puzzled.

Mouse laughed. "Didn't you know? We're both mad collectors. Coins and stamps mostly, because they're easy to lug around."

Frowning over them, Amy reminded benRabi of Alyce. So many of their facial expressions were similar. "It looks like you're mad everything. Chess. Archaicism. Collections. Football and women."

"That's him, not me," benRabi said.

"What about people?" Amy asked.

"Aren't women people?" Mouse countered.

She shook her head. She was a Starfisher, and Starfishers could not understand. Even Archaicism was just a hobby for them. Landsmen plunged themselves into things because they did not want to get involved with people. People hurt. The growing closeness between Mouse and benRabi, and the apparent friendships that had taken shape among the other foreigners, had confused Amy. She did not recognize their lack of temporal depth.

A critical difference between Confederation and Starfisher relationships was that of durational expectancy. The idea of a close relationship that could be severed quickly, painlessly, as easily as it had been formed, would not occur to a Starfisher. But they lived in a closed, static culture where a severely limited number of people passed through their lives. Friendships were expected to last a lifetime.

BenRabi was leery of the morrow. The isolation of the landsmen, far out in a remote residential cube, had minimized cultural friction during the week. But Kindervoort, for whom the outsiders had become a pet project, planned to make recreation day a gigantic college smoker, with floods of Seiners being exposed to landside ways.

Still trying to gentle everyone in, Moyshe supposed. Kindervoort was a rather thoughtful, admirable cop. He might get to like the man yet.

## TEN: 3047 AD

### The Olden Days, A Victory Celebration

"Max! You're beautiful."

"Don't sound so damned astonished, Walter."

"Oh. I didn't mean… I just never saw you dressed up before."

"Quit while you're ahead, friend. By the way. I notice you've changed a little too, Commander." She stared pointedly at the double sunbursts on his high collar. "I thought you said you were a dip."

"Naval Attaché. You know that."

"No, I didn't. Naval Attaché. Isn't that the same thing as head spy? Bureau of Naval Intelligence?"

Perchevski reddened. "Not always. Some of us…"

"Don't mind me, Walter." She smiled. "I'm just thinking out loud. That would explain some of the mysteries about you."

"Mysteries? About me? Come on, Max. I'm as mysterious as a pumpkin. Here we are."

A Marine accepted his ID badge, poked it into a slot. He eyed a readout screen somewhere out of sight. "Thank you, sir. Is this Miss Travers, sir?"

"Yes."

He consulted the screen again. "Thank you, sir. Have a nice evening, sir. Ma'am." A door slid open.

"Ma'am?" Max asked. "Do I look that old?"

"Come on, Max."

"Isn't he going to check me?"

"He did. You're all right. You don't have a bomb in your purse."

"Thanks a lot. What do they do to you in Academy? Why can't officers be polite like that nice young Marine?"

"You were just complaining… Max, you're sure contrary tonight. What's the matter?" He handed his over-tunic to the Marine corporal in the cloak room, helped Max with her cape.

"I'm scared, Walter. I've never even been near the Command Club. I don't know how to talk to Senators and Admirals."

"Know something, Max?"

"What?"

"I've never been here before either. We'll lose our virginity together. I'll tell you this, though. Admirals and Senators put their pants on one leg at a time, same as us, and they'll paw your leg under the table the same way I do."

"Male or female?" She seized his arm as they entered the huge Grand Ballroom. Her grip tightened.

"Both, the way you look tonight." He slowed. The place had no walls. An all-round animated hologram concealed the room's boundaries. Portrayals of Navy's mightiest ships of war lay every direction but downward. Perchevski automatically scanned the starfields. He saw no constellations he recognized.

Max's grip became painful. "I feel like I'm falling, Walter."

Local gravity had been allowed to decline to lunar normal to reinforce the deep-space effect.

"Somebody's really putting on the dog," Perchevski grumbled.

"Commander. Madam," said another polite Marine, "may I show you to your seats?"

The place was thronged. "Of course. How many people going to be here tonight, First Lance?" He was getting jittery. He still did not know why he was one of the elect.

"Nearly two thousand, sir. Here, sir." The Marine pulled a chair for Max.

"But…" He had scanned the faces of his tablemates. His jaw refused to continue working.

A few of them he knew personally. The Chief of Staff Navy and the Director of Naval Intelligence he recognized from the holonetnews.

Max recognized them too. She leaned and whispered, "Who the hell are you really, Walter?" She was so awed she could not look at the high brass.

Perchevski stared at his place setting, just as awed. "I'm starting to wonder myself."

"Thomas?"

Only one man alive insisted on calling him by that name. Perchevski forced his gaze to rise and meet that of his boss. "Sir?" He flicked a sideways glance at Mouse, who was eyeing Max appreciatively while whispering to his own ladyfriend.

"How are you doing, Max?" Mouse asked.

"You too, Yamamoto?"

"Thomas, the CSN and DNI want to be introduced."

"Yes sir." He evaded Admiral Beckhart's eyes by fixing his gaze on the one seat still vacant. He moved around to shake hands with the brass while Beckhart murmured the introductions.

"This is the man," Beckhart said. "He made it all go."

"Congratulations, Commander," the CSN told Perchevski. "And thank you. I understand you'll receive the Swords and Diamonds. Not to mention the prize."

Perchevski could not conceal his bewilderment.

*They've got to be talking about the operation,* he thought. *Swords and Diamonds to the Lunar Cross, right?* More chest hardware. With another medal and fifty pfenning he could buy a cheap cup of soy-coffee. Or pay half a Conmark without.

"Thank you, sir. I'd rather have my vacation, sir."

His boldness startled him even more than did his bitterness.

The DNI peered at Beckhart. "Up to your tricks with the troops, Admiral?"

"Ma'am?"

Perchevski grinned. The mission was worth it after all, just to get here and see that look on Beckhart's face.

"This man obviously doesn't have the faintest damn notion of what he's doing here."

Perchevski threw oil on the flames by nodding behind his boss's back.

He entered his commander's presence only rarely, which was just as well. The Admiral brought out the contrariness in him.

"It'll be clear soon enough," Beckhart said. "I just thought it would be a nice surprise. Go back to your friend, Thomas. I see she knows Mouse."

As Perchevski departed, he heard the DNI snap, "And see that they get some time off. The whole human race can't keep your pace."

"Yes, Ma'am."

Perchevski winced. He would get time, all right. And he would pay for it. Beckhart would get it back with interest.

"What was that about?" Max asked. "You looked like they were talking about the firing squad."

"They're going to give me a medal. There's something about medals… They just don't seem adequate."

"For surviving a virus?" She wore a sarcastic grin.

The high brass fell silent. People began to rise. Mouse abandoned the finger game he had been playing with his companion. Perchevski turned. "Jupp!"

Von Drachau looked old and haggard. His face had grown pasty since last they had met. "Hi, Tom." He greeted no one else at the moment.

The holograms faded. Perchevski spied the news crews and cameras they had concealed. "I begin to understand," he muttered.

"What?" Max asked.

"Lady, you're about to see the full might of the Luna Command propaganda apparat in action."

Von Drachau dropped into the empty chair. "Mouse," he said by way of greeting. "Tom, you seen Horst-Johann?"

"Sorry, Jupp. I haven't had a chance," Perchevski replied. "Was it bad?"

"From hunger. And they drag me down here without a chance to…" He considered the seniority of the rest of his tablemates, closed his eyes, leaned back.

"Who's he?" Max whispered.

"Jupp von Drachau. We were classmates in Academy."

"Was he in on the same thing you were?"

"Yeah. Sort of."

Navy stewards began serving dinner. It was a smorgasbord sort of meal, with the diners offered a chance to select from trays bearing bits and pieces from different Confederation worlds.

"Whatever you do, don't miss the January wine," Perchevski told Max. "They always let you have a little at these things."

"Thought you'd never been here before."

"Mouse has."

"Mouse?"

"Yamamoto."

"Oh? You know him too?"

"We were classmates too."

The holo cameras started whining. They faded behind a new holo scene.

This one was no animation. It was a speeded recording of events that had taken place inside a warship's situation-display tank.

Green friendly blips were approaching a huge chunk of asteroidal material circling a white dwarf sun. More white dwarves blazed in every direction. Perchevski could almost feel the heat, the smash of the solar winds.

"The Hell Stars," he murmured. "That's where it was."

The asteroid began sparkling. Large red blips scuttled away behind the cover of a storm of red pinpoints.

Fast green blips raced after them.

The asteroid coruscated.

"Christ!" Perchevski said.

"What?"

"The place was an arsenal."

Max did not understand. She was a Navy brat, but had not done Service herself. "What's going on, Walter? Or whatever your name is."

"That's where Jupp was. It's a display record of a battle."

The Confederation warships began their assault. Jupp had had his share of firepower.

The guests munched complacently while watching the memory of the death of a Sangaree station.

The fast boats trying to carry children to safety did not outrun Navy's blood-hungry hounds. Nor could the station's defenses stand up to the pounding delivered by a heavy siege squadron. But the Sangaree fought like a cat cornered by dogs, and left scars on von Drachau's command.

Here, there, Navy's professionals commented on the action like detached spectators at a ball game. Perchevski glared at his plate.

Von Drachau, he noted, was less excited than he.

The steward kept bringing the courses. He had to remind Max to drink her wine. The vintages of January were Confederation's finest and rarest.

The Sangaree persisted despite an overwhelming attack. It seemed impossible that they could have survived so long, let alone have continued fighting back.

Take no prisoners. That was the general order to all command grade officers who engaged Sangaree.

*Christ, we're bloodthirsty*, Perchevski thought He looked around. His neighbors were enjoying the spectacle even though they had no idea what it was all about.

Mouse looked like he was poised on the brink of orgasm.

How that man could hate! The Marine assault boats went in in time for dessert.

Hand-held camera recordings replaced the sterile display replay. Marines stalked Sangaree and their hirelings through smoky, ruined corridors. The fighting was hand-to-hand and bitter.

The camera technicians seemed inordinately fond of torn corpses and shattered defensive installations.

An assault team blew its way through an airlock.

Beyond, running for kilometers, brightly lighted, lay the hugest artificial environment farm Perchevski had ever seen. A voice boomed, "Sithlac fields."

The holos expired. Lights came up. A spot trained on the DNI. She rose. "Ladies and gentlemen. Comrades in arms. That is what tonight is all about. An operation in the Hell Stars that destroyed the biggest stardust production facility we've ever located. The raid was carried out twelve days ago. Police forces throughout The Arm are rounding up the people who processed and sold the drug produced on that asteroid."

She continued with a Navy-aggrandizing speech that Perchevski strove to ignore. Her theme was one of thank God for the Bureau's vigilance and determination.

The CSN said the same things in other ways, and praised von Drachau and the fleet people who had acted on the information the Bureau had supplied.

The hows and whys of the intelligence coup got no play. The details could not be divulged for security reasons. The agents responsible would receive decorations.

"You're a dip, eh?" Max whispered.

Perchevski shrugged. The near-worship in her face astounded him.

"I had a kid brother, Walter. He got hooked on stardust."

"Oh." He checked the time and was surprised to find that it had not been dragging after all.

The CSN insisted on presenting Captain von Drachau to Confederation's billions. Jupp accepted his decorations reluctantly.

"Instant celebrity," Perchevski mused. "Instant millionaire. And they won't remember his name in six months."

"Why're you so sour?" Max demanded. "You ought to be kicking your heels. Look what you did."

"I know what I did. I was there. Let's talk about something else. What about that Polar Flight airmail set you've been promising me for the last two years?"

"I bet you get a ton of prize money. How much? Do you know yet?"

"No. I didn't know about the raid till tonight."

"You'll be able to buy my whole shop."

"Probably." He had won prize money before. He was, by most standards, a wealthy man. He did not realize it. Money did not mean much to him. He could buy whatever he wanted when he wanted it, so economic problems never intruded on his life.

"Aren't you excited?"

"No."

"I am. When are we going to the Darkside digs?"

"I don't know. I think they're going to put me to work." He had come to a decision. He was going home. To his birthworld. One last time. Maybe there, where not one person in a billion gave a damn about Sangaree, or the March of Ulant, or McGraw pirates, or anything else going on offworld, he could get away from himself.

And maybe he could refresh his memory of just what it was that had sent him into a life he so loathed now. Maybe he could relearn what the choices were.

The show for the benefit of the holonets wound down. Then came the private postmortem, when he and Mouse shook hands with the mighty and received their medals and prize-money estimates.

Max patiently waited it out.

"You should have gone home," he told her when he finally broke away. "You can't spend your life waiting for me."

"I wanted to. I'm coming with you." She squeezed his hand.

"Sonofabitch," he said softly. His mood skyrocketed.

He had been firing on her for years. She had teased and led him on with smiles and gentle touches and had never given in. The occasional friendly date was as close as he had ever come.

Max made it a rewarding evening after all.

# ELEVEN: 3048 AD

## Operation Dragon, *Danion*

BenRabi groaned when he cracked an eye and saw the time. Noon already. He had wasted half his recreation day.

He flung himself out of bed and into the shower. Minutes later he was shuffling his *Jerusalem* papers, trying to find where he had left off.

The door buzzer whined. "Damn! I just got started. It's open."

The door slid aside. Jarl Kindervoort, Amy, and a half dozen unfamiliar Seiners grinned at him. They wore gaily colored period costumes. Moyshe laughed. "You look like refugees from a blood-and-blades epic." Except for one little fellow way in the back, grimy-gruesome in Billy the Kid regalia. "What the hell? Is King Arthur aboard?"

"It's recreation day, Moyshe," Amy said, using that smile that melted him. "We decided to drag the old grizzly out of his den."

How could he stay angry in the face of that smile? It was so damned disarming and warm. "I was going to work on the story." She had been impressed by his being a published author. "Anyway, I haven't got anything to wear." He realized they were offering him something. He grew wary.

"Eh?" Kindervoort asked, cupping his ear. "What's that? No matter, Moyshe. No time for it. Come on. We're late for the party now."

Amy chanted, "We're late, we're late, for a very important date…"

Kindervoort caught Moyshe's arm, pulled him through the doorway. He ignored benRabi's protests as he led him along a passageway crowded with young Seiners in wild costumes, zigging and zagging through to the common room serving as the landsmen's cafeteria, gymnasium, rec room, and lounge. It was a big place, but today Moyshe felt the walls pressing in. He had never seen it so crowded.

Most of the landsmen were there, lost among five times as many curious Seiners. The mixer had been going awhile. It had gotten organized. Not far from the door, at a long table where a dozen chess games were in progress, benRabi spied Mouse and the harem he had recruited.

"Where does he find the time?" he murmured.

Kindervoort and Amy herded him toward the table.

"Hey," Mouse said. "You dug him out. You have to use explosives?"

"He gave up without a fight," Kindervoort replied, laughter edging his voice. "Who should he play first?"

"Now wait a minute…"

"Get serious, Moyshe," Mouse snapped. "You're going to go Roman candle freaker if you stay locked up. Come on out and say hi to the world. Go on down there and beat the guy at the end of the table."

There was a tightness around the corners of Mouse's eyes. And an edge to his voice. Moyshe recognized a command. He moved down the table.

He did not like being pushed, but Mouse had a point. The mission was not dead. He would not get his job done sitting in his cabin.

He took the empty seat opposite the youth at the foot of the table, smiling wanly. His opponent had black. Moyshe opened with king's pawn. Four moves. "Checkmate." He could not believe it. Nobody fell for a fool's mate.

"Good, Moyshe," Amy said over his shoulder. "Tommy, wake up. Moyshe isn't a subtle player. He's more your kamikaze type."

BenRabi turned. "Really?" She was leaning on the back of his chair. Skullface Kindervoort and his troops had vanished.

"From the games I've seen you play."

Tommy's mouth finally closed. The swiftness of his defeat had shattered him.

"Let's say that's just for practice," Moyshe said. Tommy smiled weakly.

"Too generous of you," he murmured. "I deserved what I got."

BenRabi beat him again, easily, but took longer. Then he moved up the table, playing Seiner after Seiner, quickly, and one landsman whom he had beaten before. The Starfishers, while enthusiastic, were even less subtle than he. They played the game like checkers, going for a massacre. He won every match he played.

"Break time, Amy," he said. "I'm getting calluses on my butt."

"That was kind, what you did for Tommy," she said as she guided him toward the refreshments line.

"What's that?"

"Giving him a second chance. Playing badly on purpose."

"I did that?" He was glad they had dragged him in. The noise, the excitement of new people… It was infectious.

"You did. I know something about the game. Tommy's eager, but a little short. You know." She tapped her temple. "He's my second cousin. I feel sorry for him. Someday he'll realize that he won't ever beat anybody. It'll really hit him. The only thing he can really do better than anybody is handle the animals."

"Animals?" benRabi demanded incredulously.

"Sure. The zoo animals. In Twelve South, over by Sail Control. We've got the space for it. That's one thing we don't lack. We've got botanical gardens and feral forests and football stadiums and all kinds of space wasters. Our ships are built to be lived in."

"You remind me of somebody," he mumbled, remembering Alyce. Alyce had had that same elfin nose, those same high cheekbones, that same slim, small-breasted body.

"What?"

"Nothing." He tried to cover up by downing half a cup of steaming coffee. It scalded him. He sprayed the man in front of him. He mumbled apologies, felt small, and rubbed his lips and tongue.

Amy guided him away before he humiliated himself.

Swinging a hand to indicate the crowd, he said, "Reminds me of an Archaicist convention. For which read madhouse. Does this go on every week?"

"Except last week, when they were getting ready for you to come aboard. You should see it during sports season."

"How do they find people to play those games? From what Mouse told me..."

"People isn't the problem. Every residential cube has teams. They can pick and choose their players. It's a big thing, being a sports hero. Specially if you make one of the All-Star teams that play against the other harvestships. We've got every game you can imagine. You ever try nul-grav handball?"

"I've played. Maybe not by the same rules... Mouse and I play sometimes."

"Who wins?"

"He does. Most of the time. I don't have the killer instinct. I just play for fun."

"He's always dead serious, isn't he? Completely determined. And yet he seems to enjoy life more than you."

He scowled. "What is this?"

"Sorry. Where was I? Oh. There's even an Olympics. And intership games whenever we're in The Yards, and Fleet games while we're harvesting."

"The yards?"

"Enough said. That's secret stuff."

He did not press. But the agent in him red-tagged her words.

Amy led him to a cluster of tables under a banner proclaiming: COLLECTOR'S CORNER. It was quieter there. The people were older and less flashily dressed. Moyshe spied coins and stamps and other odds and ends of milemarks from Old Earth's past. Coin and stamp collections had been popular, lightweight links with the motherworld during early space days, when mass and volume had been critically important.

"Not a nibble," he overheard one man complain to another. The listener nodded tautly, as though he were hearing it for the *n*th time. "Told you it would be a waste of time, Charley. They're all hedonists." The speaker glared at a raucous group of Archaicists. "We won't see one thing new before next auction."

His table caught benRabi's eye and interest. The man had laid out a display of British coins and stamps. "Excuse me, sir."

"Yeah?" the complainer growled. Then he recognized Moyshe as an outsider who might have something to offer. BenRabi could see excitement rising in him. More companionably, "Sit down. Sit down. Name's George. What's your field?"

"Victorians. Tell me, how does a Starfisher come by..."

A quick, conspiratorial smile flashed across the man's face. "I would've bet you'd ask that, friend. I got lucky one time. I bought this unclaimed trunk when I was on The Big Rock Candy Mountain. Opened it up and, Holy Christ!" George launched a narrative which included the minutest detail of his lucky day. Collectors were that way, and every one had his story.

Moyshe studied him. How had he gotten down onto a Confederation world? Why? Was this another tidbit that should be red-tagged? Did Starfishers make many surreptitious visits to the worlds of their hunters?

"I didn't know if I'd run into any collectors out here," Moyshe said, "but I brought my trading stock just in case. I'm more into stamps than coins. British and American and German. If you know anybody. I've got some good stuff."

"Know anybody? Look around you. See all those birddogs on point?"

*I'm a champion fool,* Moyshe thought suddenly. *I could retire on my collection if I could sell it at market. Hell. I'm rich.*

Prize money had a way of piling up. He only used his to support his hobbies.

"Come on, friend. Sit. How many times do I have to tell you? Paul, get the man some coffee." All warmth now, George practically forced him into a chair. Moyshe surrendered. Amy attached herself to its back.

*She must be assigned to me, the way she's sticking,* benRabi thought. *It's not my overwhelming charm keeping her here.*

"Like I said, I'm George. Grumpy George, they call me. But I kind of grow on you after a while."

"BenRabi. Moyshe benRabi. I was noticing this stamp here..." He and George swapped stories for an hour.

"I'm glad you dragged me over here," Moyshe told Amy afterward.

"Good. I'm glad you're enjoying yourself." Her tone said she was not having fun.

"What're you doing tonight?" he blurted. He felt as nervous as a youngster trying to make his first date. "About the ball, I mean. One of the Archaicist groups is having that American Deep South Civil War thing..."

She smiled a sad smile. "I don't have any plans, if that's what you mean. But you don't have a costume."

"Is it mandatory?"

"No. You know Archaicists. They'll put up with anything to interest people in their pet periods. That one's already popular. The American ones are here. Our ethnic roots mostly go back to North America. Are you asking me?"

"Yeah. I guess."

"Good." She laughed. "I'll pick you up at eight."

"What? Shouldn't the man?..."

"Not when he's a landsman. The rules. You'd get arrested if you went running around looking for me."

"Oh. All right. What now?"

"There isn't much happening. Unless you want to join the Archaicists, or go to a ball game."

"Let's just circulate." He might pick up something interesting.

They milled in the press, watching several Archaicist performances, Mouse handling the Tregorgarthian youths, a fencing tournament, and the endless chess matches. Life aboard *Danion* was little different from that aboard a warship on extended patrol. The limits just were not as narrow.

Amy introduced Moyshe to scores of people whose names he forgot immediately. "This is getting to be like an overgrown cocktail party," he observed. "I hated them when I was line. You *had* to attend. They're the reason I decided to be a spy. Spies don't have to be nice to people they don't like."

Amy looked at him oddly.

"Just joking."

"Your friend is good at everything he does, isn't he?" She had become impressed with the way Mouse had handled the Tregor-garthians.

"When he gets interested in something he gives it everything. He's got a knack for switching on and off to complete commitment."

"And the girls. How does he find the time?"

"I don't know. If I did, I'd be cutting a swath myself."

His answer did not satisfy her. She kept trying to pry something out of him. She wasted her time. He had been in the spy business so long that the information shutdown was reflexive.

"You want to find out about Mouse, go to the horse's mouth," he finally told her.

"I don't think so, Moyshe."

He smiled. Mouse would talk about himself all night, not tell a word of truth, and seduce her three times in the process. "Probably not. We're different, him and me. I'm the type that would rather observe."

Amy linked her arm with his. "Observe for me, observer."

"About what?"

"You came to watch Seiners. Tell me about us. What do we look like to you?"

"Uhm. Happy. At peace with yourselves and the universe. Here's a thing. About laughter. It's different here. Not anything like at home. Like your souls are part of it. Like my people only laugh to push back the darkness. The guy who was doing the comedy routine?"

"Jake?"

"Whatever his name is. The one who told the story about Murph, the guy who knew everybody. He even made me laugh. And you know why? Because he was poking fun at things I wouldn't even have thought about. Or wouldn't have the nerve to criticize. I'm a moral coward."

"Whoa. What're you talking about? What brought that on?"

"I just started thinking about my boss. Very dignified gentleman. When he wants to be. All the big-timers are in Luna Command. Only their dignity is almost always pomposity in disguise. Ever since I was a midshipman I've had this fantasy about being the king's secret agent. I'd go around disguised as Joe Citizen. I'd keep a list. Whenever a civil servant or sales person was obnoxious, I'd put their names down and the king's men would come and get them. I'd also be a sort of wandering clown who made pompous bigwigs expose themselves for what they were. The Bureau would be my first target."

"You have hard feelings against the people you work for?"

Moyshe did not answer. The intensity of Amy's question scared him off. She was too keen, too tense, too eager all of a sudden. "Let's change the subject."

She did not press. A while later she suggested, "Why don't you go back to your writing now?"

"Trying to get rid of me?"

"No! That's not what I meant. Did it sound like that? I'm sorry. I just thought you might feel better now."

He reflected for a moment. "I do. Maybe it'll go better. I hate to admit it, but I've had a good time, Amy. Thanks."

He allowed her to escort him to his cabin, where he immediately attacked his story. It went well.

He hardly seemed to have begun though, when Amy pushed his buzzer. "Moyshe. Wake up," she called from the passageway.

"It's open. Time already?"

In she bounced, charmingly dressed as a southern belle, in lots of pink and petticoats. "Been going good? You've got papers everywhere." She had a Confederate uniform over one arm, and swords and things under the other.

"Smoking."

"I borrowed some things… What's the matter?"

For an instant he had seen her as Alyce. His past hit him like a tsunami.

Her smile persisted, but did not ride her voice as she asked, "Moyshe, what's behind you?"

"Nothing. That costume for me? Give it here and I'll change."

"I've been watching you, Moyshe. Something's eating you. Don't let it. Puke it up. Get it out where you can stomp on it, chop it up, and kill it."

That was the difference between Amy and Alyce. Alyce would never have asked. She would have waited till he wanted to talk.

"What about you?" he demanded. "Want to tell me what's behind you?" Best defense is a good offense, he thought, mocking himself.

She ignored it. "Tell me something." She spoke softly, with concern, just as she had done that day on the shuttle.

"I have walked with joy down the passion-shaded avenues

Abounding in the City of Love. My heart was young,
And She was beside me; together were we,
And in that was my totality."

"Czyzewski," she observed. "Yes. I read too. It's from *Sister Love.* They say he wrote it before he went into space and lost his mind—if a guy who brags about a love affair with his sister isn't crazy already. What do you mean by it, Moyshe? Is an old love affair bothering you? That's silly. You're not fifteen..."

"I'm perfectly aware of that. Intellectually. 'I was then, stark in the gardens of the moon,' " he quoted out of context. "Now I'm a tired old man, far from home, futureless, with no friend but a chess-mad Archaicist triggerman I never see except during working hours..." *Hold it,* he thought. *The mouth is playing traitor here.*

"Give me that costume. Let me get ready. Please?"

"All right." She put a lot into those two words. It reminded him of the professional mother who had taken care of him occasionally while his natural mother had chased ghosts of vanished Earths. She had been able to say the same words the same way, implying that nothing good could possibly come of whatever he planned. She had been able to say almost anything in a way that made it sound like he was condemning himself to the clutches of the Devil, or some equally nasty fate.

"Well. You make a striking officer," Amy said when he returned from the bathroom. "If you had a beard you'd look a little like Robert E. Lee."

"Yeah? Can you do something about this damned sword? How the hell did they get around without falling on their faces all the time?"

She giggled as she made adjustments. "What?"

"Just wondering how many Jewish generals there were in the Confederate Army."

"There're a lot... Oh, you mean that Confederation. I don't get it. Why should that be funny?"

"You have to know the period."

"Well, you've lost me. I only know it from military history at Academy. I can tell you why Longstreet did what he didn't do at Gettysburg, but not what religion he was. Anyway, I'm not Jewish. And you know it."

"What are you, then? Do you believe in anything, Moyshe?"

Poking again. Prying. For her own sake, he guessed. Fisher Security probably would not care about his religion.

He wanted to make a snappy comeback, but she had struck too close to the core of his dissatisfaction. At the moment he did not believe in anything, and himself least of all. And that, he thought, was curious, because he had not had these kinds of feelings since coming out of the line. Not till this mission had begun. "The Prophet Murphy," he said.

"Murphy? I don't get it. Who the hell is Murphy? I expected death and taxes."

"The Prophet Murphy. The guy who said, 'If anything can possibly go wrong, it will.' My life has been a testimonial."

She stepped back, shook her head slowly. "I don't know what to make of you, Moyshe. Yes I do. Maybe. Maybe I'll just make you happy in spite of yourself."

"Blood from a turnip, Lady."

He had had enough talk. Taking her arm, he headed for the ball, for the moment forgetting that he did not know where he was going. Then he saw that she had brought an electric scooter. The Seiners used them whenever they had to travel any distance. There were places in *Danion* that were literally days away by foot.

Red-faced, he settled onto the passenger seat, facing backward.

They did not exchange a word during the trip. Moyshe suffered irrational surges of anger, alternating with images of the gun. That thing scared the hell out of him. He was no triggerman. It seemed to have less contact with reality than did his wanting.

He had become, on a low-key, reflexively suppressed level, convinced that he was going insane.

Time seemed to telescope. The unwanted thoughts would not go away. His hands grew cold and clammy. His mood sank…

Amy swung to the passage wall, parked, plugged the scooter into a charger circuit. It became one of a small herd of orange beasts nursing electrical teats. "Good crowd," he said inanely, taking a clumsy poke at the silence.

"Uhm." She paused to straighten his collar and sword. "Come on." Her face remained studiedly blank, landside style. It was a bit of home for which he was ungrateful.

The ball seemed a repeat of the morning's get-together. The same people were there. Only a hundred or so were in appropriate costume. Twice as many wore every get-up from Babylon to tomorrow, and as many again wore everyday jumpsuits.

Moyshe froze just inside the doorway.

"What is it?" Amy asked.

"I'm not sure. I don't have the right, but… I feel like something's been taken away from me." Had all those Vikings and Puritans and Marie Antoinettes stolen his moment of glory? Had he been bitten by the Archaicist bug?

"It's our history, too, remember?" Amy countered, misunderstanding. "You said everybody's roots go back to Old Earth."

A hand took Moyshe's left elbow. "Mint julep, sir?"

BenRabi turned to face Jarl Kindervoort, who wore buckskins and coonskin cap. *Dan'l Deathshead,* he thought. *Scair 'em injuns right out'n Kaintuck.*

"The damn thing fits you better than it does me," Kindervoort observed.

"It's your costume?"

"Yeah. Let's see what they've got at the bar, Moyshe."

Amy had disappeared. And Kindervoort's tone implied business. Feeling put-upon, benRabi allowed himself to be led to the bar.

That was another unpleasantness. The setup was Wild West, with a dozen rowdy black hat types attached, busy making asses of themselves with brags and mock gunfights. Acrid gunsmoke floated around in grey-blue streamers.

Of all the period crap that Archaicists bought, Moyshe felt Wild West was the worst. It was all made-up history, a consensus fantasy with virtually no foundation in actual history.

His mother's first Archaicist flier had been Wild West. It had come during his difficulties at Academy, when he had desperately needed an anchor somewhere. She had not given him what he had needed. She had not had the time.

To top it off, the Sangaree woman was there. She had assumed the guise of The Lady Who Goes Upstairs.

"Appropriate," benRabi muttered. Her awesome sexual appetites had grown since The Broken Wings.

She was watching him with Jarl. Was she getting a little worried? Wondering when he would turn her in? He smiled at her. Let her sweat.

There was a stir at the door. "Jesus," benRabi said. "Will you look at this."

Mouse the attention-grabber and most popular boy in class, with no less than six beauties attached, had just swept in outfitted as a diminutive Henry VIII.

"We're lucky this isn't a democracy," Kindervoort observed. "Your friend would be Captain by the end of the year, riding the female vote."

Moyshe ignored the pun. Sourly, he said, "Aren't you?" He was getting irritated with Mouse's antics. The man was flaunting his successes… Envy was one of benRabi's nastier vices. He tried to control it, but Mouse made that hard.

He faced the bar, found himself staring at some horrid-looking swill in a tall glass. "Mint julep," Kindervoort explained. "We try to drink according to period at these things." He sipped from a tin cup. The gunfighters were tossing off straight shots. At bar's end a hairy Viking type waved an axe and thundered something about honey mead.

"Bet it all comes out of the same bottle."

"Probably," Kindervoort admitted.

"It's your ballpark. What do you want, Jarl?"

Kindervoort's eyebrows rose. "Moyshe, you're damned hard to get along with, you know that? Now you frown. I'm getting too personal. How do you people survive, never touching?"

"We don't touch because there're too many of us. Unless you're Mouse. He grew up with lots of elbow room and not wanting for anything. I don't expect you to understand. You couldn't unless you've lived on one of the Inner Worlds."

Kindervoort nodded. "How would you like to get away from all that? To live where there's room to be human? Where you don't have to be an emotional brick to survive?" He took a long sip from his cup, watching Moyshe over its rim.

He had to wait a long time for an answer.

Moyshe knew what was being offered. And what it would cost.

The demons of his mind rallied to fiery standards, warring with one another in an apocalyptic clash. Ideals, beliefs, desires, and temptations stormed one another's strongholds. He struggled to keep that armageddon from painting itself on his face.

He was good at that. He had had decades of practice.

It occurred to him that Kindervoort was Security, and Security men did not deal in the obvious. "Get thee behind me, Satan."

Kindervoort laughed. "All right, Moyshe. But we'll talk about it later. Go on. Find Amy. Have a good time. It's a party."

He vanished before Moyshe could respond. Amy appeared on cue.

"Rotten trick, Amy Many-Names, letting that vampire get ahold of me." Kindervoort's retreat raised his spirits. He felt benevolent toward the universe. He would let it roll on awhile.

"What did he do?"

"Nothing much. Just tried to get me to defect."

She just stared at him, apparently wondering why he was not shrieking with joy. Seldom did a landsman receive the opportunity to become a Seiner.

It was human nature to think your own acre was God-chosen, he realized. And Amy's was one he would not mind entering—though not on Kindervoort's terms. He was not in love with Confederation or the Bureau, but he would never sell them out.

"Let's dance," Amy suggested. "That's what we came for."

Time drifted away. Moyshe began to enjoy himself. He discovered that he was spending the evening with a woman who mattered more than the bag of duffel with sex organs she had been when they had arrived.

Somewhere along the way one of Amy's cousins invited them to a room party. No longer tense and wary, he said, "Why not? Sounds good." A moment later he and Amy were part of a gay crowd on scooters, shooing pedestrians with rebel yells. The partiers were mostly youngsters recently graduated from the creche schools, almost as new to the harvestship as Moyse. In a small group, confined to a cabin, he found them less reserved than the older Seiners he met while working.

They seemed to have Archaicist tendencies oriented toward the late twentieth century youth cults. At least the cabin belonged to someone fond of the approximate period. Moyshe could not identify it for certain.

Liquor flowed. Smoke filled the air. Time passed. Quiet in a corner, with Amy most of the time but sometimes without, observing, he gradually settled into a strange mood wherein he became detached from his environment. The bittersweet smoke was more to blame than the alcohol. It was dense enough to provide a high without his having to toke any of the odd little cigarettes offered him.

Marijuana, someone called them. He vaguely remembered it from childhood, as something the older kids in his gang had used. He had never done dope himself.

His companions coughed and gasped and made faces, but persisted. The drug was part of the period cult. He drifted farther from reality himself, floating free, till he swam in a mist of uninhibited, irrational impressions.

The touch of a woman on his hand—sail on, silver girl—and the flavor of whiskey on his tongue. Dancing light, harsh in a distant corner, all shadows and angles beside him. His fingers slipped into the warm place at the back of Amy's neck. She purred, moving from the arm of the chair into his lap. He thought sex… No. He was not drunk enough to forget Alyce. Fear arose. Shadows grew, beckoning. In their hearts lurked dark things, wicked spirit-reavers from the deeps of the past come to stalk him along the shores of the future. There was a magic at work in that room. He and Amy were suddenly alone amid the horde.

Alone among the golden people, all of them ten years their junior, each with a newly minted shiny innocence—on some becoming tarnished. He did not care.

They talked, she a little deeply, and he with scant attention. He was not ready to explore her yet. But it seemed, from hints she dropped, that their pasts might read like sides of the same coin. An unhappy affair lay behind her, and something physical, sexual, that she was not yet ready to yield, was troubling her now. He did not press. His own midnight-eyed haunts were lurking in the wings.

On. On. Near midnight, in a moment of clarity, he noticed her left-handedness for the first time because of the way she offered him a can of Archaicist-trade beer. Left-handed, pop the top, shift hands, offer with a bend of the wrist because he was right-handed. He marveled because he had not noticed it earlier. He was supposed to be an observant man. It was his profession. October thoughts died as his interest increased and he became aware of the intenseness of Amy's every move.

She laughed a lot, usually at things that were not funny. Her own fanged shadows were closing in, memories that she had to exorcise with forced mirth. She was trying to keep her devil out of sight, but he found its shaggy edges familiar. It was a cousin of his own.

While a dozen people silently considered the songs of someones named Simon and Garfunkel, or Buddy Holly, he discovered how nicely they fit. She spent an hour in his lap without making him uncomfortable. His left hand touched the back of her neck, his right lay on the curve of her left hip, and her head rested nicely on his left shoulder, beneath his chin. Her hair had a pale, pleasant, unfamiliar scent.

Weren't they a little old for this?

Shadows in the doorways, shadows on the walls. Don't ask questions. He listened to her heartbeat, three beats for his two.

He shivered as his monster shuffled closer. Amy moved, wriggling nearer. She chuckled softly when he grunted from the pain-tweak of her bony bottom shifting in his lap.

The partiers began drifting out, off to their private places, to be lonely, or frightened, or together till the reality of morning swept them back to work and today. Soon there were just three couples left. Moyshe shivered as he lifted Amy's chin. She resisted a moment, then surrendered. The kiss became intense. The shadows retreated a bit.

"Come on," she said, bouncing up, yanking his arm. They darted into the passageway, boarded the scooter, and flew to his cabin. She went in with him, locking the door behind her.

But the time was not yet right. They spent the night sleeping. Just cuddling and sleeping, hiding from the darkness. Neither was ready to risk anything more.

She was gone when he awakened. And his wants and haunts were strangely quiet. Where would they go from here? he wondered.

# TWELVE: 3047 AD

## The Olden Days, The Motherworld

Perchevski shuffled from foot to foot. He was too nervous to sit. He had not realized that going home would unleash so much emotion.

He glanced around the lounge. The lighter would be carrying a full load. Tourists and business people. The former were mostly Ulantonid and Toke. They huddled in racial clumps, intimidated by Old Earth's xenophobic reputation, yet determined to explore the birth world of Man. The Toke nerved themselves with bold talk. Their every little quirk or gesture seemed to proclaim, "We are the Mel-Tan Star Warriors of the Marine Toke Legion. We are the Chosen of the Star Lords. The delinquents of a decadent world cannot frighten us."

But they were scared.

No enemy could intimidate the Toke. The Toke War had proven that. Only the stroke of diplomatic genius that had made a place for them in Service, and a place for Toke in Confederation, as equals, had saved the Warrior Caste from extinction.

*It's a pity we can't work something like that for the Sangaree,* Perchevski thought.

But there had been no hatred in the Toke War. It had been an almost clinically unemotional contest for supremacy in the star ranges of the Palisarian Directorate.

The Ulantonid were less bellicose than the Toke. Their war with Confederation had been unemotional too. Another blood-flavored wrestling match for supremacy.

These looked like a Catholic group headed for Rome, Jerusalem, and Bethlehem.

"Shuttle Bravo Tango Romeo Three One is now ready for boarding for passengers making a Lake Constance descent. Passengers for Corporation Zone will please assemble at Shuttle Bay Nine."

"I'd like to meet her," said a stranger near Perchevski.

"Who's that?"

"The woman who does the announcing. She can put her shoes under my bed anytime."

"Oh. The voice." It had been a soothing, mellow, yet suggestive voice. Similar voices did the announcing in every terminal Perchevski had ever visited.

The tourists and business people boarded first. Luna Command made a habit of doing little things that avoided irritating civilians. The individual Serviceman was supposed to remain unobtrusive.

Only one check on Luna Command's power existed. The operating appropriation voted by a popularly elected senate.

The Toke Marines stood aside for Perchevski, who had come in his Commander's uniform.

It was a long, lazy twelve-hour orbit to Lake Constance and Geneva. Perchevski read, slept, and pondered the story he had recently begun. He tried not to think about the world below.

The holonets could not begin to portray the squalid reality that was Old Earth beyond the embattled walls of Corporation Zone.

The shuttle dropped into the lake. A tug guided it into a berth. Perchevski followed the civilians into the air of his native world. He had come home. After eight years.

Geneva had not changed. Switzerland remained unspoiled. Its wealth and beauty seemed to give the lie to all the horror stories about Old Earth.

It was a mask. Offworld billions cosmeticized the Zone, and Corporation police forces maintained its sanctity at gunpoint. The perimeters were in a continuous state of siege.

There were times when Luna Command had to send down Marines to back the Corporation defense forces. The excuse was protection of Confederation's Senate and offices, which were scattered between Geneva, Zurich, and the south shore of the Bodensee.

Once there had been a social theory claiming that the wealth coming into the Zone from the Corporations headquartered there would eventually spread across the planet. A positive balance of trade would be created. And the positive example of life in the Zone would act as a counter-infection to the social diseases of the rest of the planet. Change would radiate from Switzerland like ripples in a pond.

The theory had been stillborn, as so many social engineering schemes are.

*No one here gives a damn*, Perchevski reflected as he entered his hotel room. All that kept Earth going was trillions in interplanetary welfare. Maybe the whole thing should be allowed to collapse, then something could be done for the survivors.

The motherworld's people still played their games of nationalism and warfare. They loved their Joshua Jas. And they flatly refused to do anything for themselves while Confederation could be shamed into paying support.

The too often told tale of welfarism was repeating itself. As always, provision of means for improvement had become an overpowering disincentive to action.

Perchevski spent his first day at home doing one of the guided tours of the wonders of Corporation Zone. With his group were a few native youngsters who had been awarded the tour as contest prizes.

They surprised him. They were reasonably well-behaved, moderately clean, and not too badly dressed. A cut above the average run, and not unlike kids elsewhere. The Security guard was not called upon to practice his trade.

The tour group lunched in the restaurant at the Nureyev Technical Industries chalet atop the Matterhorn.

"Excuse me, Commander."

Perchevski looked up from his sausage and kraut, startled. A girl of sixteen, a tall, attractive blonde, stood opposite him. He was eating alone. His uniform had put off everyone but two Toke Marines, who were still trying to explain their need to a cook who was appalled at the idea of permitting raw meat out of his kitchen. He suspected the Marines wanted to stay near him for a feeling of added security. The Toke were a strongly hierarchical people, and among them warriors were the most respected of castes.

"Yes?"

"May I sit here?"

"Of course." He was stunned. She was one of the prize winners. Most Old Earthers so hated the Services that even the best intentioned could not remain polite.

*Is she a prostitute?* he wondered.

Whatever her pitch, she needed time. She was so nervous she could not eat.

She suddenly blurted, "You're Old Earth, aren't you? I mean originally."

"Yes. How did you know?"

"The way you look at things. Outworlders look at things different. Like they're afraid they'll catch something, or something."

Perchevski glanced at the other prize winners. Disgust marked their faces. "Your friends don't…"

"They're not my friends. I never saw any of them before yesterday. How did you get out?" Words tumbled out of her all strung together, so fast he could hardly follow them.

"Out?"

"Of this. This place. This world."

"I took the Academy exams. They accepted me."

"They didn't stop you?"

"Who?"

"Your friends. The people you knew. I tried three times. Somebody always found out and kept me from going. Last time three men stopped me outside the center and said they'd kill me if I went in."

"So there's still hope," Perchevski murmured. He knew what she wanted now.

"Sir?"

"I mean, as long as there's somebody like you left, Old Earth isn't dead. You've made my trip worthwhile."

"Get me out. Can you get me out? Anything is better than this. I'll do anything. Anything you want."

She meant it. Her desperate promise was so obvious it hurt.

He remembered his own desperation at an even younger age. When you chose the unpopular path you had to cleave to it with fanatical determination. He was moved. Deeply.

"I entered every contest there ever was just so I could get this far. I knew they wouldn't keep me from coming here, and I thought maybe I could find somebody…"

"But you were too scared to do anything when you got here."

"They were all outworlders."

"You leave Earth, you won't meet anyone else. I've only run into two or three Earthmen in twenty years." He eyed the group with which the girl had been traveling. The youths seemed to have caught the drift of her appeal. They did not like it.

"I know. I'd get used to it."

"Are you sure?…"

Three young men drifted to the table. "This slut don't belong here, Spike."

Perchevski smiled gently. "You just made fuck-up number one, stud. Don't get smoked."

That startled them. One snarled, "You'll shit in your hand and carry it to China, Spike."

"May I be of assistance, Commander?"

The Toke Marine dwarfed the three youths. Adam's apples bobbed.

"I don't think so, Fire Cord. I'd say the Banner is secure. The young men have said their piece. They were just leaving."

The Toke Major glared down. At two and a quarter meters and one hundred thirty kilos he was a runt for a Star Warrior. His aide, though, was the kind they put on recruiting pamphlets meant for circulation through the Caste Lodges. He stood quietly behind his officer, filled with that still, dread equanimity that made the Star Warriors unnerving to even the most hardened human Servicemen.

"'Go you silently, Children of the Night,'" Perchevski quoted from an old song used as a battle anthem by half the youth gangs on the planet. "You, especially, talking head."

The slang had not changed much. Unlike the Outworlds, Old Earth had become locked into static patterns.

The youths understood. There had been a time when he had been one of them.

They left, strutting with false bravura. Perchevski thought he caught a glint of envy in the spokesman's eye.

"Thank you, Fire Cord." The Security man, busy talking shit to a restaurant girl, had missed the encounter.

"We share the Banner, Commander. We will be near."

"Fire Cord?"

"Sir?"

"Don't call them on their own ground."

"This is my third visit, Commander."

"Then you know." He turned to the girl again, who seemed petrified. The two huge, leathery-skinned Marines moved to the nearest empty table.

The girl finally blurted, "Why did you come back?"

"I don't know. To remind myself? Looking for something I left behind? Roots? I'm not sure. I wanted to see my mother. It's been eight years."

"Oh." She sounded envious. "I couldn't find out who my parents were. I never met anybody who did know. Not my age, anyway."

He smiled. "Do you have a name? After that scene, you'd better stay close to me or the Marines. Well have to call you something besides Hey Girl."

"Greta. Helsung. From Hamburg. Are they real Star Warriors?"

He laughed softly. "Don't let them hear you ask a question like that, Greta from Hamburg. They're as real as the stink in the sink. I'm Commander Perchevski. If you don't change your mind, I'll take you to see somebody when we get back to Geneva."

"I won't change it. Not after all the trouble I had..."

He peered at her intently. This was too breathtaking, too real, too dream-come-true for her. She did not quite believe him. He could almost hear her thinking he would use her, then dump her.

The use temptation existed. She was fresh and beautiful.

"I mean it, Greta. And don't be scared. You're young enough to be my daughter."

"I'm not a child. I'm old enough..."

"I'm aware of that. I'm not young enough. Eat your knockwurst. The meat came all the way from Palisarius."

"Oh, God! Really? I didn't know what I was ordering. I just asked for something that I didn't know what it was. Just for something different. They didn't show any prices. It must be awful expensive." She looked around guiltily.

"So don't waste it." Then, "Price doesn't matter to most people who eat here. If they couldn't afford it, they wouldn't come. Go on. Enjoy yourself."

Her tour expenses would be covered. Luna Command would pick up the tab. The Services sponsored the contests that gave Zone vacations as prizes. Some inspired social theorist had decided to fish for Old Earth's Gretas, for the one-in-a-million children who had adventure in their genes and dreams in their hearts.

The program was as successful as the normal recruiting procedures. It gave interested youths a chance to escape peer pressure. Computers watched and cross-checked the contest entries. Undoubtedly, someone would have contacted Greta if she had not come to him.

He eyed her and thanked heaven that someone out there still cared.

He felt pretty good.

Greta remained nearby throughout the tour, milking him for every detail about outside. Her former companions were not pleased, but the Fire Cord was always too close for their nerve.

Terrorism was a popular Terran sport. Toke, though, refused to be terrorized. They bashed heads. Their reputation did not make them immune, but it did force the natives to respect them.

Perchevski took the girl to the Bureau's front business office that evening. "A potential recruit," he told the night desk man, who recognized him from a holo portrait that had preceded him down. "Greta Helsung, from Hamburg. Treat her right."

"Of course, Commander. Miss? Will you take a seat? We can get the paperwork started."

"It's that easy?" she asked Perchevski.

The desk man replied, "You'll be sleeping on the moon tomorrow night, Miss. Oh. Commander. You're leaving?"

"I have an eleven-thirty to Montreal."

Greta looked at him in silent appeal.

"Will you sponsor, Commander?"

He knew he shouldn't. It meant accepting legal and quasi-parental responsibility. The Admiral would be furious… "Of course. Where do I print?" He offered his thumb.

"Here. Thank you." Something buzzed. The desk man glanced to one side, read something from a screen Perchevski could not see. "Oh-oh." He thumbed a print-lock. A drawer popped open. He handed Perchevski a ring.

"Why?" It was a call ring. It would let him know if the Bureau wanted him on the hurry up. It would give them a means of following his movements, too.

"Word from the head office. Ready, Miss Helsung?"

"Greta, I'll see you in Academy." He wrote a number on a scrap of paper. "Keep this. Call it when you get your barracks assignment." He started to leave again.

"Commander?"

He turned. Soft young arms flung around his neck. Tears seeped through his uniform. "Thank you."

"Greta," he whispered, "don't be scared. They'll be good to you."

They would. She would be treated like a princess till her studies began.

"Good-bye. Be good."

Four of the tour youths caught him outside. He had to break one's arm before they got the message. He was nearly late for his flight. He had to wait to shift to civilian clothing till after he had boarded the airbus.

North American Central Directorate showed his mother living at the same St. Louis Zone address. He went without calling first, afraid she might find some excuse for not seeing him. Though their intentions were friendly enough, their few visits had been tempestuous. She could never forgive him for "turning on his own kind."

The passage down the last light canyon was like a journey home along an old route of despair.

The playgrounds of his childhood had not changed. Trash still heaped them. Kid gangs still roamed them. Crudely written, frequently misspelled obscenities obscured the unyielding plastic walls. Future archaeologists might someday go carefully through layer after layer of spray paint, reconstructing the aberrations of generations of uneducated minds.

He labored to convince himself that this was not the totality of Old Earth.

"Some of it's worse," he murmured. Then he castigated himself for his bigotry.

Sure, most Terran humanity lived like animals. But not all. There were enclaves where some pride, some care, some ambition remained. There were native industries. Earth produced most of its own food and necessities. And there were artists, writers, and men of vision... They just got lost in the barbarian horde. They formed an unnaturally small percentage of the population.

Not only had risk-taking been drained from the gene pool, so had a lot of talent and intelligence.

The average I.Q. on Old Earth ran twenty points below Confederation mean.

Perchevski overtipped his driver. It was enough to convince the man that he had conveyed some criminal kingpin. Crime was one profession where a man could still win some respect.

His codes still opened the building's doors. After all these years. He was amazed.

It was another symptom of what had become of his motherworld. Terror had become so ubiquitous that no one tried very hard to resist anymore.

His mother was drunk. She snapped, "You're not Harold. Who the hell are you? Where's Harold? Nobody comes here but Harold."

He looked past her into the space where he had spent most of his childhood. Three meters by four, it was divided into three tiny rooms. It had seemed bigger back then, even with his father living at home.

He said nothing.

"Look, brother... Holy Christ! It's you. What the hell are you doing here?" She sounded angry. "Don't stand there looking. Get in here before somebody burns us."

He slipped past her, plopped himself down on the same little couch that had been his boyhood bed.

The apartment had not changed. Only his mother had. For the worse.

It was more than age and unrelenting poverty. It was a sliding downhill from the inside.

She had begun to go to fat. Her personal habits had slipped. Her hair had not been combed in days...

"Let me clean up. I just got outta bed." She vanished behind the movable screen that made a bedroom wall. "What have you been doing?" she asked.

"Better I should ask you. I sent letters." And hard Outworlds currency. Neither had drawn any response.

"I never seem to get around to answering."

At least she did not make outrageous excuses, like not being able to pay a writer. He knew she took his missives to a reader. She cared that much. But not enough to reply.

"I did write twice. Once right after you were here last time, and two or three years ago, after your father was killed in the Tanner Revolt. I didn't care anymore, but I thought you might."

"He's dead?"

"As a stone. He got hung up in the Revanchist Crusade. They were getting pretty big. Then most of them got themselves killed attacking Security Fortress."

"I didn't get the letter. I didn't know." He had never heard of the Tanner Revolt or Revanchist Crusade. He asked about them.

"They were going to turn things around. Bring back the golden age, or something. Unite Earth and make it the center of the galaxy. A lot of people think you Loonies were behind it. They say the whole Archaicist thing was started by your meddling."

Archaicism had had its infancy on Old Earth concurrent with his own. If it had been more social engineering, the plan had backfired. The motherworld had not been awakened by the glory that was. It had merely found a new way to escape the reality of now.

The romantic pasts were popular. Men liked playing empires. Women liked glamour.

Men died when groups like Stahlhelm, SS Totenkopf, or Black September ganged up on Irgun or Stern… The smallest and most obscurely referenced groups were the most dangerous.

The ladies seemed to prefer Regency Balls, French Courts, and seraglio situations.

A search for uniqueness combined with the need for belonging had driven people to probe the remotest corners of Earth's history.

During his flight he had watched a live newscast of a raid on Mexico's Aztec Revivalist Cult. The police attackers had battled their way into the temple too late to save the sacrifices.

Perchevski's mother returned. She wore an outfit that looked ridiculous on a woman her age. The blouse was see-through. The skirt fell only to mid-thigh. He concealed his consternation. No doubt this was her best.

"I don't get into that kind of thing. Not my line. I do know a few guys who make a hobby of trying to save this dump from itself."

She did not like his attitude. "What are you calling yourself this time?"

"Perchevski. Cornelius Perchevski." He stared at her, and saw Greta forty years from now. Unless… If the kid enlisted, he would feel his own life-choice was justified. He would have rescued someone from becoming this…

"What are you into?" he asked. "I don't recognize the period."

"Beatles and Twiggy."

"Eh?"

"Twentieth century. Seventh decade. Anglo-American, with the beginning in England. One of the light periods."

"Youth and no philosophy? I gathered that much, though I'm not familiar with it."

"It's all the rage now. It's so very outré. So clish-clash with itself. So schizophrenic. You speak English, don't you?"

"We have to learn. Most of the First Expansion worlds have some memory of it."

"Why don't you stop all that foolishness? All those ugly Outsiders… You could do well teaching English here. *Everybody* wants to learn."

*Here we go,* he thought. *She's picking up where she left off eight years ago. It'll only get worse. Why did I come here? To punish myself for getting out of this hell-hole?*

She recognized the look on his face. "It's news time. Let's see what's happening." She whistled a few bars of a tune he did not recognize.

The editing was unbelievable. This Archaicist group had done this. That one had done that. The Bay Bombers had beaten the Rat Pack 21-19. There wasn't a word about von Drachau, or anything else offworld, except mention of a Russian basketball team trouncing the touring team from Novgorod.

"Big deal," he muttered. "Novgorod's gravity is seventy-three percent of Earth normal. They'd have to play midgets for it to be fair."

His mother flared up. She hated foreigners almost as much as she hated Outworlders, but the Russians were, at least, good Old Earthers who had had the sense to stay on the motherworld…

He tuned her out, again wondering if he had a masochistic streak.

Would she try to understand if he explained how much in the middle he was? That Outworlders disliked Old Earthers just as much as she loathed them? That he had to reconcile those attitudes both within himself and with everyone he met?

He did not think she would help. He knew her cure. Give it up. Come back home. To squalor and hopelessness…

"Mother, I am what I am. I won't change. You're wasting your time when you try. Why don't we go out somewhere? This place is depressing."

"What's wrong with it? Yes. All right. It's a little old. And I have the extra credit over S.I. basic to move. But it's so *big*… I like having all this room to knock around in. I wouldn't have that in a new place."

Perchevski groaned to himself. Now came the Mama Marx self-criticism session during which she would confess all her failings as a Social Insuree. Then she would segue into her shortcoming as a mother, ultimately taking upon herself all responsibility for his having gone wrong.

He shook his head sadly. In eight years she should have found a new song. "Come on, Mother. We did this last time. Let's go somewhere. Let's see something. Let's do something."

She dithered. She fussed. It was getting dark out. Only rich Old Earthers, who could afford the armor, went out after the sun went down.

"Here," he said, opening his bag. "I've got my own house now. I brought some holos to show you."

The pictures finally penetrated her façade.

"Tommy! It's beautiful! Magnificent. You really are doing all right, aren't you?"

"Good enough."

"But you're not happy. A mother can tell."

*Holy shit,* he thought. *I'm grown up twice over. I don't need that.* "You could live there if you wanted."

She became suspicious immediately. "It's not in some foreign place, is it? Those mountains don't look like the Rockies or Sierras."

"It's on a world called Refuge."

"Omigod! Don't do that! Don't talk that way. My heart... Did I tell you that the medics say I have a weak heart?"

"Every time you've ever needed an excuse for..." He stopped himself. He refused to start the fight.

"Let's don't fight, Tommy. We should be friends. Oh. Speaking of friends. Patrick was killed just last week. He went out after dark. It was so sad. Nobody can figure out what made him do it."

"Patrick?"

"That red-haired boy you were friends with the year before you... You enlisted. I think his last name was Medich. He was living with his mother."

He didn't remember a Patrick, red-haired, Medich, or otherwise.

He did not belong here. Even the memories were gone. He had changed. The kid who had lived with this woman was dead. He was an impostor pretending to be her son.

She was bravely playing the game, trying to be his mother. He was sure there were other things she would rather be doing. Hadn't she been expecting a Harold?

Maybe that was why they tried to keep people from going. They became somebody else while they were gone.

"Mother..." His throat clamped down on the word.

"Yes?"

"I... I think I'd better go. I don't know what I came looking for. It's not here. It's not you. It's probably something that doesn't exist." The words came rumbling out, one trampling the heels of the next. "I'm not making you happy being here. So I'd better just go back."

He tried to read her face. Disappointment fought relief there, he thought.

"I'm an Old Earther when I'm out there, Mother. But I'm not when I come back here. I can see that when I'm here. I guess I should just stop remembering this place as home."

"It *is* your home."

"No. Not anymore. It's just the world where I was born. And this is just a place where I lived."

"And I'm just somebody you knew back when?"

"No. You're Mother. You'll always be that."

Silence existed between them for more than a minute.

Perchevski finally said, "Won't you even consider coming to my place?"

"I couldn't. I just couldn't. I belong where I am, being what I am. Useless as that is."

"Mother… You don't have to get old out there. We have a rejuvenation process…"

She showed genuine interest when she asked, "You've recovered the secrets of the immortality labs?"

"No. They're gone forever. All this process does is renew the body. It can't stop nerve degeneration. It's been around for centuries."

"How come nobody's heard about it?"

"Here? With Earth overpopulated and everybody doing their damnedest to make more babies? Some people probably know, though. Some maybe even benefit. It's not a big secret. But nobody here ever listens about Outside. Everybody here is part of this big conspiracy of blindness."

"That's not fair…"

"It's my world. I have the birthright, if I want, to point a finger and call names. Are you going to come with me?" He had begun to think about Greta. That was making him mad.

"No."

"I'll leave in the morning, then. There's no sense us carving each other up with knives of love."

"How poetic!" She sighed. "Darling, Tommy. Keep writing. I know I almost never answer, but the letters… They help. I like to hear about those places."

Perchevski smiled. "It must be in the genes. Thanks. Of course I'll write. You're my number-one lady."

# THIRTEEN: 3048 AD

## Operation Dragon, *Danion*

BenRabi muttered: " 'Aljo! Aljo! Hené ilyas! Ilyas im gialo bar!…'" Over a joint with stripped threads.

"What the hell?" Mouse asked.

"A nonsense poem. By Potty Welkin. From *Shadows in a Dominion Blue.* Goes: " 'Nuné! Nuné! Scutarrac… ' "

"Never heard of it. Think we ought to cut new threads?"

"Let's put in a new fitting. It was a political protest thing. Not one of his biggies. It was a satire on Confederation. The poem was his idea of what a political speech sounded like."

"What's that got to do with anything?"

"It's just the way I feel this morning. Like a poem without sense or rhyme that everybody's trying to figure out. Including me. There. That's got it. What do we do next?"

Beyond Mouse, Amy consulted her clipboard. She had been staring at him with questioning eyes. "A cracked nipple in a lox line about a kilometer from here."

"Uhn." BenRabi tossed his tool kit into the electric truck, sat down with his legs dangling off the bed. Mouse joined him. Amy took off with a lurch that bounced spare fittings all over the truckbed. She had been angry and uncommunicative all week.

Moyshe had been as wary himself, as unsure. He *thought* she was upset because he had not tried to seduce her.

Mouse had let it be for three days. Now, whispering, he asked, "What happened between you two?"

"Nothing."

"Come on, Moyshe. I know you better than that."

"Nothing. Really. That's the trouble." He shrugged, tried to change the subject. "I still can't believe we're inside a ship. I keep feeling we're back in the tunnels at Luna Command."

"What did you mean by that poem?"

"What I said. People keep trying to figure me out. So they can use me."

The ship *was* a lot like Luna Command, with long passageways connecting the several areas that had to be big to function.

"I don't understand," Mouse said.

"Who does? No, wait. Look. Here's Skullface, trying to get me to cross over..."

"So? He tried me too. He's trying everybody. Looks like part of their plan. I just told him I couldn't meet his price. I don't know anything that would be any good to him anyway. So what's the big deal? It's all part of the floor show. We've been through it before."

*But there's something different this time,* benRabi thought. *I've never been tempted before.* "Why was she hustling me?" He jerked his head toward Amy.

Mouse laughed wearily, lowered his head, shook it sadly. "Moyshe, Moyshe, Moyshe. Does it have to be a plot? Did the Sangaree woman burn you that bad? Maybe she likes you. They're not all vampires."

"But they'll all get you hurt," benRabi mumbled.

"What? Oh. You ever stop to think maybe she feels the same way?"

BenRabi paused. Mouse could be right. Mouse knew how to read women, and it paralleled his own impression. He wished he could assume a more casual, no-commitment attitude in his personal relationships. Mouse managed, and left the girls happy.

"Speaking of women. And her." The Sangaree woman gave them a bright gunmetal smile and mocking wave as they glided past her work party, "What to do?" She had been less obnoxious since Mouse's recreation-day demonstration, but had not abandoned her plot.

"Just wait. We're making her nervous. You think old Skullface knows about her? We might make a few points by stopping her when she moves."

"It's a notion," Mouse said, becoming thoughtful. As they rolled to a stop, he suggested, "Why don't you come by for a game tonight?"

His partner was still very much devoted to the mission, Moyshe realized.

Amy plugged the truck into a charger circuit. "That woman. Who is she?"

"Which woman?" Mouse countered, tone idle.

BenRabi scanned the area. It looked like the site of a recent elephant riot. The passage had been open to space. Liquids had frozen and burst their pipes.

"We'll be here a week, Amy. How come we didn't bring any replacement pipe?"

"They're sending a Damage Control team up after lunch. They'll bring what we need. We just worry about the lox line now. It's got to be open by noon. You didn't answer my question, Mouse."

"What's that?"

"Who's that woman?"

BenRabi shrugged, said, "Maria Gonzalez, I think."

"I know her name. I want to know what's between you three."

BenRabi shrugged again. "I guess she hates spies. A lot of people have scratched us off their Christmas lists." Avoiding her eyes, he handed Mouse a wrench.

"Who does she work for?"

The question took him by surprise, but he was in good form. "Paul Kraus in atmosphere systems. He could tell you whatever you want to know."

Mouse chuckled.

A muscle in Amy's cheek started twitching. "You know what I mean. Answer me."

"Take it easy, Amy," Mouse said. "Your badge is showing."

'What?"

"A little professional advice, that's all. Don't press. It puts people off. They clam up. Or play games with you, leading you around with lies. A good agent never pushes unless he has to. You don't have to. Nobody's going anywhere for a year. So why not just lie back and let the pieces fall, then put them together." He had selected the tone of an old pro advising a novice. "Take our situation. Give me a twenty-centimeter copper nipple, Moyshe. You know we're Navy men. We know you work for Kindervoort. Okay..."

"I what?"

"Don't be coy. Torch, Moyshe. And find the solder. You give yourself away a dozen times a day, Amy. The greenest apprentice wouldn't have fallen for that left-handed wrench thing."

BenRabi chuckled. Amy had torn through all three tool kits trying to find the mythical wrench. Then she had gone down to Damage Control and tried to requisition one. Somebody down there had gone along with the gag. They had passed her on to Tooling…

Amy had been given a crash course in plumbing, but she had not learned enough to fool the initiate.

Fury reddened her face. It faded into a soft smile. "I told him I couldn't pull it off."

"He probably didn't expect you to. He knows we're the best. Doesn't matter anyway. We're out of it now. Just a couple spikes here working. Okay, we know where we stand. Where's the flux, Moyshe? So why don't you do like we do? Don't push. Pay attention. Wait. It'll come in bits and pieces. No hard feelings that way. And that closes Old Doc Igarashi's Spy School and Lonely Hearts Club for today. Be ready for a surprise quiz tomorrow. Ow! That's hot."

"Watch the torch, dummy," Moyshe said. "This T pipe is an odd size. We'll have to choke it down to two centimeters somehow."

"Here," Amy said. She made a checkmark on one of the sheets on her clipboard, handed Moyshe a reduction joint with a number tag attached. "Special made. See. I'm learning." She laughed. "No more questions. Mouse. Moyshe. I feel better now. Not so sneaky."

"Good for you," Mouse said.

*Danion* suddenly groaned and shivered. BenRabi whirled, looking for a spacesuit locker. Mouse crouched defensively, making a sound suspiciously like a whimper. "What the hell?" he demanded. "We breaking up?"

Amy laughed. "It's nothing. They're shifting mindsails and catchnets."

"Mindsails?" BenRabi asked. "What's that?"

Her smile vanished. She had, evidently, said too much. "I can't explain. You'd have to ask somebody from Operations Sector."

"And that's off limits."

"Yes."

"Got you."

The shuddering continued for a half hour. They lunched while waiting for the Damage Control people. Amy began to lose her reserve toward benRabi. Soon they were chattering like teenagers who had just made up.

Mouse did a little poking and prodding from the sidelines, as skillfully as any psychologist, maneuvering Amy into inviting Moyshe out next recreation day.

BenRabi went to Mouse's cabin after supper. They played chess and, lip reading, discussed what Moyshe was putting down, using the venerable invisible ink trick, between the lines of his drafts of *Jerusalem*. They also attacked the problem of the Sangaree woman, and found it as stubborn as ever.

Recreation day came, with all its mad morning chess tournaments and its afternoon sports furor, its Archaicist exhibitionism, and its collectors' excitement. BenRabi concluded some business with Grumpy George, got deadlocked over some stamps, and managed a handsome cash settlement on some New Earth mutant butterflies he had brought along for trading.

That evening he and Amy attended another ball. This one was Louis XIV. He went in his everyday clothing. Amy, though, scrounged a costume and was striking. From the ball they went to her cabin so she could change. They had been invited to another party, by the same cousin.

"How did you people get involved in the Archaicist thing?" Moyshe asked while she was changing.

"We're the originals," she replied from her bathroom, her voice light with near-laughter. She had been mirthfully happy all day. Moyshe, too, had been feeling intensely alive and aware. "It starts in creche. In school. When we act out history. We haven't really been around long enough to have any past of our own, so we borrow yours."

"That's not true. We all have the same history."

"I guess you're right. Old Earth is everybody's history if you get right down to it. Anyway, it's a creche game. A teaching method. And it carries over for some people. It's fun to dress up and pretend. But we don't live it. Not the way some people do. Know what I mean?"

"You remember Chouteau? That Ship's Commander who brought us here? He had as bad a case as I've ever seen."

"An exception. Look at it this way. How many people go to these things? Not very many. And they're most of the Archaicists aboard. See? It's a game. But your people are so serious about it. It's spooky."

"I'll buy that." Curious, he thought. In these two weeks he had seen nothing culturally unique to the Seiners. They lived borrowed lives in a hash that did not add to a whole. His expectations, based on landside legends, rumors, and his Luna Command studies, had been severely disappointed.

But Amy had a point. He had encountered only a narrow selection of her people. An unusual minority. The majority, remaining aloof, might represent something different.

She came from the bathroom. "Zip me up, okay?" Then, responding to a question, "We're not complete borrowers. It's partly because you're just seeing a few people, like you say. And partly because this is the fleet. You wouldn't judge Confederation by what you saw on one of your Navy ships, would you? The Yards and creches are different. Except when we're working, we try to make life a game. To beat the boredom and fear. Can't be that much different for Navy men. Anyway, you're not seeing the real us, ever. You're just seeing us reacting to you."

What were these Yards? They kept slipping into Seiner conversation. Did the Starfishers have a world of their own, hidden somewhere out of the way? It was not impossible. The records revealing the whereabouts of scores of early settlements had been destroyed in the Lunar Wars… He was about to ask when he recalled Mouse's advice about pressing.

There was much, much more to the Seiner civilization than anyone in Confederation suspected. The bits he and Mouse had collected already would be worth fortunes to the right people. If he kept learning at this rate…

They were going to give him another medal when he got back. He could see it coming. He would rather have that damned year off.

The party was a carbon of the previous one. Same people. Same music. Same conversation and arguments. Only he and Amy were different. They watched their drinking and tried to understand what was happening to them.

The partiers were younger than he or Amy, and uncomfortable with the gap, though Amy's cousin did her best to make them part of things. Moyshe never felt unwelcome, only out of place. He supposed he had been as much an anomaly before, but had been too preoccupied to notice.

Had Amy manipulated the invitation? If so, why? Another Kindervoort ploy? Both Jarl and Mouse seemed eager to push them together.

Why did he question everything? Even the questioning? Why did he feel that he was losing his grasp on his place in the universe?

They cuddled. They drank. The shadows closed in. They probed one another's pasts. He learned that she had once had an abortion after having been tricked into pregnancy by a man who had wanted to marry her, but whom she had loathed. He resisted the temptation to ask why she had been in bed with him in the first place.

He also learned that she was afraid of sexual intercourse because of some failing in herself. What? She shied away from explaining. He did not press.

Time marched. The sun of the party zenithed and hurried on. He and Amy stayed till everyone else had gone.

They feared leaving more than overstaying their welcome. That room locked them into a cell with well-known walls. Their interaction was defined by rules of courtesy toward their hostess. The limits would expand a pale of hurt.

Yet courtesy demanded that they leave before Amy's cousin found their presence painful.

The subtle differences between weeks coalesced and came to a head when they reached benRabi's cabin. Amy was frightened, unsure. So was he. This time, they knew, something would happen. The Big It, as they had called it when he was first becoming sexually aware.

Like kids, they were eager and afraid. The pleasant sharing they wanted carried with it a big risk of pain.

Thus did the sins of the past leave their marks. Both were so frightened of repeating old mistakes that they had almost abandoned trying anything new.

Moyshe watched the processes of his mind with mild amazement. The detached part of himself could not comprehend what was happening. He had survived affairs.

Even with the Sangaree woman. Why this retrogression to the adolescent pain and confusion of the Alyce era?

There was a long, pale, tense moment when the night balanced on the edge of a double-edged blade. Amy stared at him as he slowly dismounted from the scooter. Then, with a grimace, she jammed the charging plug into a socket.

Moyshe yielded to a surge of relief. She had saved him the need to make a decision. She would bear the blame if anything went wrong.

They remained nervous and frightened. The tension had its effect in temporary impotence and difficult penetration. They whispered a lot, reassuring one another. BenRabi could not help remembering the first time, with Alyce. Both of them had been virgins.

Now, as then, they managed the main point only after trying too hard. Experience made it easier from there.

The truly cruel blow did not fall till the ultimate moment.

At the peak instant Moyshe felt a flood of hot wetness against his groin, something he had thought the exclusive domain of pornography.

Amy started crying. She had lost bladder control.

Ego-mad with that stunning proof of his manhood, benRabi laughed and collapsed upon her, holding her tightly.

She thought he was laughing at her.

Her nails ripped his skin. Angry words filled the air. She tried to knee him. He rolled away, baffled and babbling.

Hair streaming, wet with their sweat, trailing a damp, wrinkled sheet, Amy fled into the corridor. By the time benRabi got into his jumpsuit and started after her, she was a hundred meters down the corridor, scooter forgotten, trying to wrap herself in the sheet as she fled.

"Amy! Come back. I'm sorry."

Too late. She would not listen. He started after her, but gave it up when people began coming out to see what was going on.

He went back and pondered what he had done.

He had given her a gut-kick in a festering wound. This must have happened before and have caused her a lot of grief. This was why she had been so frightened. But she had come to him anyway, hoping for understanding.

And he had laughed.

"Fool," he said, flinging a pillow against a wall. Then, "She should have warned me..." He realized that she had, in her timorous way.

He had to do something before her anger ossified into hatred.

He tried. He really tried. He returned her clothing with a long, apologetic note. He called, but she would not answer. He visited Kindervoort and asked his help, but that seemed to do no good.

Their paths no longer crossed. She did not return to work. He could not corner her and make her listen.

The sword had fallen.

His new supervisor, another of Kindervoort's people, was a small, hard character named Lyle Bruce. Bruce was uncommunicative and prejudiced. He was intolerant and grossly unfair. Repairs had to be done his way even though he was less skilled than Amy.

Mouse and benRabi took it all and smiled back. So Bruce tried harder. "His turn in the barrel will come," Mouse promised. "This is just some test Kindervoort is putting on."

BenRabi agreed. "He won't last. I'll sweet him to death."

BenRabi was right. Next week Bruce was replaced by a man from Damage Control. Martin King was not exactly friendly, but neither was he antagonistic. He was a prejudiced man controlling his prejudices, for the good of *Danion.* He did nothing to hamper their work.

At shift's end one day he told Moyshe, "I'm supposed to take you to Kindervoort's office."

"Oh? Why?"

"He didn't say."

"What about supper?"

"Something will be arranged."

"All right. Let's go."

Kindervoort's office was a place comfy-cozy in nineteenth-century English decor. Lots of dark wood, scores of books. A fireplace would have set it off perfectly.

"Have a seat, Moyshe," Kindervoort suggested. "How's it going out there?"

BenRabi shrugged.

"Dumb question, huh?" He left his chair, came around his desk and sat on its corner. "This isn't really business. Relax." He paused. "No, that's not all the way true. Everything gets to be business, sooner or later. I want to talk about Amy. You willing?"

"Why not?" After all, this was the man he had come running to when things had fallen apart.

"It's personal. I thought you might be touchy."

"I am."

"And honest. I'll be honest too. I want to help because you're my friends. Not close, but friends. And I've got a professional interest, of course. There's going to be more of this kind of trouble. That's bad for *Danion.* I want to find ways to smooth things over."

*Nicely rehearsed speech,* Moyshe thought. "You want to use me and Amy as guinea pigs?"

"In a way. But it's not just an experiment. You're what counts in the end."

Moyshe fought his reaction to Kindervoort's appearance. He pushed back the anger and resentment this interference stimulated…

Swirling visions of stars and darkness. The image of the gun flaming on a black velvet background. He had never had it so strongly, nor in such detail. Fear replaced anger. What was happening? What did this deadly vision mean to his unconscious mind?

"Moyshe? Are you all right?" Kindervoort bent over him, studying his eyes. His voice was remote.

BenRabi rumbled for an answer. His tongue betrayed him. Ghosts had begun dancing inside his head. He could not focus his attention.

A burning crowbar drove through his right eyesocket.

"Migraine!" he gasped.

It was so sudden. None of the little spots or the geometric figures that were the usual warnings. Just the ghosts, the guns, and that curiously familiar stellar backdrop.

BenRabi groaned. The devil himself had him by the skull, trying to crush it down to pea size.

Kindervoort bounced back around his desk, took something from a drawer, dashed through a door into an adjoining bathroom, returned with pills and water. BenRabi watched with little interest. The pain had become the dominant force in his universe. There was just him and it… And now voices.

He heard them, faint and far away, unintelligible but real, like snatches of conversation caught drifting down a hallway from a distant room. He tried to listen, but the agony made a flaming barrier against concentration.

"Moyshe? Here're some pills. Moyshe? Can't you hear me?"

A hand grabbed benRabi's chin, pulled back. Fingers forced his mouth open. Dry, bitter tablets burned his tongue. Water splashed him. A hand covered his mouth and nose till he had no choice but to swallow. The hand departed. He gasped for air.

He had not screamed. Not yet. Because he could not. The pain was killing him, and he could do nothing but cling to its shooting star. Down it went, down into darkness…

Seconds later he recovered, the pain vanishing as quickly as it had come. With it went the ghosts and voices. But he remained disoriented.

Kindervoort was seated behind his desk again, talking urgently into an intercom. "… exact time you went on minddrive." He glanced at his watch. "Were the comnets open? Thanks." He switched off. His expression was grave.

Moyshe had to have more water. He felt as dry as a Blake City summer. He tried to rise. "Water…"

"Stay there!" Kindervoort snapped. "Don't move. I'll get it." Glass in hand, he rushed into the bathroom.

BenRabi fell back into his chair, shivering both from shock and coolness. He had sweated out a good liter. The painkiller, which hit the system as fast as a nerve poison, worked perfectly but did nothing to ease nervous exhaustion. He would not be able to move for a while.

Several glasses of water and a blanket helped. When he felt human enough to talk again, Kindervoort went on as if nothing had happened. "Moyshe, I think it's important that we work out something between you and Amy. Both on the personal and social level."

"Uhm."

"Will you talk to her?"

"I've been trying for a week and a half."

"All right. Easy. Easy." He thumbed his intercom. "Bill? Send Miss Coleridge in now."

Amy burst through the door. "What happened? I heard?..."

Softly, so Moyshe could not hear, Kindervoort explained. Amy's concern became mixed with dismay. She moved to benRabi. "Are you all right?"

"I'll live. Unfortunately."

"Moyshe. Moyshe. What're we going to do?"

"I'm going to say I'm sorry," he murmured.

The apologies and explanations came easy with the edge off their emotions, though Amy remained sensitive. Her problem, as Moyshe had suspected, had caused her a lot of grief.

Kindervoort thoughtfully absented himself. In an hour or so they concluded a cautious truce.

# FOURTEEN: 3047 AD

## The Olden Days, Academy

Perchevski stared out the window as the airbus banked into its Geneva approach. Something was happening down by the lake. A cluster of flashing red lights hugged the shore.

"Ladies and gentlemen, this is your pilot. Air Traffic Control has asked me to relay a Security Service warning. There's trouble on the northbound traffic tube. Terrorists have occupied Number Three Station. They could try to retreat through the tubeway or take passenger hostages. The tube is open, but you'll have to use it at your own risk."

Perchevski watched the flashing lights and darting gnat figures of Zone police till the bus dropped too low. Later, as he crossed the tarmac to a waiting hovercar, he heard the shooting. An occasional explosion drowned the titter of light weaponry.

"They're putting up a fight," said the rating leaning against the groundcar. "Sir."

"Sounds like. What do they want?"

The rating shrugged, opened the passenger side door. "I don't think anybody asked, sir. The Zonies don't bother anymore. They just shoot them and get ready for the next bunch." He closed the door, moved to the pilot's side. "Company office, sir?"

"Yes. Who are they? How did they get in?"

"A new mob, sir. Call themselves the Ninth of June. I don't know what it means."

"Neither do I."

"They broke through at Checkpoint Ahrsen yesterday. Usual surprise attack. Another mob hit there the day before and the Zonies didn't get everything put back together fast enough. They always find a way. We had a bunch come in by hot air balloon last year."

Perchevski left the car for the office where he had helped Greta Helsung catch her rainbow. He checked in, said he was returning to Luna Command, and glanced over what they had on the girl. An hour later he was headed for the lakeside launch pits. He drew the same driver. This time the rating regaled him with a saga concerning his conquest of a "pink patch lady." She had loved him so much she had *almost* enlisted.

"Pink patch" people were Old Earthers who worked in the Zone but lived outside. The uniform patch was their entry permit. Each was Kirlian keyed to prevent terrorist use.

Perchevski was back in his lunar apartment before bedtime next evening. He took a pill and put himself out for twelve hours. Old Earth and his mother had been a miserable mistake.

He did not check his calls right away. He did not want to risk finding a summons from the Bureau.

There was none. The only messages were from Max and Greta. Max was missing him. Greta was scared and lonely and amazed by everything.

Perchevski reacted to Greta's call first. He remembered how frightened and lonely he had been when he had come to Academy. Even hating home, he had been dreadfully homesick.

He made a call to Academy Information, learned that Greta had been assigned to a training battalion, but the battalion had not begun training. The rigorous discipline of Academy would not isolate her for weeks. She could have visitors. She would be allowed a weekly visit from her sponsor after she began training.

"Things have changed since my day, Lieutenant," he told the woman handling his call.

"Since mine, too, Commander. We're getting soft."

"Maybe. Seems like a step in the right direction to me. I'll be there this evening. I'd appreciate it if you'd let me surprise her."

"Whatever you say, Commander."

"Thanks for your time, Lieutenant."

He settled back in his bed, stared at the ceiling, and wondered why he was sponsoring a kid he hardly knew. Sponsorship was serious business. His reponsibility under Lunar law equaled that of a parent.

"Will you sponsor?" the man had asked, and he had responded without thinking.

How could he do right by Greta? In his line of work... Maybe Beckhart would move him to a staff post.

"Old buddy, you backed yourself into a corner this time. How do you get into these things?"

Ah, what was the worry? Greta would be locked up in Academy for four years. She would have no chance for anything but training and study. His sponsorship would not amount to anything but quotations in her files. She would reach the age of responsibility before she graduated.

Maybe he knew that unconsciously when he agreed.

He called Max. No answer.

He donned his Commander's uniform and took the high-velocity tube to Academy Station. The tube passed through the core of the moon. Academy was Farside.

Though he still used the Perchevski name, he had abandoned the Missileman's uniform after High Command had announced von Drachau's raid. There seemed little point to the pretense.

The Bureau apparently agreed. No one had called him on it.

The tubeways were the gossip shops of Luna Command. There strangers whiled away the long transits by dissecting the latest in scandal and rumor. It was there that Perchevski first heard the March of Ulant discussed seriously.

Max had talked about it, of course. But Max was a civ. Max had been retailing fourth-hand merchandise. The people he overheard were Planetary Defense Corps general staff officers from worlds far centerward of Sol. They were in Luna Command for a series of high-powered defense strategy seminars.

Cold fear breathed down Perchevski's neck. The *what* might be debatable, but he could no longer deny that something spooky was going on.

He had been seeing the colorful and sometimes odd uniforms of the local forces everywhere he had gone lately. There were even a few from worlds not part of Confederation.

No wonder there were rumors of war.

He checked in with the local office when he arrived. He was wearing the ring, of course, but redundancy of action and mistrust of technology were Bureau axioms. A staff type told a computer terminal where he was, then in boredom resumed watching a holodrama. He caught a bus to Academy's visitors' hotel.

Academy was an almost autonomous fortress-state within the fortress-world of Luna Command. Nearly ten percent of the moon's surface and volume had been set aside for the school, which trained every Service officer and almost half of all enlisted personnel. Academy contained all the staff colleges, war colleges, and headquarters of special warfare schools which kept the Service honed to a fighting edge. At times as many as two million people taught and studied there.

Perchevski had spent eight years in Academy, glimpsing the outside universe only rarely. Passes had been few in his day. Going out usually meant having to take part in some very active training exercise. There had been no time left over for sightseeing.

He was supposed to have graduated as a dedicated, unquestioning Confederation warrior. He supposed even the best systems made mistakes.

He enjoyed his venture into the old, familiar halls, remembering incidents, recalling classmates he had not thought of in years. He was amused by all the bright, freshly scrubbed young faces behind those snappy salutes.

Greta's battalion was quartered not far from the barracks his own had occupied. He spent an hour ambling through school days memories.

It was late when he located the officer of Greta's Training Battalion. The date-letter designation on the door could be interpreted to tell that Greta's was the forty-third officer candidate unit activated in 3047. He whistled softly. They were taking candidates at a wartime rate.

There must be something to the rumors.

Nothing else would explain why Greta had been assigned to an officer training unit almost instantaneously.

A rating was closing the office. "You the officer looking for the Helsung girl?"

"Yes, Chief. Sorry I'm late."

The petty officer muttered something sarcastic.

"That attitude going to relay itself to the middies, Chief?"

"Sorry, sir. It's been a bad day."

"Where can I find her?"

"Alpha Company. Room Twenty-five. We're just starting the battalion, sir. It's one of your remedials, for candidates without a Service background."

"Thanks, Chief. Go ahead and close up. I'll only stay a few minutes."

Perchevski entered the barracks block. Generations of midshipmen had passed through it. The air was heavy with age. And human scent. He found A Corridor and followed it, glancing at the name tags on the cubicle doors. He located HELSUNG, GRETA: HAMBURG, EARTH, paired with JAMES, LESLIE from someplace on Sierra called Token Offering. No one answered his knock.

He followed the noise of a holoset on to the company commons. Some twenty youngsters were watching holo or playing games without enthusiasm. Homesickness thickened the air.

Greta sat in a vinyl-covered armchair. She had heels pulled up against her behind. Her arm embraced her knees. She had an air of infinite sadness, of unspeakable loneliness.

A ten-year-old with a boarding school voice snapped, "'Ten-shut!"

"As you were, people."

Greta hurled herself at him. She flung her arms around his neck. "I didn't think I'd ever see you again."

"Easy, girl. Don't break anything." He felt better about himself suddenly. It was great to have someone glad to see him.

"How come you're here? I thought you were going to see your mother?"

"I did. We were both disappointed."

"Oh. I'm sorry."

"It's all right. I didn't expect much. Come on. Sit down. How's it going? What do you think of the moon?"

"I haven't seen anything yet. Everything's bigger than I thought it would be. What's happening back home?"

"Nothing new. Homesick?"

She shook her head.

"Fibber. I was here too, remember? And I still get homesick. That's why I go back sometimes. Of course, I came up with Neil Armstrong…"

"Don't tease me."

"All right. Tell you what. I talked to your company commander…"

"Old Greasy Hair? I hate him already."

Perchevski laughed. "You'll hate him a lot more before you're done. He's going to be your father, mother, priest, god, and devil. Look, do you want to see the rest of the moon? You won't have a chance after classes start."

"Don't you have something better to do? You've got your job, and your own friends…"

"I'm on vacation. Sort of. And I don't have many friends here."

"I don't want to put you out." A skinny little black girl with pigtailed hair, wearing a ragged woolen smock, was staring at them. "Oh. Leslie. Come here. This is Leslie James, Commander. My roommate."

"Hi, Les. Where is Token Offering? I visited Sierra once, but I don't remember it."

The girl said something into a mouth full of fingers and retreated.

"She's shy," Greta said. "Her parents must be dead. She came from an orphanage."

"We're all orphans, one way or another. Navy is our family."

Greta looked at him oddly. Then, "Can we take her with us if we go?"

"Uhm. You're starting to understand already. I don't know. It might be complicated. I'll ask if you want."

"I think so."

"Okay. I'd better go. It's past visiting hours. I just wanted to see how you were. I'll be back tomorrow."

She squeezed his hand. "Thank you. For everything." Her hands were soft and smooth and warm.

He spent the evening entertaining fantasies he would never pursue.

The inside man never ages. He spends the rest of his life in love with the soft, smooth, warm girls he knew when he was young and just becoming aware of what marvelous creatures females are.

"Where do you want to go, girls?" They were at Academy Station. Perchevski was watching Greta try to people-watch without being offensive. Oddly uniformed folks surrounded them.

"I don't know," Greta replied.

Luna Command was no sightseer's paradise. It had no spectacular ruins or monuments. The real sights were outside, the mountains and craters of the surface.

He took the girls to Tycho Dome and for a ride on one of the surface trains. He treated them to the best restaurants and hotels. Greta's response was gratifying, Leslie's remote.

He ran out of ideas after two days. All but the alien digs, and he had promised those to Max.

Max could take the pressure off. She would have ideas… He took the girls to her shop.

"Hello, Walter," Max said. Her voice was chilly. She stared at Greta. Greta did not notice. She was engrossed in the showcases.

"Hi, Lady. Anything for me?"

"Same old stuff. Is that what you've been doing since you got back?"

"Come on, Max! She's sixteen. Greta, come here. I want you to meet Max. Max, Greta Helsung and her friend Leslie."

Greta was not imperceptive. "Hi, Max. The Commander is my sponsor."

"Your sponsor? You never told me you had a kid, Walter."

"I'm a man of mystery, Love."

"How come she calls you Walter? Your name is Cornelius."

"Because he's a man of mystery, dear," Max replied. "Everybody has a different name for him. He's some kind of spy. I don't think he knows his real name himself."

"Max…"

"Wow! Really?"

"Yes. Really. Max, you talk too much. I came here to see if you still wanted to go to the Farside dig."

Someone entered the shop behind him. Max said hello.

"Hi, tall, blonde, and desirable. Thomas? Is that you? What the hell are you doing here?"

Perchevski turned.

Mouse had come in. He gave Greta an admiring once-over. "That's right. You know Max, don't you? Max, I really want that Manchurian collection, but you're going to have to come down on it. It's just not worth twelve thousand."

"I can see what you want. Hands off. She's your buddy's kid. And I can get fifteen if I send it out to Amonhotep." To Greta she explained, "This is one of your old man's buddies. He's a spy too."

Perchevski shook his head. "She's in a Roman candle mood today, Mouse. I come in to ask her out and she plays mad dog with me. I didn't know you were a collector."

"Lot of things we don't know about each other." That seemed to close the subject.

"Mouse and I were in the same battalion in Academy," Perchevski told Greta.

Mouse gave the girl another admiring look. She moved closer to Perchevski, as if feeling for a protective shadow. Mouse smiled gently and resumed arguing with Max.

Perchevski wondered how he could demonstrate, to her satisfaction, that she was not in competition with inconquerable youth.

"Max, you want to go to the Farside digs or not?"

"When it's convenient."

"Are you really a spy, Commander?"

"I guess you could put it that way, Greta. How about after work, Max?"

"You sure you won't be busy?"

Perchevski closed his eyes, took a long, deep breath, released it. Be patient, he told himself.

"What's your real name?" Greta asked. Mouse watched, his expression unreadable.

"Honey, sometimes I'm not sure myself. Don't worry about it. It doesn't matter. If you need to get in touch, just call the number I gave you. If I can't get back to you, one of my friends will."

"But…"

"Forget it. Subject closed. Max, are you going to the digs or not?"

"You don't have to get snappy, Walter. Yes. I'm coming. What about you, Mouse?"

"Me?"

"Yes. You want to see that new chamber? They think it might shed some light on the Sangaree. There're some primitive murals that might be of human origin. On a Noah's ark theme, with spaceships. Or aren't you the culture type?"

"Sure. Why not?" He looked at Perchevski as if in appeal.

"I don't know, Mouse. Maybe it's the change." Why was Mouse attaching himself? Because of the Sangaree remark? Or because the Old Man wanted somebody to keep an eye on him? After what had happened on The Broken Wings, Beckhart would be wondering about him.

The girls slept during the tube trip. Perchevski and Mouse played chess on Mouse's pocket set. Prodded by Max, Mouse related several anecdotes about Perchevski while saying nothing about himself. Perchevski let him set the limits.

Max did not seem the least interested in his former partner.

Both men loosened up on sips from a flask Max dug out of her jumpsuit. "Emergency rations," she claimed.

"Good thinking," Perchevski told her.

"What is this? A class reunion?" she demanded toward trip's end.

Mouse and Perchevski had begun playing remember when. They were reliving the Great Sunjammer Race of '29, in which they had crewed a ship and had beaten the best starwind yachtsmen in Confederation. That fluke victory was one of the brightest of Perchevski's memories.

He and Mouse had been a team then, almost friends, and for a few days afterward they had been closer than ever before or since.

"Those were the days," Mouse said, ignoring Max. "Wish we could be kids forever. Think we could do it again?"

"Getting too old."

"Nah. I think I'll check it out. Just for the hell of it. Want to try it? If I can find a ship?"

Perchevski laughed. "Better find the time off, first. We're almost there." The capsule had begun decelerating. "I'll wake the girls."

They reached the digs an hour later.

The one-time alien base was being unearthed, studied, and explored at a snail's pace. The xenoarchaeologists had been working for decades, and might be at it for centuries. They sifted every grain of lunar dust, and preserved it. They did not want to miss a thing, even through ignorance.

Thus far the base had revealed more about humanity's past than it had about its builders.

The scientists had concluded that the station had served both scientific and military purposes, and had been occupied continuously for at least ten millennia. It seemed to have been abandoned approximately eleven centuries before its discovery, just as Mankind teetered on the brink of its first tentative step into space.

Perchevski and his companions began with the museum of recovered artifacts, most of which were everyday items comparable to human combs, tableware, worn-out socks, pill bottles, broken furniture, and the like. The aliens had taken their fancy hardware with them.

"Ooh!" Greta said as they approached a group of wax figurines. "They were ugly."

"Notice anything about them, Greta?" Perchevski asked.

"Besides ugly?"

"Yes. Look at how they're dressed. Think. All the legends about little people. Gnomes, dwarves, elves, leprechauns… The kobolds, where you come from." The largest alien figurine stood just a meter tall.

"Yeah. You're right. You know there're still people that believe in them? One time, I guess I was ten, we went on a field trip to the Black Forest. There was this old caretaker, a kind of forest ranger, who told us all these stories about the kobolds in the woods."

Max interjected, "I think it's more interesting that they resemble the spacemen of the UFO era."

Everyone looked at her. "Oh, it's not my idea. I just liked it. It was on the educational channel one time. In the old days people used to see what they called flying saucers. Sometimes they claimed that space people talked to them. They described them like this. But nobody ever believed them."

"Where are they now?" Leslie asked.

"Nobody knows," Perchevski replied. "They just disappeared. Nobody's found any other traces of them, either. Ulant got into space before we did, and they never ran into them."

"What if they're still watching?" Mouse asked.

Perchevski gave him a funny look.

"Spooky idea, isn't it? Let's look at that new chamber. Max says they found some stuff there that isn't just cafeteria or rec room equipment."

Maybe not. Perchevski could not guess what it might have been. The chamber was large and well-preserved, with most of its furnishings intact and in place. "Parallel function ought to result in parallel structure," he said. "Meaning you ought to be able to figure what this stuff is." All he recognized were the faded mural walls, which looked somewhat Minoan. He would have bet his fortune they had been done by human artists. Those he could see seemed to tell some sort of quest story.

"It's a solarium," Greta said. "Without sun."

"A hydroponics farm?"

"No. That's not right. Hydroponics is different."

"What?"

"What I mean is, it's almost like the Desert House at the State Botanical Gardens in Berlin. See how the beds are laid out? And those racks up there would hold the lights that make plants think they're getting sunshine."

Mouse laughed. "By Jove, I think the lady has something." He indicated a small sign which proposed a similar hypothesis. It also suggested that the painters of the murals might have been humans who had become proto-Sangaree.

Mouse suddenly gasped and seized his left hand in his right.

Perchevski nearly screamed at the sharp agony surrounding his call ring.

"What's the matter?" Max and Greta demanded.

"Oh, hell," Perchevski intoned. "Here we go again."

"Let up, you bastards," Mouse snarled. "We got the message. We're coming, for Christ's sake. Business, Max. We've been called in. And I mean in a hurry. Thomas?"

"I'll kill him. Just when… Max… I'm sorry."

"What's going on?" she asked again.

"We have to report in. Right now. Could you take the girls back to barracks?"

"Business?" She sounded excited.

"Yeah. The bastards. Mouse, they said no more team jobs."

Mouse shrugged.

"I'll get them home," Max promised.

Perchevski kissed her, turned to Greta. "I've got to run out on you, Honey. I'm sorry. I really am."

"Thomas, come on. The Old Man means it."

"Wait a minute, damn it! I don't know how long I'll be gone, Greta. If you need something, call my number. Or get ahold of Max. Okay, Max?"

"Sure." Max did not sound enthusiastic.

"Thomas!"

He waved a hand, kissed Max again, then Greta, and trotted off after Mouse. Greta called a sad, "Good-bye, Commander."

He was angry. He was ready to skin Beckhart with a butter knife.

The chance never came. He and Mouse were seized by Mission Prep the instant they hit Bureau territory.

The training was intense and merciless, and the explanations impossibly far between. It went on around the clock, waking and sleeping, and after a few weeks Perchevski was so tired and disoriented that he was no longer sure who he was. Tiny, unextinguishable sparks of anger were all that kept him going.

Education passed him to Psych. Psych eventually passed him to Medical. For a week every opening of his eyes meant he was fresh off another operating table. Then Education took another go at him. While he recovered he had to read. And when he slept computers pressure-injected information directly into his brain.

Dragons in the night. Golden Chinese dragons. Starfishers… What the hell was it all about? Who was Moyshe benRabi? What was becoming of Cornelius Perchevski?

Sometimes he screamed and fought them, but they were as stubborn as entropy. They kept right on rebuilding their new man.

This was the most intensive, extensive prep he had ever undergone.

He saw Mouse just twice during the whole prep period. They shared the intense hypno-teaching sessions briefing them about Starfishers, but did not intersect again till they met in their master's office. Perchevski thought they were prepping for different missions. Till the Admiral got hold of them personally.

"Boys," Beckhart said, "you've just gone through hell. And I did it to you. I'm not proud of it. It hurt me as much as it hurt you. I don't like operating this way. You'll just have to take my word that it's necessary. And I know what you think about that, Tommy. I don't blame you. But give me the benefit of the doubt, and try to trust me when I tell you that it's imperative that we bring the Starfishers into Confederation as soon as possible."

Such was the opening barrage in a one-way discussion lasting more than three hours. Beckhart talked endlessly, and never answered even one of the questions Perchevski thought pertinent.

He once protested, "You promised no more team jobs."

"And I meant it when I said it, Tommy. But this is the most hurried hurry-up job we've ever had. The CNI told me to put my best men in. She picked you. My God, Tommy, it's only for a couple of weeks. You can't put up with Mouse that long?"

"It's the principle…"

Beckhart ignored him, veering instead into another track.

Almost before he knew what was happening Perchevski found himself aboard a warship bound for the nether end of The Arm. For a world that was, galactically, only a stone's throw from The Broken Wings.

He did not like that. It seemed to be tempting fate too much.

There wasn't a thing he *did* like about this mission.

They hadn't even let him say his good-byes. Bureau thugs had surrounded him from the moment he had departed Beckhart's office…

"Hey, Moyshe," Mouse said cheerfully, within an hour of their going aboard, "Let's go up to the wardroom and play some chess."

# FIFTEEN: 3048 AD

## Operation Dragon, *Danion*

*Danion* became as comfortable as an old, well-worn shoe.

"Fact is, it's getting downright dull," Mouse complained toward the end of the third month.

"What?" benRabi demanded. "All those ball games, and you up to your ears in women, and you're bored?"

"You got it, partner. Like the man in the joke said, women are fine, but what do you do the other twenty-three hours of the day?"

Amy made a remark that Moyshe did not catch.

"If that's how you feel," Mouse replied, laughing, "you can carry your own damned books."

They were moving her into Moyshe's cabin. BenRabi was not overwhelmed by the idea. Nor was he sure how it had come about. It had just sort of fenced him in, pushed by Amy and Mouse till the move actually began and he still had not said "No!"

He preferred living alone. Sharing struck him as synonymous with imposition. Amy's mere presence foreordained increased demands… At least he would have someone around when the headaches came.

Mouse and Amy kept bickering. Mouse was teasing, but Amy sounded serious. She did not like Mouse much.

BenRabi's migraines came several times a week now. He was scared. The voices and visions… He thought it might be a tumor, but the Seiner doctors would not take him seriously. They gave him pain pills and told him not to worry.

He had been on continuous medication the last ten days. He was pale, dehydrated, weak, and shaky.

Amy seemed to be the only one who cared, and she would not say why.

His old downdeep fear that he was going mad seemed ever more creditable.

*This is a hell of a time to take a live-in lover,* he thought, dumping an armload of clothing. The relationship was paraplegic.

The inexplicable recurring memory of Alyce did not help. It frightened and disoriented him.

There was no reason for that old, dead affair to obsess him.

It was just another symptom of whatever was happening to him. But it was damned scary.

On The Broken Wings he had, almost, been the tough, hard character he had been portraying. Now, less than a year later, he was a spineless, whimpering… Disgusted, he tried to kick a chair across the cabin. It did not move. All shipboard furniture was bolted down.

He resumed work in grim silence.

"Moyshe, I need your help," Mouse said a month after the move, voice sounding a plaintive note.

"What? How? I'll do whatever I can." He glanced over his shoulder to make sure Amy remained in the women's head. He was surprised. This tone did not fit his partner at all.

"Figure out a way to keep me from killing her."

BenRabi followed Mouse's gaze. It was fixed on the Sangaree woman like the cross hairs of an assassin's rifle scope.

"She's working on me, Moyshe. She's got me working on myself. I've been having trouble sleeping. I just lay there thinking up ways… Thinking about her being right down the passage. It's because of the mess on Blackworld. I can't get it out of my head. And I thought I had it under control."

"You too? What the hell did Beckhart do to us?"

Amazing, Mouse's finally owning up to a connection with the Shadowline War. He must be under real stress.

"Self-discipline, Mouse. That's the only answer I've got. And maybe the notion that you ought to save yourself for a bigger target. She's not worth getting burned over."

"She's the queen in the game. And the stakes are as big as they can get, Moyshe. Watch her. I've never seen anybody so sure they had a winning hand. She's got a royal flush in spades look."

"You're mixing metaphors."

"Metaphors be damned, Moyshe. I need help."

*Jesus,* benRabi thought. *Here I am halfway to the psycho ward and my partner is crying for me to keep him out. Are we going to have one nut stand guard over the cracks in the other's noggin?* "Let's take it to Kindervoort, then."

"Oh, no. This stays in the family. Jarl doesn't get anything free. How's your head doing?"

"The docs keep saying there's nothing wrong. It don't sound right. I mean, how come I hurt so goddamned much? But maybe it's true. For a while I thought it was a tumor and they were just jollying me so I wouldn't panic. But the scans didn't show anything when I finally got them to let me see them. Now I think something external is causing it."

"Allergy?"

"No. I can't explain yet. It's just barely a suspicion so far."

That suspicion did not leaf out, blossom, and bear fruit for months.

Time lumbered forward. Mouse worked himself into the shipwide chess finals. BenRabi had a falling out with the collector crowd, among whom he had been a brief, bright star. They were older, more prejudiced people, and unable to tolerate his alienness indefinitely. He trudged onward in his laborious relationship with Amy.

He tried to make it work. He sincerely believed he was giving it an honest go, and for a while the curious Alyce memories and attendant mental oddities withdrew, but he never saw any long-term hope.

He even abandoned his writing in order to give her more time. "I just don't feel like writing," he lied. "It isn't me anymore."

She protested, but with such restraint that he began to resent her presence during moments when he could have written.

Turn around twice and there went another month into the file cabinets of time. And here was Mouse with another. "Moyshe, I think I need help."

"Stay out of her way."

"Not the Sangaree woman this time, Moyshe. Another one."

"What else?"

"Carrie just gave me the word. That Sally I was going with… She's peegee."

"Come on. You're shitting me. People don't get pregnant unless… Oh, my."

"Oh, my, yes. Unless they want to."

Moyshe fought a grin.

"You laugh and I'll kick your head in."

"Me? Laugh? I'm sorry. It's just that… What do you want me to do?"

"Shee-it, Moyshe. I don't know. Talk to me. I've never been up this tree before."

"What is it? She figure you'd do the honorable thing?" *Why are you doing this to me, Mouse? I had a handle on the Alyce thing.*

"That's the name of the game. That's the way they do things here. And the way they lay their little traps. Straight from Century One."

"No law says you've got to give her what she wants, though. Kiss her good-bye." That was how he had failed Alyce, so long ago. He had not found the strength to say no until it was too late.

"I don't like to hurt anybody's feelings."

"That's the chance she took, isn't it?" How come it was so easy to say, but so hard to do? "I don't see how anybody could believe in a marriage that started out that way anyway. Go on. Tell her to kiss off."

"Easier said than done, Moyshe."

"I know. Advice is that way. Here's some more, while we're at it. Take your own precautions so it doesn't happen again."

"That much I figured out for myself." Mouse went away. He returned within the hour, shaking his head. "She couldn't believe that landsmen don't give a damn if a kid's parents are married or not. But I think I finally got through to her."

For a while Mouse's social calendar was less crowded. But only for a while. The ladies seemed incapable of remaining away.

"Tell me something, Amy," benRabi said one afternoon. "Why are we here?"

She started giving him the standard story.

"That's not true. *Danion* didn't really need us. Certainly not a thousand of us. Even with only two hundred we'll finish up six months early. Your own Damage Control people wouldn't have taken much longer. So what's really going on?"

She would not tell him. She even refused to speculate. He suspected, from her expression, that she might not know, that she was beginning to ask herself the questions that were bothering him.

His came of a long line of thinking sparked by snippets of information and flashes of intuition that had begun accumulating on Carson's.

"Correct me if you can fault this hypothesis," he told Mouse when Amy was out of hearing. "We're guinea pigs in a coexistence experiment. They've got something big and dangerous going and they thought they could hire outside help to get through it. I'd guess they expect heavy fighting. Our job descriptions all deal with damage control. But the experiment was a failure. No takers."

"I wouldn't know, Moyshe. You've got your head working. Who were they going to fight? Not us."

"Sharks?"

"Maybe. But it doesn't add up. Still, I'm not much good at puzzles. How's your head doing?"

"Real good. Why?"

"I thought so. You're more like the old Moyshe lately." They completed the last scheduled repair three weeks later. From then on there was little to do.

One day a long-faced Amy announced, "They just told me. Starting Monday you'll be assigned to Damage Control. To the emergency ready room at D.C. South. I'll take you over and introduce you."

"Breaking up the team, eh?" Mouse asked. "Where are you going?"

"Back to Security." She did not sound pleased.

BenRabi felt a guilty elation. Though he loved Amy, he did not like having her around all the time. He felt smothered.

The damage control assignment was a crushing bore. "A fireman in a steel city would have more to do," Mouse complained. A few days later, he cornered benRabi in order to update him on his own snooping.

"Our fleet commander looks like a maverick. He won't bow down to Gruber of Gruber's Fleet as the head honcho Starfisher. He wants to do things his own way. The other fleets treat this one like an idiot cousin."

"That why the Old Man targeted Payne's Fleet?"

"No. He just jumped on a chance to get somebody onto a harvestship. You were right about the experiment, by the way. It was something Gruber put Payne up to. I get the impression that now he's using the failure as an excuse to go haring off on some adventure of his own as soon as we're done harvesting."

"Speaking of which. Amy says it's the best they've ever had. They're going to hold their auction after we leave."

"Kindervoort still on you about crossing over?"

"He mentions it sometimes. Came to the cabin last week." Did Mouse suspect that he found the offer tempting?

Sports season became crazier than ever as playoff time approached. For Moyshe it was all bewildering color and madness. Mouse, of course, was right in the thick of it. Football was his latest passion. He could quote records and statistics by the hour. BenRabi studied the game just so he could carry on a conversation.

Their lives, increasingly, became frosting, sugar-bits having nothing to do with their assignments. They had come here to find starfish. Despite a thousand doubts and distractions, benRabi kept his wavering cross hair sighted near his programmed target. He even resumed wrestling with *Jerusalem* so he could keep his invisible notes.

Sharing quarters with an agent for the other side constantly hampered him. He was not so naïve as to believe that Amy had been struck deaf and blind by love.

He had come aboard thinking starfish were a wonderful concept, a miraculous hook on which to hang modern myths and legends. They had been one with the lost planet Osiris and the fabulous weapons of Stars' End. Now he knew that the hydrogen streams teemed with "life." The fairy magic was gone, but still the fantastic fish were something to play with during his long hours of waiting for an emergency that never arose.

The starfish, the leviathans of the airless deep, were more fields of force and the balances between them than they were creatures of matter. The longbeards of the breed could be three hundred kilometers long and a million years old. They might occupy thousands of cubic kilometers, yet have fewer atoms in them than a human adult. In them atoms and molecules functioned primarily as points upon which forces anchored. Here, there, a pinpoint hawking hole left over from the big bang formed the core of an invisible organ.

The fabric of space and time were the creature's bone and sinew. He could manipulate them within himself. In essence, he built himself a secondary universe within the primary, and within that homemade pocket reality existed as tangibly as did men in their own reality. The part of a starfish that could be detected was but a fraction of the whole beast. He also existed in hyperspace, null space, and on levels mankind had not yet reached.

Those beasts of the big night were living fusion furnaces. They fed on hydrogen, and enjoyed an occasional spice of other elements in the fusion chain. At first

Moyshe had wondered why they did not gather where matter was more dense, as in the neighborhood of a protostar.

Amy told him that the field stresses around stellar masses could rip the creatures apart.

A starfish's stomach contained a fire as violent as that at the heart of a sun. Not only did fusion take place there, but matter annihilation as well when the beast browsed on anti-hydrogen with that part of him coexisting in a counter-universe.

BenRabi did not speculate on the physics. He was a field man. A supernova seemed kindergarten stuff by comparison. He simply noted his thoughts in invisible ink and hoped the Bureau's tame physicists could make something of them.

"Mouse, I've run into a philosophical problem," he said one morning. "About the fish."

"You've lost me already, Moyshe."

"I've gotten onto something that's turning my thinking inside out."

"Which is?"

"That this isn't your usual man/cattle relationship. It's a partnership—if the Fishers aren't the cows. The fish are intelligent. Probably more intelligent than we are." He looked around. No one was listening. "They have what they call a mindtech section in Ops Sector. Somehow, they communicate with the starfish. Mind to mind."

"Where'd you get that?"

"Around. Keeping my ears open. Adding things up."

"So the ugly old psi theory raises its head again. Out here. You know what the Old Man's scientists will say about that?"

"They'll have to loosen up those stiff necks. But what I think is interesting is the research possibilities."

"Research?"

"Historical research. The fish have been in contact with other races. And some of them are over a million years old. That's a lot of remembering, I'm thinking."

Like oceans, the hydrogen streams supported a complete ecology, including the predatory "shark," the starfish's natural enemy. There were a dozen species. Even the biggest and most dangerous was much smaller than an adult starfish. However, like man and wolves, several of the species hunted in cooperative packs. They could even pursue their prey through hyperspace.

Packs shadowed all the great herds. They struck when a fish straggled. Sometimes, when driven by hunger, they tried to cut individual fish from the herd. And occasionally, when their numbers reached a certain critical mass, a whole pack went berserk and threw itself at the herd.

The starfish were not helpless. They could burp up balls of gut fire and sling them around like granddaddy nuclear bombs. But sharks were fast and the burping was slow. A starfish under attack seldom had a chance for more than one defensive attempt. He had to count on the help of his herdmates, who might be under attack themselves. Thus inadequate, the starfish sometimes needed allies to survive.

When the earliest Seiners had located their first starfish herd the shark packs had been expanding rapidly. That first herd had been threatened with extinction.

Its fish had touched the minds of those early Seiners, had found in them a hope, and so had contacted them and had made a bargain. They would produce ambergris in quantity in exchange for human protection.

"There're times when I think they're trying to touch me," benRabi told Mouse, after rehearsing what history he had learned.

"What makes you think that?" Mouse seemed excited by the idea.

"Probably just my imagination." He was reluctant to tell Mouse that he sometimes dreamed of vast, swimming spatial panoramas, oddly alive with things never seen by human eyes. Dragons flew there, and played, with a ponderousness unmatched even in Old Earth's vanished whales. Each time he dreamed the dream, he wakened with a screaming migraine.

"So those first Fishers armed themselves," he said, resuming his history lesson. "The fish taught them to detect the sharks. The herd slowly recovered."

But the sharks, in their slow fashion, reasoned. They learned to associate casualties with the hard things shepherding their prey. In the middle thirties they had begun getting harvestships as well as herds, forcing the Seiners to defend themselves before they protected their allies.

This past year they had begun attacking the ships first, and cooperating between packs of different species.

Their numbers were still expanding. Soon, the Seiners feared, they would be numerous enough to attack and destroy whole harvestfleets.

No ships had yet been lost, but the attack on *Danion* had demonstrated the reality of the peril.

The Starfishers believed themselves at war, and feared it was a war they could not win. They were too few and too weakly armed.

"Packs are migrating here from deeper in the galaxy," Moyshe concluded. "I suppose because of a depleted food supply there."

"That's it?" Mouse asked.

"What'd you expect? It's hard to get anything out of Amy. She may be sleeping with me but she doesn't forget that I'm the other old enemy, the landsman. About the only other thing is that they're desperate for more and better weapons. They might have something cooking there. Any time I mention weapons, Amy changes the subject fast."

In fact, she usually left the cabin. That scared him. Something big was going on and she did not want to risk giving him a hint.

Her behavior confirmed the feeling he had had from the beginning. This was no ordinary harvest.

*Danion* had been under drive for weeks. Moyshe's suspicions had become stronger. Harvestships seldom went hyper. The fish did not like it.

Were the beasts following the fleet?

Nobody was talking. Even the friendliest Seiners had little to say anymore.

The year was winding down. He had learned a lot, but still nothing concrete, nothing of genuine advantage to the Bureau and Confederation. Was the mission going to end up a wild goose chase?

Playing spy-vs.-spy in the bedroom with Amy had become agonizing. Yet he had to pursue his tradecraft. He had to try to learn, and he did not dare relax.

He could not forget the Sangaree woman. She was still there, and still very much involved in her own mission.

Whatever her game was, it was in its final moves. She had resumed pushing Mouse, hard, confident of her strength.

The drives had been dead a week. *Danion* had reached her destination. Whole new sections of the ship had been closed to landsmen. The Seiners who came and went there were more closed-mouthed than ever. Some, whom Moyshe considered friends, would barely acknowledge his greetings. Whatever they were doing, they wanted no hint to get back landside.

Work schedules went to shift-and-a-half. There were no exceptions. BenRabi and Mouse just spent that much more time being bored.

"Whatever it is, it's dangerous," Mouse said. "They're all scared green."

"The shark packs are collecting. Like ten times thicker than they've ever seen."

"I watched one of the Service Ship crews come in this morning. They rotated with an alternate crew."

"Fighting?"

"Just exhausted, I think. I didn't see any stretchers. But Kindervoort's thugs ran me off before I could find out anything."

Despite Kindervoort they gleaned their bits of information. "They're in a race against time," benRabi told Mouse. "I heard one guy say they wouldn't get a chance to gamble if the sharks hit aggressive mass before they finish their experiments."

"What did he mean? Are they working on some new weapon?"

BenRabi shrugged. "I didn't ask. But I sure wouldn't mind knowing what they're risking my life for."

One evening, after a workday spent within taunting distance of the Sangaree woman, benRabi and Mouse tried to relax over a chessboard.

"You're shook up again," Mouse observed while staring at his pieces. "What's up? Trouble with Amy?"

"That's part of it. I've only seen her twice all week. She just comes in long enough to shower and change."

"So? She's not sitting on the only one in the universe. The little redhead, Penny something, from New Earth…"

"She's young enough to be my kid, Mouse. Only a couple of years older than Greta."

Mouse flung his hands up in mock exasperation. "What's that got to do with it? She's willing, isn't she?"

"Maybe. But I think I'm more a father image…"

"So indulge in a little incest."

"It doesn't matter anyway. Sex isn't the problem."

"What? It's always a problem. One way or another." Mouse chuckled. He chuckled again as he ambushed Moyshe's queen. Moyshe could not keep his mind on his game. The *want* had returned, mildly, along with that damned thing with the gun. "What *is* the problem, then?"

"The way people are treating us? I guess. They're so scared they won't have anything to do with us."

"Check. Check there too. Part of it's the Sangaree woman, Moyshe. She's telling stories on us again. Trying to isolate us. I wonder why? One move to mate."

They batted possibilities around. Moyshe so loathed the one that occurred to him that he refused to mention it right away.

His game grew increasingly poor. He became irritable. The *I want* grew stronger, louder, mocking him, telling him that he was on the threshold of its fulfillment and was too blind to see it.

"I can't hold off much longer," Mouse said, taking a pawn with a savage grab. "Next time she gouges me, or the next, I'll bend her, and damned be the consequences."

"Please don't. We're almost home. We've only got five weeks to go."

Mouse slaughtered a knight. "You think we should let her set us up?"

BenRabi glanced at Mouse's emotionless face, back to the disaster already developing on the chessboard. "I yield." The more he reflected, the more he was sure he knew what Marya was planning. He stood abruptly, scattering chessmen. "We may have to."

"Have to what?"

"Bend her. For our own good. I know what she's doing. We ignored the obvious. Suppose she has the same kind of tracer we did? They've got the technology. And suppose she has control and didn't turn it on till after the Seiners stopped worrying about things like that?"

"Got you. Let's not bend her. Let's just chop the tracer out." Mouse returned his chessmen to their box with loving care, then recovered a wicked homemade plastic knife from beneath his mattress. "Let's go."

BenRabi thought of a dozen reasons for putting it off, but could not articulate a one. It was time Marya was put out of the game. She was too dangerous.

They were halfway to her cabin when he stopped, struck by a sudden thought. "Mouse, what if she's expecting us?"

"Doesn't seem likely."

"You can't overlook anything in this business."

"That's true. Let me think a minute."

For months they had known that the Seiners sometimes listened in on them. When they did not want to be overheard they carefully lipread one another, never verbalizing anything that might excite an eavesdropper.

"I think I made a mistake bringing this up in your cabin."

"Yeah. Maybe. But it's too late to cry. If she bugged us, she bugged us."

"What're you going to do?"

"I'm thinking. I don't got a whole lot of use for Pyrrhic victories, you know."

They continued talking quietly, ten meters from Marya's door.

Three Seiners on a flying scooter squealed round a corner and skidded to a stop at Marya's door. They wore Security patches. One moved toward Mouse and benRabi, hand on his weapon, then stood easy. They tried to look like curious bystanders. The other Security men eyed the door.

"Looks like we get it done for us, Mouse."

"They're not thinking!" Mouse growled. BenRabi's heart pounded out a flamenco. These guys were too sure of themselves.

They overrode the door closure. A pair of explosions greeted them. One man fell in the doorway. The other flung himself inside.

The one facing Mouse and benRabi whirled, charged into the cabin too. His face had gone grey.

They heard grunts and a cry of pain. "Homemade gunpowder weapons!" benRabi gasped. "Nice welcome she had for us."

Mouse looked up and down the passageway. "Come on. Before we draw a crowd."

BenRabi did not know what Mouse planned, but he followed. Mouse went in the door low, scooping the weapon from the hand of the dying Seiner. BenRabi scrambled after him, seizing another fallen handgun.

The Sangaree woman had her back to the door. She was struggling with the last Security man. Her left hand darted past his guard, smashing his windpipe. He gagged. She followed up with a bone-breaking blow over his heart.

BenRabi's grunt of sympathy warned her of enemies to her rear.

"Slowly," Mouse said as she started for the Seiner's weapon. "I'd hate to shoot."

For once she had no instantaneous retort. Mouse's tone made it clear there was nothing he would hate less than killing her. Emotional pain twisted her face when she turned. Once again, from her viewpoint, they had out-maneuvered her—and this time might be fatal.

Her agony turned into a strained smile after a moment. "You're too late." The smile broadened. It became anticipatory. "They're on their way by now."

"Moyshe, get that man in here and close the door. How bad is he?"

"He's gone."

"Better be nice," Marya said as benRabi forced the door shut. She had the sense to keep her voice neutral. To survive, to enjoy her victory, she had to overcome the obstacle she had made of Mouse. "They'll be here soon. You won't want them mad at you."

"This one's gone too," benRabi said. "The other one might make it. Marya, don't think the Seiners will hand over a harvestfleet because a few raidships turn up."

She smiled that gunmetal smile.

He remembered ruined merchantmen left in the wake of Sangaree raiders. They would come with enough gunpower. There would be no survivors.

An alarm began hooting. It was a forlorn call to arms.

"General quarters, Mouse. She's for real." The borrowed weapon seemed to swell painfully in his hand. A part of him was telling him it was time he finished what he had started on The Broken Wings.

# SIXTEEN: 3049 AD

## Operation Dragon, Combat

Time telescoped, then coiled around itself like some mad snake trying to crush itself. It detached Marya's battlefield cabin from the macro-universe, establishing an independent timeline. Ten seconds became an eternal instant.

BenRabi was afraid.

Something clicked inside Mouse. He slipped into assassin's mind. BenRabi vacillated between answering the alarm and staying to restrain the organic killing machine.

*Danion* shivered. Moyshe recognized the feel of service ships launching.

"I'm going on station, Mouse. Keep her here till Jarl's people come. And keep her alive."

Mouse nodded mechanically. He was easily guided while in assassin's mind—if Psych had keyed him to accept your direction. He would be upset later. He wanted to show the woman the death of a thousand cuts, or something equally grisly.

He was on his way back to the real universe already. "Take the guns, Moyshe. Hide them."

"What about?…"

"This." He tapped the plastic knife thrust through a tool loop on his jumpsuit.

"All right." BenRabi collected the weapons. He hid them in Mouse's cabin, then headed for Damage Control South.

"What's up?" he asked one of his teammates when he arrived.

"Sangaree raidships. They say there's at least fifty of them. That's scary."

"In more ways than one."

"What do you mean?"

"That their show is being put on by a consortium. No one Family has that kind of muscle. The last time they put that many ships together was for the Helga's World thing during the Shadowline War."

The Seiner regarded benRabi with a puzzled fearful frown. Moyshe was talking foreign history.

Moyshe found his fellow landsmen in a low-grade panic. They had no faith in Seiner arms. And they were sure the Starfishers would fight. He did not understand till he heard the Seiners themselves second-guessing Payne.

Fleet Commander Payne had refused to negotiate or back down. He had told the Sangaree that he would fight to the last harvestship.

"What're we fighting *about?*" Moyshe asked plaintively.

His Seiner companions refused to enlighten him.

He felt that touch of panic himself. He never had wanted to die with his boots on. Not since he had given up boyhood daydreams. He had no interest in dying at all. Not for several thousand years.

Time moved with the haste of pouring treacle. He knew the Sangaree ships were maneuvering in the darkness outside. Outgunned service ships were moving to meet them. The death dance had begun.

Moyshe stood facing the dark gate with all the unanswerable questions still banging around in his mind. The nature of his want remained the biggest, closely followed by the meaning of the gun thing.

He started worrying about Amy. Where was she? Would she be safe? "Stupid question," he muttered. Of course she was not safe. Nobody was safe today.

Then he saw her standing at the tool crib. What was she doing here? She spotted him, started his way.

"Where's Mouse?" she asked.

He explained quickly.

"Good," she said when he finished. She tried to remain cool, but a tear formed in the corner of one eye. She brushed at it irritably. She had caught some of the groundside uninvolvement disease from him, he thought. Why else would a Seiner hide her emotions? Three men had died. It was a sad affair.

She said, "I'll call Jarl. He may not have sent anyone else down."

Moyshe resumed his seat, stared at the deck tensely, counting rivets and welds. When would the Sangaree missiles arrive?

The attack, when it came, was not Sangaree. The dull-witted sharks, confused and distressed by the sudden appearance of so many more ships, reached emotional critical mass. They attacked in all directions.

Scraps of news filtered in from Operations Sector. Some were good, some bad. The Sangaree were having a hard time. But the sharks attacking the harvestfleet were concentrating on *Danion*.

In the sea of nothing the service ships were killing, and sometimes being killed by, sharks. The Sangaree vainly fought an enemy invisible to their equipment while, foolishly, continuing to try for a position of vantage against the harvestfleet. There was a wan hope in that, Moyshe thought. The sharks might take care of them. But, then, who would take care of the sharks?

*Danion* shivered continuously. All her weaponry was in action, firing on Sangaree and sharks alike. BenRabi grimaced as he wondered just what the monster ship mounted.

He waited with his team in the heart of the great mobile, he smelling their fear and they his. Amy quivered like a frightened rabbit in the crook of his arm. Alarms screamed each time the sharks penetrated the defenses, but D.C. South received no emergency calls.

Courage brewed beneath the fear. There was no tension between landsman and Seiner now. They were united in defiance of an unprejudiced death.

*Danion* rocked. Sirens raked their wicked nails over a million blackboards. Officers shouted into the confusion. A damage-control team piled aboard an electric truck and hurtled off to aid technicians in the stricken sector. Behind them the mood gradually turned grim as the fear, unable to sustain itself indefinitely, faded into a lower key, an abiding dread. Each technician sat quietly alone with his or her thoughts.

The damage reports began arriving. Nearly ten percent of *Danion*'s population were either dead or cut off from the main life-support systems. More trucks left. Survivors had to be brought out before the emergency systems failed.

And there Moyshe sat, doing nothing, awaiting his dying turn.

Somewhere in the big nothing the Sangaree raidmaster decided he had had enough. His fleet took hyper, bequeathing the Starfishers his share of ghostly foes.

"Suits," said the blank-faced Fisher directing D.C. ops when the news arrived. He foresaw the end.

They drew spacesuits from the emergency lockers. BenRabi donned his while thinking that this was the first time he had worn one seriously. Always before it had been for training or fun.

He wondered why Mouse had not yet shown. Was he in the sector cut off? He asked Amy.

"No. There's no damage there yet. Jarl probably hasn't had a chance to do anything. Our people should all be manning weapons."

*Danion* screamed, whirled beneath them. Moyshe fell. His suit servos hummed and forced him to his feet. The gravity misbehaved. He floated into the air, then came down hard. The lights weakened, died, returned as emergency power entered the lines.

A shark had hit *Danion*'s main power and drives.

Somebody was yelling at him. Amy. "What?" He was too upset to listen closely, heard only that his team was going out. He jumped at the truck as it started rolling. Seiner hands dragged him aboard.

Twenty minutes later, in an odd part of the ship devoted to fusion plant, his team captain set him to securing broken piping systems. Whole passageways had been ripped apart. Gaps opened on the night. Sometimes he saw it, starless, as he worked, but thought nothing of it. He was too busy.

Hours later, when the pipes no longer bled and he had time for sloth, he noticed a vacuum-ruined corpse tangled in a mass of wiring, dark against an outer glow. That gave him pause. Space. It was what he was not supposed to see, so of course he had to look. He walked to the hole, saw nothing. He pushed the corpse aside, leaned out. Still nothing. No stars, no constellations, no Milky Way. Nothing but a tangle of harvestship limned by a sourceless glow.

He stood there, frozen in disbelief, for he knew not how long. No stars. Where were they that there were no stars?

The harvestship rotated slowly. Something gradually appeared beyond tubing, spars, and folded silver sails—the source of the glow. He recognized it, but did not want to believe it. It was the galaxy, edge on, seen from beyond its rim. His premonitions returned to haunt him. What, outside the galaxy, was near enough to be reached by ship?

Far away, another harvestship coruscated under shark attack. *Danion* had shuddered to several while he worked, but none had been bad. There was an explosion aboard the other vessel. Gases spewed from her broken hull. But his eyes fled her, hurrying on to the coin-sized brightness rising in the direction of rotation.

It was a planet. Self-illuminating, no sun. There was only one such place…

Stars' End.

Certain destruction for all who went near.

What were the Seiners doing? Were they mad? Suicidal?

Something broke, something blossomed across the face of the galaxy, a hundred times brighter, a fire like that of an exploding star. A harvestship was burning in a flame only a multidimensional shark could have ignited. They were growing more cunning, were spraying antimatter gases that totally devoured. In a corner of his mind a little voice asked, as a Fisher would, if that vessel's death had served the fleet. Were sharks dying there too?

His gaze returned to Stars' End. All his myths were hemming him in. He did not doubt that the Sangaree would return. It was not their style to back down when the stakes were high, and there was more on the line now than a source of ambergris.

He knew why the Seiners had come here. As did all who sought Stars' End, they wanted the fortress world's fabulous weapons. For centuries opportunists had tried to master the planet. Whoever possessed its timeless might became dictator to The Arm. No modern defense could withstand the power of Stars' End weaponry. Nor could sharks. The weapons were the salvation for which Payne had dared hope.

What a faint hope! BenRabi knew there was no way to penetrate the planet's defenses. Battle fleets had failed.

A hand touched his shoulder. A helmet met his. A voice came by conduction. "We're pulling out. *Danion*'s been hit inboard of us. We don't want to get trapped here." In those words Moyshe imagined great sadness, but little of the fear he felt himself.

They managed to reach D.C. South again only by trekking several kilometers afoot through regions of ship that looked like they had been mauled by naval weaponry. Moyshe found it hard to believe that the wrecking had been done by a creature he could not see.

A room had been prepared for them to relax in, with snacks and drinks, and secure enough so they dared shed their suits.

Mouse was there, wounded and bleeding.

"Mouse! What the hell!…"

"I should've bent her straight off, Moyshe. She got to me. Tricked me. Now she's into it somewhere."

It was a big and confused ship. She could disappear easily. "How?" Moyshe examined Mouse's left arm. It was angled. Mouse had gotten a tourniquet on somehow.

"Thing like a hatchet." Mouse's face was drawn and bloodless, but he did not protest benRabi's rough hands.

"She must've caught you napping. That don't sound like you."

"Yeah. We were playing chess…"

"Chess? For Christ's sake…"

"She's pretty good. For a woman. Nailed me when I was moving in for a mate."

BenRabi shook his head. "Are you for real?"

He could picture it. An overconfident Mouse suggesting a game to kill time, getting too deep into alternate moves to react quickly. Stupid, but in character. "How many times have I told you it was going to get you into trouble someday?"

"God damn, Moyshe, don't mother me. Not now. Do something about the arm, eh? Nobody around here is interested. I could lose it. And these clowns don't do regeneration surgery."

"Amy? Where's Amy Coleridge?" benRabi asked. He found her. "You seen Mouse? He needs a doctor bad."

"I saw him come in. There's one on the way. The woman?"

"Yeah." What was Marya doing now?

This was the price of not having let Mouse have his way on The Broken Wings. On his hands was the blood of a friend; in his mind a nagging gunmetal smile. Whatever feeling he might have had for her, or she for him, they were of enemy tribes. That was the overriding rule. In the end, neither could give quarter.

"I'll take care of it, Mouse," he whispered to his friend. "You keep Amy busy." He rose. "Keep an eye on him, will you, love? I'll be back in a couple minutes."

She asked no questions, probably assuming he was off to the toilet.

From the tool crib he drew an old Takadi Model VI laser cutting torch. It was a light-duty one-handed tool meant for sheet metal trimming. The crib attendant asked no questions.

He slipped out of D.C. and into an empty office nearby. It took just minutes to make the modifications he had been taught in a Bureau school. He created an unwieldy lasegun. Then he stole a scooter and took off.

He had tried to think like the woman while modifying the torch. He presumed that she would not know the attacks were shark and not her own people's. She would do something to neutralize the ship without damaging it. Her specialty dealt with atmosphere…

She would head for Central Blowers. She could take out Operations if she could cut its oxygen supply.

He hurtled through passageways, impatiently trying to remember the way to the blower rooms. Fate seemed determined to stall him. Damage compelled long detours. He had to wait on emergency traffic. People kept stopping him to tell him to get a suit on. The scooter, low on power, slowed to a crawl. He had to walk a kilometer before he found another unattended.

But he eventually reached his destination and instantly knew that he had guessed right. Dead men guarded the closed blower room door from within. Their weapons, if they had been armed, were gone. Moyshe glanced at the thing in his hand. Would it work?

The blower room was vast. It served only *Danion*'s core, but still was a wild jungle of massed machinery and ducting. A lot of air needed moving and scrubbing…

She was in there somewhere, trying to kill them.

Half an hour departed with antelope fleetness. He wandered among the brobdingnagian machines and found nothing. *Danion* kept shivering but the battle had become so old that it no longer caught his attention. An overpowering fatalism had set in now, a feeling that he was completely powerless in the greater situation.

But, damn! it was a long skirmish.

Weariness preoccupied him. He had been through twenty hard, emotionally draining hours.

He finally located the huge ring of consoles from which *Danion*'s core oxygen levels and humidities were controlled.

He crawled, he climbed, he attained himself a perch on a high catwalk from which most of the controls were visible. He saw only empty seats where a dozen technicians should have been stationed. Corpses lolled lifelessly in two more. A body lay like a broken doll on the aluminum grate decking.

She had been here. What was she doing now?

The question answered itself. She appeared as if spontaneously generated, moving among the boards, selecting cutoffs.

BenRabi aimed his makeshift weapons.

"Marya… Maria…" Her names ripped themselves from him against his will. She had been closer to him, in some hidden part of him, than he had realized.

Her head jerked up, turning, startled. Her eyes were narrow and searching. That mocking smile exploded across her face. "Moyshe. What are you doing here?" She hunted him with jerkily moving eyes, her hand hovering near a holstered, captured weapon. She was afraid. And she wanted to shoot.

"You're trying to kill us," he croaked.

What a stupid thing to say. Of course she was. Why was he waiting? *Pull the trigger, pull the trigger*, he screamed at himself.

He had done it a million times in imagination. All those images of the gun… *Go! Go!*

He couldn't. It was real this time. It was not some insane, inexplicable daydream oozing from the nether pits of his mind. Had the gun thing ever had anything to do with real weapons?

She stepped over a dead Seiner. "Moyshe, how can you say that? Not you. You'd be repatriated."

Repatriated to Hell, maybe. Her lie was a kilometer tall. After The Broken Wings and von Drachau's raid? She was going to have his guts on her breakfast toast if he did not do something.

She crossed his aim repeatedly, but he just could not end it. It had seemed so easy when he had been angry. It was easy for Mouse… wasn't it? Sweat beaded on his forehead as he tried to force his trigger.

His aim fell.

The movement gave him away. Her smile gave way to clashing-sabers laughter. Her weapon leapt into her hand. Her hand rose.

He reacted. Her shot reddened metal where he had crouched. But he was moving, across an open space. His finger was frozen no more, though he fired wild, scoring a section of console. He dove into the shelter of a huge machine. Disinterested, it went on grumbling to itself. Like a lot of people, it would do nothing till it was hurt, and then it would just sit there and scream.

Her shouts mocked him. He did not catch her words, but they did not matter. She was taunting him, trying to get him to give himself away again. Beams licked here and there, probing his cover, making metal run like tongues of candlewax.

He was scared. He had swum too deep this time. He had taken the dive he had feared since his assignment to Beckhart.

In an instant of insane gallows humor he told himself that death would certainly end his psychological woes.

But both he and the woman were too confident of his inability, his uncertainty, his lack of commitment. Something within him cracked. Something hatched from an egg of darkness lying in his deeps. He suddenly knew that there was something he could believe in, something worth fighting for. It had been trying to break through from the beginning.

He grinned, then laughed at the ludicrous irony of life. His Grail. He had found it here on the marches of Hell, as he was about to die. This ship, these Seiner people…

In marveling stupidity, he stepped into the open. The woman was so startled she hesitated. He did not. He shot first. His hand was steady, his aim flawless. Just as they had taught him.

The madness of the moment faded. He felt as empty as he had on the day he had entered the Blake City spaceport. Had he found anything after all? Or had his gun-need just thrown up a light-show of justification?

He was standing over her when Kindervoort's people arrived. He did not know how long he had been there. The battle had died away while he waited. And he had reversed all the switches she had thrown, though he did not remember doing so. Operations was getting its desperately needed oxygen.

He was crying when they found him. He had wondered about that for a long time. Mouse sometimes shed tears afterward, as if the new corpse were that of a favorite brother. He supposed Mouse spent his stored emotion then, while it was safe, while no one could grab a handle on his soul.

Someone pried the torch from his bent rod fingers.

"Moyshe?" Amy asked. "Are you all right?"

He seized her, held her. She was a warm fire in a cold, dark, and lonely cavern. She let him cling for a second, then pulled away, retaining a grip on his arm. She seemed a little distant, a little frightened. And who wouldn't be, after what he had done? "Come on. You've got to talk to Jarl."

He nodded. Yes. Kindervoort would want to know all about it. Old Doctor Deathshead would poke and prod and try to pry open the lid of his soul. Even on a battle day Kindervoort would want to keep an eye on the blood of his ship. That was all people were to *Danion*. The harvestship was the real living thing here. The folks inside were just specialized cells.

He let Amy lead him away, but looked back at Marya as he went. They were taking pictures and nattering into recorders. Medics were piling bodies onto stretchers. Techs were weeping over the damaged console and impatiently trying to cajole readouts on atmospheric quality… But he had eyes only for Marya.

Marya. She was dead now. He could ease up and let her be more than just "the Sangaree woman."

He did not know why or how, but he must have loved her in some odd, psychotic way. Or maybe he was in love with the death she had symbolized. But, now that she was lying there, sprawled inelegantly, brokenly, he felt a little freer. And a little sadder.

Kindervoort's office was hectic. People came and went hastily, crowding its outer reaches. The chaos was probably typical of every office aboard, Moyshe thought. There would be plenty of work for everyone.

Kindervoort pushed through the crowd. "Moyshe. Amy. Come on in the office." He broke trail. Settling behind his desk, he said, "Thank God for this lull. I was in-suit for eleven hours. The damned things drive me crazy. Give me claustrophobia. You all right now, Moyshe? You look a little pale."

BenRabi sat with his elbows on his knees, staring into infinity. He shrugged.

"For a long time you had me worried, Moyshe," Kindervoort said. "You seemed so solitary, so introspective, so ineffectual. Not exactly up to advance billing. I don't know what I expected Beckhart's top man to be, but you weren't it. Not till today. Then you acted when you had to. Intuitively, quickly, correctly, efficiently. The way I was told to expect. And in character. All on your own. Except maybe you told Mouse?"

Kindervoort had steepled his fingers in front of his mouth. He seemed to be thinking out loud. "Now tell me what happened. An unedited version."

Moyshe started talking. It helped. He began at the beginning and told the whole story, presuming Jarl had enough details to catch any major deletions. He tried to be objective.

Kindervoort nodded, occasionally doodled, once made a call for corroboration. He asked Moyshe to go over several things twice. It was a brief and gentle holiday compared to a Bureau debriefing. He had Amy call to make sure Mouse was getting medical attention.

BenRabi left out nothing but the hiding of the weapons.

When he concluded, Kindervoort asked, "Did today change anything for you? You ready to cross over now?"

Moyshe considered it. Hard. He wanted to be part of what he had found here. But he could not. Not on Kindervoort's terms. "No, Jarl. I can't."

Amy was disappointed. He expected her to be. The signs were unmistakable. She had plans. Bells and white satin, a regular Archaicist extravaganza.

"Why'd you go after Gonzalez, then? We would've gotten her eventually. Maybe too late to have saved Ops, though," he conceded.

BenRabi could not bring himself to answer truthfully. Landsmen did not avenge friends. They had no friends to avenge. And he did not want them to know that a prime rule of the Bureau was that you let no blow against one of its people slide. "That's why. It meant my neck too." Briefly, he sketched what had happened on The Broken Wings.

"I wish you'd done it for us… If you change your mind… I really want you on my team, Moyshe."

"Not on your terms."

Kindervoort looked perplexed. He started to say something, but was interrupted by a comm buzzer. He pressed a button, said, "Kindervoort, Security." He stared at Moyshe, frowning.

"LeClare, Contact," a tiny voice said. "You got a landsman named… let's see… benRabi, Moyshe benRabi, down there?"

"Right. He's here with me now."

"Good. Been trying to track him down all over. He the one with the headaches?"

"The same."

"Has he been Warner tested, do you know?"

"No. He's landside."

"But he's a marginal?"

"I'd guess a strong full. Looks to me like repeated and intense spontaneous contact reaction."

Moyshe began to feel like a sample on a microscope slide.

"Good. I'm sending a man to pick him up. Priority Alpha. The Old Man's okay. The paperwork will come down later. Off."

"Off," Kindervoort said, puzzled. He leaned back, studied Moyshe speculatively, finally said, "Well. Things change. Desperate times, I guess. I just hope they know what they're doing. Moyshe, when you're finished in Contact I want you to get plenty of rest. Amy, see that he does. Then report back here."

Moyshe looked from one to the other. Both seemed shaken, disturbed.

What the hell was going on? That comm exchange made no sense at all, but it had gotten these two as antsy as a cat in heat. What was a Warner test? Why were his migraines so important? He studied Amy. His thoughts drifted back to the attack he had suffered after being switched on. She had become as nervous then.

He had tried a dozen times to discover why she thought his migraines important. She would not tell him.

They were important to *him*, heaven knew. They had become one of the central features of his life. He had had scores since coming aboard. So many that he had become conditioned to recognize the slightest warning symptom. He gulped his medication instantly.

For a while, though, he had not been bothered much. Till *Danion* had come here. He had been eating the pills like candy the past few days, at regular intervals, not waiting for symptoms to begin. What did it mean?

"Well," Jarl said, "I've got a ton of work. Have to sort things out, count the bodies, inform the next of kin. Amy, turn him over to Contact, then get some sleep. This break probably won't last."

She took benRabi's hand, guided him to the door. Why was she so quiet? Because of Marya?

As he was about to close the door behind him, Kindervoort called, "Moyshe? Thanks."

# SEVENTEEN: 3049 AD

## Operation Dragon, Mindteching

The man who came for Moyshe, when he arrived meteorically on a fast orange scooter, wore a jumper of a style Moyshe had never before seen. It was black, trimmed with silver, instead of being the off-white of the technical groups. It was an Operations group uniform.

The man looked and smelled as if he had not changed for a week.

"Trying to find a man name of…" He checked a card. "BenRabi. Moyshe benRabi. What kind of name is that?"

"A literary allusion," Amy replied. "This's him here."

"Right. Teddy Larkin, Contact Support. Who're you?" He was brusque. And tired. He appeared to be on the verge of collapse. Moyshe felt sympathetic. He was on his last legs himself.

"Amaranthina Amaryllis Isolte Galadriel de Coleridge y Gutierez. Security," she snapped.

"Oh. All right, let's go, benRabi." He headed for his scooter.

Moyshe did not move. He was fighting his temper. Larkin's rudeness might be excused, intellectually, because he was tired, but emotionally Moyshe could not let it slide. He had the feeling that Larkin was this way all the time.

Larkin reached his vehicle, noticed that Moyshe was not tagging along dutifully. "Come on, grub. Get your ass…"

BenRabi was there. And Teddy was yon, seated on hard steel deck plating wondering what had hit him.

There was no forgiving his remark. "Grub" was the Seiner's ultimate epithet for landsmen. BenRabi moved in. He was ready to bounce Larkin all over the passageway.

Amy's touch stopped him. "Go gentle, you ape," she snarled at Larkin. "Or yours will be the second big mouth he's shut today."

Larkin took it as a wisecrack, started toward Moyshe.

BenRabi bounced him off the bulkhead and floor a couple of times.

"I meant what I said," Amy told Larkin. Her badge was showing now, literally. "How was your air supply this afternoon?"

"Eh?" Larkin's eyes widened. His face grew pale.

"Yeah. You see what I mean," Amy told him.

Moyshe slowly relaxed. "Have the covers turned down when I get home, Love," he said, blowing a kiss. He did it to irritate Larkin. Would you want your sister to marry one? "I'm going to sleep for a week." He settled himself on the scooter's passenger seat. "Ready when you are, Teddy."

He had to hang on for his life. The scooter seemed designed for racing. Its driver was a madman who did not know how to let up on the go-pedal.

"What's the hurry?"

"I get to get me some sleep when I deliver you."

A big airtight door closed behind them the instant they entered Operations Sector. Sealed in, Moyshe thought. An instant of panic flashed by. Nervous, he studied his surroundings. Ops seemed quieter, more remote, less frenzied than his home sector. It looked less touched by battle. There was no confusion. People seemed more aloof, more calm, less harried. He supposed they had to be. They had to think *Danion* past defeat. The fighting may have stopped, but it was not finished.

Larkin braked to a frightening, squealing stop that almost threw Moyshe off the scooter. Larkin led him into a large room filled with complex electronics. "Contact," Larkin muttered by way of explanation.

The battle had reached this place. Acrid smoke hung thick here. It still curled up from one instrument bank. Ozone underlay the stench. Casualties awaiting ambulances rested along one wall. There were at least a dozen stretchers there. But the hull had remained sound. There were no suits in evidence.

Larkin led Moyshe to the oldest man he had yet seen aboard *Danion*. "BenRabi," he said, and instantly disappeared.

Moyshe examined his surroundings while waiting for the old man to acknowledge his presence. The vast room looked like a crossbreed of ship's bridge and lighter passenger compartment. The walls were banked with data processing equipment, consoles, and screens whose displays he could not fathom. Seiners in black, seated shoulder to shoulder, manipulated, observed, and muttered into tiny mikes. The wide floor of the room was occupied by corn-rows of couches on which more Seiners lay, their heads enveloped in huge plastic helmets which twinkled with little telltale lights. Beside each couch stood a motionless pair of Seiners. One studied the helmet lights, the other a small, blockish machine which looked uncomfortably like a diagnostic computer. A constant pavane of repairmen moved among the couches, apparently examining the empties for defects.

BenRabi finally spied something familiar. It was a spatial display globe that lurked blackly in a far corner. Centered in it were ten golden footballs apparently representing harvestships. He supposed the quick, darting golden needles represented service ships. They were maneuvering against scarlet things which vaguely resembled Terran sharks. The tiny golden dragons at the far periphery, then, should represent distant starfish. Stars' End would be the deeper darkness biting a chunk from the display's side. He saw nothing that could be interpreted as Sangaree. He hoped they would stay gone, though it was not their style and he did not expect it.

"Mr. benRabi?" the old man said.

"Why dragons?"

"Image from our minds. You'll see."

"I don't understand."

Instead of responding, the old man plunged into a prepared speech. "Nobody explained this to you, did they? Well, our drives are dead, except for minddrive. The sharks can't kill that till they get to us here, or till we stop getting power from the fish. But we're in trouble, Mr. benRabi. We do have minddrive, but the sharks mindburned most of my techs." He indicated the nearest stretcher. A girl barely out of creche smiled in vacant madness. "I've lost so many I'm out of standbys. I'm drafting marginal sensitives from the crew. You're subject to migraine, aren't you?"

Moyshe nodded, confused. Here they came with the headaches again.

He had suspected for several months now… But the implications were too staggering. He did not want to believe. The psi business had been discredited.

Maybe if he remembered that hard enough this man and place would go away.

"We want you to go into rapport with a fish."

"No!" Panic smote him. He did not entirely understand his response.

A niggling little demon named Loyalty, to whom he seldom listened, urged him to surrender for the sake of information. Beckhart would reward him with a shovel full of medals.

He thought of sudden, terrible headaches, and of frightening, haunting dreams. He recalled his fear that he had made involuntary contact with the starfish. "I couldn't."

"Why not?"

"I don't know how."

"You don't need to. The techs will put you in. The fish will do all the work. All you do is serve as a channel."

"But I'm tired. I've been up for…"

"Tell me a story. So has everybody else." He gestured impatiently. A couple of technicians, hovering nearby, approached. "Clara, put Mr. benRabi in Number Forty-three." Both techs nodded. "There's nothing to be afraid of, Mr. benRabi."

Moyshe wanted to protest being pushed around, but lacked the will. The technicians pressed him into a couch. He surrendered. Undoubtedly he had been through worse.

The technician whom the old man had called Clara reminded him of the professional mother of his childhood. She was grey-haired, cherry-faced, and chattered soothingly while strapping his arms to those of the couch. She placed his fingers on grip-switches before she started on his legs.

Her partner was a dark-haired, quiet youth who efficiently prepared Moyshe's head for the helmet. He began by rubbing Moyshe's scalp with an unscented paste, then he covered benRabi's short hair with a thing like a fine wire hairnet. Moyshe's skin protested a thousand little tingles that quickly faded.

*I'm taking this too passively*, he thought. "Why are you strapping me down?" he demanded.

"So you can't hurt yourself."

"What?"

"Take it easy. There's nothing to be afraid of. It's just a precaution," the woman replied. She smiled gently.

*Damn*, he thought. *Better be two shovels full of medals.*

"Lift your head, please," the younger Seiner said. Moyshe did. The helmet devoured his head. He was blind.

His fear redoubled. A green ogre with dirty claws shoved nasty hands into his guts, grabbed, yanked. His heart began playing a theme for battle drums. Words came echoing through his mind, Czyzewski's, from his poem "The Old God": "… who sang the darkful deep, and dragons in the sky." Had Czyzewski had starfish in mind?

Moyshe felt his body growing wet with fear-sweat. Maybe the contact wouldn't work. Maybe his mind wouldn't be invaded. That had to be the root of his terror. He did not want anything looking inside his head, where the madness lay behind the most fragile of barriers.

It had taken him all year to get it under control… Guns, dragons, headaches, improbable, obsessive memories of Alyce, continuous instability… He did not dare go under. His balance was too delicate.

Guns! Did the image of the gun have anything to do with the Stars' End weaponry? Was it some twisted symbol his mind had created for a part of the mission that Psych had not wanted him to remember?

Somewhere, a voice. "We're ready, Mr. benRabi." The old woman. It was an ancient trick for calming a man. It worked, a little. "Please depress your right side switch one click."

He did. He lost all sensation. He floated. He saw, smelled, felt nothing. He was alone with his tortured mind.

"That's not bad, is it?" She used the voice of the professional mother this time. His cunning, frightened mind made it that of the woman of his youth. He remembered how she had comforted him when he had been afraid.

"When you're ready, depress your right switch another click, then release it. To withdraw you have to pull *up* on your left switch."

His hand seemed to act on its own. Down went the switch.

The dreams he had been having returned: space swimming, the galaxy wrong in color, Stars' End strangely misty yet bright. Things moved around him. He remembered the situation tank. This was like being bodiless at the heart of the display. The service ships were glimmering needles, the harvestships glowing tangles of wire. The sharks were reddish torpedoes in the direction of the galaxy. Far away, the starfish looked like golden Chinese dragons. They were drifting toward him.

Moyshe's fear faded as though a hand had erased it from the blackboard of his mind. Only an all-encompassing wonder remained.

Gently, warm, friendly as a loving mother, a voice trickled into his mind. "I do it. Starfish, Chub." There was a wind-chimes tinkle of something like laughter. "Watch. I show me."

A small dragon rose from the approaching herd, did a ponderous forward roll. Shortly, "Oh, my! Old Ones don't like. Dangerous. This no time for fun. But we winning, new man-friend. Sharks afraid, confused. Too many man-ship. Running now, some. Many destroyed. Big feast for scavenger things."

The creature's joy was infectious, and Moyshe supposed he had cause—if the sharks were indeed abandoning herd and harvestfleet.

Funny. His conscious mind was not questioning, just accepting.

His fear remained, down deep, but the night creature held it at bay, infecting him with its own excitement. When did the power thing start? he wondered. It had already, the starfish told him. He did not feel anything other than this creature Chub exploring the ways of his mind like a kid on holiday exploring a resort hotel.

"Shark battle won, mind battle won," the starfish said after a while, when Moyshe finally had himself under control. "But another fight coming, Moyshe man-friend. Bad one, maybe."

"What?" And he realized, for the first time, that he really was talking with his mind.

"Ships-that-kill, evil ones, return."

"Sangaree. How do you know?"

"No way to show, tell. Is. They come, hyper now. Your people prepare."

BenRabi did not want to be out here during combat. He felt exposed, easy prey. Panic began to well up.

The starfish's control did not slacken. He soon forgot the danger, became engrossed in the wonders around him, the rippling movements of retreating sharks, the ponderous approach of dragons, the maneuvers of the shimmering service ships as their weary crews prepared for another battle. The galaxy hung over everything like a ragged tear in the night, vast in its extension. How much more magnificent would it be if it could be seen without the interference of the dust that obscured the packed suns at its core? Nearby, Stars' End waited, a quiet but furious god of war as yet unconcerned with the goings-on around it. Moyshe hoped no one aroused its wrath.

"Coming now," his dragon told him. Spots appeared against the galaxy as Sangaree raidships dropped hyper. Down in his backbrain, behind his ears, Moyshe felt a gentle tickle. "More power," Chub told him.

The raidships radiated from their drop zone in lines, like the tentacles of a squid. They soon formed a bowl with its open side facing the harvestfleet. It was an obvious preliminary to englobement.

The distant, decimated shark packs milled uncertainly. They withdrew a little farther. They were not yet wholly defeated.

A ball of light flared among the Sangaree. A lucky mine had scored. But it made little difference. The power and numbers remained theirs.

Only a handful of service ships remained combat-worthy. Even the halest of the harvestships had lost some main power and drive capacity to shark attack. Minddrive and auxiliary power were insufficient for high-stress combat maneuvering.

BenRabi sensed something changing. He cast about, finally saw the great silver sails that had been taken in before the earlier fighting spreading between *Danion*'s arms and spars. The ship looked so ragged, so injured, so vulnerable… A blizzard of debris drifted about her, held by her minuscule natural gravity.

The Sangaree maneuvered closer but held off attacking.

"Trying to talk First Man-friend into surrender," Chub to benRabi. "Creatures of ships-that-kill want herd without fight."

"Payne won't give up," he thought back.

"Is true, Moyshe man-friend."

The starfish drifted closer. They were almost upon the Sangaree. They meant to join the battle this time, though cautiously. Their enemies still watched from afar, looking for another chance to savage fleet and herd.

"Fight soon, Moyshe man-friend."

The slow, stately dance of enmity ended. The negotiations had broken down. The Sangaree struck fast and hard, firing on the service ships to show their determination. The service ships dodged. Suddenly, there were missiles everywhere, streaking around like hurrying wasps. Beam fire from the harvestships wove gorgeous patterns of death.

And Moyshe became depressed. He had done his Navy fleet time. He could see the untippable balance written in the patterns. There was no hope of victory.

Chub chuckled into his consciousness. "You see only part of pattern, Moyshe man-friend."

In the far distance a starfish crept close to a raidship. The vessel's weapons could destroy the dragon in an instant—but the ship stopped attacking. It simply drifted, a lifeless machine.

"We do mind thing," Moyshe heard. "Like Stars' End, with much power. We stop ships-that-kill like human eyeblink, so fast, if no guns, no drive field to fear."

A second raidship fell silent, then a third and a fourth. Moyshe felt less pessimistic. The raidships would be locked into an overcommand directed by a master computer aboard the raidmaster's vessel. That master computer would be burning up its superconductors trying to adjust fire fields to accommodate the losses. If it became the least hesitant, the least unsure of its options…

A too-cautious starfish burped a ball of gut-fire. The micro-sun rolled through space sedately, devoured another raidship.

"Bad, Moyshe man-friend. Old Ones angry. Will give away unsuspected attack."

The Sangaree hemisphere closed steadily. Its diameter rapidly dwindled. The harvestships threw everything they had, fire heavier than anything benRabi had ever witnessed, yet were barely able to neutralize the incoming. Offensive capacity seemed to have been lost.

The starfish mindburned another raidship, and proved Chub and the Old Ones right. The fireball had given them away. Moyshe felt the deep sadness of his dragon as one of the herd perished beneath Sangaree guns.

The starfish threw a barrage of fireballs before beating a hasty retreat. Sangaree missiles broke up most of them.

The globe closed around the harvestfleet. It tightened like a squeezing fist. A desperate ship's commander, piloting a three-quarters dead service ship, knocked a small hole in the globe by ramming a raidship and blowing his drives.

"They'll know they were in a fight," Moyshe thought. There was no response from Chub.

The Sangaree stepped up the attack. Their ships began piling up toward Stars' End. Moyshe suddenly intuited their strategy. "They're going to push us into the sharks!"

Again there was no response from his dragon, unless it were that wind-chime tinkle he caught on the extreme edge of his sensitivity.

The Sangaree seemed to have managed some equipment adjustments during their absence. They appeared to have no trouble detecting the sharks now. And, since detecting the starfish attack, they were having no trouble keeping the dragons at bay.

Chub returned to his mind suddenly. "It works well, Moyshe man-friend. Be patient. Will have little time to chat. Is hard to think thoughts in commanders of ships-that-kill, and in machines-that-think. Sangaree minds twisted. Different than man-minds." The dragon faded away.

What was this? he asked himself. Were the fish trying to control the Sangaree?

The raidships massed thickly, then pushed hard. The sharks grew agitated, as if dimly aware that they were about to be drawn into the inferno. The starfish began drifting their way, as if to cover the fleet's retreat.

"Be ready, Moyshe man-friend!" It was a sudden bellow, and all the warning he received.

The trickle in the root of his brain suddenly became a flaming torrent. It hurt! God, did it hurt! Searing, the power boiled through him, into whatever *Danion* used to control and convert it, and out to the silvery sails. Moyshe followed the flow for an instant, then became lost in an ocean of pain.

The harvestship began moving *toward* the massed raidships, all weapons firing, not aiming, simply trying to erect an irresistible wall of destruction. The compacted Sangaree were unable to bring all their firepower to bear. They wavered, wavered.

A raidship blew up. It left a momentary hole in the fire pattern. Another vessel began to come apart.

Service ships were doing the same. One harvestship ceased firing. Her auxiliary power was exhausted. Sangaree missiles began picking her apart.

BenRabi felt that infinite sadness again.

The enemy drifted backward, not really retreating, just being pushed inexorably. It could not last, but the harvestfleet's ferocity, for the moment, was greater than the raidfleet's.

Afar, the starfish suddenly struck at the sharks, who scattered in dismay. The strike was pure bluff on the dragons' part. A determined shark attack would have destroyed the herd in minutes.

Something screamed across benRabi's mind, a mad voice babbling, shrieking fear and incoherencies. Its power was such that it inundated his pain. He made no sense of the mind-touch, other than warning and terror.

Phantoms, grotesqueries from the most insane medieval imagination, gathered in space around him. Things that might have been gargoyles and gorgons, Boschian nightmares writhing, all fangs and talons and fire, became more real than the battleships. Every one of them shrieked the message, "Go away or die!"

*I've gone completely insane,* he thought. *My mind has snapped under contact pressure. They can't be real.* He screamed.

Then the warm feeling came, soothing, gently calming his terror, pushing the madness away. His dragon told him, "We succeed, Moyshe man-friend. Maybe win." Then, darkly, "Monsters are Stars' End sending. Fear and visions are Stars' End mind-thing. Planet machine is mad. Mad machine uses madness weapons. Soon, other weapons.

"Look, Moyshe man-friend!"

Shielded by Chub's touch, Moyshe turned his attention to a Stars' End grown huge with their approach. The Sangaree were silhouetted against the glowing planetary disk. The face of the world had become diseased behind them. It was spotted blackly in a hundred thousand places.

The disk was receding. The harvestfleet was on the run, scattering as fast as it could. Moyshe suspected that, had any been able, the harvestships would have gone hyper. That could not be accomplished on minddrive.

The Sangaree could not jump out while locked into their master battle-computer. Breaking lock and getting up influence took time.

Two thousand kilometers closer to the fortress world's weapons, they were trying. With the desperation of the condemned they were breaking lock, scattering, throwing out defensive missiles, trying to get up influence.

They did not have time. The mad world's weapons reached them first.

"Close mind!" Chub shrieked. "Get out! Not need power now. Save mind!"

How? He couldn't remember. It became another nightmare, of the sort where all efforts to elude pursuit were vain.

Feeling returned to his left hand. Another hand rested upon it, pulling upward. The reality of the Contact Room returned.

He could feel his helmet, the couch beneath him—and a tremendous sense of loss. He missed his dragon already, and in missing Chub he understood Starfishers a little better. Maybe the contact was one reason they stayed so far from the worlds of men. The fish-Fisher thing was a unique experiential frontier.

Perhaps only one in a thousand Fishers would ever experience contact, but that one could share the vision with his blind brethren... He had suffered a range of emotions out there. Only one thing had been missing while Chub was in his mind. The ordinary, everyday insecurity which so shaped human life.

He was drowning in his own sweat. And he was shivering cold, as if his body temperature had dropped while he was linked. The room surrounding him was silent. Where were his technicians? Was he alone? No. Someone had helped him get out.

The thoughts, reflections, fears flashed by in scant seconds. Then:

His head exploded in a thundering migraine, the most sudden and terrible of his experience. It obliterated all conscious control and thought. He screamed. He fought the straps that held him, the helmet that stole his vision. He became pure trapped animal.

*Danion* shuddered, staggered, staggered. Vaguely, through the agony, he heard screams. Loose objects rattled around. Gravity surged and faded. Mind monsters momentarily broke through the pain, taunting him with visions of Hell.

The Stars' End weapons had found the Sangaree. The fringes of their fury had brushed the harvestfleet like the cold breeze of the passing wings of death. And he was pinned here, helpless, in agony.

Slowly, slowly, the breeze faded. The screams died with it—all but his own. Excited chatter surrounded him. He could distinguish no words. His head was tearing itself apart. Once, when he was a kid, it had been almost this bad. He had nearly killed himself smashing his head against a wall.

Someone finally noticed him. His helmet came off. A needle stung his arm. The pain began fading.

The room was nearly dark, so weak were the lights. Gravity had been reduced to half normal. *Danion* was rationing power.

The faces crossing his field of vision seemed unconcerned with *Danion*'s condition. They were exuberant. There was laughter. Little jokes flew.

"We've won!" motherly Clara told him. "Stars' End killed them."

*Not all*, Moyshe thought, though he said nothing. One or two had made hyper in time.

The Seiners had just moved up the Sangaree vendetta list, perhaps surpassing Jupp von Drachau.

"But we lost four harvestships," the younger half of his tech team told him. "Four harvestships." He was having a hard time believing that.

It was a victory day, all right, but one which left the Seiners little to celebrate.

Blessed darkness enfolded Moyshe. He fell into the blissful sleep of the needle, a sleep untroubled by fearful dreams.

# EIGHTEEN: 3049 AD

## Operation Dragon, the Change

He ignored the shoulder-shaking as long as he could. Finally, sleep-slurred, he muttered, "Wha'd'ya wan'?"

"Get up, Moyshe. Time to go to work. There's a million things to do."

So. Amy, he thought. Altogether too businesslike for a girl who thought she should be a wife. He opened an eye, checked the time.

"Five hours? What the hell kind of rest is that?" he grumbled. "How the hell did I get here? I was in Contact."

"It's been eleven hours. The clock's unplugged. To save power. They brought you down on a stretcher. I thought you'd been mind-burned..." She threw herself on top of him, clinging with desperation. "Moyshe, I was so scared..."

"All right. All right. I survived," he grumbled. He still was not accustomed to the Seiner habit of showing emotion.

She reached under the sheet, tickled him. "Come on, Grump. There're things to do."

He threw his arms around her and rolled her over, his mouth seeking hers.

"Moyshe!"

He smothered her protest with a kiss. "It's been a week, lady."

"I know. But..."

"But me no buts, woman. The hump-backed crocodiles of entropy are gnawing at the underbellies of our allotted spans. I'm not going to waste an opportunity on tinkering with a piece of pipe."

"Moyshe! What kind of talk is that?"

"Shut up."

"Yes, Boss."

They dressed hurriedly afterward. Amy decided on a fresh coverall.

"Now, what's the hurry?" Moyshe demanded.

"You've got to get back to work. Moyshe... We really are desperate this time. We're in a decaying orbit around Stars' End. The mindsails went in the spillover from whatever killed the Sangaree. We'll hit the boundary in two days unless we get the drives working."

"Boundary?"

"Limit of approach. Stars' End starts shooting if a ship passes it."

"I wondered why we're alive."

"Only the Sangaree violated it. The machine is very literal. Anyway. We're due on shift in three hours, and Jarl needs you to take some tests first."

"Can't they wait?"

"He said today."

"Might as well. I'm awake now. Where's Mouse?"

"Hospital block. He's doing okay."

Hospital block was fifteen kilometers away. Maybe more if there were detours. Moyshe knew he had to move fast. "We'll go there first."

"Why?"

"To see Mouse."

"But the tests!"

"Damn the tests. I want to see Mouse. You coming?"

"Not anymore. Hey! Wait!"

They ran to a scooter, laughingly fought for the controls. Moyshe made a point of winning. He did not trust her to take him where he wanted to go.

He whipped down the passageway, scattering cursing pedestrians. The wind in his face exhilarated him—till he remembered what had happened. Memories of what he had done kept him quiet till he reached the hospital block.

Bluff and bluster got him past nurses who believed they were running a monastery.

They wandered the ward where Mouse was supposed to be confined, unable to find him.

Feminine laughter suddenly rippled through the passageway. "What do you think?" Moyshe asked.

"Wouldn't bet against it," Amy replied. Her good cheer had not faded.

Moyshe followed the laughter to a small private room where he found Mouse making friends with his nurse. BenRabi began to wonder why he had come. It did not look as if Mouse needed him. Then he understood. He had not come for any good, businesslike reason. He just wanted to see how Mouse was. And that was silly. Landsmen did not behave that way.

Mouse was fine, needless to say.

"What're you doing in here?" Moyshe asked, embarrassed because he was interrupting. "There's work to do."

Mouse grinned, winked. "Moyshe, everybody gets a vacation. Besides, I had to meet Vickie here. Darling, say hello to my friend Moyshe."

"Hello to my friend Moyshe."

"Isn't she something? Been trying to find out if those long lean legs are as fine as they promise to be. Those work outfits just don't do a thing for a woman."

"How are you, Mouse?" benRabi asked.

"Like the man said before they closed the coffin, as well as can be expected under the circumstances." He whipped his top sheet back. His arm and shoulder were heavily bandaged and in a partial cast. "They'll have me back on light duty in a couple of days. Unless I can blow in that dainty ear there and get somebody to keep me here."

Vickie giggled.

"Well, good. I just wanted to check. Sorry I interrupted. Behave."

"Don't I always?" Mouse chuckled. "Hey, Moyshe, go by my cabin and make sure nobody's run off with the silverware."

"All right."

"See you in a couple days."

"Yeah." BenRabi withdrew, Amy on his heels. "Damn!" he told her. "I feel silly."

"What? Why?"

He shook his head. He could not explain. Not to her. A Seiner would never understand what he meant when he said he and Mouse had passed a point of no return and become genuine friends. Amy did not have the background to comprehend what that could mean to a landsman.

She was worried. "Thinking about what Jarl is going to say when we show up late?" he asked.

"Uhm." She remained thoughtful as they stalked the sterile white corridors. "What're the tests for?"

"I don't know. Just some tests."

He caught a whiff of untruth. He was not supposed to learn their purpose. He always hated that kind of test, though people were always taking them back home: IQ, emotional stability, prejudicial index, social responsiveness, survival index, environmental response, flexibility, adaptability, the government's euphemistically labeled Random Sample Report...

Bureau agents suffered bombardment with them during briefing and debriefing. They even had a test to test one's resistance to testing. His was strong. He did not like having people look inside him. He did too damned much of that himself.

"Wouldn't be the famous Warner test, would it?"

She did not respond. He tried a couple of different tacks, could not get a rise out of her, so gave up.

They had to make a detour returning to the scooter. Their planned path was blocked with casualties just in from one of the dead harvestships.

"It's bad, Moyshe," Amy said looking down that long hallway of stretchers. "They've been bringing people in since the shooting stopped. They may never get them all out of the wrecks. They're falling in toward Stars' End too."

"Where are they going to put them? We'll end up having to sleep standing up."

"We'll find something."

"Reminds me of my senior year midshipman cruise," he said. "There were war scares that summer too. The Shadowline War and the Sangaree. And somebody had found a McGraw world. The fleet was tied up. Academy contracted our shipboard astrogation training to private carriers."

Memories. That had been the summer he had ended it with Alyce...

"Tell me about it."

"Eh? Why?"

"Because I don't know anything about you. You never talk about yourself. I want to know who you are."

"Well, I got the worst billet on the list. Some people didn't like me. It was a raggedy-ass Freehauler on the Rim Run from Tregorgarth to The Big Rock Candy Mountain to Blackworld, then Carson's, Sierra, and The Broken Wings. Broomstick all the way, with crazy passengers. The Freehaulers carry some real weirdos. Between The Broken Wings and Carson's, coming back, we got jumped by McGraws. My first taste of action."

After he had been silent a few seconds, she asked, "What happened?"

"It was a complete surprise. McGraws don't usually bother Freehaulers, but Navy was pushing them hard and we were carrying weapons for Gneaus Storm..." Why was he telling her this? It was none of her business. Still... Talking kept his mind off the upcoming tests.

"Go on, Moyshe."

He did not doubt that details of the incident were in Kindervoort's files.

"*Tinker's Dam*—that was the ship—had a cranky drive. Just a hair out of synch. The Freehaulers couldn't afford to tune it till after the run. So the McGraws couldn't phase in and pull us into normspace. They tried putting a warning shot across our nose. The drive did one of its tricks, phased in with theirs, and dragged us both into the explosion. The McGraw was destroyed. *Tinker's Dam* was hurt pretty bad, but we kept one section airtight. I was trapped there with this crazy family from some First Expansion world. They hated everybody, and Old Earthers and aliens especially. And it was up to me and a Ulantonid radioman to find out where we were and call for help. Took three weeks to rig a transmitter, and three more months before anybody caught our signal. It was miserable. There I was, nineteen years old, scared to death, and all that on me… Hey! Where are we?"

Chagrined, Amy replied, "I was listening. I guess we took a wrong turn. We'll have to go back."

Back they went till she found a passage that would take them in the right direction. It led through a women's intensive-care ward. The casualties were out where the harried nurses could examine them at a glance. There were at least three hundred women crammed into a ward meant for fifty. "It's really bad, isn't it?"

"They're moving the walking wounded into the residential blocks."

Moyshe stopped suddenly, stricken. The face of the final patient, confined to a burn tank, was one he had not expected to see again. "Marya!"

She was alive, and inside her tank, amid the jungle of tubes, she was aware. She met his gaze, tried to communicate her hatred. Her I.V. monitor fed her a little nembutol.

"Moyshe? What's the matter?"

He pointed.

"You didn't know?"

"No. I thought she was dead."

"She would have died if we hadn't gotten her here so quick."

"But…"

"You used the torch from too far away."

"I see."

She dropped the subject, realizing he wanted done with it.

He should have realized that Marya would not go easily.

Did she have a partner? The answer was critical. His life might depend on it.

And if he survived here, Marya would come after him landside. He was winning the battles, but the war remained in doubt.

He did not look forward to their next encounter.

"What's the rush, suddenly?" Amy asked. He was almost running.

Kindervoort was not pleased with his being late, but he shuffled Moyshe into a testing room without remonstrance. "This's benRabi."

Psych types took over. Moyshe suffered through the old parade of idiot questions. Since childhood he had been trying to beat them with random answers—which was why his test sessions always lasted so long. The computers needed a big sample to pin him down.

When the psychs were done they turned him over to regular medical types who gave him a thorough physical. They were in love with his head. He told the life story of his migraine three times, and endured dozens of shallow and area skull scans.

They also wanted to know all about his instel implant.

He developed a sudden muteness. Bureau activities were beyond discussion.

Just when he was about to scream they turned him loose. The chief examiner apologized profusely for taking so long. There was not a hint of sincerity in his tone. Both he and Moyshe knew the time factor was Moyshe's fault.

Moyshe was told to get a good night's rest before going back to work.

He hoped they had not learned anything, but suspected that they had. Profile tests were hard to beat.

Time slipped away quickly, almost as swiftly as it did in the mad, hectic culture groundside. Moyshe returned to Damage Control. His working hours were gruesome.

Somehow, they got the drives functioning and pushed *Danion* into a stable orbit. Then the real work began. Everyone not engaged in rescue work, or in keeping the ship alive, began preparing her for a hyper fly to the Yards.

Moyshe's work was less demanding than he expected. *Danion* had suffered more damage to personnel than to plant, had been hurt more by shark attack than by Sangaree fire.

He heard rumors claiming half the harvestship's people had perished, or had been made as good as dead by mindburn. His acquaintances had been lucky. He knew no one who had been a victim. But every day, in the course of work, he encountered new faces, and missed a lot of old ones.

Every time he wakened Moyshe was amazed to find himself still alive. The battle of Stars' End was over and won, but winning had left the harvestfleet on the brink of disaster. New problems arose as fast as old ones were conquered.

And the sharks had not given up. They stalked the fleet and herd still, their numbers growing daily. In a week, or a month, they would strike again.

The fleet was in a race against time. It had to make the Yards before the sharks reached critical…

Time fled swiftly when sudden death lurked behind the veil of time, and every day passing brought Moyshe closer to an hour he dreaded, the moment when he would have to return to Carson's and his old life.

He did not want to leave.

The *I want* had not sipped at the blood of his soul since the battle, nor had he had visions of imaginary guns. He seemed to have undergone a spontaneous remission of his mental diseases. In that way the weeks were close to tranquil. His problems became more direct and personal.

He had found what he needed, a combination of things to do with belonging: a woman, a useful occupation, and a place in a society that considered him something more than a bundle of statistics to be manipulated. He could not yet quite understand what had happened, or why, but he knew he belonged here. Even if he was not yet wholly accepted.

This was what he had been seeking when he had abandoned Old Earth. Navy had given him some of it, but not enough. This was the real thing.

He had come home.

But how could he stay? There were prior demands on his loyalties. He simply could not accept Kindervoort's terms. He could not betray the Bureau.

Should he see Jarl and try to arrange something?… He vacillated. He swung this way and that. He decided and changed his mind a hundred times a day.

What about Mouse? What would he think? What would he do and say?

And all the while, like a recording mechanism, he kept making his notes for the Bureau. Sometimes he worried about getting them off the ship, but that did not much matter. Writing them down fixed them in his backbrain, from which the Psychs could dredge them with narcohypnosis.

Assuming he went home.

Assuming he wanted them recovered. He had not wanted this mission back when, and wanted it even less now. By carrying it out he might destroy something that had become dear.

He was in a proper mood for concluding *Jerusalem.* And he had found just the quote for summation:

> *The world was all revenge and thou hadst said:*
> *"It is a seething sea!" Earth had no room*
> *For walking, air was ambushed by the spears,*
> *The stars began to fray, and time and earth*
> *Washed hands in mischief…*
>
> —*Firdausi* (Abul Kasim Mansur)

All *Jerusalem*'s characters had perished while trying to seize their hearts' desires. *Farewell, old companions*, he thought.

So much for that. It had been a pretentious trial of modern literature anyway. He did not like the thing anymore. Only his suicidal mood had let him finish quickly, rather than with the intimate detail he had planned originally. Sometimes he felt so like his own creations, denied anything but a deadly end…

Ten days remained on his contract when he received the second summons from Contact. Jarl Kindervoort relayed it personally.

"I'd really rather not do any more mindteching, Jarl," he said. "I'm not trained for it, and I'm perfectly happy where I'm at."

"I'd rather you didn't myself." Kindervoort seemed caught in a baffled daze. "You know too goddamned much already. But orders are orders, and these came from the top."

A chill breeze swept Moyshe's cabin. He knew too much... Would they let him go? If they did... Kindervoort was capable of arranging a deep-space accident that would silence the returning landsmen.

Would Jarl's superiors authorize an incident? Starfishers were feisty, but did not go out of their way to provoke Confederation.

"What's going on, Jarl?"

"I don't know. And I don't like it. They've shut me out. They want you reassigned to Contact. That's all I know. I'm just a messenger boy. Grab yourself a scooter and go. Here's your pass."

"But I don't want to..."

"You're still under contract. You agreed to perform whatever duties were assigned."

"Damn. All right. Right now?"

"Right now."

Moyshe reached Contact a half hour later. He found the same old man in charge. "You'll be working with Hans and Clara again, Mr. benRabi. Strictly basic contact exercises. I don't know which fish your rapport will be. They decide that for themselves."

"Why am I here? There's no point in this. I'm leaving the end of next week."

The man acted deaf. "You'll probably link with several fish during the coming week. They like to get different perspectives on a mind before they decide on a permanent partner. Hans. Clara. Mr. benRabi is here. Go ahead with the basic program."

"Now wait a goddamned minute..."

The old man walked away, pursuing a black-uniformed electrician whose repair work did not please him.

"Good morning, Moyshe," Clara said. "Good to have you back. How have you been?"

And the youth, Hans, said, "We'll be your regular support team. They've given us Number Fifty-one..."

"Who the hell does that guy think he is? When I speak to somebody I expect them to answer."

"Take it easy," Hans suggested. "He does that to everybody. You'll get used to him."

"He's a dreadful boss," Clara said. "Just dreadful. But we won't have him much longer. They're booting him upstairs. Why don't you show Moyshe our station, Hans. I'll get us all some coffee."

"What do *you* think is going on?" benRabi asked Hans. He sat on the end of the Contact couch. "I've got no business being here."

Hans shrugged. "I haven't the faintest. They just told us you'd be our new mindtech, that we should start breaking you in. Clara thought you'd decided to stay. Didn't you?"

"What's that?" Clara asked.

"Say that Mr. benRabi decided to stay with *Danion.*"

"Yes. Hasn't he?" She handed Moyshe a cup of coffee. "Black?"

"That's fine. No, I'm not staying."

"I don't understand." She seemed confused.

"Neither do I. I tried to tell them somebody screwed up. Nobody would listen. You know how things go. When their minds are made up…"

"I'd better check," Clara said. "There's no point going ahead if it's all a mixup."

"Do that."

She returned fifteen minutes later looking more puzzled than ever. "They said go ahead."

"Dammit, why?"

"I don't know, Moyshe. That's what they told me."

"It just doesn't make sense."

"Thought you were a soldier," Hans said. "Thought you were used to taking orders you didn't understand."

"I knew they made sense to the man who gave them…"

Hans smiled.

*Made sense to the man who gave them.* He barely heard Clara when she said, "We'd better get started. We're behind schedule."

So Beckhartism existed here too. He must have that look of the born pawn.

Try as he might, he could see no way the Seiners could profit from training him as a mindtech. Not if he was going back.

"Ready, Moyshe. Same drill as the other day. It shouldn't bother you this time. We won't be drawing power. Just go out and float. Try to open to the fish and get the feel."

Hans slipped the helmet over benRabi's head. Clara's voice came through, warm and gentle.

"Remember, one click down on the right for TSD, Moyshe. Two for Contact. Up on the left to come back. Go when you're ready."

He pushed the right-hand switch without knowing why.

The womblike comfort of total sensory deprivation enveloped him. He let it take him, carrying off the aches and fears of reality. He ran through a mantra several times, trying to take his mind into the same nirvana his flesh occupied.

This was nice. A man could lower his guard here, could relax his vigil against the universe. Nothing could reach him…

Wrong. His hindbrain, the ancient brain that had crawled out of the sea of Old Earth a billion years ago, could not tolerate an extended absence of stimuli. It became claustrophobic.

"You're staying in TSD too long, Moyshe," Clara said from a thousand kilometers away. "That's not good for your mind."

He depressed the switch again.

Weirdly distorted and colored space formed around him.

He was falling toward a milky scar some cruel god had scratched on the face of darkness. Logic told him it was the galaxy, that it looked both solid and fuzzy because his brain was trying to translate something seen in hyper into conventionalized images.

What *was* he seeing? Tachyon scatter? Gravitation? The frenzied dance of the gluons that cement all matter? The scar was most intense toward the galactic core, which would have been concealed by dust clouds in norm space.

Long pink streaks, like the fire of ruby lasers, winked past him, arrowing to a point of convergence centered on the heart of the galaxy. A barrage of golden tracers skipped along inside the circle of pink lines. Sharks and starfish skipping along with the harvestfleet?

He extended his attention till he detected several egg-shapes of St. Elmo's fire, with cometary tails, that had to be harvestships in hyper transit. He searched, but could find no trace of Stars' End. The fortress world had been left behind. The Seiner gamble had failed. That episode had ended. Payne's Fleet was running for the Yards…

"Hello, Moyshe man-friend."

BenRabi felt a rush of elation as he recognized Chub. It became a feeling of, "I'm home! This is where I belong."

"You came back, Moyshe man-friend."

"Yes. I didn't think I would. You survived the battle. I'm glad." The starfish's mental fingers slithered into his mind, bringing comfort. He did not resist.

A feel of laughter accompanied, "Me too, Moyshe man-friend. You came to learn to be linker?"

"I guess."

"Good. I teach. Me, starfish Chub, best teacher ever. Make you best linker of all time. Show Old Ones. We begin. You study universe around, try to see, tell me what you see."

Moyshe did as he was told.

"No. No. See everything at once. Forget eyes. Forget senses of flesh entire, let universe soak in, be one. Forget self. Forget everything. Just be, like center of universe."

It was the prime lesson he had to learn, and the most difficult one for the beginning mindtech. He tried valiantly, hour after hour, but it was like forcing sleep. The more effort he invested, the more remote his goal became.

He heard a faint voice calling. "Moyshe? Moyshe? Time to come out now."

He did not want to go. This being outside, this being free, this made everything he had endured worthwhile. At Stars' End death had been leaning over his shoulder. Here, unthreatened, he found himself closer to heaven than anything else he could imagine. It was almost a religious experience, like a first space-walk EVA, or a first orgasm.

Reluctantly, he commanded his left hand to lift.

All the aches and pains of mortal flesh crept back into his consciousness, and for an instant he understood those people who sought the false nirvana promised by drugs and religion.

Something stung his arm as the helmet slid off his head.

"Just a precaution," Clara told him. "You shouldn't have much of a contact reaction, but we never know for sure."

The agonies of the flesh receded. His incipient migraine died unborn. "That was something," he said. "I didn't want to come back."

"You've got the true linker touch, then," Hans told him. "They never want to go and they never want to come back."

"Eat big and get a lot of sleep," Clara said. "Contact takes more out of you than you think."

He shared three more extended sessions with Chub, and they became solid friends—within the limits of two such alien backgrounds.

His fifth training link brought him in touch with a creature calling itself a Judge of the Old Ones. The Judge was nothing like Chub. It was completely and truly alien. It entered his mind as coldly as a serpent, digging, exploring, till he felt like a bug under a microscope. It made no effort to teach him, nor did it chat, nor conceal its task of determining if he was fit to link with starfish. Moyshe was glad to break that contact, real-world pains notwithstanding.

He went into contact with the Old Ones twice more, and each was as chill and phlegmatic as the Judge. These were the passionless creatures Czyzewski must have had in mind when he had penned "The Old God." Their minds were exactly what benRabi imagined a god's to be.

Then there were two glorious, rollicking, fun days with Chub, who had been appointed his "permanent" link. Irreverent, Chub made the most libelous observations about the Old Ones Moyshe had encountered. BenRabi countered by trying to teach the starfish the concept of humor.

And then it was over. The dream came to an end.

"Good-bye, Moyshe man-friend," Chub said, setting benRabi's mind to echoing sadness. "I will think of you often, stranger than any man-friend."

"I'll remember you, too, Chub," Moyshe promised. "Try to catch me when I reach out in my dreams." He ripped upward on his exit switch.

Clara and Hans thought he was in pain and tried to give him a second pain shot, but he pushed them away. He let the tears flow. Then he hugged Clara. "Good-bye." He took Hans's hand. "I'm going to miss you both."

They stood and watched as, slump-shouldered, he shuffled out of Contact for the last time.

# NINETEEN: 3049 AD

## The Homecoming

The days were gone. And with them most of the hours. He was down to his last few and still he had not contacted Kindervoort, still he had not found the courage to seize what he wanted. While he had slept *Danion* had dropped hyper preparatory to launching a service ship.

The starfish and sharks would be orbiting the remnants of the harvestfleet. Chub would be out there watching for the little steel needle that would take him away forever.

He lay in his bunk and remembered story time at the creche where he had lived as a small child. All those tales had had heroes who had never been indecisive, never been terribly afraid. But they had all come from a remote and probably unreal past.

There was little room for the self-assured Mouse types in this kaleidoscopic modern universe. Nowadays timidity was pro-survival.

He often wondered if Mouse was genuinely as cool as he appeared. He *had* to be bothered by something beside takeoffs and landings.

In two hours the service ship would leave for Carson's. What could he do? What *should* he do? He knew what he wanted, knew what Amy wanted, but still he teetered between the new commitment and the old. To betray Bureau secrets for personal gain, he felt, would constitute a self-betrayal.

It looked like he had picked up a bunch of new haunts to replace the ones he had conquered. The new ones at least made more sense.

His remaining time dwindled to an hour. His things were packed. He prowled his cabin like a beast caged, unable to remain still. And Amy sat on her bed, motionless, alternately sulking and subjecting him to verbal assaults. He had to get out, had to get away…

He went looking for his partner. Maybe Mouse could help. Paranoia had its merits.

They had seen little of one another after benRabi had begun mindtech training.

Mouse answered his door with pleased surprise. First thing he said was, "I was just going to look for you." His one hand was shaking. "Want to play a game while we're waiting?"

"All right." They could help each other. A game or two might relax them both.

"How's Amy taking it?"

"Like a trouper. A storm trooper." Mouse was awfully excited. His shakes were not always confined to his bad hand. Moyshe paid no attention. The usual pre-fly jitters, he thought.

"Did you hear what I found?" Mouse bubbled. "Been after it for years. I finally got it off one of our own people, a guy who carried it for luck." He displayed an ancient bronze coin with a hole in the middle. BenRabi judged it to be at least two thousand years old, Oriental, in good condition, but comparatively common. Certainly nothing special. Mouse's excitement began to puzzle him.

"Nice, I guess. Amy's really taking it worse than I expected." He glanced at the coin again, because Mouse kept shoving it in front of him. "You sure it isn't fake?"

"She'll get over it. They always do if you've loved them right. No, it's not fake." Mouse seemed disappointed about something. "You take white."

BenRabi tried to broach his problems over his almost ritualistic opening. "Mouse, I want to stay here."

Mouse looked at him strangely, as if with mixed emotions, as if he had been expecting this but hoping for something else. He fingered his coin nervously, replied. "Let's talk about it after the game. How about a drink? You look like you could stand to unwind."

A man about to undergo high acceleration and temporary weightlessness should not imbibe, but benRabi agreed. He needed something. Mouse went to a cabinet, got a bottle of something pre-mixed. While he hunted glasses, benRabi examined the cabin. Almost everything that was Mouse was gone, all the memorabilia that for a time had made the place his home. Everything but the ubiquitous chess set.

A glass broke. Mouse cursed, gathered the pieces, cursed again as he cut himself. "Why the hell aren't these things made out of plastic?"

"I wish you wouldn't use your bad hand." Then benRabi saw why he was. With his good hand Mouse was smearing something gooey over Security's bug. He then brought the drinks, resumed the game.

It was a slow one. Mouse was off his usual confident form. He had to study every move carefully. He kept fingering his coin as if he wanted to wear it out before boarding the service ship. BenRabi downed his drink, and several more, began to relax, to turn off the troubled part of his mind. He got involved in the game. For once he was holding his own. Mouse, despite his studiousness, remained remote, disturbed, and inattentive.

Mouse suddenly unleashed a series of rapid moves. BenRabi's queen went, and then, "Checkmate!"

The alcohol no longer helped. The defeat, so small a thing but so inevitable, suddenly became an analog of benRabi's whole life. His depression deepened.

A moment later, while fumbling the pieces into their box with his bad hand, Mouse said, "I kept this out so we could play on the way home. But now you say you want to stay."

"Yes. This is what I've been looking for…"

"I was afraid of that." Mouse turned. His fumbling had not been without purpose. His good hand clutched a Fisher weapon salvaged from Marya's cabin.

"You should've figured, Moyshe. You should've run to Kindervoort." Mouse was playing the game to its end. "Wheels within wheels, you know. We're still working for Beckhart. I can't just leave you."

Maybe he had known, down deep, he thought. Maybe he had come here so Mouse could make his decision for him.

"Psych programed you to cross over. So you could get where I couldn't. They might even have known about Stars' End. That's what that gun thing makes me think of."

Moyshe glanced at the coin turning in Mouse's bad hand. Strange that he had never mentioned wanting one of that type. Maybe it was a hypnotic key. Maybe it had opened the full mission to Mouse's memory.

"It was meant long term from the beginning, Moyshe. We need ambergris for the fleet. All of it. For the war."

"War? What war? Nobody takes the Ulantonid rearmament business serious. You told me it was manure yourself."

Mouse shrugged. "You were a remote data-collector. One of my missions was to be your keeper. Most of the rest was window-dressing and obfuscation."

Though it was a club-footed effort, Mouse was trying to do more than just explain. He did not like what he was doing. He was trying to convince himself.

Yes. They had grown too close. Far too close. They cared.

"We're friends, Moyshe. So let's fly gentle, eh?"

Yes, gentle. As in chess, he was outskilled here. He was the half of the team trained and programed for the "soft" work. Mouse always handled the "hard." Friendship or no, Mouse would bend him if he did not cooperate. Mouse was the perfect agent. He let nothing stand in the way of getting his job done.

BenRabi searched his partner's face. He saw the pain there. *Maybe*, he thought, *Mouse doesn't want to go back either.* But Mouse's nature would leave him less choice… It would be stupid to push him. He tended to overreact under stress.

BenRabi's shoulders slumped. He surrendered. Back to being a chip in the stream.

A dread voice rang through *Danion*, godlike, calling all departing landsmen to Departure Station for payoff and checkout. Mouse pocketed his weapon, said, "Sorry, Moyshe."

"I understand." But he did not, not really.

Mouse nodded to the door. "Let's go."

They went. Moyshe gave him no trouble, even when the opportunity arose. He had given up completely.

*No home at all*, he thought. *Guess I'll never have one. I'll just go on being a chip in a universe like those Sierran flood rivers. I'm back where I started.*

He stared at the lock that would open on the service ship. One long step through and he would come out in the terminal on Carson's. How much would things have changed during their absence? Greta would have grown…

Greta. "Mouse, I forgot to get something for Greta. I've been gone a whole damned year… I got to bring her something."

"Mr. benRabi?" A man pushed through the crowd, some of benRabi's belongings in hand. "You left some of your things."

Moyshe recognized him. He was one of Kindervoort's people. Had they found his notes? "Mike, do I have time to get a souvenir for my daughter?"

Still talking about Moyshe's forgetfulness, Mike stepped between benRabi and Mouse. Landsmen milled around them, talking excitedly of home, rushing to the paymaster when their names were called. BenRabi paid no attention. He was fascinated by the sudden despair on Mouse's face.

"The weapon, please?" Mike said.

Several men surrounded them now. Kindervoort himself was approaching, having just left a nearby office.

Mouse surrendered the gun meekly, consternation becoming a weak smile.

"Told Beckhart it wouldn't work," he said loudly. "But he never listens to the man in the field..."

There was a stir. Shouts. Screams. Mouse hit benRabi with a flying tackle. Mike grunted, twisted, came down atop them, an expression of incredible surprise fixed on the unburned half of his face. The shouting redoubled. People tried to run. A handgun flashed again. Security men tried to reach the source of fire.

"Wheels within wheels," Mouse said into benRabi's ear, his voice coldly calm. Kindervoort, kneeling beside them, looked at him questioningly. "This was mine," Mouse told him. "I figured he'd have a fail-safer in."

Fail-safer. That was a trade name for a man hyped and programed to do everybody in if a mission went bust. Fail-safers seldom knew what they were. Usually they were innocents dragged in off a street somewhere and run through the Psych mill. Even after assassinating agents about to defect or to be captured they seldom knew what they had done, why, or for whom.

BenRabi had never considered himself, Mouse, and this mission that critical.

"Sorry, Moyshe. I didn't think I should tell you. Made it look better, you believing."

*Is he telling the truth?* Moyshe wondered. *Or is he playing the ends against the middle? Is he just bending with the breeze, hoping to keep his skin?*

"We had to spot him before we could cross over, and this was the only place to do it. It's too late for him now. He can't hunt us down." Mouse shrugged, then smiled. So did benRabi.

He chose to believe. He did not want to stay here alone.

That was why he had had so much trouble deciding. Amy was not enough. Chub was not enough. The Seiner culture itself was insufficient. He had needed that one extra, Mouse, his heartline to the past.

Kindervoort's men returned. "You get him?" Mouse asked.

"Somebody did. He was dead when we got there. Looks like a nerve poison."

Kindervoort regarded them oddly, appraisingly. "Fail-safer for a fail-safer? Your Admiral is bizarre, but I've never heard of that before."

*Unusual?* Moyshe thought. *It's unprecedented. It doesn't make sense.* But what the hell? It was over now. He was home free.

Home, after all, and with a good woman— Amy was running toward him, through the crowd, pale with worry—and a friend. Life, it seemed, had finally taken a happy turn.

"Are you ready now?" Amy asked anxiously, after having made sure he was unharmed.

"Ready? For what?"

"To cross over, stupid. Are you, darling?" She seemed afraid his stiff-neckedness would persist.

It did. "Seems like I don't have much choice. But I won't talk."

"Talk?" Kindervoort asked. "What do you mean? About what?"

"About the Bureau. About its policies, its goals, its mission, things I might know that you'd want to know. I won't tell you. The man who was Commander Thomas Aquinas McClennon is dead. Everything he knew died with him. Don't try to call him back from the grave."

"That's what's been bothering you?" Kindervoort asked. "Moyshe, Moyshe, why didn't you say so? I wondered what the hell was stopping you. It was so obvious you wanted to come over. There never have been any conditions. Never. I'm sorry you got that impression. Hell, anything I want to know you don't—otherwise Beckhart never would have risked you."

BenRabi considered. It made some sense. But there were things he could tell... The hell with it. He would take the chance. He put an arm around Amy, pulled her close to him. "Thanks, Jarl. Mouse. Oh. Say, Jarl. Is there time for me to get a real Starfisher souvenir for my daughter?"

"Daughter?" Kindervoort and Amy said together.

"What daughter?" Amy demanded. "You said you weren't ever married."

"I wasn't. She's not really my daughter. A girl I met on Old Earth. I sponsored her. That's sort of like adopting a kid... She doesn't know where I'm at or what I'm doing or anything."

"Find something quick," Kindervoort said. "The service ship is going to space in twenty minutes."

"Hey, Moyshe," Mouse said. "Throw this in." He offered the coin with the hole in the center. "Tell her to mail it to the Admiral."

"A little personal message, eh?"

"You might say."

"Come on, Amy. Give me an idea."

"How come you never told me about this girl? What's her name anyway?"

Mouse watched them go, smiling wanly. That was not going to be a classic love match. But it did not have to be. It only had to last a few months more.

His mission was complete. But a Bureau man did not leave his comrades behind. And a Storm never abandoned a friend.

# STARS' END

# BOOK ONE
## THE HIGH SEINERS

# ONE: 3049 AD

## The Main Sequence

The death cry of an exploding sun illuminated a starfleet the likes of which few men had ever seen. There were six great starships in the convoy. The smallest was forty kilometers long.

No drive glow enveloped those ships. No ion wake marked their passing. They were drifting. But they met the flash front of the nova with an inherent velocity approaching three-tenths the velocity of light.

Each of those starships looked like a mobile created by a sculptor, looked like someone had visited a planetary junkyard, had welded scraps together, and then had flung the results at the farthest star. Those ships were all angles, tubes and planes, globes, cubes, and what appeared to be silver sails. Whole forests of antennae bristled on the humped mountains of their backs.

Random chunks of debris accompanied the ships, thrown out from jagged wounds in their flanks. Wisps of atmosphere leaked from those great rents, twinkling in the nova light. Smaller ships, like blowflies, fluttered around the rawest injuries.

There had been a battle. A battle at Stars' End. Its fury and magnitude would have beggared the imagination of men who hadn't ever been out among the stars.

These limping, crippled starships were the survivors.

The great lens of the Milky Way sprawled before the starships, cold and silver and bright. Their noses were aimed toward its heart. Like a dying man crossing a desert, the starfleet was dragging itself toward healthier climes.

A patch on the smallest ship began to glow, throwing color back into the ocean of night. It was not a happy color. It was the dull, dark red of venous blood, the red of senescent suns. It brightened, became more intense.

The other ships drifted away. Fate had overtaken their little sister. She was about to lose control of her fusion plant. They did not want to be too close to the explosion. The smaller blowfly-vessels flitted away, carrying evacuees.

For a moment the smaller starship yielded a light which rivalled that of the nearby nova. Fragments as big as pyramids hurtled outward, adding to the clutter traveling with the fleet. The remainder of the ship began tumbling slowly, now little more than a disemboweled corpse. The little ships darted in again, swarmed around the remains. Signals leapt across the ether. Any survivors? Anyone at all? There was no answer from the wreck. But the little ships went in anyway.

Moyshe benRabi slapped the withdrawal switch beneath his left hand.

Agony smashed into his head. A demon slapped a pair of icehooks into his temples and yanked. He screamed. "Clara! Shot!"

He did not feel the needle bite his arm. Its prick was too tiny a pain. He knew it had happened only because blessed relief hit him seconds later.

Hans pulled his helmet. The youngster's face was drawn. Clara patted sweat from his face with a towel. "Bad, Moyshe?" she asked.

"The worst. I can't reach him anymore. He's out there without protection… And we just lost *Jariel.* They couldn't contain the anti-matter leak. The Service Ships went back… I don't think they'll find anybody to evacuate."

Hans asked, "Drink, Moyshe?" The youth's voice was tremulous. He had had a sister on *Jariel.*

"Something. Please. I must have sweated a couple of liters. They get through to Gruber yet?"

Clara shrugged. "I haven't heard." She was a plump, grandmotherly, greying woman with rosy cheeks. Her appearance reflected her personality. She was a book which could be read by its cover. BenRabi was in love with her, in a filial way.

"We've got to have help. We can't hide in this nova storm forever. The particle wave is on its way. It'll shred our screens."

"Payne says we're going out. Soon as *Jariel* is evacuated. The sharks will have to take their chances."

"Oh, damn."

"What do the starfish say?" Hans asked, returning with a fruit drink. He was putting on a brave face. He had been in the fleet long enough to learn how to wait for good news or bad. They would let him know about his sister.

BenRabi swung his feet to the deck. "Like I said. I couldn't get through. Too far."

"Maybe somebody else did."

"Somebody with more experience? I don't think so."

Hans was just nineteen, hardly out of creche. He had not yet hardened to all the realities of the harvestfleet.

"Well just have to do it Payne's way. Fight our way through." BenRabi began shuddering as his body reacted to the massive dosage of anti-pain drug. Clara swept a blanket around his shoulders. It did not lessen the chills.

They still did not know for certain that they had won the battle of Stars' End. They knew only that Payne's Fleet had held the battle space, had survived, and had begun making its way home. They had not been attacked again, yet, but it was only a matter of time till the struggle resumed.

"Look at me," benRabi whispered. "I can't stop shaking."

"Go home," Clara told him. "Get some sleep."

"We might break through. They might need me to go on minddrive. Just let me stretch my legs." He picked at his arm where the needle had broken his skin. The strain of the emergency had begun to show on his flesh. He was getting tracks.

He collapsed when he tried to stand.

"Take him home, Hans," Clara told the youth. "Lester. Help Hans load Moyshe onto a scooter, will you?"

"What's going on?" benRabi demanded as Hans halted the flatbed electric truck outside his quarters. For a moment he did not know where he was. "Why did you?…"

"What happened?" a woman demanded. Worry strangled her voice.

"He passed out," Hans replied. "Just needs rest."

"I told him…"A thin, pale, nervous face outlined by short blonde hair entered Moyshe's vision, peered down into his eyes. "What's the matter with you, Moyshe? You think you're a superman? Give me a hand with him, Hans. I'll tie him in bed if I have to."

"Somebody's got to…" benRabi protested.

"You aren't the only somebody on *Danion.* There's nobody like a new convert. I love him, but sometimes he drives me up the wall."

"Take care of him, Amy."

"Don't worry. I've got too much invested in this idiot."

They dropped benRabi into his bed. It surrounded him with a womblike comfort. He felt vaguely guilty. He shouldn't be sleeping while other mindtechs were still trying to make contact.

Amy sat on the edge of the bed. He was asleep long before she finished cussing him out for not taking better care of himself.

She was still hovering around when, six hours later, the cabin comm buzzed. She answered, "Amy Coleridge, Security."

A grey-framed face appeared in the little screen. "Good morning, Lieutenant. Is benRabi there?"

"Commander. Sir. Yes sir." Her voice dropped an octave and seemed to snap to attention. "He's sleeping, sir. But I can wake him if you really need him."

"No. Don't. I wanted to speak to you, Lieutenant. I'm on my way down to see you."

Two minutes later there was a knock on the cabin door. The Commander must have been on the way when he'd called her.

"I've just read your report on benRabi."

"You did? Why? It was just a routine report."

The Commander brushed her question aside. "We may need him for something more than Contact. Coleridge, I want to ask you a question. I want a considered answer."

"Sir?"

"Is your report honest? Did you let your feelings affect it?"

"No sir. Yes sir. I mean, it's honest, sir."

"You're sure he's become a Seiner without reservation?"

"He has a few. He grew up different. But he's committed, sir. Almost too much. That's the way he is."

"Will he stay committed? Under pressure? He's changed allegiances before."

"Before? When, sir?"

"When he left Old Earth."

"That's not the same thing. Earth is part of Confederation. He just joined the Navy."

*Danion*'s commander reflected. "True. But, considering the way Old Earthers look at these things, it indicates a flighty nature. All right. Enough about benRabi. What about his cohort?"

Amy's colorless eyebrows crinkled over her pale blue eyes. "That's more difficult, sir. Mouse is more complicated."

"Are you sure you're not projecting a lack of understanding? His psych profiles make him look pretty simple. Almost black and white. He seems to have hung his whole existence on his hatred for the Sangaree."

"Then why did he stay here? He could've gone back to Confederation with the others. He can't fight Sangaree out here."

"I've been wondering. That's why I asked."

"I can't tell you, sir. He's all facade to me. All charm and silliness. I can't tell when he's serious and when he's joking. The only feeling I get is that the man I'm seeing isn't the real Masato Storm."

"Are you involved with him, too, Lieutenant?"

"Sir!"

"Answer me."

"No, sir! I am not involved with Mr. Storm."

"Makes you part of a vanishing breed, then. Seems he's bedded half the single women on *Danion*."

"He attracts a certain kind of woman."

"Oh?" The caller smiled. "But not you?"

She was a long time answering. "The temptation is there. He has an animal magnetism. There's curiosity about what everyone else sees in him. But nothing is going to happen. I don't like him very much."

Her answer seemed to satisfy the Commander.

"We're entering a new era, Lieutenant. A time of changes. Our isolationism is under attack. The sharks are wearing us down. The Stars' End idea was a debacle. We're going to have to adjust. Either that or bend over and kiss our tails good-bye. Those two might be useful. They have unusual backgrounds. We don't have a secret service to speak of. They could build one. But that would mean trusting them. And they weren't born Starfishers."

"A lot of us weren't, somewhere along the line. My father…"

"I know. We're all refugees. Thank you, Lieutenant. Consider this discussion exclusive. Don't mention it to anybody. And if you learn anything that might have a bearing on the matter, call my office. I'll have your name red-tagged to my personal recorder. I'll call you back."

"Yes sir."

The Commander left as quickly as he'd arrived. Amy sat and stared into the shadows of the room.

After a while she lifted her thin frame and drifted into the room where benRabi was sleeping. She stared down at him with an expression approaching awe.

She had never seen or met the Ship's Commander before, except in public address announcements.

Her Moyshe, her last chance man… He might amount to something after all.

She would not have become involved with the foreigner at all had her self-image not been pit-deep. She could not make herself believe that she deserved a good man, a real Starfisher. She had expected to watch her life drift away from the foot of a social and career ladder.

The Commander's call changed everything. She would have to get Moyshe moving. And make sure his friend Mouse did not lead him astray.

The differences between the Confederated life that benRabi had chosen to leave and the lives of the Starfishers were deep.

The Starfishers, the High Seiners, spent their adult lives aboard these vast harvestships, drifting the deep-space hydrogen streams, gleaning the droppings of an almost intangible spacebeast they called a starfish. A whole ecology existed in the interstellar rivers. It was vast and slow, in keeping with the low random collision of the molecules from which their type of life had gradually evolved. That life was invisible to the eye or radar. The atoms constituting the "bodies" of the interstellar creatures could be scattered over cubic kilometers.

Starfish were more vast than harvestships, yet the matter in them could be compressed into a volume smaller than that occupied by the body of a ten-year-old. The atoms were as much foci for forces as part of the life process itself. And most of the creatures of the ecology existed, in part, in hyperspace and another, congruent universe.

At the starfish's heart a tiny fusion flame burned.

Starfish swept up hydrogen and random molecules and occasionally passed a node of hard waste. The nodes were incalculably precious.

The Starfishers called them ambergris. Ambergris was the foundation of their economy.

The nodes were used in instel communicators. There was no substitute. The Seiners controlled the only supply, and, consequently, the market and price.

Countless were the organizations which would pay almost any price for near-instantaneous communication across interstellar distance.

Moyshe benRabi and Masato Storm had been sent among the Seiners to try to find a way for their employers, Confederation Navy, to seize the harvestships and ambergris industry. They had succeeded and failed. They had found the information…

And had elected to become Starfishers themselves.

The hydrogen streams boasted a complex ecology. It included the predatory "shark," which subsisted principally upon starfish. Evolution had equipped starfish with only one truly credible defensive weapon. Intellect.

Deep-space evolution had begun eons before the condensation of Old Earth's sun. The modern starfish species had a remembered history spanning billions of years. They had seen countless planet-born races come and go. They knew the value of their waste.

Over the past thousand Terran years, an eye's blink in the life of a starfish, shark numbers had exploded insanely. A new species was coming into being. It reasoned feebly, bred obsessively, and hunted in cooperative packs which now, sometimes, numbered as many as a thousand predators. The survival of the starfish species had come into sudden doubt.

Their Old Ones had deliberated with almost immoderate haste. A decision had been reached. They turned their intelligence to finding a means of contacting the tiny, hard, warm creatures who lived in the metal shells questing around their wakes.

They had struck a bargain with the original Starfishers. Ambergris in return for the protection of human weapons. It had been a good bargain. The sharks had been kept at bay for two hundred years.

Another mere blink of Time's eye.

Then the ever more numerous sharks had developed the tactic of assailing the protectors before the protected.

*Danion* had enlisted landsmen as emergency replacements for heavy casualties suffered during one such attack. Her leaders had hoped to draw high quality technicians who might be seduced away from their lives in Confederation. Instead, they had attracted scores of spies sent in hopes of capturing control of a harvestfleet. Confederation's Bureau of Naval Intelligence had sent senior field agents Moyshe benRabi and Masato Igarashi Storm.

The two had found what promised to be a home.

Sirens wailed throughout *Danion.*

Amy jerked out of her seat. "Moyshe! Battle stations! We must be coming out of the flash wave."

BenRabi surged out of the bedroom, climbing into his jumpsuit as he came. "Let's go, honey." He dragged her into the passageway outside, where a pair of electric scooters nursed charger sockets. He seized one, she the other. "See you, love," he said as he sailed away.

He pulled to the center of the passage and opened the scooter up. The walls blurred past. People were running in the pedestrian lanes. Scooters hurtled at him from the opposite direction. There were near collisions at every cross corridor. A voice like that of a god kept booming, "Battle stations. Battle station."

Damn, damn, damn, Moyshe thought. I shouldn't be going back under so soon.

Five vast and tangled ships began nosing out of the intense nova light. The blowfly vessels still swarmed around their wounds, and between them and the derelict tumbling along in their midst, guarded by their shell of fire. One by one, the five great ships rolled to present their heaviest weapons outward from a common center.

# TWO: 3049 AD

## The Contemporary Scene

A ship came into being slightly below the surface of a dust lake rilling a crater on a nameless moon circling a world far in toward the center of the galaxy. The most centerward world of Ulant lay a thousand light years rimward. No human being had traveled this part of space before.

Astronomers on the primary, had they been watching, would have been astonished by the geyser which exploded from the crater's flat dust face.

No astronomers were watching. They, like soldiers, wives, derelicts, and children... like everyone who lived on that world, were engaged in a death struggle so demanding they had ceased caring whether their satellite existed.

The ship that bobbed to the dust's surface looked like a giant doughnut with a beer can shoved through the hole and held in place by thin straws. One tall vane, like a shark's fin, rose from the torus, leaning away from the cylinder. A globe surmounted it.

The whole vessel was dead black. Not even a hull number broke its lack of color.

It was a tiny ship. The beer can was just sixty meters tall. The outer diameter of the doughnut barely spanned sixty-five meters. The curves of the vessel were broken only by a handful of antennae, two missile launch bays, and the snouts of laser and graser batteries. She was a deadly little beast, designed solely to kill.

She was a museum piece. Literally. And the nastiest little shark of a warship ever conceived by the mind of Man.

She was a Climber left over from the Ulantonid War. She had been dragged from the War Museum at Luna Command and reactivated especially for this mission.

She was the first Climber to space since the war's most desperate days—because Climbers were almost as deadly to their crews as to the enemies they stalked. Only the absolute imperative of racial survival would see them used in combat again.

Luna Command had that much heart. The Climber Fleets had been too destructive of the minds and bodies of their crews.

The little ambushers had changed the course of the Ulantonid War. And had filled the sanitariums of Confederation with walking wounded, the few survivors of service within their sanity-devouring fields of concealment.

The Climber generated a field in her torus which drove her into a dimension beyond hyper-space, called Null, where she remained virtually undetectable till she returned to Hyper or Norm to attack.

Climbers in schools had destroyed whole Ulantonid fleets.

This Climber had the most remarkable crew of any Navy had ever spaced.

Her Ship's Commander was Manfred, Fleet Admiral Graf von Staufenberg, First Deputy Chief of Staff of Confederation Navy. He had seen Climber duty toward the end of the war. The ship's First Watch Officer was Melene Telle-eych Cath, Defender Prime of Ulant, or Minister of Defense. Her Operations Officer was Ulant's Principal Peacemaker, or Chief of the General Staff, Turone Wahl-chyst Forse. Her Gunnery Officer and his leading mates were Star Lords of the Toke. One was the Star Lord who commanded Confederation's Marine Toke Legion. The others ranked him in the Caste of Warriors.

There was no man or woman aboard, of any of five races, who ranked below the equivalent of Admiral or General, and none of them were not decision-makers.

A well-placed missile could have crippled the defenses of humanity and all its neighbors.

Admiral Wildblood, the lady who directed Navy's Bureau of Naval Intelligence, and Admiral Beckhart, who ran her department of dirty tricks, had two of the more menial assignments in Operations. One watched the hyper detection gear, the other the passive radar scans.

Star Lords and all, they slept in hammocks slung from the Climber's central structural member, or "keel." They shared the one toilet and did without the shower that had never existed. In Climb they used portable chamberpots and smelled one another's stinks as had the Climbermen of an age gone by.

One and all, they had come to see for themselves the growing disaster Ulantonid explorers had been bemoaning for years.

They had seen film. They had questioned witnesses. In some cases they had begun to act. But they had had to see with their own eyes before they could finally believe.

They had to watch the war going on below. On the primary of the moon.

A race from farther in toward the galactic core was systematically exterminating every sentient creature it encountered. The natives of this world were their latest victims.

The people aboard the Climber came of races which had fought bitterly in the past. There was little love among some of them now. But never, in the most desperate, heated days of their contention, had any considered eradicating their enemies. Their wars had been tests of racial wills, with territorial causes.

This world was the fourth assailed by the centerward race since its discovery by Ulantonid explorers. The first three worlds were lifeless now. The aggressors even shunned their use as bases.

Even the Warriors of Toke could not comprehend the destruction of intelligent life simply because it was intelligent.

The Warriors believed battle to be a crucible for purification of the soul, a road to honor and glory, grimly majestic and godlike. For them combat was almost an end in itself. They fought one another when there were no outsiders.

They were perfectly aware of the distinction between victory and obliteration. They were as appalled by the excesses of the centerward race as were any of their shipmates.

They had come to see for themselves. And the grim truth burned in the Climber's display tank.

The world's atmosphere was alive with spiderwebs of coherent light. Energy and particle beams hacked air and space like the flailing swords of a thousand ancient armies. The planet people had the technological edge. The exterminators had the numbers and determination. Their ships clouded the stars.

They had overwhelmed the world's off-planet protection months ago. Now they were pounding the on-world defenses, and were making their initial landings.

Star-bright, short-lived pinpoints speckled the world's surface.

"They're using nuclears!" Ulant's Defender growled. Even during their war's bitterest hour, neither human nor Ulantonid had violated each other's worlds with nuclear weapons. By tacit agreement those had been confined to vacuum.

"They know we're here," Beckhart called out. "Seven destroyer displacement ships are headed this way."

"Very well," Graf von Staufenberg replied. "Melene, most of that looks like it's happening in the troposphere. They're probably not pushing one in a thousand warheads through to the surface."

The Star Lord who commanded all Star Lords boomed, "Every one through destroys. The defense net weakness. Soon it will be two of a thousand. Then four."

"Not to mention what the radioactivity will do in the long run. Makes you wonder why they're forcing it with landings. Here. This south tropic archipelago. They've punched an open corridor down there."

"Hell of a defense," someone muttered. "Damn near as tough as Stars' End. I wouldn't want to try breaking it."

"How long till those destroyers are pushing us?" von Staufenberg asked.

"They're humping it in Norm. Four or five minutes for the closest. Looks like some other stuff starting to move, too."

"Can't we do anything?" the D.N.I. demanded.

Von Staufenberg replied, "We could bloody a few noses. It wouldn't change anything. We couldn't do that with a hundred Climbers. There're just too damned many of them. Okay, let's give the people in the other compartments a look. I want everybody to see it. We'll have some decision to make on our way home."

"The Warriors have decided," said the Star Lord of the Marine Toke Legion.

"He speaks for Toke," his non-Service superior added. "For Toke there can be but one decision. We will come to them here. Alone if we have to."

"It's not that easy for me, Manfred," Melene said. "We're an adventurous species but I'm handicapped by democratic traditions and faith in peace. We don't organize quickly or well."

Von Staufenberg chuckled. "You did before."

The Defender was older than he. She had been a soldier throughout the Ulantonid War.

"I expect we will again. We can do anything when we decide to pull together. It's the decision process that's so abominably slow."

"Your decisions were made years ago, Melene," Beckhart growled from his radar boards. "Don't try to snow us. I can give you the names and hull numbers of a hundred new construction ships you've got tucked away in places you never thought we'd look."

"Admiral Beckhart?" von Staufenberg queried.

"I have my sources, sir. They're rearming as fast as their shipbuilding industry can space hulls. They come off the line looking like commercial ships, only they've got drive potential up the yang-yang, and they never get delivered to any of the transport outfits. They disappear for a while, then turn up somewhere else with guns dripping off them."

"Why wasn't High Command informed of this, Beckhart?"

"Because my sources are in the Defender's office. And I knew why they were rearming. You wouldn't have bought it. Half of High Command is still trying to refight the Ulantonid War. I let it go on playing that game because people were seeing enough of those new ships to get nervous and start us a secret building program of our own. So we're on our way too."

"Beckhart... Your logic baffles me. Totally baffles me. I have the distinct feeling that you'll have to explain it to a Board of Inquiry. What else have you hidden from us?"

"You want an honest answer, or one that will please you?" Beckhart did not make many friends. He retained his position principally because no one else could do his job as well.

"Beckhart!"

"Several things, sir. Ongoing operations. If they work out, we'll be in good shape for meeting these monsters."

"Monsters?" Melene demanded. "There's no evidence…"

"Melene, the Admiral is a xenophobe. In fact, he doesn't like people very much. Tell me what you're doing, Beckhart."

"There's a chance I'm on the threshold to the solution of the Sangaree problem. Some new data was on its way in before we left. I'll probably want to borrow von Drachau again."

"What else?"

"Still too tentative for discussion. A possible breakthrough in communications and weapons technologies. I won't discuss it now. Not here."

"Beckhart…"

"Security privilege. Sir. Log it if you like."

Von Staufenberg wheeled on the Director of Naval Intelligence. She shrugged. "You won't get anything from me, either, Manfred."

"Damn! All right, let's get moving. Time's running out, and everybody's got to have a look at this."

Climbers were the most cramped vessels since Gemini. Circulating the forty-odd beings aboard was a slow, uncomfortable process.

"She's about to start shooting," Beckhart said of the nearest destroyer. "She has. Missile swarm. We have four minutes to hide."

"How do you like that? Didn't even try to find out who we were or what we wanted."

"This is the Ship's Commander," von Staufenberg said into the public address system. "We're under fire. Engineering, stand by to go Null." Thirty seconds before the swarm arrived, he ordered, "Take her up to ten Bev. First Watch Officer, a gesture is in order. Program me an attack approach on the vessel shooting at us."

The Ulantonid's feathery antennae stirred, quivered. The action was comparable to a human's pleased chuckle.

The Star Lords were in Weapons Department already, hoping they would be allowed to play with their deadly toys.

"One missile," said von Staufenberg. "Right up her wake."

It was the classic Climber attack strategy. Drives were a warship's soft spot. They simply could not be designed so that thrust apertures could be shielded as well as the remainder of the vessel.

The dust in the crater flowed together suddenly, smashing in like the Red Sea on Pharaoh's chariots. The doughnut ship had vanished.

"Take her all the way to forty Bev," von Staufenberg ordered. "I doubt they know enough to look for our Hawking Point, but let's get that cross-section down anyway." One of the curiosities about the Climber was that no other race known to humanity had ever developed it. And for humans it had been an accidental by-product of other research.

Twenty-three minutes passed before the First Watch Officer reported, "Attack position, Commander."

"Weapons, Ship's Commander. One missile. Stand by. Detection, when we go down I want you to get the ranges and vectors on everything you can see. We'll do what we can. And I want the tape rolling. Ship's Services, vent heat while we're Norm. All right. Everybody ready? Take her down, Engineering."

Heat accumulation was the biggest weakness of the Climber. There was no way to shed heat in Null. And a Climber often had to stay up for days while enemy warships hunted her.

The Climber was no warship in the slug-it-out sense. She was a hit-and-run fighter dependent on surprise for her effectiveness.

The Defender Prime brought them down just four kilometers behind the destroyer. The Climber rocked. The missile accelerated at 100 g. It arrived before the destroyer knew it was coming.

"One for the good guys," Beckhart grumped as the Climber went up again.

"What was that?" von Staufenberg demanded.

"Admiral, you're giving them valuable information just by blowing them out of space. You're telling them we can do it. You'll get them wondering how. Head home before we give them any hard data. Let's save the surprises for when they'll do some good."

Von Staufenberg reddened. There was no love lost between him and Beckhart.

"He's right, Manfred," the Defender Prime interjected. "You almost wasted the Climber advantage by committing them piecemeal during the war. They would have more effective if whole fleets had appeared suddenly. We would not have had time to adapt."

"Of course. Of course. I was thinking with my guts. Program a course for the mother, Melene."

Climbers did not have a long range. A mother ship awaited this one a hundred light-years homeward. A small armada protected her.

This Climber's crew regarded themselves highly.

# THREE: 3049 AD

## The Main Sequence

BenRabi slammed his scooter through the entrance to Control Sector. Seconds later the massive shield doors rumbled shut behind him. The section was totally self-contained now. No one could come in or leave till those doors lifted.

Moyshe stopped in a long, squealing slide. He jumped off, slammed the charger plug into a socket, ran through the hatch to Contact.

"You made it," Clara said. "We didn't think you would. You live so far away. Here. Catch your breath."

"My scooter was smoking. Better have it checked, Hans." He settled onto a fitted couch.

"Ready?" Clara asked.

"No."

She smiled at him. Hans started massaging an odorless paste into his scalp. Clara slipped her fingers inside what looked like a hairnet.

"You never are. I thought you liked Chub."

BenRabi chuckled. "Chub, I like fine. He's good people. But I'd like him a lot better if he could walk in the door, stick out a hand, and say, 'Hey, Moyshe, let's go grab a couple of beers.' "

Chub was the starfish with whom benRabi usually linked.

"Xenophobe."

"Crap. It's not him. It's that out-of-body feeling..."

"Wrong, Moyshe. You can't fool old Clara. I was babying mindtechs before you were born. And you're all alike. You don't want to go out because it hurts so much to come back."

"Yeah?"

"Ready," Hans said.

Clara slid the net onto Moyshe's head. Her fingertips were soft and warm. They lingered on his cheeks. Momentary concern clouded her smile.

"Don't push yourself, Moyshe. Get out if it gets rough. You haven't had enough rest."

"Since Stars' End there isn't any rest. For anybody."

"We won," Hans reminded.

"The cost was too high."

"It was cheaper than losing."

BenRabi shrugged. "I guess you people see things different. I never would have gone in the first place."

"You took your whippings and smiled, back in Confederation?" Hans asked. "I never heard of that."

"No. We calculated the odds. We picked the right time. Then we ganged up. We didn't just go storming around like a rogue elephant, getting hurt as much as we did hurt."

"Oriflamme," Hans countered.

"What?"

"That's what they call Payne sometimes. It's something from olden times that has to do with not taking prisoners."

"Oh. The oriflamme. It was a special pennon that belonged to the King of France. If he raised it, it meant take no prisoners. It had a way of backfiring on him."

"Hans," Clara said, "Moyshe is an Academy man. He can probably tell you how many spokes in the wheel of a Roman war chariot."

"Take Poitiers, for instance…"

"Who?"

"It's a place. In France, which is on Old Earth…"

"I know where France is, Moyshe."

"All right. One of the big battles of the Hundred Years War was fought there. And you could say that the French lost because of the oriflamme. See, they caught the English in a bad spot. Outnumbered them like ten to one. The Black Prince decided to surrender. But the French raised the oriflamme. Which pissed the English, so they proceeded to kick ass all over the countryside. When the dust settled, the French were wiped out and Louis was in chains. There's a lesson in there somewhere, if you want to look. Namely, don't ever push anybody into a corner where he can't get out."

"You see what he's doing, Hans?" Clara asked.

"You mean trying to educate us until the all-clear comes through? You're out of luck, Moyshe. Lift your head so I can put your helmet on."

BenRabi raised his head.

His scalp began tingling under the hairnet device. The helmet devoured his head, stealing the light. He fought the panic that always hit before he went under.

Hans strapped him in and adjusted the bio-monitor's pickups.

"Can you hear me, Moyshe?" Clara asked through the helmet's earphones.

He raised a hand. Then spoke: "Coming through clear."

"Got you too. Your boards look good. Blood pressure is up, but that's normal for you. Take a minute in TSD. Relax. Go when you want."

His, "I don't want," remained unspoken.

He depressed the switch beneath his right hand one click.

The only senses left him were internal. Total Sensory Deprivation left him only his aches and pains, the taste in his mouth, and the rush of blood. Once the field took hold, even those would go.

In small doses it *was* relaxing. But too much could drive a man insane.

He flicked his right hand again.

A universe took form around him. He was its center, its lord, its creator… There was no pain in that universe, nor much unhappiness. Too many wonders burned there, within the bounds of his mind.

It was a universe of colors both pastel and crisp. Every star was a blazing jewel, proclaiming its individual hue. The oncoming storm of the nova's solar wind was a rioting, psychedelic cloud that seemed to have as much substance as an Old Earth thunderhead. Opposite it, the pale pink glimmer of a hydrogen stream meandered off toward the heart of the galaxy. The surrounding harvestships were patches of iridescent gold.

A score of golden Chinese dragons drifted with the fleet, straining toward it, yet held away by the light pressure of the dying star. Starfish!

BenRabi's sourness gave way to elation. There would be contact this time.

He reached toward them with his thoughts. "Chub? Are you out there, my friend?" For a time there was nothing.

Then a warm glow enveloped him like some sudden outbreak of good cheer.

"Moyshe man-friend, hello. I see you. Coming out of the light, hello. One ship is gone."

"*Jariel.* They're still evacuating."

"Sad."

Chub did not seem sad. This fish, benRabi thought, is constitutionally incapable of anything but joy.

"Not so, Moyshe man-friend. I mourn with the herd the sorrows of Stars' End. Yet I must laugh with my man-friends over the joys of what was won."

"The ships-that-kill weren't all destroyed, Chub. The Sangaree carry their grudges forever."

"Ha! They are a tear in the eye of eternity. They will die. Their sun will die. And still there will be starfish to swim the rivers of the night."

"You've been puttering around in the back rooms of my mind again. You're stealing my images and shooting them back at me."

"You have an intriguing mind, Moyshe man-friend. A clouded, boxy mind, cobwebby, atticy, full of trap doors..."

"What would you know about trap doors?"

"Only what I relive through your memories, Moyshe man-friend."

Chub teased and giggled like an adolescent lover.

By starfish reckoning he *was* a child. He had not yet seen his millionth year.

BenRabi simply avoided thinking about starfish time spans. A life measured in millions of years was utterly beyond his ken. He only mourned the fact that those incredible spans could never touch upon worlds where beings of a biochemical nature lived. The stories they could have told! The historical mysteries they could have illuminated!

But starfish dared not get too near major gravitational or magnetic sources. Even the gravity of the larger harvestships felt to a starfish much as rheumatism to a human being.

They were terribly fragile creatures.

While Chub teased and enthused, Moyshe turned a part of his mind to his private universe again.

Red torpedoes idled along far away, across the pink river, against the galaxy.

"Yes," Chub said. "Sharks. Survivors of Stars' End called them here. They will attack. They starve. Another feast for the scavenger things."

Smaller ghosts in a mix of colors shadowed both dragons and torpedoes. They were Chub's scavengers.

The great slow ecology of the hydrogen streams had niches for creatures of most life-functions, though their definition in human terms was seldom more than an approximation. A convenient labeling.

Moyshe yielded to nervousness. Chub reached into his mind, calming him…

"I'm learning, Chub. I can see the river this time. I can see the particle storm coming from the sick sun."

"Very good, Moyshe man-friend. You relax now. Sharks come soon. You watch scavenger things instead. They tell when sharks can't wait anymore. They get dancey."

Moyshe laughed into his secret universe. Starfish believed in doing things with deliberation, as might be expected of creatures with vast life spans. Young starfish tended to be restless and excitable. They were prone to flutter impatiently in the presence of their elders. The Old Ones called it "getting dancey."

Chub was dancey most of the time.

The Old Ones considered him the herd idiot. Chub said they regretted exposing him to human hasty-think while he was still young and impressionable.

"Is a joke, Moyshe man-friend. Is a good joke? Yes?"

"Yes. Very funny." For a starfish. The Old Ones had to be the most phlegmatic, humorless, pragmatic intelligences in all creation. They couldn't even grasp the concept of a joke. With the exception of Chub, benRabi found them a depressing mob.

"I was lucky to become your mind-mate, Chub. Very lucky."

He meant it. He had linked with Old Ones. He compared it to making love to his grandmother bare-assed on an iceberg, with a crowd watching. Drawing Chub was the best thing that had happened to him in years.

"Yes. We half-wits stick together. Venceremos, Comrade Moyshe."

BenRabi filled the universe with laughter. "Where the hell did you get that?"

"Your mind full of cobwebby memories, Moyshe man-friend. One time you play revolutionary on hard matter place called Dustball."

"Yeah. I did. About two weeks. Then it was duck bullets all the way back to the Embassy."

"You live much in few years, Moyshe man-friend. Ten times anyone else linked by starfish Chub. Many adventures. Think Chub would make good spy?"

"Who would you spy on?"

"Yes. Problem. Very difficult to disguise as shark."

"That's another joke, isn't it?"

"Yes. You still spying, Moyshe man-friend?"

"Not anymore. I'm not Thomas McClennon anymore. I'm Moyshe benRabi. I've found me a home, Chub. These are my people now. You can't spy on your own people."

"Oh. Saw shadows in your mind. Thought maybe secret spy-stuff lurked. So. Hey! Maybe someday you go spy on hard matter place people? Be double spy."

"Double agent?"

"Oh. Yes. That right words."

"No more spying, Chub. I'm going to be a mindtech."

"Dangerous."

"So is spying. In more ways than you'll ever understand."

"Hurts-of-the-heart dangers, you mean?"

"I don't know why they tell you you're stupid. You're a lot smarter in a lot of ways than most people I know. You see things without having to have them explained."

"Helps, being starfish. People can't look inside, Moyshe man-friend. You have to tell. You have to show. You not the kind of man to do that."

"Yeah. Let's talk about something else, huh?"

"Running out of talk time, Moyshe man-friend. Scavenger creatures getting dancey. You not paying attention?"

"I still haven't got the hang of seeing everything at once."

That was one of the beauties of the mindtech's linked universe. He was not subject to the limitations of binocular vision. But he did have to unlearn its habits.

Blind people made better techs faster. They had no habits to unlearn, no preoccupations to overcome. But blind people who suffered from classical migraine were scarce.

Scarlet torpedoes edged toward the fleet. They were not yet wholly committed. Hunger still had not banished good sense.

Sharks were slow of wit, but they knew they had to get past the harvestships to reach their prey.

That was the whole point of the starfish-Starfisher alliance.

"Can't visit anymore, Chub. We're not going on mind-drive, so I'll have to help fight."

"Oh, yes, Moyshe man-friend. Shoot straight. I help, putting right vectors in your brain."

"All right." Aloud, into his helmet, benRabi said, "Gun Control."

A second later his earphones crackled. "Gun Control, aye."

"Mindtech. In link and free to assume control of a sector battery. Sharks will attack. Repeat, will attack."

"Shit. All right, buddy. But never mind the sector battery. Master Gunner says he wants you to feed the main battle tank. Think you and your link can give us good realtime input?"

"Yes," Chub murmured deep in benRabi's hindbrain.

"Yes," Moyshe said. And wondered why. It was not something he had ever tried.

"Monitor?"

"All go, Gun Control," Clara's voice interjected. "Green boards all across. I've just keyed the translator. You can bring the computer on-line whenever you're ready."

"Stand by for draw, Linker."

"Moyshe," said Clara, "don't take any chances. Key out if it gets rough."

"Drawing, Linker."

For an instant benRabi felt as though some intangible vacuum were sucking his mind away. A smatter of panic quickly yielded to Chub's soothing.

Moyshe relaxed, became a conduit. He became an almost disinterested observer.

The scavengers suddenly grew dancey with a vengeance.

"Attack imminent," benRabi muttered.

Those pilot fish were excited because they would feast no matter what the outcome of battle. They would be perfectly content nibbling dead shark or dead starfish.

A dozen crimson torpedoes suddenly misted, stretched into long, fuzzy lines, and solidified again near the starfish herd.

A hundred swords of light started carving them into scavenger food. Sharks were easy meat for particle beams.

"Teach them to try end run through hyper," Chub whispered.

The starfish herd had not bothered to dodge. They would not begin maneuvering till the protection of the human ships began breaking down.

It might not hold, benRabi reflected. Five vessels could not establish a sound fire pattern. There would be blind spots. Big holes. To fill them would mean risking hitting your own people.

The shark packs milled. They had not yet found workable tactics for assailing a fleet of harvestships.

Their intellectual slowness was the only hope for starfish and Starfishers alike. Something had happened to the sharks. Their numbers were expanding almost exponentially. They were becoming ever more desperate in their quest for something to eat.

Their prey, historically, had been the stragglers of the great starfish herds. The feeble and injured and careless. But now they assaulted the strong and healthy as well, and had even begun turning on their own injured. Even the firepower of a harvestship could not hold the massed packs at bay when hunger heterodyned into a berserk killing rage.

"Not look so promising as you thought, Moyshe man-friend. All going to come at once, from everywhere, crazy. Just killing and dying."

There was dread in Chub's thought. Moyshe was dismayed. Even in the hell that had been the battle at Stars' End the starfish had not lost his good cheer.

The starfish's prediction proved correct. The red torpedoes suddenly exploded in every direction. Moyshe had seen the same reaction among humans. The first had been by a band of fair-weather revolutionaries who had heard the police were coming. Another time, a terrorist had lobbed a hand grenade into a crowded theater.

But the sharks were not fleeing. The instant-insanity had seized them. They were spreading out to attack.

They arrowed in on the harvestfleet. Laser and particle beam swords stabbed.

*Danion*'s fire was deadly. The realtime simulation from the minds of a man and a starfish linked gave the weapons people a fractional second's advantage over their brethren in ships relying on normal detection systems.

The shark wave rolled round *Danion* like a breaker around a granite promontory. They could have worn her down in time, had they had the patience of the sea, and the sea's resources for endlessly sending in another wave. They had hurt her bad at Stars' End. It only took one shark getting through, with its multi-dimensional fires, to ravage a whole section of ship. But this horde was more limited in its numbers and more driven by hunger.

"Oh, Christ," benRabi swore as an explosion ripped a huge chunk from a sister ship. A shark had gotten through there. The service ships, still evacuating *Jariel* and trying to plug the holes in the fire pattern, swarmed toward the fragment. Clouds of frozen water vapor boiled round it as atmosphere poured out.

A shark flung itself into the starfish herd.

The great night beasts were not defenseless. One burped a ball of the nuclear fire that burned in its "gut," flung it with Robin Hood accuracy. The shark perished in the fading flash of a hydrogen bomb.

One predator was gone. And one starfish was disarmed for hours. It took the creatures a long time to revitalize their internal fires.

BenRabi had seen the peaceable starfish use the same weapon against Sangaree raidships at Stars' End.

"Fur is flying now, Moyshe man-friend." Chub was straining for humor. "We doing all right, you and me. Maybe your Old Ones decide you not stupid after all." Left unthought was Chub's hope for the same reaction from his own Old Ones.

By way of support benRabi replied, "This is a new era, Chub. It's going to take hastiness and danciness to survive."

"Sharks coming again."

Once more *Danion*'s weaponry scarred the long night. Moyshe wondered what some alien would think if he happened on its unconcealable mark, a thousand years from now, a thousand light-years away.

Both sides had used retrospective observation techniques during the Ulantonid War. A battle's outcome might be fixed, but it could be studied over and over from every possible angle.

The second assault was more furious than the first. BenRabi stopped trying to think. He had to give his whole attention over to following the situation.

More sharks dropped hyper, drawn by no known means. The rage took them, too. They attacked everything, including wounded brethren floundering around the battle region.

This was the root of Chub's fear. That more and more sharks would be drawn till they simply overwhelmed everything.

It was the future foreseen by both starfish and Starfishers. The terror that herd after herd and harvestship after harvestship would be consumed was the force that had driven the maverick commander of this fleet to hazard the defenses of Stars' End.

The arrivals slowed to a trickle. Chub thought, "We going to win again, Moyshe man-friend. See the pattern? The glorious pattern. They waste their might devouring their own injured."

BenRabi searched his kaleidoscopic mind-link universe. He saw nothing but chaos. This, he reflected, is the sort of thing Czyzew-ski was thinking about when he wrote *The Old God.* So much of Czyzewski's poetry seemed reflective of recent events. Had the man been prescient?

No. He was far gone on stardust when he did the cycle including *The Old God.* The drug killed him less than a month after he finished the poem. The images were just the flaming madness of the drug burning through.

"Don't you get tired of being right?" he asked when the first sharks fled.

"Never, Moyshe man-friend. But learned long ago to wait till event is certain, predestined, to make observation. Error is painful. The scorn of Old Ones is like the fire of a thousand stars."

"I know the feeling." For some reason the face of Admiral Beckhart, his one-time commander, drifted through his universe. Here on the galactic rim, fighting for his life against creatures he had not suspected existed two years earlier, his previous career seemed as remote as that of another man. Of another incarnation, or something he had read about.

The assault collapsed once the first few well-fed sharks fled.

The starfish had suffered far less than their inedible guardians. Not one dragon was missing from the golden herd defended by the harvestships. But another ship had been injured severely.

A traitorous thought stole across Moyshe's mind on mouse-soft feet.

Chub was less indignant than he expected.

On a strictly pragmatic level, the starfish agreed that getting out of the interstellar rivers would be the best way to conserve Starfisher ships and lives.

"They'll never go, Chub. The harvestfleets are their nations. Their homelands. They're proud, stubborn people. They'll keep fighting and hoping."

"I know, Moyshe man-friend. It saddens the herd. And makes the Old Ones proud that they forged their alliance so well. But why do you say 'they'?"

"We, then. Part of the time… *Most* of the time I'm an outsider here. They do things differently than what I learned…"

"Sometimes you miss your old life, Moyshe man-friend."

"Sometimes. Not often, and not much, though. I'd better tend to business." He had to focus his attention to force his physical voice to croak, "Gun Control, Mindlink. The sharks are going. They've given up. You can secure when the last leaves firing range."

"You sure, Linker? Don't look like it in the display tank."

"I'm sure. Let me know when I can stop realtiming. This is my second link in eight hours."

"Right. Will do." The man on the far end seemed impressed.

Clara's voice broke in. "Are you all right, Moyshe? The strain getting heavy? We can bring you out."

"I'm okay. For a while. I remember what I am. Just be ready to hit me with that needle."

At Stars' End *Danion* had lost half her native, trained mindtechs because they had stayed in link too long, or had been mindburned by sharks breaking through the defensive fire screen. The best guess was that the former had become lost in the special interior universe of the linker. Dozens occupied a special hospital ward where doctors and nurses had to handle them like newly born babies.

Their bodies lived on. Their minds, it was hoped, might sometime be retrieved.

In all the history of the High Seiners no lost linker ever had been recalled.

The Starfishers were living on hopes these days. Stars' End had been one, for weapons capable of shattering shark tides.

BenRabi did not understand how the Seiners had hoped to accomplish what generations of madmen, fools, and geniuses had failed to do. Stars' End was a fortress unvanquishable.

It was a whole world, Earth-sized, that was a fortress. Or planetary battleship. Or whatever. It could be approached by nothing. The technologies of its defenses were beyond the imaginations of any of the races aware of its existence. Its builders had long since vanished into the abyss of time.

Generations of men had lusted after the weapons of Stars' End. Thousands had died trying to obtain them. And the fortress world remained inviolate.

Why had the Seiners been convinced that they would have better luck?

"You were right, Linker. Computer says they're pulling out. Going to let you off realtime now. We can handle it from here without."

"Thank you, Gun Control."

The sense of drain stopped abruptly. BenRabi's universe reeled. Chub reached in and steadied him. "Time to break, Moyshe man-friend. You losing sense of reality and orientation in space-time."

"I'm not lost yet, Chub."

"You all say so. No more you can do here, man-friend."

The crackle of reality beginning to fall into shards rose from benRabi's hindbrain. It pushed a wave of terror before it. Chub did nothing to soothe him.

"Clara! The needle. I'm coming out."

He slapped the switch beneath his left hand.

They were waiting for him. The agony persisted for only a few seconds.

That was bad enough. He screamed and screamed. It got worse every time.

# FOUR: 3049 AD

## The Main Sequence

They put him into Hospital Block this time. He was under sedation for three days.

Two people were at his bedside when the doctor came to bring him out. The thin, pale, blue-eyed woman with the nervous hands was Amy. The little Oriental with the presence of an iceberg was benRabi's friend Mouse.

Amy would sit for a minute, picking at her jumpsuit, shifting this way and that. She would cross and uncross her legs, then would rise and pace around for a minute before sitting again. She did not speak to Mouse. Most of the time she deliberately tried to distance Storm from herself and Moyshe. It was almost as if she saw Mouse as a competitor for benRabi's affection.

The men had shared missions under fire. Sometimes they did not like one another much. Their backgrounds were day and night. Centuries of prejudice had erected walls between them. Yet an indestructible bond had been forged and hammered on the anvils of shared peril. They had guarded one another's backs and saved one another's lives too often to let go.

Mouse waited without moving, with the patience of a samurai.

He was a dedicated Archaicist. He had just encountered his own ancient heritage and, in imagination, was trying the samurai role for size. The code and conduct suited the warrior within him.

But it did nothing for the libertine. And Mouse was a classic of that genre, at least with the opposite sex.

Masato Igarashi Storm did nothing by half measures.

The doctor coughed softly.

"Will he be all right?" Amy demanded. "He'll come out okay? I know what you told me, but…"

Mouse's facial muscles moved slightly. His wan expression spoke volumes about his disgust at her display.

The doctor was more patient. "Just an enforced rest, Miss. That's all it is. There's nothing wrong that rest can't cure. I hear he did a hell of a job feeding realtime to Weapons Control. He just pushed himself too far."

A look flickered across Mouse's stony face.

"What're *you* thinking?" Amy demanded.

"Just that he's not usually a pusher."

Amy was ready for a fight.

The doctor aborted it by giving benRabi an injection. He began to come around.

Mouse seemed indifferent to Amy's response. But not oblivious. He was an astute observer. He just did not care what she thought.

"Doc," he said, "is there any special reason for sticking with this kind of medical setup?"

The woman held benRabi's wrist, taking his pulse. "What do you mean?"

"It's primitive. Almost Archaicist obsolete. They had sonic sedation systems before I was born. Easier on the patient and staff both."

The doctor reddened. Mouse had been out of the hospital only a few weeks himself. He had spent a month recuperating from a severe wound received from a Sangaree agent who had tried to seize control of *Danion*. He was not pleased with the quality of medical care, and made no secret of it. But Mouse hated all doctors and hospitals. He could find fault with the finest.

BenRabi had tracked the Sangaree woman down, and had shot her…

Mouse had the nerve to stand toe-to-toe with the Devil and tell him to put it where the sun doesn't shine.

"We have to make do with what we can afford, Mr. Storm."

"So I've been told." Mouse did not pursue it, though he thought Seiners pleading poverty was on a par with Midas begging alms on a street corner.

BenRabi opened his eyes.

"How you doing, Moyshe?" Storm asked, trampling Amy's more dramatic opener. His presence there, betraying his concern, embarrassed him.

The fabric of centuries takes the stamp; they mark the children indelibly. Their legacy remains as invisible and irresistible as the secret coded in DNA. The young Mouse had learned that Old Earthers were pariahs.

Mouse's family had been in Service for three generations. They were part of Confederation's military aristocracy. BenRabi's forebears had been unemployed Social Insurees for centuries.

Neither man considered himself prejudiced. But false truths sown in the fallows of childhood, planted deep, continued to sprout unrealistic real-world responses.

BenRabi had begun bridling his prejudice early. He had to survive. There had been only two Old Earthers in his Academy battalion.

He needed a minute to get his bearings. "What am I doing here?" he demanded.

"You needed rest," Amy told him. "Lots of it. You overdid it this time."

"Come on. I can take care of myself. I know when…"

"Crap!" the doctor snapped. "Every mindtech thinks that. And then they turn up here, burned out. I change their diapers and spoon feed them. What is it with you people, benRabi? You all got egos two sizes too big for a small god."

Moyshe was fuzzy. He tried to say something flip. His tongue felt like it was wrapped in an old sock.

He saw tears in the doctor's eyes. "Did you lose someone at Stars' End?"

"My sister. She came out of creche just before you landsmen came aboard. She was only seventeen, benRabi."

"I'm sorry."

"No, you're not. You're a mindtech. Anyway, sorry doesn't help. Not when I have to take care of her every day. She was just like you, benRabi. She knew she could handle it. She wouldn't listen either. None of them would. Not even the controllers, who should've known better. They put her back in with only four hours' rest."

BenRabi kept his mouth shut. What could he say? He had been introduced to Contact during the battle at Stars' End. The main Contact room had been a shambles. Dozens of mindtechs had given everything to save *Danion*.

He never would have seen Contact, or even have discovered its existence, had those linker casualties not been cruel. In those days he had been a distrusted landsman, a convicted enemy spy who was screened from all Seiner secrets. They had drafted him into Contact only because he might give *Danion* a millimeter's better chance of surviving.

He had made his decision to cross over after Stars' End, virtually in the hatch of the ship designated to return the landsmen contractees to Confederation.

He had waited too long. Half of his personal possessions had departed with the ship. He had not recovered them. The service ship crew had gotten into a row with Customs. The bureaucrats had retaliated, seizing everything not bolted to the ship's frames.

BenRabi took Amy's thin, cool hand. "How've you been, darling? You look tired. How long has it been?" She felt so cold… She was a spooky woman. Why had he fallen in love with her?

He always fell for the strange ones, the neurotic and just plain rotten ones. Alyce, in Academy… What a loser she had turned out to be. And the Sangaree woman, Marya, who had been a vampire in the midst of his last two missions.

"I'm all right now that I know you'll be okay. Moyshe, please be more careful."

She seemed unusually remote. BenRabi glanced at her, at Mouse, and back again. More problems with Mouse? Her dislike for his friend had taken a quantum leap recently.

Mouse did not talk much. The inevitable chess board had accompanied him, but he did not offer to play. Amy's presence restrained him. Chess was one of his great passions, rivaling his passion for seducing a parade of beautiful women.

"Hey, Mouse. Ever wonder what Max is doing these days?" Referring to someone they had known before coming out here was the only way he could think of to pull his friend into the conversation.

"Probably getting richer and wondering why we don't come into her shop anymore. I don't think Beckhart will bother giving her our new address."

"Yeah." BenRabi laughed. "He should have heard the news by now, don't you think? Or pretty soon. He'll foam at the mouth." For Amy's benefit, he explained, "Max was a friend of ours in Luna Command. She ran a stamp store."

"Best hobby shop in the moon," Mouse said.

Amy did not respond. She simply could not comprehend what these two got out of accumulating small bits of paper that were ages old and required jeweler's grade care.

And stamps were not the only thing. Between them they seemed to collect everything. Coins. Stamps. All kinds of ancient miscellanea. Mouse had little wrought-iron trivets and other old-time dohickeys all over his quarters. The one collection she could appreciate was Moyshe's butterflies. He had a frame of exotics on his wall. They were incredibly beautiful.

The Seiner ships were ecologically sterile. Only their zoos contained nonhuman life, and that the large, well-known mammals.

Amy had no hobbies of her own. She read for relaxation. She had acquired the habit from her mother.

Mouse even managed passably with a clarinet, an antique woodwind seldom seen anymore. He claimed to have learned from his father.

"What about Greta?" Mouse asked. "You think the Department will take care of her?"

Amy jumped at the name. "You never did tell me about Greta, Moyshe."

"That was in another life."

They were lovers, but they did not know one another well. BenRabi did not like stirring up the snake pit of people's pasts. There was too much chance of finding something nasty. It was there in every life.

But he answered Amy's question. "I told you before. She's a kid I met the last time I was on Old Earth. The last time I visited my mother. She wanted out. Her friends wouldn't let her go. I arranged it for her. And ended up sponsoring her."

"Sort of like being a foster parent," Mouse explained.

"Guess she'd be eighteen now. I haven't thought about her in ages. You shouldn't have mentioned her, Mouse. Now you've got me worried."

"Hey, don't. Max will look out for her."

"Maybe. But that's not right, putting it on somebody else. Is there any way I could send her a letter now and then, Amy? Just to let her know I'm all right and thinking about her? I'd let you or Jarl write it if you wanted. You could even run it through the crypto computer to make sure it's innocent."

"This's just a kid?" Amy demanded.

"Yeah. She reminded me a lot of me when I came off Old Earth. Awful lost. I thought I could help out by sponsoring her. And then I kind of ran out when the Bureau sent us out here. I told her we'd be back in a couple of months. It's been almost fourteen."

"I'll ask Jarl. He lets a little mail go out. Some of us have relatives outside. But it's slow."

"That doesn't matter. Amy, you're a jewel. I love you."

"Well, if you're going to get mushy," Mouse said, standing. "I've got to run. A citizenship class. It's from hunger, Moyshe. Me and Emily Hopkins and this fascist bastard of a teacher… Maybe I'll hurt the arm again. Get back in here so I can miss a few too. Behave. Do what the doctor lady says. Or I'll wring your neck." He made his exit before Moyshe could embarrass him with many thanks-for-comings.

"You're awful quiet today, honey," benRabi said after a while. Perhaps if the doctor had not been there…

"I'm just tired. We're still doing double shifts and barely keeping our heads above water. We're going to be in the Yards a long time. Assuming *Danion* doesn't fall apart before we get there. Assuming the sharks don't knock us apart."

"You've mentioned these Yards about fifty times and wouldn't tell me about them. Do you trust me enough now?"

"They're what the name sounds like. Where we build and fix our ships. Moyshe, you're not going anywhere for a while. Tell me about you."

"What?"

"I met you the very first day. Way back on Carson's, when you signed your contract. We lived together for months before I even found out you've got a daughter. I don't know anything about you."

"Greta isn't my daughter, honey. I just helped a kid who needed somebody..."

"It's almost the same thing, isn't it?"

"Legally, I guess. On paper. They'd have trouble making it stand up in court."

"Tell me. Everything."

There was little else to do but talk. He talked.

The doctor, lurking in the background watching suspiciously, had made it clear that he would be stuck here for a while.

"All right. Let me know when it gets boring."

He had been born in North America on Old Earth, to Clarence Hardaway and Myra McClennon. He had hardly known his father. His mother, for reasons he still did not understand, had elected to raise him at home instead of burying him in the State Creche. Only a few Social Insurees raised their children.

His early years had been typical for home-raised S.I. children. Little supervision, little love, little education. He had been running with a kid gang before he was eight.

He had been nine when he had seen his first offworlders. Spikes, they had called them. These had been Navy men in crisp dress blacks diligently pursuing the arcane business of offworlders.

Those uniforms had captured his imagination. They had become an obsession. He had started keying information out of his mother's home data retrieval terminal. He had not had the education to decipher most of it. He had started teaching himself, building from the ground up toward the things he so desperately wanted to know.

At ten he had quit the gang so he would have more time to study. Halfway through his eleventh year the revelation had come. He *had* to get into space. He had approached a Navy recruiter clandestinely. The man had arranged for him to sneak through the Academy exams.

He never would have made it had there been no special standards and quotas for Old Earthers. He would have gotten skunked had he been in direct competition with carefully prepared Outworlders, many of whom had grown up in the military life. Half the officers in Service were the children of officers. Service was a complete sub-culture, and one that was becoming increasingly less connected with and controlled by the over-culture. He had had motivation.

At twelve he had run away from home, fleeing to Luna Command and Academy. In six years he had climbed from dead last to the 95th percentile in class standing. At graduation he had taken his Line option and been assigned to the Fleet. He had served aboard the destroyers *Aquitaine* and *Hesse,* and the attack cruiser *Tamerlane,* before requesting Intelligence training.

Following a year of schooling the Bureau had assigned him as Naval Attaché to the Embassy on Feldspar. He had had a half dozen similar assignments on as many worlds before his work attracted the attention of Admiral Beckhart, whose department handled dangerous operations, and tricks on the grey side of legal.

He had taken part in several tight missions, and had reencountered his former classmate, Mouse. They had shared several assignments, the last being to join the Starfishers to ferret out information that could be used to force the Seiners to enter the Confederation fold.

Some of it Amy had heard before. Some she had not. She was not satisfied. Her first comment was, "You didn't say anything about women."

"What do you mean? What's that got to do with anything?"

"Everything, as far as I'm concerned. I want to know who your lovers were and how come you broke up. What they were like…"

"You'll shit in your hand and carry it to China first, Lady."

He was still a little dopey. He did not realize that he had said it aloud till he began to wonder why she had shut up so suddenly.

After one stunned gasp Amy blew out of the room like a tornado looking for a town to wreck.

The lady doctor came out of the background, took his blood pressure. "She's pushy, isn't she?"

"I don't know what's got into her. She wasn't like that before."

"You've had an interesting life."

"Not really. I don't think I'd do it the same if I had it to do again."

"Well, you could, couldn't you?"

"I don't understand."

"Rejuvenation. I thought it was available to everybody landside."

"Oh. Yes. More or less. Some of the brass have been around since Noah landed the Ark. But Fate has a way of catching up with people who try to slide around it."

"Wish we had it out here."

"You don't look that old."

"I was thinking about my father. He's getting on now."

"I see. How soon can I leave?"

"Any time, really. But I wish you'd wait a couple hours. You'll be weak and dizzy."

"Mouse was right about sonic sedation."

"I know. But I don't write the medical budget. Good luck, Mr. benRabi. Try not to see me again."

"I hate hospitals, Doctor."

He did. His only stays had been at Bureau insistence, to modify him mentally or physically.

He did a few minor exercises before catching a public tram home.

Amy was waiting. "Oh, Moyshe. That was stupid of me. You were right. Those things aren't any of my business."

She had been crying. Her eyes were red.

"It's all right. I understand." But he did not. His cultural background had not prepared him for personal nosiness. In Confederation people lived *now*. They did not consider the past.

"It's just that I feel… Well, everything's so chancy the way it is between us."

Here she comes, he thought. Hints about getting married.

Marriage was important to the Seiners. In Confederation it was more an amusing relic, an entertainment or daydream for the young and the romantic. He could not reconcile his attitudes with Seiner seriousness. Not yet.

The Starfishers had won his loyalty, but they could not make him a different man. They could not make him reflect themselves merely by adopting him.

Was Mouse having the same trouble? he wondered. Probably not. Mouse was a chameleon. He could adapt anywhere, vanish into any crowd.

"I have to go to work," Amy told him. Weariness seemed to be dragging her down. "You'd better get some rest yourself, honey."

After she left he took out his stamp collection and turned the well-thumbed album pages. Mouse had opened a Pandora's box by mentioning Max and Greta. After a while he pushed the album aside and tried to compose a letter to the girl.

He could not think of much to say.

# FIVE: 3049 AD

## The Contemporary Scene

Admirals and generals did not have to endure the usual waiting and decontamination procedures getting into Luna Command. The security checks were abbreviated. No staff-grade officer had gone sour since Admiral McGraw had turned freebooter following the peace with Ulant. Admiral Beckhart entered his office just three hours after his personal shuttle berthed a little south of the Sea of Tranquility.

He had not spared the horses, in the vernacular of another age. The mother had dropped hyper midway between Luna and L-5. The first message he had received had been code-tagged, "Personal presence required immediately. Critical."

Either the bottom had dropped off of the universe or McClennon and Storm had come home with their saddlebags dripping delicious little secrets.

The Crew, as he called his hand-picked brain-trust, were in the office when he arrived.

He raised a hand. "As you were. What have we got?"

Jones asked, "You don't want to shower and change?"

Beckhart looked ragged. Almost seedy. Like a derelict costumed as an Admiral.

"You clowns sent a Personal Presence, Critical. If I've got time to shit, shower, and shave, you should've said it was urgent."

"Maybe we were hasty," Namaguchi admitted. "We'd just scanned the crypto breakdown. We were a little excited."

"Breakdown? What the hell's going on?" Beckhart tumbled into a huge chair behind a vast, gleaming wood desk. "Get to the point, Akido."

Namaguchi jerked out of his seat, flipped a square of manila across the gleaming desk.

"Numbers. Your handwriting hasn't improved."

"The Section's doing up a printout. That, sir, is what Storm had for us."

"Well?"

"Morgan Standard Coordinate Data, sir. A stellar designation. Took us two days to convert it from the Sangaree system."

"Sangaree?... Holy Christ! Is it?..."

"What we've been waiting for all our lives. Where to find their home star."

"Ah, god. Ah. It can't be. Two hundred years we've been looking. Cutting and dying and generally carrying on like a gang of fascist assholes. So it paid off. I bet my butt on a long shot and it paid off. Give me the comm. Somebody give me the goddamn comm."

Jones eased it across the desk. Beckhart punched furiously. "Beckhart. Priority. Hey! I don't give a damn if he's banging the Queen of Sheba. Personal, Critical, and I'm going to have your ass for breakfast if you don't... Excuse me, sir." His manners improved dramatically.

"Yes, sir, it is. I want a confirmation of our position on Memorandum of Permanent Policy and Procedure Number Four. Specifically, Paragraph Six."

A long silence ensued. Beckhart's cronies leaned closer and closer to their chief. The man on the other end finally said something.

"Yes, sir. Absolutely. I have the data in my hand, sir. Just decoded. Give me von Drachau and the First Fleet... Yes, sir. What I want is a blank check for a while. I can get started tomorrow."

More silence.

Then, "Yes, sir. I thought so, sir. I understand, sir. Thank you, sir." Beckhart broke the connection. "He wants to take it up with the Chiefs of Staff."

"They're going to back down now? After all the lives we've spent?"

"Commander Jones. Do you *realize* the enormity of what I just dumped on him? Let me draw you a picture. I interrupted him while von Staufenberg was briefing him on what we saw centerward. Which was about what we expected to see, and as pretty as a barge loaded with dead babies. Some psychopathic race is doing its damnedest to kill off anything sentient it can find. Then I horn in and ask for a confirm on Memo

Four slash Six. Which is a vow to exterminate the Sangaree whenever we find out where the hell they're hiding their homeworld. We're supposed to be the good guys, Jones. The things he's looking at right now kind of tend to put the damper on the fires of that good old-time anti-Sangaree righteousness."

"I don't see the problem, sir."

"Pragmatically it doesn't exist. Having seen what's going on centerward, I'd say Four slash Six is a strategic imperative. We've got to get those bloodsuckers off our backs fast. They ate us alive during the wars with Ulant and Toke. Any time there's a dust-up between non-Confederation worlds they come on like jackals. Raidships in swarms… Not to mention the price we pay in stardust addiction. Hell, half the fleet is tied up protecting shipping. Four slash Six would free those ships. And if we burned the Sangaree, the McGraws would close up shop. Those are the arguments in favor. Akido. Take the Devil's advocate."

It was an old game. Namaguchi knew his commander well. "Sir. How in God's name can we go to the people of Confederation—not to mention our allies—with the news that we've destroyed a whole race? Just when we're about to pump them up with moral indignation so we can justify a preemptive strike against a species we claim is guilty of the identical sin? Let me understate, sir, and say that the positions are inconsistent. Let me say, sir, that we're on a quick slide down into a moral cesspool. We would, quite simply, be the biggest hypocrites this universe has ever seen."

"Shit," Jones responded with no great force. "There isn't one in a thousand of them would ever see the inconsistency. They'll cheer about the Sangaree going down, then go sign up for the war against these centerward creeps. Akido, you're giving Mr. Average Man too much credit. He can't even follow his credit balance, let alone weigh a moral one."

"Charlie, that attitude is going to destroy Luna Command. And when we go, Confederation goes. When Confederation goes, the barbarians come in. In the words of the Roman Centurion Publius Minutius, speaking of the legions, 'We *are* the Empire.' "

"Just a minute," Beckhart interjected. "Akido. Come over here." He pushed the comm across the desk. "Punch up the library and get me an abstract on this Minutius."

"Uh…"

"I thought so. Another one of your out-of-the-dark authorities."

Namaguchi chuckled. It was a favorite trick. His boss was the only man who caught him every time. "Actually, old Publius probably said something more like, 'Which way to the nearest whorehouse, buddy?' But I'll stake my reputation on the fact that some Roman soldier said it somewhere along the way. It was true. The army *was* the Empire."

"You don't have any reputation to stake, Akido," Jones quipped.

"The army got a lot of help from the fact that everybody in the provinces went along with a lot of tacit rules, Akido," Beckhart remarked. "We're getting off the subject. What about McClennon's report?"

"They're still working on it. First abstracts should be up any time now. The key thing we've gotten is that the Starfishers did go after Stars' End. So you guessed right on that one, too."

"I didn't guess. I had inside information."

"Whatever. That's where Storm came up with the Sangaree data. Raidships hit the harvestfleet there. They came out on the short end. The point is, the Seiners were sure they could pull it off. The battering the Sangaree gave them is what kept them from trying."

"How soon will those boys be done debriefing? I want to see them."

Silence hit that room like a cat jumping on a mouse. It stretched till it became an embarrassment.

"Well?"

"Uh..."

"Not one of your more endearing traits, Akido. I don't need protecting. Out with it. Who got hurt? How bad was it?"

"It's not that. Sir, they didn't come back."

"They're dead? How did they?..."

"They're alive. But they crossed over."

"They what?"

"Remember, McClennon was programmed for it."

"I know that. It was my idea. But he wasn't supposed to make a career out of it. He didn't de-program? What the hell was wrong with Storm? What's his story? Why didn't he bring Thomas out?"

"We're working on it, sir. Interrogating returnees. When we can lay hands on them. They scattered after they hit Carson's, before we knew we had a problem. Near as we can tell, Storm stayed behind because he didn't want to leave McClennon there alone. The programming must have broken down. McClennon asked to stay. They kept Storm from bringing him out."

"I see. That would be like Mouse. Don't leave your wounded behind. He's too much like his father. I knew Gneaus Storm. When you get to the bottom line, it was his sense of honor that got him killed. Well, I've got my honor too, even if it's a little discolored around the edges. I don't leave my wounded behind either. Akido, I want those boys brought out."

Jones snorted.

"Charles? What's biting your ass?"

"I was just thinking that anybody who cared as much about his troops as you put on wouldn't have thrown them back in the furnace before they'd cooled off from The Broken Wings. And you hit them with that one before they'd cooled off from..."

"Hey! Charlie, it's my conscience. I'm the one who's got to live with it."

"Storm could handle it. He didn't get the deep Psych-briefings. But McClennon... You probably overloaded the poor bastard. He was goofy at his best times."

"That's enough. Right now, right here, we finish crying about Storm and McClennon. That understood? We start figuring out how to get them back. And in our spare time we worry about the Four slash Six. And come bedtime, if you get tempted to waste time sleeping, start figuring how we're going to get a hammerlock on the Starfishers before they get their hands on Stars' End."

"Sir?" Namaguchi inquired.

"One of you clowns told me they were sure they could get in. You know what happens if they do?"

"Sir?"

"We bend over and kiss our asses good-bye. Because we're dead. We can hope, but we'll still be in the line to the showers."

"I don't follow your reasoning this time."

"You're not looking at the whole picture, that's why. The gestalt, if that's the right word. Look. If they get those weapons before we do, they can tell us to go pound sand and make it stick. We won't get control of ambergris production, meaning the Fleet will have to do without adequate instel communications, meaning its chances against those centerward things will go down to zit. They aren't your candy-ass Ulantonids, planning to give us a fair shake after they whip us."

"On the other hand," Namaguchi suggested, "if we get the Fishers under the gun in time, we'll not only be able to equip the Fleet, we'll have the potential of the Stars' End weaponry. Assuming it's adaptable."

"There," Beckhart told the others. "You see why Akido is the Crown Prince around here. You take a stick and whack on him long enough and he actually starts thinking. Let's do a little brainstorming, gentlemen. Along the lines of turning our liabilities into assets."

Jones suggested, "Regarding the Four slash Six paradox. The right leak of the right info at the right time at the right place might give Luna Command a public opinion base that would make the kill a matter of popular demand. There are some real pros in the Public Information Office. They've done a hell of a job creating a climate of trepidation with hints about trouble in the March. Suppose they let a little truth wriggle out now? Just enough so people start asking what kind of horror we're covering up by giving our friends from Ulant a bad press. There isn't anything the public won't swallow quicker than a good conspiracy theory. Especially a cover-up conspiracy."

Beckhart chuckled. "What is this? Two brains working in one room? At the same time? Gentlemen, that's a first. So. We've got a couple of things to work on. Will they let us orchestrate the show?"

"Why don't we just do it? It wouldn't be the first time."

"But it could be the last. We've reached a crossroads. We—and I mean everybody in Luna Command—are going to have to fine-tune the Luna Command machine. It won't have the internal tolerance for playing games with each other. We don't have much time to get ready for this centerward race… That plan is simple. We're going to hit them first, hit them hard, and keep hitting them with everything we've got."

"The way Ulant did us?"

"Exactly. The Prime Defender's General Staff is doing the planning, based on their intelligence. She'll modify it daily, keeping as close to the realtime situation as she can. We come up with something, it'll be programmed in. If the centerward crowd do something unexpected, that'll go in too. They've sent out a whole fleet of self-destruct equipped, instelled scout ships to keep track of what's happening."

"Sir, that strategy didn't work for Ulant before."

"It may not work this time, but it's the best shot we've got. Ulant's intelligence analyses paint a pretty grim picture. The numbers... You'll see the tapes. While you're watching, remember that you're only seeing one battle fleet. Ulant has identified another four. They just seem to skip from star to star behind a swarm of scouts, coming out the Arm, scouring every inhabited world of any sentient life." The comm hummed. Beckhart stabbed it with one finger. "Beckhart. Yes, sir."

The sound was uni-directional, the picture flat-faced television. The others could not hear, nor could they identify the caller. After listening awhile, Beckhart said, "Very well, sir," in an unhappy tone. He punched out.

"That was the C.S.N. They've decided to go with Four slash Six. But they're not going to let us run it. He said they'll use von Drachau, but R and D will have operational control."

"R and D? What the hell?"

"What have they got going over there? What don't we know?"

The comm hummed again. Beckhart answered, said, "This one's for you, Charlie."

Jones sat on the edge of the vast desk, turned the comm his way. "Go ahead." In a few seconds his tall, lean, black frame began quivering with excitement. "Good. All right. Thank you."

"Well?" Beckhart growled.

"One of my Electronic Intercept people. They just picked up a message from the Starfisher Council to Confederation Senate. Routine request for clearance to hold an ambergris auction. They asked for The Broken Wings. Usual rules and mutual obligations. The same request they send whenever they hold auction on a Confederation world."

"The Broken Wings is close to Stars' End. Any other reason to be excited?"

"Payne's Fleet is going to sponsor."

Beckhart stared at his hands for more than a minute. When he looked up his expression had become beatific. "Gentlemen, the gods love us after all. Cancel all leaves. Cancel any computation capacity loans we have out. Pass the word that we're going on overtime. Everybody, including the janitors and shredder operators. I've got a feeling we'll find a rose in this dungheap yet." He laughed demoniacally. "Eyes open and ears to the ground, gentlemen. Everything that comes in from now on—and I mean *everything*—goes into the master program for correlation. And have the programming teams start working backward. I want the biggest and best goddamned model outside the High Command Strategic Analysis. Let's see if we can't do this all up in one big, pretty package."

Beckhart departed his desk and unlocked his personal bar. He took out glasses and the half gallon of genuine Old Earth Scotch he saved for occasions of millennial significance. "A toast to successes and victories. Hopefully ours." He poured doubles.

# SIX: 3049 AD

## The Main Sequence

The five great harvestships barely moved. Their velocity relative to the debris was a scant three kilometers per hour. Gnatlike service ships flitted before the head and flanks of their line, nudging any flying mountain that threatened collision.

It was almost an embarrassment, the way those swift monsters of the spatial deeps had to crawl. Elsewhere they could have sprinted off and left light lagging like a toddler behind an Olympic runner. Here they could not match the pace of a lazily strolling old man.

Those battered survivors of Payne's Fleet had been making the passage for a week.

The dense boulder screen gave way to a less crowded region occupied principally by asteroidal chunks the size of small moons. The harvestfleet accelerated. The line dispersed.

"Well, you kept asking about the Yards," Amy told benRabi. "We're there." She indicated the viewscreen they had been watching.

"Yes, but…" All Moyshe saw was a big asteroid illuminated by *Danion*'s powerful lights. A few smaller boulders drifted around it. Not one star was visible in the background. All outside light was screened by the dust of the nebula.

*Danion* seemed to be stalking that big asteroid.

"But what?"

"There's nothing here. We're in the tail end of nowhere. I expected a hidden planet. Maybe even Osiris. Something First Expansion. Strange cities, drydocks…"

"Planetary docks? How could we take *Danion* into atmosphere? Or lift her out of a gravity well? Most of your Navy ships wouldn't try that."

"But you'd have to have thousands of people to work on a ship this big. Tens of thousands. Not to mention a hell of an industrial base, and one all-time grandfather of a drydock."

"The dock's right in front of you."

"What? Where?"

"Watch and see."

He watched. And he saw.

A gargantuan piece of rock began separating from the asteroid. In time it exposed a brightly lit interior vast enough to accept a harvestship. Diminutive tugs swarmed out. Some pushed the cork. Some hurried toward *Danion* like eager bees to a clover patch.

BenRabi saw a glow in the remote distance. Another asteroid was opening its stone mouth.

"We're going inside?"

"You got it. You catch on quick, don't you?"

"Smart mouth."

"They'll lock the door behind us. Then they'll flood the chamber with air. The work goes faster that way. And the dock will hide us from any snoopers who wander by."

"Who would come poking around in a mess like this? That would be asking to get fine-ground between those flying millstones."

BenRabi was less surprised by the existence of the nebula than by the Seiners' willingness to hazard it. Similar asteroidal shoals existed inside several dust nebulae.

"But they come anyway. Moyshe, this's the Three Sky Nebula."

"No. Not really? Yes. I guess you're serious."

One of the most dramatic actions of the Ulantonid War had occurred in the outer shoals of the Three Sky Nebula. After the war, the repatriated human survivors had circulated stories of having seen abandoned alien ships there. Some had been wrecks, some had appeared to be intact.

Three Sky had won an immediate reputation as a Sargasso of space. The treasure-seekers, xeno-archaeologists, and official investigators who went there hunting the alien ships were seldom seen again.

"The expeditions… There must have been fifteen or twenty that disappeared. What happened to them?"

"We interned them before they could stumble onto something and run home to report it. They're doing what they came to do. They just can't go home."

"Why risk setting up here if the traffic gets so heavy?"

"The risk isn't that big. We don't have visitors very often. Not when they always disappear. And, of course, it's such an unlikely place to look for us."

"Still… There's been talk at Luna Command, off and on, about sending a squadron to back up an investigation. In case it's McGraws or Sangaree that have been getting the others."

"If that happened, we'd fight. And we'd win. Only a fool would attack what we've made out of Three Sky. We've been here since before the Ulantonid War. That's a lot of time to get ready. It'd be almost like guerrilla warfare. We think we can hold off Confederation if we ever have to."

"I think you're a little over-optimistic. For people who don't have the muscle to duke it out with the sharks. I'll let you know for sure after I've looked things over."

"Why do you say that?"

"Because I haven't met a Seiner yet who had the least idea of just how big and strong Confederation is. Or how tough Luna Command can be when they put their minds to it. Or that your weapons systems are prehistoric relics. *Danion*'s got a ton of firepower, but one Empire Class battleship could carve this whole harvestfleet up like a side of beef and never get in a sweat."

"I think you're probably too impressed with your Navy. Our shortcomings were calculated into our defense plans."

BenRabi decided not to argue. Each of them was telling the truth as he or she knew it. "Are the creches here?"

"Some. All of them will be someday. It's a big job, civilizing a nebula."

"Mainly an engineering problem, I'd think."

"Yes. But it takes time and money. Especially money. We have to buy everything we can't manufacture ourselves. Which means we have to wait for the auctions because our credit is pretty slim."

"Ah. I begin to see why the good doctor was making do with primitive equipment."

"We've colonized more than seven thousand asteroids, Moyshe," Amy proudly declared. "But we've only just begun. They're all cramped. The harvestships are cramped. Our other hidden places are overcrowded. We've been taking in Confederation's dropouts for two hundred years. The ones who didn't become McGraws or run away to the outworlds."

Outworlds was a word as relative as *yonder*. For benRabi, born an Old Earther, it meant anything off Old Earth. Around Luna Command it meant any planet not one of the original seven founders of Confederation. Those seven usually called themselves The Inner Worlds. But out on the fringes of Confederation outworlds were human planets not signatory to the federal pact. BenRabi was unsure which meaning Amy wanted to convey.

"You didn't answer my question," he said. "Why here?"

"Because of the industrial advantages. The stories those internees took back were true. There's a lot of salvageable stuff here. We've identified over thirty thousand wrecks and abandoned ships. Built by seven different races."

"Really?" He ticked fingers. He could name five, not counting humanity. Six if he counted the prehistoric race that had built Stars' End. "I'll give you human and Ulantonid. From the war. Who were the others?"

"I thought you'd wonder why they'd be here."

He frowned at her. Was she trying to bait him by showing off her superior knowledge? Savoring one minuscule advantage? He knew more than she about almost everything and she seemed to take it as a personal affront.

"I imagine because it's a good place to lay an ambush. That's why *Carolingian* came here during the war."

Her smile shrank. "Yeah. And because it's close to the obvious space lanes. Moyshe, there've been battles here for ages. Probably for millions of years. Or even billions.

Except for the wrecks from the Ulantonid war, which I didn't even count, none of the ships here were built by any race we've ever met. They were all extinct before man ever left Old Earth. Or at least they were gone from this part of the galaxy. They all predate any of the races we have encountered."

"Ask the starfish about them."

"We did. We're not stupid. But they don't have much to tell. They don't pay any more attention to hard matter races than we do to bacteria. Less, really, because we're curious and they aren't. We're pretty sure one bunch of ships, though, belonged to a race that moved the ancestors of the Sangaree from Earth to wherever it is their homeworld is."

"Ah? Don't let Mouse know about that. He'll drive you crazy trying to get to them."

Only in this century had geneticists surrendered to the popular notion that Human and Sangaree sprang from the same root stock. The man in the street would not believe in a parallel evolution so similar that it could produce a being indistinguishable from himself. Scientists had demurred, citing no evidence on Old Earth for extraterrestrial intervention…

Then the abandoned alien base beneath the moon's dark side had been discovered. Some major rethinking had been necessary. Then had come confirmation of reports that the human female could, occasionally, be impregnated by the Sangaree male.

The most famous—or infamous—of Sangaree agents, Michael Dee, had been half human.

"Mouse will be protected from himself."

BenRabi studied her. She wore an oddly ferocious expression.

"Amy, I've been here almost fourteen months and you're still springing surprises on me. When are you going to run out?" He stared into the hollow asteroid and awaited her response.

"Moyshe, what happened to the people who built Stars' End?"

"We'll probably never know. Unless somebody cracks its defenses."

"We'll do that. We're going back. That was a rhetorical question."

"Wait a sec. Back? To Stars' End? After what happened? You're out of your minds. You're all raving lunatics."

She laughed. "Moyshe, they left their ships behind when they disappeared. Right here. God knows how many of them there are. Three Sky occupies a cubic light-year. We haven't explored a tenth of it. They had their yards and secret places too. Most of the ships we find were theirs. They were the people who transported the Sangaree, we think. We have explorers who don't do anything but hunt for their hideouts. Every one we find is one we don't have to build for ourselves."

He spoke to the engulfing maw in the viewscreen. "She's serious."

"Absolutely, darling. Absolutely. Oh, we're not really *sure* that it was the same race that did all three things. But the computers go with the probability. See, these are mostly good ships, Moyshe. They aren't derelicts. Some of them still have a little emergency power left. They try to scare us off with mind noises the way Stars' End does. And they have parts missing. Somebody took off all their weapons. I wish we had a whole army of xeno-archaeologists and anthropologists. It's really interesting. I always go see what they're working on whenever we come in. The scientists don't go very fast. They're mostly ones we captured, so they aren't real enthusiastic about helping us out. They train some of our people as aides, sometimes. Old folks and birth defect types who can't do much else."

"That don't make sense. People don't abandon good ships, Amy. Where did they go? Why? How? And if they did build Stars' End, *why*?"

She shrugged. "They weren't people, Moyshe. Not our kind. Don't judge their motives by ours."

"I wouldn't… though some ideas would seem universal. Just thinking questions out loud."

"The questions are why I wish we had more scientists." She switched the viewscreen over to a stern camera. *Danion* was well into the asteroid's interior. "They could be the same creatures that did the tunneling at Luna Command. But were they really? Is there a connection between the moon and Three Sky and Stars' End? Were we meant to find Stars' End and Three Sky? Is it all some kind of big puzzle that we're supposed to figure out? Is it a test?"

"You think they were planning to come back?"

"Who knows? The questions are all a hundred years old. The answers haven't been born. And if we ever do answer any of them, then right away we're going to ask three more.

"Anyway, those old ships are our main reason for being here. Some we fix up and use. They make good service ships. If they can be adapted. We scavenge some for materials to build harvestships. We only buy outside if we have to. Usually the Freehaulers make our purchases landside, for a commission, and make delivery to an asteroid at the edge of the nebula. They think it's just a way station. They don't ask questions. Too many questions is bad for business. They don't try very hard to follow us around, either. They're good people."

"Is that a cut?"

"If you think so."

"I suspected the Freehaulers. I know they had something to do with me and Mouse getting caught. How's chances of me getting to look at one of those ships? I know a little about xeno-archaeology."

A girl's face crossed his mind. Alyce. She had been his Academy love. She had been a recorder at the alien digs in the moon. She had taught him a little, and the Bureau had taught him more.

Sooner or later, the Bureau touched every base.

"You'll have to ask Jarl. I don't think he'll let you, though. We're going to be awful busy repairing *Danion*. Plus you've got your citizenship classes and your beer nights with Mouse."

"Now don't start that again. He's my friend, and that's the way it's going to stay. It don't hurt for him and me to play a couple of games of chess once in a while. You can come keep an eye on us if you think we're cooking up a plot against the Greater Seiner Empire, Lieutenant."

She ignored his sarcasm. "I don't feel like it. I always..." She stopped before she began waving the red flag. Their positions were inflexible. Argument would be pointless. "Moyshe, we've got to get *Danion* whipped into shape fast. The fleets are coming in. As soon as they're all here we're leaving for auction and another crack at Stars' End."

"Stars' End. Stars' End. That's all I hear anymore. And it's completely insane. We can't stick our necks in that noose again, Amy. Look what it cost last time. And remember, I was there too. I was outside with the starfish. I know what that planet can do."

"We've got to have those weapons, Moyshe. You saw the casualty reports. You saw the extrapolations. What the sharks are doing now is going to look pacifistic in ten years. We're talking survival, Love. And you're still thinking power politics."

"You'll just get yourselves killed."

"Either way, then. But we'll handle Stars' End. Honest. The fish really do know how to open the way. They found the key while we were there before."

"Huh?" He had not caught a hint from Chub. "The Sangaree, or Confederation..."

"They'd better come toting their guns if they want to steal it from us, Moyshe. Because they'll have a hell of a fight on their hands. There's a lot of us, honey. And we're looking for a fight. People have been pushing us ever since I can remember. We're tired of it. Once we get those weapons..."

"And sharks, darling. Don't forget the sharks. Oh, it's bound to be a gay party. How do I get transferred to a ground job?"

"You don't." She laughed. "I just heard a couple hours ago. You're going to be transferred to Security for the auction project."

She did not tell him that the auction project would be a pilot for a more ambitious program. If he and Storm performed well and faithfully they would be given joint chieftainship of their own espionage outfit. She did not think her own boss, Jarl Kindervoort, knew yet. The Ship's Commander seemed reluctant to discuss it with the man.

"Auction? That's Mouse's special haunt. How'd he get stuck with it, anyway?"

"It's going to be yours, too. Our new mindtechs will start coming aboard in a couple of days. And you'll move over to the project."

"Why?"

"Because you know The Broken Wings."

"Yeah. And I want to forget it." His previous mission, as a Bureau agent, had taken him to The Broken Wings. It had been a nasty affair.

"That's where the auction's going to be held. They already sent the permission request. It's just form from here on."

"Form? What you want to bet the place is crawling with Confies and Sangaree? You people stirred up some bad feelings…"

"She hit you pretty hard, eh?"

"What?"

"The woman. The Sangaree woman. That Marya Strehltsweiter."

"What? How did you?… Mouse. Shooting off his mouth."

"He didn't exactly volunteer it. And he told Jarl, not me. I found out when I was looking through the files for something else."

"All right." His heart hammered for no reason he could justify to himself. So he had gotten involved with the woman. He had not known she was Sangaree then. "It's over."

"I know. I knew that a long time ago. Mouse wrote that report after you shot her. I guess he thought it was important for Jarl to understand what you were going through."

That did not sound like Mouse. "She would've killed all of us. Sooner or later. I had to do it. I never shot anybody before."

"Especially somebody you still halfway cared about, eh?"

"Yeah. Can we drop it?"

"Did Mouse really do that? Inject her children with stardust?"

"Yes. Mouse plays for keeps. He doesn't have trouble with his conscience. Not the way I do."

"You really think the Sangaree will be at the auction?"

"They'll be there. They hold a grudge the way Mouse does. Amy, I don't want to get involved in that. I'm happy where I'm at. I like linking. Chub is a good friend. I was just scared there at first. I've been getting to know the other members of the herd… Hell, sometimes I go in just to bullshit with Chub."

BenRabi could relax with the starfish as he could with no human. He did not feel naked when he let the starfish see what he really felt and thought. Chub made no value judgments. His values were not human. He had, in fact, helped Moyshe make some small peace within himself.

Parts of his mind remained inaccessible to the starfish. Whole sections were hidden behind rigid walls. Moyshe could not guess what might lie there. He could sense nothing missing from his past.

Seiner life was changing Mouse, too, he reflected. Storm was becoming even more sure of himself, more bigger-than-life than he had always been. BenRabi could not pin it down. One or two nights a week playing chess together was not the same as sharing a minute to minute life under fire.

Mouse was an operative born. He had changed allegiance, but not professions. He had become part of Jarl Kindervoort's staff.

Flying easy. That was what benRabi had been doing since his release from the hospital. The only pressure he faced was Amy's near-militance in hinting about their getting married. Under Chub's ministrations his neuroses were scaling away. He had come to the Seiners with a great many.

"Not much more to see," Amy told him. The rearmost cameras were inside the asteroid. The tugs were guiding the cork back toward the entrance.

"What? Oh. I'd better go say good-bye to Chub."

He reached Contact almost as quickly as he had the day of the last battle. "Clara. Where's Hans?"

"He's off. We don't have anything going."

"I want to go in. They're telling me I'm going to be transferred."

"You can't. We're closed down, Moyshe. They'll be cutting power in a minute. Heck, the herd should be out of range by now."

"Clara, I probably won't ever get another chance."

"Ah, Moyshe. It's silly. But all right. Get on the couch." She prepared his scalp and the hairnet device in seconds. The helmet devoured his head almost before he could catch his breath.

He shifted to TSD, then onward.

The colors of the nebula were incredible. It was a dreary place to the eye, completely dark unless illuminated artificially. In this internal universe Moyshe could reach out and touch all the specks of it, the clouds of luminescent dust, the glowing asteroids majestically circling the nebula's center in their million-year orbits. He could even sense the protostar down in the nebula's heart, lying patiently in its time-womb, gathering the sustenance it would need to blaze for eons.

"Chub!" his mind shouted into the color storm. "Are you there? Can you hear me?"

For a time he thought there would be no answer. The herd lay far off the bounds of the nebula, beyond the pain threshold of its diminutive gravitation.

Then, "Moyshe man-friend? What is happening?"

The link was tenuous. He could barely discern the starfish's thoughts. He could not locate the creature with his inner sight.

"I came to say good-bye, Chub. They say I'm not going to be a mindtech anymore. You were right. They want me to go back to being what I was."

"Ah. I am saddened, Moyshe man-friend. I am saddened because you are sad. We have been good friends. I am pleased that you thought it important to let me know. So many linkers just disappear. Perhaps this last time we can break through those barriers, Moyshe man-friend."

But those corners of benRabi's mind would not yield.

"Moyshe." Clara's voice seemed to come from kilometers away. "They're going to shut the power off. You've got to come out."

"Farewell, Moyshe man-friend." BenRabi could feel the sadness in the starfish.

"Go softly, golden dragon," he whispered. "My heart flies with you down the long dark journey."

Chub's sadness welled up. Moyshe could not stand it. He pounded the switch beneath his left hand.

There was very little pain. He had not been under long. "I don't need it, Clara." He pushed the needle away.

"Moyshe. You're crying."

"No."

"But…"

"No. Just leave me alone."

"All right."

He heard the hurt in her voice. He struggled off of the couch, pulled her to him. "I'm sorry. Clara, I haven't known you very long. But you've been a good friend. I'll miss you. And Hans, too. Tell him to behave."

"I see that he does. He's my grandson."

"Oh. I didn't know." What had he heard about Hans's sister? Or was it mother? She had been lost with *Jariel.* Clara had never let on.

"There're a lot of things you don't know, Moyshe benRabi. About people. Because you never get around to asking."

"Clara… Clara, come visit. Will you?"

"Yes."

"Promise? Amy would love to meet you."

"I promise. Now get out of here before somebody calls the boss and wants to know what the hell's going on up here."

"Thanks, Clara. Thanks a lot. For everything."

His return trip was less precipitous. He was not eager to get home. Amy was bound to be waiting with some unimaginative new approach to the subject of marriage.

# SEVEN: 3049 AD

## The Main Sequence

"What's the occasion?" benRabi asked. He had come home to find Amy clad only in a negligee. She had been playing body games all week. He supposed she was holding out in hopes lust would make him propose. She was going to be disappointed. He was not seventeen.

The tactic did not bode well for their relationship. There was no future in any relationship where one party practiced extortion upon the other. No one endured that for long. And benRabi had had his fill of it from Alyce, way back when.

Was this why he was so reluctant? Because Amy came on like a spoiled child?

Why *did* he resist it? If he was to make a life here he had to surrender to the culture. This one had scant tolerance for prolonged bachelorhoods.

Older singles tended to get shoved beyond the social fringes. He was out there now. And Mouse, for all the charm he exuded, was slipping too. The ladies were not buzzing round so much anymore. He had made it too clear that he was available for good times only, not for long times and old-style fidelity.

If Amy was the best available, why not?

Part of it was habit. He had been a loner for too long, caught up in a profession where responsibilities to anyone else made a deadly liability. That was why, through mission after mission, he had fought his growing friendship for Mouse.

He had failed at that, and Mouse had too. They saw so little of one another nowadays… That was a pity. Just when they had given in to it, life had taken a twist and spun them along separate paths.

That would end with his transfer to Security, wouldn't it?

"There's a bright side to everything, I guess," he murmured.

Thinking about Mouse, he remembered their last evening together. He could have sworn Mouse had been hinting that he should do something about Amy. It was a damned conspiracy!

Why the hell would Mouse want him married? Mouse did not believe in the institution.

He should take the plunge. But not too soon. He could not let Amy get the idea that she could manipulate him.

He sat with his head in his hands, scurrying around the slot-tracks of an uncertain mind. The tracks did not always follow sane routes. There were moments when he did not know who or where he was. Sometimes he did not understand what was happening, or why. Sometimes he woke up thinking he was back on The Broken Wings, or in Luna Command. There had been a night when he had called Amy Max while they were making love… And a time when he had thought she was Greta… Frightening though they were, those had been isolated incidents. So far.

He and Amy made love fiercely, desperately.

She started getting dressed immediately afterward. "What's going on?" he asked.

"You forgot? We're supposed to have supper with the Sheik and his harem."

"One thing I'm going to tell you right now, woman. And you better understand it. That man's my friend. Learn to fly with it." He had forgotten the dinner. Completely. There wasn't a ghost of memory to be found anywhere in his head.

They joined Mouse and his shrinking clutch of dollies an hour later. BenRabi found his eye roving. Mouse had several honeys he would not mind topping himself. He dared not let Amy notice him looking. Any woman who got that jealous of a male friend…

This affair is headed for trouble, he thought.

Kindervoort appeared suddenly.

Jarl Kindervoort was a tall, lean man who reminded benRabi of Don Quixote, or the Pale Imperator in Czyzewski's novel, *His Banners Bright and Golden.* Like Amy, and most *Danion* Seiners, he was pale, blond, and blue-eyed. BenRabi liked him as a person and found him physically repulsive. It was a combination he did not comprehend.

He did not quite understand Kindervoort's position in the *Danion* scheme either. Kindervoort was, apparently, Amy's immediate superior. Amy was only a Lieutenant, a low-grade officer, yet her boss seemed to speak for *Danion*'s whole Security force. The ship had a population matching that of a fair-sized city. Could the police force be that small?

Kindervoort had high cheekbones and a lantern jaw. They gave him a death's head look. His pale eyes were seldom happy. He could have given Mouse lessons in cold stares. Yet he was a genuinely warm and caring person. He asked, "May I join you?"

"Sure, Jarl," Mouse said. "Glad to have you." Amy and benRabi nodded. Kindervoort settled down, plunged into his meal tray. He did not join the table banter. Neither did benRabi, though Amy brightened for a while and kept up with Mouse in a thrust and parry duel of the risqué and outré.

During his dessert Kindervoort asked, "You told him yet?"

"What? Oh. I forgot," Amy replied.

"Told me what?" benRabi asked.

"We're moving you to Security. Starting tomorrow. For the auction project."

"Oh. That. I know."

"Who told you?"

"I'm not stupid, Jarl. I may act it, but I'm a trained professional. I can see the signs and add the numbers."

"Ah. Exactly. That's why we want you on the auction thing. You're a professional. And you know The Broken Wings. Payne's Fleet has gotten the shove into the barrel this time. Payne thinks *Danion* should provide the protection for our auction crew. Off the record, I'd guess we get the auction because Gruber doesn't want any Payne people with him at Stars' End."

"What? Stars' End? Christ! I'm starting to hope a rogue singularity comes romping around and gobbles up that goddamned gun-runner's pyramid like a big fat chocolate cherry."

"Moyshe! What in the name of…"

"Jarl, you people are crazy. Every last one of you. I won't stand around on the steps of the Senate screaming 'Beware the Ides of March!' but only because none of you whackos have got the sense to listen. It's going to kill you. Can't you get that through your thick heads? But what do I care? You're only taking me down with you. All right. What do you want me on The Broken Wings for?"

"Security shift leader down in Angel City. Night shift. I picked your men already. I want you to start drilling them tomorrow. The feedback we get says it might get hairy."

"What'd I tell you?" benRabi told Amy. To Kindervoort, "At the risk of sounding inane, why me?"

"You and Mouse both. Because you know the city."

"Yeah. And he gets stuck with the other shift? Twelve hours at a crack. Wait. It's only nine on The Broken Wings, but that's bad enough, watch and watch with some guy around every corner waiting to burn you. You know what you're asking us to walk into?"

"What?" Kindervoort would not meet his eye. He knew.

"Mouse killed her kids. I shot her here. And you let her get away. She'll be there if she has to walk halfway across the galaxy. When she hears our fleet is going to handle it… It won't matter if she can get her people's okay. She'll come, Kindervoort. With every goddamned thing she can lay hands on. Come to think of it, the Heads will probably back her even if they don't like it. They're going to be damned hot about what happened to the raidfleet at Stars' End."

"Anything else bothering you, Moyshe?"

"What?"

"I'd like to hear all your objections now. So we can get them out of the way ahead of time."

"All right. Why trust me? I'm the man you caught leading Navy ships to your herd, remember?"

"Three points. One, you're a convert. I saw your test results. Two, the Ship's Commander recommended you. And the third I'd rather keep to myself."

BenRabi tried to remember all the tests he had taken, both before and after deciding to remain with the Starfishers. They had seemed standard, but he might have missed something. "Typical security-type job? Three hours' sleep and ten minutes for personals every day? Need them or not?"

"Probably." Kindervoort smiled.

His smile did not have the desired effect on benRabi. Moyshe saw it as grim, not friendly.

"Then I'd better settle my affairs. Because I don't expect to get through this one alive. I was going to put this off a few days. Mouse, want to be best man? Jarl, you can stand witness. Everybody's invited. I'll put on a party in my room afterwards. If we can come up with anything drinkable."

Nobody said anything for several seconds. Mouse stared blankly. Kindervoort managed to appear both surprised and amused. Mouse's girls just looked puzzled.

Amy showed a half dozen quick reactions. Lack of comprehension. Stunned disbelief. Shock. Distress that threatened to become anger. "It isn't fair," she murmured. She wanted a pompous, ostentatious Archaicist affair with all the splendor of old-time royal weddings. "You're making fun of me." Their friends knew how badly she wanted him to propose.

He had to reassure her quickly.

"Jarl, can we get it done now?"

"We could start in ten minutes if you're serious."

"Go ahead."

"Moyshe, that isn't fair!" Amy cried. "You never even asked me! And I'm not dressed for it and I haven't got anything to wear and…" She had a whole list of ands and buts. BenRabi and Kindervoort waited till she got them out of her system.

"Do I call or not, Amy?" Kindervoort asked.

"Oh!" She hit the table with her fists. "Yes! Yes, dammit! Call him. Moyshe benRabi, you are the meanest, connivingest man I've ever known. How can you do this to me?"

"Hey! You've been all over me about it…"

"Isn't love wonderful?" Mouse asked the air. Amy stopped bitching. Mouse had given her a look which warned her that she was pushing her luck.

The ceremony was not what she wanted. Moyshe kissed her and whispered, "If I get out alive, you'll have the real thing. The big one you want. That's a promise."

After the reception began, Kindervoort pulled Mouse and benRabi aside. "Finally got some word on that failsafer."

Back when the landside contractees had been boarding the service ship for return to Confederation a man had tried to kill them when it had become obvious that they were staying behind. He had suicided after missing. They had assumed he was a Bureau agent failsafing them.

"The autopsy finally got done," Kindervoort said. "He was Sangaree."

"Sangaree!" Mouse said it as if it were a swear word.

"Yes. And he did commit suicide. He was wearing a poison ring."

"Nobody killed him? There wasn't a second failsafer?" BenRabi shook his head. "That doesn't make sense."

"It didn't make sense when we thought there were two of them, and one got away," Mouse said. "Looks to me like he was Strehltsweiter's man, not the Admiral's. Makes sense in that context. She wanted us pretty bad."

"That's the way I figured it," Kindervoort said. "Till now I halfway thought it might have been a setup. To make you look more palatable. It doesn't look that obvious anymore. I'm confused, though. She was in intensive care all the time. Isolated. How did she make contact? How did she relay the order, even assuming the failsafer was pre-programmed? If you come up with any theories, let me know. I'd hate to think my own people helped her."

"Uhm." BenRabi glanced at Mouse.

Mouse shrugged. "I was sure he was Beckhart's."

"Ever heard of a Sangaree suiciding?"

"It happens. Borroway."

"Those were kids. They didn't have any other way out, and they knew too much."

"He had to be programmed."

"What's going on?" Amy demanded. "Consoling the victim, Mouse? You look like your best friend just died."

"We'll talk it out later, Mouse. No, we were just talking about something Jarl brought up. Sort of a puzzle. Let's dance, honey."

It was a zestless party. It did not last long. Neither did the honeymoon. Mouse dragged benRabi out early next morning.

"Hey. I'm supposed to be a newlywed."

"Come on. You been tapping it for eight months. Getting married didn't make it new. Jarl wants us. Time to go into training."

BenRabi spent the next fourteen hours talking about Angel City, studying maps, teaching the use of small arms in a coliseum cube that had been commandeered for the purpose.

His group consisted of twenty-five people. Mouse had another the same size. Mouse drilled his mercilessly in unarmed combat. His was the easier task. His students at least had some idea of what he was talking about.

BenRabi worked at it, but thought the Seiners were taking everything too damned seriously—despite his own admonition about how rough it could get.

He vacillated between a belief that they would find The Broken Wings hip deep in Sangaree and the opposing view, that Navy Security would be so tight that not one unfriendly would get through.

His fourth morning of teaching was interrupted by Kindervoort. "Moyshe. Sorry. Got to take you off this today. They've got a tour planned for citizenship applicants."

"Can't it wait? This auction won't, and these clowns are so bad they couldn't hurt themselves."

"I argued. I got shouted down. I guess they think it's important that you know what you're fighting for."

"Yeah? I never did before, and I did my job…"

"Oh. You're bitter today."

"Just frustrated. The more I see, the worse it looks. We're going to get hurt if this thing goes Roman candle, Jarl. We won't be ready."

"Do the best you can. That's all you can ever do, Moyshe."

"Sometimes that's not enough, Jarl. I want to do enough."

"Make a vacation out of today. Just relax. I don't think it's that important. They're supposed to show you what life's like for Starfishers who don't live on harvestships. Probably do you good to get away from Amy, too. I don't know what's the matter with her. She's even bitchy around the office anymore."

"You've known her longer than I have. You figure it out. You tell me."

Mouse stalked in. "You ready, Moyshe? I scrounged a scooter. Let's go before somebody liberates it back."

# EIGHT: 3049 AD

## The Contemporary Scene

Hel did not belong. It was a Pluto-sized twerp of a straggler planet which, like an orphaned puppy, had taken up with the first warm body it had come across.

When it did so, it set up for business too far from the unstable Cepheid it adopted. Even at perihelion in its lazy, eggy orbit it did not receive enough warmth to melt carbon dioxide.

Hel was a black eight ball of a world silver-chased by ice lying in the canyons of its wrinkled carcass. Its sun was but the brightest of the stars in its sky. No one would expect such a planet to exist, and no one would want to visit it if a suspicion of its existence arose.

Those were the reasons Confederation's Navy Bureau of Research and Development considered Hel the perfect site for a bizarre, dangerous, and ultra-secret research project.

Hel Station lay buried in a mountain like a clam in sand. Its appendages reached the surface at just two points.

The Station was not meant to be found.

"Ion?"

Marescu was a sight. His waistcoat was soiled, ragged, and wrinkled. His hose was bagged and falling. His wig was askew. His facial makeup was caked and streaked.

"Ion?" Neidermeyer said a second time, catching his friend's elbow. "You hear the news? Von Drachau is coming here."

Marescu yanked his arm away. "Who?" At the moment he did not give a damn about anything, Paul's news included. The agony was too much for mortal man to bear. He yanked a grimy silk handkerchief from a pocket, cleared the water from his eyes. Paul should not see his tears.

"Von Drachau. Jupp von Drachau. The guy who pulled off that raid in the Hell Stars a couple of years back. You remember. The commentators called him High Command's fair-haired boy. They talked like he'd be Chief of Staff Navy someday."

"Oh. Another one of your militarist heroes." Marescu could set in abeyance the worst blues for a good fight about the Services. "Fascist lackey."

Paul grinned, refused the bait. "Not me, Ion. I know you too well."

No fight? Marescu faded off into his internal reality. Damn her eyes! How could she have done it? And with that… that *blackamoor*!

"Hey. Ion? Is something wrong?"

More than normal? Ion Marescu was Hel Station's resident crank and grouch, its leading Mr. Blues and Vinegar. Most people shunned him unless work forced contact. He had one real friend, astrophysicist Paul Neidermeyer, a lady love named Melanie Bounds, and managed a certain strained formality with his boss, Käthe the Eagle. Everybody else was fair game for his vituperation.

"Von Drachau? He's Line, isn't he? Why would they tell a Line officer about this place? They planning on locking him up?"

"Ion. Man, what's wrong? You look bad. Why don't we take you down and get you a shower and a clean jumper?"

One of the curiosities of Ion Marescu was that he appeared to change personalities with his clothing. When he wore standard Navy work clothing he was almost tolerable. When he donned his Archaicist costume he became arrogant, argumentative, viper-tongued, and abnormally misty, as if half the time half of him truly did exist in eighteenth-century England.

Marescu paused before a mirror inset in the passage wall, ignoring the people trying to pass. "I do look a little ragged, don't I?" he muttered. He adjusted his wig, straightened the ruffles at his throat, thought, I wish this *were* Georgian England. I could call the bastard out. Settle this crap with steel.

But you would not have done that with a Negro, would you? You'd have gotten some friends together and played dangle the darky from a tree limb. If you could have stood the shame of confessing to your friends.

Marescu was not one of Hel Station's more polished Archaicists. The others had brought their costumes and research materials with them. He had taken up the hobby only after the isolation had begun to grind him down. He had sewn his own costume, with Melanie's help.

He was more devoted than most Station Archaicists. He prided himself on that, as he prided himself on his contrariness, his crotchets, and the perfection of his work with the test programs. He liked to think that he was the best at whatever he did—including at making himself obnoxious. He seldom noticed the compensatory sloppiness he expressed in his personal habits and hobby.

He had not researched his period thoroughly. He winged most of it. His hobby-era values and beliefs were based on hearsay.

There were those who thought the dichotomy between a perfectionist work life and slovenly play life, taken far too seriously, was indicative of deep disturbance. Admiral Adler disagreed. She felt Marescu was all showoff.

Marescu started walking. He had forgotten Paul. Neidermeyer seized his arm again. "Ion, if I can't help, who can? We've been friends for years."

"It's not something anybody can help with, Paul. It's Melanie. I got off shift early. The quark tube was acting up. The strange positives and bottom negs were coming off almost a milli-degree out of track. They couldn't inject them into their orbital shells… They shut down. She had Mitchell with her."

Neidermeyer murmured an insincere, "I'm sorry." He thought, so what? and wondered if Marescu was not getting a little too far out of touch. Maybe the staff psychologists should hear about this.

A man who started confusing the mores of now with those of his hobby period was more than a little unstable.

Ion always had been neurotic. Now he seemed to have become marginally psychotic.

"How could she do it, Paul?"

"Calm down. You're shaking. Follow me, my son. What you need is a little firewater to settle the old nerves. Eh! None of that, now. Doctor's orders. Drink up, then tell me about it and we'll scope something out."

"Yeah. A drink. Okay." Marescu decided to get blotted. "Tell me about this von Dago."

"Von Drachau. Rhymes with Cracow, like in Poland."

"Poland? Where the hell is Poland?"

"Where they raise the Chinese pigs." Neidermeyer grinned.

Marescu stopped walking. His thin little face puckered into a baffled squint. Seconds passed before the intuition that made him one of Confederation's better test programmers clicked. "The non sequitur game? We haven't played in ages, have we? Poland. Chinese pigs. Poland China hogs... Isn't that the strain they were talking about on that ag show the other day? They want to breed back to something extinct?"

"I don't know what they smell like."

"Okay, Paul. I'm all right now. Ease up. That was a weak one, anyway. Just give me the story on your mercenary hero."

Neidermeyer refused the challenge. "I don't know much. It's just something I overheard at Security. They were chasing their tails getting ready. Guess it took them by surprise. We're here. What're you drinking?"

They stepped off the escalator into soft luminescence just bright enough to prevent stumbling over furniture.

The lounge had been designed to give an impression of being open to Hel's surface. Its protective dome was undetectable. The lighting was too diffuse to glare off the glassteel. The dome itself pimpled from the flank of a mountain, overlooking dark peaks and cruel gorges. The Milky Way burned above, a billion-jeweled expanse of glory.

"Ever notice how it seems colder up here?" Marescu asked, for at least the hundredth time in their acquaintance. He stared out at the poorly illuminated skin of the dead world. The inconstant Cepheid sun hung behind a peak, limning it with a trace of gold. In its off moments that sun was little more noticeable than the brighter neighboring stars. "You pick it, Paul. I'm not particular today. But build it big."

Neidermeyer collected brandy and glasses from behind the bar. "Francis must have gone down for the Security festival," he said. A Marine with an unpronounceable Old Earther name, dubbed Francis Bacon by the research staff, usually tended bar. Security had very little to do most of the time, so filled time by trying to make the Station more endurable for everyone.

People came to Hel on a one-way ticket. Only the Director of Research and Chief of Security ever ventured off world. For security reasons there was no instel comm system available. Isolation was absolute.

"Brandy?" Marescu asked, startled. Paul was a whisky man.

"Old Earth's best, Ion. Almost makes being here worthwhile."

Marescu downed half a snifter at a gulp. "They ought to turn us loose now, Paul. We built their damned bombs. All we're doing now is piddling around with make-work."

"They won't, though. Security. Won't be any leaks as long as they keep us here."

"Paul, how could she?"

"You knew she was..."

"When I got involved? I know. I keep telling myself. But that doesn't make it hurt any less, Paul."

"What can I tell you?"

Marescu stared into his empty snifter.

"Ion... Maybe you ought to ease up on the Archaicist thing. Try to get your perspective back."

"The modern perspective sucks, Paul. You know that? There's no humanity in it. You probably laugh at me because of this outfit. It's a symbol, Paul. It's a symbol of times when people did have real feelings. When they cared."

"I've got feelings, Ion. I care about you. You're my friend."

"You don't. Not really. You're just here because having feelings bothers you."

Neidermeyer glared. There were times when being Ion's friend was work. Marescu refused to apologize. Paul took his brandy to the side of the dome. He stared at the indistinct hide of Hel. The critical question glared back from the serpent eyes of his own weak reflection.

Should Marescu be reported? Was he that far gone?

Nobody wanted to turn in a friend. The Psych people could lock him up forever. Their zoo of Hel-born mental mutations was a blue-chip growth industry.

The project was too delicate to risk its compromise by the unbalanced.

But the production team needed Ion. Nobody had his sure, delicate touch with the test systems. Best let it ride and hope he would come around. This thing with Melanie could be a positive if it jarred him back to reality.

Paul turned. He looked at a thin, short, weary little man who had a thousand years etched into his face and a million agonies flaring from his narrow little black eyes. Right decision? Those eyes were lamps of torment backfired by incipient madness.

Something rattled the foundations of the universe.

The snowy landscape glowed a deep, bloody red. The glow faded quickly.

Marescu turned an ashen color. He stumbled to the dome face, caressed it with shaking fingers. "Paul... That was damned close. They could have destabilized one of the test cores. We'd have been blown into the next universe."

Fear had drained Neidermeyer's face too. He mumbled, "But nothing happened."

"I'm complaining anyway. They ought to have better sense." Feeling the breath of the angel on his neck had snapped his streak of self-pity.

He stared into the darkness outside. A pale new light had begun etching the shadows more deeply. One brilliant point of light slid across the screen of fixed stars, growing more intense.

"They're coming in fast."

Hel's surface was screaming under a storm of violet-white light when the dome polarized. The glass continued to respond to the light beating against it, its inner surface crawling with an iridescence like that of oil on water.

"Doctor Neidermeyer? Mister Marescu? Excuse me a moment."

They turned. Marine Major Gottfried Feuchtmayer stood at the escalator's head. He was Deputy Chief of Security, and a man who appeared to have just stepped out of a recruiting commercial. He was the quintessential Marine.

"Bet he wakes up looking like that," Marescu muttered.

"What is it, Major?" Neidermeyer asked.

"We need your assistance in the arsenal. We need two devices for shipboard installation."

Marescu's stomach went fluttery. The butterflies donned Alpine boots and started dancing. "Major..."

"Briefing in Final Process in fifteen minutes, gentlemen. Thank you."

Neidermeyer nodded. The Major descended the escalator.

"So," Marescu snapped. "They'll never use it, eh? You're a fool, Paul."

"Maybe they won't. You don't know... Maybe it's a field test of some kind."

"Don't lie to yourself. No more than you already are. The damned bomb doesn't need testing. I already tested it. They're going to blow up a sun, Paul!" Ion's mouth worked faster and faster. His voice rose toward a squeak. "Not some star, Paul. A sun. Somebody's sun. The goddamned murdering fascists are going to wipe out a whole solar system."

"Calm down, Ion."

"Calm down? I can't. I won't! How many lives, Paul? How many lives are going to be blasted away by those firecrackers we've given them? They've made bloody fools of us, haven't they? They suckered us. Smug little purblind fools that we are, we made ourselves believe that it would never go that far. But we were lying to ourselves. We knew. They always use the weapon, no matter how horrible it is."

Paul did not respond. Marescu was reacting without all the facts. And saying things everyone else thought but did not say.

For the research staff, service at Hel Station had been a deal with the devil. Each scientist had traded physical freedom and talent for unlimited funding and support for a pet line of research. The Station was ultra-secret, but the knowledge it produced was reshaping modern science. The place seethed with new discoveries.

All Navy had asked for its money was a weapon capable of making a sun go nova.

Navy had its weapon now. The scientists had scrounged around and found a few Hawking Holes left over from the Big Bang, had pulled a few mega-trillion quarks out of a linear accelerator which circumscribed Hel itself, had sorted them, had stacked them in orbital shells around the mini-singularities, and had installed these "cores" in a delivery system. The carrier missile would perish in the fires of a star, but the core itself would sink to the star's heart before the quark shells collapsed, mixing positives and negatives in a tremendous energy yield which would ignite a swift and savage helium fusion process.

Navy had its weapon. And now, apparently, a target for it.

"What have you done, Paul?"

"I don't know, Ion. God help me if you're right."

The passageways were a-crawl with Marines. Marescu swore. "I didn't realize there were so many of the bastards. They been breeding on us? Where's everybody else?" The usual back and forth of technical and scientific staffs had ceased. Civilians were scarce.

At Final Process they were told to report to the arsenal instead.

They found three civilians waiting outside the scarlet door. The Director, though, was an R & D admiral in civilian disguise.

"This's a farce," Marescu growled at her. "Two hundred comic opera soldiers..."

"Can it, Ion," Paul whispered.

The Director did not bat an eye. "They're watching you, Ion. They don't like your mouth."

Marescu was startled. Ordinarily, even the Eagle did not bite back.

"What's going on, Käthe?" Neidermeyer asked.

Marescu grinned. Käthe Adler. Käthe the Eagle. It was one of those nasty little jokes that drift around behind an unpopular superior's back. Admiral Adler had a thin wedge of a face, an all-time beak of a nose, and a receding hairline. Never had a birthname fit its bearer so well.

"They're taking delivery on the product, Paul. I want you to work with their science officers. Ion, you'll prepare a test program for their shipboard computers."

"They're going to use it, aren't they?" Marescu demanded.

"I hope not. We all hope not, Ion."

"Shit. I believe that like I believe in the Tooth Fairy." He glanced at Paul. Neidermeyer was trying to believe. He was like all the science staff. Keeping himself fed on lies.

"Ship's down, Major," a Marine Lieutenant announced.

"Very well," Feuchtmayer replied.

"We'd better get lined out," the Director said. "Paul, pick whomever you want to help. Ion, you'll have to visit the ship to see what you'll be working with. I want your preliminary brief as soon as you can write it. Josip, get with their Weapons officers and draw up the preparatory specs for carrying mounts and launch systems. Have the people in the shops drop everything else."

Josip asked, "We have to build it all here?"

"From scratch. Orders."

"But..."

"Gentlemen, they're in a hurry. I suggest you get started."

"They brought the whole ship down?" Paul asked. Ships seldom made planetary landings.

"That's right. They don't want to waste time working from orbit. That would take an extra month."

"But..." That was dangerous business. The ship's crew would stay crazy-busy balancing her gravity fields with the planet's. If they made one mistake the vessel would be torn apart.

"It shouldn't take more than twelve days this way," Admiral Adler speculated. "Assuming we hit no snags. Let's go." She pushed through the red door.

The completed weapons had a sharkish, deadly look, looking nothing like bombs. The four devices were spaced around the arsenal floor. Each was a lean needle of black a hundred meters long and ten in diameter. They were longer than the shuttle craft intended to lift them to orbit. Antennae and the snouts of nasty defensive weapons sprouted from their dark skins like scrub brush from an old, burned slope.

They were fully automated little warships. The essentials of the nova bomb occupied space that would have been given over to crew in manned vessels. They were fast and shielded heavily enough to punch through a powerful defense.

The weapon remained largely theoretical. But the men who had created it were confident it would function.

Neidemeyer whispered to Marescu as they donned working suits, trying to convince his friend, and himself, that they were just gearing up for a field test. "I'm sure the money people just want to see if they're getting any return on their investment," he insisted. "You can't blame them for wanting to try their new toy."

"Yeah. Our hero von Drachau is going to take potshots at a couple of insignificant stars. Right?"

"Right."

"You're a fool, Paul."

A band of strangers entered the arsenal. They stared at the four dark needles, clearly awed and a little frightened.

"That's von Drachau on the right," Paul whispered. "I recognize him from the holo. Only he looks a lot older."

"Looks a little grey around the gills, I'd say."

Von Drachau did look depressed. He spoke with the Major and Käthe Adler. Käthe led his party around one of the missiles. Von Drachau became more impressed.

There was something about the big, terrible ones that excited a resonance in the soul. It was almost a siren call. Marescu felt it himself each time he touched one of the monsters. He was ashamed of himself when he did.

"Little boys play with firecrackers, and big boys play with bombs," he muttered.

"Ease up. Käthe meant it when she said they're watching you. Feuchtmayer isn't one of your big fans, Ion."

"I'll stay out of his way."

The days whipped past. Technicians swarmed over the pair of weapons von Drachau selected. Marescu tested systems and supervised the installation of special shipping aids. Josip brought the missiles' computation systems into communion with the battle computers aboard von Drachau's ship. Technicians designed and installed adapters and links that would fit the securing rings and launch vanes going onto the belly of the warship.

Neidermeyer prepared a manual for the science officers responsible for arming the sunkiller and monitoring its gluon pulse in passage, watching for that tiny anomaly that might forecast the expansion of a quark shell into disaster.

Marescu could not believe there was so much to do. His shifts were long and demanding. He felt a lot of sympathy for Paul, whose personal research project seemed threatened with death by inattention.

Neidermeyer watched his friend more closely than he did the gluon pulse, hunting some telltale psychological anomaly. Marescu seemed almost too much in control, and had thrown himself into his work with a near-fanaticism that bespoke a very fragile stability fighting its last stand. Yet there were positive signs. Ion had shed the filthy Archaicist outfit. He had begun devoting more time to his personal appearance…

Then it was over.

Käthe Adler joined them in the lounge. "Let the firewater flow," she proclaimed. "It's time to say the hell with it and turn loose of the brass ring for a while."

Marescu gave her an odd look.

The celebration became a premature New Year's bash.

The pressure was off. The antagonisms went on the shelf for the day. Guilts got tucked away. Scientists and technicians made shows of comradeship with the Marines. A handful of von Drachau's officers joined in, drinking lightly, listening to the jokes but seldom laughing.

"For them it's just begun," Ion murmured. He glanced around. No one had heard him.

Von Drachau was a focus of brooding gloom. He seemed to have sunk two-thirds into another universe. Ion watched him glare at Paul as if Neidermeyer were some small, venomous insect when Paul tried to strike up a conversation about the raid in the Hell Stars. Von Drachau disappeared only minutes later.

"Don't think you made an impression, my friend," Ion said.

Käthe agreed. "He's sensitive about it, Paul. He's a strange one. You should have heard the row he and Ion had."

Marescu met Paul's gaze. "It wasn't any big thing. I came on a little too strong, that's all."

"What was it?" Neidermeyer asked.

"About the morality of using the weapon," Käthe said. "Von Drachau is damned near a pacifist. Ion was pretty shook when he found out the man could adapt his convictions enough to let him use the weapon."

"Ion's problem is that he's an absolutist. He's got to have everything black or white. And he's getting worse. Is there any way we can get him into therapy without having him committed?"

"You think there's a reason to worry? His profiles keep coming up off-center, but they never show any danger."

"Sometimes. Lately… He's got a creepy feeling to him. Except for that argument with von Drachau, he's swung too far away from what he was. I'm nervous about the backswing. Like I can hear the timer clicking. He might break loose going the other way."

They had begun talking about Marescu as if he were not around for the very good reason that he was not, though neither of them had consciously marked his departure.

Käthe Adler had called von Drachau a crypto-pacifist, and Marescu had seen red. Literally. The dome and people went raggedly, liquid, and red. Then it was all clear. All perfectly clear. He had to go see Melanie and explain.

He was walking down a passageway. Time seemed to have passed. He had the distinct feeling that his head was on sideways. That mercenary von Drachau… The man had kicked the foundations out from under him. A flexible morality? How could there be such a thing? A thing was either right, or it wasn't. The nova bomb was the most evil thing yet conceived by the military mind. And he had helped midwife that evil into this universe. He had allowed himself to be seduced… He had whored himself…

There had to be a way to show them what they were doing.

He shook his head violently. Things were foggy. A band seemed to be tightening around his temples. There was something wrong. He could not force his thoughts into a straight line.

For an instant he considered finding a Psych officer.

Von Drachau seemed to laugh at him again.

"You fascist bastard!"

Christ! Some Torquemada had taken another turn on the strap. His skull was creaking with the pressure.

"Where am I?" he blurted. His feet had been moving without conscious direction. He tried to concentrate on his surroundings. "What am I doing here?"

He wanted to turn and go back. His feet kept going in the direction he was headed. His hand pushed on Melanie's door.

He was an alien, a passenger aboard a body under another's control. He was a slightly panicky observer of actions being carried out by another creature.

The little gasps and grunts lashed that devil, punishing it like a wizard's curse. He stared at the eight-limbed, twenty-toed beast. It heaved and lunged. Its four blind eyes rolled swiftly. Its three uncontrolled mouths made wet, hungry sounds.

The Ion of him silently screamed and turned inward, refusing to see any more. A darkness closed round it.

A clumsy puppeteer jerked him around, dragged him out the door and down the passageway with jerky, meandering, drunken steps. When next the Ion rider surfaced it found its steed in the arsenal, clad in its Georgian, bent over the computer board in the heavily shielded test control kiosk. The clock claimed that hours had vanished from his life. His hands and fingers were flying, a pair of pale white dancing spiders.

They were doing something dreadful. He did not know what, and they would not stop when he commanded them. He watched them like a baffled child watching slow death.

An image here, an image there, surged into his mind, playing back fragments of the missing hours. Ion Marescu crawled over a long black needle. Ion Marescu crouched beneath the needle, connecting the heavy cables that ran to the test station. Ion Marescu squeezed through the cramped interior of the black ship, removing safety chips…

"Ion?"

Paul's voice barely penetrated the thick stressglass of the booth's walls. He was screaming. Ion realized the yelling had been going on for a while. He glanced at Paul puzzledly, barely recognizing him. He did not stop working. This was the most important test he had ever run. For the first time in his life he was doing something of real worth. He had found himself a holy mission.

What was it? He shook his head, tried to clear the mists. They would not go.

His hands danced.

Käthe Adler joined Paul. They pounded the unbreakable glass with their fists. Then the woman fled. Paul grabbed a fire axe and swung away.

When Ion next glanced up, the vast arsenal floor was a-crawl with Marines. Major Feuchtmayer had his pale face pressed against the glass directly in front of him. His lips writhed obscenely. He was screaming something. Ion had no time to listen. He had to hurry.

What the hell was going on out there? the observer part of him wondered.

He finished programming the test sequences.

Each weapon had to be run through a simulated plunge into Hel's own sun. Ion usually performed the test series on a system-by-system basis, with the drive never operational and the safety chips preventing the weapon from going active. "How do we know the drive will work?" Marescu muttered. "We just take their word for it?"

Paul and the Marines stopped trying to break the glass with hand tools. Ion saw the Major laying a sticky grey rope of something round the door frame.

"Plastic explosives? My God! What are those madmen trying to do?"

His right hand depressed the big black palm switch that opened the arsenal's huge exit doors. It was through those very doors that that hired assassin von Drachau had moved his two missiles to his ship.

People flung in all directions as the arsenal air burst into Hel's eternal night. Baffled, Marescu watched their broken doll figures tumble and bloat.

His left hand danced, initiating the test sequences. The arsenal drowned in intense light. The stressglass of the booth polarized, but could not block it all. The sabotaged holding blocks fell away from the number four weapon. It dragged itself forward, off its dolly. It flung off clouds of sparks and gouged its spoor deep into the concrete floor.

"Wait a minute," Ion said. "Wait a minute. There's something wrong. It's not supposed to do that. Paul? Where did you go, Paul?" Paud did not answer.

The black needle, its tail a stinger of white-hot light, lanced into the night, dwindled. The little star of it drifted to one side and downward as its homing systems turned its nose toward the target.

"What's happening?" Marescu asked plaintively. "Paul? What went wrong?"

The eye of the black needle fixed itself on Hel's sun. It accelerated at 100 g.

And in the booth, where the atmospheric pressure had begun to fall, Ion Marescu realized the enormity of what he had done. With a shaking hand he took a suggestion form from a drawer and began composing a recommendation that, in future, all test programs be cross-programmed in such a way that the activation of any one would automatically lock out the others.

"We have influence, Commander," Lieutenant Callaway reported.

"Take hyper," von Drachau replied. "And destroy that Hel astrogational cassette as soon as you have her in the hyper arc. For the record, gentlemen, we've never heard of this place. We don't know anything about it and we've never been here."

He stared into a viewscreen, slumped, wondering what he was, what he was doing, and whether or not he had been told the whole truth. The screen went kaleidoscopic at the instant of hyper-take, then blanked.

Seventeen minutes and twenty-one seconds later the sun of the world he had just fled felt the first touch of a black needle. The little manmade gamete fertilized the great hydrogen ovum. In a few hours the nova chain would begin.

There would be no survivors. Security allowed no ships to remain on Hel. The Station personnel could do nothing but await their fate.

And nowhere else did there exist one scrap of information on the magnificent, deadly weapon created at Hel Station. That, too, had been a Security-decreed precaution.

# NINE: 3049 AD

## The Main Sequence

Mouse drove down to the same departure station that had witnessed the Sangaree failsafer's suicide. A half dozen bewildered former landsmen were there already. He and benRabi were last to arrive. All but one of the others were women.

"They haven't shown yet, Ellen?" Mouse asked.

"No. Did you hear anything? You know what it's about?"

"Not really."

BenRabi tuned them out. He walked through those last few minutes before Kindervoort's men had come to disarm Mouse and he had walked into the failsafer's line of fire. He went to the spot where he had been standing, turned slowly.

"Jarl was here. Mouse was there. Bunch of people were there... They brought Marya's intensive care unit down that way, before Jarl showed, and took her right into the service ship."

He walked through it three times. He could not recall anything new. He had been distracted at the time. He had believed that Mouse was shanghaiing him, and had not wanted to leave. Then Jarl had distracted him...

"Hey, Mouse. Walk through this with me. Maybe you can think of something."

A scooter rolled into the bay. A pair of unfamiliar Starfishers dismounted. "You the citizenship class?" the woman asked.

"Hello there," Mouse said, like a man who had just crossed a ridgeline and spied all seven cities of Cibola.

The woman stepped back, her eyes widening.

"Must be Storm," the man said. "My wife, Mister Storm."

"Well... You win some, lose some. You don't know till you try."

"I suppose not. All right. Let's check the roll, then get started. Looks like we're good. We've got the right number of heads. All right. What we're going to do is leave the ship through the personnel lock and line over to one of the work bays on one of the mooring stays. There's zero gravity in the work area so you don't have to worry about falling. Follow me."

He went to a hatchway, opened it, stepped through. The future Seiner citizens followed.

Mouse tried hanging back, to get nearer to the woman.

BenRabi gouged his ribs. "Come on. Let her alone."

"Moyshe, she's driving me crazy."

"She's prime. Yes. And married, and we don't need any more enemies."

"Hey. It isn't sex. I mean, she's fine. Like you say, prime stuff. What I'm saying, though, is this is our shot at somebody from outside."

"What're you talking about?"

"She's not from *Danion.*"

"How the hell do you know that?" BenRabi ducked through the third of the lock doors. "You've maybe been around the world here, but I don't think you've gotten to them all. Not yet. We haven't run into a hundredth of *Danion*'s people."

"But the ones we have all came from the same mold. Oh, Christ!"

BenRabi slithered out of the ship. He stood on her skin, offering Mouse a hand. In both directions, as far as he could see, were tubes, cubes, spars, bars... Hectare on hectare of abused metal. Overhead, the laser-polished stone of the asteroid arched in an almost indiscernible bow. *Danion*'s outermost extremities cleared it by a scant hundred meters.

Those hundred meters had Mouse petrified.

Mouse was scared to death of falling. The phobia usually manifested itself during a liftoff or landing, when up and down had a more definite meaning.

"You all right?"

Storm was shaking. Sweat beaded his face. He shoved a hand out the hatch, twice, like a drowning man clawing for a lifeline.

The others were hand-over-handing it along a cable spanning the gap between ship and asteroid.

"Come on, Mouse. It won't be that bad." How the hell had he gotten through all the e.v.a. exercises and small boat drills they had had to endure in Academy?

Mouse's phobia perpetually astonished benRabi. Nothing else fazed the man. Whining bullets and crackling lasers simply created the background noises of his work...

His work!

"Assassin's mind, Mouse. Go into assassin's mind." The state approximated a meditational trance, except that while he was in it Mouse was one of the most deadly men who ever lived.

Was he too much out of practice?

Mouse's shaking slowly subsided. His eyes became glassy.

"All right," benRabi said. "Come on. Slow. Take the handholds and work your way over to the line. That's good. Good. Now across to the balcony."

Moyshe spoke softly, without inflection. In this state Mouse had to be handled gently. Anything could set him off. Anyone not programmed in as Friendly could get broken up pretty bad.

The woman instructor overtook benRabi on the line. "What's wrong with your friend?"

"He's an acrophobe."

"A Navy man?"

"I know. Be real careful for a few minutes. Keep the group away. He's not very stable right now."

He got Mouse onto the balcony, with his back to the vast mass of the ship, and talked him down. In five minutes Storm was asking, "You ever meet anyone on *Danion* who wasn't blond with blue eyes?"

"Some. Not many."

"Anybody with black blood?"

"No."

"I rest my case." Mouse surveyed the harvestship. "Damn, she took a beating."

"Huh?"

"Different perspective, Moyshe. It's not up and down from here."

BenRabi scanned the battered ship. "Mouse, I think we've been set up."

"What?"

"I thought it was a little weird, coming out the way we did. I was going to ask the lady why they didn't have something better." He pointed with his chin.

A half kilometer away a telescoping tubeway connected the ship with the rock face. BenRabi soon indicated a half dozen more connections. Each was large enough to use to drive heavy equipment onto and off the harvestship.

"Think they're just working on you and me? Or the whole group?"

"Fly easy," benRabi suggested.

"It's my ass in a sling, Moyshe. I'll be your basic model of decorum."

"Are these two part of a plan?"

"Take it for granted. The question is, was it supposed to be obvious? Or are they just clumsy?"

"To quote a certain Admiral, who used to tell us what to do, 'Just lay back in the weeds and let them show their hand.' He was good at mixing metaphors."

"How's the writing going, Moyshe?"

They turned to follow the Seiner couple, who were shooing the others into a tunnel.

"I haven't written a page in months. I don't know why."

"Time?"

"That's part of it. But I always found time before."

Atop all his other hobbies, benRabi dabbled at writing short fiction. Traveling to Carson's from Luna Command, an eon ago, he had looked forward to the Starfisher mission as a vacation operation during which he could get a lot of work done. He had expected to stay a maximum of six weeks. The Admiral had promised… A year had passed, and he had completed one dreary story, the manuscript of which he had not seen in months.

Once they departed the central hollow of the asteroid they entered local artificial gravity. There was little visible difference between ship and shore.

"Oh, boy!" Mouse said. "More brand new same old thing. This is going to get boring in a few years, Moyshe."

"Sorry you decided to stay?"

Mouse eyed him momentarily. "No." His expression became a little strange, but benRabi paid it no attention.

"Look, Mouse. Kids. I haven't seen any kids since we left Luna Command."

"Hooray."

"Come on, man. Look at that. Must be some kind of class tour."

Twenty little girls around eight years old were giggling along behind an old man. The old man was explaining something in a crackling voice. Several of the girls were aping him behind his back. Some of the others were making faces at the mockers.

"Call me back in ten years," Mouse said. "I got no use for them till they get ripe."

"You have got to be the sourest…"

"It some kind of crime not to like kids? Speaking of which, I never saw you get along with any but Jupp's boy and that Greta. And she was sixteen going on twenty-six."

Jupp von Drachau had been their classmate in Academy. He was now High Command's special errand boy. He had helped with their operation on The Broken Wings. Later, it had been his assignment to provide the firepower when it had come time to seize Payne's Fleet. They had thought. His premature approach and detection had left them stranded for the full year they had contracted to work for the Seiners.

"Horst-Johann. I didn't see him last time we were in Luna Command. That's two years ago now. Damn, time flies. Bet he's grown half a meter."

Their male guide said, "People, we'll lunch in one of the worker's commons before we show you a typical creche. Don't be shy. Visit. People here are as curious about you as you are about them. We'd appreciate it if you'd stay close, though. If one of you gets lost, we'll both have trouble explaining."

"Great," Mouse said. "Still more brand new same old thing. Doesn't anybody ever eat anywhere but in these goddamned cafeterias? I'd sell my soul for a go at a decent kitchen on my own."

"You cook?"

"I'm a man of myriad talents, Moyshe. Think that's what I'll do when we hit The Broken Wings. Figure out how to make myself a home-cooked meal. And devour it in private. Not out in the middle of a goddamned football field with five thousand other people."

"You've got one classic case of the crankies this morning, my friend."

"I didn't get any last night. Besides, I'm not patient with crap, and this whole field trip is main course horseshit without the hollandaise."

The commons was as predictable as Mouse feared. So was the food. The conversation did not sparkle either, till Mouse took the offensive. "Grace, what's the point of this exercise?"

"I don't understand your question, Mister Storm."

Moyshe grinned behind his hand. The woman was sensitive to that overpowering Mouse charm. She had become as decorous as a schoolteacher by way of compensation.

"This bullshit exercise. You dragged us away from work we don't have time to get done right anyway. You run us out on a goddamned wire, then walk us all to hell and gone when we could have done the whole thing on a bus. You tell us we're going to see how Seiners live when they're not in the fleet, but you just show us the same old stuff. And since you've only kidnapped us for today, you're not really serious about showing us anything. I mean, an idiot would realize that it would take weeks just to skim the surface of a civilization like yours."

The woman's dusky face darkened with embarrassment.

"I mean, here we sit, eight former landsmen, all with that much figured out, and all of us on our best behavior figuring it's some kind of test or someone wants us off *Danion* for a while… Whichever, it's dumb. You're wasting our time and yours."

"Mister Storm…"

"Don't mind him," Moyshe interjected. "It's old age creeping up on him. He's not as tolerant of games-playing as he used to be."

Mouse grinned and winked. BenRabi grinned back.

Their guides surveyed the other landsmen. They said nothing, but aggravated agreement marked each of their faces.

"There's no point in going ahead, then," the male guide said. "Your response is data enough. Finish your meals. I'll be right back." He disappeared.

"What *is* the point?" benRabi asked.

Grace shrugged. "I just work here."

"Psychologist?"

She was startled. "How did you know?"

"I can smell them. You really married to him?"

"No." She laughed weakly. "He's my brother."

"Ooh." Mouse said it softly. Only Moyshe heard.

"You swallow something radioactive, Mouse?"

"What?"

"You just started glowing."

The lady psychologist was not immune. Mouse wangled a date before her brother returned. BenRabi did not doubt that Mouse would make the date an interesting experience.

He could not fathom Mouse's method. Even knowing they were being manipulated, knowing Mouse's reputation, women walked right in. Indeed, Mouse's reputation seemed to make him more interesting.

Their guide returned. He deposited his half-finished tray on the conveyor to the sculleries. He waited impatiently while his flock followed suit. He scowled at Mouse, who had opened up with the big guns and had Grace laughing like a teenager at stories woollier than the mammoths they antedated.

"Style," benRabi told himself. "That's what he's got."

"Excuse me?" one of the ladies asked.

"Talking to myself, Ellen. It's the only way to hold an intelligent conversation."

"You think they'll be mad at us because of this?"

"Maybe. More likely at each other. Like Mouse said, it was a dumb idea, no matter what the point was."

"Unless it's a cover."

"That's a possibility."

The man had a bus waiting outside the cafeteria. In ten minutes it reached the departure bay they had left so laboriously earlier. By then Mouse was holding Grace's hand. He had her purring and almost unable to wait till he got off work.

"Come on, Storm," her brother snapped. "Back to your assigned department. The rest of you, go back to your jobs. Grace, for god's sake…"

"Oh, shut up, Burt."

"He's got a name," one of the ladies crowed. Mouse's mutinous attitude was catching. The Seiners had tried to put something over on the landsmen and they were responding with a mocking camaraderie.

"Come on, Mouse," Moyshe grumbled. "Let's don't start anything."

"Right. At eight, Grace? Bye." Storm bounced onto the scooter he had commandeered for the ride to the departure station. Moyshe took the seat behind him.

"New worlds to conquer, eh?"

"That's one way of looking at it, Moyshe. This old one is starting to wear. They must have some kind of open contract on me. Some kind of bounty for the girl who cons me into the 'I dos.' They won't take no for an answer. Not and stay friends. Weird people."

"What the hell are you doing here?" Kindervoort demanded when they strolled into the coliseum, where he was overseeing some especially poor marksmen.

"Surprise," Mouse crowed. "The game was called on account of rain."

"What's he talking about, Moyshe?"

"It was some kind of dumb exercise. I'm sure you know what it was all about."

"I told him it was stupid."

"Who?"

"The Ship's Commander. He's up to something with you two. I don't know what."

"Remind him that one of the reasons I crossed over was because people wouldn't play games with me here. I'd have a job I knew what it was. I'd have a place in the scheme. Tell him that if the crap keeps up, I hike my ass back to Contact and chain me to a couch. He can put his auction project where the sun don't shine. It's a stupid operation too."

"Calm down, Moyshe. Just go back to your job."

When Kindervoort turned away, Mouse said, "Good to see you stand up on your hind legs, Moyshe."

"It takes me awhile to get fired up."

"Like the man said, let's go to work. We've got a long way to go with these clowns."

The next morning, whispering with motionless lips as they hurried along a crowded passageway, Mouse said, "They used the time to fix us up with a new set of bugs, Moyshe. Very good stuff. Better than anything Kindervoort stocks. The kind that hook into a stress analyzer. They're putting the big eye on us, Moyshe. From now on you'd better play safe, no matter where you are or who you're with."

"What would they be looking for? We don't have anything to hide."

"Who knows? But don't forget that they're looking."

# TEN: 3049 AD

## The Main Sequence

BenRabi was trying to clip a couple of stubborn, noxious-looking hairs out of his right ear. Amy called, "Ready yet, honey?"

"Half a minute." He had butterflies. He did not want to go. The stalls and arguments had run out, though. He had to meet Amy's family. Such as it was.

He was about to be exhibited to her mother. A prime trophy, he thought. Former landsman turned Seiner, on his way up. A prize for any single girl.

He had been getting that feeling from Amy. The new was wearing off. The magic was fading. He was becoming an object of value instead of one of emotion.

Was the problem his or hers? Was he reading her wrong? He always misinterpreted women.

"Moyshe, will you come on?"

He stepped out of the bathroom. "How do I look?"

"Perfect. Come on. We'll be late for the shuttle."

"I want to make a good impression."

"Stop worrying. Mom would be happy with a warthog, so long as I was married."

"Thanks a lot."

A flash of the old Amy returned. "Any time."

They rode a scooter out one of the connecting tubes, into the halls of the asteroid. Amy slowed to pass a series of doors with temporary plaques hung on them, reading names Moyshe found meaningless. "We're here."

The plaque said STAFINGLAS. Amy parked the scooter among a small herd nursing charger teats.

"What's that mean? Stafinglas?" Moyshe asked.

"I don't know. I think it's made up."

"That's where your mother lives?"

Amy nodded. "We've got to hurry. They'll start pumping the air out of the lock in a couple minutes. They won't let us board after they start."

Could he stall that long? He decided that would be a petty trick. Much as intuition warned him that the trip was a waste, it was important to Amy. The thing to do was grit his teeth and ride it out.

The shuttle was a small, boxy vessel useful for nothing but hauling passengers. The seats were full when Moyshe and Amy boarded. Dozens of people stood in the aisles. BenRabi recognized a few as *Danion* crewfolk.

"Lot of relatives of *Danion* people in this Stafinglas, eh?"

"Yes. The old harvestships are like family enterprises. Three or four generations have served in the same ship. It gets to be a tradition. Almost nobody ships outside their own fleet. They say that's why we're getting into this nationalistic competitiveness between fleets. There's talk about having a computer assign new crews by lot."

Moyshe smiled. "Bet that's a popular idea."

"Like the black plague."

His feet hurt and his back ached before the shuttle reached its destination. It was a six-hour passage. He spent every minute standing.

Stafinglas was exactly what Moyshe expected. An asteroid with kilometer upon kilometer of broad tunnels which served as residential streets. "I'm home," he told Amy. "It's just like Luna Command."

She gave him a funny look. "Really?"

"On a smaller scale." He wanted to tell her it was not a natural or comfortable way to live. Instead, he asked, "You ever been down on a planet?"

"No. Why?"

"Just curious." He could not explain. She did not have the experience to understand.

"Anything else I should know about your mother? I want to make a good impression."

"Stop saying that," Amy snapped. "Stick to literary things. You can't miss. Duck an argument. She's contrary as hell. She'll start a fight just to find out how stubborn somebody is."

He looked at her askance.

"We had some beauts when I was young. Nothing I did and nobody I knew was ever good enough. Talk libraries if you know anything about them. She's librarian for Stafinglas."

The more Amy talked about her mother the less he wanted to meet the woman. He had encountered dragons before. They rolled right over him.

"We're here." Amy stopped at a door, reluctant to take the last step.

"Well?"

Biting her lower lip, Amy knocked.

Four hours later they excused themselves to go out for lunch. Neither spoke till they had drawn their meal trays. As he settled at a table, Moyshe said, "Jesus, do I have a headache."

"Headache? Not here?"

"Tension headache. Not migraine." It had been bad. Much worse than he had expected. The woman was a classic. He glanced at Amy. Want to know what a woman will be like in twenty-five years? Have a good, long look at her mother.

"I'm sorry, Moyshe. I… I can't even make excuses for her. There isn't any excuse for that kind of behavior."

"Uhm. Maybe I'd better get used to it. Maybe she was just saying what a lot of people think. Me and Mouse and the others may have to live with that the rest of our lives."

"You should have fought back."

"Would that have changed anything? No. It would've kept her going that much longer."

Moyshe was still numb. As an Old Earther he had been fighting prejudice since entering the Navy. He had thought he possessed a thick hide. But never had he encountered anyone as virulent as Amy's mother. Outworlders went through the forms of equality, keeping their prejudices subtle and silent. Amy's mother was open and vicious and adamantine about hers. Neither suasion nor force would alter her thinking in the least.

She had disowned Amy before it was over.

"You want to try again?" Amy asked.

He was startled. "What?"

"She *is* my mother, Moyshe."

He reached across the table, took her hand for a second. "I know." She was doing her brave act to conceal her pain. "I know. I've got one too. And she isn't that much different."

"They want the best for you. And they think they're the ones to decide what's best." Amy gulped several mouthfuls. "Mother never was good at expressing feelings positively. Maybe that's why I'm a little weird. I spent a lot of time with her while I was growing up. She never qualified for fleet duty. That was the big disappointment of her life. Till we gave her something else to feel sorry for herself about."

Amy almost never mentioned her father. All Moyshe ever learned was his name and the fact that he had been killed in an accident here in the nebula. Apparently, despite protestations to the contrary, Amy's mother had found the accident convenient.

"We'd better not go back, Moyshe," Amy decided. "Not today. Let's give her a chance to calm down and get used to the idea."

"Okay."

They had to kill four hours before a shuttle became available. Moyshe thought Amy would use the time to visit old friends. She did not. She said all her real friends were aboard *Danion*. She became defensive. She did not want to face any more disapproval. The stay-at-home Seiners were, apparently, less cosmopolitan than the people of the harvestfleets.

Going back, Amy suggested, "If you want, tomorrow we can sneak over and see those alien ships. The research center isn't that far."

Moyshe perked up a little. "All right. That's a good idea. I've been looking forward to it. What do we do about our work assignments?"

"I'll take care of everything."

Amy took sleeping pills as soon as they reached their cabin. Despite a long, long day, Moyshe was not in the mood for bed. He strolled down the passageway and awakened Mouse.

"How'd the get-together go?" Mouse asked. And, without awaiting an answer, "That bad, eh?"

"It's a whole different world, Mouse. I thought I knew how to handle prejudice… I never saw anything like it. Her mother was the worst, but there was plenty everywhere else we went, too."

"I know. Grace took me for a little tour this morning."

"You guys got out of bed long enough?"

"Hey, you got to do something the other twenty-three hours of the day."

"So tell me. And where's the board? I've been here three minutes and I still haven't seen a chess board."

"Sorry." Mouse grinned. BenRabi had accused him of being unable to relate with the human male unless a chess board was interposed. "Guess I'm preoccupied."

"She show you anything interesting?"

"I'm not sure. You can't break the habits of trade-craft. So you look and you listen. But you don't find anything that gives you a handle on these people."

"Where'd you go?"

"To some kind of office complex first. Like a government and trade headquarters. We hunked around there for five hours. They had everything out in the open… You know, like no confidential files or anything, and nobody getting excited because you pick up a paper and read it. You take white. But there wasn't anything there. I mean, nothing anybody back home would give a damn about. I didn't see a damned thing worth remembering."

"What the hell kind of weird move is that?"

Mouse smiled. "Some Seiner pulled that on me the other day."

"And lost."

"Yeah. But I was better than him. Hey. You know what they're doing? They're getting ready to go back to Stars' End."

"That isn't any secret."

"No. But they're so damned serious. I mean, Grace and I went to this one asteroid they were making into a dry-dock. After we left the other place. I got to talking to this engineer. Her husband is on the team that's adapting a shuttle to piggyback the Stars' End weapons to orbit."

BenRabi raised his attention from the board. "Curious. Everywhere you go… They're so damned sure of themselves, aren't they?"

"Awfully. Maybe we're too sure they can't do it. Maybe they have an angle." Mouse's attention had left the board too. He seemed to have a question he was afraid to ask. Moyshe felt the intensity of it, boiling there behind his friend's eyes.

"I've got a hunch that they do. Through the starfish, somehow."

Mouse returned to the game. His unorthodox opening got him into trouble early. BenRabi had him on the ropes, but let him wriggle loose by making a too-eager move. It cost him a knight.

"You always did get too excited," Mouse observed. "How has your head been?"

"I had a headache today. Just tension, though. Why?"

"Just asking." A move later, "What I meant was that disorientation stuff you had because of the Psych program. Any trouble?"

"Not much. Not like it was. I have my moments. You know. Blanking out for a second, then coming back wondering where I am and who I am. They don't amount to anything. They don't last long enough for anybody to notice."

"Good. I was scared when you were doing that Contact stuff. Thought you might get mixed up while you were in, and come back somebody else permanently."

"You didn't, by chance, have anything to do with getting me transferred, did you?"

"I would have if I'd thought I had the drag. For your own good. But I didn't." Mouse rose, indicated that Moyshe should follow him. He stepped into the passageway, tapping his ear.

"What is it?"

"Don't want them to know I know this. The orders came from up top. Way up top. I know this woman who works in Communications. She told me a couple things she thought I already knew. Naturally, I played along."

"Naturally. If it's female, you'll go along with anything."

Mouse grinned. "One of these days I'll tell you about the Admiral sending me to pimp school. Whoring isn't the oldest profession. Pimping is. You'd be knocked on your ass if you saw what a really good pimp can do with women."

"He sent you to school?"

"Yeah. Hell, Moyshe, it's the oldest trick in the spy business. You teach a guy how to make a woman fall for him, then turn him loose on the women who work for the organization you want to penetrate."

"I thought it worked the other way around. Women seducing men."

"It's done. It doesn't work as well. Men don't respond the same to emotional blackmail."

"What did your friend have to say? We can't stay out here too long."

"Buddy, we're headed for the top. Somebody upstairs has decided we're the medicine Seiner foreign relations needs. This auction project is a test. If we come through, they'll give us a shot at setting up our own secret service."

BenRabi had had a few hints. He had formed a few suspicions. Still, he was not ready for the truth.

"A real fleetwide secret service. Inside and out. Intelligence and counter-intelligence. The works. For all the Starfishers. The way it sounds, they'll give us anything we want and turn us loose. They've got friends landside who try to keep them informed. The friends have fed them enough, the last couple of years, to get them worried about what's going on in Luna Command."

"Ah. I begin to smell the rat. We've got connections. We could turn a few of our old buddies."

"You've got it."

"How do you feel about it?"

"I was about to ask you, Moyshe."

"After you."

"All right."

"All right. It would be a challenge. We'd be going head to head with the Old Man. It would be a hell of a match-up."

BenRabi was not pleased. "I take it you're excited."

"Damned right I am. Not meaning to brag, but if we'd gone back, I'd have had Beckhart's job eventually. He said so himself. And you'd have become my Chief of Operations. He thought we had what it takes, Moyshe. You see what I'm driving at?"

"I think so." BenRabi was disappointed for a moment. There was not a shred of loyalty in Mouse. His attitude was wholly mercenary… What the hell am I crying about? he wondered. I started this side-changing stuff.

He cast Mouse a sharp glance. More and more, he suspected his partner had stayed here only because *he* had, not out of conviction. What did that mean when taken with this sudden enthusiasm for directing an organization targeted against their former employer? What had become of his obsession with destroying the Sangaree?

"So what I think you should maybe be thinking about," Mouse said, "is how we could set it up. Who we should use, where we should keep our eyes open, like that. And structure, too. You're more of a theorist than I am."

"Communications would be the big problem, Mouse." He tried not to take Mouse's chatter seriously. The obstacles to creating an effective Seiner secret service were insurmountable. "How do you run an S or K net without communications? See what I mean? We're out here and the targets are the hell and gone somewhere else.You and I were always where we could use a public comm if we had to. Or we could use the Navy nets. Say we got somebody into Luna Command. He finds out something we should know right now. What does he do? Run outside and yell real loud?"

"We'll figure it out, Moyshe. Don't worry about the details that way. Don't be so negative all the time. Instead of saying, 'It's impossible,' say, 'How can we do it?' Figure a way, then organize to fit it. Let's get back in there before they get too suspicious."

They exchanged a couple of moves. Moyshe said, "I yield. I would've had you this time except for that one stupid move."

"It was a bad opening. I deserved to get stomped. Another game?"

"Just one. Then I'd better turn in. Amy's sneaking me out for a look at their xeno-archaeological project tomorrow."

"Wish I could go. But Jarl will have fits enough about you."

The main research station was awesome.

"What they did," Amy explained, "was take over one of the drydock asteroids. So they could study the ships inside."

The planetoid was smaller than the one that had engulfed *Danion*, but still was vast. At least a hundred ships floated in its interior. Some were so alien their lines almost hurt the eye.

Around the inner face of the asteroid lay an office and laboratory level. It was roofed by a layer of glassteel. The researchers and their staffs could look up at the ships floating overhead. People in the bay could see what was going on in the offices and labs. The asteroid had been given spin along its longitudinal axis instead of using artificial gravity generators, which would have been in continuous imbalance by facing inward.

Moyshe and Amy entered through a lock in the asteroid's end, and observed briefly from a lookout there. Moyshe was impressed. The line of ships marched on till it vanished in the distance.

"They bring them in this end," Amy said. "They look them over, study them, and the ones that aren't useful they move up the line." She indicated a remote vessel. Tugs were guiding it away. "The far end is industrialized. The ships the scientists don't want they break up for raw materials or refit for us to use. Let's see if we can find a scooter."

An hour later Amy introduced him to a woman named Consuela el-Sanga. "Consuela is an old friend, Moyshe. Consuela, Moyshe might be able to give you an idea or two."

Consuela el-Sanga was a small, dusky woman in her early fifties. She bore the stamp of the preoccupied researcher, of a person who had devoted a lifetime to her curiosity. Moyshe liked her immediately, and as quickly felt a kinship. She was a shy, diffident individual in matters outside her expertise.

"Are you a xeno-archaeologist, Mister benRabi?"

"No. Amy's exaggerating. I'm not even a gifted amateur. My only claim is that I followed the Lunar digs close till a year ago. I had a friend on the project."

Darkness hit him. It had the impact of a physical blow. A woman's face floated before him. He had not seen that face in years. Alyce. Academy love. The girl who had worked at the Lunar digs...

"Moyshe!" Amy sounded frightened. "What's the matter? Are you all right?"

He held up a hand, patted at the air. "Okay. Okay. I'm okay." He shook his head violently. "Just a delayed reaction to the spin here," he lied. "I've never been in centrifugal gravity."

Inside, panic. What the hell was this? It had not happened for months. He realized he was talking, and talking fast. "I was at the digs a year and a half ago. They'd just opened a new chamber, in almost perfect condition. They thought some of the machinery might still work."

Amy and Consuela watched him carefully. "You sure you're all right?" Amy asked.

"Sure. Sure. Miss el-Sanga, what could I do to help?"

"I really don't know. We could walk you through one of the ships we think relates to the Lunar base, for a layman's opinion. We're sure there was a connection, but, because of politics, we can't work with the people there."

"It's a pity, too."

"Come along. We'll start with artifacts recovered from the ships. So you're married now, Amy."

BenRabi caught an odd note in what could have been either statement or question. He gave the women a closer look. There was a slight tenseness between them, as if there had been more to their relationship than friendship and shared interests. He filed it in the back of his mind.

"Took me long enough, didn't it?" Amy tried to sound light. She failed.

The moment of disorientation had turned something on inside Moyshe. His mind went to work agent-wise. The cameras rolled. The cross-reference computer clicked. His surroundings took on more depth, more meaning. They became brighter and more interesting. His movements became quicker and more assured.

"This is what we laughingly call the museum," Consuela el-Sanga said, pausing before opening a door. "It's not, really. It's just a storage room. Whoever those people were, they didn't leave much behind. Mostly just trash. But that's all archaeologists ever have to work with. Broken points, potsherds, and whatever else the ancients threw out behind their huts."

Moyshe moved up and down rows of metal shelves. They contained hundreds of items, each tagged with a date, ship number, inventory number, and brief guess as to what the object might be. Some were referenced to other inventory numbers.

Twice he paused, reexamined an item, said, "I saw something like this at the Lunar digs. I'd say there's a definite connection."

The second time, Consuela el-Sanga responded, "Not necessarily. Parallel function. Say a comb. Any creature with hair would invent a comb. Wouldn't you say? So the existence of a comb wouldn't prove anything but a common physical trait." And when Moyshe finished with the racks and shelves, she said, "Now into my office. I'll show you our two real treasures."

Moyshe and Amy followed her through another door.

"You haven't seen these either, Amy. We found them while you were out. They were both part of the same find."

Consuela El-Sanga took two plastic cases from her desk. She handled them with loving care.

Moyshe accepted one, Amy the other. The item benRabi held was a piece of paper that had been torn into small fragments. A very few faded marks were visible.

"Is it a photograph?" Amy asked.

"Good guess," Consuela said. "We had a hell of a time with them." Moyshe traded with Amy. The second object *was* an extremely faded, flat, two-dimensional photo. It had been torn in two.

Consuela continued, "First we pieced all the tears together. Then we did scans with low-intensity lasers and computer enhancements. We came up with these." The woman glowed with pride as she handed over reproductions of the items.

The photo, in color, was of a creature very similar to the Lunar dig reconstructions. BenRabi said as much. The other object appeared to be a handwritten letter.

"Any luck interpreting this?" Moyshe asked.

"No. We haven't even determined which direction it's supposed to be read."

"You haven't found any technical manuals or anything?"

"Not a speck. Just a few characters on nameplates, stuff like you'd find around instrumentation and doors on any ship. Any time there's more than three characters, they're arranged in matrices like these."

"Maybe they had a holographic system for reading."

"No. Doesn't go with a two-d photo. We don't think."

"Very interesting," Moyshe said, studying the picture again. "A Dear John letter? And the guy, or gal, gets mad and tears up the lover's letter and picture, but then can't bear to part with the pieces?"

"That's one of our hypotheses."

Moyshe scanned the letter. "Thirty-four different characters here. Some punctuation?"

"Don't try to figure it out in your head. Even the computers can't get a handle on it. Just think how hard it would be to break our language without a starting clue. Big letters, little letters, script, punctuation, spelling variations by dialect, different type faces, all the stylized lettering and special symbols we use for technical stuff... You see? We'd need a whole ship full of old letters, novels, and newspapers to break it. Not just a few plaques on an instrument panel."

"Don't worry, Consuela," Amy said. "We'll be into Stars' End soon. You'll find your answers there."

"If I'm lucky enough to go. They haven't picked the science team yet. I'm worried."

"You'll go. You're the best."

BenRabi looked at the woman and slowly shook his head. That Stars' End insanity again.

"I don't know what I'd do if they turned me down, Amy. It's my whole life. I'm not getting any younger. And they might use my age to keep me home."

"Don't worry. You know they can't leave you behind. There's nobody better than you. And they know how much it means to you."

"How soon, Amy? Do you know?"

"It hasn't been decided yet. But it won't be long. A month or two."

Consuela brightened. "You're sure they'll send me?"

"Of course. Don't be silly."

"That's what I am, you know. A silly old woman."

Amy enfolded her in gentle arms. "No you're not. No you're not. Come on, now. Show us one of those ships."

Consuela el-Sanga led them to a little four-place air scooter, flew them out to a vessel. BenRabi felt lightheaded in the lack of gravity. "I feel like I could fall all the way to the end," he said, staring down the length of the hollow.

The ship was one of the least alien of those in the lineup. "Form follows function," Moyshe muttered, remembering the Luna Command constructs, which had very much resembled small human beings.

The ship's lock was open. Consuela made fast, led them inside. She was small, but even she had to stoop in the passageways.

Moyshe wandered around for an hour. He finally summed up his impressions by observing, "It's not that strange. Just kind of dollhouse. Like it was built for children. You can figure out what half the stuff is. It's just parked places we consider weird."

"You said it yourself, form follows function," Consuela replied. "We've done comparative studies between these, Sangaree, Ulantonid, and our own ships. The physical requirements of bipeds appear to be universal. Scales seem to be the most noticeable difference."

"That ship two ahead of this one. What built it? A giant slug?"

"We don't know. It's funny. There's something almost repulsive about it. You have to work yourself up to it if it's your turn to study it. It's like the alienness oozes out of the metal. It's more of a mystery than the other ships. It's almost contemporary, if our dating technique is valid. It shows battle damage. It's the only one of its kind we've ever located. It was as clean as these others. One of my colleagues believes the crew were forced to abandon ship after an accidental encounter during some crisis period, like the Ulantonid War, when everyone was shooting at anybody who didn't yell friend fast enough. Curiously, though, it was surrounded by a whole squadron of our little friends here."

"Enemies?"

Consuela shrugged. "Or purely chance. The ships aren't contemporary with one another. What were they doing together? There aren't enough books to write down all the questions, Mister benRabi. It gets frustrating sometimes."

"I can imagine. Could the crew have been studying the old ships when they were attacked by a third party?"

"That's a possibility we hadn't considered. I'll bring it up…"

"Consuela?" someone shouted into the vessel. "Is that you in there?"

"Yes, Robert. What is it?"

"Somebody's looking for those people who came to see you. A man named Kindervoort. He sounded pretty excited."

"Oh-oh," Amy said. "I'm in trouble now. I thought he wouldn't notice. Consuela, I'd better call him."

She placed the call from Consuela's office. Jarl foamed at the mouth and ordered them to return to *Danion*. Now. He snarled at benRabi, "Moyshe, I don't care if you cut those nitwit citizenship classes. They're a waste of time anyway. But you're not ducking out on the training schedule. Now come back here and get your men ready. You've got the rest of your life to look at old ships. The auction is now."

Amy was quiet throughout the return passage. Once she whispered, "He's really going to give it to me," and clutched Moyshe's hand. She was shaking.

"He's an amateur," benRabi told her. "You haven't been chewed out till you've taken it from Admiral Beckhart." A moment later he grinned and added, "But if it's private, he lets you yell back."

Soon after they returned they heard that another of the great harvestfleets was entering the nebula. The news generated a fresh air of excitement aboard *Danion.*

One by one, the harvestfleets came in. Scores of fresh, eager young faces appeared aboard *Danion* as graduates of Seiner technical schools filled the billets of people lost at Stars' End. The howl and hammer of repairs went on around the clock. The excitement and tension continued to mount.

They were going back. This time in full strength, and to stay. A prideful, nationalistic, bellicose mood gripped the fleets.

Moyshe benRabi and Masato Storm pursued their instruction of the teams they would direct on The Broken Wings. Their days were long and exhausting. Moyshe often tumbled into bed without enough energy left for a good-night kiss.

He began to feel the pressure. It started to intrude into his sleeping hours. He began to dream of the girl he had left behind, so long ago. He suffered more momentary lapses of attention while he was awake.

He began to grow frightened of what might be going on back in the nether reaches of his mind.

# ELEVEN: CHRISTMAS 3049 AD

## The Contemporary Scene

Tension gripped the bridge of the attack cruiser *Lepanto.* "One minute to drop," the astrogation officer announced.

Jupp von Drachau scanned his people. They were poised like runners in the blocks, awaiting the crack of the starter's pistol. They would have to grab an enormous fund of data in a few brief minutes.

*Lepanto* was coming up to an enemy star. There was no way of guessing what might be waiting. Detection gear would not work from hyper unless initial detection had been made in norm. The cruiser was going in blind.

No one knew the capabilities of the Sangaree detection systems. Operating from norm, they would not have the same handicap. A force might be moving toward the drop zone now.

"Thirty seconds."

"Stand by, Weapons," von Drachau ordered. "Button up, people." He sealed the faceplate of his own helmet.

One quick drop to get his bearings, then a short arc in to the fringes of the Sangaree sun…

"Five seconds. Four. Three."

The figures on the bridge hunched forward a centimeter more.

"One. Drop."

"Screens up."

"Commander, heavy vessels bearing…"

"Display active."

"Three ships bearing…"

"Range to star one point three two a.u…"

"We have a local inherent velocity of…"

"Attack missiles bearing…"

"Bridge. Weapons. Launching two salvos."

The vessel shuddered and rocked. Von Drachau stared at the display tank. Six red blips had come to life there. They sped along projected curves which would bring them within spitting distance of *Lepanto.* Tiny ruby pinpoints raced ahead, toward the cruiser.

"… time to intercept forty-seven seconds…"

The hyper alarm commenced its hooted warning to the crew. "Time to hyper one minute," a voice boomed.

Someone said, "Commander, we've located the planet."

"Bring me up a visual."

"Aye, sir."

Von Drachau's command screen came to life. For an instant it displayed a computer graphic of the local solar system. The schematic yielded to a visual from an external camera. It showed a white third-crescent. The amplification rose quickly, revealing a world heavy with clouds and seas. "Looks a lot like Old Earth," von Drachau murmured.

"Yes sir."

"Are you taping?"

"We're getting everything we can, sir."

"Twenty seconds to hyper."

Von Drachau glanced at the display tank. The missile salvos were driving closer. Weapons Department was not bothering with anything but defensive fire. Considering the nature of the mission, engaging a handful of raidships was pointless. "Anything near that sun?" he asked.

"No sir. We have a lot of activity near and on the planet."

That made sense. The Sangaree would be scrambling everything in fear that *Lepanto* might be the spearhead of a thrust against their Homeworld. That was the doom they had dreaded for centuries.

"Hyper in five seconds. Four."

Von Drachau did not think these picket ships would jump with him. They should await the rest of a suspected battle fleet.

"One. Taking."

The universe shifted. Screens went blank. The display tank, cued in norm, remained active. Von Drachau stared, willing the Sangaree raidships to remain where they were.

"One minute to drop." Astrogation had programmed a very short, slow arc.

Von Drachau reached back into his soul, searching for any wisp of feeling that might bear on the orders he had to give. He did not want to do this thing. Every cell of him protested. And yet… And yet he knew too much. He knew the critical importance of obtaining results. And he had his own orders.

"Special Weapons Party, stand by."

His orders would be a formality. The pre-launch program had begun an hour ago. The only significant command he could give now would be the abort.

He checked the tank again.

"Damn!" They were coming. Their detection gear was good. They knew no one else was coming in right away. "Looks like we knocked over a beehive," he said. The six raidships from the drop zone were being joined by a horde quartering in from the planet.

"Twenty seconds till drop."

It would be a narrow squeak, making the launch and getting clear in time. And some of them would chase him all the way home… "Astrogation, program your next jump for Carson's." He did not want to lead the pursuit too close to the action on The Broken Wings.

"Sir?"

"Pull the cassette and reprogram." An attack squadron would be on station near Carson's. He could scoot in and cling to its protective skirts.

"Yes sir."

"Drop."

"Special Weapons Party, launch when ready."

There. It was too late to take it back. Too late to keep from having to live with it the rest of his life.

"Special Weapons launch in three minutes, twelve seconds," launch party captain replied.

"What's the holdup? We've got Sangaree crawling up our backs."

"Sorry, sir. A coupling jammed."

"Long range hunter missiles bearing…"

"Visuals, please," von Drachau said. His screen came to life. "Show me the star."

In a second he was staring at an endless plain of fire. Broad continental reaches of darkness lay upon it. The star appeared to be passing through a period of heavy sunspotting. But, as he remembered it, the Sangaree home star was supposed to be highly active, with exceptionally intense solar winds.

"Two minutes to special launch."

Von Drachau checked the display tank. The Sangaree were coming on in a mob. They were not organized, but there were too many of them. *Lepanto* wouldn't have a prayer in a heads-up fight.

"Astrogation, how's your program coming?"

"Five minutes, sir."

"We don't have five minutes. Make it a basal arc that'll drop us in the neighborhood. Do your fine calculation during the fly."

"Yes sir."

"... to intercept fifty-two seconds."

Von Drachau glared at the tank. They would have missiles in their pockets by launch time. Power weapons would be pounding *Lepanto*'s energy screens. "Damn!" It looked bad.

"Time to launch one minute."

The bridge watch took on that hunchbacked look of people anticipating the kiss of the whip. Sixty lousy seconds. That could make a damned short life. Mayflies lasted longer.

"... to intercept fourteen seconds."

That was close. And the next salvo would be closer.

"Astrogation. One millisecond free hyper straight linear," von Drachau snapped.

"Sir?"

"Do it!"

The alarm hooted as the ship lurched.

The Ship's Commander's screen returned to life. The Sangaree sun had moved. He could see a horizon line. It had no curvature.

Weapons Department howled. They had to reprogram.

"So do those boys over there. Special Weapons. Time to launch."

"Thirty-two seconds, sir."

"Missiles bearing two five-niner relative, one two degrees nadir. Time to intercept two six seconds."

Von Drachau sighed. That was right on the line. "Gentlemen, we're going to make it."

The bridge watch did not relax. They knew his remark was half prayer. The tank proclaimed that in its totally unambiguous display. A saturation barrage was hurtling toward them.

And it was a long, long run back to friendly space.

"Ten seconds to launch."

And there was the problem of the weapon safely reaching target. If the Sangaree sniped it, *Lepanto* would have to try again. A second pass could get hairy.

*Lepanto* shuddered and lurched. Someone yelled, "That was too goddamned close!"

"Two. One. Launch. Weapon away."

The warship lurched again. "One tenth second free hyper straight linear!" von Drachau ordered. "Detection, lock on that weapon. I want to know if it makes it."

The cruiser dodged. Von Drachau shifted attention between display tank and screen, following the weapon into the sun.

Sangaree missiles had no chance to catch it. Scores of laser and graser weapons probed for it, caressed it with their deadly tongues.

"Telemetry. How are its screens holding?"

"Perfectly, sir."

*Lepanto* rocked. Time was running out.

"She's in, sir. They can't stop her now. Her sun screens are stable."

"Astrogation, get us out of here."

"You still want an observation pass, sir?" R & D had asked them to hang around and study the results.

"The hell with that noise! Get out of here before they barbecue us."

The hyper alarm hooted. The ship twisted away into an alternate dimension. Von Drachau turned to the display tank.

"Some of them are good," he murmured. "Very good."

Four vessels had caught the trail already, and were coming hard.

"Drive. Run your influence factor to the red line."

"Sir!"

"You heard me. You'll take it over if you have to. Stand by for it."

"Yes sir."

Von Drachau glanced at the sun shape dwindling in the display tank. The weapon would be sinking toward its heart. The killing process would begin in a few hours. He turned into himself again, looking for his feelings. All he found was a big vacancy, an arid desert of the soul.

He did not think much of Jupp von Drachau just then.

# BOOK TWO
## THE BROKEN WINGS

# TWELVE: 3050 AD

## The Contemporary Scene

Lemuel Beckhart felt totally vulnerable while walking the streets of Angel City. The berg was domed, of course, but the glassteel arced too far overhead. He had been born in Luna Command and had spent most of his life there and in warships. He needed overheads, decks, and bulkheads close at hand before he felt comfortable.

Worlds with open skies were pure hell for him.

He shoved his hands into the pockets of the civilian trousers he wore. It was coming together. The timing looked good. The leaks had the commentators howling for blood.

Funny how they became raving patriots when it looked like their asses were going to go in the can too... Those people in Public Information knew their trade. They were keeping a fine balance. They were generating alarm without causing panic. They were stampeding legislative sessions hither and yon, herding them like unsuspecting cattle, getting everything Luna Command wanted. Confederation Senate was passing appropriations measures like the gold seam had no end.

The real victory was a stream of confederacy applications from outworlds that had remained stubbornly independent for generations. Well-tempered fear. That was the lever. Let them know Confederation would defend its own, and ignore the others when the hammer fell... Those cunning politicians. They were using the crisis too. Everybody was scoring on this one. Would the maneuvering and manipulation settle out in time? It was human nature to go on wasting energy on internal bickering when doom was closing in.

Those PI people... They were something. They still had not released anything concrete. The propaganda machine in high gear was a wonder to behold.

Beckhart was bemused by his own pleasure at observing a high level of professional competence in a department not under his own command.

His mood soured when he reflected on the latest news from his colleagues in Ulantonid intelligence. That centerward race... They seemed to draw some special, wholly inexplicable pleasure from killing.

The latest Ulantonid package had included tape taken on a world with a Bronze Age technology. It showed small, suited bipeds, built like a cross between orangutans and kangaroos, armed principally with small arms, systematically eradicating the natives. There was ample footage of shattered cities, burning villages, and murdered babies. Not to mention clips of cadavers of virtually every other mobile lifeform the planet boasted.

If it moved, the hopping, long-armed creatures shot it. If it did not, they dug it out of hiding and killed it anyway.

There had been no sky full of ships for this primitive world, just a stream of transports sending in troops, munitions, small flyers, and the equipment used to hunt down the wilder creatures of mountain and forest. The Ulantonid experts estimated a troop input approaching ten billion "soldiers."

Beckhart could not grasp that number. Ten billions. For one primitive world… Confederation and Ulant together had not had that many people under arms during the most savage years of their conflict.

"They've got to be crazy," he muttered.

He paused near the building where Thomas McClennon, now Moyshe benRabi, had kept the Sangaree woman distracted while Storm had torn the guts out of her Angel City operation. Christ, but hadn't those boys pulled a coup? And now they had come through again, giving him the Sangaree Homeworld.

He had to bring them out. Somehow. He refused to write men off while they lived.

He was determined. There had to be a way to apply enough leverage to force their release… If it came to that alone, and he could prise no better yield from the coming encounter, he would be satisfied.

The thing looked made to order for another coup. "Down, boy," he muttered. "First things first. You're here to get your boys back. Anything else comes second."

Still, it was coming together. The word was, the Sangaree wanted revenge. It was a good bet the Seiners would have another go at Stars' End. The rumors and leaks from Luna Command had everybody excited about an ambergris shortage. A lot of eyes would be staring down gun barrels at this end of the Arm.

He was pleased. He had choreographed it perfectly. Only he and High Command would be thinking about von Drachau. If von Drachau succeeded, the news would hit like the proverbial ton of bricks.

He strolled on to the warehouse that had headquartered the local Sangaree operation. It was a fire-blackened pile of rubble. The authorities had not cleared it yet.

"Sometimes, Lemuel, you're not a very nice person," he murmured.

He was repelled by some of the things he did. But he was sincere in his belief that they were necessary.

He was terrified of that centerward race. The hungry bunnies, he called them, for no truly good reason.

Ten billions for one world. Tens of thousands of ships.

How could they be stopped?

Why the hell were they so determined to kill? There was no logic to it.

Was there anything more he could do? Anything he had overlooked?

He lay awake nights trying to think of something. He suspected that everyone in High Command slept poorly of late, running the same perilous race courses in hopes of finding the key to escape from the nightmare.

His beeper squeaked. He raised it to his ear. "Hand delivery only, urgent, for Blackstone," a remote voice told him. He returned the beeper to his belt and walked briskly toward his headquarters.

The courier was a full Commander. He wore a side-arm, and carried the message in a tamperproof case that would destruct should anyone but Lemuel Beckhart attempt to open it. The case bore a High Command seal.

"Sit, Commander. What's the news from Luna Command?"

The Commander was a taciturn man. "We seem to be in for some excitement, sir."

"That's a fact. You came in with the squadrons taking station?" Three heavy squadrons had taken orbit around The Broken Wings. They were there at his request.

"Yes sir. Aboard *Assyrian.*"

"Popanokulos still Ship's Commander?" Beckhart placed his thumbs at the proper points on the case. Something whirred. He prised it open with a fingernail.

"Yes sir."

"How is he? He was one of my students, years ago." He was reluctant to open the plain white envelope lying within the case.

"He's in excellent health, sir. He asked me to extend his best regards."

"Extend mine in return, Commander." He initialed a pink slip for the second time, indicating that the contents of the case had been received. He would have to do so twice more, indicating message read, then message destroyed.

The Commander moved slightly in his chair. He appeared impatient to return to *Assyrian.* Beckhart opened the envelope, removed what appeared to be a sheet of plain white paper. He pressed his thumbs against the bottom corners. Invisible microcircuitry read his prints. A handwritten message slowly took form, appearing at the rate it had been written.

*L: All-time screw-up at R&D research facility. Cause unclear. System destroyed. Total loss. VD away with 2 apples. Public disclosure disaster unavoidable. M.*

Beckhart laid the sheet on his desk, covered his face with the palms of his hands.

There went a key hope. Without telling his Ulantonid opposite number why, he had asked for additional deep probes toward galaxy center, hoping to locate home-worlds that could be shattered with the new weapon. He had hoped the grandeur and viciousness of the thing could be used to intimidate the centerward race into abandoning their insane crusade.

A total loss. All the info, both on the weapon itself and what had gone wrong. Damn it to hell, anyway!

He initialed the pink slip, burned the message, and initialed the slip again. "Thank you, Commander." He handed slip and case over. "There won't be a reply."

"Very well, sir. Have a nice day."

Beckhart wore a puzzled smile as the officer pushed out the door. A nice day? Not likely. He keyed a switch on his desk communicator. "I need Major Damon."

A few days later his comm whined at him. "Yes?"

"Communications, sir." The commtech sounded choked. "Signals from *Assyrian*, sir. The Starfishers are here. Just detected."

Beckhart felt a stir of excitement. He asked, "What's the problem?"

"Sir, I… Let me feed you the *Assyrian* data, sir."

Beckhart touched a button. The tiny screen on his comm crackled to life. A series of computer data began flashing across it. Then came a schematic of a ship.

He read the size figures three times before murmuring, "Holy shit." He leaned back, said, "Communications, keep running that till I say stop."

"Yes sir."

He watched the report three times through before he was satisfied.

So those were harvestships… They were self-contained worlds. If Navy could lay hands on a few of those, and arm them with Empire Class weaponry… "Communications, page Major Damon. Tell him to come to my office."

The commander of the Marine Military Police battalion reported only minutes later.

"Major, there'll be an adjustment in our plans. Watch this." Beckhart ran the report from *Assyrian*. Damon was suitably impressed.

"Major, sit. We're going to do some brainstorming."

The session lasted the day and the night and into the next day. It ended when Communications interrupted. "Admiral, signals from *Assyrian*. Sir, they've intercepted signals between the Seiner ships. They thought you'd be interested."

"Of course I am. Give it to me."

The relay was not long. And it was both baffling and exciting. The Starfishers were going to put his own boys in charge of their auction security effort.

He had it run twice. Satisfied, he said, "Major, go get yourself eight hours. Then get back here and we'll pick up where we left off. This changes things again. We work it right, now, and we're in the chips."

After the Major departed, he had *Assyrian* open an instel link with Luna Command. He spent an hour in conference. He broke off smiling a weak smile. This auction might be more than serendipitous.

He dragged himself to his cot, hoping to catch a few hours, but could not fall asleep.

His conscience kept nagging him. Once again he would have to use men cruelly for the sake of the Services and Confederation.

He was so weary of that…

# THIRTEEN: 3050 AD

## The Main Sequence

Payne's Fleet dropped hyper a Sol System radius from The Broken Wings. *Danion* formed the point of the arrowhead of ships flashing toward the planet. Accompanying the harvestships were a hundred service ships borrowed from other fleets.

The Seiners wanted to make an impression. They believed this show of strength would rivet all eyes on The Broken Wings.

While the credit from the auction was important to them, distracting attention from Stars' End meant even more.

Almost all Seinerdom had taken hyper for the fortress world. The harvestfleets had gathered. A hundred harvestships, a thousand service ships, and untold millions of people would be involved in the effort to recover the citadel world's weapons. That gargantuan armada, bearing the hope of a nation, was avoiding traffic lanes, flying easy, awaiting word of the success of the auction diversion.

A confrontation with Confederation had to be avoided. The Seiner leadership understood the swift doom inherent in a two-front war.

A one-front war was a terrible enough hazard.

"We've got trouble," Jarl Kindervoort told his staff. "We've just received a scout report from Stars' End. The Sangaree have moved in there."

Mouse made a sound suspiciously like a purr. "Won't hurt my feelings if they get crunched again."

"Somebody's going to get crunched. The report says there're hundreds of raidships there."

Storm and benRabi became more attentive. Mouse asked, "Hundreds? That would take… Hell, the Families would all have to be working together. They don't do that."

Kindervoort replied, "They seem to have their hearts set on grabbing Stars' End."

"They aren't the only ones," benRabi muttered. He snorted in disgust, shook his head. "Who's fault is that, Jarl?"

"What do you mean, Moyshe?"

"Consider our last run-in. Consider one Maria Elana Gonzales, technician, alias Marya Strehltsweiter, Sangaree agent. Remember her? The lady who tried to kill *Danion*? I shot her and stopped her. And you nice people politely patched her up and sent her home with the other returning landsmen. Bet you she ran straight to her bosses and set this up. Nice doesn't pay, Jarl."

Mouse shifted his chair so he could stare at benRabi. He said nothing.

Once upon a time, on a faraway world called The Broken Wings, a partner of Mouse's, wearing the work-name Dr. Gundaker Niven, had stopped him from killing a Sangaree agent named Marya Strehltsweiter.

Moyshe reddened.

"Let's not cry about what we should have done," Kindervoort said. "We're here now. Let me have those situation reports, Amy."

Amy pushed a sheaf of flimsies across the tabletop. "Navy is damned interested in this end of the universe, too. Three heavy squadrons off The Broken Wings. Squadrons *Hapsburg, Prussian,* and *Assyrian.*"

"Empire Class?" Mouse asked. "All of them? They mean business, don't they?"

"There're battle squadrons at Carson's and Sierra, too. Our friends the Freehaulers couldn't get close enough to identify them."

"And no telling what's in the bushes," benRabi mused.

"Moyshe?"

"They're playing poker, Jarl. They've shown us a couple of aces face up. What you have to worry about is their hole cards. What have they got cruising around a couple of light years away ready to jump in?"

"You think they'll try a power play?"

"No. Not like that. But it might behoove us to spend a little brain power figuring what they're up to. Navy doesn't put that much power together unless they're scared they'll have to use it. You hardly ever see a patrol of more than two ships."

"You know Service thinking better than me. Why're they so excited?"

"The dispositions look defensive," Moyshe said. "And that leads us to our lack of landside intelligence. What's the Planetary Defense Forces alert level in the Transverse? Have they activated any reserves? If so, which units? We could extrapolate their fears from that kind of information."

"We have the liaison team report." Kindervoort shuffled flimsies.

Mouse and benRabi had insisted on sending a few men ahead, weeks ago.

"I've seen it," Moyshe said. "They've given The Broken Wings the usual temporary free planet status. They've pledged an open auction. The city authorities are so nervous they've called up their police reserves and asked Marine MPs to help. They expect trouble. Nobody is saying why."

The coded reports said there were three hundred privately owned ships orbiting The Broken Wings. Each had brought a negotiating team hoping to carry off a supply of ambergris. Most of the vessels appeared to be armed.

All known space was, apparently, in the grip of an undirected war fervor. No one was behaving normally. The auction had a potential for becoming a wild brawl.

"Mouse, Moyshe," Kindervoort said, "I don't mind telling you, this thing has me scared. It's too big, and it looks like it could get bigger. Be very, very careful."

"It could get too big for anybody," Mouse said. His voice was soft and thoughtful. "It could roll us all under."

For two days *Danion* and her sisters drifted slowly toward The Broken Wings, watching and listening. They kept their presence secret longer than Moyshe expected. He and his compatriots obtained two days' worth of observations.

They provided no comfort. Angel City was hell incarnate. Armies of undercover people had materialized there. They were warring with one another with a fine disregard for reason and local tranquility.

The war scare had set off a chain reaction of insanity.

As a landing team leader benRabi now rated his own office and a part-time assistant. His wife filled the assistant's role.

Till this is over, at least, I'm important, he thought. He put little stock in Mouse's theory that they were being groomed to master a Starfisher secret service. He had been able to make no independent corroboration of the claim.

BenRabi's intercom buzzed. "BenRabi here."

"Jarl, Moyshe. I need you over here."

"Now?"

"Right. Final meeting."

"I'm on my way." He gathered his papers, donned fatalism like a cloak, and stalked toward Kindervoort's office. He met Mouse outside Kindervoort's door.

"Broomstick fly," Mouse said.

"No lie. Anybody with any sense would cancel the auction."

Mouse grinned. "Not the Seiners. You got to remember, this auction is part of their big picture."

"I think they'd go ahead even if it weren't."

"Come on in," Kindervoort called. A moment later he began introducing them to the Ships' Commanders and Chiefs of Security of the other harvestships of Payne's Fleet.

The gentlemen were present only as holo portrayals. Kindervoort, Storm, and benRabi would be aboard their vessels the same way. They and the holo equipment and technicians reduced Kindervoort's office to postage stamp size.

"You bring your final reports?" Kindervoort asked.

BenRabi nodded. Mouse said, "Right here. But you're not going to like them."

"Why not?"

"They're reality-based. Meaning they recommend that you cancel or postpone."

BenRabi added, "We can't handle security with what you've given us. Not under the conditions obtaining."

"We've been talking about that. How many more men would you need?"

"About a brigade of MPs," Mouse growled.

"Moyshe, you look surprised," Kindervoort said.

"Just thinking that this isn't like working for the Bureau. You ask the Admiral for more than he gives you, he takes half away and tells you to make do. I'd say another hundred men. And two more months to train them."

"Mr. Storm. Are those realistic figures?" one Ship's Commander asked.

"Minimum realistic. My partner is one of your incurable optimists. But there is an alternative. Cancel this shore leave plan. Don't send anybody down but members of the auction team. We can set up a compound…"

*Danion*'s Commander interrupted. "Sorry. No can do, Mister Storm. We promised our people liberty. Mister benRabi, we'll give you as many men as you want. But the thing has got to be done now."

"You're going to lose people," benRabi protested. He was so irritated he stamped a foot. "Shore leave is stupid. The more people you let wander around down there, the fewer I'm going to be able to protect."

He had lost this argument several times before. The brass had promised everybody a chance to see what life on a planet was like. They would not go back on their word despite having learned that the Angel City situation was more deadly than expected.

Moyshe had begun to suspect that the complication was deliberate, and purely for the propaganda possibilities inherent in potential dead or injured tourists. If his guess was correct, then someone upstairs was as cold-blooded as his old boss, Admiral Beckhart.

"This's the way it's going to be, then," Moyshe said. "You'll have ten thousand tourists on the ground all the time. That's going to make the Angel City merchants happy and me miserable. I'll have half of a hundred fifty men if you give me the hundred I just asked for. That doesn't divide out too good, so the tourists will be on their own. If they get into trouble, tough. I'll cover auction people and VIPs. God can take care of the rest."

He surveyed his audience. He did not see any sympathy there. "You pushed me into this job," he growled. "Why not let me do the damned thing?"

Mouse backed him up. "The same goes for my shift, gents. That's the real world down there. The world of Confederation, espionage, and bad guys, I should say. Those people don't do things the Starfisher way. I've been led to believe that Moyshe and I were given our jobs because we know The Broken Wings and Confederation. And the intelligence viewpoint. I wish you'd accept our expertise. And quit trying to make other realities conform to your views about the way things ought to be."

Storm winked at Moyshe. They had taken the offensive. They had gotten in their licks.

Kindervoort said, "Let's calm down. This's no time for tempers. The job has got be be done, like it or not." Kindervoort's comm buzzed. "Security."

"James, Radio, sir. Is the Ship's Commander there?"

The Ship's Commander stepped to the comm. "What is it?"

"We've noticed an increase in coded traffic, sir. It could mean that we've been detected."

Within minutes several other departments reported similar suspicions. The interruptions kept Mouse and benRabi from arguing their case. The Ship's Commander excused himself, as did his Executive Officer. The holographic visitors faded away. The holo technicians started packing their equipment.

"Well, damned me," Moyshe grumbled.

"What do you think?" Kindervoort asked.

"It's hideous," Mouse snapped.

"Moyshe?"

BenRabi spread his hands in a fatalistic gesture. "What the hell? Nobody listens to anything I say."

"You think there's any chance they could lay hands on somebody who knows something worth their while?"

"Of course there's a chance. You've seen the damned situation reports. They mean business down there. I'm trying to do a job. If nobody will let me..."

"Moyshe, I'm not the Ship's Commander. Just between you and me, I think you're right. I argued your case harder than you think. The Ship's Commander just doesn't see the rest of the universe in anything but Seiner terms. He thinks Confederation is just like us, only working against us. He thinks this is some kind of competition between fleets. He's wrong, but he's in charge. If he wants shoreside liberty, that's what he gets. Do what you can, and grit your teeth if you lose a few. Just don't let them find out what's going on at Stars' End before we get hold of the weapons."

"That will mean fighting the Sangaree again, Jarl. Which means we won't get any back-up here if this show blows up in our faces."

"True. We're on our own. So we stall. We go slow. We keep the auction piddling along. With luck, Gruber will finish before we've lost our distraction value."

"That's candy," Mouse grumbled.

"From hunger," benRabi agreed. They had begun to slip into landside idiom again. "You're all hyper bent."

The public address system came to life. The Ship's Commander asked for volunteers willing to join the auction security effort down in Angel City.

People started showing up immediately. Amy was the first applicant.

"You're not going," Moyshe told her. "That's the final word."

She fought back. The argument became bitter.

"Lieutenant," Moyshe said, "you will remain aboard ship. That's an order. Jarl, will you support my directives?"

Kindervoort nodded.

"Damn you, Moyshe benRabi..."

"Honey, I'm not letting you get killed. Shut up and go back to work."

There were thousands of volunteers. Everyone wanted an extended vacation landside. No one believed there was any danger. Previous auctions were reputed to have been long, wonderful parties.

"You got your list?" Moyshe asked.

Storm nodded.

They had interviewed the candidates who had survived an initial screening. Each had noted the most likely names. They had agreed to take the first hundred names that appeared on both their lists.

Orbiting in to The Broken Wings, Moyshe found the recent past beginning to feel vacationlike in retrospect. He and Mouse would not make overnight soldiers of their volunteers. Even the old hands were terribly weak. Seiner lives revolved around space and ships and harvesting. They would make perfect Navy people. Groundpounders, never.

The toughest hurdle was to make them understand, on a gut level, that someone they could see could be an enemy. A given of Seiner life was that those you could see were friends. Their enemies always existed only as blips in display tanks.

"It's a hard lesson for landsmen," Mouse said. "That's why Marines stay in Basic so long. Our culture doesn't produce the hunter-killer naturally. We ought to build us a time machine so we can go recruit in the Middle Ages."

Moyshe chuckled. "They wouldn't understand what the fighting was about, Mouse. They'd laugh themselves sick."

*Danion* and her sisters went into geosynchronous orbit well above Angel City's horizon. The message was not lost on anyone. If there was too much foolishness downstairs, the fire could fall.

Moyshe, in spacesuit, wrestling a load of armaments, joined Storm for the journey to their departure station.

"Wish we had real combat gear," Mouse said. "These suits won't stand much punishment."

"Be nice."

"Get any sleep?"

"Couldn't. I kept watching the news from Angel City." Moyshe had been shaken by the reports.

"Me too. Something big is happening. There're too many undercurrents. Be careful, Moyshe. Let's don't get bent with it."

"You ever feel like an extra cog?"

"Since the first day I worked for Beckhart. There was always something on that I couldn't figure out. Here we are. And Jarl looks excited."

Kindervoort was overseeing the loading of the four lighters that would make the initial landings, in pairs at fifteen minute intervals. Storm and benRabi would command the teams aboard the lead pair.

"You're going overboard, Jarl," benRabi said as they approached Kindervoort.

"Why? The more we impress them now, the less trouble we'll have later."

"You won't impress them. Not when they have three squadrons here. Go take a look at what Operations has on those ships. Three Empire Class battlewagons, Jarl. The Second Coming wouldn't faze them."

"I smell Beckhart," Mouse said. "Something about the way things are going… He's back in the woods somewhere, poking holes in our plans before we know what they are ourselves."

Kindervoort said, "Make sure that…"

"I know! I know!" benRabi snapped. "We've been over everything fifty times. Just turn us loose, will you?"

"Go easy, Moyshe," Mouse said.

"You take it easy, Mouse," he replied, gently. Storm had begun shaking. He was thinking about the long fall to the planet's surface.

"I'll be all right when things start rolling. I'll go AM if I have to."

"Things are rolling now," Kindervoort said. "Get moving. Take your musters."

Work helped settle Moyshe's nerves. He mustered his men, checked their suits, made sure their weapons were ready, and that they had the first phase of the operation clearly in mind. He rehearsed it for himself. The lighter sealed off from *Danion.* Moyshe joined the pilot. He wanted to remain near the ship's radio.

"All go, Moyshe?" from Kindervoort.

"Landing party go."

"Pilot?"

"Ship's go."

"Stand by for release."

The pilot hit a switch. His visuals came up, presenting views of *Danion*'s hull, stars, and The Broken Wings in crescent. The planet was a huge, silvery scimitar. Its surface lay masked by perpetual cloud cover.

The Broken Wings was a very hot, very wet world, with a nasty atmosphere. Its handful of cities were all protected by huge glassteel domes.

"Dropping," Kindervoort said.

The magnetic grapples released the lighter. The pilot eased her away from the harvestship. Radar showed Mouse's boat, almost lost in the return from *Danion,* doing the same a hundred meters away.

They picked up their service ship escort and began the long plunge toward Angel City's spaceport.

Kindervoort would lead the second wave. Behind him would come armed lighters from other harvestships, ready to provide close air support if that proved necessary.

The planet grew in the viewscreens. On infrared it looked rather like Old Earth. Moyshe told his pilot, "The first survey teams thought this would be a paradise."

The pilot glanced at the screen. "It's not?"

"It's a honey trap."

A greenhouse effect made it a permanently springtime world. It was a riot with a roughly Permian level of life. Its continents lay low. Much of the so-called land area was swamp. Methane made the air unbreathable. The planet was on the verge of a mountain-building age. Three hundred kilometers north of Angel City lay a region locally dubbed the Land of A Million Volcanoes. It added a lung-searing touch of hydrogen-sulfide to the air.

The first wisps of atmosphere caressed the lighters. The escort braked preparatory to pulling out. The landing teams would be on their own the last 100,000 meters.

Mouse's boat screamed down less than a kilometer from benRabi's. Their pilots kept station almost as skillfully as Marine coxswains. They had handled atmosphere before, somewhere.

Moyshe became ever more tense, awaiting some sudden, unpleasant greeting from below. There was none. It was a picnic fly, except that it was a penetration run without thought to economy or comfort, just getting down with speed. Moyshe kept a close monitor on the radio chatter of the second wave, already in the slot and coming down.

The lighter rocked and shuddered, braking in. BenRabi staggered back to his men.

There was barely time for him to hit his couch before, with a bone-jarring smack, the ship set down. Moyshe sprang up and turned to the opening hatch, laserifle in hand. Behind him came two men with grenade-launchers, then the rest of the team.

Moyshe jumped out, dodged aside. Two hundred meters away Mouse hit tarmac at virtually the same instant. His pathfinders spread out to place the target markers for vessels yet to arrive.

The thing became anticlimactic. No one was home. The field was naked of ships and people.

Then a stiff-necked, thin old man in a bubble-top, The Broken Wings swamper's out-suit, stepped from a utility shed. "Beautiful landing, Thomas," he said on radio. "Ah. And Mouse, too. You've taught well, boys. But you had the best teachers yourselves."

"Beckhart!" Mouse gasped.

"You were expecting St. Nick, son?"

"You said you smelled him," benRabi snapped. "Mouse, raise *Danion.* Tell them to stand by on the main batteries. General alarm. Have Jarl come close circle with the air support."

"Thomas, Thomas, what are you doing?"

"The question is, what are *you* doing?" He covered Beckhart while Mouse handled the communications chores. Kindervoort came up on the suit frequency, chattering wildly. He wanted an explanation for the panic.

"I just came out to welcome you," Beckhart said. "I wanted to see my boys." All operatives were "son" or "my boys" to Beckhart. He treated them like family—when he was not trying to get them killed. BenRabi had strong love-hate feelings for the man.

He stifled his emotions. For the moment Beckhart had to be considered the most dangerous enemy around. His presence altered everything.

"What is all this?" the Admiral demanded. "An invasion? This is a free planet, Thomas."

BenRabi foresaw a sorry, sad old man act. The act that so often won the Admiral his way. One means of beating it was to throw him a hard slider. What the hell was his first name? Using it would rattle him.

"We heard there was some dust getting kicked up here," Mouse said. "Nicolas! Will you get those men deployed? What the hell do you think this is?" The Seiners were standing around gawking, stricken motionless by the sheer hugeness of the planet. How could you be military the first time you saw open spaces and an infinite sky? "We don't take chances, Admiral."

Beckhart chuckled. "There was a spot of trouble. I've got it under control."

"We heard something about martial law," benRabi said. "How does that fit with your standards of neutrality?"

"We pick on everyone separately but equally." Beckhart chuckled again. He glanced around at the Starfisher landing parties, then at the sky. "There's no violation in spirit, Thomas. I need what you're selling. You'll sell it in peace if I have to break every head on the planet. That's why I elected myself your welcoming committee. Now then, I think I've got everything ready for you. Why don't you ride in with me and tell me about your adventures?"

Mouse and benRabi exchanged glances. This was not what they had expected. It stank of Beckhart scheming. But… if the Old Man said things were under control, they were. He rarely lied, though he enjoyed razzle-dazzling you from the other room.

"Right," Moyshe said, making a snap decision. "Nicolas. Kiski. Pack up your weapons and get over here. Admiral, what's the transportation picture?" The spaceport, like any built with an eye to safety, was well removed from the city it served.

"Excellent. It should be arriving… Ah. Here it is."

A column of Marine personnel carriers rumbled onto the field.

"Did you bring the Guinness?" Mouse asked. "We might as well be sociable."

"A shipload," Beckhart replied. "And with any luck von Drachau will show up and share a few before we close up shop."

"Jupp?" benRabi asked. "Really?" He looked forward to that. Jupp was still a friend, though he was on the other side now.

He and Mouse shuffled their men into the first few carriers, advised Kindervoort of the altered situation, and left for Angel City as the second wave began rumbling down the sky.

# FOURTEEN: 3050 AD

## The Main Sequence

Beckhart's word proved good. Angel City was quiet. Central Park, a recreational area at the city's heart, had been equipped with field tents, trailers, and miscellany the Admiral had borrowed from the Corps. Storm and benRabi set up for business before noon.

"Mouse," benRabi said, "you get the feeling we're being rushed?"

"It's not a feeling, Moyshe. It's a fact."

"How do we stall?"

Men with briefcases were lining up to obtain the little catalogs Moyshe's team had brought along. "Buy time," Jarl had said. It did not look like they would be given a chance. The various purchasing agents, impelled by the war scare, wanted the bidding to begin right away.

The Marines proved to be perfect policemen. They helped immeasurably. They showed favoritism only to Starfisher tourists. The Admiral seemed determined to avoid a significant incident, and to help the local shopkeepers relieve the Seiner sightseers of all their hard currency.

Storm lost his first tourist their second day on The Broken Wings. The man turned up again before Mouse learned that he had been taken. He was none the worse for wear. He was a mess cook from *Danion* who knew nothing anyone wanted to know.

"It's started," Mouse told benRabi when Moyshe relieved him. "Make sure everybody checks in before they wander off. Check their passes. The ones we have to watch have been given a red one."

"You know who grabbed the man?"

"No. I didn't try to find out. I just passed it to Beckhart. I figure we might as well let his people do it. We'll have more people to watch our criticals."

Moyshe lost several people on his shift. There was only one incident with anyone who mattered. His people handled it perfectly, and presented the would-be kidnapper to Beckhart's Marines.

The man turned out to be a frustrated newshawk trying to get around Seiner and Confederation censors. Beckhart booted him off planet.

Days ground by, producing no insoluble problems. The auction bidding was wild. Prime ambergris nodes repeatedly brought record prices. There were rumors that Confederation meant to get a stranglehold on the trade. Outsiders and private industry wanted to grab while the grabbing was good.

That rumor made Moyshe nervous. The way the Admiral shrugged it off, he suspected the Bureau had an angle.

The war scare, if not genuine, was convincing. Confederation and Ulantonid forces were marshaling on the boundaries of the March of Ulant. People were getting scared.

Did they mean to fight one another? Or some third party? The news people were wondering too. Luna Command had been leaking one line of news one week, another the next.

News snoops became Moyshe's biggest problem. They used every trick to capitalize on an opportunity to approach real Seiners. Moyshe did three interviews himself. Someone had tipped the media that he was a former Bureau agent.

He refused interviews after someone discovered that he and Mouse had been responsible for Jupp von Drachau's famous raid in the Hell Stars.

Then Seiners ceased to be newsworthy. The sword-rattling on the frontier faded away.

Luna Command had admitted that a secret research station and its entire solar system had been destroyed. The hitherto hypothetical nova bomb had been developed there, and proven in unfortunate circumstances.

Maybe there is a God, Moyshe thought. A loving God willing to turn an insane weapon on its creators.

There was a tape of the disaster. Navy claimed it had been shot by a supply vessel entering the system by happenstance. It got hours of air play.

It was awesome, but there was something odd about it. Moyshe could not shake the feeling that it had been faked.

Beckhart seemed to be amused by the whole thing. That was not his style. Not in the face of a genuine disaster.

Moyshe was using a free minute to try digesting sixteen months of back news when Amy walked into his trailer-office. "What the hell are you doing here?" he demanded.

"That's some greeting from a husband." She pouted. "I thought you'd be glad to see me." She pulled his rolling chair from behind his desk, spun him, and plopped into his lap.

"I'm not. It's too damned dangerous."

"You must've found yourself a girlfriend. Yeah. I know all about you Navy men."

"The danger… All right. I give up." He hugged her. "Let me knosh on your neck, woman."

There was a knock. "Up, girl. Enter."

A harassed and apologetic youth bustled in. "Messages and mail," he said. "Looks like some real excitement starting."

"How so?"

"Read. Read." The messenger folded his receipt and left.

The top flimsy was a copy of a terse communique from Gruber. He had sent a strong probing force toward Stars' End. It had been driven away by a combined force of Sangaree and McGraw pirates. "Amy! Read that."

She did. "What?"

"An alliance between the Sangaree and pirates?" He initialed the copy, flipped it into Mouse's In box.

The next flimsy was intriguing. Freehauler merchantmen off Carson's and Sierra reported that the Navy squadrons there had taken hyper. He passed the copy to Amy.

"All Naval personnel here have had their liberties cancelled. Two of the squadrons up top have been told to make ready to space. What do you think?"

"The war thing about to break?"

He shrugged.

The only other item was a magazine, *Literati*, with attached envelope hand-addressed to a Thomas McClennon, Captain, CN.

It baffled Moyshe.

"I see you've been promoted," Amy said. Suspicion edged her voice. He glanced at her, surprised. Anger and fear colored her face in turn.

"What the hell?" He set the envelope aside and turned to the magazine's contents page. Halfway down he encountered the title, "All Who Were Before Me in Jerusalem," followed by the promoted name. "No," murmured, and, "I don't understand this."

"What is it?" Amy looked over his shoulder. "Am I supposed to congratulate you? I don't understand what's happening."

"I don't either, love. Believe me, I don't." He slipped one arm around her waist, turned to the story.

It was the version he had written aboard *Danion*, before deciding to become a Seiner. How had the magazine obtained it?

He threw his thought train into reverse.

He had not packed the manuscript in any of the bags he had lost when his gear had gone back to Confederation without him. Though he had not seen the manuscript since then, he was sure it was in his cabin. He had not moved it. He was absolutely certain he had not.

"Amy, remember my story? The one you never could understand? You know what happened to the manuscript?"

"No. I figured you trashed it. I didn't ask because I thought you'd get mad. I never gave you any time to write, and I know you wanted to."

He made a call to Security aboard *Danion*. Fifteen minutes later he knew. The manuscript was not in his cabin.

Thinking it safely stowed away, he had not worried about it before. He worried now.

Everything he and Mouse had learned about the Starfishers had been in that manuscript, penned between the lines and on the backs of sheets in invisible ink. If that had reached the Bureau…

"Amy, that business with the Sangaree failsafer… Come on. We've got to talk to Jarl." He grabbed her wrist and dragged her. He snatched the flimsies from Mouse's In tray.

"What are you mad about?" she asked. "Slow down, Moyshe. You're hurting me."

"Hurry up. This's important."

They found Kindervoort at a place called Pagliacci's. It was a dusky, scenty, park-facing restaurant where both Seiner and Confederation luminaries dined and amused themselves by pumping one another over pasta and wine. BenRabi pushed past the carabiniere doorman, overran a spiffy maître de, stalked across a darkly decorated main dining room, through garlicky smells, to a small, private room in the rear. Admiral Beckhart held court there these days.

He and Kindervoort were playing a game of fence-with-words. Kindervoort was losing. He was relieved by Moyshe's appearance.

Moyshe slapped the papers down in front of Kindervoort. "We've been had."

Kindervoort scanned the top flimsy. "Where're your ships headed?" he asked Beckhart.

The Admiral chuckled. "I don't ask you questions like that. But not to worry, my friends. It doesn't involve your people. Not directly." He chuckled again, like an old man remembering some prank of his youth.

Kindervoort read the second flimsy, then thumbed through the magazine. "I suppose you want me to congratulate you, Moyshe. So congratulations."

"Jarl, I didn't finish that story till a couple days before the landsmen went home. And I came into this mess graded Commander. Someone had to put the story on the ship to Carson's."

"And?"

"It wasn't me that did. I left it out of my stuff because it carried the notes I'd kept for *him.*"

"Ah. I see." Kindervoort considered Beckhart.

The Admiral smiled, asked, "This lovely lady your bride, Thomas?"

Amy favored him with an uncertain smile.

"Watch him, honey. He's another Mouse. He can charm a cobra."

Kindervoort stared and thought. Finally, he asked, "Did they get anything critical?"

"I can't remember. I think it was mostly social observations. Like that. Impressions. Guesswork."

"Sit down, Thomas," Beckhart said. "Mrs. McClennon. Drinks? Something to eat?"

"It's benRabi now. Moyshe benRabi," benRabi grumbled.

"I'm used to McClennon, you know. Surely you can't expect an old dog to learn new tricks." He rang for service. "Mrs. McClennon, you've caught yourself a pretty special man. I consider my men my boys. Like sons, so to speak. And Thomas and Mouse are two of my favorites." BenRabi frowned. What was the man up to? "So, though he defected and it hurts, I try to understand. I'm glad he finally found someone. He needs you, Missy, so be good to him."

Amy began to relax. Beckhart charmed her into giving him a genuine smile.

"There we go. There we go. I recommend the spaghetti, children. Astonishingly good for this far from nowhere." Jarl coughed, a none too subtle reminder that there was business to be discussed.

"All right," Beckhart said, turning to Kindervoort. "I'm exercising an old man's prerogative. I'm changing my mind. I'm going to spill the facts before there's a bad misunderstanding."

"Yes, do," benRabi snapped.

"Thomas, Thomas, don't be so damned hostile all the time." He sipped some wine. "First, let's swing back to the Ulantonid War. To their rationale for attacking Confederation.

"Our blue friends are obsessed with the long run. Us apes, the best we manage is a ten-year fleet modernization program, or a twenty-year colonial development project. They figure technological and sociological effects in terms of centuries. We'd save ourselves a lot of trouble if we'd take a page from their book. Thomas, sip your wine and be patient. I'm politely getting to the point.

"What I want you to understand is they roam pretty far afield in order to figure out what's coming up the day after next year."

"What's that got to do with whatever you're up to now?" Kindervoort asked.

"I'm getting there. I'm getting there. See. This right here is what's wrong with our species. We're always in such a damned hurry. We never look ahead. My point? Ulant does. When the war hates settled down and we let them build ships again, they resumed their deep probes."

"So?" Moyshe said. He was trying to fly easy, but for some reason he had a chill crawling his spine.

"Let an old man have his way, Thomas. It isn't every day I spout cosmic secrets in an Italian restaurant. Here it is, then. About thirty years ago Ulant made an alien contact. This was a long way in along The Arm. They eventually brought it to our attention.

"People, this race makes our friends the Sangaree look angelic. I've seen them in action myself. Really, words can't express it. What I mean to say is, I hope I don't have to see them again, here in our space. They're bad, people. Really bad. When they get done with a world there's nothing left bigger than a cockroach."

The Admiral paused for effect. His audience did not respond. He looked from face to face.

"That's a bit much to swallow," Moyshe said.

"It is. Of course. It took us a while to bite when the Blues brought it to us. By us I mean Luna Command. They knew better than to go to that dungheap called a Diet. For a good many years now, with the Minister the only civilian in the know, we've been working with Ulant to get ready."

BenRabi recalled his visit to Luna Command before drawing the Starfisher assignment. The place had gone completely weird. The tunnels had been filled with rumors of war, and crowded with military folk from a variety of races and scores of human planets beyond Confederation's pale. Even then there had been the smell of something big in the air.

"Then this confrontation with Ulant is a smoke screen? A light show cooked up with Prime Defender so she and you people could con bigger appropriations? Admiral, the first lesson pounded into me at Academy was that the Services don't make policy."

"Yep. And it's the first lesson an officer unlearns, Thomas. One of my staff boys quoted me a Roman soldier a while back. 'We are the Empire.' Thomas, the Services *are* Confederation. Those of us who have gotten old in our jobs take that to heart. We make policy. Me, I shape the whole Confederation outlook. I'm doing it right now, by talking about this. It's no big thing, though. The news is starting to break.

So many people are in the know now, truth can't hide. In three months every citizen will have seen tapes documenting the murder of the world I visited... I can run that tape for you if you want. Just come over to headquarters sometime. Then you won't think I'm blowing smoke."

"I don't think it, I know it." But Moyshe was not sure. He had known the Admiral for a decade. He never had seen the man more excited, or more intense. He had assumed an aura, the way Mouse did when he talked about Sangaree. "You talk like a man who's found religion."

Beckhart nodded. "You're right. I'm getting carried away. But I've seen it. It doesn't make any sense, and that's why it's so damned scary. They hop from world to world, like galactic exterminators... I'm doing it again. Sorry."

"Why are you telling us now?" Kindervoort demanded.

"Trying to shed some light on what we're doing. We're going to make our first spoiling strike before the end of the year. We have just a couple of things left to straighten out before we move."

BenRabi had a sudden, intense feeling of danger. Startled, he glanced over his shoulder. There was no one behind him.

Beckhart's explanation, mad as it sounded, did tie the Bureau's frantic behavior into a neat ball. "What's still on your job list?" Moyshe asked. He glared at Beckhart, daring him to say something about Starfishers.

The original assignment now made military sense. Communications were the backbone of the fleet. Every ambergris node obtained would improve Navy's combat efficiency.

Beckhart surprised him again. "Sangaree, Thomas. The worms that gnaw from within."

Moyshe's mental alarms jangled. "You don't expect the Sangaree to be a long-term problem?"

"No. Thanks to Mouse."

"What?" Kindervoort and benRabi spoke together.

"Why were you sent to the Starfishers, Thomas?"

"To locate you a starfish herd. To get Navy a source of ambergris it wouldn't have to share."

"So you thought. So you thought. Actually, incorporation was a political goal, not military. It hasn't been important to Luna Command. We've known how to find Payne's Fleet for years. That's right, Captain Kindervoort. Starfishers can be recruited. I have agents aboard *Danion.* Thomas suspected as much when he charged in here with his magazine. But there was no pressing need to incorporate you. Grabbing a fleet might have started a fatal uproar. Nowadays... If I was a Starfisher who hoped for a future in my business, I'd polish up on my Confederation studies."

Kindervoort smiled a thin, wicked smile. "I don't think we need to worry, Admiral."

Beckhart winked at Moyshe, jerked his head to indicate Kindervoort. "Doesn't know me, does he? Thomas, the mission was aimed at the Sangaree. You should have known. That's all Mouse works. Don't interrupt your elders, boy."

BenRabi had intended to ask why he had been sent along.

"I thought the Starfishers, because they deal with the Freehaulers and McGraws, might have a line on Homeworld too. My guess was wrong, but my intuition was right."

You're lying, Moyshe thought. You're editing the past to fit the needs of the present. You knew, and controlled, more than you'll ever tell.

Beckhart said, "Mouse found what I needed. He got it out of the astrogational computer of a mind-burned raidship captured at Stars' End. He extracted the data and sent it out. Von Drachau was given the attack mission. Judging from the fleet alert, he pulled it off. He's probably on his way home now, likely with a mob chasing him. The pressure should ease for you at Stars' End, Jarl. You might not have to fight your way in after all. You might say we've done you a favor."

Beckhart leaned back in his chair, grinning at Kindervoort's consternation. "You can't kid a kidder, boy. We guessed what you were up to before you got here. Our agents confirmed what we suspected."

"If you knew that," Moyshe said, "why haven't you given us any trouble? I'd think you'd jump on Stars' End like…"

Kindervoort kicked him under the table.

"Several reasons, Thomas. We're spread too thin already, guarding against their raidships if they get too excited. We've got no feud with you. And you can't do anything but get yourselves killed out there anyway. So why get excited?"

BenRabi studied the old man. Beckhart *was* excited. What else was up his sleeve? The theft of the Stars' End weaponry after the Seiners opened the planet?

Had Mouse reported their suspicion that the Seiners could manage it?

Why was the Admiral here, now, instead of in Luna Command? Stars' End would be a damned good reason.

It came down to Mouse. Had Mouse simply yielded to his hatreds and passed on the information about the Sangaree? Or was he still reporting?

Kindervoort asked, "If you're spread so thin, how could you mount a raid on Homeworld?"

"It wasn't a raid. It was a wipeout. Let's say the nova bomb disaster wasn't as complete as the news people have been led to believe. Let's suppose a couple of the weapons were taken out before the blowup. Let's take it a little further and speculate that a certain Jupp von Drachau tumbled one into Homeworld's sun."

BenRabi snapped up out of his chair, breaking Amy's sudden iron grip on his arm. He stared over Beckhart's head, into cruel vistas of self-condemnation.

A whole solar system destroyed!

"You're insane. You're all insane."

"I wish you could know how much soul-searching went into the decision, Thomas. I honestly do. And, despite the Four slash Six memo, I don't think the decision would have been made had it not been for the centerward race. Thomas? Come and see those tapes before you judge us. All right?"

BenRabi ignored him. He was back to that failsafer day again. How did Mouse get the manuscript out to Beckhart? Kindervoort had watched them every second. Beckhart's Seiner agents must have handled it while Mouse was holding everyone's attention.

He remembered a Seiner known as Grumpy George. Old George was a coin collector. He and Moyshe had done business several times. George had had a superb collection. He had claimed to have made an outstandingly lucky "blind" purchase during an auction held on The Big Rock Candy Mountain, years ago.

Any truly devoted collector was vulnerable. And George was an obsessive.

This same George had come to Angel City with the first group of tourists. He had stopped by the office to ask about hobby shops. Moyshe had passed him on to Storm. Mouse had given him a list.

"How many hobby shops does the Bureau run, Admiral?"

Beckhart's eyebrows leapt upward. "Damn, Thomas. But you always were intuitive. Just one these days. Oddly enough, it's right here in Angel City."

"In other words, the place has served its purpose."

Beckhart leaned toward Kindervoort. "You see why he made Captain so young?"

Kindervoort simply looked baffled.

An ulcer that had not bothered Moyshe for a year took a sudden bite from his gut.

Someone pounded on the door. "Mr. benRabi, are you there?"

"Come in. What's up?"

"Someone just tried to kill Mister Storm."

"What? How?"

"It was a woman, sir. She just came up and started shooting."

"Is he all right?"

"Yes sir. He took off after her. She headed into Old Town."

Old Town was that part of Angel City which had lain under the first settlers' dome. Today it was largely a warehouse district. It was the base of the city's small underworld.

"You think it's the Sangaree woman?" Kindervoort asked.

"Marya? A grudge like that is the only thing that would set Mouse off," benRabi replied.

"How could she be here?" Amy demanded.

"I'd better go dig him out," Moyshe said. "If it's all right with you, Jarl?"

"It's your shift. Do what you want."

"Amy, stay with Jarl." Moyshe told the messenger, "Find me six off-duty volunteers. Tell them to meet me outside my office. Armed."

"Yes sir."

Moyshe bent, kissed Amy. "In a little while, hon." He wished he could have been a more loving husband lately. Events had permitted them only the most brusque of relationships.

He caught Beckhart giving him an odd look. A baffled, questioning look.

What did that mean? Puzzled, he went to the door.

He paused there, glanced back. Kindervoort and Amy were sipping their drinks, lost within themselves. Poor Jarl. The pressures here were too much for him. He was becoming less and less active, more and more a figurehead. Was it cultural shock?

He would survive. He would make a comeback in his own milieu. He did not worry Moyshe.

His concern was the almost magical disappearance of the Admiral while his back was turned.

He hated to admit it. He loved that old man like a father. Their relationship had that attraction-repulsion of father-son tension. But he could not trust the man. They were of different tribes now.

He had to hurry if he meant to stay ahead of Beckhart.

He was a block from the restaurant when he encountered the first poster. It clung crookedly to the flank of a Marine personnel carrier. He trotted past before it registered. He stopped, spun around. His eyes widened.

Yes. The face of a woman, a meter high, smiled at him.

"Alyce..." he croaked.

*Wham!* Darkness slammed home. He no longer knew where or who he was. He staggered past the carrier, went down on one knee.

His head cleared. He was in Angel City... He looked behind him. There was a man following him... No. That was last time. Or was it?

For a moment he was not sure if he was Gundaker Niven or Moyshe benRabi. Somebody was trying to kill Gundaker Niven...

He shook his head violently. The mists cleared. Which name he wore did not matter. Niven. McClennon. Perchevski. BenRabi. Any of the others. The enemy remained the same.

He returned to the personnel carrier. The poster was gone. He circled the quiet machine. He could find no evidence one had existed.

"What the hell is happening to me?" he muttered. He resumed trotting toward his headquarters.

He encountered the second poster fewer than fifty meters from his office trailer. It clung to the side of one of the tents his people used for quarters. He reacted just as he had before. He came out of it clinging to a tree, gasping like a man who had almost drowned. The poster was gone.

Had it ever existed? he wondered.

The fragile stability he had constructed with Chub's help was fraying. Was he in for a bad fall?

He clambered into his trailer like a man carrying an extra fifty kilos, dropped into his swivel chair. His heart hammered. His ears pounded. He was scared. He closed his eyes and searched his mind for a clue to what was happening. He found nothing.

It had to be this contact with his past. The benRabi personality was not really him. It could not withstand the strain of the milieu of Thomas McClennon.

Then he noticed the envelope lying on his desk. The envelope that had been attached to the magazine *Literati.*

He stared as if it were poisonous. He tried to back away. One hand stole forward.

It was from Greta Helsung, the girl he had sponsored in Academy. His pseudo-daughter. It was a grateful, anxious, friendly missive, seven pages of tight script reviewing her progress in Academy, and her continual fears for his safety. She knew that he had been captured by enemies of Confederation. His friends had promised they would rescue him. They would get her letter to him. And this, and that, and she loved him, and all his friends in Luna Command were well and happy and pulling for him, and she hoped she would see him soon. There were several photographs of an attractive young blonde in Navy blacks. She looked happy.

There was also a note from an old girlfriend. Max expressed the same sentiments with more reserve.

What were they trying to do? Why couldn't yesterday let him be?

Greta had such a cute, winsome smile…

He sealed his eyes and fought to escape the conflicting emotions.

He began to feel very cold, then to shake. Then to be terribly afraid.

# FIFTEEN: 3050 AD

## The Contemporary Scene

There were fifty ships in the exploratory fleet. They had not seen a friend in two years. It was a big galaxy. They were 10,000 light-years from home, moving toward the galactic core, backtracking old destruction.

There had been eighty-one ships at the beginning. A few had been lost. Others had been left at regular intervals, to catch and relay instelled reports from the probe. Most of the ships were small and fast, equipped for survey and intelligence scanning.

The fleet was near its operational limit. Three months more, and the ships would have to swing around, the great questions still unanswered.

The advance coreward had been slow and methodical. Still, space was vast and only a fragmentary vision of enemy territory had been assembled.

The stars were densely packed here. The night around the fleet was jeweled far more heavily than farther out The Arm. The skies were alien and strange. The worlds were silent and barren.

Where were the centerward people building all their ships? Where did the killing hordes spring from?

The Ulantonid explorers had detected convoys heading rimward. They had seen a parade of dead worlds. But they had located nothing resembling a base, occupied world, or industrial operation. They had learned only that the enemy came from still farther toward the galaxy's heart.

Then, too, there had been the tagged asteroids in the dead solar systems. Huge metallic bodies three to five hundred kilometers long, all similar in composition. Eleven such rocks, marked with transponders, had been located. The Ulantonid specialists had been unable to conjecture the meaning of the tagging.

The probe fleet had established five tracks along which enemy ships advanced out The Arm. Each was a river of charged particles, ions, and free radicals.

Contact was carefully avoided. The mission was one of observation.

Remote surveillance of the charged paths showed not only the occasional outward passage of a fleet but the regular back and forth of courier vessels. That suggested the enemy had no instel capability. Which was an important deduction. The allies would obtain a tactical advantage by being able to coordinate their forces over far vaster distances.

The centerpiece of the Ulantonid fleet was its only true ship of war, a vessel which beggared the human Empire Class. It bore the name *Dance in Ruby Dawn.*

Humans named their warships for warriors, battles, cities, old provinces, lost empires, and fighting ships of the past. Ulant used the titles of poems and novels, symphonies and works of art. Each race found the other's naming system quaint.

*Ruby Dawn* carried the liaison team provided by Confederation's Bureau of Naval Intelligence. Those people had been away from home even longer than their Ulantonid shipmates.

Theirs was a grueling task. They had to survey all incoming data and isolate those bits which justified transmission to Luna Command. They had to be diplomatic with their hosts. It was too much for twelve people eleven thousand light-years from the nearest of their own kind.

An Ulantonid officer stepped into their working compartment. "Commander Russell? We're getting something that might interest you."

Russell was a short black man built like a tombstone. He almost responded, "We'll get it in a while, won't we? Where's the damned hurry?" He did not. The Blues were so courteous it made him ashamed to think of giving them a hard time.

"Important?" he asked. The Blues were showing strain too, though they were more accustomed to extended missions.

"*Song of Myrion* reported a strong neutrino source. It didn't look natural. On the other hand, it was two-thirds of a parsec from the nearest star. Control is moving probe ships in from several directions. It was felt that you would want to see the scans we're getting."

"Of course. Of course. Doris, you can get in touch through Group Voice Nomahradine. Lead on, Group Voice."

Russell did not expect anything. The Blues came up with something new twice a week. There was always a natural explanation. But someone always went along. It was part of the get-along policy. Never give the Blues offense. The squabbling and snarling had to be confined to liaison team quarters.

A communications officer greeted them with, "We might have something this time, Group Voice." He gestured. Russell surveyed the elaborate and only slightly alien equipment. One huge display pinpointed the probeships involved in the current exercise. They had taken positions on an arc one Ulantonid light-year from the neutrino source. Lines and arrows of colored light flickered in and out of existence.

Russell was astounded. The neutrino source was not a point. The lines indicated that it subtended a half second of arc, vertically and horizontally, from the point of view of each observer. He did some quick mental arithmetic. "Jesus," he murmured. "That's a globe… almost six times ten to the twelfth kilometers in diameter. That's five hundred times the diameter of the old Solar System."

The Group Voice was equally impressed. "Commander, that's one hell of an artifact."

Russell scanned the displays. There was enough mass in the region to slightly distort space! The stars behind did not show through.

"Could it be a dark nebula?"

"Too dense."

"You'll take a closer look?"

"When it's cleared up top."

"Whatever it is, it's moving. At a damned good clip."

"That's what makes us so interested, Commander."

Russell looked for a spare seat. There were none. The word was out. The place was filled with curious Blues. The Heart Of The Shield, or Fleet Admiral, made her entry. She spoke with her science officers, and included Russell as a courtesy. Russell simply listened. It was not his place to offer his thoughts.

It took three days to design a probe mission. A swarm of instrument packages would be placed in the great globe's path, well ahead, passive, hidden on old spatial debris. Care would be exercised so the ships placing the instruments would remain undetected.

It took three weeks to do the seeding. Another month passed before the globe reached the instruments. During that period scores of couriers were recorded moving to and from the neutrino source. Two convoys swarmed out toward the remote frontier.

Intense examination of space behind the Globular revealed it to be the focus of tremendous activity. Enemy ships swarmed through that trailing space. The Globular had a cometary tail of vessels falling away and catching up.

"It looks like the warfleets are clearing the way for this outfit," Russell told his compatriots.

"Aren't they working a little far ahead? I mean, it'll be thirty or forty thousand years before they reach Confederation."

"Maybe it's lag time in case the war fleets run into somebody stubborn."

"Stubborn? They could roll over anything. There're so many of them the numbers become meaningless."

"Still, there seems to be a gap in weapons and communications technology between them and us. I'd guess around two centuries. That means we'll kill a lot more of them than they'll kill of us. The Blues think they're frozen into a technological stasis. Their real weapon is their numbers. If they ran into somebody very far ahead of us, they'd suffer. They'd win, but it might take them generations. I'd guess they've been through it before, which would be why the Globular is so far behind the front."

Probes into star systems behind the Globular had shown, for the first time, the enemy actually living on planets. Billions of the little kangaroo people seemed to have been dumped, apparently to rework the worlds to certain specifications. The Ulantonid experts thought they would be taken off after the terraforming was complete.

Yet another puzzle.

More of the little creatures were occupied mining the asteroidal and cometary belts of numerous systems. Operating in hordes, they stripped whole systems of spatial debris.

The significance of the marked bodies had become apparent. The little folk were using that type asteroid as a portable world. The big bodies were mined hollow, given drives, and turned into immense spaceships. Given spin, they achieved centrifugal gravity. Built up in tiers inside, they could provide more living space than any planet. They could grow with their populations.

"They must breed like flies," someone suggested. "If they have to devour everything for living space."

"Question," Russell said. "The Blues say they leave the planets after terraforming them. Why?"

"Nothing about these things makes any sense," a woman replied. "I think we're wasting our time trying to figure them out. Let's concentrate on finding weaknesses."

Russell suggested, "Knowing why they're doing what they're doing might clue us how to stop them. Anybody think we can do that now?"

*Ruby Dawn* was a ship of despair. Hope had vanished. Its crew no longer believed their peoples would survive the coming onslaught.

"We need deeper probes," Russell said. "We have to get this far again past the Globular if we really want to know what they're doing. From here it looks like a million-year project to remodel the galaxy."

"But we can't probe that deep."

"No, we can't. Unfortunately. So we'll never know."

When the first remote instruments were activated by the Globular, everyone in the fleet made sure he or she could examine the incoming data.

Within hours the sight of lines of huge asteroid-ships, stacked tens of thousands high, wide, and deep, killed all interest.

What point to staring into the eyes of doom? Let the watching be done by machines that could not be intimidated.

The probe fleet turned toward home, pursuing the sorry knowledge it had sped ahead.

# SIXTEEN: 3050 AD

## The Main Sequence

Six of Moyshe's best men gathered outside his trailer. They had donned night-time black. They were buttoning buttons and making sure their equipment was in order. Each bore weapons, carried a hand comm, gas mask, and any odd or end the individual thought might come in handy. To a man they were still trying to rub sleep from their eyes.

BenRabi leaned against the frame of the door to his office. He was still shaky. "You guys willing to get into a fight to save my friend Mouse?"

"You're on, Chief," someone muttered.

"He's just an immigrant, you know."

"We wouldn't be here if we weren't ready, Jack."

Another said, "We're ready, sir. He's one of us now. I never liked him much myself. He stole my girl. But we got to protect our own."

A third said, "Klaus, you're just spoiling for a fight,"

"So now I got an excuse, maybe."

"Okay, okay," benRabi said. "Keep it down. Here's the frosting for the cake. I think the Sangaree woman is involved."

"Yeah? Maybe this time we'll do the job right."

"I tried before. I didn't get a lot of support."

"Won't be nobody to feel sorry for her this time, Captain."

Moyshe started, looked the speaker in the eye. He saw no offense was meant. He and Mouse did have brevet-commissions as captains of police, with Kindervoort's regular captain's commission senior. Seiners seldom used their professional ranks and titles.

He grinned. "I think you're all fools," he said. "And I thank you for it. I'll be with you in a minute." He stepped back inside, scanned the current data on number of Seiners on-planet. The count was way down. People did not want to play tourist at night, when most everything was closed. He tapped out a red code to Traffic aboard

*Danion*, meaning something was up and no one else was to be allowed down till further word. He guessed that within four hours there would be no Seiners on The Broken Wings who were not part of the security effort. He stepped outside. "Let's go."

They whooped like a bunch of rowdy boys.

They worried Moyshe. They thought this would be fun. He had to calm them down. They could get themselves hurt.

He led them aboard a Marine personnel carrier, took the control seat himself. The engine hummed first try. He roared toward Old Town, gears crashing and tracks whining. He was so excited that, for a few minutes, he forgot to cut in the mufflers.

Rumbling through empty night streets, he tried to anticipate Mouse. Where would Storm go? That would depend on his quarry. If Mouse lost her, the warehouse important to their first mission would seem to him a likely place to pick up the track again. The Sangaree, always nose-thumbingly bold, or stupid, might be using it again.

The warren of tall, crowded old brick buildings pressed in as Moyshe plunged ever deeper into the inky silence of Old Town. The wareshouse district was a nerve-taunting area. The smell of poverty and old evil reeked from every alley and doorway. BenRabi became jittery. He put on more speed. "Almost there, men."

He swung into the street leading past the warehouse he wanted, brought the carrier to a violent, shuddering stop.

A bright actinic flash, that left ghosts dancing behind his eyes, proclaimed nasty business afoot a half block beyond his goal. The old site had not been renovated. The Sangaree obviously were not using it.

"Stand by, men. Looks like we've found him." There was another flash. He eased the carrier over so it would not block the street. "Everybody out. Stand easy."

He used a pencil to scratch a diagram on the pavement. He was amazed at how easily the Old Town layout came back. It had been years… "Nick, you and Clair come in this way. Klaus, take Mike and Will and come in from over here. Kraft and I will go straight up the street. Test your comms. Okay. Move out."

Bright lase-weapons continued their ineffectual duel. BenRabi and Kraft stalked forward, clinging to shadow, till they spotted one of the duelists.

Moyshe studied the fire patterns.

Three gunmen were besieging a warehouse. One man was shooting back from inside. He had skill enough to keep the three pinned.

"They must have lost somebody already," Moyshe guessed. The besiegers seemed to be in the grip of a crisis of nerve.

"Maybe they're keeping him pinned for somebody else."

"Maybe."

The situation looked a little strange. The man in the warehouse was not behaving like Mouse. Mouse would not waste time sniping. He preferred the attack.

"What do you see?" Moyshe asked. His man was looking around with infrared nighteyes.

“There’s just three of them. Funny. They look like pirates.”

“What? Give me those.” Moyshe took the glasses. Kraft was right. The besiegers wore McGraw jumpsuits. That made no sense. This was enemy territory for McGraws.

Could be Mouse inside, though—if they *were* pirates. They were working with the Sangaree now. Maybe Storm was hurt... Whispering to his handcomm, Moyshe moved teams into position behind each sniper. “Ready? Shoot on my mark. Shoot!”

It did not go well. The Seiners did not have what it took to do a man first hand, in cold blood. They allowed a vicious exchange of fire before dropping two of the men. The third escaped only after taking wounds no cosmetic surgeon would ever repair.

And still Moyshe worried. It seemed too easy.

He was changing. He was hardening into the paranoid hunter Bureau had made of him. He did not recognize the shift right away.

“All clear, Mouse,” he called.

Ozone stench and the smell of hot brick assailed his nostrils. Sudden steam surrounded him, rising from a puddle left by the programmed rain of the dinner hour. A quick pair of lasebolts had missed him low and high. He scrambled for cover.

“What the hell is the matter with that bastard? Has he gone hyper-bent? Give me that stunner,” he snapped at Kraft, who was too scared to move. “He must be hurt bad. Here. Take this.” He shoved his own weapon into the Seiner’s hands. “Come on. Get yourself together. You’ve got to help.” To the other teams, via handcomm, he snarled, “Draw fire, you guys. And I mean give it to him. I’m going to stun him.”

A stunning would not please Mouse, but benRabi considered the alternatives even less pleasant.

Beams on low setting tickled the ochre brick of the warehouse, bluing the night weirdly. The whole street crackled and flickered and came alive. Legions of shadows danced like spooks at midnight. The return fire became erratic and completely ineffective. Moyshe pinpointed the source, armed carefully, held his trigger stud down. “Get over there,” he growled at Kraft.

The stunner’s spine-tingling whine continued till several Seiners pushed through the warehouse’s street door.

Minutes later, from the window, someone shouted, “You got her, Moyshe.”

“Her? What the hell do you mean?”

“It’s a woman. You got her clean. Don’t look like there’s any nerve damage.”

A stunner sometimes played hell with its victim’s nervous system. Death or permanent damage could result. It did not happen often.

“Is it Strehltsweiter?”

“No. Come on over. She’s coming around.”

“What about Mouse?”

“Ain’t no sign of him.”

A woman, he thought as he started walking. What the hell? There were only two women involved in this business. Amy and Marya. The man would have screamed if this were either of them.

The Sangaree woman was on The Broken Wings, though. Of that he was convinced.

The woman was leaning out the window, up-chucking, when Moyshe entered the room whence she had been shooting. Her shoulders slumped with defeat. Moyshe watched her from the doorway. She seemed vaguely familiar from behind.

"Chief's here, lady," one of his men said, his tone not unkind.

The woman pushed herself off the sill, turned.

"Alyce!"

The name came out a strangled toad croak.

"Thomas."

Hammers of darkness pounded his brain. Hands as light as the wings of moths tried to bear him up. A voice asked, "What's wrong, Moyshe?" from several light-years away.

Despite the additional impact of seeing the woman in the flesh, the episode ended in seconds. Cold, shaking, benRabi fought for self-control.

She deposited her behind on the filthy window sill. Her breath came in shallow, difficult gasps. Her face remained curiously immobile despite its obvious effort to portray a variety of emotions.

Shock? he wondered.

He looked inside himself.

He was shocked. Shivering, he tumbled into a dusty old chair, stared at this impossible ghost of a romance past. His thoughts swooped and whirled through a realm of chaos. His soul cried in torment as it had done so constantly during his ancient introduction to the Seiners. All the demons he had thought fettered with his starfish's help were now breaking their chains and howling up from their dungeons. The inexplicable mind-symbol he called the image of the gun flashed in and out of existence like some barbarous neon advertisement for mental disease.

He did not pass out again. Neither did he regain his emotional feet. He fought what was happening in his head, fending it while trying to analyze.

There was something a little changed about all those old spooks. They were not quite identical with their predecessors. Had time eroded them? Helped them grow older and more mellow? What?

"Moyshe? What the hell is wrong?" Klaus demanded. "Woman, what did you do to him?"

Moyshe heard. He did not respond. What could he do? What could he say? To Klaus or Alyce. He had not expected to see her again, ever, even in the tight social environment of Luna Command. Certainly not out here on the fringes of Confederation, a thousand lights from the scene of their passion and pain. It was too wildly implausible a coincidence… Yet there she sat, as agonizingly real as death itself.

He ground the heels of his hands into his temples, feeling the precursor pain of a savage headache. He gripped his stomach where his half-forgotten ulcer was coming to sudden, unpleasant life. His thoughts churned and sprayed like wild white water. His very brain seemed to be sliding on its foundations. Barriers came crashing down. Viewpoints shifted. If he did not grab *something* as he whipped past, his soul would be left a fanged wasteland as lovely and desolate as a bombed-out city.

He caught a glimmer of what was happening. He shied off like a whipped dog. He clamped down, shoving a hundred mental fingers into the sodden dikes. If he could just hold on till he found Mouse…

"How are you?" Alyce asked.

Her voice was different. It was older. Less musical. More hardened by life.

Her question had no meaning. It was just noise meant to break a fearful silence. He did not immediately respond. His men watched him with wonder and uncertainty, uncomfortably aware that they were on the brink of seeing a soul laid bare.

"I'm fine," Moyshe finally mumbled. "How're you?"

"Okay, now." But she was not. She was shaking violently. It was a common reaction to stunner shock. She would be feeling as cold as he.

"Why were those men shooting at you?" he asked, trying to gain some stability by concentrating on business. "What're you doing here?"

"It was a girl, Thomas. With your hair and eyes."

"Shut her up!"

It began to twist and burn. Down deep inside, the dikes began to give. The demons howled and laughed. That insane image of the gun thing superimposed itself over Alyce's face. "Mike!" he gasped. "Take two men outside and keep an eye out for McGraws."

His second desperate attempt to achieve stability failed. The dikes were bulging inward. "Why're you here?" he squeaked.

"I thought it was all dead," she said. "I thought I'd forgotten it. But I can't, Thomas. Go away. Leave me alone."

Leave her alone? Yes. Fine. But how did he get her to leave him alone?

"Lady, the Chief asked a question," his man Nicolas growled. "Answer up."

"Easy, Nick. No rough stuff. This's personal, not business."

He spoke too late.

"Not business?" Snake-swift, the Seiner laid a hand alongside the woman's face. The blow hurled her to the floor. He caught her hair as she fell, yanked. She screamed, but her cry did not register with Moyshe.

What did was her hair, face, and throat coming away in Nicolas's hand. The Seiner raised his trophy like the shrunken, wrinkled head of a Cyclops. The unmasked woman seemed vaguely familiar, but she was not benRabi's old haunt.

"Moyshe, you done been set up."

BenRabi could not stifle a squeaky little laugh. "I done been, Nick."

Nicolas wheeled on the woman. "You start talking. What kind of game are you playing?"

"Don't bother, Nick. We won't get anything. We don't have the equipment." There were no tears in the woman's eyes now. She showed nothing but apprehension. Moyshe added, "I don't know if it would be worth the trouble anyway."

He did not need equipment. Despite the chaotic state of his mind, a strong suspicion blossomed. Someone was working on him. He had a good idea who, and why.

"Hey, Moyshe," another of the men called. "Mike says we got trouble. McGraws. A dozen or so. Out by the carrier."

He was regaining his composure. "It was a trap. But it didn't go according to plan." He turned to the woman. "The pirates weren't in the script, were they?"

To his surprise, she responded. She shook her head.

"You tell the Old Man to get him a better makeup crew. Nick, we've got to get out of here. See if you can get Kindervoort on Tac Two. Tell him I need a pickup squad. We'll let the Corps worry about their carrier."

He had cobbled together a false peace within him. He knew it would not last. He had to finish fast. He would begin crumbling again soon. The one straw too many had been thrown into the camel's back. From here on in each period of tranquility would be just one more frantic holding action doomed to eventual failure. The decay would accelerate whenever the survival pressure slackened.

He had seen it all before, in fellow agents. He was entering the initial stages of a spontaneous, uncontrolled, unsupervised personality program debriefing. It could get rough. There were so many identities in his background that he could lose his anchor to any of them.

"What about the woman?" Nicolas asked.

"Leave her. She's not the enemy."

"Moyshe," said another, "Jarl says to meet him by Jellyroll Jones. You know what he means?"

"Yeah. It's a statue in the old park. Pass the word to Mike. He knows the place. Nick, lead off. Keep close, guys." He turned to the woman. "Good-bye." He could not think of anything else to say.

She shrugged, but seemed relieved.

They slid out the back way, ran through a block of shadows. BenRabi began to worry about the time. He had been away from his job too long. How much longer? But it looked easy…

There was a shot and a shout.

A second slug ricocheted off brick near benRabi. Cobblestones became arrowheads piercing his chest as he tried to get closer to the soil.

Shades of his last visit to The Broken Wings, he thought.

His men returned the fire, their lasebeams scoring the brick of the walls of the buildings flanking the alley where the ambusher crouched.

"Come on!" benRabi snarled. "Shoot *at* him, dammit!" A fourth slug kicked chips of alley and lead into his face. He wiped at tiny pearls of blood, wondered why the assassin was concentrating on him. Was he Marya's man?

Where was Jarl? Where were Mike and his men?

"Dammit, you guys, don't you know this ain't a goddamned game?"

And where was Mouse, who had started this mess by disappearing? Emotion began to rage through him again, undirected and confused. He tried to control it, failed. His personality program resumed its dissolution. The only anchor left him was a hard, red hot anger.

A foot scraped cobblestone somewhere behind him. He rolled, shot, hit a leg. A man yelped, scrambled for cover.

The gunman with the antique firearm kept booming away. McClennon… benRabi took a second shot at his victim before he got out of sight.

Another shadow drifted into the shelter of a doorway.

Moyshe's program ceased its disintegration.

His perceptions reached a high usually stimulated only by drugs. He felt every point and angle of the cobblestones beneath him, seemed to become one with the dampness left by the programmed rain. He saw the grey and brownness of stone, the expanding sparks and yellows of another muzzle flash, heard the thud as a bullet smacked brick behind him. He smelled damp and sulfurousness of swamp the atmosphere systems could never completely overcome. He could even taste, it seemed, something salty.

Whoa! That was blood from a chip wound, dribbling into the corner of his mouth.

He edged sideways. Four meters and he would be in a position where the would-be assassin would have to expose himself to fire. He made it. The man shot. Moyshe shot back, heard a yelp. His men pursued him in his rush into that alley.

Moyshe kicked the revolver away from the would-be assassin. "This clown is as incompetent as you guys. Come on. Get your butts moving before I heat them up myself." He waved his stunner angrily.

There were shouts from the alley they had abandoned. He spun, dropped, fired quickly, followed his men. The sting of his flesh wounds drove him like a hunted beast.

Who am I now? he wondered. This isn't like me. I'm not a fighter. Gundaker Niven? Niven was supposed to be a hardcase.

The adrenaline had him on the verge of another case of the shakes. He had been through this kind of thing before, for the Bureau, but never had been able to achieve Mouse's calmness under fire. He always got scared, shaky, and constantly had to battle the impulse to flee.

Maybe that was why he had outlived several Mouselike partners.

But they, too, had been programmed to their roles.

He was doing well this time, he thought. He was showing flashes of case-hardened calm, and shooting when it was time to shoot. He had not thought himself capable of that.

Where the hell was that idiot Mouse?

After a dozen twists and turns along his journey he slowed, started trying to look like a tourist headed for the Jones monument. His men stalked along behind him.

The monument had not changed. It was the same tall bronze statue surrounded by the same small park, its boundary stockaded by imported pines and bushes. Between the trees and the statue there were a dozen lighted fountains where sea nymphs bathed in endlessly falling waters.

The park was the heart of an oasis in the desert of Old Town. Lining the streets facing it were several museums, the Opera, a library, and smart little shops which catered to the wealthy. Among them were homes belonging to some of Angel City's oldest families. The square was a tenacious place. It refused to admit that Old Town's glories had faded. Most decaying cities contained a few such pearls.

# SEVENTEEN: 3050 AD

## The Main Sequence

Jellyroll Jones, as great men went, was an accident. He never had been a hero. He came in near the foot of the list of space-age memorables. His most singular act had been that of arriving on The Broken Wings before anyone else. Native school children were taught to consider him a hero, in the mold of a space-faring Magellan, but his myths bore no relation to the truth. His discovery had been sheer happenstance, and against his will. His ship had crashed here because of damage the guns of a Palisarian Directorate police corvette had done his astrogational computer. He and his crew—the women represented by the fountain nymphs—had hidden here for a few months. Unable to take the heat, humidity, and stench any longer, they had radioed for help. The corvette had collected them. Old Jellyroll had died in prison.

Moyshe paused in a shadow. He studied the statue and the dancing tips of water columns visible above the trees.

"Jarl's on," his comm man told him.

Moyshe took the hand radio. "Jarl? Where are you? We've got people after us."

"Be there in five minutes, Moyshe."

BenRabi heard strange sounds behind Kindervoort's voice. "What's going on, Jarl?"

"Roadblock. Trouble with the natives. We're talking them down."

"Don't take too long. We're only a jump ahead."

Nicolas, hand comm against his ear, shook his head. "Mike's three blocks from here. Says they might be pulling out. Maybe they read our signals."

"Jarl, we look okay for now. They're maybe running. We'll be waiting on the north side. You get anything on Mouse?"

"Not yet, Moyshe. Out."

"Out." BenRabi returned the hand comm, studied the park through nighteyes. It seemed peaceful enough. He started toward Jellyroll.

*Flash.*

"Shit. Not again." From the frying pan into the fire twice?

Maybe not. The shot had not been directed his way.

There were more shots. Someone was fighting in there. Mouse? It looked like a baby battle, a duel, two men moving between shots. One was armed with a stunner only.

"Nick, hold on here. I'll check it out." Moyshe trotted toward Jellyroll.

The action seemed to be among the fountains beyond the statue. BenRabi pushed through the trees. He tried to spot the duelists, but they had stopped shooting. Was it over? He slipped toward the statue. Jellyroll would make a good, high observation point.

The firing broke out again. The stunner seemed to be among the far trees. The lasegun was among the fountains. The lasegunner, illuminated by the fountain lights, was moving very carefully.

Moyshe climbed three meters up Jellyroll's pedestal, slithered into a prone position between the old bandit's feet. It did make a nice vantage point, but would be hell to get away from fast. He edged forward, trying to spot the duelists.

Though the farther man was in darkness, Moyshe found him first. The nearer remained veiled by the flying jewelry flung up against the ever-shifting colors of the fountain lights. The water susurrated hypnotically as it tumbled back into the pools.

A lasebolt crackled through the branches of a pine. The gentle breeze brought smoky resin scents redolent of evergreen forests. The farther duelist snapped a shot in reply. His face was visible for an instant.

Mouse.

No doubt about it this time.

Storm clutched his left arm as he dodged to a new position. What the hell? benRabi thought. What's the fool doing out here with nothing but a stunner?

Mouse's opponent shifted position.

"Ha!" benRabi gasped. "It is her."

The Sangaree woman had had cosmetic surgery, but her catlike, sensuous movements remained unchanged. She just could not hide that deadly animal grace.

He tried to draw a bead on her. "Welcome back, sweetheart," he murmured. He was not at all surprised to see her. This was another passage in her death-dance with Mouse and himself.

She did not know another dancer was about to cut in. He grinned. A fragment of an old personality returned. He became the hard half of Gundaker Niven again.

"Ha!" She was hurt too. Her left side sported a wet, hasty bandage. Mouse had gotten close once, but had missed his kill. Surprising. That was not like him.

It said something about how good the woman was.

BenRabi got a good bead. He had no trouble shooting. The woman yowled, jumped like a broken-backed cat, collapsed on the colored concrete. Her muscles jerked spastically, then she slowly stiffened into the almost-death typical of a solid stunner shot to the head.

Moyshe looked down at his weapon. "Good shooting, cowboy. Mouse!" He shouted to make himself heard over the fountains. "She's out."

"Moyshe?" Storm called back. "Is that you?"

"Yeah." Mouse sounded weak. "You hurt bad?"

"I'll live."

Storm came into the open, stumbling toward the statue. He thrust his wounded arm into his jumper for support, carried his stunner like a revolver. He paused beside Marya, stared down. "Checkmate. Finally." His gaze flicked to the statue, back down.

BenRabi shouted, "What the hell happened? I been running myself dead trying to find you."

"She sucked me in. Showed herself, took a shot, then ran. I lost my head. I ran right into it." He glanced up again, his expression odd. "But she made a bigger mistake, eh? Let her gut override her brain." Mouse smiled wickedly. His lips stretched in a ferocious duplicate of the woman's vampire grin. "You know the funny part, Moyshe? She was working with McGraws. That's scary when you think about it."

Mouse fell silent. He stared at the woman for a long time, as if loath to end the feud.

Though benRabi did not like it, time had proven the next move necessary. She had been given two chances. Twice she had come back for more. If Mouse did not end it here, they would have the hellsbitch on their trail again, all fangs and claws once more.

She and Mouse were two of a kind, Moyshe reflected. Only death would stop either of them.

"You've got to be realistic, Thomas… Moyshe," benRabi mumbled to himself. "What's got to be has got to be."

He waited. Mouse remained reluctant. Time stretched.

Personnel carriers rumbled in the street outside the park. Moyshe looked back, expecting to see Kindervoort.

Wrong. Marines. But just as good.

Back to Mouse. Was he stalling because he did not have a lethal weapon? He could use hers. Or his hands.

Then he understood. Mouse was thinking about his Holy Grail, the hatred that had driven him so long. He would not yet know about Homeworld, but killing Marya would be symbolic of the process he had initiated. Symbolic of attaining his lifelong goal. Jupp would be the weapon… Marya might be the last of the ancient enemy he would encounter.

The end of a road is always a disappointment, Moyshe reflected.

Poor Mouse. Down deep, where he lived, he knew that when Marya went there would be nothing left to hate. His Grail, for all its distant sparkle, was just another empty cup.

"Where do we go from here, Tommy?" he asked softly.

In the shadows between Jellyroll's legs, benRabi/McClennon could do nothing but shake his head. He did not know.

Moyshe/Thomas's mind was becoming pandemoniac. The outside pressure was off. There was nothing to hold the dissociation in check. He was this man for a moment, then that. Alyce crawled through his brain like a maggot through rotting flesh. Something within him kept shrieking *I want*, and not letting him know what. Sudden storms of emotion racked him, always without detectable cause. Anger. Hate. Love. Sorrow. Joy. Despair. A moment of each, whap! like the impact of a fist, then gone, as if some storehouse had been broken open and all the containers inside dumped at random.

He wrapped his arms around his head and moaned softly.

He croaked, "I don't know, Mouse," it seemed an hour after his partner asked his question. BenRabi wanted to say, "Stars' End, and back to the high rivers," but the other characters inside kept telling him he would never see a harvestship again, would never track another herd, would never again go into Contact, would never build that secret service for the Seiners.

That Alyce creature must have been a hypnotic key, he thought. She was supposed to unlock all the spooks hidden behind the barriers Chub had been unable to penetrate. But the key had not opened the lock all the way. No more than Mouse had back when, when he had tried before their scheduled return to Confederation.

Something had shorted out. Something was trying to take him back not just to Thomas McClennon before this mission, but all the way back, to a day when he had not as yet undergone any personality programming.

He did not want to make that journey. He wanted what he had found in the high rivers between the stars. He fought. Deep inside, he howled and clawed like a wild thing tangled in a hunter's net.

There were angry shouts in the street whence he had come. The Marines were disarming his men. Ordinary precaution, he supposed. His team had been operating outside its "reasonable jurisdiction."

Mouse made his decision. It favored discretion. He stooped to recover Marya's weapon...

"Don't!" The voice was soft enough not to be heard far, yet commanding. BenRabi/McClennon shrank into the shadows of Jellyroll's legs. His Amy Many-Names had appeared. She bore a nasty little pistol. Her features were as cold as Mouse's became when he went into assassin's mind.

Mouse looked at her, saw the absence of emotion, slowly straightened. He did not drop his stunner.

"Where's Moyshe?" she snapped. "The grubs will be after him. I've got to find him first. He's suddenly the key to everything. You two never really crossed over, did you?" The words tumbled out of her mouth almost faster than her lips could shape them.

Mouse did not answer. He just stared into Amy's eyes, holding them. He clutched his weapon and waited for her coldness to thaw.

Or was he waiting for McClennon? Thomas was not sure. Mouse might be turning his own peril into some kind of test.

McClennon was sure Amy's determination would not persist. She was not trained for it.

"Where's Moyshe?" she demanded again. Her voice rose, squeaked.

"Here, Love." He eased from the shadows. "Don't move. Please?"

Her gaze darted his way, noted his stunner.

Mouse raised his weapon.

"No, Mouse. Not my wife, you don't."

Mouse stopped. McClennon's tone halted him. He swung his head for a cautious look at his partner.

"Moyshe, why?" Amy asked plaintively. Her weapon did not waver a millimeter from dead center on Mouse's chest.

"Why what, honey?"

"This betrayal. We gave you everything..."

"What betrayal?"

He could hear the *I* she was saying inside. She had opened her fortress unvanquishable to him, and now his promises appeared false. He had come to her bearing banners of love, false banners, and had raped and plundered her soul.

He could hear her pain, but hadn't any idea what had brought it on. "What betrayal?" he demanded. "What's happened?"

"The Marines are arresting everybody. 'Interning them,' they call it. Your Beckhart sent Gruber an ultimatum. We open Stars' End for Navy or he nova bombs the Yards."

No, McClennon thought. There's something twisted here. Something not quite straight. Not that Beckhart would not make the threat. He would, and would follow through for the sake of the Stars' End weaponry. He was a man who believed in his mission. But the timing seemed askew.

Or was it? The Starfishers and Sangaree were inextricably entangled at Stars' End. Beckhart was free to move against the home ground of either. It was a remarkable opportunity. Earlier, he had gloated about having hit Homeworld's sun...

Damn! Damn! Damn! he thought.

The agent part of him, the old intuition, put together everything Beckhart had, and had not, said, and threw forth one incontrovertible answer. The Admiral had been after Stars' End from the beginning. From the moment he had summoned Cornelius Perchevski from his interlude with his quasi-daughter Greta...

As Moyshe benRabi it had been his mission to come up with leverage Beckhart could use to force the Seiners to open the fortress world to Luna Command.

He had been doing the Admiral's work even when he had thought he was working against the man. Damn! Damn! Damn!

And he did have the lever the Admiral needed. Beckhart had given that away in threatening Gruber.

The Admiral needed the location of the Seiner Yards. Mouse must have told the Old Man his partner could clue him in.

Gruber would yield to the threat. Not gracefully, but he would yield. No sane man would do otherwise once the fate of Homeworld became known.

Gruber would surrender. The single most commonly known fact about Beckhart was that he was a man of his word with a threat. He would use the bomb if refused.

But McClennon was sure the Old Man was running one colossal bluff right now. He could not have the coordinates of the Yards. Three Sky was huge, even if he knew to look there. Insofar as Thomas knew, there were just three people on The Broken Wings who could tell Beckhart what he had to know. Jarl and Amy would not talk.

He was in one hell of a tight place.

The Starfishers did not call their nebula Three Sky among themselves. McClennon doubted that one in a thousand knew that landside name, and not one in a hundred of those the coordinates for the Yards themselves. Mouse did not know. McClennon had acquired the information entirely by accident, while arguing with Amy.

"Where's Jarl?" he asked. He wondered how effectively his orders had been carried out after he had alerted the fleet. Well, probably. Amy was carrying on like they were the only red pass people left.

Tears rolled as she replied, "He's dead, Moyshe. He killed himself. Only about fifteen minutes ago. I got away while they were distracted."

"While who was distracted?"

"The military police."

So. That roadblock had been a setup. And Jarl, intuiting Beckhart's thrust, had gone the only way he could to avoid checkmate.

And Amy intended eliminating another information source. Him.

Where was the harvestfleet? Had Beckhart gotten his bluff in on Payne too?

Then what would Amy do about herself? Put a lasebolt through her own brain? She was capable. She seemed a bit self-destructive.

What if Beckhart's claims about a centerward race were valid? That meant the whole human race, as well as several neighboring races, were threatened with extinction.

It seemed a lot more than Seiner freedom lay on the line.

The weight of the decision he had to make seemed as heavy as that Atlas had borne. Heavier. Hundreds of worlds might depend upon his choice... Ambergris and the Stars' End weapons. They might make all the difference.

What to do?

He leaned against Jellyroll's leg and stared at the symbols of the sides of his conflict. Which should he betray? Which should he destroy?

It was in his hands alone now, and there was no evading the decision. He could not let it ride in hopes it would sort itself out. No god from a machine would swing down on a wire to relieve him of his burden.

He had always had a yearning to become a hero, even for the few shooting star moments Confederation culture allowed. He would become one to the trillions if he delivered Stars' End and its arsenal. He would stand beside Jupp von Drachau, destroyer of Sangaree… But that would make him Iscariot to millions of Starfishers.

His fingertips sensually caressed his weapon. There lay all solutions. In the gun. The final argument. In the words of ancient Mao, "All power comes from the mouth of a gun." War and violence, he thought. A certain breed claimed they solved nothing. Those folks ignored the fact that dead men seldom argued.

He remembered a small Ulantonid nun, seen in passing in the Blake City spaceport on Carson's an eon ago, while he and Mouse had been waiting to join the Starfishers. She had served a dead man…

He was vacillating. Avoiding decision. Riding a period of stability for all it was worth.

One squeeze of a trigger would settle a trillion fates. His friend? Or Amy, his love?

Those symbols remained as motionless as the man between whose legs McClennon stood. They waited too, aware that, for the moment, he was possessed of godlike power.

Mouse had, McClennon was sure, known the ramifications for some time. Perhaps since before the mission had begun. Mouse stared at Amy's weapon, half hypnotized by the death lying there. Death had never touched him…

He had been immune for so long…

Amy was pale and growing paler. She had had time to think, to see some of the possibilities, and to grow scared. Her gun hand quivered.

Mouse began moving, almost imperceptibly bringing his stunner a little farther forward.

"Wait!" McClennon snapped. "This is silly. There's a way out."

They looked at him, their faces grave and baffled.

His finger danced on his stunner's trigger. Amy squeaked as she fell. Mouse looked infinitely surprised. Shaking, McClennon peered into the street beyond the trees behind him. The Marines seemed uninterested in the park. Good. If the men just kept their mouths shut…

He scrambled down, collected weapons, stunned Marya again. Her breathing indicated she was partially recovered, and probably gathering herself for something.

He had to keep the three of them out of the way while he twisted the Admiral's tail. Maybe he could salvage something for everybody, though Beckhart would resent it all to hell.

But, dammit! It wasn't necessary to have big winners and losers. Everybody could lose a little and win a little and come out ahead in the end.

Beckhart would give in if he could not catch up fast enough. He had to have those coordinates soon, or see his whole intrigue blow up in his face.

McClennon laughed. He was going to get the best of the Old Man, and that was as rare as roc's eggs. Still chuckling, he threw Amy over his shoulder and headed for the tight darkness of Old Town.

She would come out of this hating him, but by doing it this way he would give her more than he ever could with love.

He searched his mind for signs of instability. All the gears were in place and working smoothly. Some sort of balance had been achieved. Not a natural one, but one that looked good for a while. He was now a little of everyone he had ever been, and a little more, too.

He hoped it would last long enough.

# EIGHTEEN: 3050 AD

## The Main Sequence

"What the hell is going on, Damon?" Beckhart's voice had a saw-toothed edge. "Storm and the Sangaree woman were in that park. Storm called to say he was going in after her. McClennon's men admit he went in. You chased the Seiner woman in there. Four people. Where the hell are they now?"

"I don't know, sir," the Major confessed. "We went in as soon as we knew where to look. They weren't there anymore."

"No shit? You're aware that three of those people are professionals, aren't you?"

"Yes sir. And two of them are ours, with no reason to run."

"One of them. I'm not sure what McClennon thinks he is. It's not his fault, but he has his head on backwards and it's falling apart. He probably doesn't know who he is or who he's working for half the time. He's the one I'm worried about. He needs psychiatric attention fast."

Beckhart massaged his forehead. He was growing a bitch of a headache. Just when it looked like he had it nailed down... He had to snag Thomas or his woman before Gruber called his bluff. He had to show at the Yards before the harvestfleets extricated themselves from the standoff at Stars' End. He had to move before the Sangaree raidfleet learned about Homeworld.

"Why the hell did that idiot Kindervoort have to go and kill himself?"

"He evidently had strong feelings."

"They're a stiff-necked mob. I've never figured them out. That damned Payne is still up there making nasty talk. With three squadrons sitting on his back."

"Just pride talking, sir."

"We screwed up, Damon. If we don't find those people, alive, we're had. *We.* Do I make myself clear?"

"Abundantly, Admiral. I've got all my men digging. The local police don't have any decent tracking gear, but it's still only a matter of time."

"The shorter the time, the better, Major. High Command is breathing down my neck. The CSN has a personal stake in what we're doing. He isn't very fond of me. So don't forget that water and horseshit both go downhill."

"Message received, Admiral."

"Good. Get out there and find them. And don't forget that they're professionals."

The Marines did not turn up a trace all night. Beckhart spent the time tossing, sharing his cot with a cruel dread.

He was afraid the Sangaree woman had gotten the drop on Storm and McClennon and had spirited them out of the city. She had gotten out once before.

Time trudged along. The tension built. He began snapping at everyone around him. "Like a mad dog," he overheard one of his technical ratings say.

That hit him like ice water. It made him count ten before speaking. He had an image of himself as a reasonable, fair, and fatherly superior. His pride demanded that he treat his subordinates well.

After thirty hours he locked himself in his tiny cubicle of an office. He drank coffee, gobbled aspirin, and wondered if he was too old to start praying.

"Admiral!" an excited voice called through the closed door. "Comm call. Field channel three. It's McClennon, sir."

Beckhart slapped his drab Navy comm unit, muffing the channel selection twice. "Come on, you bastard." A moment later, "Thomas? Where the hell are you, son? What's going on? Where's Mouse? You all right?"

"We're fine. Mouse is tied up at the moment." McClennon giggled. "All three of them are."

He's gone, Beckhart thought. Cracked completely. "Where are you, Thomas?"

"Around and about. Right now I'm here."

"McClennon… Report to me immediately. In person."

"No sir."

"What? Thomas, the whole damned thing is going down…" What was McClennon up to?

"Give me one little thing, Admiral. That's all I'm asking. One thing, and I give you Stars' End on a platter."

"What the hell do you think you're doing? When did Commanders start bargaining with Admirals?"

"Captain."

"That can be rectified. McClennon, I'm tired and I'm aggravated. Don't give me any shit. Tell me where you are so I can send somebody to pick you up."

"No sir. Not till I get what I want. I've got something you need. You give me something back. You want to talk about it?"

"I'll listen, Thomas. That's all." That's all. Had anyone had sense enough to try for a fix on McClennon's transceiver? Probably not. Too much to expect of these people.

"It's simple, Admiral. I'll give you the coordinates for the Yards after you execute some instrument guaranteeing the Starfishers' independence. Recognize them as an independent political entity. Offer to exchange embassies. Offer mutual non-aggression pacts. All those kinds of things that will make it hard for Luna Command to subjugate them without a big public outcry."

"Holy shit. You're out of your mind."

"I know it." Beckhart heard McClennon's pain and fear. The man was scared silly. He knew he was on the edge. "It's getting worse. I need help, Chief. But I've got to do this first."

"Thomas, the answer is no. You know damned well that I couldn't agree to something like that even if I wanted. Which I don't, I don't have the power."

"High Command does. I'll listen on this channel. You let me know when the treaties are ready."

"Thomas, you're committing suicide. You're throwing your career away."

"Really? You mean you haven't used me up yet?"

"Thomas… You can't hide from me forever."

"I can try, Admiral. I can sure as hell try."

"Thomas, I'm going to have your balls for breakfast… Shit!" He was talking to himself. McClennon was gone.

He hurled a half-finished mug of coffee across his office. The brown liquid dribbled down the wall, onto a stack of memos that had accumulated while he worried.

Someone knocked.

"Enter."

Major Damon stepped in. "We triangulated the call, sir. No luck. He wired a standard Navy comm into a public box and made the call from a public box somewhere else."

"I told you we're dealing with professionals. But let's consider the bright side. It's a small city, and he has three prisoners to watch, feed, and keep clean. He'll make a mistake. Storm will jump him. Or we'll find him. Keep looking."

Damon left. Beckhart cleaned up his coffee mess, settled into his chair. He felt better. Almost relaxed. The worst possibilities were, for the moment, no more than ghosts of evil chance.

He made some elementary calculations. The lead time he had on the Seiners if he and they started for the Yards together. Stars' End was eight days rimward of The Broken Wings. The Yards were somewhere back toward the Inner Worlds. How long till a Sangaree courier reached Stars' End with the news about Homeworld?

The Sangaree had no known shipboard instel capacity. They communicated by courier exclusively. So his agents told him. So he hoped. The scheme depended on a long news lag and Starfisher stubbornness.

He smiled. If the fastest ship known had left Homeworld immediately after von Drachau's attack… He should have fourteen more days.

"Thomas, there's no way you can stay ahead of me for two weeks. Not in this burg."

Confidence soon yielded to doubt. High Command withdrew his Marines over his protest. The doubts grew stronger. On day seven the CSN personally called. Beckhart could conceal the truth no longer. He covered for McClennon by declining to name names.

He was loyal to his men. Thomas was no turncoat. He was a victim of his occupation and faulty technical preparation. Sooner or later every agent encountered the crisis. McClennon had had the misfortune to hit his at an historically inopportune moment.

Heads were going to roll among the Psych crew! On day eleven Beckhart came to the conclusion that the first head lost would be his own. The CSN kept making sounds like a happy executioner sharpening his axe.

"Come in, Major. I take it you're going to tell me the same old thing?"

"Unfortunately, sir. He's just not leaving any tracks. We did find a cellar this morning that someone had been using, but they were long gone when we broke in. We've covered sixty percent of the city now. We're reasonably sure he hasn't slipped back into what we've covered."

"Reasonably sure? Damon, I don't want reasonably sure. I want absodamnposilutely sure."

"And instead of sixty local police reservists, I want my battalion of Marine MPs."

"What could I do? They took them," he said into Beckhart's scowl. "I see it taking seven or eight days of searching with what we have, Major. We don't have that much time."

"The probability of contact is going up faster now, sir. He has less room to maneuver. The computers almost guarantee we'll find him within five days. The statistical profile is against him. I've had my people stop using the regular comm nets. He may have been monitoring our traffic."

"Of course he was. He's crazy, not stupid. All right. Carry on."

Beckhart leaned back, thought, Thomas, I've got to give you credit. You're good when you have to be. And, what the hell is wrong with Storm? He should have done something by now. He knows McClennon better than anybody else. He's the best man I've got.

Was the little bastard in on it? The possibility had not occurred before. Mouse was the perfect agent. You did not suspect his loyalty.

But Storm's loyalty was to his dream of exterminating the Sangaree, of avenging his family. He had no motive but habit for taking a Bureau line in this. And he and McClennon had become close friends. They had done too many missions together…

They might have cooked this whole thing up with that Seiner bitch.

"Admiral. The CSN on instel, relay from *Assyrian*."

"Oh, Christ. Again?"

"He sounds upset."

"He's always upset. Switch him through."

A moment later, "Good morning, sir."

"You found that man yet?"

"No sir. We're closing in. The computers say we'll have him any time now."

"I've got computers too, Beckhart. And a lot more input resources. I have the Sangaree raidmaster at Stars' End getting the word sometime day after tomorrow. We don't know what those people will do. Maybe go crazy. I've ordered the attack squadrons back off courier intercept. That's hopeless. They'll return to Carson's and Sierra. *Hittite* is moving up to Blackworld. Two Conqueror Class reserve attack squadrons are moving into the Twenty-First Transverse in case they break through the Twenty-Third. What concerns me more than the Sangaree, though, is what Gruber is going to do when he's free to deploy. I'd guess he'd head for the Yards. From what I've been told, if he gets there ahead of you, we lose. There's supposedly no way we can root them out, and no way to get close enough to deliver the threatened nova bomb. This isn't news to you. I repeat it in case you've lost sight of the facts. Your loyalty to your people is laudable, but..."

"I'm aware of the problem, sir. It was my intention to calculate a most probable quadrant and send von Drachau to wait there while I rooted this man out. That would give us a few extra days, added to the lead time we have because of the additional distance from Stars' End to the Yards."

"You're dealing with a stubborn man, Beckhart. You haven't found him yet, let alone gotten him to talk. You apparently know him. How long can he hold out after you take him?"

"I don't know, sir." Beckhart did not like admitting that. It was a question he had been trying to ignore. He had not come out equipped for mind probing. He had not begun to worry about possibly needing the equipment till lately.

"Why is he doing this?"

"You mean his motives? I don't know. Faulty Psych programming is what set him off. You might call it induced schizophrenia. Even he's not sure what he's doing, or why. Or even who he is a good part of the time."

"I suppose you still insist on protecting him?"

"Yes sir. I don't believe he's responsible for his own actions. I don't want him punished because of technical errors made by the people who prepared him for his mission."

"Okay, Beckhart. This is the word from High Command. Prepare to meet his demands. If you haven't got him in hand by noon Tuesday, Luna Command time, you give him what he wants."

"Sir!..."

"That's the word. We'd rather have Stars' End *and* the Seiners if we can, but Stars' End is for sure. We won't risk our shot at that weapon technology."

"Sir…"

"It's not subject to debate, Beckhart. It sounds spineless to me, too, and it's my idea. But that's the way it's going to be. If you get hold of him before deadline, we'll reevaluate our position. But only if you get hold of him."

Beckhart tried several arguments. None made any impression.

High Command's position was understandable. The very existence of the race was on the line. But still…

"Get me Major Damon," he ordered after the CSN secured. "Damon? Word from High Command. We find him by noon, Tuesday, their time. Or he gets what he wants. Do the best you can."

Beckhart leaned back, closed his eyes. He felt tired and old. He went over all the old ground. There must be a way of smoking Thomas out. He just had to look at it from the right angle.

But, oh, was it an elusive angle.

# NINETEEN: 3050 AD

## The Main Sequence

Mouse came around first. He saw McClennon sitting a meter away. Thomas wore a grave expression.

Mouse groaned. "Christ! My head. What the hell happened?"

"I shot you. Stunner."

"Why?" Storm tried to sit up. He could not. He was tied hand and foot.

"Aw, shit, Tommy. What the hell? Come on, cut me loose."

"I can't."

"What's wrong with you, man? I spent four months fixing it so we could get out. I could've left you behind… We bought the mission off, Moyshe. Tommy. With ten thousand percent interest… Damned! My head. Get me some aspirin."

McClennon had them in his hand. A plastic cup sat on the dirt floor between himself and Mouse. "Open your mouth. I gave you a little too much. All of you. I had to shoot fast. I don't have your finesse."

McClennon's face settled into tired lines. He had had no sleep. More water dribbled to the floor than passed Mouse's lips.

Mouse swallowed, but too late to avoid the aspirin's sour-bitter taste. He spat. "You'd better explain."

"I got backed into a corner, Mouse. I had to make a choice. You were on duty when the Old Man finally got around to laying the truth on the line."

"Beckhart? Our own fearless leader, who was born without a mouth?"

"Yes," McClennon repeated Beckhart's story about the centerward peril word for word.

"Did you believe him?"

"He was convincing."

"He's always convincing. That doesn't make him any less a liar. And he's the worst ever born."

McClennon was surprised. He had thought that Mouse shared his belief in the Admiral's basic honesty.

"Still, that little fable would shed a lot of light on all the weird things that have been going on around Luna Command the last four or five years. I never did buy that crap about Ulant getting ready to hit us again. You sure he was telling the truth?"

"You should have seen his eyes when he described the Ulantonid intelligence tapes. But what really convinced me was when he said they're reactivating the Climbers."

"No lie?"

"That's straight."

"Wow. What do you know about that?" Mouse shook his head in amazement. It was a difficult task, lying on his side on that filthy floor. "You were going to explain why I'm lying here in this muck tied up so I can't even scratch my butt."

"It came to a choice, Mouse." McClennon's voice grew plaintive. "Between betraying Navy or the Starfishers. When I heard Jarl was dead."

"I don't follow you, Tommy. In fact, maybe you don't either. You don't look very stable. I think we'd better get you to a Psych center."

"I know. I can see what's happening to me. Mouse, I can't stop it!" He closed his eyes momentarily. "But I'm holding it off. I have to. Because when Jarl killed himself, that only left two people who could tell Beckhart where the Yards are. And he's trying to bluff Gruber by telling him he's going to hit the Yards if the Seiners don't pony up Stars' End and the harvestfleets. Me and Amy, and maybe you, are the only ones who can give him the coordinates."

"I can't, Tommy. That's one nobody let me in on. They didn't trust me the way they did you. They weren't supposed to."

"I didn't know for sure. I might've left you behind if I had. No. I couldn't have. You know too damned much about Angel City. You would've found me."

"Tell me what the hell you're doing."

"I'm going to trade Stars' End for the Starfishers."

"What?"

"I'm going to hide till he gets Luna Command to agree to let the Seiners be. In writing. In public. Then I'll tell him where the Yards are and he can hold them up for Stars' End. That way nobody loses but me."

"You're out of your head, Tommy. You won't pull it off. He's got too much time to find you. And he'll roast you alive when he catches you."

"No. He'll be damned nice to me. He's got to get me to talk. He doesn't have any psych probe gear with him, and he'll probably hold off getting physical for a while…"

McClennon had made his decision in an instant. Every second since he had been trying to justify it and find ways to make it work. He guessed that he would have to stay missing for a week.

He had decided he would not move during that time, except to do a few things that had to be done right away. No movement, no tracks for the hunters to pick up.

"I got to piss, Tommy. Bad." Mouse examined his surroundings. "Christ! This is the hole where the Sangaree used to hide the refined stardust."

"And it wasn't in our reports. What are you going to do, Mouse? Try to jump me first chance you get? Or will you wait it out?"

Mouse just looked at him. He had donned his poker face. McClennon wore a half smile when he cut the cords binding Mouse's ankles. "Take your leak in the corner."

"With no hands?"

"They're tied in front. Or hadn't you noticed?"

A tiny smile flickered across Mouse's lips. "You've been hanging around me too long. You're getting too cool."

"Go do your business."

"This place is going to get ripe."

"I don't doubt it."

It was an earthen-floored cellar, already rank and humid.

Mouse stumbled as he walked. "Damned legs are numb." He unzipped, leaned against the wall, panted as he urinated.

A stunner blast could leave a man debilitated for days.

Mouse finished. He turned. "That's a load off my mind."

McClennon let Storm take three steps before stunning him across the thighs.

"Ah, shit, Tommy. Why'd you have to go and do that?"

"Had to."

"You're getting hard, old friend."

"It's the company I keep." McClennon looked at the Sangaree woman. She was aware now, and watching with cold gunmetal eyes. He untied her ankles. "Your turn."

She rose and took care of it without a word. She did not complain or seem surprised when he stunned her too.

Mouse demanded, "What the hell is she doing here, anyway?"

"Let's say I'm keeping a card up my sleeve." She and Mouse did not know that Homeworld had been hit. She could be told and released. Her response might make a spectacular diversion.

Amy took forever recovering, and it was with her he had tried to be most gentle.

He was sorry as soon as she did come round.

Her he had not tied. He had thought it unnecessary.

He was playing chess with Mouse, using paper pieces on a board scratched into the earth. He did Mouse's moving for him. He was losing, as usual.

"Behind you," Mouse whispered.

Clothing rustled.

He hurled himself aside, rolled, grabbed his stunner, fired. Amy moaned, fell. She dropped the length of pipe she had been about to swing. It scattered the chessmen.

McClennon could barely tie her, so badly were his hands shaking. She remained conscious but refused to talk. Neither Mouse nor the Sangaree woman made any comment

Marya did smile a thin, hard smile.

The walls seemed to push in. For an instant he was not sure where he was or what he was doing. Then, for a moment, he relived part of his first visit to The Broken Wings. His name was Gundaker Niven and he and the Sangaree woman were bedmates again.

"Tommy?" Mouse said. "Tommy! Snap out of it!"

That did it, for a few seconds. Long enough for him to see all three captives trying to gain their feet, and Mouse dead last in the race.

Cold calm washed over him. He shot all three. In the head. It was dangerous, for them, but a lot less dangerous for him if he was going into one of his episodes.

He went. And became quietly crazy for a while.

He was a Starfisher named Moyshe benRabi… A Navy Gunner named Cornelius Perchevski… A naval attaché named Walter Clark… A sociologist named Gundaker Niven… Hamon Clausson… Credence Pardee… Thomas Aquinas McClennon… A boy wandering the cluttered light canyons of a city on Old Earth and getting a stiff neck looking up longingly at the stars.

Exhaustion overcame him. He fell asleep.

He wakened before his captives. His grasp on identity and reality had recovered, but all those other men were still there inside, clamoring to be released.

He wondered if he would be able to hang on.

He needed Psych attention bad.

His stomach churned and growled. He was hungry.

Food was the weak link in his plan. He had not yet obtained any. He would have to risk capture to do so.

He checked the time. Sixteen hours had elapsed since he had spirited the three out of the park. The Admiral would not have panicked yet, he reasoned. It would be awhile before the streets became too dangerous to risk.

He stepped down the stunner's output and gave his prisoners a few more hours worth of unconsciousness. Then he took Mouse's comm and went into the streets.

He made his first stop at a used clothing store, a marginal charitable operation a few blocks from his hiding place. He purchased worn, unstylish workman's garb. He changed in an alleyway. He repeated the process in a more stylish shop, and farther away still deposited his Seiner jumpsuit in a collection box belonging to the charitable organization. He worked hard to keep the surly Gundaker Niven personality in the forefront of his mind. When he was most successful he hunched slightly, spoke crudely, and looked too tough to mess with.

He purchased a collection of small tools, then a large woman's wig which he trimmed to a style favored by Angel City thugs. He placed a small bandage on one cheek and a pebble in his shoe.

He no longer looked or moved anything like any of the people the Marines were hunting.

Mobile patrols were everywhere, astounding the citizenry with their busy-ness, but he was not stopped or questioned. They were seeking a Starfisher.

They would get organized soon, he knew. It would be difficult to evade them then.

Whenever he was safely out of sight, he used Mouse's hand comm to eavesdrop on their radio traffic.

They were confused. They had four people to find, but did not know which was doing what to whom. Their interest of the moment was to make sure no one sneaked out of the city. After the boltholes were sealed they would launch their systematic search.

He wondered if he ought not to let Beckhart stew. The confusion would give him an edge. But no. The Admiral would need time to approach his superiors.

He stole an Out of Order sign off a public comm booth and carried it several blocks to a functional booth. He hung it and began making like a repairman.

The gimmicking took longer than he expected. The comm was of local manufacture. He had to figure out the color-coding of the circuitry. Then it became a classroom exercise. He installed Mouse's comm and closed the housing in minutes. He noted the terminal number and departed.

Finding groceries required imagination. Home cooking simply was not done. Rich and poor, Angel City's people ate out or had prepared meals delivered. Most food was artificial and recycled anyway. Only a few Terran tropical plants were adaptable to The Broken Wing's atmosphere and climate. No local was gourmet enough to have invested in the genetic engineering needed to adapt a wider range of food plants.

He ended up buying field rations from a swamp dredger's supply house. The saleswoman said he didn't look the type, but asked no questions. The underworld used the swamp for its own purposes. Curiosity could be harmful to a questioner's health.

He had no local money left when he returned to the cellar. He had Seiner cash and Conmarks, both of which were negotiable, but did not want to draw attention by spending outside currency. Conmarks were never rare, but still... He searched his prisoners and confiscated their limited wealth. Most of that was Confederation's interworld currency.

They submitted sullenly. No one was talking. He did not try starting a conversation. He gave them another taste of the stunner and returned to the streets.

He found a public comm and called the booth he had jiggered. The handcomm there broadcast what he had to say.

The Admiral was not pleased with him.

Finished, he patrolled around and rented two small apartments and an office, so he would have somewhere to run if the Marines closed in on his cellar. And, finally, he braved Central Park by night to steal an all-bands tactical transceiver/scanner from the inattentive MPs.

He used an old crate for a seat and the cellar wall for a backrest. He closed his eyes and listened as the tactrans scanned the bands. He heard a movement after a while. He opened one eye. Mouse was trying to sit up.

"Tommy, you can't keep doing that. You're going to hurt somebody."

McClennon turned the scanner down. "Sorry, Mouse. But I don't have a lot of choice." He leaned toward the transceiver. It was staying busy. His call had stirred Beckhart up good.

How long would he have to stay lost?

Days passed. He lost track. One moment it seemed only a few had gone by, the next it seemed a lot. Every hour was an eon trudging wearily off into eternity.

He thought he was doing well. He had kept three willful, angry prisoners hidden and controlled for days, Beckhart had not caught a trace of him. He had driven his mental problem into a straitjacket…

That jacket was not strong enough.

He was somewhere in Luna Command. A beautiful blonde, not more than seventeen, clung to his left arm. She whispered something into his ear. She called him Commander Perchevski. He was supposed to know her. He did not. He wanted to attack her.

Another woman took hold of his right arm. She insisted his name was Walter Clark. She wanted to take him away from the blonde morsel.

The females released him and assaulted one another. They fought over his name. He kept trying to tell them they were both wrong, that he was really Credence Pardee. Or was it Hamon Clausson? Wasn't he Hamon Clausson that time on Shakedowns? He forgot the women while he tried to locate his ID badge. It had fallen off his tunic.

There it was, beneath the edge of the carpet. He yanked it out. A kid with a somber, serious face stared off the card. The kid said, "Gundaker Niven," and grinned viciously.

He screamed.

There were men all around him. Some were a little shorter or a little taller, a little heavier or lighter, but each one had stolen his face. They pummeled one another mercilessly. Whenever one broke free and charged him, the others piled on from behind.

He jumped, closed his hands around the nearest throat. "I'll kill them," he gurgled. "I'll kill them all. Then they'll leave me alone."

He fought till he had no strength left. Weary, he fell to the floor. Darkness descended.

He wakened in a dank cellar on The Broken Wings. Three people watched with the cold, hungry eyes of vultures perched over a dying thing.

He glanced at his watch. He had been out ten hours. What? They had not jumped him? They were still here? He staggered to his feet, took a step, fell as vertigo hit him.

He shook his head hard. The cobwebs broke up. They drifted away. He looked around again.

Mouse quietly proffered the stunner.

Their eyes met. McClennon took the weapon. Mouse did not say a word. He crossed his wrists and offered to be tied again.

Thomas said nothing either. Nothing needed saying. He retied his friend and sat down to wait.

The hours groaned on,

He had not expected it to take so long. How long could the Old Man hold out? Why was he being so stubborn? Giving in would not cost him much. Confederation did not control the starfish herds anyway.

He supposed Beckhart was trying to save a political coup that would help overshadow the Homeworld abomination.

McClennon had to move only once to remain ahead of the search. Then the Admiral ran out of stall time.

Von Drachau returned from Homeworld. McClennon caught the news on his scanner. He guessed that it would not be long till the news reached Stars' End. That confrontation would dissolve. Gruber would rush to defend Three Sky.

That old traitor time had turned its coat again.

He was not surprised when his hand comm crackled and Beckhart came on. "Thomas, are you listening? This is Admiral Beckhart. Thomas, are you listening?"

"I'm here. Talk." That was all he said, for fear they would triangulate his position.

"Thomas, you've got what you want. Personally guaranteed by the Chief of Staff Navy." He paused for McClennon's reply. Thomas did not speak. "Thomas, are you there?"

"I'm listening, I said."

"You've got what you want. What're you going to do about it?"

He had not thought beyond forcing their acquiescence. How could he get it nailed down, on paper, publicly, without them dragging him into some back room and running him through a psychological grist mill?

"I'll call back."

He glanced at his prisoners. He had learned that he could not serve two masters and remain loved by the bondsmen of either. Amy's hatred tortured him mercilessly. And Mouse's anger… But Mouse was helping, if only by not doing anything when he had the chance. He had allowed friendship to obscure duty, had let it make him give the benefit of the doubt.

McClennon would not have made it otherwise.

But Amy… She refused to see what he was trying to do. She called him Judas.

Marya's sullen displeasure he could bear. He had had plenty of practice. Her sultry Sangaree face became a mild, passive, resigned reflection of everything he saw in his wife.

With Mouse he had no long-run worry. Mouse would get over his anger. He would forgive the treason. They were friends.

So, he thought. Time to face the Old Man. His wolves will be at the door the second I tell him where…

"Admiral? McClennon here."

"Thomas, I don't have much time. You're getting what you want. Can we speed things up?"

"I want someone from the Judge Advocate's there."

"What? You're not being arrested. You're not even being charged. I went to bat for you, son. Just give me the word. Where the hell are you?"

"I want him to witness, not to represent me."

"Christ. Thomas, you've got my word. That's all I can give you. It would take a week to get one of those space lawyers here. Now, pretty please, will you get organized?"

Okay, okay. Maybe Beckhart was right. He was wasting time. And the man *was* giving his word…

He told Beckhart where to pick him up.

# TWENTY: 3050 AD

## The Main Sequence

Four Angel City police officers came to the door, to escort McClennon to his commanding officer. He was puzzled, but did not ask why they were doing Corps work. He untied Mouse, Marya, and Amy, and said, "Let's go, gentlemen."

He had butterflies the size of owls. They were mating on the wing.

The streets were barren. Angel City had become half a ghost town. "Where is everybody?" he asked. He had heard nothing on monitor that would explain this emptiness.

"Drafted," one of the cops grumbled.

"What?"

"Almost everybody old enough was in the Reserves. It was a good way to pick up a few extra marks. They got called up."

"This war thing must be getting grim."

"Must be," the policeman admitted. "They called up everybody in the Transverse. Navy, Marines, Planetary Defense, whatever. Not only that, they took all the equipment that wasn't nailed down."

The officers were walking their charges to Beckhart's headquarters. McClennon saw very few vehicles. "What about the gang upstairs?" he asked, jerking a thumb skyward.

"The heavies? Still there. Let's hope they hold those Sangaree. You and your buddy here, and your Admiral and his crew, are the only military people left here."

"Guess we do have to take it serious," Mouse said. "The Old Man plays games, but they're not this expensive."

McClennon could not help being startled and disturbed. This general mobilization was a distressing indicator. It suggested that Confederation meant to hurl everything but the proverbial sink into the first passage of arms.

His thoughts strayed to his homeworld. Had Old Earth been stripped of men and equipment too? If so, he had to be glad he was in the Outworlds.

That madhouse planet would descend into an age of barbarism if the policing divisions vanished. Confederation did not interfere much, but did keep the violence level depressed,

A blowup had occurred during the Ulantonid War, and to a lesser degree several other times, when the Confederate presence was weak. After settling with Ulant, Luna Command had had to reconquer Earth.

When the mailed fist vanished, the cults and movements beat swords from plowshares, eager to settle old scores.

"Mouse," he said, "it's a strange world I call home."

Storm read him at a glance. "It won't be as bad this time, Tommy. I've seen some of the standing Mobe plans. They'll do some creative drafting. Something like the ancient press gangs. They'll grab anybody loose and ship them out all over Confederation. They'll scatter them so they don't cause much trouble."

"Sounds good. Break the whole mess up if they take enough of them."

"It would tap a big manpower pool. Old Earth didn't contribute a thing during the war with Ulant."

Amy, Marya, and the policemen all watched curiously.

Even Mouse did not understand Old Earth.

Earth was the land of the timid tailor, the world cramped with a people from whom all adventure had been bred. The pioneer genes had departed long ago. The stay-at-homes were, in the opinion of the rest of humanity, the culls of the species. Even McClennon willingly admitted that his fellow Old Earthers were determined to live up to their derelict image.

The average Old Earther would faint at the suggestion of going into space. And yet he could be astonishingly vicious with his fellows...

Savage decadence? That was the way McClennon saw his native culture.

"*Lo! thy dread empire, Chaos, is restored;*

*Light dies before thy uncreating word...*" he muttered.

"What?" Mouse asked.

"From a poem. By Pope."

Mouse grinned. "Welcome home, Tommy. You're acting like my old friend again."

McClennon grunted, grabbed his stomach.

His ulcer ripped at him with dragon's claws, like something trying to tear its way out. He nearly doubled over with the pain.

"Tommy?"

"Ulcer."

"We've got to get you to a doctor."

"A little while yet, A little while. I can hold out."

"What're you going to be like afterward?"

"I've got to see it through." Only after he had fulfilled his self-appointed mission would he dare concern himself with tuckpointing the mortar of body and soul.

The weeks of waiting had brought the ulcer back to life. The anticipation had been terrible. He had defied Beckhart before, but never in anything this important.

He was terrified. What would the man do? The Admiral was fair, but would not let fairness interfere with his carrying out his own orders.

McClennon tried to banish worrying by studying his surroundings. The few Angelinos in the street seemed subdued. Their auction excitement had been replaced by trepidation.

McClennon noted one odd, common piece of behavior. Every Angelino occasionally paused to glance upward. He mentioned it to Mouse.

"Maybe they're worried about the raidfleet."

He, too, glanced upward at times, but not in search of an alien doom. He told himself he was taking last fond looks at a sun. The Cothen Zeven, the prison for military officers, lay almost a thousand kilometers below the surface of Old Earth's moon. Psychologically, it was as far removed from mainstream life as any medieval dungeon.

The self-delusion did not take. He was looking for something he had lost, something now so far beyond the sky he would never see it again. Payne's Fleet had taken hyper during the week. His Starfisher surrogate homeland was gone forever.

"In here," said the officer in charge of the police group. He led them through the entrance of a second-rate hotel.

Beckhart was tricked out full dress. He stood at a stiff parade rest as they entered. His face was corpse-like. Only an almost undetectable tightness of the eyes betrayed the anger pent within him. "Lock the women up," he said tonelessly, staring through McClennon.

Amy broke down. She exploded, mixing pleading, weeping, and outrage. Marya considered her with obvious disdain. Thomas wanted to hold her, to comfort her. He did not. Trying would only make things worse.

A bit of the true Beckhart slipped through the glacial shell. He took Amy's hands. "Be calm, Mrs. McClennon. You'll be headed home in a few days. Unless you'd rather stay with Thomas."

"Stay?" She laughed hysterically. She got hold of herself, sniffled, "I'll go home." Embarrassed by her outburst, she stared at the raggedly carpeted floor.

Past her, to Marya, Beckhart added, "I think we'll release you, too, madam." He smiled. It was that killer smile Thomas had come to know with Mouse. He saw it only when Marya's people had been done some special injury.

How we can be cruel, he thought. We're always willing to play petty torturers with our dull little knives.

Mouse understood that smile too. Von Drachau had scored! He seemed to glow. He assumed the mantle of Torquemada. He laughed. The sound of it was a little mad.

"He really did it? He broke through?" Storm spun toward Marya. "Let her live. By all means, let her live." He put on a big, cruel grin. Life for her would be crueler than death. She could look forward to nothing but flight and fear and utter lack of hope till a relentless, pitiless enemy finally ran her to ground.

Mouse told her, "Jupp von Drachau, our old friend from our younger days here, visited your Homeworld, dear."

Marya understood. Mouse had taunted her with his chance discovery during their captivity. He had mentioned the nova bomb.

She did not break. She did not give him an instant of pleasure. She simply smiled that hard, gunmetal smile, and promised with her eyes.

Nothing, ever, could more than lightly scar her outer defenses. Not after she had had to watch Mouse inject her children with the deadly drug that formed one of the foundation stones of Sangaree wealth.

The police removed the women. There was a long silence. Mouse and McClennon faced their commander. Thomas felt Mouse drawing away, closing up, becoming a Bureau man once again.

"Sit down, gentlemen," Beckhart said. "You'll have to bear with me. I'm a little edgy. The Broken Wings has been rough on me. Mouse, you go first. I want a detailed report."

McClennon's eyebrows rose. Beckhart was not going to press? What was he up to?

Mouse talked. McClennon retreated into introspection. He wrestled all the doubts he had held at bay since making his decision. The unanswerable *want* began insinuating sinister tentacles into his soul. He became increasingly confused.

"Thomas!" It was the third or fourth time his name had been called.

"What?"

"Your report on the last two weeks. I have to develop a position. You'd better think about what you'll say in your written statement, too. I tried to cover, but I couldn't. Not all the way. You'll have to stand a Board of Inquiry."

He began with Pagliacci's, lingered over the encounters with the Alyce-faces. He tried to make Beckhart understand that that deception had instigated his determination to scuttle Navy's plans for the Seiners.

"That was a mistake," Beckhart admitted. "I've made several classics during this operation. The intent wasn't malign, Thomas. I meant it as a hypnotic trigger. Way back when, before you were supposed to return to Carson's, Mouse showed you a Chinese coin. That was supposed to be your cue. You didn't respond."

"That failsafer."

"He was ours. Yes. Another of my grand mistakes." Beckhart did not apologize for the murder attempt. They were professionals. They were supposed to understand. They were living chessmen playing a giant board. "Luckily, Mouse outguessed me on that one."

McClennon wandered through his tale, trying and failing to elucidate his behavior.

"Intellectually, I know what you're saying," Beckhart interjected. "Emotionally, I can't connect. Thomas, I'm one of those fools who actually believe in their work. It may be because that's all I have. Or maybe I never outgrew my idealism about Confederation. But that's neither here nor there. You haven't given me those coordinates."

"I haven't seen any guarantees."

"Thomas, I'll promise you anything. High Command has cleared it. They've published it. We'll make it stick. Even if it costs us a Senatorial Review. We can get around those. But that's something to worry about next month. Right now we need to get a hammerlock on Stars' End."

"And then what?"

"You just lost me, son."

"What happens to me?" Does it really matter? he wondered. Who cares?

"Technically, you're under arrest till you receive a Board ruling. You put yourself in a spot. You could end up the hero or the goat of this mess. Which one probably depends on how the first battle goes. I'd just as soon forget the whole thing myself. But it's too late. They know about you back at Luna Command."

"Look on the bright side, Tommy," Mouse said. "They can't legally make you work while you're under arrest. You'll get a vacation in spite of the Bureau."

Beckhart flashed Storm a daggers look. "Can the space-lawyer crap, son. The arrest will be strictly a paper technicality, Thomas. In practice you'll be part of my staff till we sort out the Seiners and Stars' End. Mouse, you'll drag around with Thomas and me. As of now, you're his keeper."

McClennon caught a faint taste of life as he had known it before joining the Starfishers. He looked forward to the change. It might keep him too preoccupied to whine about his losses.

Poor Amy…

"First order of business, those coordinates. Then we get Thomas to a Psych team…"

A policeman came in. "*Marathon*'s stabilized orbit, Admiral. Her shuttle will be down shortly."

"Thank you."

"*Marathon?*" Mouse asked. "I thought she was in mothballs."

"She was when you left. Nothing is anymore. They're crewing the older ships with Reserves. They're replacing regular Fleet patrols. The initial battle will involve every first line ship we have."

"They sent one old cruiser to replace three heavy squadrons?" McClennon asked.

"Not exactly, *Marathon* is mine. Intelligence Admirals don't rate. Thomas, are you going to spill?" Beckhart turned to the policeman, who had remained near the door. "Officer, start moving our gear. Sergeant Bortle was supposed to scrounge up transport."

McClennon's immediate concern was that he had not had a bath. Sixteen days of grime, and he had to board a Navy ship?

"What's the program?" Mouse asked.

"First we bluff the Fishers. Then we move to Stars' End and ride herd on the scientists *Marathon* brought out. They'll supervise the Seiner teams. When I'm satisfied with progress, we space for Luna Command. After debriefing, you loaf till Thomas' Board is over. I imagine Thomas will get hung with a desk. He might even move back to the Line."

"How hard will they be on him?"

"The Board will clear him. On psychological grounds. There's precedent. But they'll want him off operations. Which makes sense, I guess. He could be burned out. He might still do commercial or diplomatic work. That wouldn't waste his training. You I don't know about yet, Mouse."

McClennon looked inside himself and could find no remorse over his potential loss of job. He did not like his profession much.

"I might retire," Mouse mused. "Captain draws a good pension." Though he smiled, the coals of lost dreams lay banked behind his eyes. He had fulfilled his goals too early in life.

"Not till after the war, you won't," Beckhart said. "Nobody retires till then. Thomas? Are you going to give me what I need? Do I have to rub your nose in our intelligence tapes first?"

"All right. It's Three Sky Nebula. Inside the wedge and pointing toward galactic center, beginning about one a.u. inside. Give me a pen." He wrote a series of numbers on a memo sheet. "There're your jump-in coordinates. From there you go ahead in normspace. I can't give you the route through the junk. People who know it aren't allowed to leave."

"Three Sky? Really? I thought it would be way outside our usual sphere." Beckhart's stiffness began to fade. He became the Admiral of old. Smiles and friendship. And willingness to spend a man's life. "The purloined letter thing. That's why ships disappear there." After a pause, "I have things to do before we leave. Meet me in the lobby in half an hour. Ready for space."

"Ready for space?" McClennon asked.

"That was a subtle hint, son. Get cleaned up. I'll have a man bring you a uniform. And try to make peace with your woman."

"Thank you, sir."

He set a record for bathing, shaving, and shifting to the clean uniform. He had ten minutes left when he finished.

One minute later he entered the room Beckhart was using as a brig. It was just a hotel room without windows, with two guards posted outside its only door. Amy and Marya sat against opposite walls, ignoring one another.

"Amy?"

She refused to acknowledge his presence.

He grabbed her chin, forced her to face him. "Look at me, dammit!" For two weeks he had been trying to make her understand. She had refused. He wanted to beat it into her stubborn head. It took an effort to speak calmly. "We're leaving in a few minutes. If you want, you can come with us."

She glared.

"We'll end up at Stars' End. I thought you might want to join your research team there. Instead of being sent straight home."

Still she glared.

"If you go back with the internees, you'll end up at the Yards. With your mother. I thought maybe you'd want to go where you had a friend."

She would not say anything.

"All right. Be stubborn." He turned to the door. "Officer? I'm ready."

"Moyshe, wait. I… Yes. I'll go."

He sighed. Finally. The first yielding. "I'll clear it with the Admiral." A wan smile teased his lips as he left the room.

It would be a long journey. Maybe long enough for him to win his case.

Beckhart did not like his idea at first.

"Sir," McClennon explained, "she's best friends with one of the senior Fisher scientists. If we can tame her, she can help sell cooperation. You keep talking about Ulantonid intelligence tapes. Use them to persuade her. We don't really have to turn her, just to open her mind."

"Thomas… I can see right through you. You don't give a shit about… All right. It's another trade-off. Bring her. But you're responsible for her."

"Tell the guards to turn her over to me."

"Go get her, will you? You're wasting time."

An hour later, they were aboard the shuttle to *Marathon.* Mouse was shaking. Beckhart was lost in dispatches that had come out aboard the cruiser. Amy had her eyes closed. She was pale and grim.

McClennon stared at her and mentally roamed fields of might-have-beens and should-have-dones. He had gotten her to admit an intellectual understanding of his actions. And her inability to differentiate between personal and social allegiances.

She could not see his betrayal of her people as impersonal. She wanted his feelings for her to have been an agent's play-acting. Somehow, that would absolve her of complicity.

She was a self-torturer.

Could he criticize her? Or anyone else? He lived his life in a self-inflicted Iron Maiden.

He and Amy had been doomed from the beginning. His program's instability had made him a natural victim for her inadequacies. They had been too much alike. And she too much like the Alyce creature programmed as one of his triggers. Maybe his ideal woman was a Marya, a cold, gunmetal woman armored at the pain points. A woman with whom it was unnecessary to exchange emotional hostages.

Had he changed during this mission? People did, but usually too slowly to notice. He did not trust the changes he saw. Too many might be artificial.

The Psychs would sort him out. A small team had come out aboard *Marathon.* Maybe when they finished he would know who he really was. He was not sure he wanted to know.

# BOOK THREE
## STARS' END

# TWENTY-ONE: 3050 AD

## The Main Sequence

The lights came on. McClennon, Mouse, and Amy sat in silence. The tapes had been grotesque. Storm finally squeaked, "Admiral… That's really what we're up against?"

McClennon peered at Amy. She met his gaze for an instant. "Moyshe," she whispered, "I think I'm going to be sick."

"It is," Beckhart promised Mouse. "It's tough to swallow. Even when you're there yourself. All that ruthlessness, for no discernible purpose, only makes it more frightening"

McClennon took Amy's hand. It was cool. She was shaking. "You need something?"

"I'll be all right. Just give me a minute."

McClennon turned, "Admiral. I've seen that kind of ship before."

"What? Where? How?" Beckhart came toward McClennon like a tiger stalking game. He seemed to have caught a sudden fever. A haze appeared on his upper lip. "Where?" he breathed.

"The Seiners have one at their xeno-archaeological research facility. You remember, Amy? I asked if it had been built by an intelligent slug? The one nobody wanted to work."

"That's right. You're right, Moyshe, It was exactly like the ships in the tape."

"Tell me about it," Beckhart said.

"There isn't much to tell," McClennon replied. "The Seiners found it in the Nebula. They considered it comparatively modern. They found it surrounded by ships left behind by the people they think built Stars' End. The same people who, I think, built the base Darkside. They assumed the ship had been attacked by accident during the Ulantonid War. I said its crew might have been studying the ships belonging to the Stars' End race. That's all."

Beckhart became thoughtful. "That isn't all, Thomas. There's always more. You just don't know it. Is there a connection? Think about it. Stars' End might be more than just a handy arsenal."

Beckhart was talking to himself, not his audience. McClennon smiled. The Admiral was making the sort of random connections that, when they paid off, caused him to be so effective.

"Thomas, I want you and Amy to talk to Doctor Chancellor's people. They came off the Lunar digs. There might be an angle."

"They should get together with Amy's friend, Consuela el-Sanga. She's more knowledgeable than we are."

"Fine. Fine. We'll arrange that. Meantime, get your brains boiling. Open them up to unexpected possibilities... Tell you what. We'll have another little get-together after dinner. With them included. *Marathon* brought me some new material. I'll lay it out then."

McClennon caught a bleak note. "Bad, eh?"

"Worse than you've seen."

Beckhart used the evening session to present the report from the Ulantonid deep probe. Afterward, he asked, "Any speculations, people?"

The science people were guarded. They wanted more data. McClennon asked, "Did Luna Command run that through the big brain?"

"Yes. And it asked for more data too. I think it has a human bias built in. It wouldn't accept the numbers. It suggested that Commander Russell be replaced by somebody less inclined to exaggerate."

"Looks to me like there's enough data to draw some first approximation inferences. Like, the Globular and war fleets represent an effort to destroy any present and potential sentience. It looks like an effort to eliminate competition and remodel the galaxy for the comfort of one race."

A scientist protested, "You can't draw those inferences. They're anthropocentric. It could just as well be a religious crusade."

"What?" Mouse snarled. "Don't be ridiculous."

"Easy, Mouse," Beckhart said, "No idea is too bizarre right now. The truth is going to be something off the wall. Brainstorm, people. Come up with as many ideas as possible, then winnow them as we accumulate more data. We shouldn't use the facts to build something acceptable. The truth may not be."

The scientists were becoming restive. Beckhart continued, "One unpalatable fact that jumps right out is that they're going to try to destroy us. Add to that their incredible numbers. Add to that the fact that the Globular is forty thousand years away. People, I think we've found us a war that will last forever."

McClennon could not handle the numbers. Forty thousand years? Eight times as long as recorded history? That was one long-term operation.

The other side had been involved for the gods only knew how long already. Millions of years?

The oddities of the alien base on the moon's dark side, the abandoned ships in Three Sky, and Stars' End itself, seemed a little less strange when seen in that light. Presuming the mysterious builders had been enemies of the centerward race, their works might constitute a counter-operation of equally cosmic scale. He tried to tote up a picture based on known factors. It did not scan. There were too many questions. What was the role of the Sangaree? What had become of the builders?

Mouse leaned his way. "This is a little much for me, Tommy. I'm just a simple-minded soldier."

McClennon grinned. "I'll go along with the simple-minded." He had spent the afternoon with a Psych team. They had performed wonders. He felt content and optimistic.

Mouse was out of sorts. He had come off The Broken Wings moody and uncommunicative. The definitive proof was that the science team boasted several attractive women. None had yet been honored by the swoop of the eagle. Amy had mentioned it in one of her friendlier moments. McClennon had not noticed it himself.

"You going to be in the mood for a game after this?" McClennon asked. Mouse had not shown much interest in chess lately, either.

"I don't think so. What's going on?" A petty officer was whispering to the Admiral.

Beckhart announced, "The Sangaree just left Stars' End. They left the McGraws to the Starfishers." He smiled. "Looks like the incidence of piracy may fall off."

"What will they do?" McClennon asked.

"We don't know. Let's hope they give it a good think. I left Strehltsweiter with a message for her bosses. Maybe Homeworld will make them listen."

"What kind of message?" Mouse demanded.

"I told them to change their ways. I said I'm not interested in wiping them out, but I will if they don't shape up. I told them I could repeat the lesson at Osiris if they insist. I let her think we know where Osiris is, too."

"Do you?" Thomas asked.

"No. I lie a lot."

For the next week McClennon split his time between the Psych and scientific teams. The Psych sessions bled the pressure off his chaotic mind. Gradually one personality—McClennon—took hold. He suffered only one minor episode.

*Marathon* dropped hyper off Three Sky. Signals from von Drachau's *Lepanto* indicated that she and her escort had penetrated the Yards. There had been a few skirmishes, but nothing serious. The Starfishers were talking, but stalling.

The Admiral observed, "Gruber is trying to fox us. He's sitting tight at Stars' End. Know what he's doing? Betting to an inside straight. He's thinking, if he can pull some of those weapons out quick enough, he can turn the tables on us."

Beckhart thereupon demonstrated his proconsular power. He contacted the Seiner leadership, told them the time. He designated it as launch minus twenty-five hours. He ordered the channel kept open and the countdown broadcast at five-minute intervals. Incoming traffic was to be recorded and otherwise ignored. Requests for delays and further negotiations consequently fell on deaf ears.

At launch minus two hours twelve minutes the Seiners of Three Sky surrendered unconditionally. Fleet Marines began occupying key installations immediately.

Beckhart summoned McClennon. "Thomas, we've finished twisting their arms here. Find your lady and ask her if she's going or staying. We space for Stars' End in one hour."

"Yes sir. Sir, I just came through Communications. The Sangaree raidfleet is still headed for Homeworld."

"Good. We'll be able to release a few squadrons, then." His eyes went glassy. "The big strike is getting closer. The Blues have picked their spot. We're waiting till the other side walks into it. Find your lady."

Amy was easily found. She would not leave her cabin unless dragged. He knocked. "It's McClennon," he said. "The Admiral sent me."

She seldom talked to him unless under pretext of business.

"What does he want?"

"We're spacing for Stars' End. You want to stay here, or go along?"

"They gave up?"

"They didn't have much choice."

She sighed. "Moyshe, I try hard to understand what's happening. But I can't. Do you think he'll keep his word?"

"I don't know. I really don't. We'll find out the hard way. He'll leave people here to establish the new order. I wish I could find out what their instructions are. What are you going to do? You have to decide quick. We're ready to leave."

"I'm going to Stars' End. Consuela is out there. They made her head of the whole team."

"Well, good for her." He did not depart immediately. She refused the opportunity he offered.

It keeps right on hurting, he thought as he stalked along the passageway. She won't even try to understand.

After relaying Amy's decision, he went looking for his partner.

He found Mouse in the wardroom, staring mindlessly into a holovision cube. He sat, "What's the matter, old buddy? Want to talk?"

Reluctantly, Mouse killed the holoshow. "Not yet, Tommy. I'm not ready."

"All right. You noticed that little blonde Lieutenant from Weapons? Tanni Something."

"From B Missiles? Primo stuff. Looks like she'd turn a man every way but loose. There's something about the little ones..."

"They say she's a Scorpio."

Mouse laughed. "You didn't fix me up, did you?" Mouse had been known to opine that Scorpio women were the hottest in the known universe. McClennon could not get him to elucidate the workings of a geocentric astrology transferred to Outworlds skies.

"Not exactly. I asked a few questions. I figured the answers might pique your interest."

"I'm interested. That little bomb is ready to go off. You can tell just by the way she moves. Blow in her ear and you're liable to start something five guys couldn't handle. But I'm also not interested. If you know what I mean."

"No. I don't. You've been celibate for a month. I thought I'd see entropy shift into reverse first."

"I got things to work out, Tommy. Can we drop it?"

"If you want. We're heading for Stars' End." As if to back him up, the ship's hyper alarm sounded

"I heard they finally gave in."

"Now all we've got to do is impress Gruber."

"The Old Man will find a way."

"He always does, doesn't he?"

"Tommy, what do you think our chances are?"

"What?"

"Our chances of coming through this thing with these centerward creatures."

"We'll never know, Mouse. It's going to go on for a long time. Our great-grandchildren's great-grandchildren are going to be fighting this war. And it's a sad thing."

"Sad? How so?"

"It may destroy us. As a race. I don't mean destroy like wipe us out. I mean put an end to what makes us what we are. I've been thinking about it a lot. You know how I get."

"You think too much." Mouse smiled.

"The human race is crazy, see. No two of us are alike. And when we form up in mobs, no two mobs are alike. We're always flying off in a skillion different directions. Everybody doing their own thing. Every culture, too. And that's a survival trait, I think. There's almost a Darwinian thing with cultures. Some die out, and others come to life. There're always some on the way out and some on the way in. The thing is, there're always a lot of different ones around. When one goes down, there's always another there to take its place."

"I'm not following you," Mouse said in a slightly amused tone. "What's that got to do with anything?"

"Look, this centerward race… To fight it we're going to have to pull together. Generation after generation. Like an anthill. We're going to turn into a warfare race. Our whole focus will be the struggle. Kids will be born to a system that will turn them into the best soldiers possible. If they're survivors, they'll work their way up and get old in harness. They'll have kids of their own, who will follow in their footsteps. After a few generations nobody will know there's any other way of life. And then, in a way, we'll be just like the things we're fighting. The diversity will be gone. And we'll be trapped in a dead end. Because every culture is a dead end eventually. I mean, what does a warfare society do after it polishes off its last enemy? Turn on itself?"

Mouse looked at him askance. "You do worry yourself about some strange things, my friend."

"I think it's a valid concern. I think we should start taking the long view now and try to retain all the diversity we can."

"So write a report suggesting a study."

"I think I will."

"It won't matter much when they wipe us out, Tommy. And from where I sit, that looks inevitable. All we can do is delay it. That'll be like trying to keep the river from getting to the sea by bailing it with a teacup."

"Maybe. Maybe."

The ship shuddered. It seemed to twist away around them. *Marathon* was on her way to Stars' End, that legendary, inviolable, virgin goddess of a fortress world that had intrigued a half dozen races for countless centuries.

# TWENTY-TWO:

## 3050 AD

### The Main Sequence

*Marathon* dropped hyper ten days after departing Three Sky. She cruised norm thirty hours before being joined by the heavy squadrons from The Broken Wings. Beckhart was afraid Gruber might still need convincing.

"There're a hundred harvestships there," Amy protested. "You know how big they are, Moyshe. Plus all the service ships. What makes anybody think a few dozen Navy ships could whip them? The whole Sangaree raidfleet couldn't."

"I hope you don't have to find out."

Mouse explained, "These ships were built for that kind of thing, Amy. All they can do is destroy. Especially the Empire Class. Other ships. Orbital fortresses. Cities on the ground. They were built to chew them up. What you Starfishers have is a bunch of ships built to do other things. Their guns were hung on them as an afterthought. Your harvestships were put together in jumbles, just growing, never designed for any special purpose."

"I still think you're all overconfident."

Both Thomas and Mouse shrugged. McClennon said, "You could be right. We're supposed to believe we're invincible." He glanced at Mouse. "Maybe that's why this centerward thing is so oppressive. It shakes our faith."

They were in *Marathon*'s wardroom. Most of the science team were there too. The countdown to hyper drop had declined past the ten-minute mark. People with no duty assignment had gathered to look at what McClennon called a thirty-first-century war god.

An untouchable world. A dead metal machine voice that shrieked against the big night, threatening anyone who came near. Stars' End. The arsenal of yesterday, more securely defended than the virtue of any medieval virgin.

"You don't need to worry," McClennon said. "If there were any chance of trouble, we wouldn't be sitting around here. We'd be on battle stations."

"The Weapons people aren't on alert," Mouse said. He was staring at a small blonde woman wearing Weapons insignia over her Lieutenant's stripes. "Watch how she moves, Tommy."

McClennon smiled. "I think he's coming around. The tomcat is coming through."

Mouse reddened slightly.

"Jesus," McClennon said softly. "You? Embarrassed?"

"I don't know, Tommy. It seems like I've changed a little. I don't understand myself."

"One minute to hyper drop," a remote voice announced. It drowned in the chatter of the wardroom.

Beckhart and the chiefs of the science team stalked in and took seats near the holo globe that had been set up at the compartment's center.

"Looks smug, don't he?" McClennon said.

The wardroom fell silent. *Marathon* dropped hyper. In moments a featureless ball filled the holo globe. Surrounding details appeared as the ship's sensors picked them up. First came the escort vessels, then the harvestfleets, then vistas of lifeless wreckage left by the fighting with Sangaree and McGraws. The planet, though, showed no changes.

McClennon had seen it before. He was not amazed. The builder race had removed any topography Stars' End may have had. It was a world machined smooth.

"Like a big-ass cue ball," Mouse murmured.

"It doesn't look so friendly when it opens up," Thomas said. He shuddered, remembering. "It gets what looks like a sudden case of acne..."

Someone sat down beside him. At the same moment he saw a Communications messenger whisper to Beckhart and pass a flimsy. What was it? he wondered.

"Commander McClennon?"

He glanced to the side and found himself face to face with the little blonde Weapons officer. "Yes," he gulped, taken aback.

"Hi, I'm Tanni Lowenthal. Weapons." She wriggled her diminutive derriere a centimeter closer.

Mouse chuckled. Thomas turned. Storm's attention seemed inalterably fixed on the holo globe. As was Amy's, though color was climbing her throat.

"What can I do for you?" Thomas asked.

"Nothing. I just wanted to meet you. Someone said you were you, so I thought I would introduce myself. You're famous, you know." She laid a hand on his. It was small and hot and felt strong. He nearly jerked away.

Mouse made a small sound again.

"It's really strange, isn't it?" the woman asked. "Stars' End, I mean."

"Very. Especially when it's in a bad mood."

"Oh. That's right. You were here before, weren't you? When you were with the Starfishers."

The conversation lasted only a few minutes. The woman abruptly said, "That's my cue. Off to the salt mines. Bye." She squeezed his hand and looked him directly in the eye for a second.

"Bye." Baffled, he looked around to see what had happened during his distraction.

Beckhart, apparently, had announced something. He had missed it. "What was that, Mouse?"

"The Seiners have it open already. We can send our people down right away." Storm was fighting laughter. He nodded toward Tanni's departing figure. "That's what you get for asking questions, Tommy. The word gets back."

Amy glared into the globe. Her jaw was tight. Her face was red. Smoke seemed about to pour from her ears. "How did that half-witted sex machine ever earn a commission?" she demanded.

Still grinning, Mouse said, "She's probably quite competent at what she does."

"I don't doubt it a bit. She looks the type."

Mouse made a little wave signal to tell McClennon to make himself scarce. Amy was ready for a scene. A scene she had no right to make, inasmuch as she had declared her relationship with McClennon void.

McClennon rose and moved nearer the Admiral. When he had a chance, he asked, "Will I be able to go down? Just to poke around?"

Beckhart looked thoughtful. "I suppose. It seems safe. They've been down for a week and nothing's happened. But wait till the science people are all down. Ask Amy to see me in my office later, will you? I think I've got a liaison job for her."

"Yes sir." He wandered back to Mouse and Amy. Storm had calmed her down. He was still grinning.

"Tommy, I think I'll take you up on that game you've been talking about. You see a table?" The new was wearing off. Ship's crew were drifting out.

"Over there. Amy, the boss wants you to come to his office when you get a chance."

He and Mouse pushed through the crowd and seized a pair of table seats. Mouse produced his portable chess set.

"I wish you'd wipe that smirk off your face. Makes you look like an idiot."

"I can't help it, Tommy. It's really funny, the way she zeroed in. Isn't she something?"

"No doubt about that. I'm wondering what."

"I couldn't decide if you were going to attack her right there or have a stroke. You can find out what, you know. She told you who she was and where to find her. Now it's your move."

Science team people began descending to the planet next working day. The afternoon of the same day witnessed the arrival aboard of a company of stone-faced Seiner dignitaries. Mouse and McClennon were assigned to make them welcome. Amy turned out to help.

Mouse asked, "What's that you're wearing?"

"My dress uniform."

"What dress uniform?"

"My police uniform. Your Admiral had it flown over during the night."

McClennon observed, "I didn't know you had one. I've known you a year and a half and never saw you wear it."

"That's where we went wrong, Moyshe. We spent all that time hiding."

He expected a difficult, delicate afternoon. He did not argue. "You may be right." He scanned a list on a clipboard. "How many of these people do you know?"

She scanned it too. "Only a few, by reputation. Gruber. Payne. They're all Fleet and Ship's Commanders."

Over a hundred names were on the list. "Mouse, we can't give them all honors." He glanced at the sideboys waiting to pipe the visitors aboard.

"No shit. It'd be tomorrow before we finished."

Amy had seen enough of the back and forth of senior Navy officers to know what they were talking about. "Don't bother," she suggested. "We don't do that kind of thing. They wouldn't know what it was. Just be polite."

Mouse went to talk it over with the chief petty officer in charge of the sideboys. McClennon stood with Amy, studying his list in order to avoid eye contact.

"You look good in that uniform," she said softly. "All those medals..."

"Beckhart likes to hand them out."

"You'll get another for this business?"

"Probably."

"Moyshe... Something I should tell you. When I said we were hiding from each other... I was hiding from you. And fooling myself. The reason I was so eager to throw a net on you..."

He glanced at her. She was showing a lot of color. "Yes?"

"It's embarrassing. I don't like myself very much when I think about it."

"Well? I don't like the things I've done, either."

"I was the Ship's Commander's special agent. I was supposed to keep an eye on you and report to him. Because he wanted to make you into the head of a Starfisher secret service. That meant you were going to be important. I wasn't important. I wasn't ever going to be. The only way I could have gone any higher was if Jarl died or left *Danion.*"

McClennon saw what she was trying to say. "It's all right. I understand. And now I know why you did so many things I thought were strange."

"Moyshe..."

"Forget it. We've got pain enough. Don't drag up any old stuff."

A red light came on over the lock housing. The ship-wide address system announced the arrival of the visitors' shuttle. It admonished all hands to remain courteous and helpful in every circumstance. The lock cycled. A great burly bear of a man stepped inside. He looked around as if expecting to be assaulted by the legions of the damned.

"Gruber," Amy whispered.

"Get him, Mouse," Thomas said.

"Me?"

"You got more balls and more suave than me." Mouse introduced himself as Captain Storm of Admiral Beckhart's staff. He introduced Thomas and Amy, then asked the Fishers to follow them.

The sideboys stood at superb, perfectly matched attention while the Seiners disembarked.

The Marine sentries at the wardroom door were military perfectionists too. They snapped to present arms.

Admiral Beckhart was waiting inside. He wasted little time introducing himself, or excusing himself for having assembled them virtually at gunpoint. He presented the Ulantonid tapes. While they ran, Mouse and McClennon passed out copies of the known data on the centerward threat. Amy distributed copies of the tapes.

The lights came up. Beckhart said, "Gentlemen, you've just seen the reason for our unfriendly behavior. I'll now answer any questions. Doctor Chancellor, Captain McClennon, Captain Storm, and your own Lieutenant Coleridge will also speak with anyone who likes."

McClennon was amazed by the reserve of the Seiner leaders. Even the worst tape scenes caused no stir. They remained obstinately uncommunicative.

*Danion*'s Ship Commander isolated Amy. They fell into heated discussion. The others asked only a few questions while Amy's interrogator worked, then conferred with Payne and Gruber.

The Fishers ignored Storm and McClennon completely.

Replying to a Gruber query, Beckhart said, "We'll be completely open with the available data. In accordance with High Command directives, you've received copies of almost everything. The centerward race threatens all of us."

McClennon told Mouse, "Ever notice the Old Man's split personality? He's three different people, depending on who he's talking to."

Mouse smiled. "We all are. More than three, usually. He's just obvious."

"Think they're buying it?"

"Payne's people are. Most of the others aren't. Gruber looks like he'll give us the benefit of the doubt." He picked lint off his dress black tunic. "We're victims of our reputation. They can't believe we're being straight."

Gruber proved willing to listen. That willingness extended the session for hours. Stewards came in, set up tables, served a meal.

Gruber finally seemed satisfied. His sub-chieftains began filing out, following Mouse to the lock.

Amy walked with McClennon. Starting at the desk, she said, "I'm going back to *Danion* now."

"Okay."

"Moyshe… I'm sorry."

"I am too, Amy. About everything. I never wanted to hurt you."

"Stay happy, Moyshe."

"You too."

She was the last Seiner into the lock. Mouse turned to McClennon. Thomas nodded.

Mouse ordered the lock cycled.

"Think it went over?" McClennon asked.

"I don't know, Tommy. I don't… Tommy? What's the matter? Chief, help me here. Stretcher. Somebody get a stretcher."

The episode was McClennon's worst yet. It took the Psych team three days to bring him out.

It had surprised him completely.

# TWENTY-THREE:

## 3050 AD

### The Main Sequence

"I don't think you should go, Thomas," the Admiral said. "Let Mouse handle it. Suppose you had one of your attacks?"

"I'll be all right. Look. Ask Lieutenant Corley. She says it'll take a week to reach another crisis point."

"Mouse?"

"Somebody has to look over their shoulders, right? Otherwise we won't know if they're getting anywhere. That's just the way those people are. They're not going to say anything till they're sure nobody can shoot them down. Scientists would rather be dragged through the streets naked than be wrong. If Tommy goes, we'll have twice as many eyes."

"All right. Thomas, you know the woman who heads the Seiner team. Talk to her. Take a recorder. I want to hear what she says."

Twelve hours later McClennon and Storm, accompanied by a pair of Marine sergeants, entered the cold metal halls of Stars' End. The dock ring of their landing bay was a good twenty kilometers below the featureless planetary surface. The plunge down the long, dark shaft had been harrowing. Mouse had lost his supper.

The Marines began horsing an electric truck off the shuttle.

Mouse walked along a steel passageway, away from the dock ring. He peered into what had to have been Ground Control in an age gone by. "Tommy, come take a look in here."

McClennon had to stoop beneath the passageway ceiling. He joined Storm. "What?" He saw nothing but a Marine sentry.

"By that console thing."

"Oh. A skeleton."

The reports said bones could be found throughout the fortress. Thousands of skeletons had been encountered.

"We're ready, sir," one of the Marines said.

McClennon snapped a picture of the bones. "All right. Mouse, let's hit Research Central first."

"Right. We'll probably get everything there anyway."

"Be charming. Consuela el-Sanga looks vulnerable."

"Am I ever anything else?"

The little truck streaked through the endless halls, down ramps, around perilous turns, ever deeper into the metal world. The Marine driver fled on as if being pursued by the shades of the builders. He shuddered visibly each time they encountered one of the skeletons. They passed through one chamber where a score of the builder folk had died.

"The bones that have touched and shaped our lives," Thomas said. "From afar, like virgin princesses."

"You getting poetic again?"

"I do when I'm depressed." He glanced at the Marines. They stared forward impassively. "And this place is depressing." The soldiers seemed to have come out of a robot factory. They had shown no reaction to the Admiral's tapes.

The driver's suicidal rush was the only evidence that either man was disturbed.

The truck swooped into a level with ceilings vaulting a hundred meters high. Brobdingnagian machines crowded it, rising like the buildings of an alien city. There was life here, and light, but it was all machine.

"I wonder what they are."

"Accumulators for the energy weapons," Mouse guessed.

"Some of them. Some of them must be doing something with the air."

"Look!" Mouse squealed. "Sergeant, stop. Back up. Back up. A little more. Look up there, Tommy. On the fourth catwalk up."

McClennon spotted the androgynous little machine. It was busy working on the flank of one of the towering structures. "A maintenance robot."

"Yeah. All right, Sergeant. Go ahead."

They descended more levels, some as high-ceilinged as that of the robot. They saw more of the mobile machines, built in a dozen different designs.

Obviously, only the builders had perished. Their fortress was very much alive and healthy. Storm and McClennon saw no evidence of breakdown.

"It's like walking through a graveyard," Mouse said, after their driver had had to wend his way across a vast, open floor where hundreds of skeletons lay in neat rows. "Chilling."

"Know what, Mouse? I think this is really a pyramid. It's not a fortress at all."

"You're not serious."

"Why not? Think about it. Can you think of any strategic reason for putting a world fort out here?"

"Sure."

"Such as?"

"Right over there are the Magellanic Clouds. Sic somebody on me willing to spend a few hundred millennia conquering the galaxy and chasing me, and I'd build me an all-time fort across my line of retreat before I jump off for a friendlier star-swarm."

"Now who's getting romantic?"

"Romantic, hell."

"They could just go around it, Mouse."

"That centerward mob don't go around anything. They'd just stay here till they cracked it open."

"Maybe you're right, but I'm going to stick to my theory."

They reached the research center a few minutes later. McClennon located Consuela el-Sanga almost immediately, and found her completely free of animosity. He was surprised.

"Why?" she asked. "I'm no Seiner. I'm just one of their captive scientists."

"I didn't know." He introduced Mouse. He wondered if Consuela had heard from Amy.

"Moyshe... That wouldn't be right, would it?"

"McClennon. Thomas. But call me whatever's comfortable."

"Thomas, this is the most exciting time of my life. We can finally compare notes with your people... It's like opening up a whole new universe. Come on. Let me show you what we're doing." Her walk had a youthful bounce despite the higher than Seiner-normal gravity.

Mouse's eyebrows rose questionably. McClennon shrugged. "Come on. Before she changes her mind."

A horde of people were at work in a nearby chamber, where hundreds of folding tables had been arrayed in long rows. Most were burdened with artifacts, papers, or the tools of the scientists and their helpers. To one side technicians were busy with communicators and a vast, waist-level computer interface.

Consuela explained, "The people at the tables are examining and cataloging artifacts. We brought along several thousand laymen to help explore. Whenever they make a find, they notify comm center. We send an expert to examine the site. The confab over there is an ongoing exchange with your Lunar dig people. The people at the console are trying to reprogram Stars' End's master brain so it can deal directly with human input."

"You found a key to the builder language?" Thomas asked.

"No. That will come after we can talk to the computer."

"You just lost me. That sounds backwards."

"It works like this: The starfish commune with the machine. They relay to our mindtechs. The mindtechs relay to our computer people. They build parallel test programs. Communications send them down. Our computer people here try to feed it back to the master brain. The starfish read the response and feed it to the mindtechs again. And round the circle. The idea is to help the computers develop a common language. So far we've only managed a pidgin level of communication. We think we're on the brink of breakthrough, though."

"Math ought to be a snap," Mouse said. "It's got to be the same all over the universe. But I can see how you'd have trouble working toward more abstract concepts."

"Unfortunately, we're using a non-mathematical interface," Consuela replied. "The starfish aren't mathematically minded. Their conscious concept of number is one-two-three-many."

"Thought you said they were smart, Tommy."

Consuela said, "They are. But theirs is an intuitive rather than empirical intelligence. But we're making headway. When our computers can link..."

"Be careful," McClennon admonished. "Be very, very careful."

"Why?"

"This is the boss machine, right?"

"So the fish say."

"Okay. That makes it big and powerful. It might be playing games with you. It's insane."

"Come on," Mouse protested. "How can a machine go crazy?"

"I don't know. I do know I was in Contact during the first battle. I got a little direct touch. It was plain out of its micro-electronic mind. I'd be afraid it could use its capacity to seize control of my own command computers."

"He's right, Captain. Thomas, we know. It's a real problem. Most of the starfish are riding herd on its psyche. Only a few are helping communicate. It seems to have several psychological problems. Loneliness. A god complex. A deeply programmed xenophobia and bellicosity... It is, after all, the directing intelligence of a weapons system."

"A defensive weapon," McClennon suggested. "Mouse laughed at this. But think about it. Is Stars' End a pyramid?"

"I don't understand."

"I'm going to wander around," Mouse said. "Don't run off without me, Tommy,"

"I won't. By pyramid I mean it serves the same function as Old Earth's Egyptian pyramids."

"A tomb? I don't think so. The idea isn't new, but it's been mostly a metaphor."

"Assume the builders knew... You don't have all the data." He explained about the centerward race and his suspicion that the builder race had been fleeing it. "Okay. They come to the end of the road. There's nowhere to run, unless they jump off for the Magellanic Clouds. I think they gave up. I think they stopped, built themselves a pyramid, put their treasures inside, and died out."

Miss el-Sanga smiled. "A romantic theory that fits the known facts. And a few you've conjured up, I think. Ingenious, Thomas. I suppose we'll be able to answer you when we complete contact with the master control."

A boyhood incident came to mind. He had discovered—independently, so far as he could discern later—that A squared plus B squared equaled C squared. He had been excited till he had explained it to a friend. The friend had laughed and told him that Pythagoras had crossed the finish line thirty-five hundred years ahead of him.

He felt the same deflation now.

"I hear you and Amy broke up."

"Yes. I didn't realize you knew."

"She called yesterday. She was very depressed about it."

"She took something personal that wasn't."

"That was the feeling I got. Her story was one-sided, but I got the impression you were trying to do what was right for everybody."

"I tried. I don't know how successful I was."

"You two shouldn't have gotten involved in the first place. Landsmen and Seiners don't speak the same language. I've been with them thirty-six years and I still have problems."

"We were both looking for something. We were too eager to grab it."

"I've been through that, too."

"Help her, will you? I never meant to hurt her."

"I will. And don't feel so guilty. She's more resilient than she pretends. She likes the attention."

"I thought you were friends."

"She was a lot more than a friend for a while, Captain. Till she met Heinrich Cortez."

"Oh."

"Hey, Tommy!" Mouse bore down on them like a mini-juggernaut. "Come here." He about-turned and steamed a reverse course.

"Excuse me, Consuela." He chased Mouse down. "What?"

Mouse stopped. "I just talked to a gal who's doing the same thing for the Fishers that we're doing for Beckhart. She was pissed. These clowns, some of them, have been here for ten days. The Fishers have eight thousand people down already. And they haven't even started looking at weapons systems. They don't even care. All they want to do is collect broken toothbrushes and sort old bones."

"They'll get to it, Mouse. You've got to give them a chance to let the new wear off. And they've got to get a dialogue going with the master control. If they manage that, it'll save time. In the long run. The machine can redesign the weapons for us. That would save ripping the old ones out of here, orbiting them, then building ships around them."

Mouse calmed himself. "Okay. Maybe you're right. But I still don't like to see *everybody* doing something else when weapons are the reason we're all here."

"What if the weapons technology requires other preexisting technologies?"

"What do you mean?"

"Go back a hundred years. Build me a pulse-graser with the technology available then. You couldn't do it. You'd have to create the technology to create the technology to construct the pulse accumulators. Right?"

"Sometimes I don't like you a whole lot, Tommy." Mouse grinned. "I'll tell the Seiner lady to be patient."

"If the Captains will excuse me?" The senior of their Marine custodians approached them.

"Yes, Sergeant?" Thomas asked.

"The Admiral's compliments, sirs, and he needs you back aboard ship immediately."

"What is it?"

"He didn't say, sir. He said to tell you it's critical."

Mouse looked puzzled. McClennon was very much so.

The news hit the busy chamber before they departed.

The starfish had had a brief skirmish with sharks. Hordes of the predators had appeared. A continuous stream were still arriving.

"Holy shit!" Thomas said. "I'd forgotten about them."

"They didn't forget us," Mouse grumbled. "Damnation!"

People swirled this way and that. The mood approached panic. Doctor Chancellor rushed over. "I heard you're going up. Take this to the Admiral, just in case." He shoved a folder into McClennon's hands. "Thank you." He dashed toward the team working at the computer. They were trying to prepare an instantaneous shutdown of the round-robin should the sharks attack.

"They should tell the idiot box to scrub the problem for them," Mouse said as they pulled away. "What did he give you?"

"His notes. They look like a cross between a journal and regular scientific notation."

"Give me some of those."

Their driver flew around worse than he had coming the other direction.

"Here's an interesting one," Mouse said. "No furniture."

"What?"

"The exploration teams haven't found any furniture. There goes your pyramid theory."

"He's right. I didn't see anything but machinery. The bodies are all laid out on the floor."

"Maybe they're invaders too?"

McClennon shrugged. "Here's one that will grab you. How big do you think Stars' End is?"

"Uhm... Venus size?"

"Close. Earth minus two percent. But the planetary part is smaller than Mars. The rest is edifice."

"What?"

"His word. I'll give you the question. Since most of the structural volume would be hollow, how come the place has so much gravity? It's a couple points over Earth normal."

Mouse sneered. "Come on, Tommy. Maybe it's the machines."

"Nope. You're going to love it. According to this, the builders, before they started building, took a little planet and polished it smooth. Then they plated it with a layer of neutronium. The fortress structure floats around on the neutronium, which may be a cushion against tectonic activity."

"Whoa!" Mouse clung to the truck as its driver made a violent turn. "How did they stabilize the neutronium?"

"Figure that out, and how they mined it in the first place, and you and me will get rich."

"What's the kicker?"

"He doesn't have one here. I think it's implied. I didn't see anything at the Lunar digs or Three Sky that would suggest that level of technology."

"So the little people *are* interlopers. Just like us."

"Maybe." McClennon had an image of Bronze Age barbarians camped in the street of a space age city.

"Keep talking. I don't want to think about the fly up."

A Navy Lieutenant awaited them at *Marathon*'s ingress lock. "If you'll follow me, sirs?"

The Admiral awaited them on the bridge. "Ah. Thomas. I was beginning to wonder."

"Is it critical, sir? We haven't slept for ages."

"It's critical. But the Seiners say it doesn't look like it'll break right away. Rest up good before you go over."

"Over?"

"I'm sending you to *Danion.* I want you to go into link and give *Assyrian* and *Prussian* a fire control realtime."

"You have got to be kidding."

"Why? My calculations show them capable of cleaning up that little mess out there. It's a chance to show Gruber what can happen if he gets tricky."

"Point. Sir, you're over-optimistic. Sharks are super deadly. They throw anti-hydrogen when they get mad. Second point. Why me? A Seiner mindtech could do the job, and probably better. They're better trained."

"I want you. I don't want some Seiner who'll adjust the data to make us look bad."

"I have to go?"

"It's an order."

"Then make it another ship. I'm liable to get lynched aboard *Danion.*"

"*Danion* is Gruber's choice. That's the ship we know. He has secrets too."

"Thanks a lot. Sir."

Mouse stage-whispered, "The ship's Legal Officer would back you if you want to refuse. You don't have to work when you're under arrest."

"I got troubles enough without getting the Old Man mad at me. Madder at me."

Beckhart glared at Mouse. "You're going with him, son. Head bodyguard. Take your two Marines. Tommy, if it will make you more comfortable, stay with the Psych people till time to go."

"I will."

*Danion* had not changed—except there were no friendly faces aboard now. Amy met them at the ingress lock. A squad of grim-faced Security people accompanied her. She installed the party aboard a convoy of small vehicles.

People spat and cursed as they passed.

"Tell me something," Mouse said. "How come everybody knows we're here?"

"This isn't Navy," Amy replied curtly.

"You keep on and I won't make love to you anymore." Mouse laughed when she turned to glare at him.

"Easy, boy," McClennon said. "We've got to get out of here alive."

Something thrown whipped over their heads.

"Did you see that?" Mouse croaked. "That was Candy… She wanted to marry me."

"Amy, have you shown people those tapes?"

"What tapes?"

"The centerward…"

Mouse nudged him. "I smell a little political skulduggery, old friend. A little crafty censorship. Old Gruber is afraid he can't keep people cranked up if they find out what's really going on."

"You're not to discuss that," Amy said.

Mouse grinned. "Oh! The Saints forfend! Never, my dear. What are you going to do about it if I do?"

"I saw Consuela yesterday," McClennon said, heading them off.

Amy softened. "How was she?"

"Twenty years younger. Happy as a kid loose in a candy store. She's hoping you'll come down."

"You went?"

"Yesterday. It's interesting. But I don't think we'll get as many answers as questions."

The convoy entered Operations Sector. A huge door closed behind them, isolating them from the rest of the ship. Mouse wondered aloud why. No one answered him. McClennon's former tech team, Hans and Clara, awaited him. Their faces were not friendly, but were less inimical than any he had seen outside Operations. Clara even managed a smile.

"Welcome back, Moyshe. You even get your old couch."

"Clara, I want you to meet somebody before we start. You never got the chance. This is Amy."

Clara extended a hand. "Amy. I heard so much about you when Moyshe was with us."

McClennon removed his tunic, handed it to Mouse. The Marine sergeants considered the couch and its technical stations, posted themselves to either side, out of the way.

The Contact room had fallen silent. People stared. Obviously, no one had been warned that Contact expected visitors.

Thomas settled onto the couch. "Clara, I'm not sure I can do this anymore."

"You don't forget. Hans."

Hans said, "You let your hair grow, Moyshe. I'll have to gum it up good."

"Haven't had time for a haircut since we hit The Broken Wings." He shuddered as Hans began rubbing greasy matter into his scalp, and again when the youth slipped the hairnet device into place. A moment later the helmet devoured his head.

"There's a fish waiting, Moyshe," Clara said. "Just go on out. And good luck."

TSD took him. Then he was in the starfish universe.

Stars' End was a vast, milky globe surrounded by countless golden footballs and needles. The three Empire Class warships became creeping vortices of color. They were at full battle stations already, with their heaviest screens up. Golden dragons slid across the distance, orbiting well beyond the ships.

And beyond the dragons, against the galaxy… "My God!" he thought.

He saw great shoals and thunderheads of red obscuring the jeweled kirtle of the galaxy. The sharks were so numerous and excited that he could not discern individuals.

"Yes, Moyshe man-friend. Will attack soon," a voice said inside his mind.

"Chub!"

"Hello. Welcome home. I see by your mind many more adventures lived, Moyshe man-friend. I see doors opened where once shadows lay."

"What in heaven… You've changed, Chub. You've become poetic."

Windchime laughter tinkled through his mind. "Have been so lucky, Moyshe man-friend. First a spy linker who taught jokes, then a she linker filled with poetry."

McClennon felt the starfish reaching deep within him, ferreting through the hidden places, examining all the secrets and fears it had not been able to reach before. "You remember fast, Moyshe man-friend."

On cue, an outside voice said, "Linker, Communications. We have an open channel to *Assyrian* and *Prussian* Fire Control. Please inform us when you're ready to begin."

Fear stalked through McClennon. The starfish reached in and calmed him. "I'm ready now," he replied.

He listened in as *Danion*'s communications people closed their nets and linked with the dreadnoughts. He heard the chatter as the Navy and Seiner fleets went on battle alert. From his outside viewpoint he watched screens develop around the Navy ships. The two giant warships began creeping toward the shark storm.

The sharks sensed the attack before it arrived. Suddenly, they were flashing everywhere, trying to reach their attackers and the ships behind them.

McClennon felt the flow from Chub go through his mind into *Danion*. He saw the response of *Assyrian* and *Prussian*. Their weapons ripped the very fabric of space. Sharks by the hundred died.

And by dozens and scores they slipped past and hurled themselves at the massed ships around Stars' End.

In ten minutes space was aglow from the energies being expended. And ten minutes later still McClennon began to feel bleak, to despair. When he recognized the mood's source, he asked, "Chub, what's the matter?"

"Too many sharks, Moyshe man-friend. Attacking was mistake. Even the great ships-that-kill of your people will not be able to endure."

McClennon studied the situation. Space was scarlet, yes, but he saw no sure indicators of defeat.

Still, starfish could intuit developments before even the swiftest human-created computer.

He began to see it fifteen minutes later. Whole packs of sharks were suiciding in the warships' screens, gradually overloading them. They were doing it to every ship.

Near Stars' End at least a dozen vessels were aflame with the fire that could burn anywhere, as anti-matter gasses slowly annihilated the metal of their hulls.

It got worse.

"Moyshe?" Clara's voice seemed to come from half a galaxy away. "You've been in a long time. Want to come out?"

"No. I'm doing fine."

"You're thrashing around a lot."

"It's all right. It's grim out here."

A driblet of fear was getting past Chub's sentinel effort. The starfish himself was in a state of agitation. His kind were being slaughtered.

It got worse.

*Prussian* was compelled to withdraw. The sharks redoubled their assault upon *Assyrian. Hapsburg* picked up the realtime link and replaced *Prussian.*

The Navy squadrons fared better than did the Starfisher harvestfleets. Their fire patterns were virtually impenetrable.

From somewhere, a voice screamed, "Breakthrough! Breakthrough!"

McClennon did not understand till much later. At the moment he thought it meant the sharks had managed their victory. It was not till Chub began exulting that he realized the tide had turned.

The sharks were turning on themselves, pairing off and fighting to the death in ponderous, savage duels. Winners searched for new victims. Here and there, a few began to flee.

Within half an hour the only red to be seen was that fading from fragments of dead shark. Space was aboil with the activity of the scavenger things that followed the sharks. Chub kept giggling like a teenager at a dirty joke. "We do it one more time, Moyshe man-friend. This time when impossible. And in grand style. Grandest style possible. Will make bet. Herd and harvestfleet will have no trouble from sharks again for age of man. So many died here…"

"Moyshe?" Clara said. "Still okay? I think we should bring you out. You've been under a long time."

A sadness came over McClennon. For an instant he could not identify its cause. Then he knew. Chub was sorry to see him go. The starfish knew that this time it would be forever.

"I don't know what to say, Chub. I already said good-bye once."

Chub tried a feeble joke. McClennon forced a charity laugh.

"Not so good?"

"Not so good. Remember me, Chub."

"Always. The spy man from the hard matter worlds will remain immortal in the memory of the herd. Stay happy, Moyshe man-friend. Remember, there is hope gainst the world-slayers too. The Old Ones tell me to tell you so. They are remembered from other galaxies. They have been stopped before."

"Other galaxies?"

"They come to all galaxies eventually, Moyshe man-friend. They are the tools of the First Race, the hard matter folk of the beginning. They do not grow old and die. They are not born as you, but in machine wombs from pieces of adults. They are created things. They do not reason as you. They know only their task."

McClennon felt the starfish struggling with concepts alien to the starfish mind. There was an aura of the extremely ancient in what the creature was trying to tell him. Chub seemed to be translating very old mood lore into the relative precision of modern human thought.

"They scourge the worlds that they might be prepared for the First Race, Moyshe man-friend. But the First Race is gone, and not there to take the worlds, nor to end the work of their tools. They were gone before the birth of your home star."

"Who built Stars' End? Do you know?"

"The little hard matter people, as you thought. Those whose bones you found. They were enemies of the First Race. They won that struggle, but still run from the tools of their foes."

"But…"

Chub knew his questions before he thought them. "They are old, too, Moyshe man-friend. They flee, and the killers-of-worlds pursue. This is not the first time they have passed through our galaxy. You do not know Stars' End. It is old, Moyshe man-friend. Older than the stones of Earth. The enemies of the world-slayers are but a ghost of what once was. They perish in flight, and decline, and always they leave their trail of traps for their foes. The herd knew them of old, Moyshe man-friend, in other ages, when the galaxies were young and closer together and our fathers swam the streams arching between them."

"You're getting poetic."

"The moods mesh, Moyshe man-friend. The moods mesh."

"Moyshe? You'd better not stay much longer." Clara's voice was more remote than ever. He began to feel her urgency.

"Linker? Communications. We're breaking lock."

"Linker, aye. Chub, I…"

"Coming to you, Moyshe man-friend. You will remember."

The starfish's message puzzled McClennon. He would remember what?

Something hit his mind. It was an overpowering wave. Panicking, he yanked upward on his escape switch. "Chub… My friend…" were his last screaming thoughts before the darkness took him.

Pain!

Overwhelming pain, worse than any migraine. His head was pulling itself apart.

He screamed.

"Hold him!" someone yelled.

He writhed against restraining arms. Something pierced his flesh. Warm relaxation radiated from that point: The pain began to lessen. Soon he could open his eyes and endure the light.

"Get back!" Clara snapped at someone. "Moyshe, how do you feel?"

"Like death warmed over. Over."

Though she looked relieved, she growled, "I told you to come out. Why didn't you?"

"Chub was telling me about Stars' End. End. About who built it, and about the centerward race. Race. It was important. Important."

"You pushed it too far."

"Give me another shot. Shot. I'll be all right. Right. How's the battle coming? Coming? What happened, anyway? Anyway?"

Hans held his arm while Clara gave him the second injection. The pain receded. It became a slight irritation over his eyes, like a sinus infection.

"They made the breakthrough with the Stars' End master control, Moyshe," Hans said. There wasn't the slightest animosity in the youth now. "You held them long enough. Once it found the key, it broke our language in seconds. It saw our problem. It did whatever it did about the sharks."

"What did it do? Do?"

Mouse stepped around where he could look into McClennon's eyes. "We were hoping you could tell us. You were out there."

"I didn't know what was happening. Happening. One minute we had no hope. Hope. The next minute the sharks sharks had been hit by a hurricane or something. Or something."

"The Empires didn't do so hot, eh?"

"They did magnificently. Better than all of Payne's Fleet Payne's Fleet did during the first battle. Battle. I think Gruber Gruber will be properly impressed. Impressed. There was just more there there than anybody expected. Expected."

Mouse frowned at him. He asked Clara, "Why is he doing that?"

"I don't know. I've never seen it before."

"Why am I doing what? What?"

"Echoing yourself."

"What do you mean? Mean?"

"How soon can we move him?" Mouse asked.

"Any time," Clara told him. "But he should stay here. Our medical people know how to handle mindtech problems."

"No. The Admiral wants him right back. Come on, Thomas. Feet on the floor. Let's see if you can stand."

"No problem. Problem." He was weak, but he could get around. Why were they all looking at him that way?

He began to remember.

"He told me I would remember. Remember."

"Who told you?" Mouse asked as he guided McClennon toward the door and conveyances waiting outside.

"Chub. The starfish. Fish. I'm beginning to. To. Mouse, I've got to see the Admiral. Admiral. I'm remembering everything the fish know about the centerward race and their enemies. Enemies." He turned. "Clara. It was good to see you again. Again. Hans. Be a good fellow. Mind your grandmother. Mother." He reached with his right hand. Surprised, Hans shook it.

"Of course, Moyshe. Good luck." He glanced at Clara.

The woman said, "Good luck, Moyshe. Maybe you'll surprise us again."

McClennon smiled weakly. "I hope not. Not. No more battles, anyway. Way. Mouse. Let's go. Go."

He was driven by anxiety. He wanted to report what he had learned before the memories slipped away.

Mouse stopped to talk to Amy before he boarded the shuttle. "Take care of yourself," he told her. "And be happy. What's happened wasn't your fault. You could say it was fate."

"I know, Mouse. But that doesn't make it hurt any less." She smiled wanly. "Greater destinies? It's probably for the best. Sorry I was such a bitch."

Mouse shrugged. "No problem. Take care."

"Take care of Moyshe." Mouse looked at her strangely.

"He's your friend, but he's the husband I'm going to remember." She leaned close, whispered, "Promise not to tell him till he's past the worst part. We've got a baby on the way."

"It's a promise. He doesn't need that on his mind too." Storm backed through the hatchway, waved, turned, found a seat. For a time he was too amazed to be disturbed by the fly.

McClennon sat opposite him, beside one of the Marines, writing furiously.

# TWENTY-FOUR: 3051 AD

## The Contemporary Scene

The Defender Prime of Ulant gave the order. The Climbers left their mother ships. Pursuit destroyers moved to positions in reserve-and-chase, ready to pounce on any courier or fugitive fleeing the battle. The Empires and Conquerors and their Ulantonid, Toke, Khar'mehl, and aChyfNth equivalents began to move. The cruisers, frigates, and bombards formed their holding screen. A gnatlike swarm of singleships put on inherent velocity preparatory to a lightning pass through the enemy, spewing energy and torpedoes and collecting to-the-minute intelligence for the Defender's master battle computers.

The centerward people were unsuspecting. Even the folk they were attacking had no idea that help had come.

Years of Ulantonid staff planning had gone into this action. It was their game. For the first time ever Confederation personnel were accepting orders from outside commanders. Even the Warriors of Toke set aside their pride and accepted direction from leaders more knowledgeable than they.

Twelve sovereign governments of five races were represented in the Allied fleet.

The Climbers materialized amid the enemy force. They expended their munitions stocks before their foes could react. They returned to their mothers to rearm.

Seconds later the singleships dropped hyper.

It took a special breed to fight the one-man scout ships. Egoists, solipsists, men convinced of their own invulnerability. Men who could not be intimidated by the knowledge that they had virtually no defense but speed and violent maneuverability.

The singleships streaked through the centerward war-fleet, spewing their hunter missiles and flailing with their lone nose-mounted energy beams. For some speed proved a liability. There were so many enemy vessels, shifting in confusion, that there were collisions.

Data flowed to the computers of the Allied fleet. The size, disposition, orientation, vectors, and velocities of enemy units began to appear in the huge displays of the Defender's command and back-up command vessels. Ships and installations belonging to the race under attack were identified and tagged friendly. Enemy command ships were identified and targeted for special attention by the next Climber sortie.

The General Staff of Ulant had planned thoroughly and well. There were no unpleasant surprises.

The heavies closed and began pounding a technologically inferior enemy.

The advantages were all to the Allies. All but one.

They were outnumbered a hundred to one.

They were a single-minded folk, those centerward creatures. When unable to fight a ship any longer, they took to their shuttlecraft and tried to land on the planet. The handful who reached the surface looked for something to kill, and kept at it till something killed them. Aboard ship and on the ground they had only a limited concept of tactics.

Tactics were unnecessary when the only strategy needed was the application of overwhelming numbers.

They seemed unacquainted with fear, and constitutionally unable to retreat. They simply fought and died and let someone else take their place.

The only ships to leave the battle were couriers departing at ten-hour intervals.

The pursuit destroyers handled them, as well as couriers coming in.

One by one, Allied warships were destroyed or injured beyond any capacity to continue fighting.

At hour forty of an action originally projected to endure about one hundred hours the Defender Prime instelled Ulant. She expressed her fear that her command was insufficient to fulfill its mission. Effective losses: twenty-four percent of commitment. Current estimated active ratios: 70-1 in the enemy's favor.

Her figures did not take into account displacements. Her ships were concentrating on the more important and dangerous enemy vessels. A significant percentage of the remaining ships were lightly armed troop transports.

The centerward people stubbornly insisted on devoting strength to their assault on the planet.

The Defender's pessimism was not unwarranted. Her one-hundred-hour report showed the Allied fleet over fifty percent neutralized. All missile stores had been expended. Breakdowns were claiming the energy weapons. She had lost the use of the last of her Climbers. Her crews were drained by exhaustion.

She disengaged.

The enemy ignored her departure. They closed ranks and continued their disrupted planetary assault.

The Defender received instructions to stand off and observe. Confederation was sending reinforcements. Convoys bearing munitions and repair spares were in space.

In the end, after a month of brutal fighting, the last centerward warship was annihilated. The Allied fleet returned home, to lick its wounds and reflect on the savagery of the encounter. The Defender departed without contacting the planets she had saved. She wanted no replacement enemy fleet finding any information on the mysterious rescuers.

A great victory, by numbers. A huge slaughter. But a Pyrrhic affair. The carefully husbanded and prepared strength of the Allies had been decimated.

At least four more warfleets were moving out The Arm. Nothing, really, had been won, except the knowledge that such a monster force could be overcome. The victory did not fill the several high commands with joy.

It simply unleashed an even more grim foreboding of things to come.

# TWENTY-FIVE:

# 3050-3052 AD

## The Main Sequence

McClennon had been relating his memories for months. "Christ, Mouse. I'm sick of it. Why can't people be satisfied with the deposition tapes?"

Mouse moved a pawn, trying to initiate a trade. "Because it's so damned fascinating. It's like meeting somebody who can wiggle his ears. You want to see him do his trick. I can't help it either. I wish I could get inside your head. Man, remembering what the galaxy looked like before Old Sol was formed..."

McClennon refused the trade. He moved a knight to support his own pawn, glanced at the time. "Four hours. I'm beginning to dread it. They'll do the whole debriefing routine. For two years of mission. And they'll stay on me about my starfish memories till they know the whole physical history of the universe."

Mouse glanced at the clock too. *Marathon* would be dropping hyper soon, preparatory to decelerating in to Luna Command. "Debriefing doesn't excite me either. On the other hand, we'll get to see a lot of people we haven't seen for a long time. They'll all be changed."

"Maybe too much. Maybe we won't know them anymore." McClennon tried to focus on his friends in Luna Command. Max would be older. Greta would be a different animal. He might not recognize her now.

His thoughts kept fleeing to the memories. He found something new each time he checked them. They were intriguing, but he could not shed the disheartening parts.

There were not just five warfleets coming out The Arm. There were eighteen. And the galaxy was infested by not one, but four Globulars. He could not console himself with the starfish view that, in the long run, the enemy was never entirely successful. He did not care that this was their third scourging of the Milky Way, that life always survived, and that sometime between the grim passages, over the eons, new intelligence arose to contest the world-slayers' efforts. He could not be consoled by the knowledge that the enemy would not reach Confederation in his lifetime.

If there was a God, He was cruel. To have allowed the creation of such all-powerful, enduring monstrousness...

"Chub thought he was giving me a gift," McClennon said. "He knew I was curious about the past. And he knew his species had information we wanted. It was a gift of despair. It just showed us how hopeless the whole thing really is."

"I wouldn't say that. You're down too far."

"Why do you say that?"

"You told me the fish said they can be stopped. That it had been done before. The Stars' End people were working on it when the plague got them."

"They were working on us, Mouse. Trying to breed some kind of killer race of their own."

Mouse shrugged. "Hi, Tanni."

McClennon glanced up into laughing green eyes.

Mouse suggested, "Why don't you take my friend for a walk? He's down again."

The woman laughed. "That's what I had in mind. Or would you rather play chess, Tom?"

McClennon grinned. "Let's flip a coin... Ouch! No fair pinching."

"Come on, you. I've got to go on station in an hour." She undulated out of the wardroom.

"Wait till Max gets a look at that," Mouse said.

"Hey. She better not. Not ever. Hear? The fireworks would make the nova bomb look pitiful."

Mouse laughed. "I'm looking forward to it, old buddy. I can't forgive you for snagging that before I did."

"You can't win them all, Mouse." He hurried after Tanni Lowenthal, Stars' End, the mission, starfish, and centerward enemies forgotten.

He spent a month in the bowels of Old Earth's moon. The mind-butchers demolished his soul and on its foundations rebuilt to saner specifications. The first three weeks were horror incarnate. He was forced to face himself by mind mechanics who showed no more compassion than a Marine motor pool man for a recalcitrant personnel carrier.

They did not accept excuses. They did not permit stalling. And even while he slept they continued debriefing him, tapping the incredible store of memories given him by Chub. They were merciless.

And they were effectve.

His sojourn among the Seiners had mellowed his memories of the cold determination of his Navy compatriots. He had come in unprepared. He was less ready to fight the reconstruction.

It went more quickly than his doctors anticipated.

When he was past crisis they opened him up and repaired his ulcerated plumbing.

He was permitted visitors on day twenty-nine.

"Two at a time," his nurse protested. "Just two of you can go in."

"Disappear," Mouse told her.

"Yes sir. Captain. Sir."

Mouse was nearly trampled by two women. He dropped his portable chess set. Chessmen scattered across the floor. "Oh, damn!"

Greta plopped her behind on the edge of the bed, flung herself forward, hugged McClennon. "I'm glad you're back. I've been calling every day since I heard. They wouldn't let me come before."

And Max, the old girlfriend, "Christ, Walter. What the hell did they do to you? You look like death on a stick."

"That's why I love you, Max. You've always got a pleasant word." He squeezed Greta's hand. "How are you, honey? How's Academy?"

She started babbling. Max got on about some new stamps she had at her hobby shop. She had been saving them for him.

Mouse recovered his chessmen, deposited the set on the nightstand, took a chair. He crossed right leg over left, steepled his fingers before his mouth, and watched with a small smile.

McClennon turned his head, trying to hide his eyes.

Softly, Max said, “Walter. You’re crying.”

McClennon hid behind his hand. “Max… It was a rough one. A long one and a rough one. I was lost for a long time. I forgot… I forgot I had friends. I was alone out there.”

“Mouse was there, wasn’t he?”

“Mouse was there. Without him… He brought me through. Mouse. Come here.” He took Storm’s hand. “Thanks, Mouse. I mean it. Let’s don’t let it get away again.”

For a moment Storm stopped hiding behind the masks and poses. He nodded.

Greta resumed babbling. McClennon hugged her again. “I’m having trouble believing it. I thought you’d have forgotten me by now.”

“How could I?”

“What am I? A sentimental fool who helped a pretty girl in trouble. We never knew each other.”

She hugged him a third time. She whispered, “I knew you. You cared. That’s what matters. When you were gone, your friends were always there to help.” She buried her head in his shoulder and blubbered.

McClennon frowned a question at Max, who said, “Your Bureau took care of her like family. She’s got to be the most pampered Midshipman in Academy.”

“And you?”

Max shrugged. “I did what I could.” She seemed embarrassed. “Well, how else was I going to keep track of you? I don’t have connections.”

“I’m glad you’re going to be all right,” Greta murmured. “Dad?”

More tears escaped McClennon’s eyes.

“Did I do wrong? I didn’t mean…”

“It’s all right, honey. It’s all right. I wasn’t ready for that.” He squeezed the wind out of her.

“Just get the hell out of my way, woman!” someone thundered in the passageway outside. Beckhart kicked the door open. “See if you can’t find a bedpan over around Tycho Crater, eh? Go on. Get scarce.”

The nurse beat her second retreat.

The Admiral surveyed the room.

McClennon stared at his professional paterfamilias.

“Looks like everything’s under control,” Beckhart observed.

“Place is drawing a crowd,” McClennon said. “Must be my animal magnetism.”

Beckhart smiled with one side of his mouth. “That’s one crime they won’t convict you of, son. Lay out that board, Mouse. I’ll beat you a game while we wait for the females.”

The game had hardly started, and McClennon had hardly gotten Greta's eyes dried. The door swung inward again. The nurse watched with a look of despair.

Tanni Lowenthal's face rippled with emotions. It selected an amused smile. "Tom. I thought I'd get here first. I guess you don't run as fast when you've got short legs." She crossed gazes with Max. The metallic *scrang* of ladies' rapiers meeting momentarily tortured the air. Then Max smiled and introduced herself. She and Tanni got past the rocky part in minutes.

Beckhart checked his watch. "Damn it, they're late. I'm going to have somebody's..."

The harried nurse stepped in. She carried a portable remote comm. "Call for you, Captain McClennon."

"Let me have that," the Admiral said. He seized the comm. "Jones? You find her? Got her on the line? All right. Thomas, your mother." He handed the comm to McClennon and returned to his game.

McClennon did not know what to do or say. He and his mother were estranged. She was Old Earther born and bred, and they had battled fiercely ever since his enlistment. Their last meeting, just before the Seiner mission, had ended bitterly.

"Mother?"

"Tommy? Is it really you?"

"Yes."

"I thought you'd been killed. When they came to the apartment... God. They say you were mixed up in this war business that's got the whole world turned upside down. The spikes are everywhere. They're grabbing people off the streets."

"I was in it a little." She had not changed. He hardly had a chance to get in a word of his own.

"They said you got married. Is she a nice girl?"

"It didn't work out. But yes, she was. You would have liked her." He checked his audience. Only the Admiral seemed to know his mother's half of the conversation.

They did not talk long. There had been little to say since he had gone his separate way. It was enough that, for all their differences, they could show one another they still cared.

McClennon handed the comm to the Admiral when he finished. "Thank you, sir."

"I owe you, Thomas. One mission and another, I put you through hell for four years. I won't apologize. You're the best. They demanded the best. But I can try to make it up a little now. I can try to show you that I didn't take it all away..." Beckhart seemed unable to say what he meant.

"Thank you, sir."

A baffled, resigned nurse opened the door. A youth in Midshipman blacks stepped in. "Uncle Tom?"

"Horst-Johann! Jesus, boy. I hardly recognize you. You're half a meter taller."

Jupp von Drachau's son joined the crowd. The boy had been closer to McClennon than his father since his parents had split. The boy was in his father's custody, and resented him for being absent so much. Thomas did not understand the reasoning behind the feeling. The boy saw Jupp more often than him... He thought of his mother and reflected that children applied a special logic to that species of adult called a parent.

He lay back on the bed and surveyed the gathering. Not a big circle, he thought, but all good friends. Surprisingly good friends, considering what he had been through the past few years... Friends whom, most of the time, he had not known he had.

He really had been way out there, lost in the wildernesses of his mind, hadn't he?

The universe now seemed bright and new, specially made for him. Even his starfish memories and his knowledge of the doom approaching from centerward could not take the gleam off.

Horst-Johann was first to leave, after a promise to visit again come the weekend. Then Mouse, who had to return to his own extended debriefing. Then Tanni, who had to get back for her watch aboard *Marathon.* She departed after a whispered promise that left him in no doubt that his masculinity had survived the hospital weeks.

Beckhart sat his chair silently and waited with the patience of a statue of Ramses.

A half hour after Tanni's departure, Max announced, "We have to leave, Walter. Greta has to get back for morning muster. You be good. And try not to collect any more little blondes."

McClennon grinned self-consciously. "You coming back?"

"For sure. I'm keeping an eye on you. You're not sneaking off on me again... It's been a long time, Walter."

Greta blushed.

"Thanks for coming. And Greta. Thank you. Come here." He hugged her, whispered, "I'm there when you need me."

"I know."

"It's important to have somebody who needs you."

"I know. I'll be back Saturday."

After the women left, Beckhart sat in silence for several minutes. McClennon finally asked, "Aren't they going to miss you at the office?"

"I'm not as indispensable as I thought, Thomas. I come back after six months in the field and find them caught up and not a problem in sight."

"What's on your mind?"

"I really said it before, about as well as I can. That I'm sorry I had to do what I did."

"Sorry, but you'd do it again."

"If something comes up. I don't think it will. Things are damned quiet now. The war has everybody's attention."

"Will we be able to do anything with Stars' End? Or what I learned from the starfish?"

"About the fish info I don't know. It does prove there's a hope. Stars' End... Our Seiner friends have gotten it straightened out. The place is almost a high-technology weapons museum. Some of the simpler systems will be available when next we engage."

"The gods are dead. Long live the gods," McClennon murmured.

"What?"

"Nothing. Nothing at all."

"A long time ago, in another life, I promised you a vacation. I sent you to Payne's Fleet instead. This time I'm sending you home. I've already sent word to Refuge to get your house ready. Take Mouse along."

"Mouse?"

"Mouse took care of you when it got tough. It's your turn. He's slipping. The Sangaree are gone. That hate kept him glued together since he was a kid."

"All right. I understand."

A mountain of paperwork was needed to close out the mission and put the Board of Inquiry into motion. The latter would be handled entirely by deposition. Thomas rolled through it. Nothing daunted him. The Psychs seemed to have rebuilt him better than original issue. He worked like a slave, and had energy left to flit from friend to friend evenings and weekends. He reminded himself of Mouse in days gone by, when Storm had been everywhere at once, pursuing a hundred interests and projects.

Mouse was the opposite. He could not finish anything.

Then it was all done. *Marathon* took them aboard and spaced for the quiet Cygnian world called Refuge, which was home for millions of retired civil servants and senior Service personnel.

But for Tanni Lowenthal the journey might have been depressing.

Going home. His showing for the mission some money, some stamps and coins for his collections, some new and old memories, and an armistice with himself. Somehow, it did not seem enough.

But he had found his friends, the people he had thought missing so long. So why was he disappointed?

There had been one soul-scar the Psychs had not been able to heal completely.

He could not forget Amy.

They had never really finished. They had not said *the end.* They had just gone separate ways.

He liked things wrapped up neatly.

Time passed. Cygnian summer faded into autumn. Fall segued into winter. Mouse and McClennon played chess, and waited, growing closer, till Mouse revealed the whole story of his past, of the origins of his hatred for the Sangaree. Gently, McClennon kept his friend's spirit from sliding away completely. Gently, he began to bring Mouse back.

The report of the Board of Inquiry, delayed repeatedly, drew no closer.

From Cygnus it did not seem there *was* a war. Luna Command had expanded its forces six-fold, and had begun building new weapons and ships, but otherwise Confederation seemed to be going on as before.

Tanni visited occasionally. Max and Greta kept in touch.

And yet…

Some nights, when the dark winter skies were terribly clear, McClennon would put aside his stamp collection, coins, or the novel he had begun writing, and would go out on the terrace. Shivering, he would stare up at stars burning palely in unearthly constellations and picture huge ships like flying iron jungles. He would think of swarms of gold dragons, and a million-year-old beast he had taught to tell a joke.

He never loved her more than he did now that she was lost forever. Mouse had told him… She might use his name to frighten his own child. She would not hate him now. She would understand. But there would be appearances to be maintained, and social winds with which to sail…

Life never worked out the way you wanted. Everyone was victimized by social equivalents of the theories of that dirty old man, Heisenberg.

The comm buzzed. McClennon answered. A moment later, he called, "Mouse, Jupp's coming in to spend a few days." He returned to the terrace. The ship burned down the sky, toward where the city's lighted towers made fairy spires that soared above distant woods. McClennon pretended it was a shooting star. He made a wish. "Want to play a game while we're waiting?"

Mouse grinned. "You're on."

"Stop smirking. I'm going to whip you this time, old buddy."

And he did. He finally did.

## Also from Glen Cook and Night Shade Books

978-1-59780-1485
Mass Market / $7.99

In *The Dragon Never Sleeps*, Glen Cook delivers a masterpiece of galaxy-spanning space opera. For four thousand years, the Guardships ruled Canon Space with an iron first. Immortal ships with an immortal crew roamed the galaxy, dealing swiftly and harshly with any mercantile houses or alien races that threatened the status quo. But now the House Tregesser believes they have an edge; a force from outside Canon Space offers them the resources to throw off Guardship rule. Their initial gambits precipitate an avalanche of unexpected outcomes, the most unpredicted of which is the emergence of Kez Maefele, one of the few remaining generals of the Ku warrior race—the only race to ever seriously threaten Guardship hegemony.

978-1-59780-0679
Trade Paperback / $14.95

The ongoing war between Humanity and the Ulant is a battle of attrition that Humanity is losing. Humans do, however, have one technological advantage—trans-hyperdrive technology. Using this technology, specially designed and outfitted spaceships—Humanity's Climber Fleet—can, under very narrow and strenuous conditions, pass through space undetected.

*Passage at Arms* tells the intimate, detailed, and harrowing story of a Climber crew and its captain during a critical juncture of the war. Glen Cook combines speculative technology with a canny and realistic portrait of men at war and the stresses they face in combat. *Passage at Arms* is one of the classic novels of military SF.

**Find these Night Shade titles and many others online at http://www.nightshadebooks.com or wherever books are sold.**

## Also from Glen Cook and Night Shade Books

978-1-59780-1003
Trade Paperback / $15.95

In the vast desert, a young heretic escapes death and embarks on a mission of madness and glory. He is El Murid—the Disciple— the savior destined to build a new empire from the blood of his enemies, who vows to bring order, prosperity, and righteousness to the desert people.

But all is not as it seems, and the sinister forces pulling the strings of empire come into the light. Who or what lies behind El Murid's vision of a desert empire?

*A Fortress in Shadow* collects *The Fire in His Hands* and *With Mercy Toward None*, which together make up the prequel series to the Dread Empire, and features an introduction by Steven Erikson.

978-1-59780-1881
Trade Paperback / $14.95

*An Empire Unacquainted with Defeat* collects all of Glen Cook's short fiction set in the vast world of the Dread Empire. With stories ranging from "The Nights of Dreadful Silence", featuring the first appearance of Bragi Ragnarson, Mocker, and Haroun bin Yousif, to the culture-clashing novella "Soldier of an Empire Unacquainted with Defeat"; from "Silverheels", Cook's first published work of fiction, to "Hell's Forge", a haunting tale of cursed pirates and strange lands, which appeared here for the first time, and also including a detailed introduction and extensive story notes by Glen Cook, *An Empire Unacquainted with Defeat* charts the development of this influential American author and the massive, multifaceted world that he created.

**Find these Night Shade titles and many others online at http://www.nightshadebooks.com or wherever books are sold.**

Glen Cook is the author of dozens of novels of fantasy and science fiction, including *The Black Company*, *The Garret Files*, Instrumentalities of the Night, and the Dread Empire series. Cook was born in 1944 in New York City. He attended the Clarion Writers' Workshop in 1970, where he met his wife, Carol. "Unlike most writers, I have not had strange jobs like chicken plucking and swamping out health bars. Only full-time employer I've ever had is General Motors." He currently makes his home in St. Louis, Missouri.